The Executioner Of God

By C. David Belt

Enterprises

ISBN: 978-1-5136-9045-2
V&E Enterprises
Springville, UT

For Cindy,
my timeless lady

"A Templar Knight is truly a fearless knight, and secure on every side, for his soul is protected by the armor of faith, just as his body is protected by the armor of steel. He is thus doubly armed, and need fear neither demons nor men."

Bernard de Clairvaux
De Laude Novae Militae

"To fight for the right, without question or pause, to be willing to march into Hell, for a Heavenly cause."

Don Quixote
Joe Darion
Man of La Mancha

"Nevertheless neither is the man without the woman, neither the woman without the man, in the Lord."

Paul of Tarsus
I Corinthians 11:11

Author's note

Nowadays, the Templars get a bad rap, in my not-so-humble opinion. These were noblemen who trained for years to become knights, long before they became Knights of the Temple. They had houses and lands and money. They had families. They had everything in life. And they left it all behind to serve God, to safeguard Christian and Jewish pilgrims in the Holy Land. They took lifelong vows of obedience, chastity, and poverty.

And they took those vows seriously. I mean, these guys were so poor (after they became Templars), at mealtimes they had to share a bowl with another knight. They were not allowed shoelaces, because shoelaces were "vanity." When they joined the order, they were expected to supply their own armor, weapons, and horses, and donate all other property to the order. And after joining the order, if the Master of the Temple determined that another Knight, another brother, needed his sword or his horse more than he did, he was expected to give up his sword (which, by the way, cost a small fortune) or his horse (which he'd spent years training). He might be supplied with another sword or horse, but it would most likely be inferior to what he had given up.

When it came to their vow of lifelong celibacy, consider this: when they left home and joined The Poor Fellow-Soldiers of Christ and of the Temple of Solomon, they were not even allowed to kiss their mother or sisters goodbye. They were not allowed to write home or receive letters or news from home for the rest of their lives.

These men gave up everything for God so they could protect the innocent.

The Templars were a cavalry of mounted knights. They were fearsome warriors who had a reputation for never retreating, never surrendering, and never leaving a brother behind. They were also profoundly religious. They prayed at least one-hundred and forty-eight times a day. They performed charitable acts for the poor. As we say today, they walked the walk.

They have been described as "warrior monks," but as I have learned in my research, these men were not monks. A monk lives in a monastery, in a cloister. The Templars did not live in a cloister. The proper term for a Templar is a "religious." In this case, "religious" is a noun. The term includes monks and nuns. It also includes Catholic priests. It could also include knights. (Not every knight was a religious, and not every religious was a knight.) Are you confused yet? Clear as mud?

Many years ago (more years than I care to admit), I served a fulltime mission for The Church of Jesus Christ of Latter-day Saints. During that time, I lived a life of obedience, (relative) poverty, and chastity. But I received regular letters from home. My fiancée (who also served a mission at the same time) and I wrote to each other weekly. And my mission lasted for only two years. Every day I served, I knew that, at the end of those two years, I would go home, see my family, marry my sweetheart in the temple of God, have children, get an education, and continue on with my life. And though it seemed long at the time, it was only two years out of so many . . . Never mind.

The Templars served for life. The order lasted for nearly two centuries. But between 1307 and 1312, due to the machinations and treachery of a greedy king and a weak (and possibly corrupt) pope, many Templars were arrested, tortured, and burned at the stake on trumped-up charges of heresy, and their order was disbanded.

It wasn't until the twenty-first century that the Catholic Church finally admitted that the persecution of the Knights Templar had been unjust. It took nearly seven centuries for the Templars to be exonerated. But in the meantime, they have been vilified by popular books, movies, and video games. Like I said, I think they got a bad rap.

I am grateful that I am not a Templar for a plethora of reasons. For example, I really enjoy being married to my sweetheart and having a family with her. I don't agree with many of the rules the Templars lived by and the doctrines they sincerely believed, but in studying them, in looking beyond the way they were so often depicted, I have come to greatly admire these valiant men who served God with faith and nobility.

On another note, I have a character named Kosminski with an unusual callsign. You might enjoy looking that name and callsign up.

One final note: obvious fantasy elements aside, I have personally witnessed all the types of spiritual gifts and miracles depicted in this book.

C. David Belt
June 2021
unwillingchild@hotmail.com

Chapter 1

Carmarthenshire, Wales: 1497 A.D.

She was caught between the devil and hell.

Black as the maw of Hell, the cave mouth loomed before Sister Mary Elizabeth. The darkness terrified her — darkness had always terrified her — causing her knees to wobble and her hands to tremble even as she clutched at the tattered, white skirts of her habit — torn as she'd fled through the forest. She'd almost fallen into the cave — the rock fissure was so well hidden — she hadn't seen it as she scrambled up the hill in her hopeless bid for escape. She wheeled, desperately seeking another path — any other path. *Not the dark!* she thought. *Anything but the dark!* But her eyes snapped back to the hound straining against its handler's leash. The dog — a *lymer*, a scent-hound — made no sound as it hunted her, its nose sniffing low to the ground, as it dragged its handler — a *berner* — by a long leash.

The lymer eats the head! she thought, fighting to control her panic. *They give the prey's head to the hound.*

But Mary Elizabeth knew that death was not to be her fate. *Death will be a kindness.*

Death will be quicker.

The setting sun caught the breastplates of her true pursuers — seven men on horseback. Six men-at-arms and, at their center, Sir Guy de Bohun, the devil who had driven her to seek refuge in the horrible abbey. Sir Guy, the fiend who would have her for his bride at any cost, whether she consented or not.

Hide in the darkness or be dragged away to a forced marriage and Sir Guy's bedchamber. Wedded to a monster.

Caught between the devil and hell, she chose hell.

Blessed Mary, Mother of God, give me courage!

Mary Elizabeth stepped into blackness.

1

She had to find a weapon. A stone. Anything to fight the hound. The hound would follow her in if its handler allowed it to.

And then she'd be trapped.

She put a hand to the tunnel wall — as much to steady herself as to feel her way in the terrifying darkness.

Was that the lymer's breath on her neck? *It's right behind me!*

"In here, milord!" she heard the berner cry. "A cave!"

The hound is outside! *Not here in the dark!* Her knees almost collapsed in relief. *Not in the dark!*

She listened for the sounds of pursuit, for other voices — for the hated voice of Sir Guy — but she heard nothing, save her own labored breathing and the blood pounding in her ears.

As she moved deeper into the tunnel, she felt ahead with her foot.

A stone! Holy Mary, give me a stone. Anything to fight with!

In spite of her fervent prayer, she found nothing. It was as if the tunnel floor had been smoothed and cleared of any debris. As if the cave were inhabited.

Trolls. Bandits. Leprechauns.

"Aye, milord," the berner shouted, his voice fainter now. "Ol' Fang an' me — we'll hold fast. Right here, milord. She won' escape!"

She dragged her right hand along the tunnel wall. The rocks under her fingers were jagged, but the ground under her feet was smooth as a goodwife's swept floor.

Spiders! There will be spiders in here!

She was certain if she so much as brushed a spiderweb with her hand, she'd scream. *Please, Holy Virgin! Let there not be spiders.*

Suddenly, her hand touched only air. Sister Mary Elizabeth fell, clutching vainly at the darkness.

Pain spiked up her knee as it struck the stone floor. Her hands, groping in the blackness, hit the ground, saving her head from the same fate. She clamped her jaws around a whimper of pain and terror. It was all she could do to keep silent.

Silence won't stop the hound!

She gathered her ragged skirts and crawled, favoring her injured knee, to the right, as she probed for the wall.

Her hand brushed against something.

Something hairy.

She heard a loud, bestial snort.

She screamed and fell back.

"Ki va là?" A voice in the darkness. A male voice. "Ditez ou mourez!"

Sister Mary Elizabeth did not understand the words, but the tone was unmistakable.

"Nomina se aut mori!" the voice demanded.

"Maebh!" she squeaked, giving her birth name and reverting to her native tongue. "I am Maebh. I mean, I am Mary Elizabeth. Sister Mary Elizabeth. I am a nun. Please d-don't kill me." The last came out as a pleading whisper.

She heard a grunt. It sounded human. "Èireannach. Tha thu Èireannach." Then he said, "You are Irish." He had spoken it in her native language, though with a foreign accent.

"Aye," she replied in the same language. "I speak some English too. Not well." *Hardly any at all.*

Another grunt. Then a sound she could not identify. Like metal rustling against metal. "I speak Irish . . . not well. My English is . . . very bad. Why are you here?"

"Please help me. There is a man . . ."

"A man? He hurts you?"

"Aye! There are seven—no—eight men. Horses. And a hound. I—"

The unknown beast snorted again, and Mary Elizabeth squeaked like a terrified mouse. She could hear the animal's feet stomping—the sound of iron on stone. *A horse?*

"Wait," he said. "Light."

Metal striking stone. A spark. A flash—almost blinding in the darkness. A flame caught near the floor.

Then the light of a single candle flooded the chamber.

"Et non erat lux," he said.

And there was light, she translated.

Mary Elizabeth shielded her eyes with her hand. When she lowered her hand, she beheld him.

He towered over her, wearing a dingy, white tabard that extended well below his knees. His blond beard was thick and long, partially obscuring the top of the red cross emblazoned on the chest

3

of his tabard. On his head, about his neck, and on his arms, he wore dark — almost black — mail. In his right hand, he carried a sword, nearly three feet in length.

Her eyes barely took in the great, black stallion, saddled and draped in dingy white, with red crosses — the beast that had frightened her so badly before. Her eyes were transfixed upon the sword pointed directly at her heart.

She began to pray. "Hail, Mary . . ." She prayed in Latin, and though she'd recited it countless times, her mind raced to the part that mattered at that moment. "Holy Mary, Mother of God, pray for us sinners now, and at the hour of our d-death. G-glory be—"

"Nequaquam enim ultra male tibi." He had spoken in Latin, but she understood the words well enough — *I will not harm thee.*

Startled, she looked up and into his eyes. Even in the light of the candle, they gleamed like hard diamonds — cold and cruel — eyes that had forgotten joy.

He lowered the sword, then handed her the candle. "Hold this," he said, reverting to her native Irish once more.

The light trembled in her hand.

Don't drop it! Not the dark again! Not trapped with this —

"Be careful," the knight said. His eyes were still cold, but his voice had softened. He turned away from her, toward a bed of wooden planks. There was no pallet, no blanket — only rough wood. He retrieved a helm — an old-fashioned helm, pointed at the top, with a brazen cross outlining the eye slits and running down the center, such as her great-great-great-grandsire would have worn. She caught the scent of old oil — olive oil. He placed the helm over his mail-covered head, but Mary Elizabeth was certain those cold eyes still glared at her through the eye slits.

He lifted a white shield bearing the intersecting lines of a simple red cross. He slid the shield's long, leather strap over his neck, then slid his left arm into straps on the back of the shield. "Órd Dubh!" he said, and the black stallion whinnied, tossing its head. "Fuirich!"

The horse snorted in response. To Mary Elizabeth, it seemed as if there was restless anger in that snort.

"Come, Sister," the man commanded, then strode past her, past the horse, out of the chamber, and into the dark. "But not close."

Mary Elizabeth followed, shielding the precious candle flame with her hand.

The tunnel ahead did not seem as dark as before. *'Tis the candle.*

Then she saw the light of the torches.

They are coming! She clamped a hand over her mouth, stifling a scream.

"I hear you, sweet Maebh!" Sir Guy's voice! That hideous voice, and speaking in her own tongue! "Come to me! Why all this trouble? You know I will have you. I've purchased you. I've paid your Mother Superior. You are mine."

"He paid your Mother Superior?" the knight hissed. "Stay here."

Mary Elizabeth halted, shrinking against the tunnel wall, the candle held before her, quivering in both hands, as if to ward off the darkness.

To the growing light, the knight challenged, "Ki va là?" He strode forward and disappeared behind a bend in the tunnel. "Ditez ou mourez!"

The challenge was answered by gasps. And then curses.

"Sui Monsieur Guy de Bohun!" her pursuer announced. "Qui estes vos? Qui oserez se mettre entre ma femme et moy?"

"Sister," the knight shouted, speaking in his heavily accented Irish, "is this man your husband? He says you are his wife."

"No!" she cried, finding courage in her outrage. "I am a Bride of Christ! I will never let that dog touch me!"

"Go," the knight said, speaking in English. "Go now and live." His voice was calm, cold as a mountain lake, though the words came haltingly. "Go or die."

"Milord," one of Sir Guy's men said, "let us flee! It is a spirit!"

"Who are you?" Sir Guy demanded. "Ghost or demon, I will have my property."

"I am"—the knight paused as if searching for the right English word—"I am Carnifex Dei."

Carnifex Dei? The butcher of God? The executioner of God?

Sir Guy laughed then. "We are eight against one! Come on then, Executioner of God. Come on and die!"

The knight began to sing —

Da pacem, Domine, in diebus nostris
Quia non est alius
Qui pugnet pro nobis,
Nisi tu Deus noster.

And though the words were not from the Mass, Sister Mary understood them.

Give peace, O Lord, in our time,
Because there is no one else
Who will fight for us,
If not Thee, our God.

She heard the clash of steel on steel, of steel on wood. Of steel squelching into softer things.

And the horrid screams of men locked in mortal combat.

She could not cover her ears—how she wanted to cover her ears!—for she knew she would drop the candle or set her headdress—her nun's veil—aflame.

And all through the sounds of death and butchery, the knight sang, sometimes in Latin, sometimes in French.

Suddenly, there were no more screams, not even the moans of the dying. There was only the song.

Crucem sanctam subiit
Qui infernum confregit.
Accinctus est potential.
Surrexit die tertia. Alleluia!

He bore the holy cross
Who shattered Hell.
He was girded with power.
He rose on the third day. Alleluia!

Then the knight was standing before her, his helm in his left hand, his shield hanging loosely from the strap around his neck, and his sword in his right hand, the point down.

He was drenched in blood. His yellow beard and his white tabard were crimson. But his sword had been wiped clean, and it gleamed in the candlelight.

His eyes were cold as the stars of heaven.

He towered over her once again.

Please don't kill me.

Holy Mary, please —

Suddenly, he knelt before her. He placed his helm on the stony floor. Then he planted his sword, point down, in the ground. He gripped the blade with one hand below the hilt. Even though the crosspiece curved slightly downward, Sister Mary realized that the top of the sword formed a cross. The knight pulled back his mail coif and shook his head, revealing his shoulder-length blonde hair under a white arming cap. His eyes locked with hers, and for the first time, she realized that his eyes were blue — blue as a clear summer sky.

His eyes sent shivers through her entire frame.

Then he closed those blue eyes and bowed his head.

And he prayed.

"Ego gratias ago tibi, O Deus, propter . . . " he prayed in Latin.

In her mind, she translated —

I thank Thee, O God, for thy mercy and for strength in combat. Thou hast given me victory this day. May my sword ever be Thy instrument of justice. In the name of Jesus Christ, Amen.

He raised his head and opened his eyes. The coldness in those eyes had vanished. He smiled and extended his hand as if to help her to her feet. "I am . . . I thank you for allowing me . . . to serve God by . . . protecting you, Sister Mary Elizabeth." He had spoken haltingly in Irish. "I am Tormond MacDonald, a Soldier of Christ."

She stared at the proffered hand. He had wiped some of the blood away from his palm, but his fingers were still stained crimson.

Tormond MacDonald, she thought. *A Soldier of Christ.*

But she also remembered the title he had used before slaughtering Sir Guy and his men. A tremor crawled up her spine, as if spiders of ice danced along her skin.

7

Carnifex Dei – the Executioner of God.

Chapter 2

Green stars glittered above them—dozens of green stars, perhaps hundreds. Mary Elizabeth knew they were not really stars, of course. They were emeralds. Rough, unpolished, but emeralds all the same. The blackness in which those green points of light glimmered was not the vault of heaven—it was the roof of the cave. And the light came not from the emeralds themselves—it was reflected from the cooking fire blazing in the center of the chamber.

The smells of burning wood and oil filled the cave. There were also the gentle, earthy scents of a stable—horse dung and urine, mingled with fresh-cut grasses—and, of course, the odor of the great warhorse itself. For its part, the midnight-black stallion—still saddled and covered in white and red—chewed on the long grass its master had cut and carried into the cave. And as the great beast ate, it eyed her as if it were considering her, weighing her, determining if she might be an enemy to be crushed under its iron-shod hooves.

There was also the toothsome aroma of roasting meat. If Mary Elizabeth tried very hard, she could imagine the meat smelled like pork. It did smell a little like pork. But she knew it was not pig-flesh roasting on that fire.

The hound would have eaten me, given the chance. Eaten my head.
Soon, I shall eat the hound. Or part of it.

She had never eaten dog, had never *imagined* eating dog, but her fearsome rescuer had assured her that *he* had consumed canine flesh on more than one occasion, and that it was tasty, if somewhat on the lean side. In spite of her fear, the thought of consuming the flesh of the hound that had so recently hunted her awakened a fierceness within her breast. *The rabbit becomes the wolf.*

Other smells wafted from the tunnel, but she did her utmost not to think about those, because thinking of those odors would only reawaken her terror. Not the reek of putrefaction—too soon for that—but the stink of a fresh battlefield.

He slew them. He slew them all.

Mary Elizabeth sat on the rough planks of the bed – or what remained of the bed. Half the planks had been chopped up to feed the fire. She nibbled on a bit of unfamiliar fruit – "dates," the knight had called them. They were sweet, but they tasted strongly of the olive oil in which they had been preserved.

Her deliverer knelt, tending the fire and the roasting meat. He had exchanged his blood-soaked tabard for a clean one – white, save for the red cross emblazoned on his chest. He said that he'd washed himself and his battle clothes in a nearby spring. The cleaned, wet tabard lay draped and drying at the end of the bed.

Its very presence made her want to retch. *He butchered them. Hacked them to bits.*

But if he were planning to kill me, he wouldn't be sharing his dinner with me, would he?

Using his dagger and a two-pronged iron fork, the knight sliced a large strip off the roasting haunch. Holding the fork with the meat impaled on it, he reached into a small pouch on the floor, then sprinkled salt on the cooked flesh. He rose, then carried the fork and the meat to her. "Careful," he said, speaking in her tongue, "it is hot."

She swallowed hard, then received the fork from his hands. "Thank you."

"Your name is Maebh?" He pronounced it strangely – "Mayff."

Maebh nodded, then shook her head. "Vuh. Vuh. May-vuh."

He nodded. "Mave. How is it" – he hesitated as if searching for the right word – "written?"

She shrugged. "I cannot read. Or write." *I'm a woman. Why would I know how to read?*

He nodded. "I see." He cut off another strip of the dog's haunch, using only the dagger and his fingers. Impaling the meat on his dagger, he blew on it a few times, then sprinkled on the salt. "The last time I ate dog, we had no salt. We had run out of salt months before. Yet, when you are hungry enough . . ." He bit into the meat and ripped off a large bite. He chewed enthusiastically, grinning. A bit of drool – the meat was too lean for the liquid to be juice – leaked from the corner of his mouth and into his long beard. He swallowed.

He pointed at the fork in her hand. "Go on. Eat. I know you are hungry."

She took a deep breath. *It would have eaten me. The rabbit becomes the wolf. The rabbit becomes the wolf.* She bit into her portion.

It was surprisingly tasty. Lean, but tasty. Hunger makes a tasty sauce, as Mam used to say. She grinned as she chewed. She swallowed, then took another bite—with far less trepidation. "Thank you," she said as she chewed. "For everything."

He shrugged. "It is my *missionem*. My *sacro missionem*. A part of it." His Irish seemed to be improving, becoming easier, the more they spoke, as if he were stretching long unused muscles. However, he frequently inserted a word or two of Latin here and there. "I am Carnifex Dei. I am sent to kill the enemies of God." He wiped his lips with his free hand. Then he tapped the pommel of his sheathed sword. He waved his dagger, then pointed at the triangular shield on the ground next to him. "You are the . . . *Bride of Christ*. By slaying your enemies, I have slain the enemies of God." He took another bite, and she heard him growl. "*Tha mi air fàiligeadh.*" He said, as if with disgust. "*A-rithist.*"

"What did you say?" *That last word. It sounded almost like . . .*
"Something like, 'Again.'"

He shook his head and pointedly looked away. "It is nothing. You are not at fault."

"At fault?" *How would I be at fault?*

"Forgive me, Sister." He growled again. "I should not have said . . ."

"Said what? How would I be at fault?" *I should not be angry. He saved my life.* More *than my life.* But she was angry.

And she was trembling. "I-I'm cold."

"It is . . . after battle . . ." He rose and moved to the end of the broken bed. He retrieved a bundle of white cloth. He unfolded it, revealing a cloak to match his tabard—snowy white, with a red cross on the left shoulder. He swirled the cloak and laid it on her shoulders. "Many new soldiers—and many old soldiers too—feel cold and"—he mimicked shivering—"after a battle. You must stay warm. You can die from this. Even with the fire. You must be careful." He passed her his waterskin. "Drink. Water. For the shock."

Mary Elizabeth shivered inside the woolen cloak — though not as much as before — and drank greedily. "Thank you. Perhaps, some of the wine?" She gestured at two small wine casks — about a gallon each — sitting beside an axe.

"No!" He grimaced. "I am sorry. I should not have spoken so harshly. But you must never touch that wine. Never. It is *sacris*. Holy."

"It is Communion wine? The blood of Christ?"

He shook his head. "No. Different. One drink and . . . 'Tis dangerous."

"Poison?"

He laughed. Softly. Mirthlessly. "Perhaps. You must not touch it."

"Why do you have it, then?"

"It is part of my mission. That is the right word? Mission?"

"Your holy mission?"

He nodded. "You must not touch it. Never drink it. Not even a taste."

"You keep saying that. I understand."

"Good."

She realized she wasn't shivering any longer. "Thank you."

He grinned. "You keep saying that."

She laughed.

Their eyes met for a moment. A long moment.

And then he looked away. "That man. Sir Guy. Who was he?"

Something about the way he'd said the word "was" sent a fresh shiver through her. As much as she had loathed Guy de Bohun, the casual manner in which the Soldier of Christ referred to the dead, unnerved her. *I am alone in the dark with a man who just butchered eight men. And he is feeding me with dog's flesh.*

"Sister? Have I said something to . . . something bad?"

She shook her head. Then her entire body shuddered. "No. I am just not . . . accustomed to . . ."

He nodded with a grunt. "I understand. He said —"

"I know what he said!" She had not meant to snap at him. She met his eyes again. He blinked, but he did not look away. "He" — she cleared her throat — "Guy de Bohun wanted to marry me. Without my consent. For my father's lands. In Ireland. But that is not all he wanted. Not *all* he tried to take from me."

"I see."

She shook her head. "No. You do not see! No one sees. Not my—" She lowered her voice. "No one but God." She bit savagely into the meat, chewing as if the act of consuming Guy's hound were somehow akin to expressing her contempt for the man who had destroyed her life.

One of the *two* men.

"Forgive me." He took his own bite of canine flesh and chewed slowly, contemplatively.

"No, Sir Knight. I ask your forgiveness, milord."

"I am no lord," he replied grinning around his food. "I was never a lord. I am the third son of a clan chief." He grimaced again. "That is the way it is said, aye? Clan chief? In Irish?"

She nodded. "Aye." She gave him a smile. "You're getting better at this."

He shrugged. "I had a friend. We used to . . . teach each other. I taught him Scottish, and he taught me Irish." He paused. "He died."

The brief statement carried with it a weight of grief, the pain of a wound never quite healed.

"How? How did he die?"

"Arrow. Through"—he pointed to his eye, then waved his finger back and forth horizontally—"the eye of his helm."

"He died in combat?"

He nodded. "On the wall. At Acre."

"Acre? In the Holy Land?"

He nodded again.

"My great-great-great-grandsire perished at Acre. In the Crusades."

His eyes fixed upon hers suddenly, with a gaze so intense, she could not look away. "What was his name?" he demanded. "Your great-great-great-grandsire?"

"Declan."

He gasped. "His full name, please."

"Declan Aidin O Broin."

He smiled then, even as he wiped away sudden tears. But his moist eyes still held hers. "Aye. You do have his eyes."

"His eyes?"

He nodded, and his mouth curled in a wistful smile. "Aye. I can see him in you."

"H-how? His eyes? How would you know?"

"He was my brother. My brother-in-arms. My dearly beloved friend. He died in my arms. On the wall of Acre."

Her teeth smote together. The chill had returned with a vengeance. *The clothes. The armor.* "Th-that was . . . two centuries ago. You could not—" She couldn't seem to breathe. She gripped the wooden crucifix at her neck as if it might protect her. "W-witchcraft!"

"Aye," he said with a grim nod. "Witchcraft indeed."

Chapter 3

Fear not, Sister." Amusement twinkled in the knight's eyes. "I, myself, am not a witch. Or a warlock. Or a wizard. I am simply a Soldier of Christ."

In spite of his assurance, Mary Elizabeth barely restrained the urge to scramble away from him. Even so, her eyes flickered toward the chamber entrance. The knight squatted between her and any possible escape. And beyond her rescuer, the great warhorse stood, blocking the exit as well. "But you said . . ."

"Oh, aye, 'tis witchcraft responsible for . . . me being here — here and *now* — with you. But I *hunt* witches." He scowled, and his eyes hardened, gleaming coldly in the firelight. "A trio of witches. And someday, some . . . *century*, by the grace of God, I will slay them. I will end their evil." He growled then — the growl of a wolf cheated of its prey. "Just not in *this* century."

He sliced off another strip of roasting meat, salted it, and stood. He stepped toward her, offering her the food.

Mary Elizabeth glanced at the fork in her hand and realized with a start that it was bare — she'd consumed every bite. She glanced again at the exit, but that was still blocked by the black horse shrouded in its white and red caparison and still wearing its high-cantle, high-pommel saddle. Her eyes focused on the proffered meat. She shook her head. "I'm not hungry."

But her traitorous stomach rumbled.

He grinned. "Go on. Take it. Running for your life — and your virtue — is hungry work. And there's plenty."

Her belly rumbled again. *Lying. 'Tis a sin.* Hesitantly, she extended the fork toward him.

But she still gripped the crucifix at her neck.

He pushed the meat onto the fork, then retreated to the other side of the fire. He cut off another strip for himself, then squatted again. As he salted his food he said, "I am not going to harm you, Sister. I will protect you."

She took a bite from the skewered meat, chewed slowly, and swallowed. She could see that he was watching her, but she did not meet his gaze. "Have you ever . . . run for your life?"

"I am a Knight of the Temple. We do not run. We do not retreat. We do not surrender." The words had the cadence of a catechism.

"You said, '*We* do not run.' But have *you*?"

His back stiffened. "Only once. And only at the direct command of Guillaume de Beaujeu, Grand Master of the Temple. When he gave me this mission. When he commanded me to escape from Acre"—he bowed his head, and his entire body seemed to hunch over—"when he commanded me to turn my back on my brothers. That is another thing we Templars never do—we never disobey an order. Never. We take solemn vows of chastity, poverty, and obedience."

"When was that? When did you leave Acre?"

"During the siege. *In Anno Domini* 1291."

Mary Elizabeth forced herself to let go of her crucifix long enough to take a drink from the waterskin. Her hands trembled, and she spilled some of the water, soaking the neck of her wimple.

"Please do not fear me, Sister." His voice had taken on a pleading tone. "If called upon to do so, I will lay down my life for you."

"Lay down your life? For me? What about your holy mission? If you sacrifice your life for me . . ."

"If that is God's will, I will submit to it. The Mamluks, the Moslems—they have a saying. *Insh'Allah*. It means, 'God willing.' If it is God's will that I fail in my holy calling, He—God—will call another Executioner. It is not for my own glory . . . *Non nobis, Domine. Non nobis. Sed nomini tuo da gloriam.*"

Not us, Lord, she translated in her mind. *Not us. To Thy name be the glory.*

"*I* do not matter, Sister," he continued. "My life . . . strange as it is . . . is *His* to spend as *He* wills. *However* He wills. *Whenever* He wills. My sword and my life for Christ."

"You . . . have not asked what year it is. I mean, right now. What year it is right now."

16

He shrugged. "I know it is not 1531." He chuckled, low in his throat, once again reminding Mary Elizabeth of the growling of a wolf. "Very well then. What year is this?"

"1497."

He growled again, shaking his head. "Thirty-four years too soon. Too long to wait. I must . . . consider . . . how to proceed. Again." The hand clutching his dagger shook as if with rage. "I must find a way to . . . Thirty-four years. Only thirty-four. If I . . . How many will die if . . ." A snarl escaped his gritted teeth.

His anger terrified her. *He would not hurt me. Surely, he would not.*

She remembered her mam, her mother—*God rest her sweet soul*—trying to calm the village farrier, a huge man, who had become enraged over a perceived slight—something about insulting his horseshoes. Her mother had spoken to the man softly, called him by his Christian name . . . *By his Christian name.*

"Tormond? Sir Tormond? Is that how I should address you?"

He laughed quietly. "Tormond. Brother Tormond, if you wish."

She forced a smile. "Brother Tormond. 'Tis an unusual name. Is it Scottish?"

He smiled then, his expression softening. "My mother was a MacLeod. 'Tis a family name on her side." He shook his head. "But 'tis not Scottish. Not truly. 'Tis Viking. The Norsemen, aye? It means 'Thor's Hammer.' A wonderful pagan name for a Christian knight, is it not?" He laughed again. "We do not change our names when we enter the Order." He gestured at her with his free hand—not the hand with the dagger. "But *you* did. Mary Elizabeth. What is wrong with Maebh, eh? I think that's a fine name. It means . . . 'cause of great joy,' does it not?"

She felt her cheeks get hot. "It also means . . . 'she who intoxicates.'"

He chuckled. "Perhaps not such a good name for a nun."

"But we all receive new names when we take our vows." She bowed her head. "When we forsake the world. When we . . . forswear the ways of the flesh." A sob burst from her.

No! I will not weep. I will not!

But weep she did.

She dropped the fork and wrapped her arms around herself in a vain attempt to contain her grief. To cage her fury.

She rolled onto the remaining planks of the rough bed, curled into a ball like a child. "Bride of Christ!" Her body trembled. "Bride of Christ. Holy. V-v-virg-gin." A strangled sob burst from her. "Holy Mary, Mother of God!"

She felt herself scooped up by two strong arms — two arms covered in metal chain. The knight held her to his white-tabarded chest, carrying her like a babe.

For the briefest of moments, the instinct to fight him — to push away from him, to gouge his eyes out with her thumbs — the instinct shook her. A sudden spasm rocked her body.

But he held her fast. Fast and firm.

And gently. So gently.

She curled tighter against his chest, pressing her face into his long, scratchy beard.

The hard rings of the mail dug into her skin, even through her thick, white habit — or what was left of it. But she didn't care.

He smelled of steel, sweat, blood, and roasted dog. But she didn't care.

Safe. She felt safe.

This man — this terrifying, uncanny warrior from another age, who had once held her dying great-great-great-grandsire, just as he was holding her now — he would protect her.

Die for me. Lay down his life.

For me.

Then she heard a crooning, comforting voice as he sang softly to her. She did not understand all the words — they might have been Scottish — but she caught a few. " . . . little child . . . angels . . . dreams . . ."

A lullaby?

His deep voice wove a soft, simple melody like a warm blanket of sound, quieting her sobs. " . . . little child . . . dreams, little . . ."

Sleep enfolded her.

And mercifully, she did not dream.

✠ · ✠ · ✠

18

When she awoke, lying on the remains of the plank bed and wrapped in the knight's cloak, the fire had burned low. The silence was absolute — even the fire did not crackle. She could no longer hear the sounds of the great warhorse.

Her rapid breathing and the terrified pounding of her heart were all she could hear.

Alone.

Abandoned.

She sat up so quickly that her head felt as if it might snap off her neck.

"Tormond?" she cried to the hollow blackness. "Brother Tormond?"

Frantically, she searched the chamber for any sign of him.

The axe was gone. The wine casks were gone. The horse was gone.

Nothing remained but the broken bed, the dying fire, the butchered remains of the hound's carcass . . . and the cloak wrapped around her.

"Tormond?" Her voice rose in pitch, becoming a shriek of terror. And of loss. "TORMOND!"

Footsteps, in the darkness, echoing in the cave. Growing louder.

Coming closer.

Tormond?

If 'twere he, would he not answer?

She stood and searched the chamber for a weapon — a stone, a stick, anything to defend herself. Her eyes lit on the spit lying by the embers of the fire — the sticks that had been used to roast the dog's haunch. The meat was missing, but the stick remained. Too thin to be used as a club, as a shillelagh, but the end had been carved to a point.

A spear. A short spear.

She snatched it up, holding the stick in both her trembling hands, pointing it toward the sounds of the approaching feet.

She scrambled to one side of the entrance — a blacker hole in the blackness.

Attack from the side. When he enters.

The footsteps slowed, then stopped.

Silence filled the cave—silence save for the thundering of her own blood in her ears.

Something moved in the darkness, rushing past her into the chamber.

She stabbed with her spear.

A flash of steel.

The wood snapped off inches away from her hand. She shrieked in terror.

"Sister!"

A strong, mailed arm enfolded her.

And even as he pulled her close, she felt him tremble.

"I could have killed you!" Tormond cried.

Mary Elizabeth trembled as well, but with anger as much as fear. "Where did you go?" *Why did you leave me?*

"I was preparing the *h-eich*. No, that's not the word. Horses? Aye? That is the word? In Irish?"

She pulled out of his embrace, shame and mortification warming her cheeks. She smoothed her tattered skirts, attempting to hide her legs. "H-horses. Aye. That is the word."

Horses? Fear seized her in an icy claw. *To travel?* "Wh-where are we"—she hoped it was *we*—she could not bear the thought of his leaving her alone—"going?"

He blinked at her as though she'd asked if water was wet. His eyes crinkled in a puzzled frown. If he'd been embarrassed by their embrace, their moment of very human weakness, he showed no signs of it. "Going? Back to your abbey, of course."

"NO!" She backed away from him in horror. "No-no-no-no-NO!"

He took a tentative step toward her, one hand extended as if to take hold of her. "Sister?"

She retreated from his hand, backing farther into the black void behind her. She shook her head violently and wrapped her arms protectively around herself. "I will not go back. Not there! Never! Never!"

He halted, and lowered his arm. "Why? I mean, why not? You would be safe there."

Fresh tears coursed down her cheeks. "Safe?" A bitter laugh burst from her lips. "Safe?" The word felt like a curse. "None of us were safe. Or protected. Not there."

His features hardened and grew cold—frosted stone in deepest winter. His left hand rested atop the pommel of his sword—but somehow Mary Elizabeth knew he would not draw, would never draw, the weapon against her. "Tell me." His voice was a cold growl. He knelt in front of her, and his eyes bored into hers. "*Insh'Allah.* My sword and my life are yours, Sister." His voice softened. "Tell me. Please."

She trembled, but not with fear.

With Tormond . . . With Brother *Tormond, I am safe.*

And so, she told him.

She told him everything.

And when she'd finished her tale, he gripped the hilt of his sword. His knuckles were white, and his voice was ice. "You will take me to this place."

Chapter 4

Órd Dubh's iron-shod front hooves crashed against the small wooden door. The sally port shattered into splinters.

Well done, my old friend, Tormond thought. He pulled the two-handed axe from its straps on the side of the horse and transferred the weapon to a loop on his belt. He loosed his dagger in its sheath. Both weapons would be ready when needed. Then he slipped his left arm into the straps of his shield, tightened his grip on his sword — the unique Templar thrusting sword, the blade wide at the base and narrow at the tip — and smoothly dismounted.

"Fuirich!" he said to his horse.

Órd Dubh snorted in protest, stamped his hooves, but stood in place as his master had commanded. Tormond knew the well-trained stallion would remain in that spot until Tormond returned. He was as certain of the warhorse's obedience as he was of his own.

Tormond glanced first at the shattered door in the side of the abbey, then turned his upper body — his great helm would not swivel sufficiently if he simply turned his head — toward the nun. "Maebh" — *Sister Mary Elizabeth! Think of her as Sister Mary Elizabeth!* — "you stay here too," he said in Irish. At least he hoped he'd said it in Irish.

Maebh nodded. In her left hand she held the reins of her own horse — a mare that had once belonged to one of the late retainers of the late Sir Guy de Bohun. She held Sir Guy's dagger in her right. Even in the darkness outside the abbey wall, Tormond could see the dagger quivering.

Please stay here. "If there is any trouble, ride away. If I don't return, ride away."

As he swiveled back to the ruined door, he thought, *She's terrified. Of course, she is. Of this place.*

But she brought me here.

That took great courage.

Glorious courage.

God give me such courage. God grant me strength.

Then he whispered the Templar Invocation of Battle, "O thou debonair, O thou meek, O thou sweet maid Marie."

Marie. Mary.

Like Mary Elizabeth.

I know why I am here, in this time. I know why God led her to awaken me. It is good for a man to know his purpose.

God grant me that I may do well this night.

Órd Dubh's smashing in of the door would alert the guard, but they would not know how many invaders there were. A hundred? A score? Or just one lone man? Yet he approached the door silently. He did not know what awaited him on the other side. And just as when he'd reentered the cave, drawn by Maebh's cries for help, he approached with caution. And stealth.

Tormond raised his triangular white, red-cross-emblazoned shield over his head and charged.

He was met with deadly steel.

Tormond caught his opponent's blade on the edge of his shield. The sword sank an inch into the linen-covered wood, trapping the opponent's blade. Tormond twisted his shield to the left, wrenching the adversary's sword out of the man's grip. Using all his strength, Tormond thrust with his sword, careful to strike the man's breastplate straight against the surface, at a perfect right angle.

The narrow tip punctured the guardsman's breastplate, penetrating his chest between the fourth and fifth ribs — straight into the heart.

Tormond quickly yanked his blade free.

With a gurgle, the guardsman collapsed to the floor.

Tormond's eyes swept the chamber — a small guard room, with armor and weapons hanging on the walls or sitting on tables, a few benches, a water barrel, candles burning in lamps — but the only guardsman to be seen was the corpse at his feet.

Tormond's shield was still encumbered by the guardsman's blade. Tormond slammed his shield at the stone wall, striking the pommel of the embedded blade. The sword ripped free of the wood and clanged to the stone floor.

His eyes turned to the chamber's door. He listened for the sounds of approaching guardsmen, but inside his helm, with his ears covered by his chain coif and arming cap, he could hear very little.

He glanced at the slain guardsman to quickly assess the armor of the age in which he found himself—a close-fitting helm with a movable visor, pauldrons covering the shoulders and upper forearms, and a breast and back plate lacquered black with a red cross painted over it.

Tormond's breath caught.

Black with a red cross—symbol of the Sergeants of the Temple.

A Sergeant? Here? In this place of evil?

But then he noticed the upper part of the cross's vertical section was bisected by a golden curve—a crescent moon turned on its back—or perhaps the horns of a cow.

Relief flooded him, sending a shiver through his body.

Nae a Sergeant. Nae my allies.

My only mortal allies.

He examined the fallen man's sword—a simple sword. Tormond scanned the room. He recognized spears and axes—single-handed with short hafts—halberds, a pair of maces, and triangular shields similar to his own. The designs were different, but they looked no more advanced than he had seen at his last waking.

The door of the guardroom slammed open.

Three guardsmen flooded into the room.

One was armed with a halberd, the other two with swords, and all three were armored like their fallen comrade.

Inside his helm, Tormond smiled. He strode into battle, singing—singing of the glory and power of his Savior.

Strength filled him, like Samson's of old.

Fulfilling his calling as Executioner of God, he advanced on the guards, a hymn on his lips as he prepared to dispatch the enemies of God to Hell.

The first guardsman, armed with a halberd—a six-foot-long combination poleaxe and spear—surged in front of his fellows. Inside the confines of the narrow guardroom, the long halberd was an awkward weapon. The guardsman had no room to swing the axe head and could bring only the spearhead to bear. Tormond deflected the spearhead with his shield, catching the axeblade at the bottom and shoving upward. Tormond then hacked with his sword at the man's unarmored thigh. The guardsman screamed and crumpled to the floor. A quick thrust to the abdomen, just above the groin, and the man was out of the fight.

The second and third guards, armed with swords — but no shields — rushed forward. They slipped in the first man's blood, became entangled in a mass of flailing limbs, and tripped over the body of their dying comrade. And once they were down, Tormond made swift work of them — a well-placed thrust to the neck of one, catching the man just below his helm, and a perpendicular thrust into the breastplate and heart of the other.

Leaving the slaughtered guardsmen in his wake, Tormond charged on, running deeper into the abbey. He followed the directions Maebh had given, working his way toward the chapel — toward the heart of evil.

He encountered no more guards as he ran, but he did encounter a pair of nuns.

They screamed and fled from him.

They walk the corridors freely. They must be part of this.

But he let them go.

He had more important prey to kill.

A tall, well-proportioned man strode into view, dressed in what must've passed for the finery of the age.

Upon seeing Tormond, the man drew his sword.

And then he turned and fled.

Nae this one. If he is here, he is certainly guilty.

Tormond transferred his sword to his shield hand, then drew his dagger. He hurled the dagger at the man. Tormond knew he must strike hard and accurately for the vertically spinning blade to pierce through the target's ribs and into the heart.

The dagger struck home.

The man fell with a strangled cry, his sword falling from his limp hand.

Tormond quickly retrieved his dagger. It was indeed wedged between a bisected rib, and it took considerable force to pull it free. Tormond wiped the blade on the dead man's fine coat. In a smooth, practiced motion, Tormond kissed the cross on the dagger's pommel, then sheathed it.

He did not say a prayer over the body. Not even a short one.

Instead, he quickly stood, turned his back on the corpse, and ran down the corridor.

He followed Maebh's instructions, recalling the map she'd drawn in the soil.

Right. Second left. Right.

And he found himself outside a huge door — the door to the chapel. A large, red-painted crucifix marked the door — a crucifix bisected near the top by the golden crescent turned on its back.

The door was unguarded on that side, though Maebh had told him there would be a guardsman on the inside of the door. With his shield hand, Tormond reached for the handle and gripped it.

He took a deep breath.

God grant me strength. Grant me courage in the face of evil.

Courage such as Maebh's.

Non nobis, Domine.

He yanked the door open.

The music of a choir penetrated through his helm — female voices singing a slow, sonorous hymn of praise to the Blessed Virgin.

The guardsman stood with his back to the door — he was on watch, not to deny entrance, but to prevent escape.

Tormond thrust his sword though the man's black-lacquered backplate and pulled his sword free even as the dead guardsman fell.

Then Tormond's eyes beheld a scene of sacrilege.

A scene of horror.

Three men — nobles, judging by their dress — sat on benches in the transept, in front of the long nave, their backs to him, facing the carved wooden screen — the rood — which separated them from the chancel, the apse, and the altar. They did not turn to look upon him — their attention was fixed on the raised platform of the chancel and the yet higher platform of the apse at the back of the chapel — and upon the altar at the center of the apse.

To the left and in front of the altar, a young nun, clad in a white habit similar to Mary Elizabeth's, knelt upon the chancel, her hands bound before her, a leather collar around her neck. That collar was attached to a wooden staff, and that staff was held by an older, stouter nun who was clearly in control of the kneeling, weeping woman before her.

To either side of the chancel, a divided choir of nuns sang a hymn, their high, melodic voices filling the vaulted chapel ceiling.

Above and behind the chancel, upon the apse, upon an ornately carved and gilded throne to the left of the altar, sat an older, large nun—the abbess, the Mother Superior of the vile order. Well-fed and clad all in white like an immense, bloated white spider, she sat presiding over her web of bondage and depravity. At her feet lay a wide, golden charger filled with gold coins—the plentiful wages of sin.

The sight of the fiendish hag would have been enough to send Tormond charging forward to attack, but it was the altar itself—the holy altar—and the sacrilege being enacted upon it that consumed him with righteous anger.

Upon the altar, on her back, lay a nun, her arms held securely by two other women in white habits. The white skirts of the victim's habit had been lifted, baring her thrashing, kicking legs. And one of the noblemen, his breeches around his ankles, advanced toward her.

The victim screamed, her voice rising above the sweet music of the choir, pleading in Latin for Heaven to deliver her.

And the Executioner of God answered her plea.

"Arrêtez!" Tormond bellowed in French as he charged up the nave.

The half-naked nobleman froze. He turned his head and stared at Tormond with wide eyes.

Tormond stormed past the sitting nobles in the transept. Ignoring the gate in the four-foot-tall rood, he vaulted the wooden screen and leaped upon the chancel. He ran past the kneeling and collared nun and her captor as he charged up to the apse and rushed toward the altar. With a mighty swing, he lopped off the head of the would-be defiler of virtue. Even as the severed head toppled to the floor of the apse, the nobleman's face bore a look of shock and disbelief.

Then Tormond wheeled upon the two figures in white who had been restraining the victim. They screamed, but had not yet released their hold on the victim's arms—as if they had been turned to stone.

Their two heads followed the nobleman's to the apse floor.

And the choir continued to sing. Their voices faltered, punctuated by an occasional scream, but they continued to sing.

The victim, suddenly freed, scrambled off the altar.

Tormond wanted to help her, but the battle had barely begun. There were more executions to perform.

Tormond turned toward the bound, kneeling nun on the chancel. He sliced the staff in two, about a foot from the collar. Then he thrust his sword into the woman still holding the severed staff with both hands, striking her through the heart. The girl was free of the staff—if not the collar—but Tormond had no time to cut the bonds at her wrists, so he placed the hilt of his dagger in the nun's trembling fingers.

The three remaining nobles were on their feet—the pompous fiends who would themselves have been at the altar with their breeches pooled around their ankles if only their gold had not been less than their dead fellow's. One was climbing over the rood to get to Tormond. One stood, trembling, his sword shaking in his hand.

The third fled toward the door at the back of the nave.

Tormond slipped his left arm from the shield. The shield hung loose at his side, held up by the guige—the long leather strap looped around Tormond's neck. He quickly sheathed his sword. Then he pulled the long-handled axe from its belt loop.

Tormond gripped the axe with both hands toward the bottom of the long, square haft. He took aim. *God guide my hands.* Then he hurled the axe toward the fleeing man. The axe toppled end over end in a high arc. He slipped his left arm back into the shield straps and drew his sword, even as the axe struck down its target. The noble crashed to the floor of the nave.

Inside his helm, Tormond indulged in the briefest of grim smiles. *Don't break my axe, laddie.*

And then another enemy of God was upon him. The first remaining lordling had cleared the rood and was charging, sword held high, toward him.

Leaving his guard open, his chest and neck exposed.

Imbecile.

Tormond easily fended off the enemy's sword with his shield, then dispatched the man with a single stroke.

The fourth and final nobleman had fallen to his knees. He held his sword above his head, gripping the single-handed hilt with both hands, waving the blade in weak, quavering arcs.

Tormond vaulted the rood and stood before the man, well out of reach of the wobbling blade.

"Pitié!" the man wailed as tears streamed down his fat cheeks and into his effeminately trimmed beard. "Pitié!"

Using his shield, Tormond batted the sword out of his enemy's hands. "Mercy?" he answered in French? "You beg for mercy?" Tormond eyed the fat purse dangling from the man's belt.

With a flick of the point of his sword, Tormond sliced open the money bag, and gold coins spilled from it. Tormond released his shield and let it dangle from the guige. He took off his helm and set it on the floor of the transept. He very much desired to look the cowardly fiend in the eyes.

With his left hand, Tormond scooped up a handful of the coins and held them before the weeping man's red-streaked eyes. "With this lucre you would have purchased the virtue of an innocent? A pure and holy Bride of Christ? And raped her upon the altar of God?"

"G-gold!" the man cried. "I will g-give you gold! This and more! Only mercy, Sir Knight! Mercy!"

Tormond fixed the man with an emotionless stare. Inside, he was seething with rage and loathing. *No. I must nae give way to hate and anger. Nae even to one such as he. I have a mission to perform. Nothing more. God grant me serenity.*

He took a deep, slow breath.

Hatred and anger evaporated like dew under the morning sun.

The choir had at last become silent.

Tormond let the gold slip from his fingers and heard it clink upon the floor. He shook his head slowly. "Mercy is not within my purview. Plead to God for mercy, for it is not mine to give."

No anger. No hate.

Only justice. The justice of God.

"Mercy!" the kneeling man sobbed. "Please!"

Tormond thrust his sword into the craven man's heart.

"Sancta Maria, Mater Dei!" a voice shrieked behind him.

Tormond wheeled about.

The corpulent abbess stood on the apse, before the throne, her hands raised above her head as if in supplication. "Sancta Maria, venite ad me in tempore tribulationis!"

Come to her? She expects the Blessed Virgin to appear? To her?

The choir began to sing once more, filling the chapel with adoration of the Blessed Virgin.

The two young nuns that Tormond had rescued huddled behind one end of the rood, clinging to each other, bleating like sacrificial lambs awaiting the knife. One still held Tormond's dagger.

Safe for now. He turned his attention on the wicked abbess.

Once more, Tormond vaulted the rood and back onto the chancel. "Who are you," he asked in Latin, "to profane the name of the Mother of our Lord?"

The vile mother superior turned her furious gaze on Tormond. "I am the Abbess of the Order of the Queen of Heaven!" Abruptly, she pointed at the altar. "Behold! She comes!"

A light blazed above the altar. The light narrowed vertically, a slash of fire in the air. Then it took shape. Curves. Colors.

The glow resolved into a woman, floating in the air above the altar. She was clothed only in a translucent robe of gossamer blue and a gold collar and earrings. And atop perfectly coifed, black hair, a crescent moon of gold, lying on its side, pointing upward like the horns of a cow. She was beautiful beyond imagining.

The singing of the choir rose in volume and pitch as if in a frenzy of religious ecstasy. "Mary! Mary! Mary! Mother of God! Queen of Heaven!"

The glowing vision extended a hand toward Tormond. Her eyes fixed upon his. And she smiled. "Come to me, my son. Embrace me."

This cannae be Mary. This cannae be —

"Tormond!" The voice came from behind him, somehow carrying over the choir. "Tormond! Behind you!" The voice had spoken in Irish.

He tore his eyes away from the apparition and spun about.

The abbess was almost upon him, her eyes blazing, a long knife raised high.

Tormond blocked the knife with his shield, then stabbed his sword into the woman's thick neck.

The abbess clutched at her ruined throat as if trying to hold in the escaping blood, dropped to her knees, then fell on her face.

Tormond whipped his head back toward the altar.

But the vision was gone. No trace remained, not even an afterglow.

That could nae have been Mary. Nae . . . like that.

"Tormond!"

Maebh entered through the small gate at the side of the rood. She sprinted toward him, her white habit skirts trailing in the blood that covered the floor. Her arms were outstretched as if to embrace him.

For a brief moment, Tormond almost hoped she would.

But Maebh stopped abruptly before she could touch him. She pivoted and rushed toward the two nuns huddling on the floor. In the blood.

She threw an arm around each, comforting her sisters. Tormond heard murmured words of consolation and grief, mostly in halting Latin, coming from three women.

Maebh's eyes locked with his. "Were you . . . in time?" she asked in Irish.

He nodded. "Aye. Barely. 'Twas . . . as you said. All of it."

"Thank you," Maebh said.

"Thank you," one of the sisters said, speaking in Welsh. At least, that was what Tormond thought had been said.

"Thank you, Sir Knight," the other rescued sister said—the one who still wore the leather collar and clutched his dagger. She had spoken in English.

Maebh rose. She took the dagger from the English nun and returned it to Tormond. "You did it." Her eyes were glowing, grateful. "You saved them."

Tormond felt heat rise in his cheeks. "God strengthened my arm. I am but His Executioner."

Maebh looked around the chapel. "So much blood." She put a hand to her mouth as if she might be sick. "But 'tis . . . 'tis done."

Tormond realized with a start that the choir had stopped singing. He turned his eyes to the two sections of the choir on either side of the chancel. *The choir.* He swallowed hard. *The choir.*

The nuns sitting in the opposing choir sections also huddled together, their eyes wide with terror.

Tormond let out a weary breath. *They are a part of this.* "My labor is not yet done." His insides roiled. They are complicit. He swallowed down bile. *God give me strength to do what must be done.* He raised his sword, and it had never felt heavier. *O God, I do not want to do this. Please give me a reason to spare them.* He advanced on one group of nuns, realizing the other group would likely flee while he was occupied.

The nuns in front of him screamed. They recoiled.

But they did not flee.

It is as if they know they are guilty and are resigned to their —

"Tormond. Please."

He felt the weight of Maebh's hand on his shoulder.

He shook off her hand. "They are part of this. They —"

He felt the weight of her hand once more. "You don't know that. How many of them were once victims? Probably all of them."

"They are part of this evil," he growled through clenched teeth. "I cannot show mercy in the face of evil. I cannot. I am the Executioner of God. That is my calling. My mission. I must do as —"

The tears spilling from his eyes surprised him.

Weeping?

He had not wept. Not in centuries.

Nae since Acre. Nae since Declan died in my.. .

"Please, Tormond. 'Tis enough. You have done enough this night."

He fell to his knees. Sword and shield dropped from his hands onto the blood-soaked floor.

And he wept.

Suddenly, gently, Maebh's arms were around his mailed shoulders. She spoke softly, her Irish voice lilting, soothing, comforting. "You have slain the enemies of God. You have protected the innocent. You have done well."

Tormond trembled, weeping like a lost child — lost and found after an eternity shivering alone in the cold and the dark.

He wept and he trembled.
And Maebh held him.

Chapter 5

The oak felt good in Tormond's hands. Comforting. Familiar. And the scent of fresh-cut wood and sawdust...

Like home.

Nae home, exactly. 'Twould only be home if Mam and Da were there. And Hamish and Caelan and Isobel. And their wee ones screaming and laughing as they played on the floor with the hounds. He smiled at the memory.

For a moment.

But they are nae but dust by now. All dead.

All gone.

Everything and everyone he had ever known. Even his brothers of the Temple. The Order itself — gone.

Dust.

Still the oak reminded him of happier times.

The wood wasn't the best. Aye, 'twas oak, but 'twas rough-cut, unpolished, unsanded, barely planed smooth. *Good enough for the bottoms of guardsmen.* A scowl twisted his face. *Especially that unholy lot.*

He'd slain more than fifty of the brutes before the night's butchery was over. After the slaughter in the profaned chapel, he'd rooted the guardsmen out of every corner of that vile abbey. He'd caught them asleep, drunken, relieving themselves, or in the very act of rapine on some poor nun imprisoned in a cell, sometimes with the girl chained in irons.

Tormond's weary, aching shoulders knotted at the memory — not the memory of the killing, but of the victims. Even once they'd been delivered, they trembled and wept — or howled. A few prayed, covering themselves in their shame. Some clung to him — though his tabard was stained with blood. Others ran, screaming, from the room in which they'd been imprisoned and assaulted.

But it was the eyes that haunted him. They couldn't see *his* eyes, not through the slits of his helm. But he had seen theirs — eyes filled with sorrow and humiliation, or worse — eyes that appeared as if their owners were already dead inside.

34

Most of the nuns he'd rescued, he was certain, would survive their ordeal. But some, he knew, would not. Sadly, Tormond had known too many women and girls who suffered the violent theft of their virtue. Not just in the Holy Land, but at home in Scotland as well. Some victims would waste away, he knew. Some would not be able to live with the shame and trauma. Though it was a mortal sin, they would take their own lives. *God, have mercy on them. What was done to them is nae their doing. And if their minds are shattered . . . forgive them, for they may nae know what they do. Take them unto Thyself, O Lord. Enfold them in the arms of Thy mercy and love.*

I came too late to save them.

Perhaps if I'd awoken sooner.. .

He growled, shaking his head. Then he sighed.

Forgive me, Lord, for my arrogance. I cannae right every wrong.

He continued to saw a plank from what had lately been a wooden bench. *Think of the oak, laddie. Think of the task at hand.*

He'd found the carpenter's tools—hammers, saws, planes, drills, nails, and a square—in a storeroom he discovered as he went around, hunting guardsmen and freeing captives.

And when he was certain he'd rooted out and executed every man in the abbey, he retrieved the tools and went to the guardroom. He removed his weapons, tabard, and armor—save for the padded gambeson and breeches—and set to work. The tools of his mission— sword, shield, axe, and dagger—were still close to hand, of course, but at that moment, he was working with other tools. Instead of destroying, he was making, repairing.

And he took joy in the making.

"Tormond," Maebh said, then quickly corrected herself. "*Brother* Tormond. Here you are!"

Tormond turned his face toward her, even as he finished the last stroke with the saw, and the newly cut board came free. He smiled at her. "Sister Mary Elizabeth." He nodded toward her. "I see you found a clean habit." *At least this habit is nae torn nor bloodstained. I cannae see her legs.* He crushed down a wistful sigh of regret before it could escape his weak, ungodly lips.

"What are you doing?" She stared at him in amazement.

He nodded his head toward the partially repaired sally port door. "I can't leave you completely defenseless here."

"Us? Defenseless?" She stepped forward, hesitantly.

Is she still afraid of me? Perhaps 'tis the beard. Unfashionably long for this century. Makes me look like a Hieland brigand. "Aye. I must at least repair the door."

Maebh took a seat on a nearby bench—one that he hadn't as yet dismembered. She put a hand to her face, covering her mouth and nose. "How do you tolerate it?"

"Tolerate what?"

She pointed at the corpses of the four guardsmen, piled up like firewood. "The stench of death?"

He shrugged as he lifted the plank and gathered nails in his hand. "I have seen so much death." *I have* administered *so much death.* "And these wretches have not even begun to stink."

"The blood. The . . . other things the dead release. It smells like a slaughterhouse *and* a dung heap."

He stuffed the long nails into his mouth, tasting iron and rust, and picked up a hammer. "I've been a soldier for a very long time." He enunciated carefully around the nails. "An overripe latrine is one of the . . . realities of army life. And blood?" He set the plank over the breach in the door, partially covering it. Then he proceeded to hammer the board into place. "I thought . . . the *women*" —even if all of them had at one point been victims themselves, he would not refer to the willing participants as *sisters*—"I thought they were set about the task of removing and burying the dead." He had given that order himself. "I left you in command. To ensure they did it." Having secured the final nail, Tormond spat the unused nails into his hand and returned to the saw.

Revulsion and no small discomfort were evident in Maebh's countenance as she glanced nervously at the dead guardsmen. "It is being done. They—the women being forced to remove the dead—simply haven't gotten to these. I—I needed to rest. And"—her cheeks colored as she averted her eyes—"I needed to make sure you are . . . well."

He smiled and nodded, even as he used the square to measure the next length of bench-board. "I am well enough. This . . . helps."

"Were you a carpenter? Before you were a knight? Before you were a crusader?"

He shook his head as he began to saw into the wood. "No. I haven't the skill. I was always a chieftain's son. A *third* son. Unlanded and . . . unnecessary. But I do know how to repair a door." He chuckled. "However, if I had to build a *new* one? By myself? It would be a very poor door indeed."

He glanced at her. She was smiling. She was quite beautiful when she smiled. She was quite beautiful even when she did *not* smile. Too beautiful to be a nun.

A bonnie lass, aye. Such lovely gray eyes.

I wonder what color her hair is under that veil.

Be wary, laddie. That way lies sin.

If the Knights of the Temple still existed, I would be required to do penance for embracing a woman and for gazing too long upon her face.

I shall perform my own penance. At the first opportunity.

He forced his eyes back to the wood and the saw, though he allowed himself to continue to smile.

But 'tis nae a sin to simply acknowledge that a lass is bonnie. And she is that.

Then his smile faltered. *Perhaps that's why she was chosen by this vile Order.*

No. "Chosen" is nae the correct word.

Acquired. Acquired *by the Order.*

"Tormond?"

"Aye?" He kept his eyes on his work.

She paused for so long, he almost looked up at her again. When she did speak, her voice carried a note of fear. "Who was that? The vision? Was she . . . the Blessed—"

"That was not the Virgin!" He growled, shaking his head vehemently. "Not Mary."

She shook herself. It was not quite a shudder. Not quite. "The Virgin would not appear . . . practically unclothed, would she? And if she wore a crown, it would not have horns. Like a cow's."

Tormond's saw attacked the wood with greater vigor. "What makes you think the Mother of God would appear in this unholy place? In that horrible ritual?" *'Twas a ritual. There was a pagan aspect to it.*

"What was that then?" Maebh asked. "Who was that . . . woman?"

"A demoness," he snarled. "From the Pit of Hell." *Lord, how am I supposed to fight demons?*

The words of St. Paul echoed in his mind. "For we wrestle not against flesh and blood . . ."

What good is my sword and my axe against demons?

"I didn't see . . . the demoness," Maebh said softly. "Not when I escaped. I escaped before Sir Guy could . . ."

He nodded. "You must have been very strong to have broken free. And very brave." *So brave. As brave as she is bonnie.* He glanced at her and gave her a kindly smile. At least, he hoped it appeared kindly.

Her cheeks flushed, but she favored him with a small, shy grin. "What is it you are always saying? God strengthens your arm? Perhaps, God strengthened my arms last night. And my legs. Especially when I kicked Sir Guy in his . . ."

He'd thought her cheeks were red before, but they were suddenly bright crimson.

Tormond chuckled. "Perhaps God *guided* your foot as well. Like a master archer's arrow to the target."

A broad smile lit her face. "Perhaps." Then the smile vanished. "I should not take joy in . . . And he is . . ." She looked away. Her eyes appeared to be fixed on the pile of corpses. She put a hand to her mouth and nose again.

"Sister, I'll not deny there is *joy* in battle. A fierce and terrible joy."

She turned her face back to him, her eyes wary, fearful — a doe that might flee at any moment.

Tormond stopped his labors and looked her in the eyes. Those soft, gray eyes, so like her great-great-great-grandsire's. "Not in the killing," he said. "Never in the killing." *The day I find joy in the killing . . .*

Her eyes softened as fear was supplanted by questioning. "Joy in what, then?"

He smiled again. A weary and wistful smile. "In doing the work of God, no matter how difficult or how fearsome that work may be." He sighed. "In knowing you might die at any moment, but if you die, you will die in His service. And He shall take you home."

"It sounds almost . . . like Valhalla. The heaven of the Vikings."

He blinked at her. "You know of Valhalla?"

She shrugged. "I have Viking blood too." The shy grin returned. "A little."

He grinned broadly at her. "But not a Viking name."

Her smile widened, and she shook her head. "No. *Tormond*," she said, emphasizing *his* Viking name. Her cheeks flushed again, and she turned her face away.

Silence filled the room—the silence of the mortuary. There were, after all, four corpses in attendance.

Tormond resumed his sawing.

After several long minutes and after two additional boards had been nailed into place, Maebh finally spoke once more. "Do you truly think the door is enough to keep men who would . . . do evil here . . . to keep them out? This door didn't keep *you* out."

"I think so. At least, at the first, it will. Ordinarily, no one would dare attack an abbey. Guards are not necessary. Normally. And those vermin"—he nodded in the direction of the piled corpses—"from the way the defenses were laid out, I suspect they were here to keep innocence inside, to prevent escape, not to keep evil out."

"Perhaps, you could stay. Here. To protect us."

Out of the corner of his eye, he could see her looking at him. Expectantly. Hopefully. But he did not meet her gaze. Instead, he shook his head. "I cannot. I have my mission. My quarry. The Witches. I must pursue them. I must slay them. I have already lingered in this century far too long."

She nodded her head. Slowly. "But we cannot stay here. Not for long. Surely, the reputation of this place is known. Other men will come."

It was Tormond's turn to slowly nod his head. "I agree. This door is but a temporary bar to *that* danger. I have been praying, Sister. Very hard. For you. For your innocent sisters here. Even for . . . the others. About what to do. Praying for the guidance of Heaven."

"And has God spoken to you?"

He glanced at her—to see if she was mocking him. But she seemed in earnest.

Tormond shook his head. "I am not one of the saints. God does not speak to me. I am but a soldier." He hesitated. "But I have . . . *felt* as if God was speaking . . . to my heart. Silently. Like a whisper in the stillness of the night."

She arched an eyebrow. "When have you had time to be still?"

He shrugged, then nodded at the mostly repaired door. "My hands may not be still, but my mind has been open to . . . reflection. And prayer."

"And what has God whispered in the stillness?"

"That you should take the gold—the wages of sin—and travel north."

She gaped at him. "Travel? North?"

He nodded. "Aye. To Scotland. The whispers tell me that this country, Wales, will soon no longer be safe. Not for nuns. Or priests. Or any religious."

"With Sir Guy gone, perhaps we could go to Ireland."

"Home? To your father?"

She shook her head. To Tormond it seemed as if she was angry at the thought. "No. Not to my father. I am . . . a Bride of Christ. And he—"

"But the Order—"

"The Order can fall into the flames of Hell!"

Her anger, the vehemence of it, surprised him. "But your vows were made—"

Though she remained seated, she straightened, drawing herself up taller. "My vows were made to God, no matter who administered them. I am a Bride of Christ." Her jaw seemed to clench. "And I will always be. I—We can find another order to take us in."

He nodded. "Aye. But not in Ireland."

"Why not? More whisperings?" Her voice held just the hint of scorn. She held her chin high, and her eyes were cold.

He met her gaze. "Aye. Ireland is not safe. Nor is England or Wales. You must away to Scotland. Where Henry does not rule."

"Henry? King Henry? Henry the Seventh?"

Tormond lowered his eyes and frowned. "I don't know. Perhaps. Or perhaps his son. I am . . . uncertain."

"But you are certain about Scotland?"

He met her scornful gaze that time. "Aye. I am certain about Scotland."

"The whisperings?"

"Aye."

The scorn drained away, as if it were leaking from her eyes in the form of tears. "I shall urge my sisters to flee to Scotland then."

Tormond smiled, then returned to his work. "I am . . . gratified that you will be safe."

"And you? Where will you go? Back to the cave?"

He nodded. "I must. This time."

"You don't *always* return to the cave?"

He laughed, low and mirthlessly. "'Tis different every time. 'Tis always a cave, aye, but not the same one."

"But not this time? This time, 'tis back to the same cave"

He hesitated. "You will keep my secret?"

"Aye!" Her answer came quickly, without the slightest hesitation.

It brought a smile to his lips. "I have allies. The Knights Templar may be fallen." He swallowed, choking on the bitter word. *Fallen. Disbanded. Falsely accused.* "The Order may be lost. But the Sergeants remain."

"The Sergeants?"

"Aye. Men who served the Order of the Temple, but were not brothers, not *religious*, like me. They were not bound by our vows. They could marry if they desired. Oh, aye, many of them were warriors. Others were craftsmen, physicians, engineers, and the like. They wore black tabards, rather than white. Still with the red cross, though." He pointed at the corpses and growled through clenched jaws. "Not with that vile, golden crescent on it."

"And they are here? The Sergeants? Among us? Still?"

He nodded and resumed his work. "Aye. In secret. They are my informants. They are my eyes and ears in my hunt. While I sleep."

"For the Witches?"

"Aye. The Witches."

"Tell me about the Witches. Please."

41

He shook his head. "No. They are horrible. And when they appear . . . there is so much death, so much evil."

She turned her face toward the dead guardsmen.

So much death. How am I any different? He growled and began to saw more quickly. *Nae. I slay the enemies of God. I dinnae corrupt and murder fools. It is* nae *the same thing.*

"Tormond? Brother Tormond?"

She was gazing at him again, and there was concern in her eyes.

"Aye?"

"What you did, here, in this place . . ."

He continued to saw. *Oak. Sturdy. Strong. And hard to cut.*

Women. Unarmed women.

At least, some of them were unarmed.

I cut down unarmed women.

The wood. The oak. That is all that matters. Think only of the wood.

"Tormond." Suddenly, she was in front of him, kneeling on the stone floor, looking into his eyes. Her gray eyes were like the sea at twilight. "This night, Tormond, you were the hand of God."

His lips twitched, but he said nothing. He averted his gaze. *The hand of God? The Executioner of God? Executioner? Perhaps the* butcher.

His mouth was suddenly dry. So dry. He licked his lips, attempting to moisten them with a tongue that felt like dry, cracked leather. He cleared his parched throat. "You. You stopped me. From killing the rest of them — the choir."

She nodded slowly. "Aye. You showed them mercy."

He shook his head. "No. That was you, Sister. The mercy came from you."

It was her turn to look away. "There must be mercy. God is merciful, is He not?"

"Aye. God is merciful." He began to saw the oak. "But I cannot be. 'Tis not my calling."

For several long minutes, silence reigned — an abstinence from words. The only sounds were those of sawing and hammering.

"Tormond," Maebh said, breaking the silence at last, "you were telling me about the Sergeants. And why you must return to the cave this time."

42

He measured out the last board, scored it, then began to saw again. "The Sergeants will leave me a message—for when I awake—telling me where to go, where I *might* find my quarry, what they, the Sergeants, have learned of the enemy. Where I might find them. Perhaps. The Sergeants know where this particular cave is. They directed me to it—to the cave. The Witches once lived there. Long ago, but no longer. That is where the Sergeants will leave the message." *Assuming they are still here, a new generation of them, ready to serve.*

Maebh nodded, her expression thoughtful. "But I woke you. Too soon, you said."

"Aye. Thirty-four years too soon." He punctuated each syllable with a stroke of the saw. *And when I awake again, I will be —*

"You will be too late," Maebh said, echoing his thoughts. "'Again,' you said. Because I woke you."

"Aye."

"'Tis my fault."

He stopped. Leaving the saw wedged in the wood, he leaned forward, and gently lifted her chin. *Her skin. So soft.* "You woke me to slay evil." He smiled, and he hoped it was a reassuring smile. "You woke me, because it was the will of God. *You*, Sister, were the hand of God."

Her gray eyes brimmed with new tears. "But your quest. Your mission."

"Someday. *Insh'Allah.*"

She nodded, and a tear slid down her cheek. "*Insh'Allah.*"

He almost—almost—reached out to wipe away her tear.

And then it came to him—like a flash of lightning out of a clear sky.

He stabbed a finger toward her. "You! You could wake me! A second time. Wake me again!"

"Me?"

Laughter burst from him. It be so clear now! "Aye, thanks be to God. You! In thirty-four years. You could return to the cave. And wake me! Just as you did. Simply touch my skin. Touch my flesh, and I'll awake!"

Touch my flesh. Unholy thoughts stabbed at his mind, like spear points. But he parried them away. *Nae now. Nae ever. I have vowed.*

And she has vowed.

And I have my mission. My holy mission.

"Touch my flesh—my hand or my face," he said again, "and I'll awake."

"But"—she averted her eyes again—"I'll be too old."

"Old? You cannot be yet twenty. You will be less than sixty years. Surely you could make the journey from Scotland to Wales. You should not be too old."

Her lips trembled. Then she nodded. And she wiped away fresh tears. "Not too old. To make the journey."

"Then you'll do it?"

She nodded more vigorously and smiled. The smile, however, did not reach her eyes. "Aye. I will."

"Thanks be to God!" He lifted his hands and his eyes toward heaven. "Thou art most merciful and kind, O Lord." He drew a cross on his chest with a finger, then turned his gaze back on Maebh. "And thank you, Sister Mary Elizabeth. You are indeed the hand of God."

He resumed his sawing. "Only one more board!"

He felt like singing. *'Twill nae be too late! Nae this time! Finally!*

Sister Mary Elizabeth rose, her face a mask of serenity, despite the trail left by her tears. "I must return to my tasks. I will see that food and wine are brought to you."

She turned and strode out of the guardroom, her back as straight as a spear.

His eyes followed her. His lips turned down in a frown. Brought to me? *Meaning—Some other nun will bring it.*

'Twill nae be her. Nae Maebh.

A pang of regret smote him.

Sister Mary Elizabeth. She is Sister Mary Elizabeth.

And when next I wake, she will be an old woman. An old nun.

Too old? She cannae have meant...

He attacked the wood with the saw, growling softly.

The oak.

Think only of the oak.

44

Chapter 6

She had won the argument—at least on the most important point—but it had not been easy. And Maebh could argue as well as any Irish lass—freely employing fiery anger and petulant begging and everything in-between—whatever was needed to get her way. Perhaps it was beneath the dignity of Sister Mary Elizabeth to engage in such an unseemly battle of words and emotions, but Maebh O Broin was determined to emerge victorious. She was determined, because it was a battle she could not afford to lose.

More importantly, it was a battle Tormond could not afford to win. Of that she was absolutely certain.

And in the end, Tormond—*Brother* Tormond, she had to keep reminding herself—saw the sense of her position. In truth, Tormond was more *stubborn* than *skillful* in his arguments. Or perhaps, it was that he simply did not know how to argue with a *woman*.

Does the man have – did *he have* – *no sisters?* she thought with a wry smile.

And best of all, every word she said was absolutely true—not that she wasn't prepared to lie if that was what it took to win. But she wasn't honest with him—not completely. And that in itself was a sin. *God will forgive me,* she thought. However, she had already recited the *Pater noster*, while counting on her rosary, no less than fifty times as they rode back to the cave—not as a penance—not precisely—but as a *precaution*.

God will forgive, but will Tormond?

The unassailable bastion of her argument had been simple. "The cave is well hidden, and I discovered it only by accident. I doubt I could find it again—not on my own."

That was the *easy* victory—well, relatively easy. Even stubborn Tormond, the fearsome and implacable Executioner of God, was forced to concede that point. No, the more difficult part was to get him to allow two more sisters to accompany them—"No woman should make the journey back to the abbey alone," she pleaded.

Tormond was caught between his need for secrecy and his chivalric code—torn between protecting his sacred mission and protecting womanly virtue. Like all Templars, Tormond was a knight long before he became a religious.

In the end, chivalry won the day, and secrecy gallantly, if reluctantly, surrendered the field. "But," Tormond said, "they will not enter the cave."

"Of course not." Maebh conceded that point easily. *Give the man a small victory,* she thought, suppressing a triumphant grin. *A small victory.*

But more important than allowing Tormond to think he won, the accompanying sisters might not *enter* the cave, but they would see the entrance. They would know where to find it—when the time came.

Maebh and the other two nuns—Sister Rebecca and Sister Ruth—rode in a line behind the knight. As it was impossible for the nuns to sit in their saddles without exposing their legs to the knees or higher—their white habits had never been designed for riding horses—each nun rode with her cloak draped over her legs. Maebh did not know the other women well. They'd all been kept locked away in cells, like sacrificial calves kept in stalls, awaiting their fate—kept away from even the guardsmen, at least until after the *initiation* that had once awaited them. At least they were innocents—like herself. And both of them were Irish.

Tormond was unaware of the fact that she could easily communicate with the other two nuns. And as long as he *remained* unaware . . .

Maebh had it all planned out in her head—planned out, but far from settled. As heatedly as she'd argued with Tormond, Maebh and Sister Mary Elizabeth had fought even more passionately on the battlefield of her mind.

I will fulfill my vow! I will. I will see them all safe to Scotland. I'll do that. And then these two can —

No! I must be the one to wake him. I promised I would.

A promise is not a vow. I vowed to take them to Scotland. I promised to —

No! I cannot betray his trust. I cannot.

But it will be thirty-four years! If Sister Rebecca and Sister Ruth know where the entrance is, surely, they can.. .

But why would you do such a thing, Maebh O Broin? He is a monk. No, not a monk – he does not live in a monastery, but he is a religious. And you are a nun. And that is the end of it. What can you possibly hope for? It can never be!

Tormond would never forgive me.

He will. Eventually.

No, he will not. And you know it. Besides, this is not about what you want. 'Tis about his sacred mission. He gave up all – family, friends, brothers-in-arms – to serve God, to fulfill his mission. And you would frustrate that? For what?

To remain with him.

To tempt him, you mean? To tempt yourself?

No! Not that. Never that.

Maebh scowled in frustration as her heart warred with her head.

She gazed down the road, at the back of the knight and his horse, and wondered if Tormond had the slightest perception of her internal struggle, of what she might be planning – of her possible duplicity. He turned in his saddle, perhaps checking to see if she was still following – and that was the only acknowledgement of her presence.

Órd Dubh, Tormond's huge, black warhorse, dragged behind him three oaken planks – wooden boards rather than the stuffed pallet Maebh had begged the knight take with him. She had lost that part of the argument, though she made one final, futile attempt as they were preparing to depart the abbey.

"A bed of planks is all a Knight of the Temple requires," he said as he finished tying up the planks behind his horse. "It is better than the stone floor, and a pallet would attract vermin." The corner of his mouth twitched as if in irritation. "And besides, the Witches sleep on a pallet. I have seen such a pallet" – he growled low – "when I found their lair . . . after they escaped me. Yet again."

"Have you ever seen them? Seen the Witches?"

He shook his head. "Not I. My predecessor – the first Executioner – he saw one of them. Once. A honey-haired woman in white. Beautiful, he told me. Enticing." Tormond glanced at her then, but his eyes moved quickly away. Had his cheeks colored? It was difficult to tell above the edges of his long, full beard. "But she escaped him. She . . . They, the Witches, always escape." He bared his teeth. "But, God willing, I will catch them and slay them. This time. Or the next. Someday. *Insh'Allah.*"

He tightened the rope. Then he moved around the horse to its front, patting the huge animal as he went. He spoke to the horse in a soft voice — in Scottish, she assumed. His voice was comforting — just as it was in the cave.

That voice made her feel safe.

She shook herself. Witches and their magical sleeping habits aside, she had to make him see that he must choose the pallet. She couldn't bear the thought of his sleeping on bare wood.

"You intend to sleep for thirty-four years on bare wood?"

"I have slept for sixty. I do not feel any . . . discomfort." He patted the warhorse's neck affectionately. "Just as Órd Dubh does not suffer after standing and sleeping for all that time. But then again, you are a stout laddie, aren't you, my old friend?"

The horse whinnied as if in agreement.

"But, Tormond — "

"It is not your decision. I am a Knight of the Temple. And I shall follow the laws of — "

"But the Temple Order no longer exists!" she snapped, her temper getting the best of her. "It has fall — " As soon as the words left her lips, she wished she could recall them.

He looked at her, his eyes unfathomable wells of bleak sorrow. Then those eyes hardened like fire-forged spearpoints. "As long as one Templar draws breath" — his voice was colder than frozen stone in the heart of winter — "as long as I draw breath, we have not fallen."

Maebh meekly lowered her eyes.

The argument was over. She had lost.

"Forgive me, Brother Tormond." She turned then, and walked slowly to her mare.

She was still angry — but not at him.

Stupid! Stupid! Stupid!

Curse my Irish temper!

She blinked back tears, resisting the urge to dab at her eyes.

I've hurt him.

He will probably never speak to me again.

Never.

Not until he awakes.

And by then, I shall be . . . old.

And he will not look at me or speak to me – not in the same way.

The thought of never again hearing Tormond's calming, soothing voice made her feel as if she had a hole in her heart—a bottomless chasm that could never be filled.

But why should I be sad about that? I am a Bride of Christ. He is a religious. There can never be –

She reached her horse and turned to mount.. .

And Tormond was there.

She nearly squeaked in surprise.

Tormond bent, lacing his fingers together. She realized he was offering to assist her in mounting the mare.

And he had smiled at her.

Thinking back on that argument, Maebh patted the pommel of the dagger in her belt. Though the scabbard was wrapped in white linen and hidden within a fold of her habit, the weapon's presence still irked her. That was another part of the argument she'd lost— Tormond had insisted she carry a dagger from the guardroom. And she finally agreed. It might be unseemly for a nun to carry a weapon, but if her safety demanded she have traveling companions on the journey back, then it stood to reason that she might require other protection as well.

She sighed. *After all we've been through, Tormond is probably correct. Who knows who or what we might encounter on the road?*

God willing, nothing and no one.

God willing? What's that phrase Tormond is always using?

"Insh'Allah," she whispered. "Insh'Allah."

The road widened a bit, so Maebh kicked her mare's sides and urged the beast forward, leaving the other two nuns and their mounts behind. Maebh guided the mare around the wooden planks dragging on the road after the warhorse. Soon, she was riding alongside the knight.

He acknowledged her presence with a nod and a smile. "Sister."

Maebh smiled back. *I wonder what he would look like if he cut his* beard. *Not shaved it off—just trimmed it so it wasn't hanging halfway down his chest?*

Perhaps he would be quite handsome.

Not that it matters. He is a religious after all.

But it would make him appear younger. Less like —

Her breath caught. *Less like my father.*

She felt her gorge rise. *No! Not like him! Nothing like him!*

The forest around her began to spin. Her stomach suddenly wanted to empty itself of her breakfast. Perspiration beaded on her face as she fought against the urge to vomit. Her hands became slick. She swayed in the saddle.

"Sister?" Concern and alarm filled Tormond's voice. "Are you well?"

She was falling.

She clutched at the high, wide pommel of the saddle. But her slick, clawing hands could find no purchase.

The hard ground seemed to rush at her.

I'm going to dash my head on a stone. And die.

She even saw the stone. On the road. Large and hard and unyielding.

Lethal.

The world had stopped spinning. Indeed, time seemed to slow as her eyes fixed on the rock that would kill her. *I'm going to die.*

But in that final moment, when death was certain, she was not afraid—she was only sad. *I shall not be there to awaken him.*

I'm sorry, Tormond.

The stone filled her vision, shooting toward her.

And then it stopped.

Or rather, she stopped.

Strong arms had caught her. Strong arms clad in mail.

She remained in his arms, still facing the ground and the stone, gulping short, rapid breaths of air.

"Sister?" He lowered her to the ground, gently setting her unsteady feet on the very stone that should have claimed her life. "Are you well?"

She clung to him, gripping his mail-covered shoulders as if she might fall again. Her face nestled in his beard.

And she shivered. *Nothing like my father.*

She nodded fiercely. *Nothing like Da.*

His beard pulled up, tickling her face. She realized he was nodding in return.

"Good," he said. "Can you stand?"

"Aye." She pushed away from him. With reluctance. "Thank you for saving me. Again." *Again and again.*

He shrugged. "I must fetch your horse." He pointed toward the mare, which had wandered a few dozen paces away. It stood, munching on grass.

As the knight strode off toward the errant horse, Maebh marveled at his steady, confident gait. *All that armor. And he walks as if it were nothing.*

She watched as Tormond slowly and cautiously approached the mare. Maebh could neither see his face nor hear his voice, but she imagined him speaking softly to the animal in his native Scottish, speaking words of comfort and assurance.

So fearsome in battle. Yet so gentle and kind.

I have known him for less than two days, and yet, I cannot imagine my life without him.

How I shall miss him.

Even if I do come back long before the thirty-four years — while I'm still young — I shall miss him until then.

As Tormond returned, leading the mare, Maebh noticed that he rolled his right arm and shoulder as if they were causing him pain, as if he were trying to soothe a hurt. When he laid eyes on her again, however, he stopped moving his arm and smiled once more.

She pointed at his shoulder as he and the mare came to a halt beside her. "Are you hurt?"

He shrugged, wincing slightly. "'Tis just . . . I do not know the right word in Irish. Fatigued? No that's not it. Pain? Aye. Pain. But it's not that bad. 'Tis just" — he shook his head, grinning — "the breastplates of this century are very thick." He tapped the pommel of his sword. "Very thick indeed. 'Tis very difficult to pierce one. You have to strike at just the right angle and" — he chuckled — "thrust with all your might. *All* your might, mind. And even then . . . If I had missed, if God had not guided my thrust and strengthened my arm . . . at best, the blade would have slid to the side. At worst, I could have shattered my arm." He grimaced then, gritting his teeth.

"You *are* hurt!" she cried, resisting the sudden urge to rub his shoulder, to relieve the pain there—not that he'd have felt it through the heavy mail—not that he would have allowed her touch. "Shouldn't you bind the arm?"

"Bind it? Oh, aye. Under other circumstances. If I had time to rest for a fortnight or more. No, the *sleep* is what I need. And the wine. While I sleep, the wine will heal all hurts."

"Is it magic, then? The wine?"

"Magic? Aye. Witchcraft, more like. But . . . I must make use of it to fulfill my mission. And count the healing as a blessing from God, even if delivered by an unholy hand."

Tormond bent, interlacing his fingers again to help her back into the saddle. "Are you well enough to go on?"

She nodded. "Aye, but . . . your shoulder!"

"Nonsense. Here. Let me help you."

She hesitated but a moment. *Do not shame him.* "Thank you."

She grabbed hold of the saddle's high pommel, placed her foot into his hands, and mounted.

He gave no further indication of pain—no grunt, no grimace.

She did her best to arrange her skirts to cover her legs as much as possible. Her cloak must have been lost when the horse ran away.

Her legs were bare to mid-thigh.

She looked about for Tormond, blushing.

And she saw him, trotting toward her with her white cloak, coming to her rescue yet again. He carefully averted his eyes as he helped her spread the cloak over her legs once more. When she was modestly covered, he turned his eyes back to her—or rather to her covered legs. He nodded as if in approval.

Then he turned to the other two nuns. "Sorores! Paratae estis? Venite. Abeamus."

In her mind, Maebh translated, *Sisters! Are you ready? Come. Let's go.*

The knight mounted his massive stallion, and Maebh once again marveled at his strength and agility while wearing the heavy mail—and with an injured shoulder. With a small flick of the black horse's reins, Tormond rode away.

And once more, Maebh maneuvered her mare to ride beside him. He acknowledged her with a nod, but no smile. He kept glancing at her with concern.

He thinks I might fall again. She cleared her throat. "How much does all that armor weigh?"

He chuckled. "Far more than the armor of this century. Plate has advanced much since I saw it on Mamluk warriors in the Holy Land." He shrugged again. "This mail weighs, perhaps, ninety pounds or so."

"Pounds?"

"Isn't that the word?"

She shrugged.

"Uh, perhaps" — he seemed to be figuring in his mind — "seven stone?"

"I see." *Seven stone? How can he move in that?*

"If I did not wear the *chausses*" — he paused — "I think you would call them mail leggings — without them, perhaps about five stone? I've fought with and without leggings. For now, though, I choose to wear them. Especially when riding. So that my legs will be protected. However, the mail on my legs makes it more difficult to mount my horse. Leaping like that, you see. Into the saddle."

Leaping? Into the saddle? That was nothing! Back in the chapel, I saw you leap over the rood!

"Interesting helms they wore," he continued, oblivious to her astonished gaze — "those guardsmen. The helms fit so close to the face. Such a helm would turn easily with the head." He patted the great helm poking out of a saddle bag. "These steel buckets do not turn with the head. At least not well." He gestured with his thumb at the hood of the mail coif that hung down from the back of his neck. "I doubt one of those close helms would fit over mail, though. Hmm . . ."

"Why do you wear such antiquated armor? Why not wear something new?"

"A very good question. I have spent all my youth and manhood training to fight in this way, with this armor. It would take me a very long time to learn to fight with new armor. And by the time I did, I would go to sleep and when I awoke, it would all be changed."

"Tell me," Maebh began, "about—" She stopped herself before she could say, *your family.*

"About what?"

"Nothing. 'Twas . . . nothing."

"Very well. Then tell me, Sister, if you will, how it is that an Irish nun comes to be in a convent in Wales? I know you were unaware of . . . what your Order was doing. I assume you were"—he paused, as if searching for the right word—"deceived?"

She shivered, then nodded.

"I see. But why Wales? Why not Ireland? Surely there are convents in Ireland?"

"There are. That is where I joined . . . the Order. The Order of the Queen of Heaven." *That was not Mary! That was not the Virgin. But surely, Mary is the Queen of Heaven, is she not?* She swallowed, then cleared her throat. "I . . . joined the Order, took my vows in Kilkenny. The very next day, the abbess told me I was to take ship for Wales—that God had called me there." She lowered her voice. "*God* had called me there."

He looked at her askance. "Take ship? Alone?"

She closed her eyes for just a second, then opened them quickly lest she fall from her horse again. She laughed bitterly. "No. I was to be accompanied by my father. My da. He was sorry, the abbess said. Repentant, she said. My da would take me to a place where Sir Guy de Bohun would never find me."

"But de Bohun *did* find you."

"Aye." Her lips twisted in rage. "Because Da betrayed me. He delivered me right into . . . right into that dog's hands."

"Your father knew?"

"Aye. Da knew all too well."

"And he knew what . . . goes on in that Order?"

She nodded, hot tears spilling from her cheeks. "He was there. I saw him. That night. With Guy. The night I was . . . upon the altar."

Tormond said nothing. He was silent for a long time.

She snuck glances at him, but he only stared ahead. His brows were lowered, and hard lines surrounded his eyes.

He slowed his horse, halting in the road.

She halted her mare as well. "Brother Tormond?"

54

"Tell me where I may find him." His voice was ice. Ice and death. "Your father. Tell me where I may find him. Find him and send him to Hell."

"No!" She extended a hand toward him, as if she could stop him. But her reach could not bridge the distance between them. "No! You mustn't!"

He turned his head toward her. His blue eyes shone with a deadly light, and his hand rested on the pommel of his sword. "I must. Your father shall not escape the justice of God."

"I don't know where he is!" It was true. She reached for him again. Her mare took a step toward the stallion.

The warhorse snapped at the mare.

The mare whinnied and snapped back, then hastily backed away.

Both Maebh and the knight struggled for mastery of their horses.

Tormond quickly brought his stallion under control.

Maebh took a moment or two longer, but when she had calmed her mount, she found Tormond staring at her.

"Has he gone back to Ireland? Does he have estates in Wales? England? Cornwall?"

"No! All our— All *his* lands are in Kilkenny. He must have gone back to Ireland. He'll be halfway to Liverpool by now."

Tormond nodded. "If I ride hard, I can catch him before he sails—"

"No, Tormond. Please!" *No more killing. Not for me.* "Leave him to God. Think of your mission!"

"With you to waken me, I could take a year to hunt him. I shall find him. I swear by—"

"Stop! Please don't swear by anything. Not to kill him. Not in my name."

He opened his mouth to protest, then shut it with a teeth-jarring snap. He drew in a slow, calming breath. "'Twould not be in your name. 'Twould be—"

"No." Her voice was calm. "Please. Let him live. God will deal with him."

"But I must—"

"Please, Tormond. For my sake. Please?"

He stared at her, his eyes hard and cold. But slowly those icy, blue eyes softened. "Very well, Sister. For your sake."

Relief flooded her, making her tremble. "Thank you."

Why should I feel relief? After what Da did?

He surely deserves —

No. Not in my name. Not because of me.

He nodded. "We need to move if you are to return to the abbey before dark." He flicked the reins on Órd Dubh, and started riding forward once more—riding toward the cave—toward their parting.

Maebh followed, the other two nuns riding silently behind.

✠·✠·✠

After the brilliant sunlight outside the cave, the feeble, wavering flame of the single candle barely seemed to penetrate the darkness surrounding Maebh. A few flecks of green caught that light, however, and it seemed emerald stars twinkled in the darkness above her.

Somehow, the scent of roast dog yet lingered in the blackness, even after nearly two days.

Maebh was grateful she could no longer smell the corpses secreted in the smaller chamber she and Tormond had passed on the way into the cave. She knew Sir Guy and his men wouldn't be rotting just yet, but the unseen carcasses still stank of dung, urine, and dried blood—they still stank of death.

Órd Dubh stood near the mouth of the chamber. The massive beast's head was lowered in a sleep so profound Maebh could neither hear nor see the stallion's breathing. As soon as the animal licked the wine—"the Witches' wine," Tormond called it—out of the knight's hand, he instantly succumbed to the magic liquid's effects. Tormond assured her that the warhorse was still alive in his deathlike slumber.

Tormond himself lay upon the three planks he'd set upon the cave floor beside the remains of the wooden bed he'd broken up to make a fire for her when she was last in the cave. *Was that truly yesterday? It seems a lifetime ago.* At the time, she was suffering from the shock of her first encounter with Tormond, so she hadn't really examined the bed. As Tormond had made his preparations for sleep, Maebh examined the bed. The posts and headboard were intricately carved, she noticed—carved with images of birds—ravens, perhaps—and of dogs. There were also symbols—circles, whorls, circles within circles, and Celtic knots. What remained of the bed was no longer wide enough to accommodate the knight in his armor— someone smaller, perhaps, but not Tormond.

He adjusted his body, squirming like a man attempting to get comfortable on an unyielding bed—like a man preparing to sleep for decades.

In his right hand, he clasped the hilt of his sword to his chest, the blade pointing toward his feet. In his left hand, he held a simple wooden cup—a cup containing a small amount—no more than a sip—of wine from one of the two small casks. A single taste, he'd informed her, was all it would take—just as it had for the stallion.

If no one disturbed their slumber, Tormond and Órd Dubh would awaken in sixty years.

I shall return in thirty-four years to awaken him. I will.
I will keep my promise.
Though I'll be so old.

His eyes gleamed in the light of the candle as he gazed at her. "Remember, once I drink the wine, I shall fall asleep. You must exit the cave immediately, quietly. Otherwise, you'll wake Órd Dubh. You must not touch either of us—neither me nor the horse. Flesh-on-flesh—'tis all it will take to wake me. To wake either of us. And if he wakes, he'll wake me."

He smiled at her, and there was gentleness and gratitude in that smile. "When the time comes, when you return, simply touch my hand. I'll awaken. Do you understand? Thirty-four years? Flesh-on-flesh?"

She opened her mouth to reply, but she didn't trust her voice, not with tears threatening to spill from her eyes. She mutely nodded instead.

"Thank you, Sister." He looked as if he might say more—she hoped he'd say more, that he'd release her from her promise—that he'd beg her to stay with him.. .

"Lead them safely to Scotland," he said.

"If I can. Perhaps they won't follow me. Or listen to me."

He gave a slight, thoughtful nod. Then he fixed her with an intense gaze. "But even if *they* will not go, *you* must go."

She nodded. "I will go."

He sighed. "Thank you." He shifted again, the mail rings of his armor scraping on the wooden planks. "Pray for me, Sister."

She nodded again, and that time, the tears spilled from her eyes. "Every Matins. Every Lauds. Every Prime," she said, listing the daily Offices of Prayer. "Every Terce, Sext, None, Vespers, and Compline. Every day and every night"—her voice caught—"for the next thirty-four years."

Her tears fell on his face. When the first drop hit him, he flinched slightly, but then his own eyes seemed to mist.

"Thank you," she said, "f-for s-saving my life."

"Oh, Sister. I—" He sighed. "I must sleep."

"Will you dream?"

He shook his head slightly. "No. But, when I awake . . . no matter how many times, no matter how many centuries . . . I will always remember you." A sad smile curved the corners of his lips. "'Til we meet again, Sister. *Insh'Allah.*"

I will be true. She'd made her choice. Her head had defeated her heart. And her heart ached. "*Insh'Allah,*" she repeated. "'Til we meet again." *I will not betray your trust. No matter the cost.*

He put the cup to his lips and drank.

His eyes closed.

The cup fell from his hand.

And silently, Maebh wept.

She knelt for a long time, so long she feared the other nuns might come looking for her.

She heard footsteps behind her.

"So that's the bastard, is it?"

The voice—that familiar voice, that hated voice—shattered the quiet of the cave.

Maebh lurched to her feet, then turned to behold—

"Da!" she cried.

Her father stood in the flickering light. Her father was a large man—strong and powerful as a bear—and just as terrifying. His clothes were travel stained and torn as if he had been following her through the forest. His face was twisted with rage and hate.

And in his hand, her father held his ring-pommeled sword. "Well, he's not so mighty now. Bewitched, is he?"

"Da! What are you—"

His hard eyes fixed on her. "And you! You stupid cow. You've ruined everything! Do you know what you cost me?" He took a step toward her. "My lands! They would've yielded tenfold. Tenfold! 'Tis what she promised me! Do you know what she'll do to me now? Do you know? Can that empty, female head of yours begin to comprehend? You were good for one thing! One thing! And I promised you to her!" He took another step toward her. "I promised you to her, you wretched little whore!"

The primal urge to flee shook Maebh, making her knees wobble. But she did not move. She did not give ground. *Protect Tormond.* Her eyes flickered toward the knight's axe lying on the stone floor, near Tormond's feet. *I'd never reach it in time. Must find a weapon. God, give me a weapon!*

"Her?" *Keep him talking. A stone!* "Promised me? To whom?"

"Mary!" her father snarled. "The Blessed Virgin, the Queen of Heaven."

Her eyes cast about for a stone. "Where are the other sisters? The ones outside?"

"Fled. Gone. Riding for their lives, once they saw me. They won't help you." He pointed with his sword at Tormond's head. "Now, move aside, stupid girl." He raised his sword and bared his teeth, growling like a bear.

"No!" *The dagger!* With trembling hands, Maebh drew the dagger from its hidden sheath. "Don't touch him!"

She saw the massive fist an instant before it smashed into her face. But even as her father struck her, she thrust the dagger into his chest.

Maebh crumpled to the cave floor. Dimly, as if hearing the faint rumble of distant thunder, she heard her father roar. A chaotic myriad of lights flashed before her eyes, but she saw the sword fall, heard it clatter on the ground.

Her father staggered, clutching at the dagger hilt protruding from his chest. He yanked it free. Blood gushed from the wound.

Vainly, her father covered the wound, attempting to prevent his life from spilling on the floor. He stared at the blood in horror.

Then his wild eyes fixed on her. "Stupid girl. You've killed me."

He raised the dagger and lurched toward her.

Maebh tried to crawl away.

But she was too slow. Far too slow.

He fell upon her, pinning her legs.

She saw the flash of the blood-covered steel, saw it arc downward, toward her.

She felt the blade pierce her abdomen.

Pain.

She had never known such pain, had never imagined such agony.

For a few moments, her entire existence was consumed with pain.

She grasped the hilt of the dagger and pulled it free of her body and let it fall.

With a scream of agony, she kicked and wriggled to free herself from under her father's corpse. All the while, blood continued to flow from her belly.

When she finally pulled herself clear, her breathing came in whimpering, rapid gasps. But somehow, the pain seemed to fade. The light in the cave also seemed to fade.

Dying. I'm dying.

Her eyes fixed on Tormond.

The knight slept on, wrapped in oblivion.

Tormond.

Tormond will save me. Touch his hand.

Flesh on flesh.

She stretched her fingers toward him.

But he was too far. Out of reach.

Her hand fell, landing on the wine cup.

The cup. Wine.

Magic.

Darkness closed around her.

She gripped the cup, lifted it.

Please. Just a sip. A single drop.

She pressed the cup to her lips, tilted it. But she tasted nothing.

Gone!

Sweetness trickled into her mouth, onto her tongue. She swallowed.

Tormond. Forgive –

Blackness enfolded her.

Chapter 7

Carmarthenshire, Wales: 1557 A.D.

Tormond awoke to absolute darkness.

And to profound, tomblike silence.

The moment he awoke, he knew he had failed.

Again.

He had failed to find his quarry. The Witches had escaped him.

Again.

And he also realized that Sister Mary Elizabeth had failed to awaken him, that without her touch — or the touch of some other living soul — the wine would have kept him sleeping for sixty years.

Twenty-six years. The Witches will have been sleeping for twenty-six years. Sleeping and hidden away.

Safe from me and the justice of God.

With a groan, he gripped the hilt of his sword and sat up. That groan was not the consequence of any physical discomfort — the magic wine had preserved him and healed his physical ailments — no, the groan was born of a soul-deep weariness.

Again.

How many more people will they kill?

How many souls will they corrupt?

He turned over and knelt, holding the sword in front of himself with both hands — the sword serving as his crucifix. The links of the mail covering his knees pressed against his flesh, even cushioned as his knees were by the padded breeches he wore between his flesh and the mail. It was painful, of course, but he embraced the pain, hoping it would bring him closer to God.

As our Lord suffered for my sins, so let me suffer in His service.

He sighed deeply and began to pray.

"Ego gratias ago tibi, O Deus, propter misericordiam tuam . . ." He continued in Latin, " . . . and for allowing me to continue in

Thy service. I have . . . failed again, O God. I have overslept. I relied on . . ." *Nae. I will nae lay blame upon her.*

"Perhaps, she has died." His voice broke. *It has been sixty years.* If nothing disturbed his magical slumber, it was always sixty years. *She is surely dead by now.* "If—If so, O Holy Father, I pray that Thou wilt take her to Thy bosom. Shelter her in Thy tender and merciful hand. Perhaps, she was ill and was not able to make the journey. Or perhaps, some other circumstance prevented her. Perhaps, she was afraid." But he could not imagine Maebh O Broin to have ever surrendered to fear. "No. Not afraid. Never that."

He paused. "O God, forgive me for my sin. Forgive me for my arrogance. Sister Mary Elizabeth would never succumb to fear. I have never seen greater courage, O God. No, not on the battlefields and nor in the sieges of the Holy Land. Ask her to pray for me . . ."

✠·✠·✠

Maebh awoke to absolute darkness.

But not to silence.

Instead of the silence of the tomb, she heard a voice. A tender voice. A familiar voice. Tormond. Pleading with the Almighty.

" . . . for my sin. Forgive me for my arrogance. Sister Mary Elizabeth would never succumb to fear. I have never seen greater courage, O God. No, not on the battlefields nor in the sieges of the Holy Land. Ask her to pray for me, for I know that Thou wilt hear her saintly prayers."

He's talking about me?

Brave? Me?

I almost betrayed him. Almost.

But I didn't —

She gasped and sat up. *Alive! I'm alive!*

"Ki va là?" His tone was menacing as he uttered the now familiar challenge, and Maebh heard the rasp of mail dragged across wood. "Ditez ou mourez!"

"Tormond!" She shrank back from the sound of his voice. "'Tis I! Maebh! M-Mary Elizabeth!"

"Sister?" Menace had been replaced by wonder. "Sister?" And by hope.

"Aye, Tormond." She laughed. "'Tis I."

He laughed as well.

63

She heard more rustling in the dark, then metal striking stone. A spark. A flash—almost blinding in the tomblike darkness—as if her eyes had not beheld light in years. In decades.

A flame caught near the floor.

The light of a single candle flooded the chamber.

"Sister!" he cried, his smile wide, teeth gleaming in the candlelight. He looked as if he might scoop her from the cave floor and embrace her.

He peered at her face. "So . . . young." His eyes crinkled in puzzlement, then widened in alarm. "What has happened? You have awoken me too soon! Is there some wrong I must—"

"Oh, Tormond!" Sudden tears spilled from her eyes. "I have failed—"

"You are wounded!" He pointed at her—at her belly. "The blood." Then he shook his head. "No, 'tis black. So black."

Maebh clutched both hands to her abdomen.

And felt a gaping hole in the skirt of her habit—no cloth— only bare flesh. Bare flesh—unmarred by any gaping dagger wound—covered by a flakey substance that crumbled to dust as she touched it. *Blood? My blood?*

Dried to powder after . . . "Sixty years." The words came out in a whisper of amazement.

"Sixty years?" His voice boomed through the chamber. "Sixty—"

Suddenly, he was kneeling before her. His eyes flickered to the wine cup lying beside her, then to the dagger—the blade of which had cankered with rust. Then his gaze locked onto her belly. "Forgive me, Sister." He extended his hand toward her stomach.

She flinched only slightly as his fingers probed her exposed flesh. Nothing improper—not a man touching a woman's exposed flesh—merely a soldier examining a comrade's wound.

A soldier's concern. Nothing more.

"No scar." He nodded, withdrawing his fingers. "Good. You bled a bit. That is why your skirt is damaged—the wool rotted away with the blood's corruption." Then his eyes went back to the rusted dagger, and he frowned in puzzlement once more. "Isn't that the dagger I found for you?" He blinked. "Surely, you did not— No. You would not—" He looked at her once more. Then his jaw dropped as his gaze moved beyond her. "Sancta Maria, Mater—" He quickly crossed himself.

Maebh turned, following his gaze.

Her scream reverberated through the cave.

Little flesh remained on the skeleton. Scraps of desiccated skin stretched across her father's skull. Straggling wisps of hair and beard lingered. Black, empty eye sockets stared at her accusingly. *Stupid girl,* they seemed to say. *You've killed me.* The lower jaw hung at an unnatural angle—motionless. Most of his clothing had rotted away or crumbled to dust—except for the boots. Her father's fine leather boots were dry and cracked, like parchment left in the sun. Withered legs—barely more than bones—protruded from the gaping tops of those boots.

The candlelight shifted, shortening the eerie shadows cast by the corpse.

Tormond must have stood. He stepped closer to the body, made the sign of the cross, then squatted in front of her father's remains.

Tormond turned his own head about, examining—not just the cadaver, but the entire scene.

"Your father." Tormond had not asked a question, merely stated a fact.

Maebh tore her eyes away from her da and focused on Tormond. "H-how did you know?"

Tormond shifted, picking an object from the cave floor.

Maebh heard the ring of metal sliding on stone.

The knight held aloft her father's sword. "Irish sword." He pointed at the pommel. "You can tell by the ring pommel." Tormond grunted. "Beautiful piece." With a contempt that belied his words, he dropped the weapon to the floor. A loud metallic clang echoed in the chamber. He gestured with a hand, sweeping it in front of the body. "From what's left of the clothes, I'd say he was a wealthy man." He grunted again. "He'd have to be wealthy to possess a sword such as that."

Maebh swallowed, suddenly feeling she might vomit. A small, distant part of her wondered if there could possibly be anything in her stomach after six decades. "He—He followed us. Followed me. Here."

"He was going to murder me," Tormond said, his voice cold as the tomb. "While I slept." Tormond turned his face to Maebh. "You stopped him." His face was cast in shadow.

Maebh could not see his eyes. "Aye." Bile rose in her throat. She felt as if she might drown in it. "I"—she swallowed, but the acid would not go back down—"killed him."

Tormond nodded. He brought the candle forward.

At last, she could see his face again.

His eyes were moist, kindly. "You're so like him."

"Like him?" The bile surged once more. "My da?"

He chuckled softly, shaking his head. "No, no, no. Not that wretched vermin. Declan. You are like Declan. Your ancestor. My friend."

Tears spilled from her eyes. The urge to retch was gone. Replaced by another urge.

A far more dangerous urge.

She desperately wanted to go to the knight, cling to him. Be held by him.

No! It cannot be. It cannot. "Wh-what? How? My eyes?"

He smiled. "Those too. But I was referring to your courage."

"Courage?" *When he was praying, he spoke of my courage.* "I'm not brave."

He laughed then. Softly, but heartily. "Oh, Sister! You stood, armed only with a wee dagger, before a man with a great sword. You! A maid. And he a man—if man he can be called. And judging by the size of his bones, a large and mighty man. And you stood between that knave and me." He shook his head, but the smile remained. "If that's not courage, I have never seen it."

"He . . . He was going to kill you." Her voice dropped to a whisper, and she lowered her face and eyes. "What else could I have done?"

"Nothing less than what you did." He extended a hand, gently placing a finger under her chin and raising her face once more.

Her eyes met his.

He sighed. "'Tis who you are."

Maebh felt heat rise in her cheeks. "I am . . ." *I am a Bride of Christ. And he is a religious.*

"You are Declan's heir. You are his legacy. You are"—he cocked his head to the side—"if you will permit me, Sister Mary Elizabeth . . . and though I may never name you so again . . . this day, I do name you Maebh O Broin, *Christi Innupta Scutae*, Shield-maiden of Christ." His eyes shone with admiration.

Shield-maiden? A thrill shivered through her.

"Are you cold?" Concern replaced admiration in Tormond's eyes. "'Tis no wonder! Your dress!"

Maebh looked down at her habit, truly looking at it for the first time.

The sleeves were gone, at least to the elbow. A large hole gaped across her chest, exposing an indecent expanse of bosom. And, of course, her belly was bare.

Everywhere the blood touched. Da's blood. My blood.
Rotted away.

One hand clutched the remnants of her bodice, the other went to her abdomen in a vain attempt to cover herself. The more she clutched at the edges of the decayed fabric, the more it seemed to crumble under her fingers. She tried to wrap herself in her cloak, but the heavy cloak had taken far more damage than her ruined habit.

Heat blossomed in her cheeks anew. She averted her eyes.

"Here, Sister," Tormond said, his voice unmarred gentleness. "Take my cloak."

She felt the cloak settle over her, covering her, protecting her. *'Tis not just the cloak. He is protecting me. Once again.* "Thank you," she whispered, clutching the cloak, white with a red cross, around her.

The loud and sudden snort of the horse startled her.

She stifled a shriek.

Tormond grinned. "Well, look who's finally awake!" He stood and strode to the warhorse. The stallion whinnied, a surprisingly low-pitched sound that echoed in the darkness.

Maebh could see the animal moving, as it stamped and shook itself—a great beast rousing from a long sleep. The white and red caparison covering the horse's body armor rippled like a flag fluttering in a wind.

Tormond sheathed his sword, then patted Órd Dubh's neck beneath the chamfron armoring the animal's head. "Madainn mhath, seann charaid." The knight's voice was gentle as he spoke to the fearsome beast. He turned his face to Maebh. "He won't be hungry just yet." His brow furrowed. "Are *you* hungry, Sister?"

Maebh's stomach still roiled from the shock of killing her father. I have just slept for sixty years. I should be hungry.

I should need to relieve myself.

But it feels as if no time at all has passed.

As if I just killed Da. Moments ago.

Sixty years? Truly?

She shook her head. "No."

"Hunger will come. Just as with any waking. But we must wait still a while before we break our long fast." He raised a finger. "First, I must see what the Sergeants have left for me."

"The Sergeants?"

He nodded. "I told you about them."

"Aye, of course." *His informants. Operating in secret. Hiding in the shadows.* "They have been here? The Sergeants?"

"One of them has, at least." He strode toward the mouth of the chamber. "He should have left me a message."

Maebh rose to her feet, gathering the crusader's cloak around herself. She followed him, carefully avoiding her father's corpse. "The message. Where is it? How will you find it?"

"Voila!" He knelt just inside the chamber entrance. "Hold this." He handed the candle to her.

As his fingers touched hers, she suppressed a sudden trembling. She felt no answering tremor from him.

She knelt beside him.

He lifted a clay pot, a foot tall and half a foot wide, from the tunnel floor. The pot was lacquered black and covered with dust. It appeared simple in design, but well made. Tormond brushed the away the dust. Maebh could see that the lid was emblazoned with a simple red cross. Rather than removing the lid immediately, Tormond tilted the pot in his hands, examining the vessel.

Why doesn't he open it?

At last, he nodded as if satisfied. "The wax seal is intact." With that, he smashed the pot upon the ground.

Maebh nearly jumped in surprise. "Why?"

"As our Lord has said, the outward vessel does not matter." He flicked aside the shards, revealing a roll of parchment. "Only what is inside."

He unrolled the parchment.

Maebh bent to look over his shoulder. It wasn't that she could read the words—she was simply a lass. Why would anyone teach a girl to read? But she wanted to see anyway.

And though she couldn't read, she knew the appearance of proper letters. And these were not proper letters. They resembled nothing she had ever seen. "Is—Is it French?" *French would look different, wouldn't it?*

"No. 'Tis— I do not know the word in Irish. It is a type of . . . secret language—aye, close enough—a secret language used only by Templars and the Sergeants."

"What does it say?"

"It says the Witches—at least one of them, the Mother—her face is unmistakable—she was sighted in one of the Bavarian duchies. Munich. This was in . . . 1543? That means their cycle of sleep was disrupted. They were awakened early." He chuckled. "Just as I was. Last time. Or perhaps they lingered an extra twelve years. And that has never happened—they have never lingered so long. At least not as far as I am aware."

Maebh frowned in concentration. "What year is it now?" *'Twas 1497. Sixty years! Has it really been so long? It seems as if it were only moments ago.* Maebh glanced quickly back at her father's wasted remains. *Sixty years.* She swallowed, then added quickly in her head. She might not be able to read, but, like any good Irish farmgirl, Maebh O Broin could figure numbers—"1557?"

He nodded, stroking his beard. "Aye. 1557. I have missed them by fourteen years. They will next awaken in 1603. That is, if nothing else disrupts the cycle."

"What will you do?"

He shrugged. "Go to Bavaria. What else can I do? I cannot wait for them to awaken in . . . forty-six years. The first Executioner— my predecessor—tried that. And still they managed to elude him. Aye, go to Bavaria and hunt for their hiding place. I'll most likely fail. I have always failed to find their lair"—he swept an arm around the cave—"unless 'twas long after they'd abandoned it."

His predecessor? That's twice now he's mentioned him. "The first Executioner?"

He nodded, though he continued to peruse the parchment left by the mysterious Sergeants. "Aye. He was a knight, but not a Templar. Not at first. He joined the Order late in life. Peredur was his name. He was Welsh. At least, I *think* he was Welsh. He also died at Acre. He was . . . quite old when he fell. He"—Tormond swallowed—"died, covering my escape. Cut down by a Mamluk scimitar, his body trampled by the cursed Muslim's horse." He growled, but a tear swelled at the corner of his eye. "He thought his life a supreme failure. He had failed to execute the Witches. Aye, he failed"—Tormond lowered his voice—"just as I have failed again and again." Tormond shook his head slowly. "But he died with more courage and honor than—" The knight sighed deeply. "God grant that I may die as well as Peredur."

Peredur? She tried the unusual name on her tongue. "Peredur. His name sounds familiar."

He blinked, turning his gaze back to her. "You are Irish, not Welsh. And not English. Lass, have you heard of King Arthur?"

She shook her head. "Arthur?" And then it dawned on her. "Not 'Arthur.' At least not in my language. He is called Artur. King Artur and his Knights of the Table."

"Aye. Artur. That would be the name."

"But what does Artur have to do with . . ."

Tormond chuckled. "Peredur came to be known, at least in the stories, by another name. Percival. I do not know how it is pronounced in Irish."

"Sir Percival!" Maebh's hands went to her mouth. "Peredur is Sir Percival? Percival and the Holy Grail?"

Tormond laughed softly. "'Twas not the Cup of Christ he sought through the centuries. 'Twas the *Witches*. The Witches who murdered Merlin."

"Merlin?" *The magician? Murdered?* "The Witches? I thought Nimue was the . . ."

"Aye. That was the name of *one* of them in that day. The Mother. That was the name she went by back then."

"The Mother?"

He nodded. "Three Witches — the Maiden, the Mother, and the Crone."

Maiden, Mother, and Crone. She gasped as understanding dawned within her. "The Morrigan!"

He cocked his head and eyed her. "You know this name?"

A chill ripped through her like a spear of ice. "Know them? They are a tale used to frighten children, to whisper on All Hallows Eve. On Samhain, when all the forces of evil walk the night." She pointed a trembling finger at him. "You hunt . . . the Morrigan?"

"Aye." He drew the word out slowly as in a weary sigh. "I hunt the Three Witches of legend. 'Tis like grasping at smoke. Like trying to slay the wind with a sword."

"It sounds so . . ." *So hopeless.*

"Hopeless?" he asked, as if he had heard her thoughts. "In the stories, Percival pursued a hopeless quest for the Holy Grail. In the end — not in the stories, but in the waking world — he died a noble death." He shrugged his shoulders. "Peredur never found his quarry, but he found eternal glory. And now I continue his quest, his holy mission. Hopeless?" He shook his head, smiling. "My hope is in my Lord. My faith is in Christ. If I live or if I die in His service, 'tis enough."

His eyes locked with hers. And those eyes hardened. "I desire nothing else in this mortal life."

Nothing else? She gave him a shaky nod. "Of course. Nothing else." *He is a religious.*

A religious.

And I am a nun, also a religious. "Nothing else." She lowered her eyes. "So, we . . . go to Bavaria?"

"I will go to Bavaria," he replied. "I will go. But first, we must —"

"You will go —" Fear skittered up her spine like a spider. "But — But I'm going with you!"

He shook his head slowly, but a kindly smile lifted his countenance. "Oh, Sister, where I go, you cannot —"

"I cannot follow you?" Her fear was chased away by another emotion — the anger of her Irish temper. "I've already followed you! Through years! Through darkness!" She pointed an accusing finger in the direction of her father's bones. "Through blood."

"Sister, I'm taking you to Scotland, there to find a suitable abbey for—"

"No! Tormond MacDonald, you will not—"

"You cannot come with me."

Anger and outrage had not worked.

And so, Maebh tried a different strategy. She recited words she'd heard read to her—read to her from The Holy Scriptures. "Ne adverseris mihi ut relinquam te et abeam: quocumque enim perrexeris, pergam: et ubi morata fueris, et ego pariter morabor. Populus tuus populus meus, et Deus tuus Deus meus. Quæ te terra morientem susceperit, in ea moriar: ibique locum accipiam sepulturæ. Hæc mihi faciat Dominus, et hæc addat, si non sola mors me et te separaverit."

Entreat me not to leave thee, she translated in her mind, *or to return from following after thee: for whither thou goest, I will go; and where thou lodgest, I will lodge: thy people shall be my people, and thy God my God. Where thou diest, will I die, and there will I be buried: the Lord do so to me, and more also, if ought but death part thee and me.*

Tormond appeared to be genuinely astonished. "You have read the Book of Ruth? You can read?"

She laughed. A little. "Of course not! I can't read any more than any other lass. Where I come from, lassies are not taught letters. Are Scottish girls taught to read?"

He laughed then. "Scottish *laddies* are barely taught to read! And usually only the sons of chiefs. Most lads learn a trade or farming." He shrugged. "Myself? I learned the sword, the axe, the dirk, the spear, the bow"—he gestured toward Órd Dubh—"and the horse. But, aye, I learned my letters. Lassies? No. They have . . . other things to learn."

Like how to manipulate men? Is that what you're a-thinking, Tormond MacDonald?

"But you"—he pointed at her—"you know *Ruth.*"

She felt heat blossom in her cheeks. "'Twas a story read to me by our parish priest. I loved that story! I begged him to read it to me again and again. I committed that one passage to memory."

"You were inspired by the story?"

"Aye! By Ruth's courage. Her loyalty. She left everything behind—her people, her tongue, her gods, even the grave of her husband. All to follow and serve her mother-in-law and the one true God. And she became the ancestress of God! Through her, came the Lord Himself."

"Is this why you became a nun?"

She averted her eyes, feeling the heat in her cheeks rise anew. "No. I . . . became a nun to avoid . . . *marriage* to Sir Guy. And then my da—" She choked on the word as she glanced in the direction of the corpse. "M-my d-da—"

"Your father tricked you, sold you into that thrice-damned order."

She nodded mutely, tears falling from her eyes.

"We shall find you a *new* order, Sister. A *holy* order."

She looked at him with pleading eyes. "But 'thy people shall be my people.'"

"My people are dead. My family. My brothers of the Temple. All dead."

"My people are dead too! Can you not understand, Tormond MacDonald? You are my people now!" *You're all I have remaining in this world!*

He narrowed his eyes. "We shall talk more of this later. But first"—he stood abruptly—"I must do my best to find you a suitable gown. I doubt I'll be able to find a nun's habit, but I shall do my—"

She shot to her feet, nearly extinguishing the candle as she wrapped the knight's cloak around her ruined habit. "You're leaving me here? Alone?"

"Forgive me, Sister, but I must. For a little while only. You can hardly travel while"—he suddenly averted his eyes—"covered in naught but, well, little more than my cloak."

She clutched the cloak even more tightly about herself, keenly aware of her near nakedness. She tried to think of any argument, any excuse, that would prevent him from leaving her behind. Alone. In the cave. With her father's—

"Don't leave me here! Not with"—she pointed to the body with a trembling finger—"him!"

Tormond turned his head and stared at the corpse. He let out a grunt—or was it a growl?—and nodded. "Very well. But your legs—I don't know how we'll keep those covered."

She gave him a puzzled look. "My legs?"

"You'll be riding Órd Dubh."

"What? No! I can walk."

He chuckled and shook his head. "No lady shall walk while I ride."

"Lady?" *He's talking about me?* "I'm no lady. Not anymore. I'm just—"

"You are a woman. Highborn or lowborn, it matters not. To a knight, to me, you are a lady." He smiled. "And so shall you ever —" He leaped to his feet, drawing his sword. "What is this?"

He strode past her, into the tunnel. "Stay back," he commanded. He paused in the passageway, looking about, peering into the darkness.

Maebh scrambled upright, her heart pounding in sudden terror. "What? What is it?" She glanced at the cankered dagger, the weapon she'd used to kill her father.

"Silence!" Tormond hissed.

Maebh nearly shrieked as Tormond rushed at her and snatched the candle from her hand.

"Someone has been here," he whispered. "They may be here still."

With sword drawn and candle held high, he quickly inspected the chamber. He patted the warhorse under the beast's neck, speaking softly in the knight's native tongue. The horse snorted, but stood in its place.

Tormond glanced at her. "Stay here." Then he left the chamber, taking the light with him.

Maebh was alone. In the dark. With the corpse.

Heedless of the order she'd been given, Maebh shuffled after Tormond, as if pursued by her father's ghost. Frightened though she was, she was forced to move slowly, feeling her way in the dark with her feet. Her hands met nothing but air, yet she waved them in front of herself.

The cloak parted, and cold air raised goosebumps on her exposed skin, making her shiver.

But modesty was the least of her concerns, and her trembling was not entirely due to the gaping holes in her habit.

Da is not here. He's not!

There is no ghost. No ghost!

Just bones. Old bones.

Not Da.

I killed him. I killed Da!

She stumbled in the darkness. Clutching at the air, Maebh fell with a shriek.

Pain shot up her knees and right shoulder as she struck the floor. Her scream seemed to echo through the darkness, coming from everywhere and nowhere at once. She forced herself to her feet, but in the darkness, she could no longer tell left from right.

She was no longer certain in which direction lay the door.

Tormond? The door? Where?

That way?

She lurched after him.

And fell again.

She caught herself that time.

Panting, almost sobbing, she tried to crawl toward the exit, feeling her way in the blackness. *Where is it? Which way? Which way?*

Her hand fell upon something—hard and leathery and hairy.

Da! Da's head!

She screamed.

She tried to fling the skull away, but her fingers clenched, seizing and gripping the very object she feared.

"Sister!"

The light returned.

And the light fell upon the skull gripped in her hands.

Her father's dark eye sockets stared up at her accusingly.

Maebh screamed again, finally casting the skull out of her hands.

It clattered as it bounced, then rolled along the cave floor.

And then Tormond was kneeling beside her, his arm around her. "I'm sorry," he whispered. "I should not have left you."

Maebh trembled. Then she melted into his embrace, burying her face in his beard. "Why did you go?"

"I'm sorry. I— Someone had been in here. In the cave. They left something behind. I had to check the tunnel." He held her more tightly. "You must have been so frightened."

She snuffled. "I heard you praying. You said I was . . . I was brave."

He laughed then. "O Sister! Being brave — it has nothing to do with — Sister, all of us know fear."

All of us? She pulled her face from his beard and looked up at him, searching his eyes in the candlelight. "Even you?"

He chuckled, then squeezed her. "When I heard your scream, I was so very . . . I should not have left you behind."

"Then . . . you will not leave me behind again?"

He sighed. Then he chuckled softly. "You know 'tis not that simple. There is the matter of your habit, your clothing."

Maebh was suddenly aware of her bare flesh pressed against his tabard. It wasn't flesh-on-flesh, but it was still improper. And so was being locked in an embrace with a man — no, far worse than a man — a *religious* man.

Maebh pulled away from him, covering herself with the cloak. "I'll be fine. I can walk. There's a village nearby. Carmarthen, I think 'tis called? Perhaps we can find something there."

He nodded. "Perhaps." He stood, sheathing his sword.

Alarm shot through her. "Where are you going?"

He reached down for her. "The intruder left something behind. A wooden chest. I am going to examine it." He grinned. "Are you coming, Sister?"

She smiled back. *That's better.* She took his proffered hand and stood, carefully gathering the cloak around herself. As she did, she looked down and beheld her father's headless corpse at her feet.

And she was afraid.

But she was with Tormond. And with Tormond, she could face her fear. *Da is not here. They're just old bones.*

With a start, she realized she was still holding onto the religious's hand, still holding onto him for support. She jerked her hand away as if his touch burned her.

In a sense, it did burn her.

I am a Bride of Christ.

Seemingly unaware of her discomfort, Tormond turned away and strode toward the chamber exit.

Maebh followed after him.

A few feet beyond the shards of the Sergeants' jar lay a small wooden chest, perhaps a foot-and-a-half in width, a foot in length, and nearly a foot in height.

Tormond knelt beside it, again giving Maebh the candle to hold. He examined the chest without touching it.

The box appeared to be simple in design, but well made. A single letter had been carved into the wood. Though Maebh had never been taught to read, she knew the name of that letter.

"*A?*" she asked. "What does it mean?"

Tormond shook his head. "I do not know." He continued to examine the box. "Sealed with wax. Just like the Sergeants' urn. But there is not as much dust on the lid. It hasn't been here as long."

She knelt beside him. "Why don't you open it?"

"It could be poisoned. A small needle, perhaps. Hidden." He drew a dagger and pointed at the box with the blade. "I must use caution."

Using the dagger, he pried open the lid.

Inside the box lay a scroll and two purses — both apparently bursting with coins — all three lying atop some green cloth.

Tormond gasped.

"What?" Maebh cried. "What is it?"

"The scroll." Wonder suffused his voice. "It bears my name. And yours as well."

Maebh dropped to her knees beside him. She stared at the scroll in wonder even as the meaning of the neat lettering eluded her. "What? How?"

"How?" He shook his head slowly. "I don't know."

"Witchcraft?" She shivered. *The chest was covered in dust!*

His only reply was a grunt.

"What name?" she asked. "For me? What name? Mary Elizabeth?"

He shook his head again. "It says, 'Maebh O Broin.'" His voice dropped to a whisper. "And beneath your name, 'Shield-maiden of Christ.'"

Maebh gasped at hearing the fierce and noble-sounding title Tormond had given her only minutes before. "It says that?"

He nodded slowly. "Aye. It does."

"How could they possibly know that name?"

He shook his head. "Either by the power of Heaven" — he, the mighty Knight of the Temple, visibly shuddered — "or by the power of Hell."

Chapter 8

Dread seized Maebh like an icy claw, causing her to tremble. But with that dread, she also felt a thrill of anticipation. *He — whoever wrote this message — knows me. Knows my name. How could that be?* "What . . . does it say?" She stared over Tormond's shoulder as he unrolled the parchment.

Tormond stared at the writing. He opened his mouth, then shut it, scowling. "'Tis Latin, but . . ."

"Aye. But what?" she prompted.

He shook his head. "Well, 'tis Latin, but 'tis also . . . strange."

"Strange? What do you mean?"

He grimaced. "It reads . . . It does not read like the Latin I learned from the priests. 'Tis as if the writer . . . He writes like Julius Caesar. I read Caesar's *Bellum Gallicum* when I was a squire."

"Who is that? Did this Julius . . . Did he write it?" *If Tormond was a squire, this Julius would be long dead, wouldn't he?*

Tormond glanced at her, then shook his head. "I don't think so. This parchment is too fresh. No, 'tis as if . . . How can I explain? Do you remember Sir Guy?"

Maebh shuddered.

"Of course, you do," he hastened to add. "Forgive me. I meant . . . When I spoke with him . . . and with the other noble vermin in the abbey . . . we spoke in French."

Maebh nodded. "Aye, you spoke in French. I couldn't understand the words."

Tormond nodded. "But I *did* understand the words. Most of them. 'Twas not easy. For me, at least. Perhaps they had the same difficulty with my words, may they all burn in Hell." He paused, shaking his head. "No. May God have mercy on their souls. Aye. Even theirs." He sighed. "Their French was . . . *newer* than mine, I suppose. Languages change over the centuries. The Latin we speak in the Mass. It is newer than the way the ancient Romans spoke it. Or wrote it. This writing" —he waved the parchment— "is like that. Like the Romans would have written. The words, the way they are" —he paused—"I don't know the word in Irish. They are arranged and formed differently."

"I don't understand."

"I'm saying, this is written as if the writer learned to speak Latin only in the ancient way."

"As if he didn't learn in the Church?"

Tormond nodded. "Aye."

"Not of the Church? Of the devil, then?" Maebh made the sign of the cross.

Tormond shrugged. "I don't know. Please. Let me read it."

"Isn't that what I've been telling you to do?" Maebh tried to keep the growing exasperation out of her voice. She tried, but . . . *Why is he making this so complicated?* "Please, Tormond, what does it say?"

Tormond pursed his lips, apparently annoyed. He muttered something Maebh could not quite catch, but she thought she heard something about "impatience."

Tormond began to read.

"'You do not know me, but I am your friend. Inside this'" — he paused—"I don't know this word. Perhaps, it means 'box' or 'chest?' Aye. Perhaps. 'Inside this *box*, you will find gold and clothing for . . . you both. It is . . .'" His brow furrowed. "'Suitable,' perhaps? Aye, 'It is suitable for this time. You must not travel as religious and nun. Tormond, you must shave your beard or cut it short. Your beard will be . . .'" He nodded. "'Your beard will be noticed.' Aye, that is what he means. 'You must be hidden. This land is torn by religious strife. It is unsafe for a religious or a nun in many parts of this kingdom. Learn the common tongue of Britannia.'"

"The common tongue of Britannia?" Maebh asked. "Does he mean English?"

Tormond nodded, then continued, "'This is the tongue that will be of most worth to you in the future. Go not to Germania. Germania holds nothing—"

"Germania?" Maebh interrupted again. "Where is Germania?"

"In ancient times, 'twas a region that encompassed many . . ." Tormond shook his head. "I think he means Bavaria. Go not to Ba—"

Maebh gasped. "How would he know you were—" She shivered. "He knew about your naming me Shield-maiden." In spite of her fear, that name still sent a thrill through her. She smiled. *He thinks me brave.* She squared her shoulders in determination. "So where shall we go?"

"Hold a moment," Tormond said. "There's more. 'Go not to Germania. Germania holds nothing for you. When next you wake, your prey will have returned to Britannia. Remain in Cambria until your next sleep.'"

"Cambria?"

Tormond nodded. "Wales. I think he wants us to stay here. In Wales." He continued reading, "'You must . . .'" His mouth worked, and he cocked his head to the side as if he were puzzling out the words. "'You must *prevent* a great evil in this land. God has preserved you for this purpose. Tormond, the shield-maiden has something vital to teach you. Keep her at your side.'"

Maebh gasped again. *Me? Teach him? What could I possibly have to teach—*

"'Maebh,'" Tormond read on, "'the soldier of Christ has something vital to teach you. Never leave him. It is the will of God that you two journey together.'"

Tormond paused, letting those words drift away into the hush of the cave.

As the silence lingered, Maebh felt a small thrill of hope.

Tormond said, "It appears, Sister, as if you get your wish." He looked at her, a smile playing at the corners of his mouth. "We are to journey together."

"I"—she swallowed—"I did not . . ." *I desire nothing more at that moment than to remain with you, but . . .* She swallowed again, then forced the words past her gritted teeth. "What if this is not of God? What if . . . this is witchcraft? Of the devil?"

Tormond made the sign of the cross. "God forbid." He paused. "But now that I think on it, Bavaria does seem a fool's errand. I have missed the prey." He frowned. "Again."

He growled, sighed, and then resumed reading, "'Trust not in any mortal who calls himself or herself holy. Trust in God the Father and in His Son, Jesus. Listen to the whisperings of the Holy Spirit. Tormond, you know His voice, for He has led you in times past. He

80

shall lead you in times to come. He shall never lead you astray. His whisperings told you to send the nuns to Caledonia." He looked at Maebh. "That means Scotland." He turned back to the parchment. "'You saved many of them, because you listened.'"

Tormond stopped reading.

Maebh waited for the knight to continue for several seemingly interminable moments. The silence closed in around her. "Is that all?"

"'Many,'" Tormond said, shaking his head slowly. "'Many,'" he repeated, scowling as if the word tasted like bile in his mouth. "But not *all*." He bowed his head. "Why didn't they listen? Perhaps if I'd stayed . . . I could have led them to Scotland myself." A growl escaped his lips. "How many died? How many did I *fail* to save?"

Gently, Maebh laid a hand on his mail-covered arm. She could feel his trembling, but she could not tell if he shook with rage or sorrow. She squeezed his arm. "I was supposed to lead them to Scotland. I. Not you. If anyone failed to—"

He shook his head. "I am a knight. I am supposed to protect the weak."

"Oh, Tormond, you cannot save everyone."

"No. I cannot." He dashed a tear from his eye. "Fighting is all I know. Fighting and killing. And killing saves no—"

"Oh, Tormond!" She was gripped with a sudden impulse to put her arms around him, to hold him. To comfort him.

But Tormond shook himself, displacing her hand, dampening her dangerous impulse. "Others lead people to salvation. My calling is to kill. To kill in the name of God. I have sometimes wondered . . ." He paused, took one shuddering breath, then continued to read, "'Tormond, my son, you have done well.'" He muttered something in his native tongue, before reading on, "'You fill me with joy and pride.'"

He stopped, staring at the parchment.

He called Tormond, "my son." But Tormond's father must be long dead. Was this written by a priest? But Tormond said 'twas not written in the language of the Church. "Is there more?"

Tormond pointed at a solitary letter, larger than the rest, and written in a bold hand at the bottom. "Only this—'A.'"

81

Maebh considered the letter. "The same as on the lid of the box. A? What does it mean?"

"'Tis . . . I don't know the word in Irish. 'Tis most likely the first letter of the writer's name—his surname, probably. One thing I do know—'tis not from the Sergeants of the Temple."

"Do you trust it? Will you . . . Should you . . . Should *we* heed it?"

Tormond sighed. "The advice is good." He cocked his head and looked her in the eyes. "What do you think?"

She blinked at him. "You're asking *my* opinion?"

He grinned. "Has no one asked you for your opinion before, Sister?"

"Not often," she muttered. "No one—no *man*, to be sure— ever cared what I thought."

He chuckled then. "From my short experience with you—at least while waking—I have not known you to keep your thoughts to yourself."

Heat blossomed in her cheeks. She lowered her gaze.

"Are all Irish lassies so free with their tongues?"

That brought her eyes back to meet his.

His grin widened, and his eyes twinkled in the candlelight. "Or just you, Sister?"

She gave him an icy stare. "Perhaps, 'tis because you foolish men will not listen. Tell me, Brother Tormond, are all Scottish men as stubborn as—as pigs led to slaughter?"

"Pigs led to—" He threw back his head and laughed, his mirth echoing through the chamber. Then he looked at her, his grin almost as wide as his bearded face. "Ah, Sister! Now tell me, pray, why should not a pig resist being led to the butcher's knife, not when he knows what awaits him? And pigs *do* know. Aye! Somehow they always know when their day has come."

Maebh felt as if her cheeks were burning.

"Tell me, Sister, is this your *own* proverb? Or did you learn it from someone else? Some other *wise* Irish woman?" He laughed again, shaking his head. "'Stubborn as a pig led to slaughter!' I *like* it!"

But Maebh was not going to back down, not when her Irish temper was hot as a smithy's forge. She stood, towering above him as he continued to kneel on the floor. "'Tis a *fine* proverb!" She cast about in her mind seeking some justification. Any justification. "A pig exists for two reasons only—to breed other pigs and to be slaughtered and eaten!"

"The breeding part, I understand," he said, grinning toothily. "Most men live but to breed—religious and priests excluded, I grant you—to breed and to eat. But not to *be* eaten. Don't you agree?"

"Oh, shut your wicked mouth!" She bent quickly, placed her free hand on his head, and shoved with all her might.

With a cry, Tormond toppled backward, landing on his back. And lying on his back, staring up at the cave ceiling, he laughed all the louder. "Ah, Sister! I haven't laughed like this in a long time. Not in centuries." He sat up, grinning at her. "I thank you. Stubborn as a pig led—" Again his mirth filled the cave.

Maebh continued to glare at him, until a titter burst from her lips. She couldn't stop it. Soon she was laughing as well. She knelt beside him, grinning as she giggled. "Well, have you ever seen a hog led to slaughter? It squeals and screams and fights as if—as if it's going to be killed!"

Fresh peals of laughter—pure, cathartic laughter—echoed in the chamber. Órd Dubh whinnied loudly and stomped a hoof as if joining in.

✠·✠·✠

Tormond, dressed in a linen shirt, a close-fitting, sleeveless, leather vest, woolen hose, and ridiculous, voluminous, short breeches—all provided by the mysterious A—sat on a large stone outside the mouth of the cave. He watched as Órd Dubh, also no longer wearing his armor—the horse's barding had been left in the cave—contentedly cropped the grass several yards away.

Tormond stood and adjusted the short breeches. They didn't even come down to midthigh. And the pants were thickly padded. Very thickly padded. "I look a fool," he muttered. "As if I'd stuck my legs through pumpkins!" He growled and sat once more on the rock. "A pox on the vanity of men!"

I hope Maebh—Sister Mary Elizabeth—fares better with her gown. He glanced toward the hidden mouth of the cave—not for the first time. A part of him—a part he dared not give voice to, not even in his most secret thoughts—was eagerly anticipating her appearance. He had tried—oh, how he'd tried!—not to imagine how she would look in clothes that weren't designed to hide her feminine curves. Clothes that might, perhaps, emphasize her bosom or her waist and hips, rather than cloak them.

Think on something else, laddie. Anything else. She's nae for you. She belongs to God.

When he'd pulled the green gown from the wooden box and held it up to the light of the candle, Maebh screeched as if she'd seen a mouse in her morning's porridge. She snatched the garment out of his hands before he could see it properly. She balled it up and clutched it to her chest as if to hide the gown, and then she snatched the accompanying linen chemise, hiding it from view. It was difficult to see by candlelight, but he was certain she'd been blushing.

The memory brought a grin to his face.

He drew his dagger and stared at the keen blade. He took a deep breath, then let out a wistful sigh. He chuckled. "What was I saying about the vanity of others, Lord? Forgive me mine. I have not truly considered the enormous beam in my own eye."

'Tis merely a beard.

He grasped hold of his beard in one hand and put the knife to his throat with the other. "Goodbye, old friend."

And he began to slice at the beard.

It was painful work. In spite of the sharpness of the dagger, the hairs of his beard pulled as he cut them. Nae unlike sheering the wool off a sheep. *What I would nae trade for a good pair of sheep sheers right now.*

Ah, well, laddie. Consider it a penance for vanity.

When he was done, he sheathed the dagger, then stared at the pile of wavy, yellow hair that had once been attached to his face. "The Lord giveth"—he shook his head with a sigh—"and the Lord taketh away." He rubbed his much-diminished facial hair. "Barely a thumb's length remains."

He gazed toward the cave again, frowning in concern. "Surely she must be dressed by now." In the time since he'd left the cave, he'd already removed Órd Dubh's barding, removed the preserving beeswax from the horse's saddle, bridle, and reins, dressed himself in those ludicrous clothes, and cut his hair and beard. And still she dawdled in the cave. *What could be taking her so long?*

He'd noticed that the gown and chemise provided for Maebh had not included a kerchief or other covering for her head. At the time, he'd remarked on it. He'd been told that, under their veils, nuns either kept their heads shaven or, at the very least, kept their hair cut very short. While, for a nun, this was a token of her vow, of forsaking vanity and femininity, Tormond very much doubted nonreligious women of the current century wore their hair in such a manner. He'd offered to improvise a kerchief. "I could cut up the remains of your habit, Sister," he'd said at the time. "'Tis ruined, after all. There's enough cloth to make—"

"No!" she snapped, clutching the gown and chemise all the tighter. "Do not concern yourself."

"But you cannot go about with a shaven—"

"No." She hadn't snapped that time, but she shook her head with vehemence. "I will attend to it." And then she told him to gather his own clothes and leave her alone, shooing him—and Órd Dubh—out of the cave.

And so, dressed in the ridiculous fashion of the day, his beard shorn—roughly shorn, to be sure, but far shorter than it had been even when he'd first joined the Templar order—he watched and waited for Maebh to appear. Nervously, he fingered the pommel of his sword and the smaller pommel of his dagger.

His hand went to the heavy purse dangling at his belt. The second purse, equally heavy, was concealed in one of Órd Dubh's saddle bags. *So much gold! And nary a single silver coin.* It wasn't as if Tormond coveted gold—he didn't. As a religious and a Templar, Tormond had taken a vow of poverty. But the Order had fallen, and without the support of the Order, Tormond knew that money could make survival in the current century—in any century—easier.

What is taking so long? 'Tis nae as if she has to brush and coif her hair.

I wonder . . . Will her hair be shaven or merely cut short? He tried to picture Maebh both ways. *I wonder what color it is.* Her eyebrows were dark—he thought—but at that moment, he wasn't certain. He'd been distracted by the color of her eyes. He'd never actually seen a nun without her veil.

When he freed the nuns in the horrible abbey, delivered them even as they were being ravished, all had been wearing — at least to some degree — the white habit and veil. *'Twas as if the fiends who defiled them preferred their victims wearing the symbols of purity. Even if those poor lassies were no longer undefiled. The villains must have enjoyed the pretense, the perverted fantasy that they were despoiling sacred virgins.*

And that thing! That apparition in the shape of a harlot! What was that? "Nae Mary!" he growled. "Nae the Blessed Virgin."

But surely those poor nuns pled with the Virgin — the true Virgin — to intercede. Surely, they —

"Tormond!" Maebh's cry sounded like the wail of a lost child.

The knight snatched up his shield, drew his sword, and dashed toward the hidden maw of the cave.

Did someone slip past me? Into the cave?

A horrible vision filled his mind — a vision of brutish men in ridiculous hose and padded short-breeches, assaulting Maebh — a dozen of them, all wearing the face of Sir Guy and leering like hyenas at their prey.

"Tormond! Help me! Please!"

He didn't cry out in response. *Let them think she's alone. Defenseless. They will nae hear me coming.*

Villains!

I'll gut them all.

God in Heaven, protect her!

Chapter 9

Tormond charged around the rock face hiding the cave entrance, sword and shield at the ready.

And there Maebh stood.

Alone and...

"Safe." He halted abruptly. His hand — and his voice — trembled slightly as he sheathed his sword and set his shield aside. "You're safe."

He had to stop himself from running to her.

Tormond drew a shaky breath. He bowed his head and shook it ruefully. "Oh, Sister! You should not have . . ." But all words of recrimination died on his lips as he took in her obvious distress.

Tears streaked down her crimson cheeks. "I can't do it!" She clutched the shoulders of her gown, which hung loosely about her. "I've tried and tried. But I can't. I can't lace it up the back. Not by myself."

"Ah!" He felt heat rushing to his own cheeks. "I see. Well." He sighed. *Another penance.* He took a step toward her. "I suppose you cannot go about the Welsh countryside half clothed." He bent his knee and gave her a courtly bow. "Your humble servant, milady."

When he looked up, she was smiling shyly through her tears. "Thank you," she said. "I wouldn't ask . . . It's not fair . . . Not to you. O-or to" — she swallowed visibly — "to me." She lowered her eyes. "Forgive me, Brother Tormond."

He shook his head again and gave her a warm smile. "There's nothing to forgive, Sister."

And then he saw her — truly saw her for the first time. Even with her gray eyes puffy, she was lovely. Her hair was —

"Brown," he whispered in awe.

"What did you say?"

He swallowed. "Your hair. It's" — *long, the color of chestnuts* — "brown." His mouth was suddenly dry.

She blinked. "My hair?"

"I thought . . . Forgive me, Sister, but I thought nuns cut their hair short or shaved their heads when taking the veil."

"Shaved?" Understanding dawned in her eyes. "Oh. Aye, well . . . not in my order." Suddenly she scowled. "Not my order." She shook her head vehemently. "No! 'Twas never *my* order." She took a deep breath. "I should say, not in *that* order. I didn't understand it at the time—I thought the same as you, that we were to have our hair shorn—but I suppose the abbess wanted us to be kept more . . ." She bared her teeth in a snarl. "So that our virtue might fetch more gold." "More gold," Tormond repeated. He found himself gazing at her in wonder. *Such a bonnie lass.*

Then he shook himself, repeating in his mind the first words from the Rule of the Templars, Number Seventy-One—

> *We believe it to be a dangerous thing for any religious brother to look too much upon the face of woman.*

Penance upon penance, laddie. Penance upon penance.

He cleared his throat. "Allow me to help you with that gown."

"Thank you." One corner of her mouth lifted in the hint of a smile. "Sir Knight."

Dinnae look too much 'pon her face, laddie.

Tormond hurried around her, averting his eyes. Still, he took in the sight of her brown tresses. *Did she comb her hair? Where did she get a comb? Or did she simply run her fingers through it?*

Never mind that. Look at her back instead, laddie.

Maebh grasped her hair, which—once Tormond got a closer look at it—appeared to have been thoroughly combed, and pulled it to the front, giving Tormond access to the gown. Though the laces hung loose, and the gown was open in back, the linen chemise covered her flesh. Tormond had never helped a woman dress—or undress—before. He'd never seen it done. No, not with his mother or his sister. Or any woman. Ever.

But you understand well enough how lacings work.

He clenched and unclenched his hands, calming his trembling fingers.

You'll nae be touching her flesh – only the lacings.

As he tightened the laces, Maebh cleared her throat. "How is Órd Dubh?"

Tormond blinked. "My horse?" *Is she simply attempting to ease the awkwardness?*

"Aye. Your horse."

"He's well. Happily eating and dreaming of—" Tormond's breath caught at what he'd been about to say.

"Dreaming of what?"

"Nothing. Just something my da used to say."

"What did your da used to say?"

"Nothing. 'Twas nothing." Tormond adjusted the laces, redistributing the tautness so her chemise was covered.

"Oh, come now. I shared my proverb with you." She giggled—a delightful, girlish sound. "Share your da's with me."

Tormond cleared his throat again. "Dreaming of mares." He tied off the laces.

"Oh. I see." Even the exposed skin of her neck blossomed with pink.

Tormond gave his handiwork a final assessment. "Is— Is't acceptable?"

"Acceptable? The proverb?"

"The laces. The gown."

"Oh." She nodded, dropping her hair to the back again, partially covering the laces. "Aye. Thank you."

Slowly she turned around, her hands placed above her bodice. "I'm sorry."

And Tormond understood why—back in the cave when she'd first seen the gown—why she'd reacted with a screech at the sight of it. The neckline was squared and . . . very low.

Poor lass. She must be mortified.

"The chemise," she said with fresh tears threatening, "it covers less than the gown. I'm sorry. I do not mean to— Forgive me."

He gave her a kindly smile, keeping his eyes on hers. On her eyes and no lower. "We shall have to trust that this is simply the fashion of the times. No more unchaste or immodest than any other well-dressed woman in Wales."

"But"—her hands trembled over her exposed skin—"it is so . . . so low."

Aye. Indeed, it is.

Another penance.

God grant me strength.

Maebh lowered her hands. Slowly.

And Tormond gave her what he hoped was a reassuring smile. *If I stare only at her eyes, she won't believe me.* He pointedly shifted his gaze away from her eyes, taking a step back, and gazing at her in total. He made certain that his eyes did not linger on her bosom. "If you will pardon my saying so, Sister, you look lovely. The gown . . . suits you."

She smiled then, her cheeks flushing. "And you . . . You cut your beard. And your hair. And you —"

A laugh burst from her. One hand went to her mouth, the other pointed at his ridiculous short pants. "You look so . . ." She laughed again.

"Absurd!" he finished for her, shaking his head and grinning widely. He joined in her laughter.

"And we," she said, her gray eyes gleaming, "shall have to trust that this is simply the fashion of the times. No more ridiculous than any other well-dressed man in Wales." She giggled again and smiled.

A man could lose himself in the tinkling of her laughter and in the brightness of her smile.

A man could.

But nae this man. Nae I.

Beware, laddie. For lying — 'Tis a deadly sin too.

And so is pride.

Remember what you are about, laddie. Remember your holy mission.

His countenance must have fallen, for hers bore a look of dismay. "What's wrong?" she asked.

"We'd best be finishing our preparations to go. And then, Sister, I have something to show you."

Something to remind us of the mission.

✠·✠·✠

"If death be a place," Tormond said, kneeling in a clearing, "then that place would be here." He made the sign of the cross.

Maebh, sitting in Órd Dubh's saddle, stared at the barren ground. All around the perimeter rose a tall and ancient forest, but the clearing itself, a dozen paces wide, was conspicuously devoid of life. Not a single blade of grass or a weed. Even the fallen leaves of winters past, so dense on the forest floor, seemed to shun the clearing, as if the spot were antithetical to the very memory of life. At the center of the void lay a large, flat stone, about a pace wide, weathered smooth over time.

Tormond placed his hand on the stone. He bowed his head in reverence, as if he were placing his fingers on a holy relic. His lips moved as if in prayer.

Maebh shivered, despite the late morning sun shining overhead. *I feel chilled to my bones,* she thought, *like death. As if I'll never know warmth or joy or love again.* "Is this spot . . . cursed?" She also made the sign of the cross.

Tormond wore a grim expression. "Aye. Cursed. 'Tis where it all began."

"The Witches?"

Tormond nodded. "Aye. 'Tis the place where they murdered Merlin and stole his secrets, his power. This spot was where they entombed him in a tree."

"A tree?"

"Aye, Sister. A tree. A monstrous tree. A tree that devours life itself."

Maebh glanced about. Suddenly the trees encircling the clearing and the shadows beneath them took on a sinister cast. She imagined skeletal branches reaching for her, grasping at her.

Out of the corner of her eye, she saw movement in the trees. She whipped her head around, staring, wide-eyed and clutching a hand to her breast.

Shadows. Only the shadows. Leaves stirring with the breeze.

But she felt no breeze.

She wetted her lips. "Where is the tree? I see no tree." She sounded irritated, angry, but she didn't care. She wanted only to be away from that dreadful place.

"It's been a thousand years since the tree stood here. 'Tis gone now."

"But surely there'd be a stump. Or-or a mound."

"There is only the marker."

"Who put it there?" she asked. "Who placed the stone?"

Tormond stood. "Peredur. When he began his quest. His mission. He harvested some of the fruit of the tree." Tormond pointed behind Maebh, and she realized he was indicating the direction of the cave, an hour's journey from where they were. "The wine. He made it from the fruit, so he could pursue the Witches through the centuries."

Maebh put a hand to her neck, as if feeling where the single drop of wine — of witchcraft — had trickled down her throat.

And then she remembered why she'd been forced to taste the wine.

I killed him. I killed Da!

The man who'd dandled her on his knee. The man she loved and worshipped when she was but a wee girl.

The man who sold her when she grew to womanhood — sold her to the Order of the Queen of Heaven.

She'd loved him, and he'd betrayed her.

And when he attempted to murder Tormond, she stabbed him.

How she hated her father! But she'd loved him too — far longer than she'd hated him.

Now he is naught but bones.

" . . . it down. Burned it." She noticed Tormond was speaking, but she'd been too lost in her own dark thoughts to listen.

"What did you say?" she asked.

Tormond gave her a kindly smile. Now that his beard had been cut short, he was quite pleasing to look upon, not as fearsome as he'd appeared. "I realize," he continued, "this is a lot to understand. All this must be a shock and a strain for you. And you just lost your father." He shook his head. "I'm sorry."

Does he know my thoughts? My heart? "Please. Tell me again. About the tree?"

He nodded slowly. "Aye. Well, Peredur, after he made the wine . . . You understand about the wine? Where it comes from?"

She nodded. "I understand." *Not fully.* "Go on."

"Peredur cut down the tree. Burned it. And centuries later, when he saw that nothing grew here, that nothing would ever grow here, he placed the stone." Tormond pointed at the stone, and Maebh recognized it for the monument it was. "He told me that he carved a cross on it—he was a Christian knight by then—but it is gone. Time has devoured it—the cross, I mean." His lips drew into a tight line. *"Tempus edax rerum."*

"Time devours all," she translated the Latin aloud. "Aye?"

He nodded. "Aye."

"Why did you bring us here?"

"Because, Sister"—he walked toward her—"I want, nay, I *need* you to understand how truly dangerous our mission is."

Our mission. He called it our *mission.*

"I understand."

He shook his head. "No, you do not." He halted, standing beside the horse. He gazed up at her, and his eyes burned with a cold fire. "We hunt death itself. Where the Witches go, they leave death in their wake. I have seen the aftermath. They corrupt men and women. They have corrupted whole villages, entire towns. Madness—pagan madness—and death is their work."

The sweep of his arm took in the barren clearing. "Nothing lives. Nothing grows. Nothing ever comes again."

She shuddered.

"'Tis why I have given up all that I know, all that I love"—he paused—"to slay them. And if you are to travel the ages with me, you will travel a long and lonely road, fraught with peril. Deadly to both body and soul. You must be prepared for that. You must steel yourself to face true evil."

Maebh's mouth was suddenly dry, and she felt a chill rip through her. But she sat tall in the saddle. "I have faced evil. And I will face it with the courage of God. I will face it"—she lowered her voice to a whisper, a whisper that she both hoped and feared he might hear—"with you."

The fire in his eyes faded, and he smiled warmly. "You are well named, Shield-maiden of Christ."

Their eyes locked, and in spite of her fear, a smile crept across her lips.

Órd Dubh snorted and pawed the ground with one massive hoof.

Tormond patted the great beast's neck. "I guess you are ready to move on, aren't you, my old friend." He extended a hand to Maebh. "Sister? May I?"

She handed him the reins.

Their fingers touched briefly, and warmth seemed to flow from his fingertips into hers.

"Come, Sister Mary Elizabeth." He smiled. "Let us see what we shall find in Carmarthen." He turned and led the horse across the clearing and into the shadows of the forest. "Perhaps we shall find out why God has preserved us for this time and place — what it is that A says we must do."

As she rode behind the striding knight, she said, "Tormond?"

"Aye, Sister?" He did not turn around.

"You must not call me that again."

He glanced over his shoulder, back at her. "Shield-maiden?"

The title sent a thrill through her. "Well, aye, but that's not what I meant."

"Ah. Sister. Sister Mary Elizabeth."

"Aye. If we are not to be known as a nun and a religious . . ."

"Very wise," he said. "I shall call you Maebh then. And you must call me Tormond."

She grinned. "I already call you that."

He nodded. "Aye. That you do."

"And who are we? I mean, to each other?"

"I see. Perhaps we are brother and sister? Traveling together?"

"Brother and sister? But we look nothing alike. No one would believe that."

He glanced at her again, a smile on his lips. "And 'twould be a lie. Then we shall be distant cousins. Once, long ago, the Scotts and the Irish were cousins. So 'tis the truth."

"But why would distant cousins be traveling together?"

"You shall be my ward then. And I shall be your guardian and protector."

You are already that. "'Tis the truth." *Or close enough to it.*

"Aye. And you are now orphaned. And so —" He froze, halting in the road. He turned to face her, his face stricken. "Sis — Maebh. I'm so sorry."

She shook her head quickly, but firmly. "No. Do not be sorry. I'm glad he's dead." She hastened to add a less than sincere, "May God have mercy on his soul."

Tormond's eyes hardened. "He was part of that evil lot. He died unshriven. God will judge him, but I do not believe those fiends will find mercy when they stand before the judgement bar of God. My mission . . . *Our* mission is not to extend mercy. Our mission is to execute the enemies of God. Never forget that."

"Aye, Tormond. I won't forget."

With that, the Executioner of God turned, and resumed leading their way through the forest.

✠·✠·✠

Sitting atop Órd Dubh's rolling back, Maebh watched with fascination as a small, blue-winged, and yellow-breasted bird perched on a tree branch overhanging the River Towy. The bird bobbed its head as it appeared to be studying the river below.

Suddenly, the bird streaked down to the water, disappearing completely beneath the surface. It quickly emerged on its flapping, blue wings, carrying a small fish in its long, pointed beak. Dripping wet, the bird flew back to the branch and perched there on its legs. The avian predator adjusted the wriggling fish until the bird had its prey by the tail. The bird then slammed the fish against the branch repeatedly until the prey was either stunned or dead. Once more the bird repositioned the fish until it had its prey by the head. Then the bird swallowed the fish whole.

Such a beautiful creature.
A beautiful killer.
Preying on the weak and helpless.
Then again, even Sir Guy was handsome.
And now, he is but moldering bones.
Like Da.
I loved Da. Once.
And I killed him.

Maebh wasn't entirely certain there was not a small part of her heart that loved her father still.

He was a monster. I had to defend Tormond.

"Tormond," Maebh called to the knight leading the horse, "the fisher bird—what is it called?"

"The blue bird? With the yellow breast?"

"Aye."

"I don't know the word in Irish. Or in English. Or in Welsh. But in Scotland, we call them *cruinne-cruinne*. Pretty things they are."

"Aye. Pretty. But the poor little fish. They are utterly defenseless."

"Aye," Tormond said, "but all life preys on other life. The fish eat insects and smaller fish. The cruinne-cruinne eat the fish. The hawks eat the smaller birds. And we? We eat them all."

She wrinkled her face in disgust. "We do not eat insects!"

He shrugged his shoulders. "I have. In the Holy Land, I ate locusts. Saint John the Baptist ate locusts. They are quite tasty when fried and dipped in honey."

Maebh's stomach—which contained nothing but water and preserved dates—roiled, threatening to empty itself. "I don't think I could ever eat an insect."

"You have eaten dog. Was it not tasty?"

"Aye," she admitted, "'twas." She grinned fiercely, finding satisfaction in the memory of eating that which had desired to eat her.

"Our mortal flesh," Tormond said, "requires us to satisfy our appetites by consuming the life and flesh of other creatures. Plants or beasts, it is all the same. Only when we die and become pure spirit are we freed from the need to consume life. The life of a religious or a nun is spent in denying the flesh, aye?"

"But that is a different kind of denial. We are denying . . . different appetites." *Like the desire of a man for a woman. Or a woman for a man.* "Not the flesh that brings life."

Tormond shrugged again. "But even there, do we not deny our appetites as much as possible? As Templars, while living together in the Temple, we tried to eat meat sparingly. Only thrice in a week if we had sufficient other food available. We also took meals only twice in a day. And there is also the fasting. And we forego slumber to perform all the offices of prayer. 'Tis all part of learning to overcome the flesh, denying the needs of the mortal body. 'Tis the higher, holier way."

"But as a soldier, did you not need to keep up your strength?"

He chuckled. "Aye, there is that. We must all be ready to fight in God's name. But we must also rely on His goodness and His strength. He is our sword and our shield" — he paused, tapping the hilt of his sword — "made manifest in our physical armor."

The woods at last gave way to lush, green grazing land, dotted with sheep and cows. Low walls of stacked stone separated individual pastures. Maebh could see the walls of Carmarthen Castle rising in the distance. *I wonder how much it has changed in sixty years.* She'd seen the castle once before, when her father brought her up the Towy, past the town, and into the forest — toward the hidden abbey and its dark and profane rites. It had been springtime then too.

To the north of the castle, rose the steeple of a church. She'd asked her da what the church was called. He chuckled at the question, then answered with a gleam in his eye, "I don't know. Perhaps St. Mary's." She asked him why he laughed. He shrugged and replied, "Soon you will know."

She shuddered at the memory.

And at the memory of a pile of bones rotting in a cave alongside a rusted knife.

Da claimed the apparition was the Virgin.

Tormond says 'twas not Mary above the altar, that it could not be the Virgin.

And whom, Maebh O Broin, do you trust more? The father who betrayed you or the man who saved you?

She smiled fondly, looking down at the top of Tormond's head. Then she grinned as she gazed at the awkward manner in which he was forced to walk in his funny, voluminous short pants, his hips swaying from side to side.

I trust Tormond with my life.

And with everything else.

As they drew near the first buildings of the town, Maebh could hear the clinking of metal on metal and saw black smoke rising from a chimney. The smithy, for so it was, seemed to be doing a brisk trade, for she heard the sound of multiple hammers and saw a farrier outside the building, shoeing a horse. A small group of men and boys lounged about on benches or barrels, watching the farrier at work. Two younger boys frolicked beside the smithy, playing at swords using sticks.

Across the road from the blacksmith's shop sat a much larger house consisting of two stories with many windows. Maebh supposed it to be an inn. It was far from the center of town, but close enough to the castle. Outside the inn slouched a pair of brutish-looking fellows, each armed with a large cudgel. Maebh recognized them for what they were—tavern guards, ready to remove rowdy patrons—but she'd never seen a tavern requiring two guards at once.

How rough must a tavern be to need two such brutes?

And as if two guards weren't sufficient, a third figure sat in a chair by the inn door—a lean woman with snow-white hair. The woman called and cackled to the men in front of the smithy. Likewise, she called to a well-dressed man on horseback, approaching from the opposite direction. Maebh assumed the rider to be well dressed and to have coin, for he wore the same style of voluminous short pants as Tormond.

Tormond and Maebh were close enough to be able to hear the woman's voice, but the words she spoke were not in a tongue Maebh understood.

Probably Welsh.

The hag persisted in her cackling, gesturing for the man to approach.

The rider halted, and the old woman shouted something through the door.

In moments, a pair of women sauntered out of the inn. They stood near the well-dressed man. One reached up and stroked the man's leg. From their mode of dress and the way they carried themselves, Maebh quickly recognized their trade.

Whores.

And that is no inn. 'Tis a brothel.

The man dismounted, fished a coin from his purse, and gave it into the outstretched hand of the old woman. She deftly hid the silver in her bodice and laughed loudly, as the man tossed a copper to one of the boys standing in front of the smithy. The boy easily snatched the coin from the air, then took the reins of the horse.

The well-dressed man put an arm around one of the prostitutes, and the two of them—the man and the woman—passed into the den of iniquity and out of site.

Maebh shuddered as memories of the abbey flooded her mind.

Could that have been me? Could that have been my fate?

"Our first task," Tormond said, mercifully interrupting her dark thoughts, "is to find an inn and secure rooms and meals. I like dates well enough, but the olive oil ruins the taste. Then we must find you a suitable horse." He grinned at her. "Órd Dubh seems to like you, but—"

He stopped, halting the horse as well, apparently seeing her expression of horror. His own expression showed concern. "What's the matter? Are you ill?"

She shook her head. "No. I am well." She nodded her head in the direction of the brothel. "Were it not for the grace of God and for you, Brother Tor—I mean, Tormond—I might have ended up in such a place."

He shook his head, and his expression sobered. "No, Maebh O Broin. You fought your way free of just such a place. You chose the possibility of death over that dishonor. And after you were safe, you led me back there to free your sisters. Though you feared that evil place and all it represented, you led me back. You are the most courageous woman I have ever known. You would never have become . . . like those poor souls."

His praise thrilled her. But that thrill was soon drowned in pity. *Those poor souls.*

She shook herself, pointedly looking away from the brothel. "And after the rooms and meals and horse?"

"I have business at the smithy."

"The smithy?"

He nodded and resumed leading the horse toward the Carmarthen. "Aye. When last I was here, the blacksmith was a Sergeant."

"A Sergeant? Of the Temple?"

"Aye. Perhaps his grandson still is. Or I suppose 'twould be his great-grandson or great-great-grandson now. But, no more on that. Others might hear."

Tormond, Maebh, and Órd Dubh entered the town and were about to pass between the smithy and the brothel with its foul wardens.

Maebh kept her eyes straight ahead or on the smithy and men and boys gathered there, pointedly avoiding looking in the direction of the brothel.

A few of the men grinned, nodded, and uttered what sounded like words of greeting or welcome, though Maebh didn't understand them. One of the older boys gave her a smile that would've been completely inappropriate—had he known that she was a nun.

She blushed and fought the renewed urge to adjust the low neckline of her gown. Instead, she pulled her hair over her shoulder, concealing the indecently exposed flesh.

"Maebh?" a voice said. "Maebh?"

Maebh turned her head toward the speaker and stared down into the wide eyes of the old woman.

The hag's mouth worked as if tasting something bitter, and then she said in Latin, "Sister Mary Elizabeth? Is that you?"

Chapter 10

No, you cannot be she," the old woman croaked, her wrinkled eyes narrowing. "Her" — the crone seemed to be searching for a word — "daughter's daughter, maybe."

The two guards, one on either side of the brothel door, though they continued to slouch against the wall, stared with a practiced casualness — not at Maebh, but at Tormond.

Maebh realized with a start, that Tormond was no longer on her left. He had crossed in front of the horse and now stood between Maebh and the crone and her two guards. Without looking at her, Tormond handed Órd Dubh's reins to Maebh. His right hand rested on the pommel of his sword, and there could be no mistaking his posture — he stood ready to fight.

"No," the old woman continued, shifting from Latin to Irish, staring intently up at Maebh, wrinkles upon wrinkles deepening and tightening around her ancient but clear eyes. "It is you. Sister Mary Elizabeth."

Maebh opened her mouth to protest, but stopped herself. *Can I lie? Even about this?*

"Don't bother denying it, girl!" The old woman snapped. "I know you." The hag made the sign of the cross, a gesture utterly incongruous, coming as it did from a prostitute. "Witchcraft or magic. I don't know. But 'tis you. You and no other."

The ancient eyes shifted to Tormond. "And you! Aye, the beard is much shorter, and you're not drenched head to foot in blood . . . But those eyes . . . So cold. So hard. No." She shook her head slowly. "No, yours is a face I could never forget."

"Woman, I —" Tormond began, but the crone cut him off with a wave of one bony, age-spotted hand.

"You spared my life that night." She eyed him carefully. "But you don't remember me, do you?"

Tormond said nothing.

"In the chapel. At the ritual, the sacrifice. I was . . . in the choir." Her eyes returned Maebh. "You stopped him." The woman

101

wagged a skeletal finger at Maebh. "He was going to slaughter us all. But *you* stopped him."

Not one of the victims.

One of them.

The old woman stood. Slowly. Painfully. Maebh could almost hear the ancient joints creaking. The crone stared Tormond in the eyes for a long moment.

And spat in his face.

"Bastard!" she snarled, sounding like a hissing cat. "You should have killed me!"

The two guards stepped forward, menacingly slapping their cudgels on their palms.

"Na!" The hag waved a bony hand at each of the guards. "Byddai'n lladd y ddau ohonoch chi."

The guards hesitated, exchanged glances, then shrugged in unison and resumed their practiced slouching against the wall.

Tormond's right hand gripped the hilt of his sword, ready to draw.

He made no move to wipe the spittle from his face.

The crone stared at Tormond without the slightest hint of fear in her eyes. "And you would, wouldn't you?" she said, once again speaking in Irish. "Eh, Crusader? You would slaughter them like sheep."

Tormond kept his silence, but his jaw tightened.

The crone laughed, soft and low and ominous. "I could denounce you. As a witch." She grinned widely, showing the few yellowed teeth remaining to her. "They'd *burn* you, Crusader. Burn you both. Aye, the good Catholic townsfolk here—they burned a heretic bishop—one of old Henry's lads, he was—nigh two years gone. All I have to do is give the word." She lowered her voice. "One word." She laughed again, her voice rising to a high-pitched cackle. "And you must be witches! Aye, you must be." She paused, narrowing her eyes at Maebh. "You've not aged a day, girl."

A small crowd had gathered around them—mostly men and boys from the smithy, but others from the town as well. They kept a safe distance, as if they understood that blood was about to be shed. As if they wanted to observe the fighting but take no part in it, except to cheer on the combatants. Faces peered from the lower windows of the brothel.

"Perhaps," Tormond said, his hand never leaving his sword, "I *should* have slain you that night. But pity stayed my hand. Pity and this good woman here. I pity you now more than ever."

"Pity?" The word came out as a croak, as if from a raven's beak. "Was it pity? Do you think 'twere merciful?" She spat again, but this time onto the dirt at Tormond's feet. "Do you know what you condemned me to? This life of-of-of . . . whoring and beggary! You pious, holy bastard!" She lowered her voice. "You witch!"

"Tormond!" Maebh whispered. "Tormond! Let's go. The crowd." She eyed the mob, but no one appeared to have understood the accusation in the crone's Irish words.

For his part, Tormond only spared the surrounding men and women a seemingly casual glance. "Woman, even if you feel I have wronged you, I don't see how I could make amends—save to end your life. And I would not slay you now, unless you threaten me or my ward." He lowered his voice as well. "Tell me, woman, are you so very anxious to die? To die in your sins, unshriven, and then stand before the judgement bar of God?"

Someone in the crowd shouted, "Beth mae'n ei ddweud?"

Another cried, "Beth mae e eisiau?"

Yet another shouted, "Mam Gwyneth!" This—apparently the crone's name—was repeated by others.

A memory stirred within Maebh—a nun with haunted eyes who'd brought her food and water in her cell. And then, on that awful night, along with other members of the satanic choir, had dragged her from her cell.

Maebh peered at the old woman. "Gwyneth? Sister"—she searched her memory for the name—"Sarah?"

The crone flinched. "Not Sister Sarah. No longer." A bit of that haunted look Maebh recalled came back to the hag's wrinkled eyes. "Gwyneth. That's my name as was. And is now again."

Rage boiled in Maebh, threatening to drown her in its bile. "You were there! Singing in that horrid choir, while others held me down on that profane altar."

The haunted look vanished as the old woman grinned toothily. Evilly. Hungrily. "I could have my boys hold you down now. Right here in the street. There's still some as would pay good silver to ravish a nun. Though, only the *first* one would have a *virgin* nun."

"Enough!" Tormond growled. He lifted his voice and shouted in a language Maebh did not understand, though she assumed it was English. His words were halting, but his voice was strong. The intent was clear.

And the crowd obeyed — they backed away, muttering.

"You called me Crusader." Tormond's voice was cold as the grave. "And a Crusader I am. But I am also a Templar."

Old Gwyneth flinched again, apparently at the word "Templar." She sank onto her chair, shielding her wizened face behind an emaciated hand.

Órd Dubh, seeming to sense his master's mood, whinnied loudly and stomped at the ground.

Tormond took a step toward the crone. "I tell you this, woman, because you should know who I am and *what* I am. And how I fight. We Knights of the Temple do not retreat. We do not surrender. We fight to the death. Always to the death." He let that word settle on Gwyneth's ancient ears. "You seem to have some influence in this benighted town. Perhaps you *could* call the people down upon us. But know you this — in the strength God, I *will* prevail. And when they are all dead or have fled before the wrath of God, fled to cower in their hovels . . . then I will *not* kill you. Oh, no. I will not. Instead, I will empty your house of iniquity. And then I will burn it. I will raze it."

Tormond towered over the cringing woman. "And you will enslave no more women and corrupt no more souls." He whispered, "Now, woman, tell these people to disperse and leave us in peace."

Maebh stared at the Executioner of God in awe and not a little fear.

The old woman lowered her hand. "Pity, Crusader? Mercy?" She lowered her eyes. "Again?" Her voice was barely a whisper. Tears fell from those wrinkled eyes. She lifted her voice and cried, "Gadewch iddyn nhw fynd! Dim ond camddealltwriaeth ydoedd. Gadewch iddyn nhw fynd!"

Amid a susurrus of murmurs, the crowd slowly parted.

Tormond took the reins from Maebh, then led the warhorse — with Maebh in the beast's saddle — out from the midst of the throng.

Once they were well clear, Tormond finally took his hand from his sword hilt and wiped the spittle from his face. He drew his dagger and handed it to Maebh. "After the inn and the meals, I need to procure you a dagger of your own."

Maebh shivered as relief washed over her. "That was incredible. You have no fear. None."

Without looking at her, he said, "I was stupid. Reckless. I should never have let us get surrounded like that. I should never have let *you* get trapped like that." He sighed, shaking his head slightly. "I'm sorry."

"But you are completely, utterly without fear."

He shook his head. "Not true. I *was* afraid. Not for my own life." He glanced back at her, and she saw what she had never expected to see in his eyes — terror. "But for yours."

For me? For my life? "But the danger" — Maebh glanced behind them — "the immediate danger, surely it has passed."

"We are being followed." He sounded as calm as if he were remarking on the pleasing shape of a passing cloud.

Gripping the pommel of the saddle with hands suddenly slick with sweat, Maebh twisted atop the horse, looking back once more. Though many in the crowd stared in their direction, none of them seemed to be following. "I don't see anyone in the street."

"Not in the street." Nothing in Tormond's casual stride or in the tone of his voice betrayed the slightest concern. "To the south, on your left. He just went behind the cobbler's shop."

Maebh's head jerked to the left. She eyed several small wooden buildings standing in a row, lining the south side of the street. The houses or shops were low and built close together, separated by narrow alleys barely wide enough for two men to walk abreast. Above the door of one such shop, she spotted the crudely painted — though still recognizable — image of a pointed, red shoe.

"Look," Tormond said, "but try to not stare." He handed the reins to her again. "And ride away at the first sign of trouble. The first sign."

Maebh turned her head forward once more—mostly forward, at least—but she kept her eyes on the alley at the far edge of the cobbler's shop.

Nothing moved in the darkness between the houses.

"I don't see—" she began.

And then she saw it—a pale face peering out of the shadows like a ghostly apparition.

"Tormond!" she whispered, glancing down at him.

But Tormond was no longer in front of the horse.

When she looked back toward the alley, Tormond was there, gripping a young man by the shirt, his sword against the youth's throat.

The boy stared at Tormond, his eyes wide with terror.

Tormond growled something in that language Maebh did not understand. But there could be no mistaking the knight's lethal tone.

"'Tis you!" the frightened youth squeaked in Latin. "You're he! You're the Executioner of God!"

Chapter 11

At those words, spoken earnestly and without the slightest hesitation, in spite of the lad's obvious terror, a chill ripped through Tormond like a jagged knife of ice. *How does he know who I am?*

"Who are you?" Tormond demanded in Latin. "Why are you following us?"

"William," the youth replied. "I am a Sergeant of the Temple."

This lad? A Sergeant?

Keeping his sword at the lad's throat, Tormond said, "Prove it."

The youth — William — blinked. Then with the slightest nod of his head, he began to raise his right hand.

"Slowly," Tormond cautioned.

William's hand moved deliberately, avoiding contact with the sword, until it came level with his eyebrow. He touched the tip of his thumb to the tip of his index finger, forming a circle, while keeping the other three fingers extended.

Tormond observed the secret salute out of the corner of his eye. "Very well." Abruptly he stepped back, pulling the sword away from William's neck.

But Tormond did not sheath the weapon.

The boy sagged, putting a hand to his throat and breathing heavily. A smile crept over his face. The smile grew until it nearly split his face in two.

He was not a handsome youth — his ears and nose were too large for that — but his smile was genuine and guileless.

No longer seeing the lad as a threat — at least not an immediate one — yet still not taking his eyes off William, Tormond spoke in Irish, loud enough for Maebh to hear. "'Tis well. He is one of" — *Maebh might nae know the Latin word for Sergeant, and 'tis nae a title to be saying so others can hear* — "one of our *allies*."

"One of —" Maebh cut off before saying the word. "Oh. I see."

Clever lassie. So quick to learn.

"What tongue is it you are speaking?" William's eyes were bright as he continued in Latin. "I don't know it. 'Tisn't Welsh or English. Is it Scottish? I would dearly love to learn Scottish. I love learning foreign tongues! Will you teach me?"

"'Tis Irish," Tormond replied, amused by the boy's eagerness. *How did I ever think he was a threat?*

Tormond sheathed his sword.

"Irish! Is that what you were speaking with old Mother Gwyneth?"

Tormond nodded. "How did you recognize me?"

William, displaying not even the slightest remnant of the terror he'd known mere moments before, pointed at the pommel of Tormond's sword. "The cross! And on the other side, the sigil of the Soldiers of Christ—two knights on one horse, signifying your vow of poverty." He looked Tormond in the eyes. "I was taught it has the motto of the Knights etched on the blade. I saw the lettering, but when you had the blade to my throat, I was too frightened to read it. But I assure you—I *can* read!"

Tormond chuckled at the boy's proud declaration that he was, in fact, literate. *'Tis an accomplishment for any commoner.* Tormond then glanced around to ensure they hadn't been overheard. "Aye. 'Not for us, Lord. Not for us. To Thy name be the glory.'"

The boy's eyes grew wide, and his mouth hung agape. "And it was given you by Grand Master Guillaume de Beaujeu himself! At the siege of Acre!"

Tormond nodded. "The same." *Grand Master Guillaume, forgive me. I have failed thus far. You trusted me and —*

"May I hold it?" William extended an eager hand toward the hilt.

"Not here. Not now."

The boy took a step back. "I understand. 'Tis sacred. A knight never relinquishes his sword. But, oh, how I'd love to hold it. Just once! I would take great care not to damage it. My father's not just a blacksmith. He's a swordsmith. And I'm his apprentice."

Tormond couldn't suppress a grin. "Not here and now, but later. I give you my word."

William's smile of wonder and gratitude lit up his countenance. "Oh! 'Twould be glorious!"

"At the moment," Tormond said, "we could use some assistance."

William blinked again, then looked past Tormond to Maebh. "We? Who is she?"

"She is my—" Tormond didn't know the word for "ward" in Latin. "She is under my protection. She is traveling with me."

"Oh!" William's youthful brow creased in apparent concern and his eyes narrowed. "I understand."

However, it was obvious that the boy did not understand, that perhaps he suspected something. Something improper.

Tormond sighed. *Well, I suppose I'd better give the laddie some explanation.* "She protected me, saved my life while I slept. Then she was forced to drink the sacred wine. And now, I owe her my life. She is part of my mission." When the boy still looked doubtful, Tormond added, "I yet keep to my vows. *All* my vows." He lowered his voice to a whisper. "And she, herself, is a nun. And she keeps her vows as well."

The lad nodded slowly, then his grin returned.

But the smile vanished again, to be replaced by wide-eyed mortification. "A nun!" His cheeks turned crimson, and his head lowered. "Forgive me, Sister. I didn't know. When I smiled at you earlier, when you rode into town. I— Forgive me, please."

Maebh said, "I forgive you," though her cheeks turned pink.

He smiled at her?

Well, Sergeants do marry. And she is a bonnie lass, is she nae? And dressed as she is . . . Nevertheless, Tormond experienced a brief flash of an emotion he had not felt in centuries—jealousy. He shook his head, dismissing such thoughts. "We are in disguise." *Ridiculous pants!*

And Maebh's expanse of bosom.

Stop that, laddie! "You could not have known."

William lifted his head, smiling once more. "You said you need my help. I am a Sergeant! Like my father and his father before him. I stand ready to help you." He looked past Tormond once more, his cheeks flushing again. "Both of you."

"Thank you," Maebh replied.

William gave them an almost courtly bow—a bow directed seemingly at Maebh. "How may I serve?"

Tormond experienced another twinge of jealousy. *Stop it, laddie! He's younger than she is!* "First, Sergeant William, do you know of a good inn?"

The boy nodded vigorously. "That I do!"

✠·✠·✠

Using a single gold coin from the mysterious "**A**," Tormond rented two rooms—located adjacent to each other—for a fortnight. The inn was named "Pen y Baedd" or, as William happily translated, "The Boar's Head." And indeed, the inn's sign bore the image of a swine's head. Tormond—through the medium of William's translation—also arranged for their meals to be brought up to their rooms.

And before the meals, a tub, hot water, soap, and towels were to be brought to each room for washing. Tormond had asked specifically for cold water to be brought to his own room, but William had advised against it. "You'll catch your death. It's bad enough to bathe overmuch anyway. But if you must bathe, use hot water. My father says it's unhealthy to bathe more than once in a month, and then only—"

"Very well," Tormond had growled, cutting him off. "Hot it shall be."

William accompanied Tormond, Maebh, the innkeeper—a somewhat portly man with more hair on his face than atop his head—and a young maid—apparently the innkeeper's daughter—up to the fourth floor of the inn. According to the landlord, that was where the finest—or at least the quietest—rooms were.

Tormond pitied the maid who would be required to haul the pails of hot water up the narrow stairs.

"Why don't you eat in the common room?" William asked.

Tormond shook his head. "No. After this morning, I think we should be seen as little as possible."

"Why?" The boy looked at him askance. "Because you had an argument with old Mother Gwyneth?"

Tormond nodded. "Aye."

William waved a dismissive hand. "She argues with any man who passes her doors and doesn't go inside. Especially if he has fine clothes and a fat purse. Like yours."

"But I was with a lady," Tormond growled. "Even were I inclined to visit a brothel, that should have discouraged her."

The youth shrugged. "'Twouldn't be the first time a woman has been forced to wait outside while her husband—"

Tormond waved a hand, cutting the lad off. "I don't want to hear about it. Let it be."

William's cheeks flushed. "I'm sorry. I have memorized the Rule as well. From Rule Forty-Three—'Let him not heedlessly dare to recall with his brother, or any other, the carnal pleasures with most wretched women.'" Then he hastened to add, "Not that I have ever entered that sinful house." And then, with a nervous glance at Maebh, "Not that I believe women to be 'wretched.' I don't."

If Maebh had taken offense, she gave no sign of it.

Tormond chuckled. "'Tis nothing. I forgive you. And you are not a knight. You are a Sergeant. You don't have to live by the Rule, as I do. You can marry and you—"

William hung his head. "How I wish I could! I wish I could be a knight like you. But I am not noble born. I could never be a knight, much less a Knight of the Temple."

"The Knights of the Temple are no more." The words tasted like ash in his mouth. The first time Tormond had awakened, he learned of the papal bull that officially disbanded the order, declaring the Templars to be heretics. He also learned of the arrest and execution of his brothers across Europe. "I alone remain. I am all that is left of the Order."

They burned Jacques de Molay at the stake. De Molay was the twenty-third and final Grand Master of the Temple.

Tormond fought beside the man at Acre, though De Molay was not Grand Master at the time. Tormond liked and respected the man.

If I had been there, if I had survived Acre, I would have been burned as well.

Burned as a heretic.

"As long as you draw breath, Tormond," Maebh said, breaking her silence as she followed behind them, "the Knights live on."

"And as long as you live," William added, standing a little straighter as he climbed the stairs, "the Sergeants of the Temple will assist you."

Tormond smiled at the boy's earnest enthusiasm.

And at Maebh's words.

✠·✠·✠

Maebh luxuriated in the hot water of the tub and in the simple, clean scent of soap. She likewise basked in the knowledge that she, herself, no longer stank like a stable boy.

She had not felt clean — truly clean — since that horrible night in the unholy abbey.

When she first realized who Gwyneth was, Maebh felt rage and loathing for the elderly prostitute.

One of them.

How many times had she been part of forcing an innocent onto that altar to be held down and raped by the likes of Sir Guy?

Or Da?

One of them.

But as she soaked in the water, a new feeling trumped her anger and hatred — pity. She felt *pity* for the wizened crone.

Gwyneth wasn't always one of them. Once she was a victim. Like me.

Or almost a victim — I escaped, but she did not.

She was robbed of her virtue. And she became one of them.

Tormond says we are to slay the enemies of God. And a whore and mistress of a brothel . . . Is she not an enemy of God?

Holy Mary, Mother of God, help me to forgive her. Truly forgive.

The water was growing colder.

The maid rose from her stool. She was a young lass of no more than twelve. She'd hauled the hot water, two buckets at a time, up the stairs and then assisted Maebh with her gown and her bath. She picked up both empty buckets and headed wearily and silently toward the door.

"No," Maebh called after the girl. When the maid turned toward her with a questioning look, Maebh said, "Na," using the Welsh word she was certain meant the same. She'd heard the word enough times to deduce its meaning. Maebh gave the girl a smile, waving her dripping hand in a halting gesture.

The maid seemed to catch her meaning, setting her buckets on the floor. She gave Maebh a shy grin, bobbed her head, and said, "Diolch."

Diolch? I suppose that means, "Thank you." Maebh smiled back. She stood in the wooden tub, trying very hard to keep from sloshing water onto the floorboards. She almost succeeded.

The maid hastened to Maebh's side with a towel, then assisted her out of the tub.

The girl began to dry Maebh, until Maebh snatched the towel away. "Scrubbing my back is one thing, child, but I can dry myself." *But you have no idea what I'm saying, do you? I must learn Welsh. Or English. They seem to speak both here.*

The maid shook her head, indicating her complete lack of comprehension. Then she grinned, bobbed her head again, and stepped back.

As Maebh dried herself, the maid dipped the buckets, one at a time, into the soapy water. Then she carried them to the window and emptied the buckets onto the street below.

"Hei!" Maebh heard a man cry from the street in a tone that spoke of indignation and surprise.

Maebh grinned as she toweled her hair. *Perhaps that word is the same in any language.*

At least, 'twas merely bathwater, and not the contents of the chamber pot.

Maebh sighed as she eyed the gown draped across the bed. The gown was immodest to be sure, but it was also lovely. And once became used to wearing it and—a wee bit—used to having so much of her bosom exposed, she enjoyed a bit—a wee bit—of maidenly delight in simply looking pretty once again.

And she *had* enjoyed the looks young William gave her.

If only Tormond would look at me that way.

She clucked her tongue and scowled. *Improper thoughts for a nun.*

But I'm not dressed as a nun. I cannot dress as a nun.
If A is to be believed, I may never dress as a nun again.
But is A to be trusted?
Tormond seems to trust him.

She looked at the gown and chemise again. She bent and sniffed at the fabric of each. And wrinkled her nose.

The gown smelled of horse, though not too strongly. However, the chemise stank of unwashed, sweaty nun.

She sighed. "'Tis all I have."

A knock came at the door.

Maebh squeaked. She snatched up the woolen blanket from the bed, dumping her gown and chemise on the floor. She hurriedly wrapped herself in the blanket. The rough wool made her skin itch, but she drew the blanket even tighter around herself.

The maid looked at her questioningly. She smiled and raised a finger as if to reassure Maebh. The girl moved to the door and asked, "Beth sydd ei eisiau?"

A muffled, if somewhat lengthy reply came through the door.

Maebh thought she recognized the voice as William's, though he spoke in Welsh.

The maid answered with "Da iawn." She opened the door just a crack. A bundle of whitish cloth was thrust through.

"Haec est matris meae!" William called out in Latin. "Donum."

A gift? From his mother? "Gratias tibi. Tibi gratias ago ei." Maebh hoped she had expressed her thanks properly, lamenting her limited command of conversational Latin.

"Ffwrdd â chi!" the maid said, closing and bolting the door. The girl turned toward her, presenting Maebh with the bundle.

Maebh unfolded the linen and discovered, to her delight, two chemises. Two *clean* chemises.

God bless you, William! And God bless your mother!

But after examining both underdresses, she discovered both were very low-cut in the front.

Maebh sighed.

The fashion of the times. Ah, well. At least they will work with the gown. My one and only gown.

Perhaps Tormond could spend some of that gold to have new ones made . . .

With the help of the girl, Maebh was soon dressed. Once clothed, Maebh produced her comb from the hidden pocket in her gown and gazed at the multicolored object.

An object of vanity. I should not have kept it. She smiled, thinking fondly of her long-dead mother's gift. *I'm so glad I did.*

I miss you, Mam.

But remembering her mother also conjured up memories of her father.

Da betrayed me.

I killed him.

She shuddered, remembering his skull with the patches of hair.

I killed Da!

"Ooh! Pert!" the maid cried. She was gazing at the comb in Maebh's hand. "Crwban?" When Maebh gave her a questioning look, the girl said a word that sounded very much like a word Maebh recognized.

Maebh smiled and nodded, repeating the almost-familiar word. "Turtle."

The girl nodded with enthusiasm.

"Well," Maebh said to herself, "I suppose I've just learned my first new English word." *A said we should learn the tongue, did he not?* To the maid, she said, "A gift from my mother. Mam."

The girl seemed to recognize that last word as well. She nodded. "Mam." She giggled.

Maebh couldn't help giggling as well. "Please?" Maebh pointed to her own hair.

The maid nodded, grinning. She took the tortoiseshell comb from Maebh and pointed to the bed.

Maebh sat, and the girl sat behind her. Gently, the maid began to comb Maebh's hair.

Maebh found herself idly wishing for a mirror in the room.

Beware, Maebh O Broin. Vanity is a sin. Especially for a woman. Especially for a nun.

✠·✠·✠

Maebh stood outside the knight's door with her dinner, a large bowl of mutton stew, in her hands. The savory aroma set her mouth to watering, and the warmth of the pottery in her hands radiated comfort. Positioning the bowl in the crook of her arm, she knocked. "Tormond?"

"Aye? 'Tis unlocked. Enter!"

She opened the door and stepped inside.

And was so astonished by what she saw that she nearly dropped her bowl.

Tormond was sitting on the floor, eating his own stew.

William was also in the room, but the lad sat on the bed, reverently holding Tormond's sword.

Two sturdy-looking stools sat unoccupied.

"What are you doing?" Maebh asked in Irish. "Why are you eating on the floor?"

Tormond did not answer. He merely averted his eyes.

Maebh turned her astonished gaze to William, pointed at Tormond, and asked in Latin, "Quid struit?" *What is he doing?* "In" — and realizing she didn't know the Latin word for floor—"terram?" *On the ground?*

William glanced at Tormond, then lowered his eyes. "Poenitentiae."

It took Maebh a moment to recall the meaning of the word. "Penance?" she asked in Irish, then spoke to the knight. "Why are you eating on the floor? As a penance? What have you done to deserve such a penance?"

Tormond shot William a look of annoyance, then sighed. "Very well. When a Templar is under penance . . . as I am . . . he must eat on the floor. 'Tis a mild penance. Think nothing of it. And don't think ill of me, please."

Maebh sat on one of the vacant stools. "But what have you done?"

"Many things."

"Such as? What sin have you committed?"

"We are all sinners."

What's he hiding? Has he committed some great transgression? Tormond? Never. "What have you done?"

"I left my hauberk—my armor—behind. If I am not wearing it while traveling, I am required to carry it in my hand."

Maebh's jaw dropped. "But 'tis ridiculous! You are not traveling as a knight. We are in disguise, remember? A said we must go in disguise. You could not carry it about. 'Twould draw attention."

He shrugged. "Perhaps you are correct. But 'tis, nonetheless, part of the Rule of the Knights Templar."

"Rule? You must still obey these rules?"

He nodded. "Aye. And I am a Templar. The last Templar. And I shall live by the Rule when I can. And when I cannot, I shall do penance."

Maebh started to protest, but thought of another tactic. "Very well. You have done your penance. Please, sit on the bed next to William. Or on a stool."

Tormond remained on the floor.

"Please, Tormond. Get up from the floor."

He shook his head. "There are . . . other things as well."

"Other things? Other sins?"

He nodded.

"Such as?"

"I would . . . rather not say."

What's he hiding? "Please, Tormond. If we are to travel together, we must be forthright with one another. Whatever you have done, it cannot be that bad." Her face twisted in a derisive sneer. "Are you supposed to carry your *helm* everywhere you go? Is that it?"

"Maebh, you must not—"

"These rules are silly. Trivial. Nonsense." When he didn't answer, she demanded, "What have you done?"

"Very well. I have . . . embraced a woman. I have gazed too long upon the face of a woman." He swallowed. "And I have enjoyed both."

A woman? Me? He means me? "I? I am the cause of your penance?"

He lifted his eyes at last and met her gaze. "You? Oh, no. No. You are not the cause. You are innocent in this. I alone bear the guilt."

My gown. My hair.

My face.

Maebh lurched to her feet. Somehow, she found the presence of mind to set her untouched bowl on her stool before she turned away from him.

Tears spilled from her eyes, coursing down hot cheeks.

She recalled William's words earlier, as the young Sergeant had quoted from the Rule . . . *"most wretched women."*

Most wretched woman. He thinks of me as . . .

"Oh, Tormond! I'm sorry. I—"

She fled from Tormond's room, from the religious she had unknowingly tempted. Once inside her own room, she latched the door, then threw herself on the bed. She buried her face in her pillow, muting her sobs.

Chapter 12

What happened?" William cried in Latin. "What did you say to her? I couldn't understand a word of it."

You told her I was performing a penance, Tormond thought. *'Tis what happened.* He shot the boy an angry look, then immediately felt ashamed. "I explained why I was under penance. I have hurt her."

Tormond set his half-empty bowl on the floor, then stood. "My sword."

The young Sergeant blinked at him without comprehending. "Sword?"

Tormond resisted the urge to roll his eyes. "I may not be able to carry my armor about with me in this town, but I must have my sword to hand at all times." He extended his empty hand. "My sword."

"Aye." William lifted the sword by the slightly curved crosspiece, carefully avoiding any touching of the blade.

Tormond grasped the hilt, lifted the weapon out of the boy's grasp, then sheathed the blade. Instinctively, Tormond reached for his dagger, to make certain it was ready as well. But of course, the smaller weapon was not there—he'd lent it to Maebh. Something about the idea of bringing a sword to talk to a lady bothered him. *But the Rule requires it.*

"Can I come?" William asked with his customary eagerness. "I want to apologize."

Tormond lifted a hand, palm toward the boy. He shook his head. "No. This is my wrong to right. Besides, I will be speaking in Irish. You won't understand."

Ignoring Tormond's warning hand, the young Sergeant rose to his feet. "Then speak in Latin! She understands Latin."

"No, young William. She understands little beyond what is spoken in the Mass or in prayer. And she speaks less of it than she understands."

The boy appeared crestfallen—his chest almost seemed to cave in on itself—but he nodded in acquiescence. "Aye, Brother Knight."

Tormond laid a gentle hand on William's shoulder. "One of your tasks, to help us with our sacred mission, will be to teach us both to speak English. Can you do that? Will you do that?"

William raised his head, his eyes gleaming. An earnest and eager smile split his face from one oversized ear to the other. "I can do that! 'Tis my duty and honor to serve the Knights of the Temple."

Tormond nodded, forcing a smile. "Good lad." The smile vanished as if it had never softened his face. "And now I must try to atone for offending one of the Lord's precious little ones."

As if a millstone were tied about my neck and I were about to be cast into the depths of the sea.

With that proverbial weight dragging at him, Tormond turned and followed after Maebh, shutting his door behind himself.

What can I say? I'd rather face a dozen armed foes than one little nun.

But I've hurt her. Wounded her.

No, I'd rather face an entire army of Moslem Mamluks than bear the thought of leaving Maebh in pain.

I'd rather face the Witches while armed with naught but my faith.

Holy Mary, Mother of God, help me know what I can say to comfort her.

Maebh's door was closed, of course. Tormond had heard it slam.

As he stood without the shut door, he could hear sobs coming from within.

He felt as if his own dagger had been thrust into his gut—thrust in and twisted.

He knocked.

And waited.

He counted off several seconds. No answer came, but the sobbing seemed to quiet. A little.

He knocked again. "Maebh? I'm sorry. I must speak with you. Please let me come in."

The only reply was silence—not even the sound of muffled weeping.

Why did she press me to tell her? Why?
And why, oh, why did I answer?
Because I was annoyed?
Nae with Maebh, surely.
Nae. I was annoyed with myself, with my own weakness.
And I hurt her.

"Maebh, I'm so very sorry. Please let me enter. Please speak with me." *Please tell me you forgive me.* He lowered his voice. "Please forgive me." It was little more than a whisper. He doubted she heard him.

"Please forgive me." The words had not come from him. They had come from her.

She must be just on the other side of the door.

He leaned against the door. "Please open." He said it softly, as softly as he had pleaded for forgiveness.

"But you would have to look upon my face."

He stood straighter. "I would gladly eat on the floor for the rest of my life. I would do it, and I would count it a blessing."

"No. I will not be the cause of your suffering."

"Eating on the floor? 'Tisn't suffering. 'Tis nothing. Maebh. We are on this mission together. God has placed us together. We must find a way to serve together. We must find a way."

Because A said we must remain together.
And the whisperings say I should trust this A.

The thought of continuing without her terrified him. "I have given up everything," he said, "in the service of God. I have given up my family. My brothers in the Order. Everything. I have known hunger, thirst, and fatigue." *And loneliness. Terrible loneliness.*

Am I truly listening to the voice of God?
Or am I simply listening to the longing of my heart.

"But you cannot look upon me. You cannot be around me." There was a pause, and when she spoke again, her voice was softer, barely audible through the door. "I am wretched. I am vile."

The imaginary dagger in his gut twisted again. "No. You are not. You are a Bride of Christ. You are holy. You are sacred."

"I have tempted you. I did not intend to tempt you."

He smiled at that. "I am a religious, but I am also a mortal man. I cannot help but be tempted." *Especially by you. I have known*

121

you less than three waking days, but already I — He shook himself. "The trick of the thing is to acknowledge the temptation — not deny it — and then to defy it." He paused. "Even our Lord was tempted. Yet He denied the devil, saying, *'Vade Satanas post me.'"* He quickly added the translation in Irish, "'Get thee behind me, Satan.'"

Silence.

"Maebh?"

"Are you comparing me to Satan?"

He almost laughed. Almost. "No. Satan intentionally sought to destroy the Lord. You have done no such thing. You cannot help being a woman. God made you as you are." *He made you lovely.* "He fashioned your flesh and your spirit." *He made you lovely inside and out.* "You are holy, because He made you holy."

"God made Eve. The original temptress."

What can I say to that? Holy Mary, Mother of God, what can I say to that?

And then he heard it — that still, small voice. That inner voice that had never led him astray. He smiled. "He made Eve. Aye, He did. And 'tis through her blessed line came our Lord into the world."

"But she —"

"And He made Mary, the Mother of our Lord."

"But I —"

"And He made *you*, Maebh O Broin. And I thank God that He did. And I thank God that He placed you in my path. I *need* you." *I need you by my side. Always.* "You must teach me something. I don't know what that may be, but A said you must."

He paused, waiting for her to answer. When the empty silence became unbearable, he said, "Maebh?"

"Do you believe A? Do you believe his words are true?"

He nodded. *She cannae see you nodding, laddie.* "Aye, Maebh. I do."

"Why? How can you be certain?"

"I feel it. In my soul."

He heard the latch lift. The door opened — just a crack, just enough to let him see one of her gray eyes. Blue and streaked with red. "I must teach you something," she said. "And you have something to teach me."

He smiled. "Please, may I enter?"

Her eye disappeared, and the door opened all the way. And there she stood.

The breath caught in his throat.

Sae bonnie.

Her eyes were puffy with weeping. But there was no denying her beauty.

Or the effect she had on him. "Thank you."

She fixed him with an angry glare, and put her fists on her hips. "If we are to serve together, I want your oath, Tormond MacDonald. Your oath!"

Tormond knew that tone. She'd tried it on him before. He suppressed a grin. "Aye?"

She stepped forward and jabbed him in the chest with her finger. "No more eating on the floor like a dog. Your sacred oath on it."

I can do this. I can.

I am the last Templar. The only Templar.

'Tis as if I am the Grand Master of the Temple. The Master can impose, approve, or suspend any penance.

I can do that. I must do that.

For her.

"Aye." He nodded gravely, but inside, he felt as if the proverbial millstone had dropped from off his neck. Dropped and plunged into the depths of the sea — the stone only, not him with it. "You have my word."

"I want your oath!" Fire blazed in her gray eyes.

"Aye." He reached again for his dagger, but of course, it was not in its sheath. He glanced about the room and spied the pommel of the weapon sticking out from under Maebh's pillow. And so, he drew his sword — slowly so as not to frighten her — then knelt before her. He held the sword point-down, gripping the blade a hand's breadth below the curved crosspiece. He bowed his head. "By the sacred iron of my sword, I swear to you, Maebh O Broin, that I shall never again serve penance by eating on the floor." He grinned, looking up at her, meeting her eyes. "Good enough?"

She continued to glare at him. "And you will never again serve penance because of *me*."

His grin widened. And he was sorely tempted to wink at her. "Tell me, lass, may I still say the *Pater noster*? I mean, should I have . . . an inappropriate thought? That is, in addition to the other one-hundred and forty-eight times a Templar must repeat the 'Our Father' each day?"

She blinked. "One-hundred and . . . Each day?" Then her eyes narrowed. "Ooh! You!" She seemed to quiver with rage. Or at the very least with supreme annoyance. "Aye." She jabbed the finger again, poking him on the forehead. "You may pray—"

"Thank you, lass." He did wink at her that time. "I have your permission to pray. You are most generous."

Her mouth gaped, and her eyes widened in obvious indignation. She began to splutter. "You! Big! Oaf! You—"

"I also swear to serve no penance save prayer for any infraction of the Rule occasioned by my service to God in the company of Maebh O Broin, Shield-maiden of Christ." *And may God grant that service may continue 'til the end of my days, 'til that glorious day when I shall be stripped of this mortal body and no more be subject to the temptations of the flesh. For I cannae bear to be parted from you, lassie.*

The anger in her eyes faded.

"Good enough?" He did not wink that time.

She nodded—slowly and definitively. "And we will have no more of this foolishness?"

Still kneeling and still clasping his sword, he nodded. "Aye. No more foolishness." *I shall be saying many prayers. So many, many prayers.*

"And you will be able to talk with me, to look upon me without . . ."

Without desire? "I cannot promise that. I shall converse with you freely, look upon you without shame, but I cannot promise I will not be tempted." *I am tempted.*

"But—"

"But I shall, with God's grace, endure it." *Because I cannae be without you.*

She smiled then, and fresh tears spilled from her eyes. "And I shall also, with God's grace, endure it."

They gazed into one another's eyes, into one another's souls. Words unspoken—words that could never be spoken, not to each other, not even to Heaven—passed between the two of them in that look. Those words—spoken so often and so casually between a man and a woman—often without sincerity.

And yet, Tormond knew—and he was certain Maebh knew as well—exactly what those unuttered and unutterable words were and what they meant.

In Irish—*Is breá liom tú.*

Or in Scottish—*Tha gaol agam ort.*

Or in Latin, simply—*Te amo.*

After those words—in Tormond's mind, at least—followed four more words. And Tormond suspected those four words would become a prayer to be repeated over and over for the rest of his mortal life—perhaps they would be repeated as often as the *Pater noster.*

Deus det mihi vim.

God grant me strength.

✠·✠·✠

Tormond stared across the nave of St. Peter's Church, at the confessional near the entrance. His own confession was complete. Maebh knelt there, whispering to the priest on the other side of the screen. *I should nae stare. If she glances this way, she'll think I'm staring at her. Trying to listen.* The distance, of course, made such sacrilegious eavesdropping impossible, even if Tormond were tempted—which he most certainly was not.

I dinnae want to know what that poor lassie might have to confess. Some of it—much of it on account of me. He leaned toward William—who was studiously avoiding watching the nun and the priest. "Are you sure this priest is privy to . . . who I am?"

William's head snapped toward Tormond. The young Sergeant's eyes were wide, his cheeks flushed, and his mouth agape. He had all the appearance of a naughty child caught filching apples from a neighbor's tree. "The priest? Father Sebastian?" He blinked, then nodded. "Aye. He is a Chaplain of the Temple. In secret, of course. We Sergeants need him as much as you Knights. As much as you, Brother Knight. And if he were not"—the boy gestured at Tormond's sword—"do you think he would have allowed you to bring weapons into the house of God?"

125

Tormond nodded slowly. "But he seemed so" — What is the word in English? — "*stupebant.* It took him some time . . . to grant me *absolutionem imponebantur.* After my confession, he was silent for a very long time."

William patted Tormond on the shoulder. "Your English is getting better. You have learned much in these past four months." William proceeded to correct the gaps in Tormond's English. "*Stupebant* is 'astonished.' And *absolutionem imponebantur* is simply 'absolution.'"

"Well," Tormond said, "I knew a little English before. A very little. And you're a good teacher."

The youth stood a little taller. "And you, Brother Knight, are an excellent student." He gestured toward Maebh. "So is she. Almost as fast as you." He smiled while gazing at her. "As for the priest, I'm certain he was simply overawed at hearing the confession of the Executioner of God."

Tormond eyed the elderly cleric. Father Sebastian's white hair was so sparse, it was difficult to tell where the shaved tonsure ended, and the man's natural hair began.

Tormond had the unnerving sensation the Chaplain was staring right back at him.

Tormond's confession had not been detailed. It had never been the custom of the Templars to confess infractions of the Rule — only true sins. Other than a few improper thoughts — improper, not lustful — the greatest sin had been that Tormond had not confessed his sins during his last waking, the sixty years prior.

I was a bit distracted last time. But still, annual confession is required.

But what does annual mean in my case?

The priest nodded, then slowly raised his bony hand to his brow, touching the tip of his thumb to the tip of his forefinger, keeping the other three fingers extended.

The Templar salute.

Tormond surreptitiously returned the salute with a slight grin. *Perhaps William is correct. The priest was — what was the word the laddie used? — overawed.*

I am but a man, Father Sebastian. A humble servant of God. Like you.

126

By myself, I am nothing.
But in God's name, I can do all things.

"I've been meaning to ask you something," William said. "Why don't you shave the crown of your head in the tonsure? Like other religious?"

"When we join the Order—" Tormond's jaw clenched. *I am the last. The last of the Order.* "When we *used* to join the Order, we shaved off all our hair, not just the crown of the head. After that, the requirement was that we not grow it so long as to be a danger in battle. Besides, a tonsure would mark me, and I must travel—we must travel *incognito*."

William nodded. "*Incognito* is 'unknown.' Perhaps, 'in disguise' would be a better term."

Tormond nodded. "In disguise. Aye."

"During King Henry's reign—when the king broke from the mother church and established his own heretic church—we had to hide Father Sebastian. His tonsure would have gotten him arrested and burned at the stake."

Burned at the stake. Like Grand Master de Molay.
Like my brother Knights.

"William," Tormond said, shaking off his dark thoughts, "you name the previous king, Henry the Eighth, and his church as heretic. But Pope Clement declared all Templars to be heretic. *I* am a heretic."

William eyed him gravely. "His Holiness was wrong."

Of course, he was. The corner of Tormond's cheek twitched in the hint of a smile. "Careful, laddie. That sounds dangerously like heresy. I hear they burn heretics in this town. Best if you not speak such things aloud."

William shuddered, then nodded. "Aye. 'Twas . . . horrible. I could never forget the screaming. Or the stench."

"You were there?"

The boy nodded again. "I kept thinking, 'That could be me.' Or my father. Or my mother."

"Or Father Sebastian."

The young Sergeant said nothing.

Tormond looked at the youth. "If they had known he is a Chaplain?"

William's eyes were downcast. He muttered something that Tormond didn't catch.

"What did you say, Sergeant?"

William bit his lower lip. He whispered, "When they burned the heretic priest . . . 'twas Father Sebastian . . . who threw in the lit torch."

Tormond's eyes widened, and the breath caught in his throat. He swallowed down bile as he looked upon the priest with new eyes. "Of all the horrors I have seen on the battlefield, even at the hands of the Muslim devils . . ." He could not bear to complete the thought. "And by the hand of a priest!"

I've made my confession. I dinnae have to speak with the man again. Soon, we will sleep, and by the time we awake, he'll have gone to stand before God.

And God will judge him.

Maebh rose from kneeling in the confessional. She wore the latest gown Tormond had commissioned for her at the dressmaker's — all blues and reds, and — despite Maebh's explicit instructions to the contrary — still cut as low over the bodice as all her other gowns.

Her eyes sought out Tormond.

And she smiled.

The horrors of but a moment before lifted from Tormond's mind. A smile crept across his own face, and he strode toward her.

The doors of the chapel were thrust open, causing Tormond to halt. In walked three figures — three persons Tormond had never expected to see in the house of God.

Mother Gwyneth hobbled down the aisle of the nave, accompanied by her two brutish guards. She was clothed in — what Tormond supposed to be — her best frock, one suitable for a feast day. Oddly enough, the brutes on either side of her were dressed in feast-day clothes as well.

Ever vigilant of threats, Tormond noted that neither guard carried a cudgel nor appeared to be wearing a dagger or other weapon.

The ancient whore cast her eyes on Tormond and sneered. Her head swiveled toward Maebh's direction.

Tormond heard the hag's low cackle.

Tormond resisted a sudden urge to confront the vile woman, to drive her from the house of God.

We are all sinners, are we nae?

Gwyneth and her entourage proceeded up the aisle, toward the altar. Though she hobbled and stooped as she went, the crone carried herself—not as a penitent sinner—but as if the church were somehow her personal domain.

Maebh hurried to Tormond's side, then whispered, "What is *she* doing here?"

"Mother Gwyneth?" William responded. "She comes to mass at least once a week."

"She does?" Tormond and Maebh had spoken as one.

"Aye," the boy answered. "But I've never seen her dressed like that. I didn't know she possessed clothes so fine."

Upon reaching the rood—the low wooden barrier separating the transept from the chancel, and thus the altar—Gwyneth and her party did not pause to light a candle or to kneel. To Tormond's astonishment, they went right up to the door of the rood, opened it, and climbed the steps to the altar.

"What's she doing?" William hissed.

Tormond glanced at Father Sebastian.

The elderly priest did nothing, said nothing to hinder the sacrilege. He merely hung his ancient head.

"Tormond!" Maebh whispered. "Do something! Stop her!" She gripped the hilt of the dagger Tormond had purchased for her from William's father, but she did not draw it.

Every instinct within Tormond screamed that he should do as he had done in that unholy abbey. *Slay them!* Instead, he pointed at the priest. "If the Holy Father will do nothing, then I shall do nothing. If he asks for my aid, my sword is his."

The priest glanced at Tormond, then quickly lowered his eyes.

"But the altar!" Maebh's knuckles were white on her dagger.

Tormond put his hand atop hers, preventing her from drawing the weapon. "Will you shed blood in a church?"

"You did!" Maebh's hand trembled. "In the abbey."

William tore his eyes away from the whore and her guards kneeling before the altar and gazed at Tormond. His eyes were huge with apparent disbelief. "B-but you are the Executioner of God!"

Ignoring William for the moment, Tormond fixed Maebh with a hard stare. "'Twas no longer the house of God, if ever it had been. And there, I fought to slay the enemies of God and to protect the innocent."

He turned his steely gaze on William. "And I would say that this house, this *church*, is no longer holy."

"But—" Maebh and William cried together.

Gwyneth's high cackle filled the church, echoing off the stone walls. "Behold! She comes!"

Tormond pointed at the altar. "Look!"

A light blazed above the altar.

A light Tormond had seen before.

And just as before, the brilliance narrowed vertically, a slash of fire in the air. The glow resolved into a woman, floating above the altar of St. Peter's Church. The woman, beautiful beyond imagining, was clothed only in a translucent robe of gossamer blue and a gold collar and earrings. And atop that perfectly coifed, black hair, she wore a familiar recumbent crescent moon of gold.

"Who is that?" William's voice was filled with awe. And Terror. "Is that the Blessed—"

"No!" Tormond and Maebh snapped together.

"'Tis a demoness of the Pit," Tormond said.

"A d-demoness?" William looked to Tormond with pleading eyes. "Slay it!"

Tormond gritted his teeth. "How, Sergeant? With a sword?"

Tormond's eyes went back to the apparition above the altar.

The demon fixed Tormond with her alluring, enticing gaze, as if she were peering into his very soul.

And she smiled.

Chapter 13

The demon's smile froze the breath in Tormond's lungs.

"Behold, Templar!" Gwyneth cried aloud in Latin, her screeching voice filling the church. The ancient whore had risen to her feet as effortlessly as if she had been restored to her youth. She raised both hands in adoration to the alluring horror above the altar. "Behold the Blessed Virgin! Holy Mary, Mother of God! 'Tis she who sustains and supports me in my hour of need. She who will punish my enemies!" The hag cackled in fiendish glee as she turned toward Tormond, Maebh, and William. Flanked on either side by her two brutish guards, she pointed a bony finger at them.

Not at *them*.

At Tormond.

"I curse you, Templar! You are dead! Dead and damned for what you did in her sacred abbey."

William tugged on Tormond's arm. "Do something! Stop her!"

"Stop her?" *Stop whom? The hag? Or the demoness?* Tormond's eyes strayed back to the demon and her captivating gaze. *So beautiful.*

Nae! He ripped his eyes away and focused on the priest, on anything other than the lovely horror above the altar. "Father Sebastian?"

The priest knelt on the stone floor, gazing in adoration at the vision. His wizened hands were held palms together in an attitude of prayer and supplication. His lips moved, and though Tormond couldn't hear the priest's words, he well knew the words of the prayer spilling from the chaplain's mouth.

"*Ave Maria, gratia plena, Dominus tecum. Benedicta –* "

Rage erupted within Tormond's gut. "'Tis not Mary!" He strode across the nave toward the priest, drawing his sword as he went.

The priest cowered before the Templar's righteous anger. The old man raised his hands defensively as if to ward off Tormond's sword.

"I'm not going to smite you, you —" *Don't call the man a fool! Our Lord forbids.*

Calm down, laddie.

Nae in anger.

Ne'er in anger.

Tormond pointed the sword toward the demon. "'Tis not the Virgin. You know 'tis not." *It cannae be.*

Gwyneth cackled, then spoke in English, "Why are you wasting your time with that pathetic worm? He's no sanctimonious man of God!" She laughed, high and loud. "The sniveling, pious wretch is one my regulars! One of my best customers!"

Tormond looked down at the elderly cleric in shock. "You?"

Father Sebastian laughed, showing gaps in his yellowed teeth. It was a nervous laugh, but there was not the slightest hint of shame in it. "Don't you see, Brother Knight?" He pointed toward the demon and the whore with a trembling, skeletal finger. "She is the Blessed Virgin. The Queen of Heaven. And Mother Gwyneth is her high priestess!"

"Aye!" screeched the crone. "And the good father comes to worship at *my* altar often enough. Don't you, dearie duck?"

The priest nodded, grinning. "Aye, Mother!" He licked bloodless lips with a pink tongue. His eyes blazed with the fires of lust. "Aye, Mother!"

Rage and disgust warred in Tormond, his stomach frothing with bile. Tormond pointed his sword at the priest. "You vile —"

"No!" Maebh tugged on his sword arm. "Tormond! No!"

"I'm not going to kill him," Tormond growled. In spite of Maebh's tugging, Tormond's sword arm had barely moved. He glared at the priest. "Leave the house of God!"

Father Sebastian cringed away, but he made no move to depart. "The Queen of Heaven has sanctified this holy house."

Maebh continued to pull at Tormond. "Can't you see, Tormond? This place is no longer the house of God! This place is . . . unholy."

I was nae going to kill him, was I? Tormond stepped back, lowering his sword.

"Come, Crusader!" screeched the hag, drawing Tormond's gaze back to the altar and the lovely demon. "Come worship at *my* altar!"

The whore, moving with an alacrity that defied her advanced years, leaped upon the altar. Cackling like a demented hyena, she squatted and began hoisting her skirts.

The words from the scripture blazed in Tormond's mind —

Et in fronte eius nomen scriptum mysterium, Babylon magna mater, fornicationum et abominationum terrae.
And upon her forehead was a name written, Mystery, Babylon the Great, the Mother of Harlots and Abominations of the Earth.

"Babylon!" Tormond roared. He strode toward the whore, determined to pull her from the altar and thrust her out of the church.

The demon extended her arms toward the knight.

And she spoke. "Come to me, Tormond." The voice was music, like the piping of a flute, the singing of a nightingale.

Tormond faltered, halted. *So lovely.*

"Come, my truest of knights." Her melodic words filled the church, making the air tingle, resonating through Tormond's body. "You have denied yourself for so long. Come to me and partake in the true worship."

The sword trembled in his hands. "No! I will not!"

Or had he said something else? *Verily I come. I come unto thee.* "No!"

"Of course," the vision said, "you do not desire to worship with this wizened, old prune, do you? Someone younger? Someone purer?" The demon pointed at Maebh. "Take the nun, my sons. Take the virgin and place her on my altar."

Gwyneth let out a triumphant crow and slid herself off the altar. "Finally! After all these years!"

The brutish guards strode forward, reaching into their tunics and producing hidden cudgels.

"William," Tormond said, "stay back. Protect her at all hazards."

"Tormond!" Maebh cried.

"Stay back," he commanded. Then he turned all his attention to the advancing men with their cudgels. "You shall not touch her." Tormond grinned, the fierce grin of a warrior facing battle. The men were larger, taller than he was, but their muscles, stature, and wooden clubs would be no match for his steel and the purity of his heart.

Tormond felt no fear.

"No fear, boys!" Gwyneth cried. "The Queen of Heaven will protect you!"

Their weapons, the two clubs, glowed with an unearthly light, the same hue of light that shone around the demon.

What is that?

Holy Mary – the true *Virgin – give me strength!*

Even as Father Sebastian cried, "Not in the house of God," with roars of savage glee, the brutes charged toward Tormond.

Lacking a shield, Tormond drew his dagger, holding it blade-up in his left hand as a parrying weapon.

And he began to sing a battle hymn —

> Give peace, O Lord, in our time,
> Because there is no one else —

And then they were upon him.

He met one blow with the dagger and the other with the sword.

And very nearly lost his grip on both weapons.

The glowing cudgels landed with incredible force. With demonic force. The huge men attacked as if with one mind, landing blow after blow.

Tormond could barely keep his feet. It was all he could do to deflect his opponents' weapons. With each strike, the clubs seemed to shine brighter and brighter. He felt as if the next pair of blows would shatter both his arms.

"See, Crusader?" howled Gwyneth with fiendish glee. "You cannot break their holy weapons!"

I cannae! I cannae break them!

I can barely withstand them.

Then dinnae try, laddie.

Both men raised their clubs as one, and swung them down.

But that time, Tormond did not meet the blow from the right. Moving as swiftly as a diving *cruinne-cruinne* bird, he ducked inside his opponents' reach.

Tormond parried the club on the left with his dagger, even as he hewed at the arm of the man on his right.

The club and the severed arm fell to the stones of the floor.

As the wounded man screamed, staring in horror and disbelief at his life's blood gushing from the stump of his arm, Tormond lopped off the other man's arm.

Tormond thrust his dagger into the heart of one of his foes, then with his sword, chopped off the head of the other.

"Murder!" the priest screamed. "Murder in the house of God!"

Remembering the horrid mother abbess and her dagger in the hellish nunnery, Tormond glanced quickly in the direction of Father Sebastian. But the old priest posed no threat. The old man cowered behind the confessional as if retreating to that ecclesiastical spot would somehow protect him.

"You killed my grandsons!" Gwyneth's anguished wail echoed off the vaulted ceiling.

Tormond wheeled toward the hag and the demon.

The crone remained, but the apparition had vanished.

The whore stumbled forward, demonic strength and agility no longer sustaining her. "Dafydd!" she wailed. "Medwyn! My boys!"

Tormond stepped back as Gwyneth splashed into the crimson pool. She grasped the severed head of one man and gazed into its lifeless eyes. She shrieked.

Clutching the head to her bosom, she turned her horrified eyes on Tormond. "Bastard! Pious bastard! You killed them. You . . ."

Tormond gazed down on the wretch as she sat, the blood of her grandsons soaking into her finest gown. He tried to find some vestige of pity in his heart for the grief-stricken grandmother, but all he felt was a profound sadness. Not for her, but for the men he had sent to hellfire. "I would have spared them had they not attacked, had they not threatened Maebh. Their deaths and damnation are on their own heads."

Gwyneth howled again. "Holy Mary! Strike this monster down!"

But no answer came to her plea.

'Twas nae Mary. He didn't bother saying it aloud. In a voice as cold as a sepulcher, he said, "Your mistress has abandoned you. In the end, the devil always abandons his children."

Gwyneth dropped her grandson's head. She placed both hands in the pool of gore, bent her head, and sobbed. Her ancient body quivered. "Kill me! Please, kill me. Just . . . kill me." Her voice dropped to a whispered croak. "Please."

Tormond took a step away from her.

"No." He stooped and wiped his sword and dagger on an unstained area of one of the dead men's tunics. "You will live. Use the time left to you to repent. Their time is past."

"Mercy, Crusader?"

He shook his head. "No. *Justice* is my mission. I fear letting you live may be a far worse punishment than taking your life. For mercy, you must turn to God."

Tormond sheathed his weapons. He began to turn about to find Maebh and William, but they already stood on either side of him. Maebh was on his right, William on his left. Maebh held her dagger as if she had been ready to use it in Tormond's defense. Of course. William, who had entered the church weaponless, held a pair of candlesticks, one in each hand.

Tormond nodded at the young Sergeant. *Brave lad.*

He turned his gaze to Maebh.

Her eyes brimmed with tears and concern. "You... are unharmed?" she asked.

He nodded. "I need a bath and a change of clothes."

She favored him with a little smile. "Aye, you do."

Her smile took his breath away. In her smile was beauty. True, virtuous beauty. *How could I ever have thought that fiend lovely?*

"What about Father Sebastian?" William asked. "Will you let him live?"

Tormond looked at the priest as the old man continued to cower inside the confessional. "Father, I suggest you find your own confessor."

The old man hid his face in his bony hands and wept like a child who'd lost its mother.

"Pray, Father," Tormond said, "that we do not meet again."

The Executioner turned his eyes away from the old priest.

"Come, my friends," Tormond said. "Let us leave this place." He smiled at Maebh and shook his head. "You were correct, Shield-maiden. 'Tis no longer the house of God."

The last rays of the setting sun gleamed through the windows, casting all in crimson shadow, as if the entire church were drenched in blood.

"There will be consequences for my actions this day," Tormond said as the three of them moved toward the exit.

"Aye," William said. "Mother Gwyneth is a person of influence in Carmarthen. But more out of fear than any other reason. Fear of her guards and her secrets. And without Dafydd and Medwyn to enforce her will . . ."

"Is it time?" Maebh asked. "Is it time for us to leave this place? To sleep?"

Have we done all God sent us here to do? "I'm not sure A would—"

Tormond was interrupted by shouting from the street outside.

Faces peeked through the windows, and figures appeared at the door.

Tormond drew his weapons. "Get behind me. Both of you."

Both Maebh and William moved to obey, but they held their own weapons ready—Maebh with her dagger and William with the two candlesticks.

From the door, one woman pointed at them. "A demoness!" she cried. "Did you see?"

"He has slain a demoness!" a man beside her shouted. "Sir Tormond has slain a demoness!"

"And Dafydd and Medwyn too!" another man cried, making the sign of the cross. "He has slain those villains!"

"Thanks be to God!" another man shouted.

Soon a small crowd of people, of all classes, high and low, of all manner of dress and trade, were streaming into the church. They raised their hands and shouted in a raucous babble. Most of the words were lost, but the smiles on the faces of many were unmistakable in their meaning.

Tormond blinked in surprise and confusion, but he did not sheathe his blades.

One woman, a small, willowy thing, who looked as if she had never had a full belly in her life, fell at his feet and threw her skinny arms around his knees, ignoring the blood on his hose. "Thank you, Sir Tormond!" She wept. "Thank you!"

A man knelt in front of Tormond as well, clasping his hands together. "Thank you, Sir Tormond! Praise be to God!"

"Witch!" a voice cried from behind him.

"Witch!" another screamed.

Tormond pulled himself out of the thin woman's arms. He turned toward the cries of "Witch!"

He turned, expecting to see accusing fingers pointed in his direction, but instead beheld the mob surrounding a screaming and thrashing figure —

Gwyneth!

"Burn her!" they cried. "Burn the witch!"

Tormond lifted his sword and roared, "Stop!"

The mob fell silent as his shout echoed from the ceiling. As one, all eyes turned to him.

"Let her go!" He lowered his voice, but his commanding tone carried through the chapel. "She is a witch, aye. But her power here is broken. Cast her out if you will. But leave her to God."

"But," said one man whom Tormond recognized as the town goldsmith, a corpulent fellow wearing clothes finer than most, "she is a wicked sinner. A witch and a harlot."

"Aye" — Tormond nodded — "that she is. And how often have you, yourself, been in her brothel, Master goldsmith? How many times have you committed sin in her house?"

The man flushed and stammered. "I-I-I—"

Tormond pointed with his sword at each man in the mob. "And you, Master cobbler? And you, stable boy? And you, Lord Mayor? How oft have you entered her house of sin? How many of you have led sinless lives?"

The men began to back away. The women as well.

The ancient whore knelt on the floor, quaking. She was covered in blood, but whether the gore was her own or that of her grandsons, Tormond couldn't tell.

"Let her go." Tormond sheathed his sword and dagger.

Flanked by Maebh and William, Tormond strode toward the cowering old woman. The crowd parted before them. *Woman, where are those thine accusers?* "Get up, Gwyneth," he said. "Go."

Gwyneth covered her head with her hands. "But they'll kill me."

"No," Maebh said, her tone gentle, "they won't. They are convicted by their own sins. And Tormond— And we will see that they do not. Now, go."

"Vade," Tormond said, "et amplius iam noli peccare." *Go, and sin no more.* He knelt before her. "Please, Gwyneth, at the end of your life, take this last chance that God has offered you." He extended a hand to help her rise.

Gwyneth lifted her bloody face and met Tormond's eyes. For a moment, her wrinkled eyes seemed to soften. But only for a moment. "I hate you."

And with that, she swatted at the proffered hand and lurched to her feet. "I hate you all!" She spat at the crowd, then fled from the church, limping and cursing as she went.

Tormond sighed in resignation. *I made the attempt, Lord. I did nae believe she'd take it, but I made the attempt.*

Maebh put a hand on his shoulder. "You did all you could."

"'Twas not enough."

'Tis ne'er enough.

Maebh offered him a hand.

He took it and stood.

He gave her a small smile as his thanks. "And now for that bath. I need to wash myself clean of their blood."

Chapter 14

Do you not fear the sheriff?" Maebh asked as they ascended the narrow stairs at The Boar's Head, climbing toward their rooms. "I know what you did was righteous and just, but yet . . ." She allowed her voice to trail off as she grimaced once again at Tormond's blood-drenched clothing. *I'll never get the blood from his hose or breeches.*

Not "breeches," she corrected herself. *Trunk hose. What a silly name!*

A silly name for ridiculous breeches.

Though Tormond had never allowed her to wash his clothes, always sending his laundry out with the maid or attending to it himself, Maebh felt a strong desire to make the offer. Again. *He faced death. He was defending me. He fought the servants of a demoness. A demoness!*

She shuddered, remembering the horrid vision above the altar—and at the memory of the lingering wish that she, herself, could be half so perfect, half so alluring. *Vanity is a sin. I do not want Tormond to think of me that way. I do not.*

With a small start, she realized Tormond was speaking to her.

" . . . noble born," he said, shrugging his shoulders. "'Tis not justice, but 'tis the way of this sinful world."

"What?" she asked, almost pausing on the stairs.

"The sheriff?" Tormond prompted. "You asked about the sheriff. And if I feared him." He did pause their climb, turning to her with a look of concern. "Are you well, milady?"

She shook herself. "I am . . . quite well." *Because of you.* She favored him with a smile. "What were you saying? Please"—*Oh, what is that word? English is so hard!*—"say it again."

He narrowed his eyes, peering into hers. "I said, the sheriff wouldn't question what I've done. I am a knight. Nobility." He lowered his voice. "If barely that." The corner of his mouth twitched in irritation. "And if there is combat between a knight and two armed ruffians, the sheriff would assume I had the right of it.

Because I am noble born. 'Tis not justice, but 'tis the way of this sinful world."

"'Tis true, milady," William added from behind them. "Sheriff Ioan will assume Sir Tormond was merely dispensing well-deserved justice. A knight may dispense justice. And those two — Dafydd and Medwyn — were a blight on Carmarthen, and no mistake."

"If so," Tormond said, his voice low and dangerous, "why did Ioan not deal with them long before this?"

The youth shrugged. "Why does any officer of good Queen Mary turn his eye away from justice?" He rubbed two fingers against his thumb. "Silver. 'Tis well known that Mother Gwyneth has slipped the good sheriff the odd half crown or two so he would ignore the misdeeds of her grandsons. And 'tis not as if the honorable sheriff were above patronizing her house."

Tormond scowled. "Perhaps, I should go and —" Abruptly, his eyes shifted down the stairs.

The maid, the innkeeper's twelve-year-old daughter, was trudging her way up, laboriously hauling two small pails of steaming water.

Tormond pushed past William. "Here now, young Mererid! Allow me to carry those."

Mererid gasped, halted on the steps, and stared at him with wide, horrified eyes. As Tormond reached for the buckets, she stammered, "N-N-Nay, Sir T-Tormond, milord! You mustn't. Father will give me the st-st-strap!" She swallowed, shaking her head so vigorously the contents of the buckets threatened to slosh over. "Please, Sir Tormond, my father would not take it kindly if —"

Tormond, ignoring her protestations, gently took the buckets from her. "Your father will not give you the" — he paused as if attempting to recall the unfamiliar word she'd used — "*strap*. I shall speak to him." He turned sideways and nodded for the girl to pass by him. "Lead on, lassie."

She stared at him, blinking in obvious incomprehension. "Lead on, milord?"

He chuckled. "I know not where you were going with these. Lead on!"

"Aye, milord." She started up the stairs once, only to pause again. She put both hands to her mouth as fresh terror filled her eyes. "But, Sir Tormond! Your clothes! They —"

He smiled. " — will need washing. I know. I'll attend to it. Now, my fair, young lassie, show me where these are to be taken."

"Aye, milord." She lowered her eyes as she passed, but Maebh could see the girl glance furtively at Tormond — and at his gory clothes — as she did so. "But, milord, I don't understand."

What is it she does not understand? Maebh thought. *His kindness?*

William descended one step toward the knight. "Allow me to —"

Tormond shook his head. "Nay, young William. 'Tis nothing. These weigh less than my hauberk." He lowered his voice to a whisper. "Which I should be carrying at all times. And yet I am not." Tormond winked at Maebh. "Think of it as a penance."

Maebh tried to glare at him, but she couldn't prevent the hint of a smile from curling her lips. *At least he's not eating on the floor.*

And his kindness to the lass is so . . . Warmth blossomed in her cheeks. *As if 'twere possible to admire him more.*

Mererid led the way up the stairs, passing the second floor, and climbing toward the third, the topmost, floor. Tormond followed behind the maid, Maebh followed the knight, and William followed the nun.

When Maebh emerged from the stairwell onto the third-floor landing, she saw the innkeeper, Master Gruffydd — Mererid's father — standing in front of Tormond's door. The portly innkeeper stood as tall and stiff as a sentry guarding the gate of the castle keep. But the man's eyes were wide in shock and mortification. "'Ere now, girl! What's a-goin' on? Guests carryin' their own bath water?" He raised a hand as if to strike his daughter. "I'll —"

"You'll do no such thing." Tormond's quiet, controlled tone communicated both danger and the possibility of painful retribution. "I insisted, Master Gruffydd. The lassie is not at fault. And if I hear that she has been punished in any way, because of *my* actions . . ." What Tormond might do in such a case apparently required no articulation.

Gruffydd nodded briskly. "No, milord! I'll not touch the child. My oath on it! She's a good girl, my Mererid is." The innkeeper hurriedly made the sign of the cross, but he gave the child a nervous smile. "A good girl."

Tormond nodded. "That she is. Now, Master Gruffydd, why are you standing in front of my door?"

"Standing, milord? Standing?" The poor man seemed befuddled by the question.

Tormond smiled—a tight-lipped smile of wearied patience. "You are standing in front of my door."

"Your door, milord?" The innkeeper looked about him as if wondering where he was. "W-W-Why, I-I-I'm guarding it. 'Til you return. I *must* guard it. Let no one enter before you return."

Tormond set the buckets down. "Why?"

"I-I p-promised."

Tormond's patience appeared to be wearing extremely thin. "To whom did you give your promise?"

Gruffydd blinked. "Promise, milord?"

Tormond's expression soured. "Aye, Master Gruffydd. Who made you promise to guard my door?"

The man's brows creased as he appeared to consider the question. He shook his head, seeming utterly confused. "I-I don't rightly know. I-I can't remember."

Tormond's eyes narrowed. "You can't remember?"

"No, milord. Only that I was to guard your door and let none enter, save it were my Mererid fetchin' your bathwater."

So, the bathwater is for Tormond. Maebh stepped closer. *How did they know he needed a bath?* "Was it a man or a woman?"

The innkeeper turned his bewildered gaze on Maebh. "A man? Or a woman?"

Maebh was tempted to grind her teeth, but she gave the man her sweetest smile instead. "Who told you, Master Gruffydd, to guard the door? And to have bathwater brought up?"

Gruffydd blinked like a confused owl. "I don't remember."

William asked, "Master Gruffydd, was he a stranger?"

The poor innkeeper was becoming visibly agitated. "I don't know. I tell you, I don't know!"

143

Witchcraft? She suppressed a shudder. *The poor fellow certainly does seem bewitched. Have the Witches been here? Here? In the inn?*

Tormond laid a hand on the man's shoulder. "Very well. You have done your duty." Tormond smiled—a kindlier smile than before. "And done it well."

The innkeeper grinned at that and stood just a little taller. He bowed his head. "Thank you, milord. Thank you!"

Tormond fished into his purse and brought out two large gold coins. He pressed one coin—a gold sovereign—into the innkeeper's hand. "Now, if you will allow me to pass, good Master gatekeeper?"

Gruffydd stared at the gold, then back up at Tormond. "Pass, milord?"

Tormond's smile widened, suddenly filled with gritted teeth. "Into my room?"

The innkeeper nodded vigorously. "Oh-oh, Aye! Of course." His fist closed around the coin. "Thank you!" He bowed to Tormond. Then he bowed again. "Thank you, milord." He stepped aside, allowing Tormond to unlock his own door. "Mererid! Quick! The water!"

The girl scurried forward.

But Tormond stopped her. "No need." Gently, he took the girl's hand and placed the second gold sovereign into it. "Thank you, lassie."

As Tormond picked up the buckets, the girl stared wide-eyed and openmouthed at the gold in her hand.

A whole sovereign! A whole pound. Twenty shillings. To her, 'twould be as good as a fortune.

"That's yours, lassie," Tormond said, with a meaningful glance at her father—a glance Gruffydd acknowledged with a hasty nod. "Buy something pretty with it."

She nodded mutely, still staring at the coin.

Tormond grinned, though the girl probably didn't notice. "And," he said, "I'll be down to carry the rest of the water myself."

She looked up at that, her fist clamping tightly around the gold. She gestured toward the buckets with her free hand. "That's the last of it, milord. I already fetched the rest."

Tormond nodded. "Thank you, lassie. Give us an hour before you bring up our supper. Will you do that?" Without waiting for an answer, he carried the buckets through the door and into the room.

"As you say, milord," the innkeeper said. "An hour." He grasped his daughter by the shoulder. "Come, Mererid, I'll show you where you can keep that safe."

Something in the man's tone caught Maebh's attention. She spun about and gripped the innkeeper's arm. "Master Gruffydd?"

The man turned and gave her the obsequious smile so typical of innkeepers. "Aye, milady?"

"That money is Mererid's."

He nodded. "Aye, milady. As you say."

"And," Maebh continued, "Mererid shall spend all of it—every farthing—as she chooses. I would be most unhappy if I were not to see her wearing the finest feast-day gown. The finest in all of Carmarthenshire." She fixed the man with her eyes. "*Most* unhappy. And so, I think, would Sir Tormond."

He nodded, shooting a quick glance past her, toward the door. "Aye, milady." He swallowed. "I understand."

"Good. I'm so glad we understand one another."

He swallowed again. "That we do, milady."

She smiled. *One more attempt.* "And who was it told you to guard the door and prepare a bath?"

He blinked, then his eyes seemed to lose their focus as if he were staring at something far away. "I don't remember." His gaze seemed to alight upon her. "My oath on it, milady. My oath."

"Maebh, William," Tormond called from the room. His voice had an air of forced casualness. "Come hither, please."

Maebh let go of the innkeeper's arm, and the man and his daughter hurried away. Maebh could hear their footsteps on the stairs as they descended.

Maebh turned and followed William into Tormond's room.

Two candles burned above the fireplace, casting shadows toward her. In the middle of the floor sat a bathtub, steam rising from it. Beside the tub rested the two buckets, wisps of steam rising from them as well.

And beyond the tub, by the hearth, Tormond knelt, his back to them.

145

Is he praying?

Seizing his chance to help, William hastened to the buckets and emptied one into the tub.

As William hefted the second bucket, Tormond said, "Close and lock the door."

William hesitated, emptying the last of the water into the bath. He glanced at Maebh.

She nodded. "I'll do it."

After she had secured the door, she turned back to the knight.

Tormond had not moved from where he knelt.

"Tormond?" she asked, taking a tentative step toward him. "What is wrong?"

Still with his back to her, he said, "It seems I've had a visitor."

"A visitor?" she asked.

William moved to stand on Tormond's left. "What's that?"

Maebh stepped to the other side of the Templar.

She gasped.

On the floor, in front of Tormond, sat a wooden box. A very familiar-looking wooden box.

And though Maebh could not read, she recognized the single letter carved into the lid —

A

Chapter 15

Maebh wrung her hands as she watched Tormond assessing the box. "Aren't you going to open it?"

He carefully avoided touching it. He appeared to be examining all sides of the chest.

"Aye," he said. "I shall, but first I must check for poisoned needles."

Just as he did the last time. "Don't you trust A?" *Trust our mysterious benefactor about whom we know nothing?*

The Templar nodded slowly, then drew his dagger. "I do trust him. I think I do. But who is to say whether this came from him?" He probed the narrow cleft between box and lid with the dagger's point.

Maebh pointed at the letter engraved upon the lid. "'Tis the very same chest!"

"Aye. 'Twould appear so."

William dropped to his haunches beside Tormond, his eyes alight with eager curiosity. "Is that the box from" — he lowered his voice to a whisper — "the Crystal Cave? The one from" — his whisper dropped even lower, barely audible to Maebh's ears — "A?"

Tormond continued prodding the lid. "I think so, but even then, how do we know 'twas removed from the cave and brought here by our benefactor?"

Maebh shuddered. "If someone else has discovered the cave . . ."

"If that be the case," Tormond said, "we can find another place to sleep."

William nodded and grinned widely. "The Sergeants have prepared a secret chamber beneath the Collegiate Chapel of St. Matthew in Rosslyn. In Midlothian."

Maebh eyed the young Sergeant. "Midlothian? Where is that?"

William opened his mouth to reply, but the knight answered first.

"Scotland," Tormond said. He lifted the lid of the box using the dagger. The lid fell open, and the light of the candles glinted off the contents.

All three of them gasped in wonder.

Save for a small parchment, the chest was filled to the brim with gold coins.

In all her life, Maebh had never seen so much gold. She made the sign of the cross. "But why? We still have plenty for our needs."

"So much," William said with an air of reverence and awe, without the slightest hint of avarice. "It must be very heavy."

Tormond nodded. "Aye. 'Twould have been a great labor for one strong man to carry it up those many stairs." He stroked his bearded chin. "Surely someone would have noticed. This chest could not be concealed under a cloak. I wonder how A got it up here?" He paused, "Assuming 'twas A."

"No wonder Master Gruffydd stood guard," William said.

Tormond retrieved the parchment from the box and unrolled it, spreading it atop the shining gold. He stared at the scroll without speaking.

Maebh could not, of course, read the scroll, but her eyes sought the bottom and spied the bold "A" written there. "'Tis from A."

"Aye," Tormond said, "'tis. But—"

"That's English!" William said, pointing at the message. "You told me A wrote in ancient Latin."

"Correct, young William," Tormond replied. "But 'tis English. And hastily written. Did you note the smudges? The crossed-out words?"

Maebh barely suppressed the urge to stomp her foot in frustration. Instead, she knelt beside Tormond, careful to avoid the drying blood on his clothing. "Will one of you two lettered men please read it to me?"

Tormond gave her a sidelong glance, but he was grinning. "Forgive me, Maebh." He read, "'Tormond, my son, you have done well, as has your faithful companion, Maebh. William of Carmarthen has also performed a great service by'"—Tormond slowed as he struggled with an unfamiliar word—"'tutoring?'"

Tormond looked up at William, who nodded.

"It means, 'teaching,'" the young Sergeant said, beaming with obvious pride.

Tormond nodded, then continued, "' . . . *tutoring* the Executioner and the Shield-maiden in the English tongue and by acting as their guide. Tormond, my son, you have made an end to a great evil in Carmarthen, but your work in this place and time is not yet complete. The prophesied wrong that must be righted is yet to come, but when the time does come, remember the evil of Béziers, commanded by a pope and committed in the name of the Almighty.'"

"Béziers?" Maebh asked, interrupting. "What is 'the evil of Béziers?'"

Tormond scowled. "Twenty thousand people slaughtered in Béziers, in France" — he paused and furrowed his brow — "three-and-a-half centuries ago. By a crusader army of *Christian* knights. At the command of the *pope*." Tormond's lips writhed as if he were chewing on something particularly vile. "The papal legate leading the crusade, an abbot by the name of Arnaud Amalric" — Tormond pronounced the name as if it were a blasphemous oath — "is reported to have given the command, *Caedite eos. Novit enim Dominus qui sunt eius.*"

In her mind, Maebh translated from the Latin, *"Kill them. For the Lord knows those that are His own."*

Kill them all?

She put her hands to her mouth, but she would rather have covered her ears.

"And so," Tormond continued through gritted teeth, "the crusaders slaughtered the whole city. Every man, woman, and child. Because *some* of the people and the ruler of the city were heretics."

"*All* of them?" Maebh did not attempt to hide the horror in her voice. "Even the innocents?"

He met her wide eyes and nodded grimly. His own eyes looked haunted, ashamed. "Twenty thousand. Slaughtered like pigs. In the name of God."

Holy Mary, Mother of God! "Where — Were *you* there? Doing the killing?"

He shook his head. "Not I. I had not yet been born."

Maebh shuddered in relief. *He was not there. He did not . . . murder innocents. He would not. He would never. Tormond could not be so . . . unjust.* "Were" — she paused — "Templars involved?"

He shook his head, scowling once again. "No, thanks be to God."

He turned his face away from her and resumed reading. "'Ask yourself, my son, had you been there, what would you have done?'" Tormond paused.

Judging by the disgust evident in Tormond's scowl and the tension in his clenched jaw, Maebh could divine the answer to that question.

Tormond took a deep breath and read on. "'Trust in the whisperings of the Holy Spirit. You will know what to do when the time comes. But tonight, you have another task to perform. You have broken the power of the demoness's high priestess in this town. However, Gwyneth's legacy of evil remains. This is not an evil that can be slain with the sword. No, to slay this evil will require other weapons. Indeed, you may not save a single soul this night, but you must make the attempt. Ask Maebh for guidance in this. She will know what you must do.'"

Tormond turned to look intently at Maebh.

Her wide eyes flitted from Tormond to the parchment and back to Tormond's intense gaze. "I? *I* will know what to do? What is he talking about?"

Tormond's brow creased as he turned his eyes back to the parchment. "It says, 'She *will* know what you must do.'" He cocked his head and met her eyes once more. "Perhaps that means that you might not know *now*, but *will* know later?"

"I most certainly do *not* know what you must do. Not now. I don't think . . ." Her voice trailed off as she shook her head in dismay.

He gave her a kindly smile. "I believe 'tis what *we* must do — not *I* alone. We are on this mission together, are we not?"

Maebh felt the heat in her cheeks. But she did not look away. "Aye, Tormond, we are."

The silence stretched out as they gazed unblinking into each other's eyes, into each other's souls.

I love you. God forgive me, but I do.

William coughed softly. "That's, uh, all it says. There is only the A at the bottom."

Both Tormond and Maebh averted their eyes, looking once again at the parchment.

"Perhaps," William continued, "if you do not know now, *Sister*" — the emphasis on her title was not lost on Maebh — "you should consider in *prayer* what it is we should do?" He paused. "While *Brother* Tormond bathes. Before supper?"

Maebh nodded quickly. *William knows. Well, of course he does. A blind man could see it — the way Tormond looks at me, the way I look at him.*

I must bind my heart.

What is it Tormond is always muttering under his breath?

Deus det mihi vim.

God grant me strength.

And what in the name of Heaven is it I'm supposed to know? How am I to know what we should do?

✠•✠•✠

As she knelt at her bed alone in her room, clasping her crucifix in both hands, Maebh pleaded with God. She had started the prayer in Latin, of course, but before long, she was pouring out her heart to the Almighty in her native Irish. And her pleading had grown increasingly frantic.

Surely, the hour is past!

"Please tell me what we are to do! I don't hear the *whisperings* as Tormond does. I am no Soldier of Christ. I'm simply a nun. I'm simply . . . me."

How does Tormond do it? How does he . . . hear what he does?

"I don't know what to do!"

She buried her face in the blanket and sobbed. "I don't know what to do."

You have pleaded. You have demanded. But you have not yet asked a question.

The words were in her own voice, but the words were not hers.

She looked up, her bleary eyes searching the room as if she expected to see a heavenly messenger.

But she saw nothing and nobody.

Ask a question? What question? She opened her mouth and whispered, "What should we do?"

She squeezed her eyes shut and listened with all her heart. *Please answer!*

But no answer came.

Did I imagine it?

I asked a question! I did!

"The message from A said I would know what to do. But I don't know anything. I'm not Tormond. I'm not the Executioner. I'm nobody. No person of consequence. Only a woman. Nothing."

You are a woman, a beloved daughter of God. You are of great consequence to Him.

Fresh tears leaked from her tight-closed eyes. These were no tears of anguish — they were tears of joy, like a light, summer shower on a parched flower. She felt warmth envelope her. It started at the crown of her head and flowed down her body, like honey.

Like pure love.

"I thank Thee. Oh, I thank Thee." She swallowed. "I love Thee."

The warmth surged.

"But . . . But I love Tormond too. I love him. And 'tis a sin."

God is love, and love, in His sanctioned place and time, is never sin.

"But I am a Bride of Christ," she whispered, "am I not?"

There was no answer, only a feeling of emptiness. The warmth was gone.

She shook herself. *No more of that. Not now. Ask another question.* "Gwyneth is defeated. A said so. But her evil remains. We are to fight this evil with weapons other than a sword. But what other weapons do we have?" She remembered the knife at her waist. "Daggers?" She shook the crucifix in her hand. "The cross?" *What do we have? Our clothes?* She considered the horses in the stable — Órd Dubh, Tormond's great black warhorse, and Fiona, the gentle gray mare Tormond had purchased for her the day after she and Tormond arrived in Carmarthen. "Horses? We possess naught else." But she realized that was not true. She thought of the bounty of gold in the chest A had provided. "Gold?"

The warmth returned.

"But money — no — the *love* of money is the root of all evil, is it not? Surely not the gold? Could it be the gold?"

That feeling of pure love intensified.

She nodded, smiling. "The gold, then! But who would need that much gold? Surely, we — Tormond and I — do not. Who would need it?" *Gwyneth's evil,* she thought. *Who has been hurt most by her evil?*

And the answer came to her, clear as sunshine piercing the clouds after a summer rain.

✠·✠·✠

Tormond had barely finished fastening the second buckle on his double-wrapped sword belt over a fresh pair of silly, puffed-out trunk hose, when there came a pounding at his door.

"Perhaps," William said as he moved toward the door, "'tis the maid with our supper?"

"Hold," Tormond whispered in command. He drew his sword and dagger.

William nodded, then backed away from the door, drawing his own dagger.

"Who is it?" Tormond demanded.

"Tormond!" Maebh's voice. "'Tis I! I have the answer!"

Maebh. His heart quickened in anticipation. Tormond nodded at William, and the young Sergeant sheathed his knife, grinned, and opened the door.

Maebh burst into the room. Smiling. And it was as if the room needed no other light than the radiance of that smile.

Tormond sheathed his weapons, then made the sign of the cross. *Another penance.*

She crossed the floor, looking as if she might throw her arms around him.

Tormond's eyes grew wide, and he took a step back. Away from her.

Away from the embrace he feared. And desired.

Maebh lowered her arms and bit her lower lip. The smile was gone, and without it the candles seemed inadequate. "I have the answer! We must—"

"Your pardon, milady. Milord." Mererid stood in the doorway, bearing a tray with three steaming bowls, a loaf of bread, a pot of butter, and three mugs of ale. She curtsied as she smiled at Tormond. "I have some nice beef stew and fresh bread. Hot from Mum's oven."

Tormond gave the girl a courtly bow. "Thank you, fair maid. You can place it on the table." He pointed at the small table, surrounded by the three sturdy chairs Master Gruffydd had provided months before, when the stout innkeeper finally realized that his wealthy and well-paying guests would never be taking their meals in the inn's common room.

The maid hurried over to the table, then placed the tray upon it. She turned toward Tormond. "Do you wish me to empty the tub now or after your supper?"

William chuckled. "No need, Mererid. I've already dumped the bathwater out the window."

Mererid appeared crestfallen. "You did?"

Tormond grinned at her. "Aye, he did. That water was tinged with blood. 'Tis something for a knight or his squire to deal with, not a maid."

Mererid eyed William curiously. "You cannot be his squire, William. You're the blacksmith's son. I've known you all my life."

William's mouth twisted in a rueful grimace. "No. I'm not. I'm more like his serv—"

"He's my, *friend*," Tormond said. He gave the girl a courtly bow. "Now, lass, if you will give us half an hour, we'll eat this tasty stew and your mother's fresh, hot bread, and then—"

"And then," Maebh interrupted, "we'll be off on a—" She paused as if searching for a word, then glanced at William, who shrugged. She looked to Tormond. "I know the word in Irish." She whispered, "Errand."

Tormond almost laughed. He grinned instead. "'Tis the same in English, lass. Errand."

"Oh!" she exclaimed. And that glorious smile returned. She turned her beaming countenance to Mererid. "Then we shall be off on an *errand*! You may clean up after that."

The girl grinned and curtsied once more. "Aye, milady. Milord. William." She wheeled and hurried from the room, closing the door after herself.

Tormond strode over to Maebh. He stopped himself just short of grasping her by the shoulders. *Surely, I was nae going to embrace her, was I?* "Out with it, lass. What's the answer? What are we to do?"

Maebh opened her mouth as if to answer, then abruptly shut it. After a moment's consideration, she said, "I'll tell you after we pray. While we eat." She dropped into one of the chairs. She closed her eyes and inhaled deeply, then sighed. "I love the smell of fresh bread!"

Tormond gaped at her in astonishment. *She has the answer! Why is she making us wait?* "If you—"

But Maebh's dazzling smile and her bright, gleaming eyes stole his breath away.

God grant me strength.

Her smile transformed into an impish grin. "Have you said your sixty *Pater nosters*, Tormond? Your sixty prayers before the meal?"

He nodded. "Aye. In the tub."

She winked—*winked!*—at him. "Then I think we've both prayed sufficiently for now." She grasped the hot loaf, before snatching her fingers away. "Ooh! 'Tis warm!" She drew her dagger and plunged it into the loaf. She hacked off a chunk, then dipped the dagger carefully into the butter dish. As she began slathering butter over the steaming bread, she gave Tormond and William a wry grin. "Aren't you going to have any? It smells delicious!"

Tormond sighed and shook his head. *She has the answer! Why the delay?* "I'll never understand women. Not if I live another thousand years." He chuckled and settled into his chair. "And I just might live that much longer," he muttered. *If the Witches go on escaping me.* He grinned at Maebh. "Slice me off a wee bit of that bread, lass. If it pleases you."

Triumph shone in Maebh's eyes. That triumph quickly melted into genuine affection—affection for him. "Now," she said, "as to what we are to do this night . . . It involves all that gold."

"The gold?" William asked, glancing at the chest which sat under Tormond's bed. "All of it?"

"Aye," she replied as she chewed a mouthful of bread dripping with butter. "All of it."

She proceeded to explain her plan.

And as she did, Tormond nodded. *A spoke true. Maebh does indeed have the answer.*

I would never have thought of it.

Nae if I lived another thousand years.

Chapter 16

Never in all his unnaturally long life had Tormond set foot in a brothel. *And yet, here I am, consorting with whores.*

Indeed, flanked by Maebh and William, Tormond stood at the center of the common room of Gwyneth's bawdyhouse, while six prostitutes sat in chairs before him, staring in disbelief at the thirty small sacks lying in a pile on the floor.

"Each purse," Maebh explained to the assembled women — it had been her idea, after all — "contains one-hundred gold crowns. That makes five purses for each of you. Five-hundred crowns. For each."

Tormond watched the prostitutes' faces as Maebh spoke. The only light in the room came from the fire on the hearth and two candles. Tormond had noted the absence of any other candles in the common room. At first, he'd wondered why so little light would be available, because this room was where Gwyneth displayed her "merchandise" — the women she rented to any man who had silver with which to pay. But after Tormond had taken a good look at the "merchandise," he understood.

The shadows — they hide much.

In the dim light, a man might not notice the haggard, pock-marked faces hidden under powder and rouge. He might fail to note the missing and rotting teeth, and worst of all, the sunken, haunted eyes. In the dim light, a man might be able to imagine those painted faces were bonnie and desirable. Two of the whores seemed pretty enough, he supposed, to catch a lustful eye — or might once have been so. He recognized those two women as the pair of whores he'd seen coming out of Gwyneth's house on the morning he and Maebh first entered Carmarthen. *Those two are the prize ponies, the ones Gwyneth trotted out to lure customers in.* The other four...

I cannae see how any man who looked closely could desire them. I suppose once alone in a darkened room . . .

Aye. And thus, laddie, the dim lights.

I wonder how many years . . . or how few . . . 'twould take to age them so?

157

Mayhap, nae a one of them is above thirty years of age, though they appear to be much, much older.

Truly, "most wretched women."

Tormond felt not the slightest stirrings of lust for any of these creatures. They inspired in him but one emotion, and that mightily — pity.

One of the women, though her hair was not yet gray, looked as old as a grandmother. "Why?" she asked, barely opening her mouth as she spoke. That practiced, close-lipped manner of speaking seemed to be intended to conceal her dreadful teeth. "Why are you a-doin' this?"

She turned contemptuous eyes on Tormond. Such a look of hatred burned in those sunken eyes that Tormond was taken aback.

She hates me. Why? I've ne'er laid eyes on her. Nae, nor she on me, as far I know. Is't because I drove Gwyneth away? Gwyneth and her protection, such as it was?

Earlier, he'd seen the older-looking woman cast the same baleful gaze on William.

Or is it simpler than that?

Aye, 'tis. She hates men. All men.

Those painted, nearly closed lips, curled in a sneer, "Ol' Mam Gwyneth—she comes 'ere all cursin' an' a-wailin' an' says as you upped an' murdered 'er boys, Ol' Bruiser an' Beater, as we calls 'em. Then she empties her coffer an' runs off for parts unknown. Leaves nothin' for us. Not like she ever gives us any money. Nah. Roof o'er our 'eads, a crust of bread, an' ale's good 'nough for the likes of us slatterns. Now, all we gots is the roof. Gwyneth's taken the rest. Even poured out the ale. Thanks to you." She looked as if she was going to spit at him, then thought better of it. "I s'pose that makes you the new master roun' 'ere."

Tormond shook his head in disbelief. "Nay. I—"

One of the younger whores sneered at him. "If you are expectin' us to whore fer you now—"

"Shut your mouth, Bess!" snapped the first woman, finally baring her hideous teeth as she snarled at the younger prostitute. "You knows 'e's just gonna dangle that money in front of us." She turned her malevolent gaze back to Tormond, and that time

Tormond was certain the hatred was directed at him alone. "An' then he's gonna just put us back to work. We won' see a bleedin' farthin'."

"No!" William spluttered. "You don't understand! 'Tis not —"

"An' what be you a-doin' here, Will-o-the-Forge?" sneered the older woman. "You ne'er set a foot in 'ere afore. You too good for the likes of us?"

Bess laughed derisively. "Is't 'cause he don' got two coppers to rub together?" She pointed at William — or rather at his groin. "Nah. 'Cause he don' got no stones!" Her cackles rivaled those of Gwyneth, her former mistress.

Tormond was about to reply when Maebh cut him off. "Enough."

"Oh," the older woman growled, "then I s'pose you're the new mistress?"

"No," Tormond said. "No mistress. No master. You're free. The money is yours. No conditions. You're free to go. Wherever you wish. And if you choose to go, I will pay for guards to protect you on your way."

All six prostitutes gaped at him, then at the money.

Bess said, "'Ere now. 'Ow does we know them sacks amn't filled wi' coppers instead o' gold? Or maybe just pebbles?"

Tormond suppressed a growl of vexation. He bent down, scooped up a purse, and extended it toward the younger woman. "Careful. Gold is heavy. That sack alone weighs more than half a stone. And they're all the same."

Bess gaped at him as she took the purse. "Curse me! 'Tis 'eavy!" She set it on her lap and undid the lacing at the top. An unmistakable yellow glint caught the firelight. "Curse me! Gold!"

Another woman snatched at the bag.

"'Ere, now!" Bess cried, slapping the other woman's hand away, safeguarding the purse like a dragon hoarding its plunder. "This 'ere's mine, Mari! Leave off!"

Three of the other women were on their knees, scrabbling for the purses on the floor. The one called Mari soon joined them. And so did Bess.

"We're rich!" one cried.

"Mine!" another screamed. "You got your five!"

"Five 'undred pounds!" Mari crowed. "A bleedin' fortune!"

"I could buy anythin'!" a third cried as she gathered her share. "I could buy me own 'ouse! An' servants! An' — an' a carriage an' horses!"

"A new frock!" Bess cried. "A dozen new frocks. One for ev'ry day o' the bleedin' week!"

"Mine!" Mari cried, clouting another woman with her fist. "Get your cursed 'ands off!"

In a moment, five women were clawing, punching, and hissing at each other like cats trapped together in a tiny cage.

"STOP!" roared Tormond, his voice like thunder in the room.

The five women on the floor froze, at least two them with their fists still enmeshed in another woman's hair. Their heads turned as one — even the two held by the hair — to stare at Tormond with wide, frightened eyes.

"Five hundred crowns each," he said in a softer tone, "is enough to buy your own inn somewhere. Or you could buy a farm. Raise chickens or — "

"Why?" the oldest woman asked. Of the six, only she had remained in her chair. She had not scrabbled for the gold nor fought with the others.

All eyes turned to her.

Her own eyes no longer burned with hatred. They had narrowed in suspicion. "Why?" she repeated. "Why be you doin' this? Wha' do you wan' of us? O' me?" She scowled. "No man ever gave me nothin', no' unless he wan'ed somethin' in return. An' if the price were too high, he just took wha' he wan'ed. Wha' do *you* want?"

Maebh shook her head, a look of utter incomprehension on her face. "Nothing. We want nothing of you. Nothing at all."

"Why?" the woman demanded once again. "I'd bed a poxy cripple for a penny or a crust o' bread or a half-pint of sour ale. But nothin' for nothin'. That's wha' me own father always tol' me, afore 'e upped an' sold me to Mam Gwyneth for two shillin's. Two shillin's. That's all I was to him. So, tell me, Sir Knight. Why?"

Maebh opened her mouth to reply, but Tormond answered first. "Because our Lord Jesus walked among sinners, among publicans and whores." Tormond walked toward the woman slowly, his hands open. He didn't dare put his left hand on the pommel of his sword to steady it as he walked lest he should frighten her. But her eyes were on his eyes—not on his sword. "Because," Tormond continued, "our Lord refused to cast the first stone at the woman taken in adultery." He knelt in front of her on one knee. *This did nae work with Gwyneth, but I must try.* "He said to her, 'Go thy way and sin no more.'"

Her lips curled in a sneer. "So tha's your price, is't? Sin no more?"

He shook his head slowly. "No price. None."

"Whorin' is all I know. Wha' if I ups an' takes your money and buys m'self another brothel? Or just stays 'ere an' runs this one? Wha' then?"

Tormond shook his head again. "No price. No conditions. You can live your life as you choose. You can do with the money whatever you choose." *'Tis nae working.* "We don't know if the woman taken in adultery did as our Lord instructed. The scripture doesn't say what she did after He told her to go and sin no more."

Her lips trembled, and her eyes grew wet. "Wh-why?" The tears spilled down her powdered cheeks, making streaks in her rouge like trickles of blood.

Tormond reached for her hands. She flinched, but allowed him to gently grasp them both. "Because our Lord loved her, even though she was a sinner. He loved her *because* she was a sinner. He loved her and He wanted her to be able to begin her life anew." He released one of her hands and gently wiped the tears from her cheeks. "What's your name, lass?"

"Angharad." She quaked with suppressed sobs.

Tormond smiled. "Angharad. A lovely name. What does it mean?"

She shook her head. "I"—she swallowed—"don' know."

"It m-means," William said, his voice breaking, "'much loved.'"

Tormond nodded. "Aye. Well, Angharad. You are indeed much loved." He glanced upward. "*He* loves you. *He* wants you to begin anew. Please, Angharad, please begin anew."

The suppressed sobs burst from her like a sudden rainstorm after a long drought. She pulled her hand free of his and threw her arms around Tormond's neck.

The

Tormond sighed softly. Another penance. He put his arms about her and held her as she clung to him and sobbed.

A penance I shall bear gladly.

✠·✠·✠

Much later that night, Tormond and Maebh at last bade goodnight to an exhausted, yet exuberant William. "I don't think I shall sleep a wink," the boy had said at their parting. "What a day this has been!"

Aye, Tormond thought. *What a day, indeed.*

The young Sergeant had, in the course of a single day and a night, experienced a world of emotions. He'd known terror at the sight of the demon and the deadly combat in the church, experienced awe and enthralled curiosity at the sudden appearance of the gold-laden chest left by the mysterious A, and felt trepidation and unholy—though natural—curiosity at entering the forbidden brothel, which sat just across the street from his home all his young life. And finally, he'd been blessed with joy at the unexpectedly moving scene of redemption within that same den of sin.

What a day.

After leaving the brothel, Tormond and Maebh had counselled with William and his father at the smithy. The Templar charged the Sergeants with arranging a safe escort for the six former prostitutes—collectively or individually—to wherever those women might choose to travel to begin a new life. At least, Tormond fervently *hoped* those women would choose to become *former* prostitutes.

With the waxing gibbous moon shining low in the night sky and a gentle breeze stirring their cloaks, Tormond and Maebh strolled back toward the inn. As had become their custom in public, Tormond offered his arm, and Maebh took hold of it. She walked on his right, of course, so he could—should the necessity arise—be free to draw his sword in her defense. It was certainly a more intimate way of walking together than would be proper for a religious and a nun, but then again, they were not known to the town as Brother Tormond and Sister Mary Elizabeth. Rather, the townsfolk knew them as Sir Tormond of Skye and his distant cousin, Lady Maebh of Kilkenny. Both names were true and accurate, as far as that went. He was a knight, and she had been born a lady.

He noted her smile—an utterly female, secret smile. A delightful smile, with no missing teeth—though the smile wasn't directed at him.

He realized he was grinning as well. "What are you thinking?"

She did not glance his way, but her smile broadened. She sighed happily. Her smile softened, then faltered and vanished. "Do you think they'll truly start anew?"

Tormond had the distinct impression that her question was a diversion, that she had been thinking of something else entirely—of what, he had no notion. "I don't know. I think Angharad will choose another life. The rest?" He shrugged. "I shall pray for them. I shall hope. We have done all we could."

She nodded, gently squeezing his arm. "Aye. We did all we could. But without the gold . . ."

"Aye. Without the gold . . . Nay, without A . . ."

Maebh nodded again, then shook her head. "Who is he? How does he know . . . the things he knows?"

Tormond shrugged. "I don't know, but I am grateful to God for sending him to guide us. Sometimes, a prayer of thanks is all we can do. May God bless him, whoever he may be." *Whatever he may be.*

Maebh made the sign of the cross with her free hand. "Thanks be to God."

They strolled in silence for a while, neither of them in a hurry to be quit of the other's company.

Once they were inside The Boar's Head, a chorus of greetings—and words of gratitude and praise—rose from the assemblage of men and women in the common room. Some raised their mugs of ale and beer with cries of "To Sir Tormond! The demon slayer! And to his fair cousin! Lady Maebh!"

I did not slay the demoness. But Tormond inclined his head toward them. "Thanks be to God."

The crowd lifted their mugs. "Thanks be to God!" Several of them added. "For Sir Tormond!" A few more added, "And Lady Maebh!"

He nodded once more. "Good night and good morrow."

With the cheers following them, Tormond and Maebh ascended the stairs.

163

When they arrived at Maebh's door, Maebh released his arm. She retrieved her key from her purse and handed the key to Tormond.

He unlocked the door, returned the key to Maebh, and then, as was his custom, drew his sword and entered the room first. A fire burned on the hearth, providing a dim light—evidence that the maid, Mererid, had been in the room and attended to the fire. Tormond scanned the room, probing under the bed with his sword. He opened and checked the wardrobe, finding naught but Maebh's empty clothes. He made certain the window was closed and latched. Only then did he sheath his sword. *How did A enter my room undetected? How did he carry that heavy chest up here with no one noticing?* Tormond winced, remembering how he and William had hauled those thirty sacks of heavy gold down the stairs and across town to the bawdyhouse.

He plucked a long matchstick from the jar beside the hearth. He lit the match in the fire, then lit the two candles on the mantle.

He turned toward Maebh.

She stood in the doorway, and that secret, intriguing, feminine smile had returned.

What are you thinking, lass?

She stepped through the doorway and into the room. The reflected light of fire and candles danced in her lovely gray eyes.

Tormond's breath caught, and his pulse quickened. Unlike the women in the brothel, Maebh was beautiful in truth. The dim light concealed no imperfections.

God grant me strength.

'Tis nae her eyes as makes her sae bonnie. 'Tis her purity, her virtue. 'Tis her soul.

And I would lay down my life, sacrifice anything to protect and preserve that precious soul.

He smiled and gave her a courtly bow. "Sleep well, Maebh."

She curtsied and replied, "Sleep well, Tormond." Her smile quickened his pulse.

Anything to protect and preserve you.

He exited the room quickly, and she closed the door behind him. He lingered in the corridor until he heard the click of the lock.

Anything.

He shook himself, then retrieved his own key from his purse. He drew his sword again, then unlocked the door. Entering the room, ready to search it as searched Maebh's room, he froze.

He immediately knew that, though the door had been locked and the window was secure, someone had been in the room. Someone other than the maid.

The empty wooden box with the bold A engraved on the lid was gone. And in its place, laid out on the floor as if by a mother's loving hand, was Tormond's armor—including helm, hauberk, coif, chausses, padded gambeson, arming cap, and breeches—as well as his shield, axe, and his white tabard with the red cross. And next to that was piled all the barding armor for his horse, Órd Dubh.

His eyes were drawn to the fireplace mantle where burned two candles. Tormond well knew the maid would kindle the fire to warm the room, but she'd never leave the candles burning. Between the two candlesticks, weighted under a small stone, sat a bit of parchment.

Tormond stepped past his weapons and armor on the floor and hurried to the mantle. He read the note.

Very well done, my son. I hope you will forgive me for doing so, but as you can see, I have fetched your weapons and armor from the cave. You will need them soon.

A

Chapter 17

The dagger in William's father's hands was a thing of beauty.

William sat in the smithy with his father, Thomas Smythe, as the senior Sergeant skillfully worked his craft. But though William had known great joy working alongside his father, the young Sergeant felt a great heaviness in his heart. *As if any chance for true happiness is slipping through my fingers.*

All his life, William had loved the smells of the smithy — hot iron, coke fire, leather, oil, and good honest sweat. Of late, however, he'd found those familiar scents to be confining, as if they circumscribed the walls of his life, castle walls that he could neither scale nor escape.

A castle . . . or a prison.

"The summer is coming to an end," Thomas, William's father, said as he sharpened the new dagger he'd fashioned. Sitting in the corner of the smithy, Thomas moved his foot smoothly up and down on the foot pedal that kept the sharpening wheel turning. "And soon 'twill be time for the Executioner to sleep once more. He and the sister." The master smith held the dagger with the blade pressed lightly against the spinning granite stone. A few sparks flew from the blade. Any spark that hit the senior Sergeant's lap instantly disappeared as it cooled against his much-charred leather apron. "The time we have prepared for all our lives will be over."

"Aye, Da, I know." William nodded. *And it weighs so heavily upon my heart.* "Tormond — I mean, Brother Tormond said — "

"'Tis well, lad. The Executioner himself told you to refer to him as Tormond. And to the sister as Maebh. Don't change that custom simply because you're in my presence."

"Aye, Da." William nodded again quickly. "Tormond said there is a task yet for him to do here. *Another* wrong to right."

Thomas turned the blade over and pressed the other edge to the spinning stone. "But you still don't know what that task might be?"

William shook his head. "No, Da. Even Tormond doesn't know."

"And you've not told me how the Templar knows there is yet another task to perform before he resumes his sacred mission."

I can't tell you. I gave Tormond my word.

"I know," his father said, shaking his head. "I know about your promise. A man must keep his word. And the Templar's commands are to be obeyed. That is what we Sergeants do. We obey. No matter the cost."

As his father lifted the dagger and inspected the blade, turning it so the edge caught the light, William extended a hand. "Here, Da. Let me sharpen it. 'Tis usually my task to do the finishing."

Thomas pursed his lips and shook his head. He didn't look in William's direction but, keeping his eyes on the work, merely switched hands, holding the hilt with his left hand, and pressing the other side of the blade against the sharpening wheel. "No, lad. This is a special commission. No hand but mine must do the work."

"'Tis a fine weapon," William said. "The gold and silver in the pommel. It should fetch a high price." He paused. He'd asked the next question before, but had never received a satisfactory answer — or any answer at all. "Who's it for?"

"High price?" His father lifted an eyebrow, acting as if he'd not heard the second question. "You might say that. Very high indeed. The highest."

William struggled to keep the annoyance from showing. His father had avoided the question every time. "Is it Sergeants business? The Council?"

His father nodded. "That it is. But" he said, cutting off William's next question, "not for your ears just yet. You will know soon enough." He turned the dagger over and began to sharpen the other side. "Aye, soon enough."

Not for my ears yet. Sergeants Counsel. Not 'til I'm fully initiated. Another year! Then I'll be old enough. I will know all the secrets, all the mysteries.

Not all the secrets of the Temple. Those mysteries are for the Knights only.

For Tormond only.

The last Templar.
How I wish I could be a Templar!
But I cannot.

"Dreaming again, son?"

William started. "What?"

His father examined the edge of the dagger, looking for imperfections—tiny spots where the light reflected on the very edge of the blade. "You know 'tis impossible. No use dreaming about it. You can never be a Knight."

I could, if Tormond would knight me.
But he won't. He can't.

I am not noble. Only Queen Mary could grant me that. "I know, father."

"You are a Sergeant of the Temple. That is a high honor. A very high honor. Be content with that."

William nodded. "I will." *I will try.*

"You told Tormond about the chamber in Rosslyn, aye?"

"Aye. I did. Do you think he—*they* will go there? This time?"

His father shrugged. "I don't know. 'Tis at the Executioner's discretion. What did he say?"

"Nothing. I told him about Rosslyn. 'Twas last week, the night after the demoness appeared. The night we went to Mam Gwyneth's house. To liberate . . . those women. But he said nothing about going to Rosslyn."

Thomas nodded. He grabbed an oiled cloth from the workbench and began cleaning the weapon. "Almost finished."

"May I see it?"

His father gave the sharpened blade another wipe with the oiled cloth, then handed it—hilt-first—to William.

The youth held the dagger up to the sunlight streaming through the slats in the smithy wall. Dust motes floated in the beams of the late morning sun that glinted off the steel. The nine-inch blade had a diamond-shaped cross section that narrowed cleanly to the sharp tip, the crosspiece curved slightly upward, and the handle was covered with wire-wrapped brown leather. A golden cross on a field of silver decorated the octagonal pommel.

"Beautiful. 'Tis fine work, Da. Very fine work. It looks very much like Tormond's dagger. Very like. Though his has no gold nor silver." William drew his thumb across the edge of the blade in several places, feeling the keenness of the edge. "Fine edge too. You said, 'Almost finished.' It appears finished to me. So, do you have only the scabbard yet to complete?"

His father did not smile at his son's praise. Rather, he sighed. "No scabbard. Not yet. That will come later. I still have to finish the pommel decoration. A small touch, yet clearly specified in the commission. I need to get a bit of gold from the strongbox. I'll finish it this afternoon, perhaps, while you're attending to the Executioner." He looked at William for a moment, then cast his eyes on the shelves of the smithy—the shelves where they stored their finished work. "Are Tormond's pauldrons finished? I don't see them."

William grinned. "Aye! I delivered them yesterday. He said he was quite pleased." William beamed at the memory. Tormond had been very pleased indeed.

Maebh had thanked William.

And she had smiled at him.

Thomas nodded. "Good lad. Always such a good lad. That will protect his shoulders and upper arms. He still insists on wearing the chain—"

"Tormond says he does not have time to learn to fight all over again—not in a full suit of plate. He insists the plate would not give him the flexibility he needs. And Maebh says she has seen him in armored combat, and 'tis as if the mail weighs naught upon him."

His father shrugged. "Aye. Whatever the Templar needs. 'Tis the role of a Sergeant. We exist to serve. We serve God and the Temple."

"Da?" William hesitated. He wasn't certain whether or not that moment was the right time to broach a particularly sensitive subject.

"Aye, son?" His father's eyes softened with affection as they met William's. He almost smiled. Almost.

His father rarely smiled.

"Tormond asked me to wake him—to wake *them*—in thirty-four years. So he can be awake at the same time as"—William lowered his voice—"the Witches. So he can hunt them and finish his mission."

Thomas nodded. "Aye."

"He said that he has made a similar request before. To the Sergeants. But they have never —"

"We *have* awakened him early." There was a sharpness to his voice. "At his request."

William nodded, perhaps a bit too quickly. "But it was too late, was it not? He'd already missed the Witches. By two years."

Thomas nodded. "Aye. Someone or something broke their cycle — awakened the Witches early."

"Aye, but . . . didn't we know they had awakened early? Didn't our spies —"

His father waved a dismissive hand, cutting him off. "Our spies were delayed. The report took too long to reach us. We didn't know. Until 'twas too late. We failed him." Thomas's lips twitched. "Again." The word came out as a growl.

"I see." *But I will not fail. I will do as Tormond asks. 'Tis the duty and honor of a Sergeant.*

His father extended his open hand to William, and the youth gave the dagger back into Thomas's keeping. "Tell me, son." Thomas met William's eyes, and sadness was in the older man's expression. A profound sadness.

"Aye, Da?"

"You're in love with her, aren't you?"

"Her?" But William knew exactly who his father meant. Heat rose in William's cheeks.

"The nun . . . who dresses like a courtesan."

"Don't speak of her that way!"

His father grunted, shook his head, then turned his sad eyes away. "She is not for you."

William glared at his father. "I know that."

"She is for —"

There was a pounding at the smithy door. "Master Thomas!" More pounding. "Master Thomas!"

Thomas stood. "Aye?" He strode to the open doorway.

There stood Huw, the cobbler's son. The boy was panting as if he'd run a great distance, but his eyes were alight with exhilaration. "We've caught another one!"

"Another what?" William asked, approaching the door.

"Another heretic!" the boy cried, as joyful as a child who'd been given a new pony.

No! 'Tis Tormond! They're going to kill Tormond!

And Maebh!

"Who?" he asked, barely able to get his lips and tongue to form the word.

Huw grinned widely, his mouth full of teeth, his eyes alight with zealous fire. "One o' them so-called protestant priests! Another one of Ol' King Henry's priests! They're bringin' 'im to the market square. They're a-goin' to burn him! At noon!"

No! Not again!

William's breath caught in his throat at the memory of the protestant bishop who had suffered death by fire. It was as if the same awful stench filled his nostrils again — the reek of oil-soaked wood burning, of hair burning, and worst of all, human flesh melting and charring. The doomed man's screams seemed to echo in William's ears once more. In his mind's eye, William saw again the fiendish glee on the face of Father Sebastian as the elderly priest cast in the first flaming torch to light the fire.

I must warn Tormond! They'll be coming for him!

William pushed past his father and shot through the door. He sprinted for The Boar's Head.

He ran as if the very Torchbearers of Hell were pursuing him.

But when William arrived at the inn, he found the common room deserted. His lungs burning with the effort, William clambered up the stairs, shouting Tormond's name. He pounded on Tormond's door, then at Maebh's, but he received no answer.

Órd Dubh! The horses! Maybe they've gone out riding.

He hurtled down the stairs, then out the inn's door, intending to head for the stable, but he flattened himself against the outer wall as he heard the thundering of hooves fast approaching. He looked and beheld a sight to inspire both terror and awe.

The great, black warhorse, barded and draped in white with red crosses, charged toward him. And atop the massive steed rode Tormond in full mail, clad in his white tabard with the red cross on the breast. The gleaming helm captured the midday sun and threw it back again as if to blind the foes of righteousness. Tormond rode with shield and reins in his left hand and his sword in his right.

171

And on the Templar's shoulders and upper arms gleamed the pauldrons William had fashioned for him.

William had but a moment to take in the sight of the Executioner of God before the horse and rider thundered past. And less than a dozen paces behind Órd Dubh galloped Fiona, the sturdy, gray mare, with Maebh in the saddle. Maebh's long skirts were drawn up, baring her legs to the knees. The nun spared but a glance in William's direction, then galloped past him, following after Tormond.

The young Sergeant stumbled after the horses, clutching at a cramp in his side, choking on dust.

When William arrived at the market square, wheezing from the exertion, he found a tremendous mob encompassing the square. It was as if the whole town had assembled. Some of them bore lit torches. A greater number brandished clubs, knives, or axes. Many of the adults carried children on their shoulders, so the wee ones might have a better view of the sport to come. The throng jeered and shouted curses and threats in Welsh and English, sounding to William's ears like a pack of wolves howling for blood.

As William pushed and shoved his way through the crowd, he recognized faces. Most of these people he knew as kind and gentle folk. At the moment, however, they resembled ghouls licking their lips in drooling anticipation of a chance to feast on the corpses of the damned.

The crowd thickened as William forced his way to the front. The mob had left a circular clearing at the center, about twenty paces wide. A dozen soldiers from the castle, wearing burnished breastplates and open-faced bascinet helms, stood, scattered about the inner edge of the circle, making a small show of holding the mob back with their halberds. For all their howling curses, the good people of Carmarthen made no real effort to push past the soldiers and their poleaxes, not even through the large gaps between the armored men. The soldiers themselves were obviously more interested in what was happening in the center of the clearing than they were in containing or controlling the mob.

Beyond the soldiers, in the center of the clearing, stood a pair of wooden stakes as thick as trees, protruding upward, atop a large pile of firewood, branches, and other wooden debris.

And lashed to those poles slumped a man and a woman, their naked flesh a mass of bruises and bloodied cuts. The woman's hair had been roughly shorn off, and she sobbed, wailing for mercy.

Between the mob and their prey, circled Tormond upon Órd Dubh. Maebh dismounted, and her riderless mare trotted back and forth, whinnying and snorting in fear. The mare, apparently spotting a small opening in the crowd, charged toward it. The crowd parted to let the terrified animal through, then closed behind the fleeing beast.

As Tormond rode round and round the place of execution, Maebh climbed up the wooden pile, working her way toward the intended victims. She stumbled, fell to her knees, then awkwardly stood once more before resuming her unsteady climb. The front of her skirts appeared dark and wet.

William caught a whiff of oil. He stared in horror as he recognized the dark stains on Maebh's skirts. "Maebh!" he cried. "The oil! You'll burn!"

"That she will!" a woman beside William crowed — Mari, the miller's wife. "The harlot!"

"Burn! Harlot!" shrieked the gleeful young lad sitting on Mari's shoulders. The child raised his little fist to the heavens. "Burn!" William knew the boy — he was barely six years of age.

Seething with anger and disgust — and spurred by terror for Maebh and Tormond — William shoved past the woman and her son.

"'Ere now, you!" Mari cried. "What do you —"

But William paid no heed as he darted into the clearing.

Maebh had cut the naked, sobbing woman free from the stake. Maebh then proceeded to the man, and began sawing at his bonds with her dagger.

A roar of anger and indignation came from the crowd, but few advanced beyond the soldiers. Those that did, hastily retreated as the Templar wheeled his black stallion toward them and brandished his sword.

Even as William began to climb the mound of oil-soaked wood, Maebh cut the naked man free. She sheathed her dagger.

"William!" she cried. "Help him down!"

Help him down? The young Sergeant got a good look at the man's bare and bleeding feet and William understood. *He'll never*

173

make it on his own. William scrambled up to the condemned man and quickly turned around. William bent at the waist. "Climb on! I'll carry you."

"Bless you!" the man cried as he clambered onto William's back. William hooked a hand under the man's legs. Those legs were slippery and coated with oil. *My back's covered with it now too. One touch of flame, and I'll burn.* Bearing his charge, William stumbled down to the verge. Setting the wretched man down, William turned back to the wood and the stakes, only to find Maebh alighting on the grass beside him, carrying the woman on her back.

Once the four of them—William, the man, Maebh, and the woman—were clear of the intended and as yet unlit pyre, Maebh ordered, "Stay behind us!" The man and woman clung to each other, she sobbing, and he gazing about in mute, wide-eyed terror. Both of them reeked of fear. And oil.

We all reek of oil.

One torch is all 'twill take...

Maebh drew her dagger once again. William drew his.

The mob howled, but none approached to light the fire.

What are they waiting for?

"HERETICS!" a thin, shrill voice screamed. "BLASPHEMERS!"

And William understood why the crowd had waited. Or rather for whom.

Father Sebastian had emerged from the suddenly silent mob. The elderly priest hobbled forward with a lit torch in his skeletal hand. He pointed with the firebrand at Tormond. "You would deliver those wicked ones from the flame of God's justice? You, Executioner?" The torch wobbled in the old priest's hand. Flaming droplets of oil fell from the torch to the grass below.

If that flame touches us . . .

Tormond maneuvered his horse so that he and Órd Dubh were between the priest and the intended victims.

Father Sebastian halted, though his head swung back and forth on his spindly neck as if he were looking for an opening, a way past the Templar.

Tormond dismounted with his sword and shield so quickly, the priest lurched back a step from the knight.

"Fuirich!" Tormond said to his horse.

Órd Dubh snorted, but stood still.

In a practiced motion, Tormond hooked his helm with two fingers of his sword hand, took the helm off, and let it drop to the grass. His head was still covered by a mail coif. "What evil have they done?" Tormond's commanding voice filled the square.

Father Sebastian's face split in a mad, rictus grin. "That man is a heretic priest. And though he claims to be a priest, he has *married* that whore beside him!"

"'Tis my understanding," Tormond said, "that under your late king, Edward the Sixth, priests were allowed to marry, that clerical celibacy was no longer required in Britain."

"Heresy!" the old priest cried. "Vile, lustful heresy!"

"Perhaps," Tormond said, "but nevertheless, this man *and* his wife serve God according to their consciences."

Spittle flew from Father Sebastian's lips as he said, "Queen Mary put a stop to—"

"And who are you, *Father*, to condemn a man for taking a wife when you, yourself—priest though you claim to be—have lain many times with the whore, Gwyneth? Who are you to condemn another for heresy when *you* have bowed down and worshipped at the feet of a demoness?"

"Lies! LIESSS!" The priest spluttered and hissed like a frightened and cornered cat. "Blasssphemy! I am a man of God!"

"Are you, now?" Tormond gestured with his shield toward the man cowering behind William and Maebh. "He believes he is also a man of God, called to the ministry."

"Heresy! He must die!"

Some in the crowd echoed Father Sebastian's words.

"Heresy or no," Tormond said, lifting his voice so all could hear, "no man or woman deserves to die merely for his or her beliefs, no matter how different or strange or misguided they may be. And no man or woman shall, so long as I am here to defend them."

Remember the evil of Béziers.

Tormond kicked at something on the ground, and William saw a small stone roll toward Father Sebastian. "Know this—if you take one more step toward them, 'twill be your last. But, if you are without sin, then by all means, *Father*, cast your first stone."

The old priest's lips writhed with inarticulate rage. With an inhuman shriek, he tried to dart past Tormond.

Tormond's blade whistled through the air.

The torch and the hand that had held it fell to the ground.

Father Sebastian screamed. He clutched at the bleeding stump of his arm. Then his eyes fell upon Tormond. With his remaining hand, the priest drew a dagger from the folds of his habit and lunged at the Templar.

Tormond parried the dagger with his shield and with a smooth, mighty slash of his sword, lopped off the old priest's head.

"Murder!" a woman in the mob screamed. The cry echoed through the crowd. They started to move forward. The armed soldiers joined them in their advance toward Tormond and those who stood with him.

Tormond quickly stepped to Órd Dubh, transferred his sword to his shield hand, and pulled his two-handed axe from the straps on the stallion's side. He tossed the axe in William's direction. The weapon stuck in the earth a pace in front of William. Taking his sword again in his right hand, Tormond said, "Defend her. Get her on my horse and get her to safety."

Tormond deftly scooped up his helmet and donned it, then turned back to the mob and the soldiers.

William picked up the axe in one hand and grasped Maebh's arm with the other. "Come!"

She shook free of him. "No." Her voice was calm. Unyielding. "I stand with Tormond. I will not leave him."

"Maebh!" William made no effort to conceal the anguish and terror in his voice. "Please!"

But she shook her head resolutely, then lifted her voice. It rang out clear as if shouted by an angel from Heaven. "I stand with Sir Tormond! I stand with God and Sir Tormond! Who will stand with me?"

The crowd shambled to a halt. The soldiers stopped also. They turned their helmeted heads, looking to one another, unsure of what to do.

William tried to force his way in front of Maebh, but she stepped around him.

"Who?" she cried. "Who will stand with me? Who will stand with the servant of God who drove the demoness from your church and your town?"

Silence reigned. The only sound William could hear was his own heart thundering in his chest. He gazed in awe at Maebh. William had never seen a queen, but at that moment, he could not imagine a queenlier woman than Maebh O Broin, Shield-maiden of Christ.

She is not for you.

"I will," a voice said. "I will stand with you."

A woman pushed her way out of the mob and approached them from the right. For a moment, William didn't recognize her. Indeed, she looked so different than she had the last time he'd seen her. Perhaps it was the gown—not stylish or ostentatious, but well made. Perhaps it was that her hair was combed. Perhaps it was the way she stood—taller and prouder than before.

And then he recognized her.

Angharad strode forth. Tears streamed down her face, and her hands trembled as if with fear. But on she came.

She drew from her girdle a thin, three-sided dagger and stood beside Tormond.

"I will!" another, higher-pitched voice cried. A maiden darted from the crowd—Mererid, the innkeeper's daughter. She was dressed in a gown so fine, it would have been suitable for a feast day. The girl came and stood between Maebh and William. She turned to William, and her lip trembled. "W-William? May I . . . h-have your dagger?"

William nodded mutely and placed the hilt in the girl's trembling hand.

"Thank you." She managed a tiny smile, then turned her attention to the mob.

William swallowed. He tightened his two-handed grip on the axe.

"And I!" Master Gruffydd emerged from the crowd. The stout innkeeper had no weapon, but he moved quickly to the corpse of the old priest. He plucked up the dead man's dagger, then Gruffydd took his stand beside—and slightly in front of—his daughter.

Mererid smiled up at her father, then her face hardened, and she held William's dagger, pointing it at the mob.

A large and broad-shouldered man pushed through the mob. William grinned at his father as Thomas Smythe approached. Without uttering a word, the senior Sergeant stood beside his son, gripping a heavy blacksmith's hammer, with grim determination on his face. His strong hand alighted on William's shoulder and squeezed gently.

Several others separated themselves from the mob. Some had daggers. Some had cudgels. Some had no weapon at all. But they came nonetheless and took up positions beside Tormond, Maebh, and William.

Two of the soldiers glanced at each other and nodded. They strode forth and joined Tormond's small army.

"For God and Sir Tormond!" Mererid cried in her clear, youthful voice. "For Lady Maebh."

"For Sir Tormond!" Angharad cried. "The demon slayer!" She appeared to be a completely different woman. She turned her close-lipped smile on the knight and said more quietly, "Sir Tormond who tol' me I could star' anew." She lifted her dagger to the air and shouted "Sir Tormond!"

Angharad's cry died away, and a hush blanketed the square.

No others came forth.

In all, Tormond's wee army numbered no more than twenty.

Twenty. Against hundreds.

We're all dead.

William gripped the axe all the tighter in his white-knuckled, sweat-slicked hands.

Tormond sang a battle hymn.

Crucem sanctam subiit,

Qui infernum confregit,

Accinctus est potentia,

Surrexit die tertia. Alleluia!

But no one answered him.

Slowly, one or two people at a time, the mob that had howled for blood turned and melted away, leaving behind Father Sebastian's corpse and a guttering torch.

The remaining soldiers lowered their halberds and slunk away.

And with their departure, only Tormond and those who stood with him remained.

Chapter 18

William, breathless after sprinting up the stairs at The Boar's Head, burst into Tormond's room without knocking. "Was there another note? From A?"

Tormond and Maebh sat opposite each other at the small table. Maebh sipped from a cup of red wine, and Tormond from a mug of ale. Tormond still wore his mail, but he had changed into a fresh white-with-red-cross-emblazoned tabard. The tabard he had worn at the market square lay draped across a chair in front of the fireplace. That tabard was wet, freshly cleaned of Father Sebastian's blood.

Tormond shook his head in answer to William's question. "No, but I must admit, I more than half expected to find such a note." Tormond grimaced as if annoyed.

"Did you find Fiona?" Maebh asked with obvious concern.

William grinned. "Aye! She's back in the stable next to Órd Dubh."

Maebh clapped her hands together. "Oh, thank you, William!" She smiled at him. And that smile smote his heart. *If only . . . No.*

She is not for me.

"It must have taken you hours," she said, her smile fading. "I'm sorry."

He shrugged. *Anything for you.*

Her brow knotted in concern. "Fiona? Is she well?"

William nodded, happy to be able to deliver more good news. "Aye. When I found her, she was happily grazing, down by the Towy. I unsaddled her and brushed her down for you."

That heartbreaking smile returned, making William's pulse quicken. "Thank you, William."

"What of the Anglican priest and his wife?" Tormond asked.

William looked around, checking the empty hallway outside the room, before shutting the door. He lowered his voice so none but Tormond and Maebh could hear him. "Safe in my mother's keeping.

She's nursing their hurts and found them suitable clothing, though nothing save a hood will cover the poor woman's hair. My father says the Sergeants will spirit them out of town and out of the country as soon as they've recovered."

"Well done." Tormond reached for his purse. "They'll be needing gold to—"

William waved a hand, cutting Tormond off. "No need. My father says the Sergeants will meet the cost."

"But, William," Maebh said, "we have gold and to spare. Your father should not bear the cost."

"He won't," William replied. "The Sergeants of the Temple have ample means."

Tormond nodded, while rubbing his short beard, his eyes taking on a look of introspection. "As I have long suspected. The Sergeants have control over the wealth of the Order."

Maebh looked puzzled. "The wealth of the Order?"

"Aye," Tormond said, "before the fall of the Templars, my order had vast wealth."

Maebh blinked. "Vast wealth? But you all took vows of poverty."

"Aye. That we did. And so we lived. But the *Order* was quite wealthy. We became the bankers—" He looked to William. "Bankers? 'Tis the word, aye?"

William nodded.

"Aye. We became bankers for the crusades. Before departing for the Holy Land, kings and knights and other pilgrims would give their gold and other valuables into the keeping of the Order at the closest preceptory, and the Order would give them a writ of receipt."

"Aye," William said. "Once there were preceptories all over Europe."

"Aye," Tormond continued, "and upon arriving in the Holy Land or upon returning from it, they could present such a writ to any preceptory and receive their gold in return."

"I see," Maebh said. "That would make it much safer to travel, wouldn't it?"

Tormond nodded. "Aye, but it grew far beyond that. Knights who joined the order donated their lands and possessions to the Order. So, whereas we lived in poverty, the Order controlled enormous wealth. Soon we were lending money as well—to kings and other nobles. 'Tis said, King Phillip the Fourth of France"— Tormond growled as he said the name—"was heavily indebted to the Templars. Very heavily. 'Tis why he and his accursed nephew"— Tormond growled again—"His Holiness, Pope Clement the Fifth, invented charges of heresy against the Order—all so his uncle, Phillip, could seize the wealth of the Templars."

"But Phillip was disappointed," William said, eagerly adding to the story. "For when he raided the treasuries, most of the gold was gone." The youth grinned fiercely. "The Sergeants had hidden it."

Tormond nodded. "Aye. 'Twas as I thought."

William waved both hands. "*We* don't use the money for ourselves! Not a farthing! Only to guard it. To serve the needs of the Order—the Templars. To serve God. When the Order returns—"

Tormond shook his head vehemently. "The Order will *ne'er* return. I am the last."

"Is that where A gets his gold?" Maebh asked, wide-eyed. "From the Sergeants?"

Both Tormond and Maebh looked to William.

"No!" the young Sergeant answered. "At least, I don't think so." He paused. "Tormond, I have done as you asked—as I promised. I have revealed naught to my father about A. Nothing. But my father asked me—after the night at the brothel—whence came all your gold? I told him that I did not know. And 'twasn't a lie, because I *don't* know! We know almost nothing about A."

"Good." Tormond scratched his beard. "Good." He fell silent.

As silence filled the room, William watched Tormond and Maebh. The knight and nun were exchanging concerned and knowing looks.

And William guessed what passed unspoken between them. "You're leaving, aren't you? Going to sleep?"

Tormond nodded. "Aye, laddie. We are. We have finished our mission here. But the Witches remain. Thus, we must sleep again."

Maebh gave William a sad smile. "For thirty-four years. Until you wake us. You will do that, won't you? We're relying on you."

"Aye." William choked on the word. He swallowed and nodded resolutely. "I will."

"You're a good lad, Sergeant William," Tormond said. "You have served well. And you have been a good friend. You are beloved. By both of us."

William fought back tears. *I will not weep. Not in front of her.* "When?"

Tears glistened in Maebh's eyes. "Tomorrow morning."

William chewed on his tongue, anything to distract himself from the grief welling up inside, anything to prevent the tears threatening to spill from his eyes. He stood abruptly. "I must inform my father." He turned, heading for the door.

"William!" Maebh's voice echoed some of the anguish he felt.

But the tears had already leaked from William's eyes. He strode to the door and departed, closing it behind himself.

As he ran toward home, toward the prison his life had become, he did nothing to hide his tears. He didn't care if the whole town saw him weep, so long as Maebh did not.

When he reached home, the sun was dipping toward the horizon. The smithy door was closed, and that was almost never the case before dusk. Panting heavily, he slowed. *Da closed the smithy early?* He scrubbed at his face with his tunic sleeve, wiping away the tears.

He went to the smithy door. He was about to push on it, but stopped himself as he heard voices from inside—his father's . . . and a woman's. William did not recognize the female voice, but the tones were sweet and unquestionably commanding—the voice of a woman to be obeyed.

"The dagger is finished?" the woman asked.

"Aye. 'Tis finished," he heard his father say. "I finished it this afternoon. It is just as requested."

So, this is who commissioned the dagger! He tried to peek between the slats of the wall, but, in his limited field of view, could see no one other than his father.

"And the sheath?" the woman asked.

"The sheath will be ready. When the time comes."

"The time," the honeyed voice said, "is tomorrow."

"So soon?" his father asked. He paused, then added, "Tomorrow. Aye. Tomorrow 'twill be."

All I must do is wait until the door opens. Then I will see who this mysterious patron is.

He stepped back, leaned against a hitching post, and waited silently. Long moments stretched into minutes, and minutes stretched into what felt like an hour. The sun sank below the horizon, and twilight enveloped him.

The door opened.

His father emerged — his father . . . and no one else. His father closed the door, put the lock in the latch, and turned the key.

Where did she go? Did he lock her inside? "Da?"

His father spun around, his eyes wide. "Son! You've returned!"

William approached his father. "What were you doing, Da? Why was the smithy closed up?"

His father's eyes narrowed, and he scowled. He spoke, but his words were harsh and low. "Council business. Not for your eyes or ears."

"But, Da!"

"No! Not now. Not here. You will know soon enough."

William bowed his head. "Aye, Da." *Where did she go? Who was she? Is she still in there?*

I'll make some excuse to enter. To fetch a tool, perhaps. Or to —

"Come along, son."

No! William tried to hide his frustration. "Da?"

"We'll not speak of this, I say." His father turned and strode toward their home, adjacent to the smithy.

"We need to talk about something else, Da."

His father stopped. He turned toward his son. "What, then?" His voice and his countenance had softened. A little.

William fought back tears once more. "Tormond. And Maebh. They're leaving. In the morning."

The older Sergeant's shoulders slumped. "I see. Very well then. As the Templar commands. Have the horses ready before dawn."

A small hope, bittersweet, bloomed in William's chest. "We're going with them? As far as . . ." *As far as the cave? More than just a quick farewell at dawn?*

His father nodded. "Aye, son. Now, come along."

I'll get to see her once more. Ride beside her. Talk with her.

Once more before the thirty-four years have passed.
Before I am old. Too old.
I'll get to see them both.

✠·✠·✠

William knelt for a long time in the cave, long after Tormond and Maebh had drunk the magic wine and slipped into their deathlike slumber. His knees ached from resting so long upon the hard cave floor, but he did not care about the pain. No, the problem was his candle. It would not last much longer, and he would soon need to leave the cave before the solitary light guttered out. William was keenly aware that he must not touch any of the other denizens of Merlin's Crystal Cave, that he mustn't stumble into them in the dark. That would awaken them, and as much as he longed to do so, he had promised that he would not awaken them until the spring of 1591, in thirty-four years. *When I shall be an old man.*

Old or no, I shall be there to serve them in my old age. To serve her.

His father's words echoed in his mind — *She is not for you.*

I know. Not for me.

The light of his candle reflected and twinkled in the tiny emeralds still embedded in the chamber roof and walls, as if hundreds of green stars shone down from the blackness of a night sky. But William had no eyes for stars or for emeralds.

William gazed upon the knight and the nun, the two people he loved most in all the world. Maebh lay farthest from him, on the boards of the makeshift bed, her head resting on a feather pillow — a gift from his mother. The nun was, of course, dressed as a noble lady in a simple yet elegant gown — a gift from Tormond — and not in a nun's habit.

And she was beautiful, the loveliest woman he had ever known. *Even if I marry — Aye, I must marry — there must be other Sergeants after me to serve God and the Temple. But even though I will marry, all women will pale before your beauty. And not only your beauty, but the beauty of your soul.*

But you are not for me.

Beside Maebh lay Tormond, positioned between her and the chamber entrance — between her and William. "To awaken first, if there be danger," the knight had said. Even in slumber, Tormond would protect her.

You'd lay down your life for her, wouldn't you, Tormond?
Aye, you would.
As would I. As would I.

The Executioner of God was, of course, clad in his full mail — including the pauldrons William had made — and in his tabard, his sword lying atop his body, the hilt in his hand. Tormond was ready for battle, even in slumber. His helm, protected against rust by a thin coat of grease, sat on the floor beside his head. The goblet, drained of the magic wine, rested beside the helm, as did a single candle, a piece of flint, and a wad of tinder for lighting the candle when Tormond awoke.

On either side of the chamber stood the horses — on the right, Órd Dubh, the great, black warhorse in full barding, and on the left, Fiona, the gentle, gray mare. Both beasts hung their heads in magical slumber. William could smell the grease that had been applied to their saddles and tack — all their equine accoutrements — to preserve them through the decades, but the scent of the *horses* themselves had faded to a memory. *As if the horses are not here at all.*

If the slumberers breathed, their breathing was too slow to be perceived by mortal ears. The only sound William could hear was his own breathing. Even that sound seemed inappropriate, almost sacrilegious, in the chamber — like irreverent laughter in a chapel — or in a tomb.

William had long since finished praying over Tormond and Maebh, pleading with God to preserve them and protect them. All that was left was for him to say farewell, then leave the cave and join his father outside.

Softly, he whispered, "I don't suppose you can hear me, can you?"

He held his breath.

Silence was his only answer.

He sighed. "Ah. 'Tis as well you can't. I suppose none save God can hear me. But I must . . . Well, 'tis almost a confession. Of sorts. Though 'tis nothing I could tell a priest — that is, if we still *had* a priest. I suppose we'll need to recruit another chaplain for the Order."

He glanced nervously at the candle. His time was running out.

Get on with it then.

"I love you. Both of you. How could I not?"

He gazed at the nun. "Maebh, you are so . . ." He shook his head. "Words fail me. I'm no bard to compose sonnets to your beauty. And were I the greatest, most skilled bard that ever lived, still I could not do you justice. But as Da says, you are not for me."

He turned his eyes to the knight. "Tormond, you are everything I could ever desire to be. Everything I can never be. You have been more of a father to me than . . ." He tried—and failed—to swallow the lump in his throat. "And you are the truest of friends."

William cleared his throat. "But, if you'll permit me to give you a bit of humble counsel, Tormond . . . I could never have said this to you if you were awake, but . . . When you have completed your mission, when the Witches are no more and there is no more need of the Executioner and the Shield-maiden . . . When that time comes . . . *marry* her, Tormond. I know she will gladly give you her consent."

Tears spilled from his eyes. "She loves you. I can see it. She is not for me." He tried again to swallow the lump in his throat and again he failed. "But I believe—may God forgive me for saying so—I believe she is for *you*."

He rose to his feet. "Farewell, my dearly beloved friends. May God guide you, strengthen you, and grant you His grace. And may God grant that the next thirty-four years will pass swiftly for me. God be with you 'til we meet once more."

And with those parting words, William Smythe, Sergeant of the Temple, turned and strode from the chamber. As he and his small candle passed out of the Crystal Cave, the last of the tiny, green points of light winked out, leaving Merlin's chamber in profound, tomblike darkness.

✠ • ✠ • ✠

William's father did not utter a word when William emerged from the hidden cave. Nor did his father speak as he and William rode through the forest back toward Carmarthen. William assumed his father was allowing him to grieve in silence. But as the two Sergeants rode into the Cursed Clearing, with its lifeless ground, barren save for the large, flat monument stone at the center, his father spoke at last.

"Dismount."

Here? William gazed about the clearing. Dread seized him like wooden tendrils wrapping themselves about him, like the branches of the Witches' legendary, life-devouring tree. In the forest beyond the dead space, shadows seemed to move under the living trees.

William certainly feared this place, but he obeyed his father. William always obeyed his father. *For God and the Temple.*

His father tied his horse's reins to a tree. He motioned for William to do the same.

Wordlessly, William secured his horse. The poor beast seemed agitated as if it wished to be gone from the wretched spot. William patted the horse's neck, attempting to lend comfort to the animal—comfort he himself did not feel. When he turned back, he saw his father kneeling a pace from the monument stone, facing it.

His father did not look at him. "Kneel beside me, son."

William did as he was told.

Thomas put his hands together in an attitude of prayer.

William did the same. *Why would we pray in such an unholy place?*

But his father did pray. He uttered the familiar supplication in Latin—

"Hail Mary, full of grace. The Lord is with thee. Blessed art thou amongst women, and blessed is the fruit of thy womb, Jesus. Holy Mary, Mother of God, pray for us sinners, now and at the hour of our death. Amen."

"Amen," William echoed.

"She comes."

What? Who? He opened his eyes and gasped.

Above the monument stone, a light blazed.

William had seen such a light before. In St. Peter's Church.

And just as before, the brilliance narrowed vertically, a slash of fire in the air.

A chill ripped through William. "Da! 'Tis—"

"Silence!" his father commanded.

The glow resolved into a woman, floating above the stone. However, unlike before, this woman was *not* scantily clad—she wore a gown of pure, snowy white, girdled at the waist, and a long, blue veil draped across her head and down her back, nearly to her ankles. Her face was calm, the very picture of virginal purity.

"Holy Mary!" William exclaimed. "Mother of God!" *It cannot be!*

The vision glanced at him for but a moment, then turned her eyes to his father. She smiled. "Well done, Thomas. Tell me — is the sheath ready?"

William recognized that voice. *The Blessed Virgin is Da's patron? Mary commissioned the dagger?*

Thomas bowed his head. "Almost."

What need would the Mother of God have for a dagger? "Da?"

"Look at the Virgin, son," his father said. "Now!'

William gazed up at the vision before him. She looked down, and her eyes met his. She bestowed on him a beatific smile. Something about that smile seemed familiar. Unsettlingly familiar.

Above the blue-veiled head, appeared a shining crescent moon of gold, lying on its side, pointing upward like horns.

"Da!" William cried. "The demoness!"

Even as he started to rise, out of the corner of his eye, he saw a flash of movement.

Something hard struck the back of his head, near the base of his skull.

For a moment, William felt white, blinding pain.

And then blackness took him.

✠·✠·✠

William awoke to agony.

His head felt as if it had been struck by a forge hammer. He opened his eyes and saw a blue, cloudless sky. The setting sun was obscured by the tall trees which surrounded the clearing, casting the dead clearing in shadow.

He groaned and sat up.

Or rather, he tried to sit up.

He could not move. His arms were pinned painfully under his back. He could feel the ropes that bound his hands and elbows together. His feet and knees were also bound. His back was stretched upon a hard, rough surface.

The monument stone! I'm lying on the stone!

Terror stole the breath from his lungs. "D-Da? Da! Help!"

189

He heard a voice — his father's voice. "Where is it? Where is it?"

William turned his head toward the sound. "Da! Help me!"

His father circled the clearing, just at the edge of the trees. He appeared to be searching for something. Frantically searching. "Where is it?"

"Da!"

His father turned toward him then. The man's eyes were wide with terror and panic. He suddenly dashed toward William. "There was supposed to be a ram!" His father wrung his hands together. "God will provide a ram! He will! He must provide a ram!"

His father knelt beside William. Tears streaked the older man's face — William had never seen his father weep, and this frightened him all the more.

His father's lips trembled. "As with Abraham and Isaac. Don't you see, son? Don't you see? God didn't *truly* intend for Abraham to sacrifice his son. An angel! Aye! An angel stopped him." A sob broke from his father, a wail of loss and grief. And of madness. "There was a ram, stuck in a bush. Caught by the horns. 'Twas a test! A test of Abraham's faith and obedience. Merely a test!" His father twisted his head left and right, searching. "Where is the cursed ram?"

"Oh, Thomas," the honeyed voice said. "God *has* provided a ram. He has provided your son. Your son who must *not* wake the Templar and the Offering early."

"NO!" William fought his bonds, but he couldn't move, he could only writhe atop the stone. He tried to look about, to see the demon, all the while pleading with his father. "Please, Da! Don't do this! I must awaken them. Thirty-four years! Please!"

"Thomas," the voice said, "it is time. Sheathe the blade."

His father looked up, gazing past William. Gazing at the demon, whom William could not see. "Aye, Holy One. I hear. And I obey." His father pulled the dagger from his belt. He held the dagger above William. "For God and the Temple."

"Da! Please!" In the midst of his peril, William's eyes became fixed on the gleaming dagger. Indeed, it was very like Tormond's, except for the gold and silver of the pommel. And in that decorative pommel, the golden Templar cross had been altered — the top of the cross bisected by a golden crescent—a crescent moon, pointing upward like a pair of horns.

"Sheathe the blade, Thomas!" cooed the demon. Even when commanding, her voice was sweet honey, laced with deadly nightshade.

His father raised the dagger. "I'm sorry, son. I love you."

"DA! NO!"

William saw the dagger plunge toward his chest.

And into his heart.

The last thing William heard was his father screaming, as if his father's mind were shattering in a madness of grief—as the demon laughed.

As death claimed him, William's last thoughts were of his friends. *Tormond. Maebh. Forgive me.*

Chapter 19

Carmarthenshire, Wales: 1617 A.D.

Tormond awoke to the sound of weeping.

Beside him, in the dark, Maebh was sobbing like a mother mourning her lost child.

Tormond sat bolt upright, gripping his sword. "Maebh?"

"He's dead! William is dead!"

Understanding hit him like a blow from a mace. "He did not wake us."

"No!" she wailed. "He didn't!"

In the darkness, her hands found Tormond. She threw her arms around him, clinging to him as she sobbed.

He laid his weapon aside and enfolded her in his arms. The embrace happened without the slightest tinge of guilt. He knew he should feel some remorse for holding her, but he couldn't muster it.

She mourns. And so do I.

The words of St. Paul came to him —

> *Propter quod consolamini invicem . . .*
> *Wherefore comfort yourselves together. . .*

"H-he was right h-here!" she cried. "Only a moment ago."

"Aye." Tormond's own eyes filled with tears. "It seems so. But 'twas long ago. So long ago." *Another sixty years.*

"He would have c-come if he were" — her voice broke — "st-till alive."

"Aye. That he would've done. At all hazards, William would've come." The tears spilled down his cheeks.

Maebh sobbed all the louder, her body quaking.

He held her as they two wept together in the black emptiness.

As he had once, centuries ago, comforted his younger sister, Isobel, after the death of her firstborn, Tormond lifted a hand and gently stroked Maebh's hair. *So soft.* He hummed a lullaby, one his mother had sung to him when he was a lad.

Slowly, her trembling eased. She laid her head on his armored shoulder.

Tormond was seized by a sudden urge to kiss her. *Surely a single kiss would be no great sin. Just a single kiss. To comfort her. To comfort us both.*

But he knew he wouldn't stop with a single kiss. And so, he continued to stroke her hair — that and no more. Though he *ached* to do more.

"Is this what it feels like?" she whispered. "To lose a friend, a dear friend, in battle?"

He drew a deep, slow breath, then let it out even more slowly. "Aye."

"How do you bear it? How do you go on?"

He swallowed. "I— You simply do it. You simply go on. There is a time to mourn and a time to fight. If the battle is not yet over, you fight on. 'Twas what I did when your . . . when Declan died. I allowed myself but a moment to weep. And then I fought on until the enemy withdrew. And when the fighting was done that day, only then did I allow myself to grieve."

"William would have come, wouldn't he?"

Tormond nodded. "Aye. He would have."

"So, we have failed again, haven't we? We are too late again. By twenty-six years."

"Aye." He sighed. "But we fight on."

She squeezed him, though he barely felt the increase in pressure through his mail. "We fight on." She pulled herself from his embrace.

He resisted the urge to hold on to her, to never let her go. "I'll light the candle." He drew his mailed legs under himself and knelt. He groped in the blackness and found the candle, the flint, and the tinder. Drawing his dagger, he struck the flint. Sparks flew, catching in the tinder. In moments, he'd lit the candle.

He turned to her. The site of her tear-streaked face almost broke him. *So lost. So vulnerable.*

So bonnie. The desire to kiss her returned, many times stronger than before.

God grant me strength.

He grasped his sword as if the weapon, the feel of it in his hand, would lend him that strength. He stood, sheathed his sword, and offered Maebh his hand to assist her up.

She took his hand and stood beside him. Her hand lingered in his for a long moment. Then she yanked it away and lowered her eyes. "I'm sorry."

So am I, lass. So am I, but nae for the same cause, I suspect. "Dinnae be sorry." He paused, then smiled. "Let's see what the Sergeants have left for us."

"Do you think A will have left anything for us?"

He shook his head. "It has been sixty years. I dinnae think —"

"Look!" She pointed with a trembling finger.

His eyes followed the direction she indicated.

Near the mouth of the chamber sat two objects — the Sergeants' customary urn and a familiar-looking wooden chest.

Órd Dubh snorted and lifted his head. Likewise, Fiona lifted her head and whinnied. Tormond strode toward the stallion and patted his neck, speaking to the warhorse softly in Gaelic. "Soon, my old friend." He caught Maebh's eye and nodded in the direction of the mare.

Maebh nodded as well. She went to her horse, patted her, and spoke words in a comforting tone — words that Tormond could not catch. Leaving the mare, she rejoined Tormond, and together the two of them approached the urn and the chest. As they drew closer, the light revealed that the urn bore upon its lacquered lid a red cross on a field of black. The chest, of course, displayed the proud letter A carved into the lid.

Tormond gave the candle to Maebh, then knelt.

Maebh knelt beside him, holding the light. "Which one shall we open first?"

Tormond grimaced in vexation. "As much as I desire to open the chest, duty before curiosity. Our mission comes first." *Though we have missed the Witches. Yet again.*

He drew his dagger and shattered the urn with the pommel. He retrieved the scroll from the shards, unrolled it, and translated the Latin. "It says, the Witches — the Maiden, at least, and her two great, black hounds — were sighted in Bavaria in 1595 — something must have disrupted their cycle again. And the Mother was sighted in London, later that year. However, the accursed tree was planted, harvested, and burned in Midlothian. As was the Burning Man."

"The Burning Man?"

He nodded. "Aye. They sacrifice their victims to their pagan god. They build a wooden structure, shaped like a huge man. And in this, their victims—their disciples—are burned alive."

Maebh gasped in horror, putting her free hand to her face. "No! How awful!"

"Aye. And thus do they reward all their disciples."

"They must be stopped! If the Sergeants know where they are, why do the Sergeants not stop them?"

Tormond growled in disgust. "'Tis nae always the Sergeants that see them. They have spies in many cities and towns of the world, and 'tis the spies that see the Witches. And the knowledge comes to the Sergeants of the Temple too late. Sometimes 'tis years after the sighting. Too late to do aught but wait the sixty years. And the Sergeants are not warriors. They serve in other roles. But once, long ago, a pair of Sergeants discovered them and attempted to stop them. One was caught and devoured by their hounds. The other was seduced, corrupted, and burned alive, along with the rest of the Witches' disciples."

He turned his face toward her, his expression grim. "'Tis why I hunt them. Alone."

"No, Tormond." She shook her head. "*We. We* hunt them. You are no longer alone." She placed one hand atop his. She did not grasp his hand. She merely laid hers there.

He did not pull away from her touch. He smiled at her. "Aye, Maebh, Shield-maiden of Christ. You are with me. And I thank God for that." *God grant me strength.*

She smiled and withdrew her hand. "So, do we go to Midlothian? William"—her voice caught, but she pushed on—"said we have a chamber prepared for us there."

His flesh tingled where she'd touched him. *I shall perform many penances this day.* "That was in 1595, so assuming they slept again that year—"

195

Maebh looked at him, her expression showing confusion. "You said the tree was planted and harvested in that year. Surely not in so short a time."

"Aye. The accursed tree is planted, grows, and bears its horrid fruit in a single year. 'Tis fed by the blood of human sacrifice. 'Tis witchcraft."

"Blood?" Maebh shuddered. "I see." She shuddered again.

"As I said, assuming they slept that year — and they would have — they should next awaken in 1655. Since we slept the whole sixty years, this would be 1617. So, they will appear again in . . . thirty-eight years. 'Tis too long to simply wait. If we go to Midlothian, to Scotland, and sleep . . ."

"We would miss the Witches by twenty-two years. That's . . . getting closer, is it not?"

He nodded. "Aye. We *are* getting closer. I think, perhaps, we should go to Midlothian. What do you think we should do?"

She appeared surprised. "You're asking me? Aren't you . . . the military commander here?"

He chuckled at her quaint assumptions. *What she means is, aren't you the* man *here,* "Aye. Any military mission must have a commander. But any commander is a fool if he does not take counsel from his comrades-in-arms, especially when he has time to do so. And we have much time, do we not?"

She smiled. "Comrade-in-arms, am I?"

How he loved to see her smile. "Aye, Shield-maiden."

"Well, then I counsel we see what A has to say, before we make a decision." She paused. "Wait. Is there more? From the Sergeants?"

Tormond turned back to the parchment. "Aye, but the rest is merely instructions on how to find the hidden chamber in Midlothian, under Rosslyn Chapel."

"Very well," she said, her expression brightening, though her eyes were still red from weeping. "Let's see what A has to say."

"Agreed." Tormond drew his dagger again and probed the wooden chest, checking for poisoned needles. He scowled.

"What is it?" she asked. "Do you suspect the box isn't from A? 'Tis the reason you gave last time."

"I'll always be cautious about poison, aye. The box could have been tampered with after our benefactor left it here. But 'tis not what concerns me."

"What, then?"

He drew a finger across the lid, then showed his fingertip to her. "I don't see any dust on the box. It could have been planted today or yesterday." He pointed with his dagger in the direction of the shards of the Sergeants' urn. "Not like that. The jar had layers of dust on it. " *As if the Sergeants put it here as soon as they learned of the Witches' whereabouts.*

But they did not bother to wake us.

Ach! William, laddie – what happened to you?

O Lord God, what happened to my friend?

Take him unto Thy bosom, O Lord, as Thou hast taken so many of my comrades.

The sound of weeping pulled him out of his silent prayer. He looked at Maebh. She was in the act of dashing tears away. She shook her head. "No. We must fight on."

He nodded. "Aye. We must."

"Open it, please." The pleading note in her voice let him know she was eager for anything to distract her — to distract them both — from their grief.

He sheathed his dagger and opened the chest.

Inside, he found two small purses of gold lying atop a mound of what appeared to be clothing. But of course, it was the scroll that caught his eye.

He picked up the parchment and unrolled it.

Maebh brought the candle closer. "'Tis in English."

He grinned. "I thought you couldn't read."

She huffed, then pursed her lips in vexation. "You know very well I cannot read. But the letters — some are big, and some are small. Latin letters are all the same size."

"You are a clever lass." *I think I shall teach you to read.*

When I have the time.

He turned his attention to the note. "'Tormond, my son, and Maebh, whom I would call daughter, had I the right to do so, I have grim news. Young William Smythe is dead. He was slain by the hand of his own father —'"

197

Maebh gasped and put a hand over her mouth. "No!" The word had emerged as a wail.

Tormond stared in horror at the words written on the vellum. *His own father? Master Thomas? The Sergeant?*

Tormond read the sickening words again. "'He was slain by the hand of his own father shortly after you began your long sleep. I am truly sorry, but I only learned of this decades after the murder.'"

Tormond growled. "Thomas shall know the justice of God."

Maebh clutched his arm with her free hand.

He looked at her and noted the fire in her eyes and her firm-set jaw. She shook her head. "No. The murderer is long dead."

Tormond nodded grimly. "You're right, of course. He'd be dead by now." He read on, "'Think not that the murderer has escaped the justice of God. From what I could learn, and this was not long after the murder, in fact, 'twas only a few days later, Thomas went mad, and within the year, had taken his own life.'"

Maebh gasped once more. She released Tormond's arm and made the sign of the cross. "May God have mercy on his poor, mad soul."

"Aye, but if he was not mad when he committed the foul deed"—he clenched his teeth—"may he burn in everlasting fire." Tormond paused, then made the sign of the cross himself.

He continued to read, "'I know this news will sorely grieve you, but perhaps, when you awake, you will have already guessed that William was dead, for he did not wake you. He was a valiant and true servant of God, according to the knowledge that he possessed, and I mourn his passing. But know this, my son and she whom I would call daughter, God knows and loves His own, even in this benighted time. I am confident that, after all that has been lost has at last been restored, William will be with God and Christ in Their kingdom. They will reward William for his valiant service. They will each embrace him and welcome him home.'"

Tormond stared at the words, rereading them. "What does he mean? 'After all that has been lost has at last been restored?' What has been lost? I don't understand."

Maebh shook her head. "Do you think he means . . . the Holy Land? Jerusalem? After another crusade restores it to Christian hands?"

"Perhaps." He shook his head. "No. That does not make sense. Why would William have to wait in Purgatory until the Holy Land is retaken? No. That cannot be it. And what does this mean? 'With God and Christ in Their kingdom?' '*Their* kingdom?' '*Their* eyes?' 'They will *each* embrace him?' A writes as if the Holy Trinity is not one God in three Divine Persons, three aspects of the same God. He writes as if They are separate. Three Individuals." He crossed himself again. "What heresy is this?"

She laid a trembling hand on his arm. "Perhaps you are—I don't know—wresting too much from these words. Perhaps, A is simply using words you do not fully understand."

"Aye." Tormond grunted. "I do not understand." He rubbed his bearded chin. "I do not understand at all."

"Tormond, has A ever led us astray? He's been right about so many things."

Tormond clicked his tongue. "No. He has never led us astray, but this— It sounds very much like pagan heresy."

Maebh nodded slowly. "Heresy."

Suddenly, a laugh burst from him.

"What?" Maebh cried. "Why do you laugh?"

He looked at her, grinning. "Who am I to condemn someone as a heretic?" He slapped his chest. "Am I not a Templar?" He laughed for a moment, before sighing. "And you are right, Maebh. A—whoever he is—and however he could be still alive to send us this fresh message—he has never led us astray. He knows things we do not." Tormond rubbed his chin again. "I must ponder this and pray on it."

Maebh nodded. "Aye. Ponder and pray. But read on, please."

He grinned, bowing his head toward her. "Aye, milady."

Sister. I should call her "Sister."

She smiled back.

And her smile stole away any thought of calling her "Sister."

God grant me strength. Reluctantly he turned back to the parchment—away from gazing at her—and enjoying the gazing far too much—and read on. "'Now as to your mission in this time, you must away to the isle of Colonsay.'"

"Where is that?" Maebh asked.

"I think he means Colbhasa. 'Tis a smaller island in the Inner Hebrides, off the west coast of Scotland. Last I knew, 'twas the home of Clan MacFie. They have strong ties to Clan MacDonald, my clan."

"'Tis a good thing, aye?"

He shrugged. "Perhaps, aye. Perhaps, nay. 'Tis possible many there will know the names of any highborn MacDonalds. They may ask the names of my kin, but what answer could I give them?"

"I see." Though it seemed to Tormond as if she did not understand, not fully. "Read on," she said.

He nodded. "'There you must preserve the life of Elspeth MacKinnon, the betrothed of Malcolm MacFie of Kilchattan. You must deliver her so that she may wed her betrothed and bear a daughter, Marian. You must not fail in this. I wish I could tell you more, but that is all I know.'"

Tormond stared at the parchment. "'That is all I know?' All he knows? How can that be?" *A is nae omniscient.*

But you did trust A as if he were all knowing, did you nae, laddie?

The candlelight wavered, so he turned his eyes to Maebh.

She trembled, her hand covering her mouth, her eyes wide. "We have followed him. Followed his instructions. And this is all he gives us?" She dropped her hand, and her eyes narrowed in anger. "How are we to find this person? This *Elspeth* person? How are we to protect her?"

Tormond shook his head. "I don't know." He squared his jaw. "We must go in faith."

"Go in faith? But how —"

"Did David know how he would slay Goliath? When David said he would go and fight the Philistine?" He shook his head. "No. David merely said, 'Thy servant will go and fight.'"

She stared at him for a long moment in silence, then bowed her head. "We will go in faith." She raised her head and gripped his arm. "We will go in faith together. A has not failed us." She shrugged. "But who is he? How is he still alive? How does he know the things . . ." She shrugged her shoulders. "I suppose I thought he knew everything."

Tormond chuckled. "So did I, lass. But only God knows everything." *Have I put my trust in the arm of flesh? Am I serving the will of God or the will of man?*

She smiled. "Perhaps A is also acting on faith."

He nodded and turned his eyes back to the parchment. He laughed.

"What is it?"

He shook his head, grinning. "It says, 'You must walk by faith.'"

She laughed as well. "Truly? 'Tis as if he knows what we are thinking, what we are saying."

Tormond read on, and his countenance fell. "'This time, I cannot go with you to guide you, to watch over and assist you as I did sixty years ago in Carmarthen. You shall have only each other and God to protect and preserve you. I must remain on this isle of Great Britain. I too have a prophecy to fulfill, and I must remain here to do it.'"

Tormond blinked, rereading. "'I too have a prophecy to fulfill?'" He looked at Maebh, and a shiver ran through him. "A is guided by prophecy."

Maebh nodded, her eyes on the parchment, her expression thoughtful. "Prophecy," she said slowly. "'Twould explain much."

He gazed at her with curiosity. "Does that not cause you concern? Prophecy?"

"Do you not believe in prophecy, Executioner of God?"

He grimaced, chagrined. "Aye. In the Bible. But . . ." He grunted and shook his head. "What am I saying? Of course, I believe. Even as the last Grand Master of the Temple, Jacques de Molay, was burning at the stake, he prophesied that King Philip the Fourth and Pope Clement the Fifth would die within the year."

"And did they? Did they die within the year?"

He nodded. "Aye. Philip was struck down by a fit of apoplexy while he was out a-hunting. And Clement?" Tormond nearly spat out the foul name. "He died of stomach" — he paused — "I think the word in English is cancer. In Irish 'tis *ailse*."

He looked to Maebh.

She nodded. "Cancer. I think 'tis correct."

He nodded. "Clement died of stomach cancer less than two months after de Molay's martyrdom. He died in agony." Tormond paused again, fighting a sudden urge to grin. *Dinnae rejoice in another man's suffering, laddie. Nae even in that accursed man's agony. Well deserved though it may have been.* "After the pope's death, lightning struck the church wherein he lay in state, burning it down, almost consuming the corpse. 'Twould seem both those evil men were smitten by the hand of God. Aye, Maebh. I *do* believe in prophecy."

He crossed himself.

So did she. "What else does it say?"

He returned his attention to the parchment. *Led by prophecy.* "'When you return from Colonsay, know that I will once again be watching over you. From afar.'"

"Like a guardian angel." Her face brightened. "Do you think that could be the answer? That, perhaps, our benefactor is an angel?"

Tormond wrinkled his brow as he considered the suggestion. "I don't know. He calls me 'son.' But he calls you — What was it?" He glanced over the message, looking for the phrase A had used. "Ach! Here 'tis. 'Maebh, whom I would call daughter, had I the right to do so.' 'Twould seem as if he has a connection to me, but not to you. If he were an angel, I don't think he would refer to me as 'son.' I would think he'd say things like, 'Thus sayeth the Lord.' Don't you agree?"

He looked to her again.

Her brow furrowed as she considered, then she shook her head. "No. I think you are correct. Guardian angel. 'Twas a foolish thing to say."

He grinned as he shook his head. "Maebh, I have come to learn that nothing you say is foolish." He paused. "Well, perhaps that proverb about the pigs." He winked.

Her jaw dropped in indignation. "Oh! You—" Her mouth snapped shut, and she glared at him. She opened her mouth again, took a deep breath, and looked as if she were about to hit him with the full brunt of her Irish temper.

Abruptly, she giggled.

How he loved it when she giggled.

"Aye, Tormond. You have me there. 'Perhaps *that* was a *bit* foolish." She smiled, and even with the lines of dried tears on her face, it seemed to Tormond as if the darkness of the cave had retreated.

How he loved it when she smiled.

God grant me strength.

He winked at her again. "Perhaps a *wee* bit foolish."

He tore his eyes away from her bright countenance and returned his attention to the parchment. "'Once again, you cannot go about as religious and nun. Scotland has broken with the Roman church and has established a national church of its own. In England, Cornwall, and Wales, the Anglican church is supreme, and Catholics are suppressed, unless they take an Oath of Allegiance to the king, and I am sure you would not so swear. A Scottish king, James the Sixth of Scotland and the First of England, Wales, and Ireland, now rules all of Great Britain and Ireland.'"

Tormond grinned. "A Scottish king rules in England." He shook his head. "Who could've foreseen that? Even when I fought alongside Robert the Bruce— But 'tis a story for another time." He read on, "'Amidst all the religious strife in this land, James has done something miraculous. He has had the Holy Scriptures translated into English and published. Now the Scriptures may be read by any man or woman who can read the common tongue.'"

The Holy Scriptures? In the common tongue? Nae in Latin?

More than a century earlier, Tormond had heard rumors of a heretical English-language translation of the Bible.

A called it miraculous.

If the Bible can be read in English, then the Bible is nae longer solely the province of the clergy and nobility.

But is that wise?

"Women?" Maebh's eyes were wide with awe. "*Women* may read the Holy Bible?"

Tormond gazed at her, noting the eager light in her gray eyes. Any misgivings he'd had at the thought of a non-Latin Bible vanished. "I must teach you to read."

She gasped. "Truly? You will teach me? I"—fresh tears spilled from her eyes—"shall be able to read . . . the word of God? Myself?"

He could not help but smile. "Aye, lass. I shall teach you, and you, Maebh O Broin, Shield-maiden of Christ, shall read the Bible for yourself."

She put a hand to her mouth again. She closed her eyes, bent her head, and sobbed.

The burning desire to embrace her, to comfort her, returned, hotter than ever. *God grant me strength.* He swallowed. *I cannae. She's weeping with joy. She does nae need comforting.* "Maebh, I—"

Careful of the candle, Maebh reached for him with her free hand. For a moment, Tormond thought she meant to embrace him — and he both feared and hoped she might — but she merely grasped his hand, even as it held the parchment. She bent her head, kissed his hand, bathing it with her tears. "Oh, thank you! Thank you, Tormond. Thank you."

"Maebh, I— Of course, I will teach you. If I had known how much it meant to—"

"It means the world to me." She laughed and sat up. She released his hand, then put her hand to her breast. "To be able to study the word of God for myself. Even if it is in this ridiculous, difficult English tongue!" She laughed again.

He laughed as well. "Then we shall see if it might be possible to purchase one of these English Bibles along our journey."

"Oh, I hope we can find one!" She pointed at the parchment. "Read the rest. Please!"

He read, "'I have provided appropriate clothes for you in this box. You will find another, much larger chest near the mouth of the tunnel. I placed it there so you would not be forced to carry it so far.'" *Carry it so far? Carry it whither? 'Tis nae as if I could carry it on my back. Perhaps I can construct a litter and drag it behind Órd Dubh?* He read on, "'The chest is quite heavy. Inside, you will find more clothing, other things you will need, including shoes. My son, you need new shoes. Yours have large holes on the bottoms. I know the Templar Order does not permit knights to wear shoes with lacings, but I hope you will accept these from me.'"

"What?" Maebh grasped his arm. She maneuvered the candle so she could see his feet. She growled in frustration. "I cannot see your shoes through the soles of your armor leggings. Why didn't you tell me you needed new shoes?" Her expression conveyed concern and hurt. "I would have bought a pair for you in Carmarthen. I would have!"

Tormond felt his cheeks flush. "I am sworn to poverty." *And to chastity.* "I didn't wish to indulge my worldly needs. And the buckles or ribbons on the shoes men wore in Carmarthen — they were . . . ridiculous."

"But I saw men wearing shoes without buckles! Or ribbons!"

He shrugged. "Those shoes had lacings. Shoelaces are specifically forbidden by the Rule of the Templars."

She stared at him, openmouthed. "Truly?"

He nodded. "Aye."

The corner of her mouth lifted in a half-smile. "Another stupid rule."

He shrugged. "Aye. Perhaps." Then he sighed. "Another rule I shall have to break." *Another penance. A daily penance.*

He read on, "'But you must not perform penance for wearing the shoes. That rule is for a bygone age. I trust and pray that you will not.'"

Perhaps he is correct. Very well. Nae penance. Nae for the shoes, at least.

"'Outside the tunnel, I have also provided a small wagon such as the mare Fiona can pull. The wagon is laden with foodstuffs and wine for your journey. You will need the wagon to transport the chest, Tormond's armor, Órd Dubh's barding, and the Witches' wine.'" Tormond shook his head in wonder. "So much. So very much he has provided for us."

"Aye, he has. Is there more?"

He nodded. "'Go with God, my son, you and your brave, faithful companion. And go with my love.'"

At the bottom, the message was signed, "A."

"Let us see the new clothes," Maebh said, grinning.

Tormond drew out the various items. "At least the pants are longer. They're still puffed out. Ridiculous. But they *will* reach to my knees."

"And," Maebh said, "that bodice will cover my —" She blushed, then she glanced at Tormond, and there was guilt in her eyes. "Tormond, I'm sorry."

He felt his own cheeks redden. Again. "I understand. We do what we must."

Her eyes brightened once more. "Let's go see what else A left for us." She stood and motioned for him to do the same. "Come! He said it was at the mouth of the tunnel." She grasped his hand and pulled him to his feet.

He could not help but smile at her eagerness and delight.

Holding the candle aloft, she pulled him down the tunnel.

He heard Órd Dubh and Fiona whinny as they left the chamber. The mare sounded frightened. "I shall return shortly, old friend."

At the mouth of the tunnel, in the near blinding, though shaded, light of day, sat a large, iron-bound chest. "Very large and heavy indeed." *'Twill take all my strength to lift it. Why not simply leave it in the cave?* The chest bore a stout lock, though the key was inserted into the lock.

Maebh released his hand, then knelt and set the candle against the tunnel wall. She reached for the key, but Tormond commanded, "Stop!"

She snatched her hand away as if it'd been burned. "I forgot. You must check for poisons."

"Aye." He examined the chest, probing with his dagger. When he was satisfied, he said. "You may open it now."

Maebh turned the key in the lock, then removed the lock and set it aside.

Tormond unlatched and lifted the lid.

Inside—just as A had said they would—they found a great mound of clothing and a pair of shoes for him, as well as two pairs of smaller shoes for Maebh. But lying in the very center, atop the clothes, lay a large, thick book.

Maebh gasped. "Is that—"

He nodded, knelt, and crossed himself. "Aye."

The brown leather cover of the book bore no name, but on the spine, a red rectangle, embossed with gold, proclaimed the title—

"HOLY BIBLE"

A sob burst from Maebh. She reached forward with trembling hands and lifted the book from where it lay. She clutched the sacred tome to her breast. Her tight-shut eyes leaked tears of joy. "I shall . . . I shall read it for myself."

Tormond bowed his head in prayer. *I thank Thee, O God. I thank Thee for this miracle.*

And I thank Thee for A.

✠·✠·✠

206

The wagon was loaded, and Fiona harnessed to pull it. Tormond and Maebh were dressed in their new clothing, leaving the previous century's garb behind. Tormond wore his new shoes — including the laces. Tormond and Maebh were ready to begin, to seek out Elspeth MacKinnon, the betrothed of Malcolm MacFie of Kilchattan, on the isle of Colonsay, and preserve her life. Somehow.

Tormond assisted Maebh onto the wagon, after she assured him yet again that she was perfectly capable of driving. After mounting his warhorse, Tormond wheeled Órd Dubh around and smiled at Maebh, bowing slightly in the saddle. "Are you ready, Lady Maebh?"

She nodded her head. "I am ready, Sir Tormond."

The knight turned his horse in the opposite direction. He pointed ahead with his hand. "Forward!" he cried as if he were leading troops into battle.

The stallion started forward.

Maebh snapped the reins. Fiona lurched in the harness, and the wagon began to roll, following after the mounted knight.

Neither of them saw the hooded and cloaked figure standing in the shadows of the cave. From within the deeper shadow of the hood, shone a pair of green eyes — green as the emeralds of Merlin's Crystal Cave. Those eyes watched Tormond and Maebh as they departed.

From the hood, from the shadow within the shadows, whispered a voice, "God speed, my son." White teeth gleamed in a wide smile. "God speed you both."

Chapter 20

Isle of Colonsay, Scotland: 1617 A.D.

Wisps of cloud as black as Órd Dubh's hide drifted across the night sky. There was no moon, the light of the flickering stars the only illumination shining on the expanse of water before Tormond and his two companions.

Tormond sat upon his black stallion, staring across the slackening tide to the sandy beach on the other side of the submerged causeway. Both knight and warhorse wore their armor, but Tormond's mail was not adorned by his white tabard, and neither was Órd Dubh's barding draped by his white caparison.

It bothered Tormond that he was not wearing the red cross upon his breast. But the nature of the mission that night demanded stealth. And that meant the white tabard was a liability.

In his left hand, Tormond held his helm, as well as the strung longbow he'd purchased while he and Maebh journeyed through Wales to the coast. Across his back, dangling from the leather guige strap, was slung his white shield, emblazoned with the simple red cross.

Órd Dubh stamped the wet sand, impatient to charge into battle.

Tormond patted the horse's neck through his armor. "Soon, my old friend. Soon." He spoke softly, in Scottish. "We must wait for low tide, else we'll nae make it across the causeway."

Órd Dubh snorted as if to express his disapproval.

Ye're as anxious as I am. 'Tis past time to slay the enemies of God. But we must wait for low tide.

On Tormond's right, sat Maebh on her gray mare, Fiona. Behind Fiona stood a shaggy, highland pony, saddled and bridled, with a long lead rein held firmly in Maebh's hand. The nun wore a simple riding frock of variegated browns and blacks. A black scarf bound her long, brown hair, protecting it from the chill, westerly breeze that blew from the sea, and keeping it out of her eyes. In her belt, she carried her dagger and a brace of snaplock pistols, loaded and ready to fire.

At least, Tormond thought, glancing at the clouds and then at the nun's firearms, *there is nae rain. Her powder should remain dry.*

As long as we dinnae get hit by ocean spray driven by a treacherous gust of wind.

O God, keep her powder dry! Those pistols are her best defense.

Tormond wished he could have procured her half a dozen pistols, and not just the pair she carried.

And please, Lord, let them not go off by accident!

He suppressed a shudder at the thought of a ball exploding through her leg or abdomen.

"That shield of yours," she said in English, "it catches the starlight. If ye intended stealth, ye've failed. 'Tis as if ye are wearing a big, white-and-red target on your back. If they have arquebuses or pistols, they'll be able to see ye in the dark and shoot ye in the back."

The corners of Tormond's mouth lifted in a smile. "Then I'd best not turn my back on the villains, aye?" He winked at her. "Thank ye, lass, for the sound advice. I dinnae know how I'd ever face the enemy without your counsel."

She glared at him. "Men! Stubborn as pigs being led to—" She cut off quickly.

Tormond chuckled. Although he couldn't discern colors in the darkness, he was certain her cheeks were reddening. "Stubborn as pigs being led to slaughter. I remember."

Her eyes narrowed even more. Then her expression melted into a smile as she laughed softly.

How he loved her smile. And her laugh. *Sae bonnie.*

God grant me strength. He smiled back.

"How can ye be a-laughin' at such a time as this?" snapped the man sitting astride his own shaggy pony on the other side of Maebh. Malcolm Macfie spoke in English, though with a heavy brogue. "We are a-goin' intae battle, man! And there are six o' the villains!" He carried a targe—a round, leather-covered wooden shield with a wicked, rectangular spike thrusting out of the center. At his belt he wore a dirk, a single pistol, and a sword with a steel basket around the hilt. He was clad in a long, dark plaid—pinned at his shoulder, belted around his waist, and extending to his knees—a brown shirt with ridiculously puffy sleeves, laced-up shoes, and knee-high stockings.

And no pants whatsoever.

The Scots of that time called the strange garment a "fèileadh mòr." The English called it a "kilt."

Tormond called it "impractical," and hoped the fashion would simply vanish in good time—perhaps when next he and Maebh awakened—vanish like dew on the heather under the morning sun.

"Six o' them," Malcolm continued, growing more agitated by the moment, "and but two of us!"

"Three," Tormond corrected. "Three of us."

Malcolm spluttered, pointing at Maebh. "She's a lass!"

"Oh, ye noticed that, did ye?" Tormond quickly suppressed an urge to smile at the man's distress. "And here I was, worried about the state of Scottish manhood." He refrained from pointing at Malcolm's skirt.

"A woman!" Malcolm continued, completely missing the subtle jest.

Tormond turned in his saddle and faced the fellow. The Templar's expression was grim. "Laddie, I ken that ye are a wee bit frightened, as well ye should be. But this woman, this lass"—he nodded his head in Maebh's direction—"has seen more combat and death than ye have ever seen. God forbid ye should ever see so much."

"But she's—"

"And when we rescue your betrothed," Tormond continued, "and we *will* rescue her—after what the poor lass has been through, after what has been done to her by that blackguard, Ian McKinnon, and his cursed brothers as well"—Tormond gritted his teeth and growled—"by her own *cousins*, she may need comfort such as only a woman can give another woman. Dinnae expect her to run into your arms, laddie. Nae after what she's been through."

Malcolm's face took on a stricken expression. "But ye dinnae know that tae be true. It could all be—"

"Laddie, ye need to prepare yourself, to steel your courage. And your resolve. McKinnon and his brothers—they've boasted of what they've done. 'Tis how we know where they are. Aye, they've boasted of their foul deeds. First, to force the promised dowry from her father, to make her — as McKinnon thinks — unfit for marriage to any but himself. Second, to humiliate ye, laddie. Ye and your whole family."

"But her father said he'd nae give the dowry, since she is" — he appeared to swallow, to choke on his words — "since she is spoiled. They cannae be waiting for that."

"Aye, and 'tis why your own kin refused to help ye save her."

And why time may be running out for the poor woman. Once the McKinnons tire of her. Once they're certain no dowry or ransom is coming.

"'Tis why ye need us," Maebh said. "'Tis why we were sent by God. To help ye and to help her. When none other would — not your kin, not even her own kin."

Malcolm nodded quickly, his lips drawn tight. "And I thank ye. I do." He bowed his head. "Forgive my rash words, *mo bhean*. I mean, milady."

She gave him a kindly smile. "There is naught to forgive. Ye are grieving and ye are worried." She gave a more radiant and knowing smile to Tormond. "But I have learned from Sir Tormond that, when ye are 'waiting on the walls,' as he puts it, ye can brood and ye can fret. Or ye can jest and sing. And ye can pray. The last three will lighten the heart before going into battle. The brooding and the fretting do no good for anyone."

Her smile and her courage sent a thrill through Tormond's chest. He smiled back, then gazed at the causeway again. "The tide has gone out. We ride. We ride in silence." He made the sign of the cross and started his stallion forward.

The others followed in silence, save for the soft clanking of Órd Dubh's armor and the squelching of hooves in the wet sand.

As they approached the opposite beach on the lesser isle of Oronsay, Tormond caught sight of a lone figure silhouetted on the low cliff above. The man on the cliff gave no indication that he'd seen Tormond and his companions.

Tormond raised his hand, and the others halted. "Ye're certain, laddie," he whispered, "there are none, save the McKinnons, on this isle? And, of course, your lady? Certain *sure*, ye are?"

Malcolm nodded.

Tormond handed his helm to Maebh, then drew an arrow from the quiver at his hip. He nocked the arrow, drew the bow — holding it slantwise so he could shoot from horseback — and placed the fletchings of the arrow against his cheek. "Fuirich!" he whispered to his horse.

Órd Dubh stood still as a stone.

God, guide my arrow. Tormond sighted down the shaft, adjusted for the breeze and the range, slowly let out his breath — and loosed.

As soon as the arrow leaped from the longbow, Tormond knew he'd missed his shot. *'Twill be to the left.* Not by much, but the breeze was stronger than he'd accounted for. Quickly, he nocked a second arrow, readied his shot — adjusted a wee bit to the right — and loosed again.

Two seconds passed — long and seemingly interminable.

The dark shape on the cliff turned as if in response to the first arrow, then fell. There was no sound until the corpse hit the water below.

No other shape appeared on the cliff.

Tormond smiled grimly. *Three against five now.*

He retrieved his helm from Maebh, then motioned forward. Tormond and his companions rode on.

Once across the tidal causeway, they dismounted and led their horses up the narrow slope from the beach. At the top of the slope, they found a pony standing, his shaggy head bowed in sleep. They gave the animal a wide berth so as not to disturb it. *Cannae have the beast running back to its masters.* They remounted and prepared to ride the three-quarters of a mile to the abandoned priory.

"What a shot!" Malcolm hissed as he rode up on Tormond's left.

Tormond waved him to silence, glancing at the lone pony with trepidation. The beast slumbered on. *I thank Thee, O Lord, that Thou didst guide my second shot true. And I thank Thee for giving me a grandsire who taught me the longbow in my youth.*

Non nobis, Domine. Non nobis. Sed nomini tuo da gloriam.

Not for us, Lord. Not for us. To Thy name be the glory.

They rode between low, barren rock formations on either side of the only feasible road — a narrow track. They went at a quick trot, but they did not gallop. *We must hurry, aye, but I dinnae wish to weary the horses.*

They had but one sentry on the cliff. He'd have only needed to watch at low tide. There could be no danger at any other time. But then he'd ride straight back. We must be there before he's expected to return.

If the other five are all together, 'twill be easy. If they are nae together, we may be pursued.

And we must wait 'til the next low tide to escape.

After they'd gone less than half the distance, the rock formations on the left gave way to open grass. The road forked with a branch going off to the west, while the other fork continued south.

Tormond hesitated but a moment at the fork. *Please, O Lord, let them be all together at the priory.* He crossed himself again and chose the west branch of the road.

Before long, the buildings of the long-abandoned priory appeared ahead, seeming to rise out of the dark ground. Tormond could see a glow winking through the arched eastern window of the stone chapel.

They lit a fire in a chapel with no chimney? Who would be so daft as to do that? How is the smoke to escape?

Perhaps, the roof has a hole in it. The place has been abandoned for more than sixty years. With no monks to maintain the place, 'twould be in disrepair.

Must be a peat fire. I have nae seen a single tree on this wretched island.

But why would they choose the chapel? 'Tis probably the least defensible building.

But ye do know why they chose it, laddie, d'ye nae?

Aye, ye do.

From what Malcolm had told him, the best approach would be from the southern door. But there was also a northern door that led to the rectory, and through that door the blackguards might escape. But Tormond was less concerned that one or two might escape — momentarily — than he was about what the villains might do if he didn't kill them all quickly enough.

The true danger lies in what they could do to the lass, once they know we're here, once they know they're cornered. Slit her throat, like as not.

We must be quick. Very quick.

As soon as Tormond's eyes could discern the low wall encircling the monastery—what the Scots of the time called a "dyke"—he halted. He motioned for Maebh to wait where they were, well short of the dyke.

Her lips were tight, and she breathed loudly through her nose as if to show her displeasure. But she nodded. She knew her part in the plan, and he had no doubt she would carry it out with exactness.

Thank ye, lass. I dinnae need two women to protect. Nae yet.

Malcolm dismounted and handed his pony's reins to Maebh.

Tormond, however, remained atop Órd Dubh. For one brief moment, he considered leaving his longbow and quiver of arrows with Maebh. *For extra protection.*

Nae. She'd nae have the strength to draw the longbow. And she's nae trained to shoot it.

But she knows how to fire those pistols, if it comes to that.

If it comes to that, O Lord, grant that her powder be dry, and her aim be true.

Tormond gave his steed a gentle nudge with his heels, and the stallion started forward slowly.

Malcolm followed on foot, his sword drawn and his spiked shield at the ready.

Tormond listened for the sounds of men reveling in their cups. But he heard nothing except the cry of a lone seagull and the soft clopping of the stallion's hooves.

Perhaps we shall come upon them in their sleep.

The arched window in the east end of the chapel grew more distinct. It bore not even the remnants of glass—if it ever had any. It was tall and wide and open and—

Tormond hissed softly in annoyance.

He motioned Malcolm forward.

The young Scotsman strode quickly to stand on Tormond's left. His pale, bearded face gleamed in the starlight as he gazed up at Tormond with a worried expression. "Why have we—"

"The window," Tormond whispered as he pointed at the chapel. "Ye did nae tell me 'twas so low to the ground."

Malcolm looked puzzled. "Aye? So?"

Calm yourself, laddie. He's inexperienced. He did nae think 'twas important. "A man could escape through that. Easily."

"Aye? So?"

Tormond fought the urge to growl in annoyance. "So, we now have three exits to cover."

Malcolm's countenance fell. "Ach. Nae. And there are but two of us."

Tormond shook his head. "Three, laddie. Three." *But I did nae want her to be so close to the fighting.*

He set his jaw and turned his horse back toward Maebh.

She started her horse forward, leading the two ponies behind her. When she pulled up beside him, Tormond halted. She raised an eyebrow. "Change of strategy?"

He nodded grimly. "Aye. Ye must ride up to the dyke there." He pointed toward the low stone wall. "Stay *outside* the dyke, mind. Then ye must dismount and shelter there. Behind the wall."

She nodded, not a hint of fear in her gray eyes. "What do ye need me to do?"

Good lass. Brave lass. "There are three exits. Three, nae just the two we planned for. Have both pistols ready. Shoot any man who comes out of the window."

She nodded again. "I will."

"Wait until he is silhouetted against the light, but fire while he's still in the window. Remember to close your eyes when ye shoot. So it does nae blind ye."

She grinned. "I remember. I'm a better shot with these hellish devices than ye are, Sir Knight. And I can shoot with both hands."

He grinned back. *'Tis true.* "Aye, but 'tis one thing to shoot a tree and quite another to shoot a man."

Her grin vanished. "I have slain a man before."

Aye. Her wicked father. He nodded. "Aye, lass. Ye have." He paused. "And make certain sure 'tis nae the lass."

She nodded. "I'll be certain." Her grin returned—a fierce grin, such as Tormond had seen on many a Crusader riding into battle. "Come on, then. Let's go rescue Elspeth."

Tormond wheeled his horse and rode slowly back toward Malcolm and the priory.

And the coming battle.

In his mind, he sang a battle hymn.

As the three of them approached the dyke, Tormond pointed to the north.

Malcolm nodded, crouched low, and trotted away quietly, along the dyke, with his sword and shield ready.

Tormond offered one more quick, silent prayer that the lad would obey his orders to the letter—to enter the rectory from the north and not attack until he heard the signal.

Just see that none escape that way. Leave the rest to me.

Ye must live to marry Elspeth and be a father to Marian.

'Tis what A prophesied.

But the prophecy does nae mention whether Maebh or I will survive...

Please, O Lord! Keep Maebh safe!

Maebh dismounted, then led Fiona and the two ponies to the dyke. Tormond watched as she removed a stone from the top of the low wall and set it on the ground. She gathered the three sets of reins—the mare's and the two ponies'—and wrapped them around the stone. Drawing her two pistols and kneeling, she peered intently over the wall at the chapel window.

Tormond looked to the north in time to see a dark figure—Malcolm—clamber over the dyke. Malcolm crouched low once more and hurried toward the rectory.

When Malcolm disappeared behind the rectory wall, Tormond began to count slowly in his head. He would give the young Scot to the count of one hundred to be in position before beginning his approach.

One. Two. Three.

As he counted, he heard the bleating of sheep, and the neighing of several ponies. The neighing was not coming from Maebh's direction—coming instead from somewhere within the priory grounds.

Tormond continued to count.

By the time he got to forty, Tormond heard a voice from the chapel, speaking in Gaelic. "Seamus isn't back yet, and 'tis almost time for the ritual. Angus, go outside and see if ye can spot him coming."

If they hear Órd Dubh's hoofbeats, Angus will nae come outside.

Malcolm probably isn't in position, but I can wait nae longer. Tormond donned his helm. He dropped the longbow and quiver to the ground, then pulled his shield around from his back, slipping his left arm into the straps. He gripped the reins with his shield hand, then drew his sword.

He kicked the warhorse's flanks, and the black stallion charged forward.

Tormond rode through the dyke gate, then straight for the chapel's southern door.

Through his helm, coif, and arming cap, Tormond thought he heard a woman screaming, "No!"

Horse and knight stopped just short of the door. Órd Dubh reared, then crashed his mighty hooves against the door. The wooden barrier exploded into splinters.

Tormond leaped from the saddle. Landing squarely on his feet, he charged through the wreckage of the door.

He saw a flash and heard a boom.

The ball struck him in the left shoulder, spinning him halfway around and nearly knocking him off his feet.

Shot! He had felt the impact, but no pain. *Hit my pauldron.*

Tormond stumbled, then wheeled to the right, just as he saw another muzzle flash and heard another boom. But he felt no impact.

Missed!

He charged forward.

There were five of them. And the lass.

She was lying atop the altar before the window, held down by two strong men. Just as Tormond had seen one hundred and twenty years before in the horrid abbey, the victim was fully clothed, though her skirts had been pulled up, exposing her legs. A third man stood near the end of the altar as if he were approaching her to "complete" the vile ritual. Two other men—the ones who shot at him—had drawn steel. One a sword and the other a dirk.

Tormond sprinted toward the swordsman. He caught the sword with the top edge of his shield. The blade embedded itself in the wood, sticking fast. Pain shot from Tormond's shoulder and down his shield arm. Grunting from the pain, he hacked at his opponent's left shoulder.

The man screamed and fell to the ground.

Tormond quickly rid himself of the shield with the embedded blade. He spun to his right, just in time to parry the second man's dirk, then he swung his sword in an arc and struck deep into the man's side.

The wounded man dropped to his knees, clawing at his own entrails.

Three more.

The woman, having escaped her captors, cowered in a corner behind the altar.

Two of the remaining men had drawn their dirks.

One had drawn a pistol from his broad kilt belt. He aimed it at Tormond's chest.

Distantly, Tormond could hear pounding coming from the northern door. It was securely bolted with a heavy wooden bar.

Malcolm cannae help me.

I'm a dead man.

"Dog!" the man with the pistol cried. "Ye killed my brothers!"

"Just shoot him, Anndra!" one man shouted—the one who'd stood ready to ravish the girl.

The pistoleer ignored his brother. Instead, he waved the snaplock at Tormond. "Did ye kill Seamus too? Tell me!"

"Shoot him!" the third man cried, pointing his dirk at Tormond with a trembling hand. "Shoot the bastard, Anndra!"

"Shut it, Ian!" the pistoleer, Anndra, cried. "Did ye kill Seamus?"

Tormond noted the name of the man with the dirk. *Ian. The one who abducted the lass.*

Ignoring the pain in his shoulder, Tormond removed his helm.

He could definitely hear Malcolm pounding on the northern door, desperately seeking entrance.

Tormond glanced quickly up at the great cross hanging above the altar. The crucifix was not adorned with a depiction of the dying Christ. But above the crosspiece was a recumbent crescent moon.

Tormond grinned with a fierce baring of teeth. "She's nae the Blessed Virgin, ye ken."

Anndra blinked. "What did ye say?"

Still grinning, Tormond said, "Ye serve a demoness. Ye, Anndra, and Ian, and . . . whatever your name is, laddie." He waved his shield arm, forcing himself not to grimace as pain shot down his arm. "This—this ritual. Ravishing a woman on the altar of a church. 'Tis all to serve a demoness."

He began to chuckle, low in his throat. *Let them think I'm a madman. Just let me get closer.* He took a step toward Anndra. "Ye're all damned for what ye've done."

"Shoot him!" Ian cried. "Shoot him! Shoot him!"

"Shoot, Anndra!" the other man screamed.

Tormond took another step forward. He glanced at the girl. "Run, lass. Run. God has delivered ye from these dogs. Out that door, now. Be careful of my horse."

The girl hesitated for only a moment before jumping to her feet and running for the southern door.

Tormond did not spare her another glance. He focused all his attention, all the force of his will on Anndra. And the pistol.

The firearm shook in Anndra's hand. "Look me in the eyes before I blow your brains out. Did ye kill Seamus? Is he dead?"

Tormond knew he could not hope to close the gap in time. But he took another step anyway. *At least the lass escaped. At least we saved her.*

Be safe, Elspeth.

Goodbye, Maebh.

I love ye. God forgive me, but I do.

"Dog!" Anndra shouted.

Tormond heard the boom.

But he did not see the flash.

Anndra toppled forward, the unfired pistol falling from his hand.

Maebh stood, framed in the window.

She had already drawn her second pistol.

"I'll handle these two, Maebh!" Tormond shouted in English. "Attend to the lass!"

Maebh nodded and disappeared.

The as-yet-unnamed man dropped his dirk and fled, running for the door.

"Órd Dubh!" Tormond called over his shoulder. "*Marbh!*"

The man bolted through the open doorway.

Tormond heard Órd Dubh scream—not in pain, but in fury. He heard another scream—a man's scream. Then he heard a loud double-thud, followed by a squishing sound like the smashing of a melon.

And then silence.

Tormond chuckled, shaking his head. He looked at Ian. "I told the lass to be careful of my horse. I guess your brother did nae listen."

Ian fell to his knees. He clasped his hands together and raised them in supplication. "Mercy!" he cried, tears streaming from his eyes.

"Oh, laddie"—Tormond shook his head—"I am the Executioner of God. I dinnae show mercy to defilers of women."

CRACK!

The northern door burst open, and Malcolm stumbled into the chapel, nearly falling on his sword. He quickly righted himself, and his wide eyes swept the room.

His eyes alighted upon Ian. "Villain!" Malcolm raised his sword. "Where is she? Where's Elspeth?"

Ian shook his head. His whole body trembled as he knelt, cowering. "I d-dinnae know!"

Malcolm advanced on his enemy. "Where's Elspeth!"

"She's right here." Maebh had reappeared at the window.

Elspeth clung to her, sobbing like a wee child clinging to her mother.

"She's safe, Malcolm," Maebh said.

We did it.

Nae. Nae we.

Thou hast done it, O God. I thank Thee.

Elspeth is safe.

Maebh is safe.

'Tis all that matters.

Malcolm glanced from Elspeth to Ian. The wild look faded from his eyes, and they narrowed. An icy rage burned there. "Give him a sword." He looked at Tormond and growled. "Now."

Tormond nodded. He strode to his shield with the sword stuck in the edge. Tormond wrenched the sword from the white-and-crimson shield. He carried it to Ian and set it on the stone floor within the villain's reach before stepping back.

Ian stared at the sword as if it were a viper.

"Pick it up." Malcolm's voice was cold as the frost in a graveyard. "Pick it up and fight me. Or is it only women ye'll raise a hand tae, aye? Ye thrice-damned coward?"

"Ye'll just kill me anyway." He turned his wretched face to Tormond. "Or if nae, *ye* will."

I should kill him. He deserves it, certainly.

Tormond glanced at Elspeth. Her wide eyes were locked on Malcolm.

Nae. She needs to see Malcolm *fight him. To see Malcolm fight for her.*

"If ye will fight him," Tormond said, "and if 'tis a *fair* fight, I will nae interfere. And if ye should win, I shall let ye depart alive. Ye have my sacred word on it." Tormond sheathed his sword.

Ian hesitated. His trembling ceased. A slow, wicked grin spread across his tear-streaked face. He grasped the hilt of the sword and stood. "He said a fair fight. I've got nae but sword" —Ian drew his dirk—"and dirk. Ye have a targe and a pistol. Now how is that fair?"

Malcolm laid his spiked targe on the flagstones. The rectangular spike pointed to the chapel ceiling. He pulled his pistol from his kilt belt and set it carefully on top of his round shield, then drew his dirk. He assumed a fighting stance, sword and dirk at the ready.

With a savage roar, Ian leaped at him, slashing with his sword.

Malcolm met him steel for steel. He thrust with his dirk, causing Ian to jump back.

Ian dropped to a fighting crouch and grinned. "I've *had* her, ye ken. All of us have had her. Every night. For months." He licked his lips. "She *loved* it. She squealed like a bloody English whore." He drew the last word out slowly as if relishing the taste of it in his mouth. "Is that nae the right of it? Aye, Elspeth?" He laughed. "A born whore. Best I ever had."

Malcolm's icy rage was gone. His mouth twisted, and he roared. "Ye'll nae speak of her so! Ye'll—"

But Ian was upon him again. Slashing with the sword.

Malcolm barely managed to parry with his dirk. He swung his sword wildly, but Ian ducked underneath, thrusting with his dirk.

Malcolm twisted away, attempting to gain space in which to bring his sword to bear.

Tormond fought the urge to step in and cut the blackguard down. *Hold, laddie! Let Malcolm fight for her.*

Ian laughed and slashed again.

Malcolm parried with his dirk. He managed to bring the steel basket hilt of his sword down upon Ian's head with an audible crack.

Ian cried out, dropping his weapons and clutching at his head. He stumbled and fell to the floor, landing on Malcolm's shield.

The tip of the spike poked up through Ian's belly.

Ian twisted, thrashing with his arms, trying to free himself.

His legs did not move at all.

Malcolm advanced slowly, his sword pointed at the man who had stolen and violated his beloved.

Ian froze and stared up at his enemy.

"Hold, laddie," Tormond said. "Ye dinnae need to finish him. He's done for."

Malcolm looked to Tormond with stricken eyes. "But he—"

"Look at his legs, man. They dinnae move. That spike has gone straight through his spine. See the blood? Even if he were to live, he'd be a cripple for the rest of his miserable life. And he'd nae be able to hurt another woman. Ever again. But I tell ye, laddie. He will nae survive this night."

"But he—"

Tormond put his left hand on Malcolm's shoulder, gritting his teeth against the pain. "Listen to me, laddie. There's a bonnie lassie outside, waiting for ye. Ye've shown her how very much ye love her. Ye've fought for her. In spite of everything that has befallen, ye've fought for her. She knows ye still want her."

Malcolm lifted his face, and tears spilled from his eyes. He looked toward the window.

Tormond looked as well.

But Maebh and Elspeth were no longer there.

Tormond felt a brief moment of terror.

"Malcolm!"

The voice came from behind them. From the southern doorway.

Elspeth was there.

And so was Maebh.

Tormond shuddered with relief.

Malcolm dropped his weapons and opened his arms. "Oh, Elspeth."

She ran to him and threw herself into his arms. Sobbing. Clinging to him. "Ye came! Ye came for me!"

"Oh, my dearie!" Malcolm cried, kissing her face, her eyes, and finally her lips. "I would hae come sooner! But I could nae find anyone to help me. I could nae fight all six alone." He kissed her again. "But then God sent me help."

"But, Malcolm"—Elspeth lowered her eyes—"I am soiled. Impure."

Malcolm kissed her forehead. "Nae tae me. Nae e'er tae me. Tae me, ye will always be pure."

"But they have taken—"

Malcolm shook his head. "They have nae taken anything that truly matters. They have nae taken your heart, my love. That will always be mine."

Maebh came to stand at Tormond's right side. She slipped a hand into the crook of his elbow and leaned her head on Tormond's armored shoulder.

"But," Elspeth began, "Malcolm. I cannae bare ye children. I am . . . barren. I must be."

"Hush," Malcolm said. "Dinnae say such things."

Elspeth shook her head. "If I have nae conceived"—she sobbed—"after all these months . . ."

Maebh lifted her head from Tormond's shoulder. "But ye will conceive."

"How—" Elspeth looked to her. "How could ye know that?"

"There is a prophecy," Maebh said. "Ye will have a daughter, at least."

"Prophecy?" Elspeth's eyes filled with fresh tears. And something else Tormond suspected had been missing there for a very, very long time—hope. "A daughter?"

Tormond nodded. "Aye. A daughter. And ye shall call her name Marian."

Elspeth sobbed anew. "Thank ye! Bless ye! Bless ye both!"

"Kill . . . me!"

All eyes turned toward Ian.

His breathing was labored and shallow, and blood spread from him onto the floor, leaking away in tiny rivulets between the flagstones. "Kill me. Please!"

Elspeth broke away from Malcolm's embrace.

"Elspeth?" Malcolm's voice trembled with new anguish.

But she held up a hand. "Nae, my love. I must do this. Myself."

She stepped slowly, deliberately, toward her tormentor. She halted near his head, looking down on him, then spat in his face.

Ian flinched. "Elspeth?"

She stared at him with cold eyes. "Ye are nothing. Ye have nae power over me anymore. Ye have taken— Nae. Ye have taken *naught* of consequence. Malcolm says that to him" —she swallowed— "to him, I am *pure*. I pray ye and your cursed brothers roast in hell with Judas himself as your tormentor."

Ian coughed, and blood flew from his mouth. "Kill me."

Elspeth pointed at Ian's side and the barrel of the pistol sticking out from there. "Ye have a pistol under your back. If ye can work it free, ye might end your own suffering a wee bit sooner. I dinnae care."

Malcolm was at her side, pulling her gently away from the wretch on the floor. "Come, my heart. Let us begone from this horrible place."

Elspeth turned away from Ian, placed her hand into Malcolm's. And she smiled at him.

"Oh, and, Ian," Malcolm said without turning around, "ye can keep the targe. And the pistol. Consider them a gift on the occasion of my wedding." He picked up and sheathed his sword and dirk. He snatched up two of the snaplocks dropped by Ian's dead brothers. "I'll take these instead."

Tormond also bent, careful not to dislodge Maebh's hand from his arm, and picked up his shield. He grimaced from the pain and at the two-inch-deep gash at the top. *I'll need to put some glue in that. To prevent it from splitting.*

Then the four of them left the chapel, while Ian's pleas for a merciful death followed after them.

But none of them paid the wretch the slightest heed.

As Tormond, Maebh, Malcolm, and Elspeth rode away from the abandoned priory and into the night, they heard a single gunshot.

And after, there was only silence.

Chapter 21

Tormond poked his fingertip into the dent in his left pauldron — the spot where that piece of plate armor had stopped the pistol ball. He thought of his murdered friend.

Thank ye, William. Ye saved my life, laddie. Had the ball hit my chain, for certain sure the mail rings would've shattered and been driven into my flesh.

Aye, well, deeper *into my flesh.*

And it could've shattered my shoulder.

The bleeding wasn't bad. In fact, Tormond was certain it had stopped. Mostly.

I'll have to mend the mail and the gambeson.

And stitch up the wound.

Perhaps, I should consider getting a breastplate as well?

With the rapid pace at which firearms are improving, who can say if, in sixty years, even a breastplate *will stop a bullet?*

Perhaps there'll come a day when armor will nae be effective at all.

He made the mistake of shifting his left shoulder and grunted in pain.

"Ye *are* hurt!" Maebh was at his side — though she had never been far from it, not even to tend the fire — putting a hand to the pauldron. "Take that thing off right now, Tormond MacDonald. Let me see exactly how bad this 'trifling' wound is."

He waved her away. "No need, lass. We dinnae have the time."

She gave him such a glower as would've made any Irish goodwife proud. "Stubborn as a pig, ye are!"

He noted with a smile that she had stopped short of the phrase about "being led to slaughter." He noted also that she was beginning to pick up some of the speech patterns the Scots — including himself — used when speaking in English. Especially when her Irish temper was up.

She wagged a finger at him. "Ye said yourself that the tide won't go out for another hour or more. We have time right now, so take off that armor and let me have a look at ye. Or I'll fetch Malcolm *and* Elspeth" — she pointed at the reunited lovers, sitting on the opposite side of the beach fire, holding hands, and whispering to each other — "and we'll take it off ye by force, whether ye will or no!"

Aye, ye have me there, lass. I dinnae think I could stop ye.

The clouds had cleared somewhat, and Maebh's face seemed to shimmer in the starlight. Even the angry lines around her eyes were softened in that muted glow. And she was —

Sae bonnie. How could I ever refuse ye anything, lass?

God grant me strength.

He gave her a wicked grin. "Very well, *mother.*"

Her lovely, angry eyes narrowed even more.

He got to his feet and grunted as a spike of agony shot from his shoulder and down his arm. *Perhaps I've broken something after all. 'Tis nae anything the Witches' wine cannae fix.*

When I can get back to the wine, that is. But 'twould mean sleeping in Wales again.

Painfully, he lifted his left arm and began to unbuckle the pauldron straps under it.

Maebh watched with concern written plainly on her face as the left pauldron dropped to the sand of the beach.

But when he tried to reach for the right pauldron with his left hand, a hiss of pain escaped his clenched teeth.

She was on her feet in an instant. "Let me help!" She went to him quickly and fumbled at the buckles and straps. "I'm sorry," she whispered as her fingers struggled with the unfamiliar task.

"Sorry for what, lass?"

"This is . . . improper. So" — she seemed at a loss for the English word — "*pearsanta,*" she finished in Irish.

Intimate, he translated in his mind.

Ye are helping me to undress, after all.

"'Tis nothing." He lowered his voice to a whisper. "Nuns have been tending the wounded for centuries."

She nodded as the last strap came loose, and the right pauldron joined its fellow on the sand. "I am a nun." There had been an edge to the simple statement that did not escape Tormond's notice.

Does she . . . regret her vows?

"Bend over," she commanded.

He complied, letting his arms dangle, gritting his teeth against the pain in his shoulder.

She grasped the knee-length hauberk mail below his posterior and pulled it up and over his back. The hauberk slid off his back, over his neck, and down his arms.

He groaned as he was relieved of the weight of the mail. He straightened up, painfully. "Thank ye, lass." He reached for the lacings at the neck of his padded gambeson.

She swatted his hand away. "Stop that." She untied and loosened the lacing. "I'm going to help ye. I'm a *nun*." She had fairly growled the last word. "Bend over again."

He complied. *Ye are a nun, lass. And I am a religious. We must ne'er forget that.*

She pulled the gambeson off him. And his sweat-soaked linen shirt.

As he stood straight once more, he heard her gasp. "No!"

She was staring at his shirt in horror. From his vantage point, he couldn't see the front of it, he couldn't see the blood, but there must've been a large stain indeed for her to react so. Then her eyes went to him. Or more specifically, to his left shoulder.

Her hands, clutching his shirt, trembled. "Tormond!"

He looked at his wound. The bruise covered his entire shoulder, extending a good hand's breadth down his arm and his chest. The wound itself didn't look ugly. Not *so* ugly.

He grinned at her. "'Tis a wee laceration, is all."

She shook her head as she lowered his shirt. She extended a quivering hand toward the wound. In an instant, her expression of horror vanished, replaced by determination. "'Twill fester. Do ye have anything in your saddle bags to clean and stitch up the wound?"

He grimaced, but not at the thought of her having to stitch his wound. "Aye. Needles and stout thread."

"What about something to cleanse it?"

Tormond shook his head. "I have nae wine." When she gave him a dubious glance, he said, "In the Holy Land, we used wine to cleanse wounds. Wine or vinegar."

"I suppose ye did not think to bring vinegar either?"

He shook his head.

She pursed her lips into a frown. "I suppose seawater will have to do."

"I have whiskey!" Malcolm was on his feet and fishing around in the sporran at his waist—the leather pouch that dangled in the front of his kilt. Elspeth stood as well. She clung to Malcolm's arm as if she couldn't bear to be parted from him for a moment.

Malcolm produced a small, silver flask, grinning. "Always keep a wee bit for emergencies. 'Twill sting like the very de'il, but whiskey's the good for all as ails ye."

Maebh strode to him quickly and snatched the flask from his outstretched hand. "Thank ye." She turned back to Tormond and muttered, "Praise be to the Almighty for Scotsmen and their love of whiskey."

Tormond eyed the flask with a grimace. "I'm nae certain—"

"'Tis whiskey or seawater," Maebh said, untying her kerchief. "Ye decide."

Tormond glanced toward the sea that separated them from the opposite shore and thought of all the sand awash in the water. He turned his eyes back to Maebh, seeing her determined look. "Whiskey." He chuckled and gave her a wink. "As if ye were truly giving me a choice."

A knowing smile curled the corners of her mouth as she pulled her kerchief from her head. The breeze whipped at her hair in a way that made her even more beautiful to his eyes. She unstopped the flask and poured the contents onto the kerchief, then she dropped the empty flask to the sand. "I'm told this will sting." Her smile became an apologetic frown. "I'm sorry, Tormond."

He grinned. "Do your worst, lassie."

She pressed the kerchief to the wound.

He hissed. *Like the very de'il!* Tormond crossed himself. *Forgive, O Lord, for my mentioning . . .* him.

"I'm sorry." She wiped at the wound. "I wish I could be gentler. I do." Tears threatened in her eyes.

In spite of his pain, he gave her a tender smile. "Maebh, your touch is as light as goose down on a moonlit breeze."

She raised an eyebrow, though her eyes remained focused on her task. "Light as goose down on a moonlit breeze? Now tell me, wise Tormond MacDonald, how that makes any sense at all?"

He gritted his teeth as she dug a little deeper into the wound. "'Twas the best I could come up with in the moment."

She chuckled, though tears spilled down her cheeks. "And is this how ye speak tenderly to a maid? These are the words ye'd choose?"

"I would nae know. I have nae experience. 'Tis well I became a religious, aye?"

She opened her mouth as if to answer, but shut her lips again. Finished with the wound itself, she began to wipe the rest of the blood away.

"Dinnae bother," he said. "Just clean around the wound. Once ye bind it up, I'm just going to put the rest back on again."

She looked at him, clearly surprised. "Surely not! 'Tis all bloody!"

"Modesty forb—" Small, twinkling lights caught his eye, as if a dozen yellow stars had fallen from heaven and settled onto the far beach. "'Twould seem as if there be some opposition to our return to Colonsay." He tilted his head in the direction of the opposite shore.

She turned her head and looked. "Torches? What makes ye think they'll oppose us?"

"They stubbornly refused to aid Malcolm in rescuing his poor lass. I dinnae think they await on yonder shore to welcome us back."

She took in a deep breath through her nose, then let it out slowly. "I suppose not."

"I'll fetch my stitching pouch." He strode toward Órd Dubh and his saddlebags. He dug through them, retrieving a small leather pouch and two white bundles—one large and one small.

When he returned, Maebh eyed the bundles. "Why would ye need those? Why did ye bring them at all?"

He shrugged. "The whisperings." He dropped the bundles on the sand. "When I face them, 'twill be in my vestments. Órd Dubh as well. Those craven naysayers shall face the wrath of an offended God."

"But your wound!"

He handed the pouch to Maebh. "Best be quick about your stitching."

✠·✠·✠

As Tormond, Maebh, Malcolm, and Elspeth neared the end of the causeway, riding in single file with Tormond in the lead, a dozen Scottish warriors rode highland ponies down the Colonsay beach to meet them. Or, as seemed more likely, to bar Tormond and his party from coming ashore.

Tormond carried his strung longbow in his left hand and his helm in his right, guiding Órd Dubh with his knees and heels, as he assessed the arms of the opposing force. In addition to the lit torches in their hands, each man bore sword and targe—some with spikes and some without. Tormond suspected more than a few carried pistols in their kilt belts. *Best to assume they carry at least one firearm apiece.* The warriors were arranged in a wide line as they rode—a formation more suited to intimidate—and possibly to surround—than to make a direct attack.

Tormond had no illusion that he could defeat all of them. He was fairly certain he could cut a path through their center, but he doubted he could hold the gap long enough for his companions to ride through and away to safety. He had no fear of death, nor for the lives of Malcolm and Elspeth—they would, he knew, live to marry and have a child—but he feared for Maebh. *Should nae have brought Maebh along.*

If ye had nae brought her, laddie, ye'd be dead, fallen to Anndra MacKinnon's pistol. She saved ye, laddie.

Aye, and now I must save her.

In the torchlight, Tormond recognized the face of each man present. Most of them he and Malcolm had approached, seeking their aid in Elspeth's rescue. And to a man, each had refused.

Ian Macfie, Malcolm's father, rode in the center. To his right rode Lauchlane MacKinnon—The MacKinnon, chief of Clan MacKinnon—and to his right, Angus MacKinnon, Elspeth's father. Angus had refused to pay the ransom and had told Malcolm that he'd withhold his daughter's dowry as well. Although, looking at Elspeth's father, it seemed to Tormond as if the man looked less resolute, more conflicted than before. *Perhaps seeing his daughter has made him doubt his decision?*

Tormond had expected to see other members of Clan Macfie and Clan MacKinnon. But the man whose presence surprised him was Finlay MacKinnon—father of the six brothers Tormond, Maebh, and Malcolm had slain—the six brothers who abducted and raped poor Elspeth.

Ian Macfie, Malcolm's father, pointed his torch as if it were the burning finger of accusation. "Come no further, MacDonald! Ye'll nae bring that whore onto this island!"

"Ye'll nae speak of her so!" Malcolm bellowed from behind Tormond. "She bears no blame in this! No shame! 'Twas all Ian MacKinnon and his damned brothers!"

"Bastard!" Finlay MacKinnon spurred his pony forward. "Where are my sons? What hae ye done wi' my bonnie lads?"

Tormond pressed his knees against Órd Dubh's sides, halting the horse. *Let him come to ye, laddie.*

Then, perhaps, 'twill be a mere eleven *to one.*

Tormond raised his helm, ready to don it. "Your sons, Finlay MacKinnon? I have sent them all to Hell. Perhaps ye should have taught them to nae defile Scottish maidenhood. Rapine—'tis a grievous sin, ye ken?"

Finlay was a mere handful of yards away. "All? Ye hae murdered them *all*?"

"All," Tormond said. "And 'tis nae murder to execute the justice of God, to slay raping dogs."

"Bastard!" Finlay drew his sword.

Quickly, Tormond placed the helm on his head. He plucked an arrow from his quiver, nocked it, ignoring the agony in his shoulder as his stitches ripped. He drew his bow, aimed—adjusting for his helm—and loosed before Finlay MacKinnon had closed half the distance between them.

With a strangled cry, Finlay dropped to the sand, an arrow in his heart. His riderless pony galloped away, down the beach.

Tormond readied another shaft and aimed it directly at the MacKinnon chief.

But Tormond did not fire.

Lauchlane MacKinnon froze, his hand on the snaplock pistol in his belt. His eyes were wide in wonder. And fear.

At least half a dozen pistols were now trained on Tormond.

"If any of ye shoots," Tormond cried, enunciating to be heard and understood despite his helm, "The MacKinnon is dead."

"And I," Maebh cried in a steady, commanding voice, "will shoot ye, Ian Macfie, and ye, Angus MacKinnon. And both your children will be fatherless."

Tormond could not see her, but he was certain Maebh had drawn both pistols and aimed them at Malcolm's father and Elspeth's father. He grinned inside his helm as he felt a thrill of admiration.

Brave lass.

He could, however, see the pistols aimed at him waver as their wielders could not decide whom to shoot.

"And I will shoot *ye*, uncle," Malcolm shouted. "Though, it should be ye I shoot, father! Perhaps, ye did nae have the courage to come with me to rescue Elspeth, aye? But now ye have the courage to bar my lady from her home?"

Ian Macfie scowled. "I told ye, lad, if ye go after that whore, ye'll never spend another night under my roof. Ye have defied me, and for that—"

"Ye need have no fear o' that, father," Malcolm replied. "I'll nae set foot inside the house of a spineless coward. Elspeth is mine. She's to be my bride. And she is nae a whore. The next man who says so—"

"She enticed them, lad," The MacKinnon said, speaking with quiet conviction.

"'Tis a lie!" Elspeth cried. "I did nae entice them! I did nae entice any man, much less that pile o' cur's droppin's, Ian MacKinnon!"

"What witness have ye of this charge against her?" Maebh shouted. "Have any had the courage to come forward and utter such lies?"

The MacKinnon said, "Finlay said—"

"Oh, aye! Finlay!" Elspeth barked a scornful laugh. "*He's* your witness, aye? Finlay MacKinnon, himself, tried to force me at Michaelmas! In the very kirk! D'ye nae remember the scratches on his face? I gave him those. *I*! And he still bears the scars. Ye all know it. And ye can ask Mari, his wife! Aye, ask his widow. She saw. And he beat her for it! For the mere *seein'* of it! Where d'ye think she got those two black eyes? From her cur of a husband, that's who. Now that she has nae reason to fear him any longer, she'll tell ye! And nae a week after his cursed sons dragged me off to Oronsay, a-kickin' and a-screamin', ol' Finlay himself came out to force me while his sons held me down!"

The assembled MacKinnons and Macfies seemed shocked by Elspeth's words.

Even Tormond was surprised by the vehemence of her tone. *Where has this feisty vixen been a-hiding?* He grinned inside his helm, in spite of the pain shooting through his shoulder into his bow arm. *Keep the bow steady, laddie. Dinnae show weakness.*

But holding the bow steady was becoming nigh impossible to do.

"Ye brave men, ye!" Elspeth continued. "Oh, aye, ye have the hearts of lions, ye do! Ye come down here to prevent me from a-comin' ashore, from soilin' your island, but nae a one o' ye had the *stones* to come deliver me!"

"Silence! Ye lyin' bitch strumpet!" roared Elspeth's father, Angus MacKinnon. He bared his teeth in a snarl. "If ye were a-kickin' and a-screamin', as ye say, ye'd have fled from them. Ye'd have run away and come home."

"I did!" Elspeth was defiant. "I escaped, but there's nowhere to go on that wee island. Nae way off, save this one way alone. And ye damn well know it, ye cowardly —"

"That's enough of that," The MacKinnon said. "We'll nae be spoken to like that by the likes of ye. Angus, restrain your daughter."

"She's nae daughter o' mine!" Angus declared.

"The next man," Malcolm cried, "who says another word of insult 'gainst my Elspeth, I'll shoot him down. Do ye hear me? I swear by almighty —"

"Ye'll be banished," his father snarled. "Banished from Colonsay and from the clan!"

"Oh, banished, is't?" Malcolm replied. "And by whose authority, pray tell, would I be banished? The Macfie, Malcolm Macfie, himself is a-hidin' away on Dùn Eibhinn. Tell me, *father*, did ye go to the hill fort this night and ask our clan chief to banish me?"

"Ye are nae son o' mine," Ian Macfie retorted.

"And ye are nae father o' mine, ye damned coward."

Tormond could feel the strength in his bow arm failing. *I must end this, and soon.* "I saw the dried blood on her ankle, where the chains scraped her flesh—the chains with which she was bound when they did nae have her stretched on the kirk altar. I saw the Brothers MacKinnon as they were about to perform the ritual."

"Ritual?" The MacKinnon blinked. "What ritual be this? That smacks of witchcraft."

"Nae witchcraft," Tormond replied, "devilry. 'Twas a Luciferian rite in worship of a demoness."

"Demoness?" MacKinnon eyed him dubiously. "What proof have ye of that?"

"We've seen the ritual before," Maebh replied, and Tormond noted with pride that there was not the slightest hint of fear in her voice. "And the demoness."

"I say again, MacDonald," the MacKinnon chief said, "what proof have ye?"

"The recumbent crescent moon," Tormond said, "bisecting the top of the great crucifix in the priory chapel. Ye can go and see it for yourself. Two men hold the victim upon the altar of a kirk under that foul symbol, while one man after another rapes the sacrifice—"

"Hold!" The MacKinnon raised a hand—the hand that had been resting on his pistol. "I've seen this cross with the horns afore." There were murmurs among the MacKinnons and the Macfies. "I've seen it, I say!" To Tormond he said, "Lower your bow, MacDonald." He raised his voice so all could hear. "Nae man shall fire 'pon ye." He turned to Ian Macfie. "I said, nae man shall fire. Lower your weapons, lads!"

Slowly, each man who had a snaplock trained on Tormond and his group, lowered and stowed their pistols.

Tormond eased his bow. *Nae a moment too soon. I dinnae think I could've kept it drawn any longer.* He kept the arrow nocked, though he wasn't sure he could draw the bow again.

Or lift his left arm.

The MacKinnon dismounted and strode, kilt flapping with the sea breeze, to the corpse of Finlay MacKinnon. He knelt on the sand, ripped open the dead man's shirt at the neck, and yanked at something inside. He held an object aloft, turning it so those nearby could see—a medium-sized silver crucifix, with a golden crescent moon bisecting the top, the ends pointed upward, like the horns of a cow. "See! Here's the proof MacDonald spoke true."

The chief stalked up and down the line of riders, displaying the demonic symbol. "Finlay and his sons were in league with a demoness! D'ye hear what I say? We have done Elspeth MacKinnon an injustice! A grave injustice." He stopped in front of Ian Macfie and Angus MacKinnon and brandished the corrupted crucifix at Elspeth's father. "Angus MacKinnon, ye shall beg your daughter's and her betrothed's forgiveness. And ye *will* give her the promised dowry. D'ye so swear before Almighty God and these here present? D'ye swear on the sacred iron of your dirk?"

Angus MacKinnon sheathed his sword, then drew his dirk. "Aye, that I will." Holding the dagger by the blade, by the sacred iron, he bowed his head. "I so swear it." He sheathed his dagger, then made the sign of the cross. He lifted his head. And through the slits in Tormond's helm the Templar could see tears on Angus's face.

The MacKinnon next addressed Malcolm's father. "Ian Macfie, will ye also so swear to beg your son's forgiveness?"

Ian Macfie scowled at the MacKinnon chief. "Ye have nae right to command me thus. Ye are nae my chieftain."

The MacKinnon shook his head, but he still held aloft the demonic cross. "Nae, laddie. I dinnae have the right to command ye. But ye have still done your son and his bride a wrong. We were *all* wrong to refuse this lassie aid. Ye need to beg —"

Ian Macfie spat at Malcom. "Ye are nae more my son. The de'il take ye all." With that, he wheeled his pony and rode away.

"And ye are nae more my father!" Malcolm cried.

Elspeth's father dismounted. He laid his weapons on the sand, then walked slowly toward his daughter. Tormond removed his helm, turned his horse, and watched as Angus MacKinnon knelt on the sand beside Elspeth and her pony. Elspeth did not flinch or draw away when Angus put a hand upon her foot. He lifted his head. "Oh, Elspeth, my poor darlin' lass. What ye must have been through . . . Will ye forgive a foolish old man his sins against ye?"

Elspeth dismounted and raised her father from the sand. She embraced him. "Aye, Da! With all my heart, I forgive ye!"

Angus, his face buried in his daughter's curls, said something Tormond could not catch.

Father and daughter wept together.

All the while, Malcolm, sat his pony tall and proud.

Ye must forgive him as well, laddie.

Angus raised his head and turned his face to Malcolm. "Malcolm Macfie, can ye also forgive?"

Malcolm's proud shoulders slumped. "If Elspeth can forgive ye, then so do I."

Angus said, "Ye shall always have a place with us, Malcolm Macfie. I have ye to thank for my daughter's safe—for my dear one's return."

"Thank ye," Malcolm said, then he added, "Thank ye, Da."

Angus smiled. "Come! Let us all go home. The night is wanin', and we'll all be a-wantin' fire, food, and whiskey." He pulled out of his daughter's embrace and clapped his hands on her shoulders. "And to welcome my darlin' lassie home!" He paused, turning to Tormond and Maebh. "But first"—once again, he knelt, this time facing Tormond—"I dinnae know where ye came from, Tormond MacDonald, and ye, Maebh O Broin—out the mists of the past, maybe—but whence e'er 'twas, I thank God for ye both. Ye have saved my darlin' lass and shown an old fool he has much to learn. Will ye join me in my house and feast with me? 'Twould seem we have a weddin' to prepare, soon as may be."

Maebh bowed her head, "We would be honored, Ian Mac—"

"But," Tormond interrupted, "we must ride hard for the harbor at Scalasaig." He gestured north with his right arm—with the arm that he was increasingly and alarmingly coming to think of as his "good" arm. "We must take ship this very day."

Must get back to the Witches' wine. If I lose the use of my shield arm, I'll nae be able to fulfill my mission. And I'll nae...

I'll nae be able to protect her.

When did protecting Maebh become as important as the hunting of the Witches? Nae, more important than the hunting of the Witches?

Maebh looked at him with curious eyes. Curiosity turned to concern. She swallowed. "Aye. We must take ship on the next tide."

✠·✠·✠

"Tomorrow morn?" Maebh glared at the captain of *The Maid of the Isles*, trying very hard not to raise her voice at the sturdy little man. "Four days, ye said, perhaps three, with favorable winds. It has been Six. *Six*, Master MacLeod." She pointed toward the shore off the bow. "I can see the Welsh coast, man!" She'd done it. She'd raised her

237

voice. She'd let her temper—and her fear—get the better of her. "Why wait 'til tomorrow?"

Aiden MacLeod stood barefooted before her in the twilight, looking more like a common sailor than the master of a ship. He had his hands on his hips and glared right back at her. "I said, yer *ladyship*, when ye and Sir Tormond hired my vessel, that we'd make all possible speed. And I did say three days wi' favorable winds, but we have nae *had* favorable winds, now, have we? We've been fighting a southerly wind—a headwind, mind—near the whole voyage."

"But the lights of Newport are right there! Ye can see it. And we've paid ye well. Very well."

"Aye, ye have, and I'll nae deny it. But yer gold cannae change the tides, ye ken? Only God can do that. And to my knowledge, the Almighty has ne'er done so for any man or woman. It be too shallow. We'll dock when 'tis safe to do so."

Only God can change the tides.

Maebh crossed herself.

Forgive me.

But I'm just so frightened!

MacLeod's scowl softened. "He's . . . bad, aye?"

Maebh closed her eyes and nodded. "Aye."

"There be doctors in Newport. I know a leech, a good one, who—"

"Nae!" Tormond lurched out of the door of the captain's cabin, which he and Maebh had commandeered for the voyage. His skin was pale and damp with sweat, his eyes sunken, but his cheeks burned with fever. He swayed as he staggered toward them, pitching with the ship as it fought wind and wave. He was bare-chested, save for the crimson-and-ochre-stained bandage about his shoulder and the sling that held his left arm immobile. And yet, he still carried his sword and dagger at his belt. The man slept with the sword—Maebh had seen him sleep each night in their shared cabin with the weapon clutched to his chest as if it were the only thing anchoring him to the world. "I'm beyond the help of leeches. I need more help than any doctor can give."

MacLeod nodded. "I'll dock as soon as I can. But 'twill be long after dark."

Maebh gave the captain a sad smile. "I know ye will do the best ye can. Forgive my harsh words. As ye said, only God can change the tides."

The captain sighed. "Aye, milady." He raised his head and shouted at the mate standing by the helmsman on the quarterdeck. "Ho! Hobbes! Rig for all speed. We push on for Newport tonight! I mean to catch the midnight tide!"

"Aye-aye, captain!" Hobbes replied. Then the mate began shouting orders to the crew of the caravel ship.

"Thank ye, captain," Maebh said.

MacLeod nodded. He placed the knuckle of his curled forefinger to his brow in salute. "Milady. Milaird." He stomped up to the quarterdeck to supervise the mate, even as the mate supervised the rigging of the sails.

"Now, ye, *milaird*," Maebh said, striding quickly to Tormond and taking firm hold of his right arm, "back to your berth with ye."

He shook his head. "I must tend to Órd Dubh."

"I can tend to the horses." She pulled him toward the cabin door. Tormond gave her little resistance. *He's so weak! 'Tis like pushing about a new kitten.* "I think Órd Dubh likes me better anyway."

Tormond chuckled, and she could hear the horrible rattling in his lungs. "'Tis because ye give him apples. And ye speak so kindly to him." He gave her a weak, tender smile. "As ye do to everyone."

Except when my temper is up.

When she got him into his narrow berth—one of two in the captain's quarters—she touched his hand, the hand gripping the hilt of his sword as the weapon lay on his chest. She noted the whiteness of his knuckles in the failing light. *He clings to the sword as he clings to life.* The heat of his flesh was worse than before. She forced herself to remain calm—on the outside. She lit a candle and placed it on the low table beside his bed. She wetted her kerchief with water from a bottle and wiped his forehead, attempting to cool him. The wound stank, and she could see dark veins snaking away from under the bandage.

Please, Tormond, hold fast. Please be strong. Think of your sacred mission.

Don't leave me.

I love ye so.

Don't ye dare die until ye realize how much, how dearly I do love ye.

'Til I can tell ye myself. Aloud. With my own lips. Without shaming ye.

"I'm trying," he whispered.

Her hand froze on his burning forehead. "Did I say something? Aloud?"

He chuckled again, then coughed. Pink spittle flew from his lips. "Nae, but I know what ye are a-thinkin'. Ye are a-thinkin', 'Hold fast, Tormond. Be as stubborn as . . . as a pig . . . being led to slaughter.'" He winked at her, and his lips curled in a weak grin. "'Tis what ye were . . . a-thinkin'."

She forced a smile. "Ye have me to rights, Sir Knight. 'Tis precisely what I was a-thinking."

He closed his eyes. "Maebh?"

"Aye, Tormond? What is it?"

He swallowed and opened his eyes again. "Thank ye, lass. Thank ye for . . . all ye have done."

"'Tis nothing." *Oh, Tormond, don't ye dare die! Ye must live. Ye must.* "Tormond?"

His eyes fluttered open, then focused on her face. "Aye?"

"Ye must fight. Ye must hold fast."

"I will. And I shall live, *insh'Allah.*"

She nodded. Hot tears spilled from her eyes. "*Insh'Allah.* God willing."

He coughed again. Violently. When the fit subsided, he whispered, "Maebh?"

"I'm here, Tormond."

"Please . . . will ye pray for me?"

"Oh, Tormond! I pray for ye always! *Always!* Ye know that!"

"Nae, lass. 'Twas nae my meaning. I meant . . . I have nae . . . finished my prayers. I lack yet . . . thirty-two *Pater nosters* to say this day. Will ye . . . say them for me?"

"Aye, Tormond!" She gripped his hand—his sword hand.

And he released the hilt of his sword to grip her hand. Weakly.

Maebh began to recite the Lord's Prayer as night fell. "*Pater noster qui es in caelis sanctificetur nomen tuum . . .*" She recited without thinking of the words, but at the end of each line, she silently offered up her own silent prayer, line by line, pleading with Heaven.

Our Father, who art in heaven, hallowed be thy name.

O, Father, save Tormond! Spare his life. Spare him!

I know I'm not supposed to love him, but I do. He has become my life. I would forsake my vows if he asked me to marry him. I would gladly marry Tormond MacDonald.

But I will remain a nun and celibate all my days if that be the price of his life. If that is what Thou askest of me, I will do it gladly. To save him.

Or take my life. Take my life, not his. Please.

Please. Anything Thou dost require — that I will do. Anything!

Just, please, please spare —

THUMP!

Maebh jumped, squeaking in alarm. Tormond didn't flinch.

The cabin door slammed open.

And framed in the doorway, silhouetted against the rising crescent moon, stood a tall figure, hooded and cloaked.

From beneath the deep shadows of the hood shone a pair of eyes, green as emeralds.

"Who are ye?" Maebh cried, drawing her dagger and lurching to her feet in the cramped cabin. She brandished the dagger at the figure. "If ye touch him, I'll—"

"Oh, put away the knife, girl," a melodious yet stern voice said, a voice to be obeyed. "Put it away before you hurt yourself. I'm here to help him, to save him. So, get out of my way. Quickly now. He's nearly gone."

Maebh felt a sudden urge to do exactly as she was told. But she did not lower her dagger. "Who are ye?"

"Maebh," the figure said, "I don't have time to argue with you. *He* doesn't have time."

A chill ripped through her. "H-how do ye know my name?"

The figure laughed softly. "I know all about you, Maebh O Broin, Shield-maiden of Christ. And I know all about Tormond MacDonald, the Executioner of God. And, my dear one, the man you love more than life itself is dying."

Maebh's jaw dropped. "A?"

The figure nodded. "Yes. Now, please let me save my son."

Chapter 22

Save him, please!" Maebh stepped aside, allowing the hooded figure to pass in the narrow cabin. *If ye are* able *to save him,* she thought, though she dared not voice her doubts aloud. "I prayed for help."

The hood was thrown back by a pair of pale, feminine hands, revealing a face of rare beauty. Pale, flawless skin. Full, red lips. A mane of curling red hair. Striking green eyes. "Yes," the woman said. "You prayed for help, and God has sent me." She unfastened and removed her cloak, then handed it to Maebh. "Guard the door, child. See that no one disturbs us."

The woman, "*A,*" was clad in a gown of dark green with long, full-length sleeves. The gown was fashionably cut, but not ostentatious—more like that of the wife of a well-to-do merchant than of a highborn lady. She would not stand out on the streets of Newport, except for one unusual anomaly—over her shoulder she wore a buckled leather strap—a baldric—that stretched across her body to a scabbard containing a short sword with a bone-white handle and a round wooden pommel. She gathered her skirts and pushed past Maebh. This proved awkward, given that both women wore the full, wide skirts of the time.

The woman knelt at Tormond's side.

Tormond, for his part, seemed unaware of her presence. His breathing was shallow, rapid. He moaned. "Maebh. Maebh?"

"I'm here, Tormond!" Maebh answered. "I'm here. H-help has come."

The woman did not look at Maebh—all her attention was on Tormond—but she said, "I warn you, dear one, what you are about to witness will both confuse and frighten you. But you must trust me as you have trusted me in the past. I have never led you amiss."

Frighten? Maebh was more than frightened—she was terrified. "I do trust ye. Just, please! Please, don't let him die!" Tears spilled from her eyes as she tangled her hands in the woman's cloak.

242

"I will save him. But guard the door. And no matter what you see, don't scream. And don't interfere."

Maebh tossed the cloak onto her berth as she moved quickly to the door and placed her back against it.

"Maebh?" Tormond's voice was shockingly weak.

"Hush, my son," the woman said, her voice soft, kind, and unmistakably filled with love. She opened her mouth wide, baring her white teeth. Maebh saw two of the woman's teeth extend, sharp and glinting in candlelight.

Maebh put a hand up to cover her mouth, stifling the forbidden scream. "What? What are ye?"

"Tormond's only hope," the woman said. She placed her red lips on Tormond's throat. And bit down.

Tormond uttered a small cry. His eyes flew open, wide with shock and pain.

"Tormond!" Maebh cried as terror ripped through her. "What are ye—"

Suddenly Tormond's eyes relaxed, seeming to lose their focus, and closed once more. He sighed, his pale lips curving in a smile. His breathing eased.

"What are ye doing?" Maebh took a step toward Tormond and the woman with her mouth affixed to his neck. "Are ye"—the thought was chilling, monstrous—"*drinking*? Drinking his blood?"

The woman held up a warning hand, even as she pulled her lips away from Tormond's neck, exposing two small wounds, each leaking a trickle of blood. "Only a very little. I would not take any, but 'tis the fastest, most effective way to get it into him."

"What?" Maebh shuddered. "Get what into him?"

"My spittle. The Seed. It will make him whole, fight the poisoning in his blood." She grimaced, her lips working in disgust. "The festering— It spoils the taste."

Maebh clenched both hands over her mouth in horror.

The woman bent her head once more and replaced her lips on Tormond's neck.

He was moaning now, as if with unspeakable, forbidden pleasure.

As terrified and confused as she was, Maebh felt a flash of an unfamiliar and ugly emotion.

Jealousy. She fought the urge to push the lovely, fearsome woman away from Tormond.

Smiling in his delirium, Tormond mumbled something — something Maebh wasn't quite sure she'd heard correctly. He moaned and repeated the words. "Maebh. Is toil leam thu."

Maebh knew those words, though they had been spoken in Tormond's native Scottish. The words were similar in Irish — *Is breá liom tú*. She'd heard those words repeated over and over between Malcolm and Elspeth on the beach on Oronsay as the reunited sweethearts gazed into each other's eyes —

I love ye.

The woman known to Maebh and Tormond as A lifted her lips from the Templar's neck. She licked the twin wounds with her tongue, wiping away the two trickles of blood.

Maebh watched in astonishment as the two circular wounds on Tormond's neck closed and disappeared — as if his neck had never been punctured.

The woman stared at Tormond's face for a few moments, then smiled softly. "Yes. That should do it. He's out of danger. His pallid color will pass as his healing body generates new blood." She sighed in satisfaction, then grimaced as she licked her lips. "Ew. That was . . . awful." Gingerly she removed Tormond's bandage, stained with crimson and a sickly yellow from the festering of the wound. "Now to see to the shoulder."

"What are ye?" Maebh asked. "Are ye as . . . Abhartach, the" — she didn't have the slightest idea what the word was in English — "*neamh-mairbh*, from the tales of Ireland?"

The woman laughed softly. "Abhartach? The undead?" She shook her head. "Do I appear undead to you? I can assure you that I am very much alive." She wrinkled her brow and nose as she examined Tormond's wound. "Ew. So, this is what has caused all the trouble. Shot, was he? But he must have been wearing that bit of plate armor, I suppose — the pauldrons young Sergeant William made for him. And 'tis a good thing too."

Maebh nodded as she wrung her hands. "I tried to sew it up. I did. Twice. But the stitches kept tearing."

The woman probed gently at the wound with her slender fingers. "You did the best you could. The flesh was too badly damaged and too tight over the muscles beneath. But the flesh is looser now. Yes, I can heal this." She grimaced again. "The bone is fractured too, but 'twill heal right enough." She pulled her red hair back, bent her head over the wound, and placed her lips over it.

Once again, Tormond began to moan as if with pleasure.

The jealousy returned. *She's helping him. Healing him. Don't think about the fangs or the drinking of the blood. And how ye want to pull her away from him.* "But, if ye are not . . . undead, then what are ye?"

After several long moments, the woman lifted her head. She pressed her fingers to the wound, spat on it, then pressed the edges of the mangled flesh together. "I suppose your Irish legend of Abhartach is close enough to the truth. Yes, I have heard the stories, though I never met him. I am a Daughter of Lilith."

Maebh gasped and started forward.

The woman chuckled. "Fear not, dear one. I long ago forsook the path of evil I had once freely chosen. And now I avoid all other Children of Lilith at all costs, save to defend the life of a mortal. I'm still a Daughter of Lilith, yes, but I am what my kind call a Penitent. I no longer prey on the innocent." She sighed. "Though to sustain myself—for I must drink human blood to survive—I do take the blood of the guilty—murderers, rapists, and such. I take only from the truly wicked."

She removed her hands from Tormond's shoulder. There was no longer any sign of the wound—the flesh was unblemished as if Tormond had never been shot. Even the remains of the bruise and the black tendrils were fading before her eyes. "He'll heal now. With some good food, wine, and rest"—she smiled at Maebh—"and your tender care, he'll be his old self in a day or so. My son will soon resume slaying the enemies of God as he is meant to do. With you, dear Maebh, forever at his side."

"Truly?" Maebh dropped to her knees beside the woman and grasped Tormond's hand. His flesh no longer burned with fever. He squeezed her hand—apparently by reflex—and already some of his strength seemed to have returned.

Maebh sobbed with joy. She pressed her lips to his hand and kissed it, bathing it with her tears. "Tormond! Oh, Tormond! Ye shall live!"

Maebh felt a hand on her head, gently stroking her hair. Just as her mother had done long ago.

"Yes, dear one. He shall live. He still has many prophecies to fulfill. You both do."

Maebh heard a quiet sob. She looked up.

The Daughter of Lilith was weeping.

"Why do ye weep?"

The woman let out a ragged laugh and brushed away a tear. "Oh, I confess I was afraid as well. I was so worried I wouldn't be in time to save him. I know what the prophecies say, but I do have my moments of doubt, especially where my children's welfare is concerned. I've" — she paused — "failed so many of my children in the past. So very many. I cannot be everywhere I'm needed. I came as soon as I saw your ship, as soon as the sun went down." She smiled sadly. "I could not come before that."

"How? How did ye get here? Aboard the ship?"

The Daughter of Lilith shrugged. "I flew, of course. But I cannot move about in the sunlight. I *burn* in the sunlight."

"Ye can fly? Like an angel?"

The woman laughed. "Yes, I can fly. All my kind can fly. But I am no angel."

Maebh laughed nervously. "Of course not. Ye have no wings."

"Oh, I have wings when I fly. They simply appear. But, child, angels do not have wings. Only —"

"But of course, angels have wings!" Maebh protested. "To say otherwise is heresy."

The woman sighed. "Oh, child, you have so much to learn."

So much to learn? Perhaps, but . . . Angels do not have wings? "But why do ye call Tormond your son. Are ye . . . his mother?"

The woman smiled down at Tormond and stroked his cheek lovingly. She shook her head. "No. Not even his grandmother."

Maebh looked from the woman's face to Tormond's, searching for any resemblance. She saw none. "His distant ancestor then?"

"No. Females of my kind cannot bear children."

"Why then do ye call him son?"

"Because long ago . . . so very long ago"—fresh tears streamed down her cheeks—"I was married to Tormond's ancestor, my beloved husband. I have watched over my husband's descendants ever since. But there are so many now. I cannot possibly protect them all." An angry, bitter look spread over her lovely features. "And I can only come out at night."

"Your husband? He was . . . like ye? Is he still alive?"

The bitter expression gave way to a sad, sweet smile. "No, dear one. He was mortal. And he died long ago. I have been alone since then. I will never marry again, for I will never love another—not as I love him. And someday, when all is restored, I will be his wife again, and he will be my husband."

"How long ago?"

"It has been nigh fifteen centuries since my beloved died. In nine years, it will be fifteen centuries. We were together as man and wife for twenty-four wonderful years. And I *will* see him again. Someday. And I *will* be his wife again. When the true church of Jesus Christ is restored in its fullness."

"Restored?" *What heresy is this?* "The *true* church?"

The Daughter of Lilith gave Maebh a sad smile. "Oh, dear one, do you think this pale remnant of Christianity is Christ's church? With all its pagan rituals and praying to dead saints, rather than to God the Father? Where priests indulge the sins of rich men in exchange for money? They lack the priesthood, the authority of God." She shook her head. "This poor shadow of the past. It is all lost."

"Surely, ye speak of the Churches of Scotland and of England and the other heretical protestant churches, not of the Holy Catholic Church?"

"The Catholic Church?" The woman raised an eyebrow. "The same church that allowed you to be stretched upon an altar so your chastity could be offered up in sacrifice to a demoness?"

Maebh shook her head in protest, shuddering in horror at the memory. Tormond, grasping her hand, seemed to shudder as well. She glanced quickly at him, but his eyes were still closed. "That was the Order of the Queen of Heaven! Not the holy mother Church!"

"Oh, dear one, such abuse of nuns has been occurring for centuries—not of all, certainly, but of far too many. *One* is too many. Priests are often the worst abusers."

"No! It cannot be. 'Tis monstrous!"

"Do you think your order—"

"'Twas not *my* order!" Maebh had nearly spat out the words. "I would never have joined them if I had known of—"

"Please forgive me. My choice of words was ill considered." The woman nodded. "You are correct, of course. It was not *your* order. But consider, dear one, what happened to the visiting priests who 'ministered' to that order? Who took confessions? Surely, they knew of what went on inside the abbey. And they did *nothing* to stop it. Some of them participated in it."

"No!"

"Oh, yes, they did. And what happened when the church discovered that Tormond had executed the abbess and the guards and liberated the captives? What happened then? What did the church do? Did it seek out the other abbeys where innocents were being held captive and abused? Did it put a stop to this abomination? No. They hid up their sins. They simply moved the guilty—and the victims—to new abbeys, to new locations where they could continue their blasphemous rites."

Maebh was weeping again. "No. Ye lie. Ye must be lying." But her words lacked conviction.

The Daughter of Lilith laid a gentle hand to her cheek. "Oh, dear one, I have not lied to you. I have never lied to you. I have only ever spoken the truth."

"But I believe in God! I believe in my Lord Jesus Christ!"

The woman smiled. "Yes, my dear one. Believe in God the Father and in His Son, Jesus Christ, and in the Holy Ghost. I too believe. I too *know* They are real, They live. I know that Jesus suffered for our sins to redeem us from Hell, that He died for us and rose again on the third day to bring about the resurrection of the dead." She smiled through her tears. "He has atoned for my sins—even for *my sins*, as black as they were. He is my Redeemer. He is your Redeemer." Her expression sobered. "Yes, believe in Them, and not in that corrupt church—the church that burned the faithful Templars, the Soldiers of Christ, at the stake, to satisfy the greed of the King of France."

"So, ye are A."

Both women started, then turned their eyes to Tormond.

He was awake. His eyes were bright and alert, unclouded by fever and pain. And those keen eyes were focused on the green-eyed woman.

The woman nodded. "I am, my son."

Tormond gave Maebh's hand a gentle, tender squeeze before pulling his hand away.

Maebh fought the urge, the *need* to hold on to his hand. But she let him go.

He gripped the hilt of his sword. But he made no aggressive move. He sat up slowly, not as if he were in pain, but as if he did not trust the strength of his limbs. He turned his gaze toward their mysterious benefactor. "Thank ye for saving me."

The Daughter of Lilith gave him an apologetic smile. "I'm sorry I could not do it sooner. I—"

He interrupted her with a slight shake of his head. "Then I was nae dreaming." His eyes narrowed as he scrutinized the woman. "The stories . . . the legends are true?"

The woman raised an eyebrow. "So, you heard all that."

"Most. I think. I thought 'twas but a fever dream at first."

She sighed. "I suppose that is just as well. You would have discovered all of this . . . in time."

"That is the second time ye have referred to the Holy Trinity as 'They,' as if God the Father, God the Son, and God the Holy Spirit were not one God. As if They were separate. Why do ye say this?"

Maebh stared at him in astonishment. "This? *This* is what ye ask about?" She found her temper rising. A wee bit. She lowered her voice and imitated his Scottish brogue. "Nae, hello, 'A!' So, ye are a monster, are ye nae? Will I become a blood-drinking monster as well now? My thanks to ye for healing me, but tell me—how 'tis that a creature of darkness who drinks the blood of the living can be a servant of God?" She glared at him, dropping the accent. "I could think of a thousand things to ask that do not touch on points of doctrine!"

Tormond didn't spare Maebh a glance. He continued to stare silently at the green-eyed woman.

A smiled. "I understand, my son. You need to know if you have been deceived, if I speak blasphemy. You need to know if you can still trust me, if you can — or should — still follow my counsel."

Tormond nodded slowly.

Her smile widened. "Ever the Soldier of Christ, are you not? Ever the strategist, considering your next move, your next battle."

One corner of his mouth twitched in the hint of a smile. "Aye."

"Very well, then," she continued. "But first let me assure you and" — she looked at Maebh — "your faithful and courageous companion that you, my son, will *not* become as I am. You would have to *choose* that path, and I know you would never do so."

Maebh shuddered. "No, he would not." *No one would. But if one must choose that path, that would mean...*

The Daughter of Lilith smiled. "Of course, you would not. You would never knowingly choose evil. As once I did." She sighed. "In answer to your question, my son, I was baptized — by immersion, not by pouring a bit of water over the head — and 'twas done by one having authority from God — in *Anno Domini* one hundred and two. That was nearly fifteen centuries ago. The Church was already in decay at that time, already in the beginnings of the 'falling away' prophesied by the Apostle Paul . . . and by others. But my husband, he who baptized me, was one of the last remaining elders, one of the last true bearers of the priesthood of God after the order of His Son. My husband taught me the true gospel of our Lord Jesus in its uncorrupted form, even as the church around him crumbled. I remember the truth. I was there. I have seen it all."

She shook her head sadly. "Heresies — oh so many false beliefs — have crept in over the centuries. For example — since you mentioned it — the false doctrine of the Trinity did not become accepted throughout Christendom until more than two centuries had passed since my baptism. Men assembled in a great council and debated — *debated* — the nature of God. As if *man* could define the nature of *God*. That particular bit of nonsense — the Trinity — won out. No, my son, from the beginning, God the Father and His Son and the

Holy Spirt have been three separate Persons, one in divine purpose, but three distinct Individuals."

"I see." But it was obvious to Maebh from Tormond's expression and tone of voice that he did not see. Maebh wasn't sure she understood—or believed—either.

"Think, my son," the woman continued, "to Whom did our Lord pray in the garden in the midst of His sufferings? Did He pray to Himself? No. He prayed to His Father in Heaven." She leaned toward Tormond and fixed him with her eyes.

Suddenly, she jerked, as if she had caught herself doing something she should not. "No." She averted her eyes. "I must not look directly in your eyes—not when speaking of such things. It is the nature of my kind that we have powers of *Persuasion* over mortals. No. If you are to believe, it must be of your own accord, not because I will and wish it so." Still looking away, she said. "Listen to your heart, my son. And you too, Maebh. What do your hearts tell you? What do the whisperings of the Holy Spirit tell you?"

As Maebh listened with all her heart, she felt something stir within her—a thrill, a joyful burning. She had felt it before. It started at the crown of her head and flowed down her body—the warmth and sweetness of pure love.

Tormond shuddered. A smile spread across his face, and he nodded. "Aye. Ye speak the truth. I do believe ye." His eyes brimmed with unshed tears. "Every blessed word."

His hand sought Maebh's once more. He turned his face to her. "Maebh?"

She nodded, smiling as the tears streamed down her face. "I too. I believe," she whispered. Her eyes locked with his for a long, joyous moment.

Tormond tore his gaze away from her and looked intently on the Daughter of Lilith who had saved his life. "I have one more question."

The woman raised an eyebrow and smiled. "Only one?"

He chuckled softly. "Aye, truth be told, I have many. But I have one *burning* question, if I may be so bold."

The woman winked at him. "When have you ever *not* been bold, my son?" She straightened, squaring her shoulders. "Very well, ask your burning question."

251

"We cannot go on simply calling ye A. Pray, what is your name, milady?"

The Daughter of Lilith smiled wistfully. "He called me that— my husband did. He called me 'my lady.'" Her eyes shone with love as if recalling the memory. "My name is Aquillius, or rather, that is my husband's family name and now mine. Hence the A. You may call me Branwen."

Chapter 23

When will we *finally* slay the Witches?" Tormond asked Branwen, the Daughter of Lilith, as he stirred the fire. It was the second night of their journey to Merlin's cave to retrieve the buried casks of magic wine. He and Maebh camped in a small clearing of a wood in Wales. Branwen joined them just after sundown, bringing with her a brace of freshly killed rabbits for Tormond and Maebh's supper, as well as two apples for Órd Dubh and Fiona. The toothsome smell of roasted cony filled the clearing. The Daughter of Lilith did not join them on the first night of their journey, and she informed them that she had "other tasks" to attend to. Tormond suspected one of those tasks involved taking sustenance "from the truly wicked."

The concept was something Tormond still wrestled with — attempting to reconcile the loving, kind, and devout Christian — but not Catholic — woman who had saved his life with the Daughter of Lilith who drank the blood of the living.

Branwen, clad in a light green gown — green seemed to be her favorite color — sat on a tree stump and stared into the flames without answering, and Tormond wondered if she'd heard his question.

Tormond exchanged a glance with Maebh, and she seemed as uncertain and as confused as he. They had come to trust the lovely and uncanny creature of darkness as much as they had the mysterious words on the parchments bearing the signature "A," but Branwen had not been as forthcoming that night as she had been on *The Maid of the Isles*.

I sense good in her, whatever she is. And I feel her love. When I look in her eyes, 'tis as if I'm looking into my own mother's eyes.

And the whisperings — they tell me to trust her.

Maebh shifted on the stone upon which she sat. "Branwen? Did ye —"

"I heard you." Branwen met his gaze. Her mouth twitched in a flicker of a smile. "My hearing is far better than yours." She sighed. "I don't know the answer. Not yet."

"Not yet?" Maebh asked. "Ye are guided by prophecy, are ye not?"

Branwen turned her patient gaze on Maebh. "Indeed I am. But the prophecies are not my own. I did not receive them myself. They are my husband's." As she mentioned her long-dead husband, her voice took on an unmistakably tender note.

Whenever she mentions him, her centuries-dead love, she gets a wistful look in her eyes. 'Tis as if her love for him still burns as bright as it did when he was alive. His eyes flickered to Maebh, and he felt an all-too-familiar longing for what could never be. "But ye have them, aye?" he asked. "The prophecies?"

Branwen nodded. "I have them. I copied them from his scroll long ago." Her eyes took on that wistful look once more. "He jokingly called it *The Book of Marcus Scribonius.*"

Scribonius? I thought his name was Aquillius.

A question for another time.

Branwen sighed. "And I've had centuries to study them, but . . ." She shook her head slightly. "I don't always know what they mean. Some are more . . . obscure than others." She shrugged. "Even my beloved Marcus did not understand most of them, unless they had already come to pass."

She smiled at Tormond. "Indeed, some of the prophecies about you are the plainest of the lot. He actually mentions you — and you, Maebh — by name. Though he renders your name 'Tormond, Son of the Donalds,' and yours, 'Maiv of Broin.' He wrote in Latin, of course. And I think that was as close as he could come to it. But not everything is so easily understood. Fortunately, in your case, I have sixty years between your awakenings to ponder and pray on which prophecies apply at which time."

"But about the Witches?" Tormond persisted.

"Ah, yes, the Witches." Branwen cocked her head. "All I have been able to discern from the prophecies is that you shall pursue them through the centuries until you awaken in the top of the mountains." She paused. "That's what it says, 'the top of the mountains.' It says that only then will your mission finally be fulfilled."

Maebh scowled. "But the top of *which* mountains?"

254

Branwen shook her head. "I do not know. But I do know that you yet have many tasks to fulfill, many wrongs to right before you get there."

Tormond scowled. "So, not for some time yet." *Possibly not for centuries.*

He glanced at Maebh and saw that she was looking at him. There was sadness in her eyes. *Not for centuries.*

"I understand part of your difficulty, however," Branwen said. "You're out of cycle with your prey. I can help with that. I can awaken you in 1655."

Maebh gasped, clasping hands together. "'Twould be wonderful!"

Hope surged in Tormond's heart. "Aye!" The *Sergeants have not been able to, but this creature of darkness can.* "I thank ye." *Ye cannae imagine how grateful I am.* But his newborn hope faltered. "Assuming the Witches dinnae have their cycle interrupted yet again."

Branwen gave him a sad smile. "I cannot control their cycle, but I can awaken you. That much I *can* do."

He nodded. "I will be content—and oh, so grateful—for that."

A bit of grease fell from one of the roasting rabbits. It struck the wood, then sizzled and flared. Tormond watched as Maebh stood and approached the fire. She drew her dagger and gently poked at the conies. "I think supper is ready." She bent and lifted the spits from the fire. She presented one spit to Tormond, then turned to Branwen. "I would gladly share, but I don't suppose . . ."

Branwen's nose wrinkled in disgust. "Thank you, but no. Mortal food makes me ill. Ew. Even the smell."

And the thought of what ye eat turns my stomach as well. "But I thank ye, milady. Fresh meat is a boon to us."

Maebh, who had been sitting farther away, took a seat next to Tormond, sharing his fallen log. "Forgive me, Tormond. 'Tis so Branwen doesn't have to smell our food."

Ye dinnae have to make apologies to me, lass. I dinnae mind your company. I should, but I dinnae mind in the slightest.

Secretly, he relished having her close.

Branwen smiled, inclining her head toward Maebh. "That is very thoughtful of you, dear one." She beamed at Tormond. "Is she not a fine lady, my son?"

He smiled. "The finest."

Maebh's cheeks darkened as she blushed.

Tormond looked across the fire at their benefactress. It seemed to him as if Branwen and Maebh exchanged a secret, knowing look. And for the second time, he wondered if Maebh was regretting, or perhaps, reconsidering her vows.

Dinnae think on such things.

God grant me strength.

Using her dagger, Maebh pushed her rabbit onto a flat stone in front of them. She cast aside her empty wooden spit, then took Tormond's spit and likewise removed the stick from his rabbit, laying the cony on the stone next to hers.

"Thank ye, lass."

She smiled at him, and that smile smote his heart, evoking in him forbidden desires.

Eat! Think on something else. He ripped a haunch from the rabbit and sank his teeth into the hot, savory meat, letting the juices run into his beard.

Think of the mission.

Branwen will awaken us in 1655.

Then we should be awake when the Witches are active and engaged in their evil.

And once they are slain, perhaps then Maebh and I could...

Dinnae think on it!

'Twill nae be for centuries yet.

Which mountains, I wonder? If Branwen does nae know . . .

Around a mouthful of roast cony, he asked, "What do the prophecies say about the Witches, about how we will catch them, about how they can be defeated?"

Branwen shook her head. "Very little, I'm afraid. At least, not so far as I've determined. The Holy Spirit may yet show me some passage in my husband's book that may shed light on your prey. I will have a few decades to pray and ponder on it before —"

Her head snapped up, and she seemed to sniff the night air. She stood abruptly.

"Branwen?" Maebh asked, but Tormond reached over with his left hand and gripped her wrist to silence her.

Careful, lassie. We still dinnae ken everything about what Branwen is, about what she's capable of. Not fully.

Tormond felt Maebh's hand atop his. She took a firm hold on his hand, but she did not tremble.

She should be frightened. We both should be.

But we trust Branwen. She has guided us and —

Branwen's lips opened in a snarl, showing her gleaming, white teeth. Two of those teeth lengthened, becoming fangs.

Tormond gasped. So did Maebh.

The teeth! Maebh told me, but.. .

God, preserve us!

God, preserve Maebh.

Branwen's eyes narrowed and hardened, but they were not focused on Tormond or Maebh. Her head swiveled back and forth, and she sniffed like a predator scenting prey.

With his right hand, Tormond gently eased his sword in its sheath, loosening it, preparing to draw it. If necessary.

If she attacks, strike at the neck. Branwen said 'tis the surest way to slay one of her kind.

The Daughter of Lilith's green eyes seemed to burn with rage. And they suddenly focused on Tormond. "Yes, my son, draw your sword." Her voice was cold as a frozen river in midwinter. "Prepare to defend yourself and your lady."

Tormond leaped to his feet, drawing both sword and dagger.

Maebh stood beside him, her own dagger at the ready.

Branwen shuddered, and drool spilled from her fanged mouth. "I must go. I smell evil blood." White, feathered wings unfurled behind her, as if they had sprouted from her back. Suddenly, she shot into the air, then disappeared behind the tops of the trees.

The great wings made no sound and he felt no rush of wind from their flapping at the air.

"Get behind me," Tormond whispered to Maebh. "Guard my back."

"Aye," she replied as she quickly moved with a rustle of her skirts.

He peered into the woods, but could see nothing moving in the darkness under the trees. Briefly, he wished he had his longbow or his shield. But he dared not retrieve them from the wagon.

Órd Dubh, tethered at the edge of the clearing, stamped at the ground. Fiona, next to the great warhorse, whinnied nervously.

"We'll make our stand here," Tormond said. "By the fire."

"Together," Maebh replied.

Tormond listened to the night sounds — the gentle wind sighing in the treetops, the hoot of an owl, the snorting of the horses, the crackle of the fire.

A scream rent the night. A very *human* scream. Of terror.

It had come from the left. Tormond wheeled, facing the sound.

Another scream, that time from the right. Tormond wheeled toward the second cry.

Maebh moved with him, keeping her station at his back.

The next scream came from behind them.

It was followed by another and another.

Men were shouting all around them, but the screams — they seemed to be progressing in a circle. *As if we are surrounded and Branwen is picking them off one by one.*

Tormond heard the unmistakable sound of steel striking steel. But he heard that sound of combat only once.

A final cry of mortal terror.

And once all cries died away, the only sounds were the sighing of the wind in the trees, the snorting and stamping of the horses, the crackling fire, and Tormond's and Maebh's rapid breathing.

Branwen emerged from the trees. Her light green gown bore several large, dark, wet-looking stains. Tormond was certain they were blood. In her hand she carried her short sword. The blade dripped blood from its sharp point.

And blood was on her lips.

She strode confidently into the firelight. "The danger is past." She again took her seat on the tree stump as if nothing of any import had passed. She licked her lips, removing most — but not all of — the blood from her face. She gave them a beatific smile. Gone was the feral rage that, but a few short minutes before, had possessed the fearsome Daughter of Lilith. "Sheathe your weapons. Sit, my son, dear one. Enjoy your meal." She sighed contentedly. "I have certainly enjoyed mine."

Tormond and Maebh did as they were instructed, but not before crossing themselves.

I trust her. She has never led us astray. I do trust her.

I must.

She could slay us before I could draw my sword.

Branwen raised her sword, and Tormond shuddered with revulsion as he watched her lick the blood from the blade. When she had finished, she gazed lovingly at the gleaming weapon as if it were a cherished treasure. "I cannot truly remember what mortal food tasted like, but the memory of the sweetest honey cannot compare to the intoxicating sweetness of *evil* blood."

Tormond and Maebh exchanged horrified looks. When they looked back at Branwen, she appeared to be both amused and annoyed. "Oh, don't look at me like that. There were eighteen of them. You would never have been able to defeat them all, my son, not even with the help of the Shield-maiden. And, dear one" — Branwen looked pointedly at Maebh — "the things they planned for you, before they slit your throat . . ." She pursed her lips. "I'm sorry. I shouldn't have mentioned that. But 'twas true. I overheard a couple of them whispering as they approached."

She looked down at her skirts and groaned. "Another gown ruined. I'll never get this much blood out." She sighed and, finding an unstained patch on her skirt, dried her sword.

"Cold water." Tormond was surprised at his own words. He cleared his throat. "Cold water. Before ye use the lye soap. I've used it often to remove blood from my cloak and tabards. And they're of white wool."

Branwen shook her head as she sheathed her sword. "Ah, my son. This" — she indicated her skirt — "is silk. Not wool."

"Just add a bit of salt to the water. My mother" — Maebh's deep blush was apparent, even in the firelight — "she had a silk gown. The only one she ever possessed. She was — She wore it once when her menses had already started. My da insisted. Some of the blood leaked. It was very . . . embarrassing." Maebh's blush deepened all the more. "But one of the maids showed her how to get the blood out."

Branwen chuckled. "Well, I must say, in all my unnaturally long life, I have never heard of that before. A little salt, is it?" She grinned and inclined her head. "I thank you, dear one." She let out a sad sigh. "All the lovely gowns I have cast away over the last few centuries . . ." She pointed at the rabbits. "But eat your food before it gets completely cold."

Tormond didn't feel particularly hungry, but he had learned long ago to eat whenever God provided the opportunity. *Must keep my strength. To fight.* He ripped a foreleg from the roasted rabbit. "Your sword. I've never seen its like."

Branwen patted the round wooden pommel affectionately. "My husband's. Roman. *Gladius Hispaniensis.* Or more commonly, simply a *gladius.* I am never without it." She smiled sadly. "I plan to be buried with it."

Buried with it? "But ye are immortal, aye?"

Branwen waved a dismissive hand. "Immortal, yes. But that doesn't mean I cannot die. And one of the prophecies does say that I will die. Someday, when my mission is over. When I am finished protecting my family. And then"—a tear fell from her eye—"then I will at last be reunited with my beloved Marcus. And with my beloved sister, his first wife." She wiped away her tear, then gazed into the fire. "But that day is yet far off. And thus, I wait. And I serve. Alone."

Pity swelled in Tormond's breast as he thought of Branwen— of her facing the centuries alone. *Alone? I too know what it is to be alone. And I was alone.*

Until God sent Maebh to me.

Beside him, Maebh stirred. "'It is not good that man should be alone,'" she quoted.

Branwen gazed upon her and smiled. "Nor the woman. You have been reading the Bible I gave you."

Maebh nodded. "Slowly. I am yet learning to read, and I am not very skilled at it. I am still in Genesis."

Tormond grinned. "Ach! Dinnae listen to her. She's a very fast learner. She just spends too much time going over and over every passage of scripture."

Maebh blushed. "Not *every* passage."

Branwen smiled. "Just the passages that matter, no doubt."

Must guide the conversation away from this — away from talk of man and woman being alone. "Who were they? The men you killed? Did any escape?"

"Common brigands. Murderers." She glanced at Maebh. "Defilers of women. And no, none escaped."

"How could ye know they were evil?" Maebh asked. "Before they approached?"

"I could smell their evil blood, the blood of men who have committed great evil, great violence. The same would be true of any who have murdered."

"But I," Tormond said, "I have led a life of violence. I have killed many. So very many."

Branwen shook her head. "My son, you have never shed innocent blood. If you had, I would be compelled to take your blood, if not your life. I myself have slain so many. But I have never shed innocent blood. Never. Not even when I was . . . Not even before I met my husband, before I was baptized and washed clean of my sins, through the grace of my Redeemer, Jesus Christ. In some ways, we are much alike, you and I, Tormond MacDonald, Executioner of God."

Alike? I and this creature of darkness? This paradox of darkness and light? "But ye are . . ."

"A monster? A demoness?" Branwen smiled. "Yes, I have been called that. My husband called me a night demon. And, in truth, I was." She paused, then spoke as if to herself. "Later on, when we were married, he called me *his* lovely night demon." She sighed. "Don't you see, my son? I, who was the very vilest of sinners, even *I* can be saved by the grace of Lord Jesus, because I was willing to repent and call upon His name and rely on His love. Love" — she turned her green eyes to Maebh — "*true* love can conquer all things. In God's time."

An uncomfortable silence befell them.

Surely, she speaks of the love of Christ for mankind. Nae the love of a man for a woman.

Maebh cleared her throat. "Branwen?"

"Yes, dear one?"

"Ye said Tormond and I . . . that we have something to teach each other. What is that? What could I possibly teach him?"

"Oh, Maebh." Branwen's eyes softened in the firelight. "Dear, dear Maebh. You have already begun to teach him, and he you. You are already better than you were. Both of you."

Tormond was unable to swallow the lump that had suddenly taken up residence in his throat, but he looked at Maebh. "I am . . . a better man" — he hastened to add — "a better Soldier of Christ, since ye came into my life, Maebh O Broin."

Tears coursed down Maebh's cheeks. "Oh, Tormond, I — " She turned her face away.

Abruptly Tormond stood. "I must gather more wood for the fire." He turned and headed toward the edge of the clearing.

"Tormond!" Maebh's anguished voice followed him as he strode into the forest, but he did not turn back.

As he left the women behind, he heard Branwen's clear voice, though she seemed to be speaking only to Maebh. "Give him time, dear one. He's not yet ready."

Time? Time for what? Not ready for what? To forsake my sacred vow?

I made my vow freely. I made it to God. And God has not released me from it.

Celibacy is the higher way. It is!

Then why, laddie, do ye torture yourself with her presence?

"Because," he whispered to the darkness, "I cannot go on without her."

Alone. Like Branwen.

He gathered wood as he ventured farther and farther from the clearing.

He spotted a thicker broken branch and stooped to pick it up, but as he did, his eyes alighted on the corpse.

The man lay on his back, his dead eyes staring at the trees above. Staring at nothing. The hilt of a broken sword lay near his hand, the severed blade lay a couple feet away. His neck still bore the twin wounds of Branwen's bite, but the bite wasn't what killed him. He had been gutted, the offal lying on top of him and all about — evidence of Branwen's sword and fury.

"What a waste." The voice came from Tormond's right.

Tormond drew his sword and dagger and wheeled to face the stranger.

Standing a few yards away, the man was tall and fashionably dressed for the time in a tight-waisted coat with lace cuffs and a wide, circular lace ruff at the neck, a short cape draped over his left arm, voluminous knee breeches, stockings, and shoes with large, puffy rosettes. On his head, he wore a tall, flat-topped, wide-brimmed hat decorated with feathers and ribbons. The man had no beard, not even the neatly trimmed mustache and short beards so common among the nobility of the time. At his side, he wore a two-handed longsword.

"Who are ye?" Tormond challenged, pointing his weapons at the stranger.

The man raised an eyebrow. "You think you can match swords with me, mortal?" He laughed.

Mortal? Tormond's blood seemed to freeze in his veins. *A Child of Lilith? Like Branwen?*

The man sauntered toward Tormond, apparently undaunted by Tormond's sword and dagger. "I came here to feast on the sweetness of pure evil." He stuck out his lower lip as if he were a pouting child and shook his head. "And all I find is one very foolish—but sadly, also very *innocent*—mortal." He let out a dramatic sigh. "But I suppose you will just have to suffice." He licked his lips as his fangs extended. "For you see, my paltry supper, I have worked up *such* an appetite."

Chapter 24

Come on then, mortal." The stranger leered at Tormond like a cat grinning at a mouse it has trapped, his fangs gleaming in the moonlight. "Show me your" — he gave a derisive chuckle — "*skill* with a blade."

Tormond stood his ground. "I'll nae attack an unarmed man. Draw your sword."

The man rolled his eyes. "And I thought the Chivalric Code was passé. Oh, very well. As you wish." In the blink of an eye, the longsword was out of the scabbard and in his hands. The movement was so quick, Tormond didn't see the stranger draw his weapon. The man gave Tormond a mocking, courtly bow, but his leering grin never wavered. "With chivalry satisfied, sir, *en garde!*" Casually, the man took a combative stance suitable for a two-handed weapon, but he did not attack.

Tormond knew in that moment that he was facing his death. *So fast. I cannae hope to beat him.*

Sancta Maria, Mater Dei —

Then remembering Branwen's instruction to pray only to God, *God in Heaven, protect Maebh. And protect Branwen.*

Perhaps, if I can warn them...

He lifted his voice in a battle hymn.

Crucem sanctam subiit,
Qui infernum confregit —

The stranger raised an eyebrow. "I have not heard that song for centuries. Not since I was a Templar."

He was a Templar? It was Tormond's turn to sneer. "Ye're nae a Soldier of Christ. Ye're a Son of Lilith."

The man's grin vanished, and his face seemed to drain of blood. "Who told you that name?" His lips curled in a snarl, and his fangs glinted. "None are privy to that name save those Chosen to join our ranks. And if you were Chosen, you would not dare challenge me. Who told you? Who betrayed the Great Secret? Tell me!"

"I did!" a voice cried.

Suddenly, Branwen was there, behind the man, her sword drawn.

Faster than a striking viper, the stranger wheeled and swung his longsword at Branwen.

She met his attack with her short sword.

A rapid, arhythmic cacophony of steel striking steel filled the forest. The movements were so fast, Tormond could barely follow them. He watched in mute awe as the two immortal combatants thrust, slashed, and parried at a blinding speed. The clash of weapons produced no sparks, as if the swords themselves were impervious to damage, despite the violence of the blows.

Branwen was clearly at a disadvantage. The longsword afforded her opponent a much longer reach, and she seemed to be hampered by her voluminous skirts. Compared to her male opponent, she appeared to move more slowly, her skirts swaying and turning. Repeatedly, she was forced to give ground, stepping back again and again, then appeared to rally, driving her enemy back.

Maebh dashed into view, carrying a pistol in one hand and a dagger in the other. She halted and gaped at the incredible scene.

Tormond moved to protect her, knowing his defense would likely fail in seconds if the immortal predator prevailed. He could do nothing to help Branwen.

Maebh was attempting to aim her snaplock at the enemy, but both Branwen and her opponent moved so quickly in their deadly dance that Tormond knew Maebh would not be able to get a clear shot. She looked to Tormond, her eyes wide with fear and doubt.

He shook his head, and she lowered her weapon.

We cannae do a thing to help.

Maebh has nae fear for herself, only for Branwen.

Brave lass.

Branwen screamed.

Tormond's attention snapped back to the combatants.

To his horror, Tormond saw that the stranger had thrust his blade through Branwen's heart. But the man did not move, he simply held the sword immobile, as if he were waiting for her to die.

Tormond leaped forward, swinging his sword.

The stranger pivoted, his triumphant grin faltering as he spied Tormond. A moment later his head—and its foppish hat—toppled to the forest floor. The headless body stood for a brief moment, then it too fell, the hands still grasping the longsword, pulling it from Branwen's chest.

Branwen also collapsed to the earth.

In an instant, Maebh dropped her weapons and knelt at Branwen's side, throwing her arms around their benefactor's shoulders. Maebh rocked back and forth and began to wail. "Branwen!"

Tormond bowed his head in grief. *She sacrificed herself for me. She was immortal.*

Or she was supposed to be.

He sheathed his dagger, then dropped to his knees. He held his sword by the blade in front of him, its point on the ground.

He offered up the Prayer for the Dead.

"Requiem æternam dona ei, Domine. Et lux perpetua luceat ei. Requiescat in pace. Amen." *Rest eternal grant unto her, Lord. And let light perpetual shine upon her. May she rest in peace. Amen.*

As he took his right hand from the blade and made the sign of the cross, Maebh screamed.

His head snapped up as Maebh shrank from Branwen.

Branwen was sitting up, breathing and grimacing.

Alive?

"That hurt!" the Daughter of Lilith said. She rubbed at her chest, her hand covering her torn and blood-drenched bodice. "Healing is almost worse than the pain." She stuck her fingers into the hole in her bodice—there was no hole in her chest. She looked down and scowled. "Now the gown truly is ruined." She lifted her head and looked from Maebh to Tormond. She stuck out her bottom lip in a pout worthy of a vexed little girl whose feast-day frock has been soiled. "I'm afraid a bit of salt in cold water won't remove *this*."

She sighed, then gave Tormond an apologetic smile. "I suppose I have you to thank for my deliverance?"

266

Tormond nodded. He opened his mouth to speak, but no words came out. He pointed mutely at the severed head — and the corpse that had been so recently relieved of it.

"Yes. I see." Branwen smiled at him and inclined her head. "Thank you, my son." She turned to Maebh, extended a hand, and pushed back an errant lock of hair from Maebh's face. "I'm sorry I frightened you, dear one."

Remarkably, Maebh did not flinch. "Ye were dead!" she managed to choke out.

Branwen shrugged and rocked her head from side to side. "No, I was not. If I were dead, I wouldn't be speaking to you now."

Tormond pointed at Branwen's chest. "But he put the blade through your heart. I witnessed it."

Branwen nodded. "Yes, he did. But he didn't leave it there long enough to kill one of my kind. A few more seconds, and my heart would not have been able to Heal — not before I died in truth. But you saved me in time." She extended a hand to him.

Tormond stared at the hand, blinking without understanding the gesture. It took Tormond an awkward moment to realize she was allowing him to help her to her feet. He stood, took the proffered hand, and gently assisted Branwen up.

Branwen brushed leaves and dirt from her posterior for a moment before giving up with a grimace. "Why bother? I shall have to change into something else soon enough, and I didn't bring a spare gown with me. I wasn't expecting a fight." Her grimace turned into a sly grin. "If I had, I would have dressed to suit the occasion. Perhaps next time, I shall be better prepared."

Tormond chuckled nervously. He extended a hand to Maebh and helped her to stand as well. The pair of them exchanged looks of dread.

Branwen laughed. "Look at you two! If you are going to spend any time in my company, you will need to become accustomed to the idea that I am *extremely* difficult to kill."

Tormond, who had not sheathed his sword, pointed the weapon at the corpse. "What of him? Will he suddenly . . . resurrect? Like ye?"

"I didn't resurrect." Branwen chuckled. "You beheaded the villain. There's no coming back from that. Not even for my kind.

Even were you to place the head immediately back upon the neck, 'twould not Heal. 'Tis the surest way to kill a Child of Lilith. You can pierce the heart, of course, but you must leave the blade or spear in the heart long enough for the rest of the body to die."

She cocked an eyebrow. "I fought a man once—a Son of Lilith—whose heart was on the *right* side of his chest, not the left. I stabbed him through the chest." She shrugged. "Did nothing. Yes, it hurt him, but there I was, waiting for him to die. He actually laughed at me as I held my sword in his—"

Her voice cut off abruptly, and her eyes went wide with horror. "The sword!" She spun about, looking wildly for her dropped weapon. When she spied the short sword, she bent and snatched it up. She hugged the blade to her chest and sobbed. "Oh, Marcus! *Marcus!* I thought I'd lost it!"

Reverently, lovingly, she wiped the blade on a relatively clean patch of her skirt.

Tormond noticed she did not lick off the blood that time. *Perhaps she cannae consume the blood of immortals?*

"'Tis all I have left of him," Branwen said. "Of my beloved husband." She gazed at the blade, and tears spilled from her eyes. "I have his words, to be sure, his prophecies, but not in his own hand. Only my copy. The original scroll is lost to me. I know not where it is. Or if it still exists." She sheathed the sword in the scabbard at her hip before wiping away her tears and smiling tenderly at Tormond. "And, of course, my son, I have his precious descendants. To look after, to guard." She caressed his cheek. "And in your case, my time-lost son, to guide." The tenderness in her smile faded to sadness. "For yet a little while."

Branwen sighed. "Come, children. Let us go back. Your dinner is getting cold." She stooped and retrieved Maebh's pistol and dagger from the ground. She smiled at Maebh. "And you, dear one— You came to save me as well. And perhaps"—she winked—"to save Tormond?"

Maebh blushed—mere shadows on her cheeks in the moonlight. "I could do nothing."

Branwen handed the weapons to Maebh. "But you came. You hazarded your life to save us. You are so courageous." She inclined her head toward Tormond. "I expect nothing less of him, the fearsome Executioner of God. But you are . . . You are *worthy*."

Maebh's blush deepened.

But Branwen's praise for Maebh filled Tormond with pride. *She is indeed worthy.*

"But ye," Maebh said, "ye were *fearless*. His sword was so . . . and he was taller than ye. And he was a *man*!"

Branwen threw back her head and laughed. "Oh, dear one!" She shook her head. "I am far from fearless! But then, 'tis easy to be brave when I know that I shall not die until I have fulfilled *all* my husband's prophecies — at least the ones concerning me." She sighed. "You see, I know I cannot die until my mission is accomplished." She raised her hand and waggled a finger. "And the prophecies of Marcus are never wrong."

Tormond glanced again at the corpses on the ground — the beheaded Son of Lilith and the brigand that Branwen had killed earlier. "What of the dead?"

Branwen scowled contemptuously at the bodies. "Leave them for the crows and ravens." She looked as if she might spit on the dead. "Clean your sword, my son." She pointed at the headless corpse. "Use that vermin's cape."

Tormond knelt and did as instructed, then stood and sheathed his blade.

With Branwen leading the way, they walked toward the light of their campfire.

Tormond held his sword arm bent and slightly away from his body. He risked a glance in Maebh's direction.

Maebh smiled and slipped her hand into the crook of his elbow. For a moment, she leaned her head against his shoulder. Together, they followed Branwen through the trees.

Tormond grinned. Automatically, he began to recite the *Pater noster* in penance.

Branwen glanced at them and smiled. "That was a lovely prayer you said for me, my son. Even if I was not yet dead."

Tormond felt heat in his cheeks. "'Twas merely the Prayer for the Dead. 'Twas nothing."

"Still," Branwen replied, "'Twas lovely even so." She paused. "But you must not pray to the Lord Jesus. You must always pray to

God the Father. Pray in the name of Jesus — that is essential — but pray only to the Father. And, my son, pray from your heart. No more of these memorized prayers."

Caught off guard by her words, Tormond nearly stumbled. "Memorized prayers? The Prayer for the Dead?"

"Yes," Branwen said as she continued walking, "and the 'Our Father.' How many times have you recited it today? Hm?"

Tormond did stumble that time. He would have fallen if Maebh had not been supporting him. "The *Pater noster?*" *I'm not supposed to say the Pater noster?* "I still have forty repetitions to say this night. Before I sleep. But that . . . That is the way our Lord taught us to pray!"

"That is the *form* only, my son. Pour your heart out to God. He wants to hear what comes from your heart, not, as our Lord said, 'vain repetitions.'"

"But how am I to perform penance? If there are no priests left to whom I can confess my sins and receive absolution . . ."

Branwen stopped, causing Tormond and Maebh to halt as well. "Penance? Penance for what? What sin have you committed this night?" She stared him in the eyes, and it seemed to him as if she were staring deep into his soul.

I am enjoying the company of a woman. I am enjoying Maebh's touch on my arm. Her closeness. But he said nothing. Such an admission would only cause Maebh pain.

"We all sin," Branwen said. "All of us. But unless the Lord has forbidden a thing . . . Perhaps some things you might *think* are sin are indeed not. Perhaps some things you *fear* are actually *holy* in the sight of God. Remember the words of our Lord — 'But in vain they do worship me, teaching for doctrines the commandments of men.'"

And with that, Branwen turned and strode toward the firelight.

Tormond stared after her, his mouth gaping, then turned his gaze to Maebh. "What does she mean? 'The commandments of men?'"

But Maebh did not look at him. Rather, she looked straight ahead as she squeezed his arm.

On her face, she wore a familiar—uniquely feminine and utterly frustrating—smile.

Chapter 25

Maebh was awakened by a caress — the feather-light touch of rough fingers on her cheek. Her eyes fluttered open, and she beheld Tormond kneeling beside her. And he was smiling.

In the light of the candles, his face seemed to radiate with joy.

Her newly awakened heart raced at the sight. She beamed back at him, basking in his joy.

"She did it," he said. "Branwen did it!"

"Branwen?" Maebh's smile faded as she glanced around. Her eyes lit upon the alluring Daughter of Lilith standing behind Tormond.

"I'm here, dear one," Branwen said. She wore a gown with a neckline that left her shoulders bare, and it's puffy sleeves reached just past her elbows. Her skirts were padded and far wider at the hips, but less voluminous than those she'd worn in 1617. The gown's pale blue silk made her green eyes all the more striking.

A momentary flash of resentment and jealousy toward the lovely immortal overcame Maebh, followed by shame. Heat blossomed in her cheeks.

"Aye!" Tormond gave her an enthusiastic nod. "She has awakened us. 'Tis 1655!" Suddenly, his grin was all teeth. "We can *finally* hunt down the accursed Witches."

She forced herself to smile again. "Aye. Of course." She was surprised at the lack of enthusiasm in her voice. *I should be as joyful as Tormond. When this is finished, when his . . . when our mission is finished . . .* She could not even voice the secret hope in her mind.

He blinked, his grin vanished, and his eyes narrowed as if in confusion. He offered her his hand to help her to her feet. "Milady?"

At least he's not calling me "Sister." Not in front of her.

Stop that. Branwen doesn't deserve my resentment. She has been a true friend and ally.

272

When Maebh took the proffered hand, Tormond's smile returned. He helped her sit up. Still holding his hand, she swung her legs and capacious skirts off the wide stone bed upon which they'd slept. She allowed Tormond to pull her to her feet.

Tormond gave her a courtly bow before releasing her hand.

Maebh felt a pang of loss when his hand no longer touched hers. "Thank ye, Sir Tormond," she muttered.

She glanced around the chamber, taking in their surroundings again—a large, subterranean chamber cut by hand out of the light gray sandstone, lit by half a dozen candles burning in sconces carved into the walls. The horses still slept at the far end of the chamber with their heads down—Órd Dubh standing a few hands taller than Fiona.

Against the right wall sat their armaments—Tormond's long-handled axe, shield, longbow, and quiver of arrows. Maebh spied a brace of pistols, her powder horn, and pouch of lead shot. The pistols hadn't been there when they went to sleep. The firing mechanism looked different—simpler than the snaplocks she'd carried before. In addition, Maebh saw her treasured Bible, Branwen's customary chest—probably containing clothing suited to the times and a generous supply of gold—a much larger wooden chest that Maebh did not recognize, and, of course, the two small casks of magic wine, with the goblet atop one.

Carved into the left wall was a tall, shallow alcove with an altar and a hassock for kneeling. Both the altar and the hassock were carved from the same living rock as the alcove. Atop the altar stood a simple, golden crucifix. Beyond the horses, the chamber terminated in an arched passageway—tall and wide enough to lead the horses through—and beyond that, shallow, wide steps leading up and out of the artificial cave.

As Maebh took in their surroundings, her thoughts returned to Branwen. *She has never looked upon Tormond in that manner. Aye, she looks upon him with love, but 'tis the love of a mother for a son. That and no more.*

And she is so obviously devoted to her husband. Her dead husband.

But compared to her, I am . . . plain. Like a scullery maid in the shadow of the Queen of Faerie.

273

Her lips twitched in irritation. *Enough of that, Maebh O Broin. For shame. We have a mission to perform. A sacred mission. And we'll not finish it 'til we awaken in "the top of the mountains." And as impressive as this chamber is, 'tis not in "the top of the mountains."*

"What did ye say?" Tormond asked. He and Branwen stared at her.

Did I say that aloud? "I—I was merely s-saying, 'tis not 'the top of the mountains.'" She swallowed. "We'll not catch the Witches here. Not this time."

"No." Branwen smiled wistfully as she shook her head. "Not this time. Not here."

Tormond bared his teeth. "But we are awake in the same year as they, aye?" He turned his hopeful face to Branwen. "The same cycle as they, aye?"

The immortal shrugged. "That I cannot say. I do not have . . . the *resources* your Sergeants possess to spy out their whereabouts."

Tormond scratched at his short, yellow beard. "Aye. Ye have the right of that." His eyes brightened. "But what have the Sergeants left for us this time?" He strode through the sandstone chamber, his head swiveling left and right as he searched for the customary urn, lacquered black with a red cross painted at the top.

When he reached the end of the chamber, he peered up the ascending passageway. "But where is it?" He looked to Branwen, a mixture of concern and hope on his face. "Did ye see it when ye came down here, milady?"

Branwen shook her head. "No, my son." Her gaze flitted around the chamber as if she were nervous.

Why is she unsettled?

Tormond pursed his lips. "'Tis yet early in the year. Perhaps the Sergeants have nae espied them as yet."

"Perhaps," the Daughter of Lilith mused. "'Twould stand to reason they might not yet know."

"And"—Maebh could not quite hide the irritation in her voice—*Tormond used to consult only with me, not her!*—"we have not awoken in the prophesied place. So, we won't catch them up 'til then."

"'The top of the mountains.'" He repeated, then gazed at Branwen. "'Twill nae be 'til then, aye? Ye are certain sure?"

He clings to the hope that 'twill be this time. He wants our mission to be over.

As do I.

But do we hope for the same thing? And for the same purpose?

Branwen sighed. "The prophecies are never wrong." She winked at Maebh, and her full, red lips lifted in a half grin.

Maebh trembled as a thrill ran up her spine and into her head. *She knows something. Something she's not ready to tell Tormond.*

Something only for me.

Heat rushed to her cheeks again.

If a woman could die from blushing, I'd have perished long before this.

Branwen's half grin blossomed into a full smile as she observed Maebh's pink cheeks — which, of course, only made Maebh blush all the more. The immortal winked again.

What is it? I do wish she'd tell me!

"So!" Tormond clapped his hands, then he rubbed them together briskly like a hungry man anticipating a tasty meal. "If we must wait for the Sergeants to report, what do ye have for us, Milady Branwen? What do the prophecies say we must do in this place and time?"

"That I'll happily tell, my son," Branwen said. "At least as far as I'm able. But if you don't mind, *above* ground?" She grimaced at the sandstone ceiling, and a shadow — *fear?* — seemed to dim her lovely, immortal eyes.

Of what is she afraid? Of being down here? Under the earth?

"I have left suitable clothing for both of you." Branwen pointed at the chest with the large A engraved on the lid and then at the larger chest beside it. "And gold, of course. Maebh, the larger box is for you. I'm afraid you'll find the gowns of this time to be" — she patted the wide, cushioned skirts of her own gown — "a bit bulkier than what you've worn before." She sighed. "But 'tis the fashion of times. You — and I — must not draw attention that marks us as different from other ladies of this time and place." She gestured at Tormond. "The same is true for you, my son."

Branwen glanced toward the chamber exit, then back to them. "And, children" — she indicated the shrine — "I'm certain you'll want to thank the Almighty for His mercy and blessing. When you are finished with your prayers *and* properly dressed, you'll find an inn to the northeast from where you'll come out, after you exit the chapel above. Simply follow the road. 'Tis the only one leading from the chapel. I'll meet you there."

She whirled about and headed for the stairs.

"Wait!" Maebh called after her.

Branwen turned back toward them. "Yes, dear one?" Her smile was tinged with impatience and discomfort.

"I thought ye could not . . . move about in sunlight?"

Tormond nodded. "Aye. Ye said ye'd burn."

Branwen laughed and gave a dismissive wave of her hand. "Oh, that. You are correct, of course, and I am grateful for your concern. But fear not for my sake. 'Tis already dark outside. I waited 'til the sun had set to wake you this night. I've told Master Hamish to expect you. There'll be water and fodder for your horses in the inn's stable. And I've engaged two fine rooms for you. Supper will be delivered to the two of you in Tormond's room. I'll join you there."

She turned to leave, then stopped once more. When she turned back, she grinned at Tormond. "My son, as for *your* clothing, I have left instructions — including drawings — on how to wear it all." Her green eyes twinkled in the candlelight. "And, Tormond, I'm certain you'll look quite dashing in it." She gave him a mischievous wink. "So very fashionable." Then, with a swishing of her wide skirts, she quickly disappeared up the stairs.

"Instructions?" Bewilderment twisted Tormond's features. "Drawings? Surely a man's garments cannae be so intricate as to need all that."

Eager to see whatever lovely gowns Branwen had provided for her, Maebh hurried to the larger chest, knelt, and lifted the lid. The topmost gown — or at least the bodice of it — was a light green, the color of seafoam. She squealed with girlish delight as she lifted it from the chest. "Such a pretty color!"

"Aye, 'twill bring out the color of your bonnie eyes." Tormond said as he knelt before the smaller chest. His glance was fixed on her. "It suits ye, lass."

She blushed. But Tormond did not. *It no longer embarrasses him when he compliments me.*

'Tis progress!

276

He resumed unpacking his chest. He'd already set aside the bags of gold. He held up a wide, black leather belt with a large silver buckle, then a silver brooch with an amethyst in the center and a large pin protruding from the brooch. He examined it and wrinkled his nose. "Such finery. 'Tis nae fittin' for a man to wear, even be he a clan chief." He grunted, grimacing in disgust. "And silver. Does she nae ken a Templar is to shun the wearing of silver?" He shook his head, then tilted in it the direction of the still-sleeping warhorse. "I'm nae to even put silver on Órd Dubh's bridle, much less wear it myself."

Maebh lifted the light green skirt of the gown from her chest. It had the same wide hips she'd seen on Branwen. She smirked. *Bulky, indeed. With such skirts, how am I to sit a horse?*

"What's this?" Tormond unfolded a length of wool cloth, woven in a pattern of crisscrossing red and black. The garment appeared to have no shape at all, as if it were uncut, as if it had come fresh from a weaver's loom. The Templar appeared completely befuddled. "How am I to wear . . ." He glanced down into the box.

Maebh followed his eyes. A large sheet of paper lay there, and it was indeed covered by drawings and instructions written in Branwen's bold hand.

Maebh barely stifled a giggle. *So that's what she meant!*

"Ach, nae!" Tormond exclaimed. "Nae!" He laid aside the cloth and rummaged in the chest. "And there's nae a thing to wear underneath it!" He growled. "I could almost *throttle* the woman, though I cannae say as she'd notice. I dinnae know if she needs to breathe at all. She *does* need to breathe, does she nae?" He growled again.

Maebh put a hand to her mouth to cover her grin.

A pained expression appeared on Tormond's face. "'Tis one of those things, aye? One of those ridiculous kilts!"

Maebh could contain herself no longer, and her peals of laughter filled the chamber.

✠·✠·✠

Branwen greeted them with a mischievous smile when Maebh and Tormond entered Tormond's room at the inn. "I think you look quite bonnie, my son."

Maebh nodded, grinning widely. "Aye. Quite bonnie, laddie."

Tormond scowled and shut the door behind them. "I look silly."

Branwen strode toward the fire, her skirt swirling behind her. "On the contrary, my son. You are dressed like half the men in the common room." She sat in a chair by the fire, adjusting her wide skirts as she did so. "Or didn't you notice?" She pointed at Tormond, but looked at Maebh. "Does he not have fine calves, dear one?"

Heat rose in Maebh's cheeks. Again. "Indeed, he does." Though she was blushing, she also took far too much pleasure in Tormond's discomfort. And she did enjoy admiring his legs.

Her smile faded. *Still, I do not like to hear her making such an observation about his legs.*

Tormond growled. "I do not appreciate being treated like the prize bull at a village fair! Kilts! How unmanly."

Branwen rolled her eyes. "Have you seen the breeches the foppish noblemen wear these days? They are so loose and so wide and have so very many layers, they resemble a lady's skirt and petticoats! Only they stop at the knees. I've even heard them referred to as 'petticoat breeches.'" She shook her head. "Unmanly?" She grinned. "Did you know, my son, that the Romans—at least of my husband's time—and, I suppose, *my* time as well—considered breeches of *any* kind to be unmanly?"

Tormond's scowl vanished, and he blinked. "Truly?"

Branwen nodded. "Truly."

Tormond wrinkled his nose as if with distaste and pointed at the door behind himself. "Ye mean to say, that ridiculous fellow downstairs . . . I thought he was . . . deep in his cups, and the townspeople had dressed him in that ridiculous manner as a jest."

Maebh had taken notice of the strangely dressed young man as well, though she'd not come up with an explanation such as Tormond's. She'd merely thought the man's mode of dress odd.

Branwen nodded. "Oh, yes, he was quite inebriated—I can attest to that. But he is the mayor's eldest son and heir. And he follows all the latest fashions of Europe."

"The mayor's son?" Tormond raised an eyebrow. "What about the king? Does he follow these strange fashions?"

278

Branwen sighed. "The king? We have no king right now. We have a Lord Protector. And no, Oliver Cromwell is a Puritan—a religious sect that is very somber in their mode of dress." She winked and raised her hand beside her mouth conspiratorially as if she were about to communicate a particularly juicy bit of gossip. "The Puritans think music and dancing are sinful." She shook her head and smiled. "Lord Protector Cromwell would *never* wear petticoat breeches."

"No king?" Maebh gaped in astonishment. "How does this Cromwell rule, then?"

Branwen waved a dismissive hand. "By the will of Parliament, supposedly. But they'll not oppose Cromwell, or he'd simply disband them. Or take his army and slaughter—"

A knock at the door interrupted Branwen. She nodded toward the noise. "'Twill be the maid with your supper." She sniffed the air, then wrinkled her nose in disgust. "Definitely your supper. Go ahead, children. Eat. And while you eat—" She grimaced. "Oh, but it *does* stink!"

Maebh sniffed the air and detected the mouth-watering aroma of mutton stew. She sighed happily. "Smells utterly delightful to me."

Branwen shuddered in disgust. "'Tis not blood."

Maebh shuddered as well. Her appetite had vanished completely.

✠·✠·✠

"Enough about politics and"—Tormond glanced down at his kilt again, his lips twitching in obvious irritation—"fashion." He had just finished a second bowl of the savory stew. "If we'll not slay the Witches this time, what *are* we here to do?"

In spite of Tormond's encouragement for Maebh to "build up her strength" after their decades-long sleep, Maebh was not hungry at all. She had forced herself to eat half a bowlful of stew and to sip a bit of the fine red wine, but that was all she could manage. *Branwen consumes naught save Blood. I knew that, but . . .* Maebh shivered in revulsion.

She suppressed the urge to make the sign of the cross.

As the two mortals ate, Branwen sat apart, gazing into the fire. She fingered—or rather caressed—the round wooden pommel of her sword. Her husband's sword.

Maebh's revulsion turned to pity and sadness.

She has been alone for centuries.

Tormond and I sleep in between. The centuries pass quickly for us.

We may not be man and wife, but . . . at least we have each other.

I cannot imagine being truly alone *for centuries. If I couldn't be with Tormond . . . even if merely as . . . companions, comrades, fellow servants of God.. .*

But . . . if we became as Branwen is — a Son and Daughter of Lilith — we could hunt down the Witches. We would no longer have to worry about missing them. We would no longer be bound by time. We could find them, slay them.

And then, at last.. .

If I were to become as Branwen is, would I be as alluring as she?

Would Tormond look at me, desire me? As a woman?

Cease such wicked prattle, Maebh O Broin! Don't even consider such things.

"Are we to execute this Lord Protector?" Tormond asked. "Put the rightful king back on the throne? Is that what the prophecies direct?"

Branwen blinked. "Execute Cromwell?" Her lips twisted as if his name tasted foul in her mouth. "No! I see nothing in the prophecies directing you to interfere in the matters of kings and queens. Or of Lord Protectors."

Tormond opened his mouth to speak, but Branwen held up a hand to stop him. "And, yes, my son," she said, "I know about what you did at Bannockburn." Pride glowed in her eyes. "That was . . . magnificent. Marcus would've been very proud of you. As am I."

"Bannockburn?" Maebh asked, glancing from Tormond to Branwen and back. "What did ye do at Bannockburn?"

Tormond pursed his lips, seemingly vexed. "'Twas nothing."

Maebh turned to Branwen for the answer. "What did he do at Bannockburn?"

Branwen lifted an eyebrow and cocked her head to one side. "Nothing?" Then she turned her gaze on Maebh. "He says, 'Twas nothing.' What do you think, dear one?"

Maebh chuffed out a laugh. "When Tormond refers to one of his deeds as 'nothing . . .'" She shook her head. "Like as not the piled-up corpses of his enemies formed a wall around him. And that wall of corpses was probably the only thing stopping him from slaying a hundred more."

Branwen laughed and clapped her hands. "Oh, my son! Did I not say you need her at your side?" She beamed at Maebh. "Dear one, you are so very wise for someone so young. So very discerning."

Tormond's cheeks turned crimson, and he looked away, glowering. "I did nae slay so many as that," he muttered. His voice dropped to a whisper. "Nae at Bannockburn, at least."

"So" — Maebh grinned and leaned conspiratorially toward Branwen — "what great, miraculous deed did he perform at Bannockburn?"

Branwen stood and pulled her chair away from the fire, dragging it over to the table. She sat once more and leaned toward Maebh. "I was not there, of course, for the battle was fought in the daylight, but" — she lowered her voice to a loud whisper such as an actor might use on a stage — "I *heard* that Tormond singlehandedly turned that battle in favor of the Scots. 'Twas in the year 1314 — I'm sure you must have been awakened early — "

"'Twas nae *singlehandedly!*" Tormond exclaimed with indignation. "I had thirty Sergeants with me!"

Branwen winked at Tormond. "*Almost* singlehandedly, then." She grinned at Maebh. "You see, dear one, Robert the Bruce, King of Scotland, was *badly*, badly outnumbered, fighting for Scottish independence against Edward the Second, King of England. The numbers I have heard on each side were — "

"I lead *one* cavalry charge against the English flank!" Tormond snapped. "One charge! 'Tis all!"

Branwen nodded. "You and your contingent of Sergeants arrived, unbidden and unheralded, at a critical moment and broke Edward's heavy cavalry. Edward himself was forced to flee, coward that he was." She leaned forward. "*You*, Tormond, Knight of the Temple — *you* delivered Robert the Bruce and Scotland from the tyranny of a very wicked man."

Tormond scowled, anger burning in his eyes. "And I lost four men in that charge. Those Sergeants *followed* me. They followed me and they died because of it." His hands were balled into fists on the table, his knuckles white.

Maebh placed a hand atop one of his. "Men — good and bad — die in war." The tension in his hand eased. "At least they died fighting for a good cause."

He bowed his head. "Aye. 'Twas a good cause, for certain sure. But 'twas nae *their* cause." His mouth twitched as if in irritation. "Oh, aye, they were all Scots to a man, they were — same as myself — but 'twas nae my place, nor theirs, to serve any earthly king. We are to be servants of God, nae of men." He crossed himself. "I am sworn to give God the glory and do His holy will, and nae to gratify my own" — he glanced at Maebh, and then quickly lowered his eyes, but the guilt in those eyes had been unmistakable — "my own selfish desires."

Selfish desires? As in defending your homeland?

He pulled his hand from under hers.

As in loving me?

"'Twas folly," Tormond muttered. "Sin."

"My son," Branwen said, her voice soft and tender, "Marcus prophesied your deed at Bannockburn."

Tormond's head snapped up. "He did?"

Branwen nodded. "Yes, he did. And so long as you —" Her voice cut off, and her eyes widened. "So *that* is what he meant!"

"What?" Maebh and Tormond asked together.

"Marcus said —" Branwen paused, and her lips moved as if she were reciting silently. Reciting or translating in her head. "Yes! He said, 'He shall deliver his people, yet he shall count it for sin.' Tormond! 'Tis you! And then he said, 'Say unto that man, did not I, even the Lord God, lay down my life that men might be free?'"

Maebh sensed the truth of the words as a tingle rippled throughout her body. "Tormond, it *is* ye."

A smile slowly spread across Tormond's face. "I did well then?"

Branwen laughed and clapped her hands. "Yes! You did very well!"

Maebh beamed at him. "Very well indeed!"

Tormond seemed to shudder. "I thank ye, milady. Ye dinnae ken how long that has weighed on my soul. I have sought to do penance for wielding my sacred blade in that earthly battle." He bowed his head, crossed himself, and recited the Templar motto as a prayer. "Non nobis, Domine. Non nobis. Sed nomini tuo da gloriam."

Branwen nodded. "I like that one. 'Not for us, Lord. Not for us. To Thy name be the glory.' You go on repeating that one. 'Tis not 'vain repetition' if you mean it with all your heart."

Maebh laid her hand atop Tormond's once more, and he did not pull away. "Aye, he does mean it! With all his heart." For a moment, she locked eyes with him. "Ye are a good and faithful servant of God." *And I would follow ye anywhere, Tormond MacDonald. Into the Pit of Hell itself if ye lead the way.*

"And ye," Tormond said, staring intently into her eyes, "are the finest, the bravest, the truest soul—" He stopped, and his eyes went wide. "That is to say, ye are—" He swallowed. "I thank ye, lass, for serving alongside me." He blushed and looked away, appearing to fix his gaze on the fire.

But he did not move his hand from under hers.

Her cheeks warmed. She glanced at Branwen, and the lovely immortal gave her a knowing smile.

"'The top of the mountains'" Branwen mouthed, "Later." She winked, then said aloud, "My son, you asked why you are here."

Tormond's head jerked in Branwen's direction. "Aye? What are we to do?"

Maebh leaned forward, studying the immortal woman's face, awaiting her pronouncement on their current mission.

Branwen's eyes narrowed, and she pursed her lips. "This particular prophecy is more obscure than most concerning you."

"What does it say?" Again, Maebh and Tormond spoke as one.

"It says, 'When first they shall awaken in a northern land without a king,'"—she paused—"that sounds like Scotland and now, but that's not the obscure part. It says, 'When first they shall awaken in a northern land without a king, the Executioner and the Shield-maiden shall deliver the damned soul from the Pit of Hell.'"

Branwen leaned forward, her expression grave. "Well, children? Are you willing to ride into Hell?"

Tormond locked eyes with Maebh. "Will ye follow me into Hell, Shield-maiden?" Maebh shivered, but squeezed his hand. "As Ruth said, 'Whither thou goest, I will go.'"

Chapter 26

Branwen sat on the roof of the inn, listening with her enhanced hearing to Tormond's prayers. Praying from the heart. No recited prayers. She smiled to herself. *You're learning, my son.*

She gazed at the night sky. The absence of the moon made the stars seem brighter. It was glorious.

Do you remember, Marcus? That night in the woods in Cambria? The night we both nearly died of the cold, shivering in our wet clothes? The night we sat before the fire, I in my wet shift, and you in your wet subligar, waiting for my gown and your toga to dry?

'Twas a night such as this. The stars above, a steady breeze.

You held me, keeping me warm. You stroked my hair, comforting me in my endless loneliness.

And when you realized I was starving, you let me Feed from you. Just a little. Just enough to restore myself.

'Twas the night I truly fell, Marcus. I fell hopelessly, madly, eternally in love with you.

I knew you were pledged to marry Maelona, that you loved her, that you would be true to her. And you were true to her. And I loved you all the more, because of it.

That was the night I knew I would wait for you. Until Maelona had passed beyond the veil. Until you were free to marry again. No matter how long it took, I would wait.

And I did wait for you, my love.

After our clothes were dry, I carried you aloft.

She closed her eyes and sighed. She flung her arms wide. "And how we flew!"

Her skin tingled at the memory of that lovely, heartbreaking night. A tear escaped from her tightly closed eyes.

"I miss you, Marcus." *It never gets easier, my love. Not even after all these centuries.*

I still ache for you.

She put her hand on the wooden pommel of his sword, caressing it as Marcus had once caressed her hair. *Someday, Marcus.*

Someday, beyond this veil of sorrow, when I have fulfilled the final prophecy, we shall be together once more.

Though I wait another thousand years.

Alone.

She could hear Maebh reading from her Bible inside the inn. Branwen recognized the story. It was near the end of the Book of the Judges — the decimation of the tribe of Benjamin. *Not a pleasant story at all.*

Most of Judges isn't pleasant.

But soon she'll be in Ruth. Again. I know it's one of her favorite stories. Branwen smiled. *She quotes it frequently.*

The breeze shifted, coming from her right.

"You are a good girl, Maebh O Broin. A good woman. Good and true and brave. You are good for *him*. I look forward to the night when I can finally call you my —"

The sweet, nigh irresistible scent of evil blood blossomed in her nostrils.

Her head snapped to the right, to face the wind. Her fangs extended, and drool filled her mouth. The familiar rage burned within her, hotter than a smith's forge. *Kill! Drain him! Rip him to shreds! Send him straight to Hell.* Her wings sprang into existence, and she shot from the inn roof, flying like an arrow from the bow, following the airborne spoor of her prey.

✠·✠·✠

Dougie Seton watched from behind the stone well, running his thumb across the edge of his sgian dubh. The meticulously honed blade of the wee stocking knife was indeed sharp. Perfect for Dougie's needs that night.

Soon. She'll come out soon. Tae fetch water frae the well.

He'd promised the Lord above — and himself — that the previous little whore would be the last.

But then he'd seen *her*. That very afternoon, behind the silversmith's shop. Fetching water from the well. She'd looked at him and smiled.

Perhaps, she thought 'twould appear a shy smile. But I kenned better.

The little harlot. The wanton eyes. Mincing as she goes. Enticing a man. Aye, she kens precisely what she be a-doing.

285

Aye, she'll nae be a-tempting another virtuous, God-fearin' man, nae after this night.

She was just the right age too—ten or eleven or twelve at the most—just on the cusp of womanhood, before the corruption of her sex, before the foul changes began. Dougie wanted her. He desired her.

He burned for her.

And that is why she must die. Before I succumb tae temptation. Before I give in tae sin.

Slide the blade across her throat and 'twill all be over.

And as the light faded from her eyes, he'd kiss her lips as he'd kissed the others.

His breathing quickened, and his pulse pounded in his ears.

The back door of the shop opened, and light streamed into the night. Out she came, bucket in hand. Just as he knew she would.

Dougie hunched down, out of sight. He licked his lips in anticipation.

Wait 'til the door be closed, sae none can see her in the dark. Wait 'til the wee harlot be drawing from the well, 'til her head be down. She'll nae let go of the rope — nae even when she sees me, when she sees my knife.

He heard the hollow splash as the bucket struck the water. The girl grunted as she hauled on the rope.

Dougie grinned widely as he slowly crept around the well, keeping low and silent.

He was almost upon her. He tensed, poised to leap, the sgian dubh ready. *One slice, and 'twill all be over.*

She'll nae have time tae scream.

More's the pity.

I'll take my kiss and —

Dougie saw the angel.

She swooped out of the night sky on white wings like a hawk, then alighted on the ground between Dougie and the wee harlot. The wings vanished as if they'd never existed. Her face was twisted in rage, and she snarled, exposing her gleaming fangs.

But it was her eyes that transfixed him. Green as emeralds and burning with loathing—loathing for him. Loathing and hunger.

Dougie's mouth opened to scream, but his tongue froze to the roof of his mouth, and no sound escaped his lips.

Never taking her eyes off Dougie, the angel said, "Run, lassie."

The little whore stood where she was as if immobilized by fear.

"Inside! Now!" the angel growled.

With a squeak of terror, the girl—Dougie's righteous prey—dropped her bucket, turned, and fled.

Dougie's bladder emptied itself onto his kilt.

The angel lunged toward him, and something struck Dougie on his right arm, just below the wrist. The angel stepped back, and Dougie looked down.

His hand hung at an unnatural angle, the knife fallen from his useless fingers.

Pain exploded in his arm.

Dougie's tongue was finally loosed—he screamed. High and loud and shrill. Like a wee girl.

The angel gripped him under his arms, her wings suddenly reappearing, and she lifted him into the air.

Dougie looked at the receding ground. The lights of the village below them dwindled, growing at once closer together and more distant. Then he looked into the blazing eyes of the angel.

Her mouth opened wide. Drool dripped from her fangs. She bent her head, placing her lips on his neck.

He screamed again as her fangs pierced his flesh. There was new pain...

And then there was ecstasy.

Dougie moaned as the pleasure spread quickly from his neck, throughout his body. The pain in his arm disappeared, though his hand still dangled uselessly. He clutched at the angel's shoulder with his good hand. "More," he pleaded. "More. Please." He felt his strength, his life ebbing as she drank. He reveled in it.

But she did not take more. Instead, she licked his neck where, but moments before, her teeth had pierced him. She pulled her head back and stared into his eyes with an intensity that bored into the depths of his soul.

Dougie lost himself in her furious gaze. Rapture filled him, as sweet as the ecstasy he'd known when she was draining him of life.

He'd never seen anything so lovely as those fierce, searing eyes. As long as he could remember, Dougie Seton had thought adult women loathsome, deformed—not like the young lassies he lusted after, the wee harlots who tempted him. But he was so very wrong, so blind. *Now I have seen* true *beauty, true perfection.*

"What have you done?" she snarled. "Confess your sins, you despicable, little worm!"

Aye! I am a worm. Anything ye command. Anything to please ye.

And Dougie confessed. He told his new mistress everything. Each and every murder. He did not glory in the details as he once had, neither did he feel the slightest bit of remorse. No, he only wanted to confess. Because she asked him to confess.

As he listed every lass he'd killed, the angel's rage seemed to burn brighter.

Sae bonnie. I love ye.

He told her of the kitten and puppies he'd tortured and slaughtered when he was but a wee lad.

"Enough!" she growled.

Dougie ceased his confession. Because she commanded it. He gazed at her in adoration and longing. "Aye, milady."

"Do not call me that! You are not worthy to call me that, you fiend, you loathsome monster."

"As ye command."

"I should kill you. I *want* to kill you. With every fiber of my body, I want to give you the death you so richly deserve." She quivered, shaking him.

He could only smile. "Please, mistress. As ye wish."

She shook her head, and the green fire in her eyes dimmed to a smoldering. "I should kill you. But I won't."

Please. Please kill me, if 'twill make ye happy. I live for ye. I'll gladly die for ye.

"You will never harm another living soul. Never. Do you understand?"

The words seared into his soul. "Aye! I understand. I'll never harm another living soul."

"Do you know the home of the High Constable?"

He nodded with joy. "Aye! That I do!"

"Good. 'Twill save me the trouble of taking you there."

Vaguely, Dougie realized they were no longer flying. His feet were on the ground, and her hands had released him. Her hands, but not her eyes. He swayed unsteadily, like a drunken man.

"You will go there. You will run. You will turn neither to the right hand nor the left. And when you arrive, you will knock and demand to see the High Constable."

Something I can do to please her! He nodded, beaming. "Aye! That I will!"

"You will confess to the High Constable—all your crimes—every lass you've murdered. And you will go on confessing until the High Constable believes you, until you are dancing at the end of a rope. But you will never tell a living soul about me. Not a single word."

Nae a single word! What joy! *I can die for ye!* "Aye. Anything for ye, mistress!" How had he ever thought womanly curves disgusting?

She nodded, then licked his blood from her perfect, ruby lips. She let out a sigh. "So sweet."

Her wings appeared once more, shining like the moon.

And then the angel was gone, soaring into the sky.

An agony of loss, more profound than any he'd ever known, smote Dougie's heart. He ached for her presence, for her touch. He sobbed in grief, for he knew he would never see her again. She would never feed from him again.

But I can still please her. He smiled blissfully.

He ran—turning neither to the right nor to the left—straight for the High Constable's home.

And when it came time to dance at the end of a rope, Dougie Seton knew he would truly dance with all the vigor he possessed. *Anything for ye!*

✠·✠·✠

A rapping at her window startled Maebh.

Branwen was outside, her wings flapping.

Maebh's heart thundered in her chest. *I'll never become accustomed to the sight of her flying!*

What would it be like? To be able to fly? Like a bird?

To be forever beautiful?

With trembling fingers, Maebh reverently closed her treasured Bible, setting it aside.

Ruth will have to wait.

Maebh hastened to unfasten the latch and open the window.

"Thank you, dear one." The Daughter of Lilith glided into the room. Her wings passed through the window casement and the walls as if those wings were immaterial – or the walls were. As soon as her slippered feet rested on the floor, the white wings vanished. "I'm pleased that you are still awake."

Maebh blushed. "I was reading." Then she gasped, putting hands up to cover her reddened cheeks. "Forgive me!"

Branwen blinked. "Forgive you? For what?"

The heat in Maebh's cheeks burned all the hotter. "My blushing. Does it not . . . increase your thirst?"

Branwen chuckled and waved dismissively. "Oh, child! No! I mean to say, you *do* look delicious – so healthy and pink – but I have already dined tonight. Feasted on the blood of a murderer." She winked. "'Twas very sweet."

Maebh shuddered. "Did ye . . . *kill* him?"

Branwen grimaced and shook her head. "No. I don't kill unless I must. Such as that night in the Welsh forest. There were too many of them to deal with one at a time, so I killed to defend you and Tormond. I *wanted* to kill this one tonight, but I did not. 'Tis the nature of my kind – we have a nigh irresistible urge to send the guilty unrepentant and unshriven to Judgment. No, I left him very much alive. I simply *Persuaded* him to surrender to the High Constable and there confess his murders. All of them." She waved dismissively again. "Let the law punish him according to his crimes. He'll harm no one else. I saw to that."

Maebh shuddered, then glanced in the direction of Tormond's room. "Do ye wish me to fetch Tormond?"

Branwen shook her head. "No. I wish to speak to you alone, dear one. Just betwixt we two women."

Alone? Suddenly, Maebh's palms were moist. *Surely, I do not fear her. She would not harm me. But what would she have to say to me alone?*

Branwen pointed to the bed. "May I?"

Maebh nodded quickly.

The Daughter of Lilith glided to the narrow bed, then, arranging her wide skirts, sat near the foot of the bed.

She is so beautiful, so elegant. Maebh wished she hadn't already stripped down to her shift in preparation for sleep. "Wh-what do ye wish to talk about?"

Branwen patted the bed with one delicate, mighty hand. "Please. Join me."

Maebh quickly moved to the bed, very much aware that when she walked, she could not match Branwen's stately grace. She sat and turned toward the lovely immortal. "Aye, milady?"

Branwen smiled. "No need for such formality, child. It makes me feel truly ancient. Please. As I've told you before, call me Branwen."

Maebh grinned back at her. "Of course. Branwen"

Branwen reached over and took Maebh's hand. "I truly do wish you could call me by yet *another* name."

Maebh blinked. "Another name?"

Branwen sighed. "I wish you could call me . . . Mother. But . . ."

"Mother?"

Branwen shook her head sadly. "But not yet."

"Because I am not"—Maebh swallowed the lump that suddenly constricted her throat—"not of your kin. Your husband's descendants."

"Correct, dear one. You are not." She winked and squeezed Maebh's hand. "Not yet."

Tears threatened in Maebh's eyes. "No. Nor ever will be." She bowed her head, and the tears fell. "I am a nun. And he a religious. And 'tis unlikely 'twill ever be otherwise."

Branwen leaned toward her. She stroked Maebh's cheek, then lifted her chin. "Look at me." When Maebh did not immediately comply, Branwen added, "Please?"

Maebh lifted her eyes and met the woman's gaze.

Branwen smiled, and Maebh was astonished to see tears on the immortal's cheeks. "I had to wait too," Branwen said. "I waited fifty-one years. Marcus was seventy when we married, when he was free to marry again. Even then, I gave him a year and a day to mourn his first wife, my beloved sister-wife." She sighed. "I'm waiting again, of course. 'Til that glorious day when we shall be together once more. And I will continue to wait for as long as it takes. Because he is worth the waiting."

Maebh looked away. "But I'm not . . . immortal like ye."

"Perhaps not, but"—Branwen tilted her head and eyed Maebh curiously—"you don't seem to have aged a day since I first began observing you and Tormond. Perhaps, my eyes are deceiving me—though I doubt they do—but I think it could be an effect of the Witches' wine. From what I understand, the Witches do not seem to age either. Each time they are spotted, they appear the same. And they have been doing this far longer than either of you."

Maebh met her eyes again. "Ye think Tormond and I are . . . immortal?"

Branwen grimaced. "No, I don't think so—nor should you wish to be. Trust me on this, Maebh. But I think, as long as you take the magic draft, you will go on without aging. When you stop—as Sir Peredur, the first Executioner did—you will begin to age once more."

Maebh nodded. "But for now . . ."

"For now, dear one, you still have time. He loves you. I am certain of it. And I am certain that you know it as well. And you love him. I know you do."

Maebh hesitated, then nodded. "Aye! With all my heart! But 'tis a sin! We have taken vows before God!"

Branwen chuckled. "Oh, dear child, God never intended for there to be religious, monks, and nuns. Celibacy before marriage, yes, of course, but marriage is the highest order, not the cloister. The Almighty created Adam and Eve—men and women—to love each other, to cleave to each other. To become one flesh."

Maebh turned her eyes away, shedding bitter tears. "Tormond does not believe that."

Branwen smiled. "He will."

Maebh snapped her eyes back toward Branwen. *Could it be true? She has hinted at it before.* "Truly? He will?"

Branwen nodded. "Yes, he will. In time."

Maebh suddenly found it difficult to catch her breath. "A-a prophecy?"

Branwen's smile widened, and she nodded again. "Yes. After you awaken 'in the top of the mountains.' After your mission is fulfilled."

Maebh's heart felt as if it would leap from her chest. "Truly? Marcus prophesied this?"

Branwen nodded, then her eyes took on a faraway look as she quoted, "'And when their mission is completed, the Executioner of God and the Shield-maiden of Christ shall wed and be sealed together for eternity in My holy house.'" Her eyes focused on Maebh once more. "That's what Marcus wrote. I don't know if I'll live to see it, but 'twill happen. I promise."

A joyful sob burst from Maebh, and she flung her arms around Branwen.

Branwen patted Maebh's back, and Maebh could feel that the immortal trembled with weeping as well. "And then," Branwen said, "I shall truly be able to call you my daughter."

"Thank ye!" Maebh cried. "Oh, how I thank ye!"

The two women, the mortal and the immortal, held each other as they wept.

After what felt like a very long time, they separated. Maebh took both Branwen's hands in hers. "Thank ye, Branwen."

Branwen smiled sweetly. "'Tis what I came to tell you. To give you hope."

"And now, I *do* have hope!"

"Good. Will you wait for him?"

Maebh nodded with joyful vigor. "Oh, aye! I will wait for him! For as long as it takes!" She paused, beaming. "Because he is worth the waiting.

Branwen looked toward the ceiling, her expression wistful. "For as long as it takes."

"Branwen?"

The immortal met Maebh's gaze again. "Yes, dear one?"

"Ye say that Marcus is never wrong."

Branwen nodded, then shook her head. "Never."

"Then if Marcus is never wrong, I *will* be your daughter. Someday. And ye *will* be my mother. Someday."

"Yes, dear one. You *will* be. And I *will* be."

"Then, please, may I call ye mother? Now?"

Fresh tears spilled from Branwen's eyes. "Yes! Oh, yes! And may I call you Daughter? Now?"

"Aye, Mother!" She threw her arms around Branwen. "Oh, aye!"

The mortal daughter and the immortal mother held each other and shared in joyful tears.

✠·✠·✠

Dougie Seton's dungeon cell was cold and wet and stank of human waste. But it wasn't just the cell—Dougie, himself, stank of his own waste. He had removed his urine-soaked kilt and wrapped it around himself as a plaid—a blanket. The irons around his legs siphoned heat away from his body. He shivered in his wet plaid, and his teeth chattered.

But he really didn't mind the chill and the stench. No, he did not.

Dougie was happy. His life had purpose. He was confessing his murders over and over. Joyfully. Gleefully. He did not glory in the memory, but merely in the telling. He knew full well that no one was listening to him confess at that moment, there being no guard immediately outside his cell door, but that mattered not a wit. Dougie was acting as his beloved angel had bidden him do. And serving her was all that truly mattered.

They'd brought him bread and water. And he'd eaten and drunk. Aye, though he continued to confess between and around mouthfuls. Dougie ate and drank, because he knew he needed to keep his strength up—he had yet one final task to fulfill.

I must have strength to dance at the end of a noose, aye?

He grinned and recommenced his litany of crimes from the beginning.

And so, he shivered and confessed and ate and drank what he was given.

She will be sae pleased with me.

294

Chapter 27

Months 'tis been, and nary a sign! Tormond clenched his jaw as he paced the wooden floor of his room at the inn. He paced, but he was sorely tempted to stomp. *This is the correct year! Where are they?* His left hand gripped the pommel of his sheathed sword, his right, the hilt of his dagger. He longed to draw the sword — not because he wished to threaten the stout man leaning with his back against the door as if the closed portal were the only thing keeping the fellow upright — no, Tormond simply longed for the comforting feel and heft of the sacred weapon in his hands. The sword was an anchor in a raging sea of confusion and doubt, a constant reminder of his duty, his sacred mission, and his unholy targets — targets that seemed to be forever beyond his reach.

Why am I sae angry? All I'm doing is frightening the Sergeant. And I need the Sergeants — we need them — if we are e'er tae succeed.

But winter is almost here! The Witches will be sleeping soon!

Master Hamish, innkeeper and — secretly — Sergeant of the Temple, wrung his hands, reminding Tormond of Pontius Pilate vainly attempting to wash away his guilt, his impotence, and his utter failure to uphold Roman law to protect the guiltless Christ. "Please forgive me, Brother Executioner."

Will ye stop apologizing, man? Tormond thought. *I neither need nor want your apologies. Just do your duty!* He glanced briefly at Maebh as she sat in a chair by the fire, serenely reading her Bible. At least, she *appeared* to be serene and untouched by Tormond's vexation.

Do your duty, Sergeant. As I must do mine. "Nowhere, ye say?" He wheeled toward the man, finally letting go of his weapons and flinging his arms wide in frustration. "Nowhere in all the British Isles?"

The man flinched as if Tormond had raised a fist. "Nowhere in all Christendom, Brother Tormond."

"Tell us, Master Hamish," Maebh said, calmly looking up from the scriptures, "how ye can be so certain? Ye say ye are the Spymaster of the Temple. How is it your vast army of spies can find no trace of the Witches?"

Hamish's eyes flashed briefly in Maebh's direction, and Tormond was certain he saw resentment, even contempt in the Spymaster's gaze. And worst of all, lust.

But the Sergeant answered her not a word.

Tormond's hands itched to draw his sword. *Nae, I could strike the man down with my bare hands if I wanted to.* Instead, he fixed the innkeeper with a fierce glare. "Know this, Sergeant Spymaster, when the Shield-maiden of Christ asks ye a question, she asks with *my* authority. She speaks as my comrade-in-arms in this sacred mission." His arm swept the room in a wide arc. "In *our* sacred mission." He pointed at the man. "In *your* mission." He took a step toward the Spymaster. "And ye *will* give her answer! And ye will do so with all deference and courtesy." He spoke through clenched teeth and tight-drawn lips. "D'ye ken my meaning, Sergeant?"

The fellow's knees smote together, and he resumed wringing his hands. But he turned his wide-eyed face to Maebh. "F-forgive me, Shield-maiden." He bowed his head in deference. "I meant no disrespect."

Well, there be a lie.

Tormond growled softly as he made the sign of the cross. *Forgive me, O Lord, for my unkind words.*

Well, my unkind thoughts, *at least.*

Even though they be accurate.

"All is forgiven," Maebh replied, and though Tormond was not looking at her, he could easily imagine the kindly smile on her face. "Now, if ye please, Sergeant," she continued, "how can ye be certain sure the Witches are nowhere in all of Christendom?"

She is patient. And kind, even in the face of Hamish's contemptible behavior.

She knows just how to handle him . . . now that I've put a wee bit of holy fear into the man.

Tormond almost grinned. Almost. *She has much to teach me indeed.*

"Well, Sister," Hamish began, his eyes flitting between Maebh and Tormond, "they—the Witches, that is—leave behind certain traces. Every time, 'tis the same. The Mother—the Witch with the malformed visage—seems to conduct most of their public business, even if she goes about veiled—as she often does. So, she cannae pass unnoticed. And she has nae been seen. There has been no Burning Man, nor ring of lifelessness left after the accursed tree is burned. No mass slaughtering of their acolytes."

He turned his face to Tormond and pointed toward the window and the light of the lowering sun. "The pigeons have come in from all of Europe, Brother Executioner! There has been no word, no sign."

"Europe, ye say?" Maebh asked. "What about other shores? The Holy Land? Egypt? Other Mohammedan lands?"

Hamish shook his head. "No, Sister. The Witches have never ventured beyond the ancient Celtic lands."

"The Celtic lands?" Maebh asked.

"Aye," Tormond said, "the lands once occupied by an ancient race called the Celts. This includes all of these isles and most of the lands of Europe." He mouthed, "Branwen's people." Aloud, he said, "Our pagan ancestors."

Understanding brightened her eyes, and she nodded.

Hamish nodded with obsequious enthusiasm, obviously standing on more familiar ground. "Aye, Sister. The Council of Sergeants has long speculated that"—he paused, and his voice took on the cadence of an oft repeated theory—"the Witches can only find disciples among people whose forebearers once practiced the same foul, pagan rites as they—the Witches—do themselves. And they need disciples for their blood sacrifices."

"I see." Maebh's brows knit together. "Perhaps, then, Spymaster," she said slowly, "they have followed those who have sailed from these isles? To the New World, perhaps?"

The innkeeper nodded. "Aye, we have considered that. Indeed, we have. We sent Sergeants across the ocean. This very summer."

Tormond resumed his pacing. "The New World. Where have ye sent them? To which colonies?"

"Virginia and Massachusetts Bay, but those men were to spy out all the British colonies. And New Amsterdam. We also sent a man to New Sweden. And La Florida and the Caribbean Isles. The southern spies—the Spanish and French colony spies—have returned, but they saw no sign. The English and Dutch colony spies have not returned, nor has the Swede. But even if they found the

Witches, and if they returned and brought us word this very day, 'twill be November soon. 'Twould be too late in the year for ye to set sail. Ye'll nae find a ship willing to launch 'til the spring. If they *do* bring word, if they confirm the Witches be there, ye'd still be forced to sleep once more and cross the ocean sixty years hence."

Tormond growled low in his throat. *Sixty years hence. 1715.*

And we've yet to fulfill the prophecy Branwen spoke of – to "deliver the damned soul from the Pit of Hell."

Whate'er that means.

We cannae leave this place before we've accomplished that.

He stopped pacing once more. "Sixty years hence." He was surprised to realize he'd said it aloud. He gazed at Maebh. Her lovely gray eyes gazed back at him. Those sweet, tender eyes spoke mutely of sadness. And of longing.

Forbidden longing.

Her lips drew into a tight, thin line, and her eyes hardened. She nodded resolutely. "Sixty years hence." The corners of her mouth hinted at a smile. "Master Hamish?"

The Spymaster ceased wringing his hands and faced her. "Aye, Sister?"

Though she'd addressed the Sergeant, her gaze still focused on Tormond, and her eyes seemed to twinkle. "Can ye tell me, are there mountains in the New World?"

God grant me strength.

✠·✠·✠

Dougie Seton gleefully recounted the litany of his murders as he felt, rather than saw—there was so little light in the High Constable's dungeon—the approach of night. His throat was raw, and his voice no more than a hoarse whisper as he proclaimed his sins, though nobody heard him—the dungeon guards had retreated to the end of the corridor months before, unable to either shut him up or ignore his ceaseless, blissful confessions. Even in his sleep, Dougie was certain he continued to recount each and every lovely throat slitting, describing with delight how the hot blood would spurt onto the ground as he kissed the writhing lips of each wee harlot.

But in his dreams? Even while his cracked and bleeding lips moved and his voice rasped as he recited his qualifications for Hell,

298

he dreamed only of her. His true love. *How had I ever thought those young lassies to be tempting? Only my love is beautiful. Only* she *is desirable.* His true love would be here soon, he knew. She came every night, just after sunset, standing outside his cell door and glaring at him with those lovely green eyes, with that angelic loathing and magnificent rage.

And every night she would ask him the same question. "Why have they not yet executed you, filth?"

And Dougie would shrug his shoulders and briefly—oh, so briefly—interrupt his recitations to answer, "Soon, Mistress! Soon I will dance for you!"

She would then turn away with a twirl of skirt and petticoats—how he would love to kiss the hem of that skirt!—and stalk down the corridor, past the oblivious guard, as Dougie resumed his never-ending confession.

Soon! She will be here soon!

Footsteps approached. It was the guard with Dougie's gruel and water. He did not drool with anticipation—his mouth was too dry to salivate anymore—and he could not smell the food—all scents were overpowered by the reek of his own waste.

But the small slot at the bottom of his cell door didn't open. Instead, Dougie heard the rattling of keys in the lock. The door opened, and the blinding light of a single candle streamed in. Dougie squinted to shield his eyes from the painful light.

But he still recited his sins.

The guard stood in the doorway, but neither entered nor blocked the way.

Have they come to hang me at last? Dougie's heart leaped in anticipation.

The guard reached inside his breastplate and pulled out a crucifix on a chain. The small crucifix was bisected near the top by a recumbent crescent moon. "Come, O Blessed Mother!" the guard cried.

Light blazed in the cell, and for a moment, Dougie could see nothing save the dazzling light. He blinked back tears and stared. In the midst of the light was a woman, radiating glory, as she floated a foot above the cell floor. She was clothed in a translucent robe of gossamer blue and a gold collar and earrings. Atop on her hair was a recumbent crescent moon of gold—like the horns on the guard's crucifix.

She spoke, and her honeyed voice filled him with pleasure such as he had never known. "Cease your prattling, Dougie."

Dougie obeyed, suddenly freed from the compulsion that had ensnared him for months. He fell to his knees and worshipped her. *How did I ever call that green-eyed witch beautiful? All beauty pales before this goddess!* Hastily, he crawled forward to kiss her feet. *So close!* He scrambled toward the vision of perfection, reaching for her.

"Do not touch the Blessed Virgin!" a voice barked—the guard.

But it was too late. Dougie's momentum had carried him forward, and his grasping hand fell *through* her foot, clutching nothing but air.

"Arise, Dougie Seton!" the Blessed Virgin commanded.

Dougie clambered to his feet. He gazed at the woman in adoration. "Please!" he croaked. "How may I serve Thee?"

She smiled, and the beneficent beauty of her smile smote his heart. "First," she said, "I will heal you of your affliction." She put a hand to his dry lips. He could not feel her touch—not so much as a stirring of the air—but instantly the agony in his throat was gone as if he had not been speaking without ceasing for half a year. The pain was gone.

Or was it?

Some tiny, distant part of Dougie's mind suspected the pain was still there, that it had only been masked by the ephemeral touch of the alluring vision. But he shoved that aside. "I thank Thee, O Blessed Mary." His voice was restored! He hesitated, however, fearing he'd offended her. "Thou art Mary, Mother of God?"

Her enchanting eyes appeared to laugh. "I have been called by many names during the millennia since Adam and his bitch were cast out of the Garden, since their children first groveled and worshipped me. But 'Mary' will do quite nicely. Or you may address me as Queen of Heaven."

"Aye, my Queen!" Dougie cried. "How may I serve Thee?"

"Oh, you have served me well, my son, for most of your life, though not in the *precise* manner to which I am accustomed. But I have one last task for you to perform."

"Anything!"

She smiled again, and Dougie trembled in a paroxysm of ecstasy. "Dougie, do you remember the little strumpet who escaped you?"

He nodded fiercely, his hands itching to hold a knife, to slit the wee harlot's throat while he kissed her writhing lips.

"Do you remember the winged demon bitch who robbed you of your righteous prey?"

He growled, his cracked lips stretching in a rictus grin. "Aye, that I do!" *The winged whore bewitched me!*

The Queen of Heaven smiled as she placed an insubstantial hand upon his head as if to bestow a blessing. Or an ordination. "I want you to kill them both for me. Can you do that?"

"Oh, aye, my Queen!"

"I am pleased, my son. But before you kill the young whore, the girl, I want you to *take* her. Take her *properly*. That is the *true* form of worship. You'd like to do that, wouldn't you?"

At last! All the pent-up, unfulfilled desires of a lifetime of forbidden lust seemed to explode within him. He would finally have the release he craved. He could die happy. "Aye, my Queen!"

"First, you must slay the winged demon. The fallen Daughter of Lilith. Only then, after you have slain the Daughter of Lilith, will you have your heart's desire—the child. You will take the child, and when you have worshipped me through her, you will spill her blood. Do you understand?"

"Aye, my Queen!" But then the green eyes of the winged demon burned in his memory, and Dougie was suddenly afraid. "H-how am I to kill"—*What had she called her? The fallen Daughter of . . . something?*—"the other one? The winged witch?"

The vision grinned, then pursed her lips as if to kiss him. "Ooh, my son, I will show you the way. I will give you the means. I will show you the place."

The Queen of Heaven spun halfway round in the air. As she turned, her form altered. Suddenly, she was fully dressed in fine clothes such as a noblewoman might wear, and she no longer glowed. She floated down to the floor, then looked at him and gestured with an alluring hand. "Come, my child."

Dougie hesitated. "But if she bewitches me again?"

The Blessed Virgin turned back to him, smiling sweetly. "Ah, yes. To do that, she would need but to look into your eyes. No, my son. That will not do at all. Thank you, Dougie, for pointing out the flaw in my plan." She turned toward the guard, though she gestured at Dougie. "Simon, my son, pluck out his eyes."

"My eyes?" Dougie cried.

The guard—Simon—grinned and entered the cell. He reached for Dougie's head with his left hand, while aiming his right thumb at Dougie's left eye. "With pleasure, Holy One. Are you sure I cannot cut out his tongue as well? I heard enough from this one to last me all my life."

The Virgin shook her lovely head, smiling sweetly. "Just his eyes, Simon."

Dougie shrank back in horror. "B-but how shall I see?"

The glorious vision smiled. "Fear not, child. As I healed you just now, once your corruptible, mortal eyes are gone"—she licked her perfect lips—"I shall give you *spiritual* eyes."

The guard placed a strong, implacable hand at the back of Dougie's head, then the guard's thumb plunged toward Dougie's eye.

Dougie screamed. And when Simon took his other eye as well, Dougie screamed once more, louder than before.

Suddenly, the agony was gone, and an eerie warmth filled Dougie Seton's empty sockets.

He could see perfectly. All was bright and new. 'Twas as if he had never truly seen the world before.

At the center of his world was his new love, his new joy. The Queen of Heaven turned away once more. "Come. Follow me."

✠·✠·✠

Both Tormond and Maebh gazed out the window, eagerly watching the sunset, Maebh holding Tormond's arm. She leaned her head against his shoulder. "The sun sets earlier each night."

Tormond closed his eyes and breathed in her scent—the honeyed smell of the beeswax soap he'd bought for her, the fragrance of her soft hair. *We should nae be so . . . familiar. Nae so close.* And yet he did not shy away from her. "Aye," he sighed, "autumn has begun. See?" He inclined his head. "The leaves are turning."

She nodded, still resting her head against his shoulder. "Soon all the trees will be bare and brown." She sighed. "Brown is such an ugly color."

He glanced briefly at her hair, the color of chestnuts. "I'm rather fond of brown. Sometimes, I believe 'tis the bonniest color in all of God's creation." *Daft fool! She'll know precisely your meaning.*

She lifted her head and turned her face toward him, though he didn't meet her gaze. He dared not after what he'd said. Out of the corner of his eyes, however, he saw the ends of her mouth curl in that maddening, secret smile of hers.

Aye, she knows.

Ye're a daft fool, Tormond MacDonald!

And ye are playing with unholy fire.

But as irritated as he was at his lapse in judgment, he still mourned the loss of the pleasant, intimate pressure of her head against his shoulder.

He cleared his throat softly. "Branwen will be here soon."

Maebh nodded. "Aye, and then we can tell her of Master Hamish's . . . report."

"Why would the Witches go to the top of a mountain?" he mused aloud as the last light of the sun vanished and as twilight shrouded the room. "Surely, they'd nae find enough people to seduce, corrupt, and murder to serve their vile purposes in such a remote place."

Maebh pursed her lips. "It doesn't say the top of *a* mountain. It says, 'the *top* of the *mountains*.' As in, the top of more than one mountain."

"But how can they gather their disciples at the top of more than one mountain at the same time? It makes nae sense."

Maebh shrugged. "I don't understand either. But then again, neither can I make sense of the prophecy we are to fulfill here. How are we to descend into the Pit of Hell? And to deliver the damned soul fr—"

A knocking at the door interrupted them.

Tormond and Maebh jumped, separating from each other, like naughty children caught filching apples.

Tormond went to the door and flung it open to reveal Master Hamish bobbing in the corridor, holding their supper tray. The tempting aroma of roast beef, gravy, and boiled potatoes and carrots wafted into the room.

"Here's your supper, milaird, mila—" The innkeeper blinked like an owl. "Why are ye all a-standing here in the dark?" His eyes searched the room. "And where is Mistress Branwen? Does she nae join ye around suppertime each night?"

Tormond shook his head, grateful for the darkness so the guilty flush in his cheeks wasn't so obvious. "She's a bit late tonight."

Maebh shrugged. "I'm sure she'll be along shortly."

Master Hamish stepped into the room and placed the tray on the small table. "'Tis a pity she ne'er eats here. Or stays here. I've nae notion of where she stays when she's in Rosslyn." He lowered his voice and muttered, "As if my house is nae good enough for a highborn lady." He straightened and rubbed the small of his back. "I should nae hae said such a thing." His eyes grew wide, and he looked genuinely afraid. "Ye'll nae tell her I said such ungracious words, aye?"

Maebh smiled and shook her head. "Oh, Master Hamish, ye may sleep easy on that. We'll—"

She was interrupted by the sound of running footsteps pounding down the corridor. A boy—Master Hamish's son, Daniel, barely ten years old—appeared in the doorway, out of breath. "Da! Da!" he panted. He held forth a cylinder the size and color of a small bone. "Just arrived! From London! Afore sunset! I ran all the way . . . from the loft. It's got the Seal on it!"

A tiny red cross was painted in fine lines over a black dot on the miniscule tube.

"Here now," Hamish said, snatching the tube from his son, "let's us have that." He examined the seal, nodded, then broke the bone in half. He extracted and unrolled a thin message scroll.

Maebh took hold of Tormond's arm again. "What is it?"

The boy, still panting, stepped into the room and closed the door. "'Tis from Gravesend!" He grinned joyfully. "That pigeon . . . the one this come in on . . . she was dispatched to the port. In London, milady!"

"Hold your tongue, laddie," snapped his father.

Daniel's mouth snapped shut, and he nodded quickly. The boy gave Tormond the Templar salute, touching the tip of his forefinger to his thumb and extending the other three fingers.

Tormond quickly returned the secret signal, then turned his eyes to the Spymaster. "What does it say, Sergeant?"

Hamish looked up from the message. "'Tis as we feared. But 'tis good news as well. The Witches be in Virginia!" He grimaced. "Or rather they *were* in Virginia. When our man arrives from London, I'll get a full report. Well, at the least, we'll know where to look for them next time."

Tormond nodded, both relieved and frustrated. "At least we'll know where to start." He grimaced. "In sixty years' time."

Another pounding of footsteps sounded in the corridor—heavier than before. A tall, broad-shouldered man burst into the room. Tormond recognized him as a local blacksmith and a Sergeant.

"Hamish!" the man huffed, clearly out of breath.

"What is it?" the innkeeper, the Templar, and the nun cried as one.

"Callum!" the man answered. "I was to relieve him . . . on guard . . . at the entrance to the . . . chamber!"

The newcomer, glanced at Tormond and gave him a shaky salute. "Brother Templar!"

"Speak, laddie!" Tormond commanded, but he did return the ancient salute. "What of this Callum?"

The man nodded. "Aye. Callum's dead! Slain. And there's someone down there. In the chamber!"

Tormond gripped the pommel of his sword and pushed his way past the Sergeants.

"Where are ye going?" Maebh cried after him.

Tormond did not slow as he sprinted down the corridor, but he shouted back, "To saddle my horse! Bring my axe!"

✠·✠·✠

Branwen steeled herself for the ordeal to come, the trial she had endured each night for months. *Must resist the rage, the need to slay him. To drink the nectar of his sweet corruption. To drain him. Then to rip his head from his body!*

She shuddered even as she flew to the High Constable's dungeon from the secret hill cave where she Slept during the days. *Think of something else.*

Think of Marcus.

But at that moment, the memory that stood forth in her mind was of the night centuries before—the night when she ripped the head from the neck of the wicked man who stabbed Marcus. She could almost smell the decapitated man's blood as it—

Think of something else! Think of Tormond and Maebh.

She pictured the two of them, sitting in Tormond's room, eating their supper. She imagined seeing Tormond's armor and Órd Dubh's barding secreted in the large wardrobe and the Witches' wine hidden under Tormond's bed.

Maebh will be reading her Bible. And Tormond – he'll be pacing. Or praying. Or –

But her thoughts shifted back to the foul beast in the dungeon. She thought of her brief, nightly visits to ensure Dougie Seton was still safely locked away where he could harm no other little girls. *Why has his execution been delayed so long?*

Her mouth filled with drool, and her fangs extended at the happy fantasy of executing Dougie Seton herself.

No! Brace yourself!

You will not kill him this night. Leave it to the justice of the law.

The infernally slow justice of the law.

By force of will, she spat out her drool and made her fangs retract.

Not tonight. I will not kill tonight. Not unless I must.

Almost there. I should be smelling his evil blood any time now. If the wind shifts.. .

And the wind did shift, coming from the direction of the dungeon. However, the breeze didn't carry the scent of evil blood. Only the putrescence of misery, unwashed bodies, and human waste.

She halted, hovering in the air. *Have they hanged the fiend at last?*

She flew to the execution grounds, but saw no scaffold there. *Surely, they would not have beheaded him – not in this age. These days, that style of execution is reserved only for nobility.*

Branwen circled the town, but though she could catch faint whiffs of him on the night air, she could not determine from which direction the scent came. *Surely that fool of a High Constable didn't release him, did he?*

She heard voices below her—a man and a woman calling, "Morag! Morag! Where are ye, lass? Morag!"

Below Branwen, a father and mother frantically searched in the darkness for their lost daughter. Branwen recognized the place— the silversmith's shop, the well of water—the spot where she had rescued that young girl from the monster, Dougie Seton.

The wind shifted again.

And she caught the scent—faint, but steady, and coming from the south. She wheeled and sped southward, following Dougie Seton's evil blood.

The mouth-watering fragrance came from a small, stone building set in the side of a low hill. The windowless structure, built to resemble a small stable, had two tall, wooden doors—tall and wide enough to lead a warhorse through. Near the structure stood a covered water well likewise surrounded by stones.

Inside, she knew she'd find a man—a Sergeant of the Temple—dutifully, if perhaps drowsily, guarding the entrance to a tunnel leading down into the earth. Beyond that tunnel, carved into the sandstone bedrock, lay the secret, man-made cave where Tormond and Maebh had slept for decades.

However, one of the two great doors hung ajar.

And the sweet smell of freshly spilt blood—human, but not *evil*—emanated from the door.

The guard. Probably slain. By Dougie's hand.

But if the murderer is...

Branwen alighted outside the entrance, her wings vanishing as she touched down. Her fangs extended, and drool spilled from her lips.

But she did not enter the door. Instead, she trembled.

No! Not in there.

Not under the ground. In the dark.

Not again.

It was as if she could once more feel the incalculable weight of earth and stone crushing her. Shattering her bones. Mangling her flesh. Suffocating her.

Healing. Tearing. Breaking. Healing. Tearing. Breaking.

Over and over and over in an endless cycle of agony.

Two years.

Two years she'd been buried alive as she slowly — an inch, sometimes no more than a hair's breadth in a day — clawed her way out of the earth to freedom.

Two years of hell.

Almost sixteen centuries had passed since her agony, and yet, if there was anything Branwen, immortal Daughter of Lilith feared, it was being crushed and buried in the dark.

And burning in the rays of the Sun.

Again.

"No." Her voice came out as a quavering whisper. "No. Please. Not that. Not again."

Her ancient torment had begun, not in darkness, but in fire. When she'd deliberately exposed herself to the burning rays of the Sun. Flesh burning. Cracking. Sizzling. Her eyes melting in their sockets. Her tongue flaming in her mouth after she could no longer scream in her agony.

But she had done it willingly. She had chosen to sacrifice herself.

To save them. To save Marcus and Maelona.

Another scent emerged from the cave, not as strong as Dougie's evil blood. But she knew that scent and what it portended.

Oil.

Barrels and barrels of it by the smell.

She also detected the horrifying stench of burning.

The oil? Aflame?

No. Different. Burning pitch.

She gasped. *The fool has a lit torch!*

Laughter — mad laughter — emanated from the depths of the earth.

"Are ye coming?" Dougie's voice. She knew it well. She'd heard it reciting his murders in great detail each night since she'd caught him and foolishly delivered him over to mortal justice.

Since the night she'd chosen *not* to kill him.

The fiend laughed again. "I've got her! The wee whore. I've got her again. Down here." He cackled. "Down here, ye winged bitch. And this time . . . this time, I'll take her *proper*. Show her for the whore she is. Then I'll slit her throat. Aye, I will!"

Please, God. Not this. Not underground. Not the burning.

Branwen dropped to her knees. "Please," she whimpered, "not again."

"Ye should hae killed me when ye had the chance!" Dougie's voice taunted, sing-songing from the darkness. "But ye did nae kill me, did ye? And now, whate'er happens to this wee whore . . . 'twill all be on yer head." He paused. "Go on, ye wee harlot. Scream!"

A child's scream of terror blasted from the depths. The shrill sound ripped into Branwen like a jagged blade in her gut.

Enough! She snarled in fury as she gathered her courage. She welcomed the bloodlust. *Father in Heaven, let my rage be stronger than my fear.* She spat the drool from her mouth. *Give me courage. Like my Marcus.*

Please.

With a quaking hand, she drew Marcus's sword, casting the baldric and scabbard aside.

If I survive this night, I'll come back for them.

If I survive.

Don't think. Just act.

Save the girl.

Slay the monster.

Wings sprouted from her back, and she flew into the darkness.

Into the Pit of Hell.

Chapter 28

With her ephemeral wings extended, Branwen hurtled down the sandstone tunnel with Marcus's sword held before her like a lance. The tunnel seemed to close around her, threatening to crush her, to bury her. Again.

Not again! Please, God, not again!

Down she flew, fighting panic and terror. The light of the as-yet-unseen torch glinted off the oil-drenched stairs all the way to the bottom.

'Tis everywhere!

If he drops that torch.. .

She flew into the chamber, ready to attack.

And halted abruptly in the air.

A pool of black oil, fully a dozen feet across, lay at the foot of the stairs. At the edge of that pool stood Dougie. He clutched the terrified girl to his chest with one arm, holding a small knife at her throat. Blood already trickled from a throbbing vein in her neck where the point of his sgian dubh had pricked her skin.

In his other hand, he held the lit torch. Droplets of burning pitch fell from it like fiery raindrops, landing inches away from the oil.

Branwen knew Dougie didn't need to deliberately drop the torch to set the chamber ablaze. *If I move too quickly, if I seize the torch, and it flings just one of those drops of flame.. .*

Stop him! Persuade *him.*

But when she looked from the torch to his eyes, she knew her power of Persuasion would be useless.

His hollow eye sockets glowed with fire, as if a pair of stars had been cast down from the heavens and had taken up residence there. Blood trailed from those otherwise empty holes like tears of crimson.

His mouth was frozen in a rictus grin of madness. His head turned ever so slightly in her direction. "There ye are, ye winged bitch!"

Can he see with those lights? "Let the child go!" she commanded, hoping the strength of her voice alone might give him pause.

Dougie merely laughed, low and guttural. "I dinnae have tae listen tae ye. Nae any longer."

Still hovering in the air, her wings beating in furious silence, she circled slowly around the fiend and his prey. All the while the sweet evil of his blood screamed out to her. *Kill him! Send him to Hell!*

As she circled, Dougie turned with her.

He can see me.

When Branwen reached the other end of the chamber and hovered in front of the stone bed, she stopped. Terror and blood-rage warred within Branwen for mastery, but she forced her fangs to retract.

Perhaps if I can lure him away from the oil.. .

But though Dougie faced her, he had not retreated from the oil and the threat of fiery holocaust.

"P-please, holy angel," the girl whimpered, "s-save me!" The child didn't struggle in Dougie's arm, but the monster increased the pressure of his knife. The trickle of blood from her neck thickened and flowed faster, staining her blouse. Her tear-streaked face was a ghastly, sepulchral white.

Kill him! Kill him! KILL HIM!

Branwen gave the child what she hoped was a reassuring smile. "I will, lassie. I will save you." *But how?*

"Save her?" Dougie sneered, and his empty sockets blazed all the brighter. "Ye cannae save yerself!"

Branwen gazed into Dougie's glowing eye sockets and licked her lips. "Come to me, Dougie," she cooed. "Do you remember the pleasure? The bliss of my lips on your neck? You can know that joy again. Come to me."

Dougie's maniacal grin faltered. He lowered the torch slightly.

"Come to me, Dougie. Know my touch and —"

Another light bloomed in the chamber — unearthly and unholy.

The demon floated before the stone altar. Her radiant beauty surpassed anything Branwen had ever beheld in all her long life.

Suddenly, the centuries-old memory was back, searing her mind—the terror and agony of the tortures she'd endured in Arawn's subterranean temple. She could feel the sword twisting in her gut over and over as her body repeatedly healed itself only to be stabbed and mutilated again.

A cry of horror and remembered torment burst from her, and her wings vanished. Branwen fell to the chamber floor.

She clutched Marcus's sword with both trembling hands, attempting to draw strength from her love for her long-dead husband. *I will not fail. I will not give in to despair.*

Marcus prophesied I yet have a mission to fulfill. I will not die this night.

My time has not come.

Branwen clung to that thought like a drowning woman to a raft made of rotting wood.

Please, God. Not again!

The demon's voice echoed in the chamber. "See, my child? She is powerless. She is nothing."

Branwen forced herself to her feet, hampered by her capacious skirt and petticoats. She kept her eyes away from the demon. She did look at Dougie. Instead, she focused solely on the child who was staring at the apparition in horror. "Don't be afraid, lassie," Branwen said, willing her voice to be calm, forcing it to hide the terror that nearly consumed her. "Don't look at that thing. Look at me. Can you do that, lass? Can you look at me?"

The girl's wide eyes focused on Branwen.

"Aye, lass," Branwen said. "I won't let him hurt you. I promise." *I can snatch away the torch or I can snatch away the child. If I go for the torch, he'll slit her throat. If I go for the girl, he'll drop the torch.*

The torch or the child?

"Enough of this," the demon said, her voice honeyed venom. "Take the girl, Dougie, my love. Take her now and worship me in the only true way."

Torch or child? Torch or child?

"Aye!" Dougie cried. "At last!" In his lust-fueled eagerness, the madman flung the torch away.

Dougie had made Branwen's choice for her. She shot forward, reaching for the knife and the girl.

Even as Branwen ripped the weapon and the child out of Dougie's grasp, the torch splashed into the oil. "NO!" she screamed.

Flames erupted, racing up the stairs.

Cutting off escape.

NOT AGAIN!

Dougie Seton stumbled, falling backward into the flames. He screamed in agony as he thrashed in the hellish fire.

Red flame and black smoke filled the chamber.

And the demon laughed.

✠·✠·✠

Tormond leaped from the saddle, sword at the ready. "Fuirich!" he commanded, and Órd Dubh stamped and tossed his head as if in acknowledgement of the order to remain in place. Tormond drew his dagger as well, holding it blade-up as a parrying weapon, and advanced cautiously toward the ersatz stable hiding the tunnel entrance.

As he advanced, his foot struck against something, and he glanced down. A short, black-leather scabbard, decorated with brass and attached to a slender leather baldric, lay discarded on the ground. Empty.

Branwen's scabbard.

She's inside there.

And she went in prepared for battle.

One of the stable doors hung open, and a dim glow emanated from within.

The scent of oil hit him, flooding his mind with horrific memories—vats of burning oil dumped from parapets, landing on men, setting them ablaze with unquenchable fire. Burning men, screaming in agony as they ran from the flames—flames that were a part of them, flames they could never escape until long after the burning oil had consumed their flesh.

Tormond had seen friends, brothers suffering in blazing, mortal agony.

He had seen enemy soldiers dying in the same the horrific way.

Both sides—Muslim and Christian—had used the brutal tactic when defending their strongholds. A living human pyre was a sight Tormond had fervently prayed he might never see again.

Fainter than the scent of oil came another all-too familiar stench—death. Even with all the men Tormond had slain over the centuries—and he'd slain many, so very many—the reek of freshly spilled blood and entrails made his stomach threaten to empty itself.

That'll be Callum, the hapless Sergeant guard.

O Lord, have mercy on his soul.

Tormond probed the darkness beyond the door with his sword, but met no resistance. The blade glinted dully from the faint light within.

If there be someone inside, they'll already know I'm here.

Nae sense in waiting.

Tormond leaped through the doorway, blindly slashing with his sword and stabbing with his dagger. But no foe stood to oppose or ambush him.

His eyes quickly scanned the ersatz stable.

The dead guard lay facedown in his gore. A small table and an overturned stool were the only furniture. The single horse stall was empty.

Tormond approached the faintly glowing tunnel mouth.

"NO!" The scream of terror exploded from the tunnel, followed by roaring flames and searing heat.

Tormond jumped back from the mouth of Hell.

"Branwen!" he shouted, but the only answer he received was the roar of the fire.

Must get to her!

But even if I could get down there, how could I get her out?

"Fly, Branwen! Fly out!"

But would she survive the flames?

Casting his weapons aside, he wheeled and dashed for the well outside, then halted. He knew with gut-churning certainty that water would not quench oil-fueled flames—only sand or earth could do that.

"Please, Lord! Show me how to save her!"

A desperate plan blossomed in his mind.

Maebh galloped toward him on Fiona. Maebh abruptly halted beside Tormond's horse and scrambled from the saddle. Tangled in her skirt, she fell to the earth before he could catch her. She landed hard, her gown billowing out around her.

But in her hands, she clutched his axe.

Thank ye, Lord! "Thank ye, lass!"

He ripped the axe from her grasp. "Water!" he bellowed, his command barely audible above the roar of the inferno. "From the well!"

He turned and hacked savagely at the door hinges.

✠·✠·✠

The girl in Branwen's arms shrieked.

Branwen was frozen in mute horror as Dougie Seton rose from the flames, somehow still mobile, somehow still alive. He reached for the demon as if pleading for deliverance. Or oblivion.

The demon waved a hand in contemptuous dismissal. Then she vanished, abandoning him.

He took two steps, then collapsed.

And he moved no more.

Get-out-get-out-get-out-GET-OUT!

Branwen released the child. For a second, the immortal braced herself, ready to fly up the tunnel.

She'd burn. She'd endure unspeakable agony.

But she'd make it out.

Maybe.

Her wings appeared.

"No!" the girl screamed. "Don't leave me!"

Branwen might survive the flames. She might, if she were very, very quick.

But the girl would not.

The wings vanished, and Branwen enfolded the child in her arms, attempting to shield the girl from the heat. "I've got you." Branwen scrambled to the back of the chamber. Holding the child, she crouched behind the carved sandstone bed. "I won't leave you."

The girl clung to her neck with immense strength born of mortal terror.

"Let go, child," Branwen shouted. "Put your face near the floor. The air is better there."

To Branwen's relief and astonishment, the girl obeyed, lying facedown on the floor gulping in lungfuls of the relatively cooler air.

"Good lass." Branwen stretched out beside the child.

Even down here, the air won't last long.

We're both going to die.

"Good lass," Branwen said again, tears falling freely from her eyes. "Brave lass."

I'm going to die down here. Under the earth.

Branwen sobbed in despair. *Marcus! You were wrong, my love.*

A ghost of a smile curved her lips. *I'm coming, Marcus. I'm coming home.*

She sobbed anew. *But you were wrong. I'm going to die* here. *Not when...*

The last prophecy won't be fulfilled.

If only I could have saved the child.

God, please let the girl's passing be swift.

The flames howled like an enraged dragon.

But above the roar of the fire, another sound emerged, growing louder. And faster.

Bop. Bop. Bop. Bop. Bop-bop-bop-bop-BOP-BOP-BOP-BOP!

Branwen popped her head above the bed and stared in disbelief.

Through the fire and smoke, a shape appeared to be sliding down the tunnel, like a child riding a sled down a hill of flaming snow.

The sled popped out of the blazing maelstrom and slid across the floor. It stopped when it collided with the stone bed.

The sled itself was burning all around the edges.

But atop it, apparently unscathed by the flames, sat Tormond.

He stood, rising from the center of the burning sled like a phoenix of legend, rising from its own ashes. He stooped, and — as if possessing more-than-mortal strength — lifted a large, flat, rectangular slab and heaved it clear of the flames.

Then Tormond himself leaped clear.

He was wrapped from armpits to knees in his kilt as if he were rolled up in a blanket. Smoke rose from the woolen cloth.

Not smoke. Steam.

He quickly unwrapped the sodden cloth from around his body, leaving himself clad only in his long shirt, then he tossed the kilt to her. "Take off your skirt!" he shouted. "It'll only burn. Wrap yourself in the kilt. Quick, woman!"

316

Branwen recognized the large, flat object he'd ridden down the tunnel and through the fire—one of the wooden doors from above.

"Wrap yourself, woman!" he ordered. "Then ye can fly the two of us out of here on that!" He pointed at the flat object he'd tossed clear of the flames—the second door from up above. "I'll ride," he said. "Ye'll fly. But be swift, wom—" Tormond coughed, hacking in the befouled air.

Branwen ripped off her skirt and petticoats, leaving her legs covered in naught save her shift. "*Three* of us," she cried, a savage grin on her face. "Three!" She snatched up the wet kilt and the girl, and before Tormond could object, she thrust the child into Tormond's arms, then wrapped the steaming, sopping woolen blanket around both Tormond and the girl, bundling them together.

Branwen lifted the two of them and set them down upon the second wooden door slab—the door that was *not* burning. "Lie down," she ordered, then pointed at the door handle in the middle of the slab. "Hold on tight." She handed Marcus's sword to Tormond. "Keep this and the girl safe. And hold your breath!"

Tormond nodded, still coughing, but he obediently lay upon the door, protectively curling his body around the girl, and clutching both the sword and the door handle. "Fly!" he croaked. Then he and the child sucked in deep breaths and held them.

Branwen lifted the laden door slab over her head, and taking a brief, terrifying moment to steel herself for the agony to come, she flew, carrying the door with Tormond and the girl atop it.

Branwen shot into the inferno.

✠·✠·✠

Tears streaming down her face, Maebh ripped off her skirts and petticoats, then she poured the pail of well water on them, soaking the garments thoroughly. Clad only in her shift and bodice, she hastily lowered the bucket once more and drew another pail of water from the well. She carried both the pail and sodden skirts toward the doorless stable entrance.

"O God! Please protect them! Bring them back to me." A sob ripped unbidden from her throat. "Please! Please bring him back to me!" *Even if he's burned and scarred—I don't want him to be burned and* scarred — *for his sake, not mine — but even if he is, I will love him and cherish him all my days.* "Just please, please bring him back to me!"

She was only dimly aware that Hamish and the other Sergeant had come running up, calling both her name and Tormond's. It was difficult to hear anything other than the roaring flames. She could only stare at the Pit of Hell. And wait.

The ground under her heaved violently, nearly knocking her off her feet. The tunnel entrance trembled, and she heard a low-pitched rumble.

The tunnel! Collapsing!

"TORMOND!" she screamed.

A jet of flame shot out of the crumbling tunnel, flew over her head, and crashed to the ground several paces beyond her.

She spun, and still carrying the wet skirts and the bucket — and trying desperately not to spill the water — she lurched toward the wreckage.

Tormond rose from the flaming ruins. He was still wrapped in the kilt and carried Branwen's short sword. But he was oddly misshapen to Maebh's eyes.

Then Maebh discerned the smaller form clutched to his chest under the plaid.

A child? A child was down there?

Tormond dropped the sword and tore savagely at the blanket, loosing a young girl of no more than ten years of age. The girl collapsed to the ground, apparently unharmed. "Help her!" Tormond commanded, but he was not speaking of the child.

On the ground lay a still-smoldering figure. Branwen's skin was blackened and bubbling, and she writhed in mute agony. The reek of burnt flesh assaulted Maebh's nostrils as she poured the bucket out over the convulsing body. The water hissed and steamed, and Maebh felt wet heat rising from Branwen. Maebh then spread her wet skirt and petticoats over Branwen, seeking to cool the charred woman further.

But once Maebh had done all she could, she could only stand by and witness the woman's suffering. Maebh felt completely helpless.

What more can I do? Help her, O Lord! Save her! Heal her!

Branwen spasmed and let out a scream, and that horrible, night-rending cry seemed to carry the agony of all the damned in Hell. Blackened skin cracked and fell away, as Branwen's flesh reformed, healing itself. Red hair sprouted from her once-more-pink scalp and rapidly grew to its previous length. Her entire body appeared to be fully restored.

Branwen convulsed and screamed once more.

And then she sobbed.

"Sergeants!" Tormond turned to the two wide-eyed men. "Off with your kilts! Now! Cover the lady afore she freezes! And the wee lass too!"

Neither man moved to obey, their eyes filled with horror. Hamish's lips moved as if he were reciting a desperate prayer. The other Sergeant extended a quavering hand toward Branwen's trembling, half-naked form. He pointed with two crossed fingers — the ancient ward against witchcraft.

"'Tis nae witchcraft, ye daft fools!" Tormond stomped toward them, his long shirt barely keeping him covered. "She be a servant of God, I say! Now, off with the kilts, or I'll rip them off ye myself!"

"Aye, Executioner," Hamish said. The other Sergeant muttered a similar reply. Then both Sergeants hurried to obey.

Soon all three men were kiltless, and the girl and Branwen were wrapped in stout woolen cloth. The Sergeants turned their eyes decently away. Maebh sat on the ground and held the girl to her bosom, crooning words of comfort. The child clung to Maebh, trembling and softly weeping in her embrace.

Branwen, however, huddled in her blanket, alone and sobbing, comfortless.

"Be off wi' ye," Tormond commanded the Sergeants. "Fetch more blankets." The men wheeled and ran back to the inn as if all the hosts of Hell pursued them.

For a moment, Tormond helplessly watched the immortal woman's suffering. Then his eyes brightened, and Tormond stooped, reaching for Branwen's sword. As he bent, his shirt lifted, exposing part of his backside.

Heat rushed to Maebh's cheeks, and she quickly averted her eyes.

"Your sword, milady," Tormond said.

Maebh risked a glance back at Tormond and beheld him kneeling before Branwen, extending the weapon hilt-first toward her.

To Maebh's astonishment, Branwen did not take the treasured sword. Instead, she shook her head, her body rocking forward and back. "Unw-worthy."

Unworthy? To take the sword?

"Nae, milady," Tormond said, his voice reverently soft, "ye are *most* worthy. Ye did well this night. Ye saved the lass."

Branwen shook her head again as she continued to rock like a lost child. "P-p-pit of H-hell," she sobbed. "D-damned s-soul."

The prophecy!

But who is the "damned soul?" The girl? Surely not.

The child in Maebh's arms stirred and pulled away from her. Maebh acquiesced, letting the girl go. The child stood and, keeping the blanket wrapped around herself, wiped away her tears. She walked quickly over to Branwen, then wrapped her thin arms around Branwen's neck. "Dinnae weep, holy angel. Oh, dinnae weep! Ye saved me. Ye stayed wi' me. I was so frightened. And ye stayed wi' me. "

Branwen loosed her arms from the blanket and embraced the child. "Oh, wee one! You owe your life — not to me — but to this brave man here and his noble companion. And to God. Always to God." She paused, then lifted her eyes to the stars. "Father in Heaven, I thank Thee this night that Thou didst send Tormond and Maebh to save us from the Pit. I thank Thee that Thou hast saved this sweet, innocent child and this" — she choked out another sob — "this d-damned soul." She paused. "In Christ's name, amen."

Herself? Branwen is the "damned soul?"

Tormond glanced at Maebh, then turned his gaze back to Branwen. "Surely, milady," he said, "ye are mistaken. How could ye think ye are damned?"

Maebh also stood and hurried over to Branwen. She knelt beside the immortal woman. "Mother?"

Branwen turned eyes, red from weeping, to Maebh. "Daughter?"

With a gentle hand, Maebh wiped tears away from Branwen's tear-and-soot-stained cheek. "Ye are . . . the noblest, truest soul I have ever met." Maebh glanced at Tormond. "Ye *and* Tormond, that is."

She turned her gaze back to Branwen and locked eyes with the woman. "The noblest, truest souls on God's earth. Ye are *not* damned, Mother."

Branwen dropped her eyes. "When I was . . . in the pit, when I thought I was going to die, I"—she swallowed—"doubted. I lost faith. Without faith, I am . . ."

Damned?

"Truly?" Tormond's voice sounded almost as if he were amused at the thought. "Ye are saying ye had a moment of doubt, aye? Then I am damned as well, for I struggle every day to cling to my faith. Every single day. Sometimes it feels as if I am clinging by only my fingernails."

Tormond? Tormond struggles with his faith?

"But Marcus's prophecy," Branwen objected. "Surely this was it. This was the fulfillment. That was the Pit of Hell. And I was— I am the damned soul."

"Ach, nae!" the girl cried. "Dinnae say such wicked things! Ye are a holy angel of Heaven."

"Perhaps," Maebh ventured, "in those moments when all seems lost, in the moments when we feel as if God has abandoned us—"

"God never abandons us, Daughter," Branwen corrected. "He *never* abandons us. I . . . forgot that."

Maebh smiled. "Precisely. When we *feel* as if He has abandoned us, when we lose hope, perhaps for that moment, we *are* damned." A tear spilled from Maebh's eye. "And then, in our darkest moments, He redeems us *again*. Or maybe, 'tis the *same* redemption— I know not. But in that moment of despair, 'tis when we feel God's holy love anew."

Fresh tears fell from Branwen's eyes, and she smiled. "And then how sweet is that holy love!" Branwen gently pulled one arm away from the girl and wrapped it around Maebh, pulling her close. "Oh, Daughter! Thank you!" She paused. "And thank *you*, my son!" Branwen laughed softly. "I'd embrace you as well, Tormond, if I thought for one moment you might not die of shame."

Tormond's cheeks darkened.

Maebh almost laughed as well at Tormond's embarrassment.

Tormond bowed his head and again presented the short sword to Branwen. "Your sword, milady."

Branwen shook her head as she broke from Maebh and the girl's embrace. "No, my son." She took the sword and clutched it to her breast. "'Tis *Marcus's* sword. Now and forever."

She closed her eyes, squeezing out fresh tears. "Oh, Marcus!" She let out a wistful sigh. "It seems, beloved husband, that we must wait yet a while longer."

Branwen turned her head, looking toward the smoke issuing from the mouth of the collapsed tunnel. "And it appears, my children, that you will have to find another place to sleep for the next sixty years. Perhaps, back to Wales?"

Tormond's cheeks darkened again. "At least, in Wales, I'll nae have tae wear those ridiculous kilts."

Chapter 29

Gravesend, Kent, England: May 3rd, 1715 A.D.

The sun!" Maebh pointed to the window in alarm. "Mother! The sun has risen!" She jumped up from her customary chair near the hearth in her room at the Amsterdam Inn, snatching up her cloak.

Tormond too was on his feet, hurriedly removing his knee-length coat. He and Maebh nearly collided in their haste as he leaped to cover the window with his coat and Maebh scurried across the room, nearly tripping on her hooped skirts, to where Branwen sat near the empty wooden wardrobe. Maebh lifted her cloak to cover the Daughter of Lilith and shield the immortal from the sun's deadly rays.

Branwen, however, laughed and clapped her hands.

Has she gone mad? Maebh thought as she attempted to protect Branwen. *She'll burn!*

But Branwen caught the cloak and gently wrested it from Maebh's hands. She shook her head, grinning. "Oh, Daughter, I thank you for your concern, but I am quite safe here, in this corner" — Branwen waved a dismissive hand — "in the shadows." She nodded toward Tormond. "You can put your coat back on, my son. In this age, some would consider removing your coat in the presence of ladies to be positively indecent." She chuckled.

Tormond, hesitated, then lowered his coat from the window. Dawn streamed in through the east-facing window, but the rays of sunlight hit the wall on the far side of the wardrobe — well away from Branwen. "Is't only *direct* sunlight can harm ye?" he asked.

Branwen laughed again. "Oh, there are a great many things that can harm me." She handed the cloak back to Maebh. "Thank you, dear one. But, yes, Tormond, the Sun can only harm me if his rays shine on me directly." She waved vaguely toward the ceiling. "Why, on a cloudy or rainy day, I can even walk abroad — hooded and cloaked and wearing gloves, of course." She smiled sweetly at them, but a twinkle of mirth remained in her emerald eyes. "But I thank you for your concern." The twinkle vanished, and her eyes glinted with sudden tears. "And your love." She drew in a tremulous breath, then sighed. "Thank you for sitting up all night with me. How I shall miss the two of you, my darlings."

Maebh opened her mouth to speak, but a lump suddenly took up residence in her throat, making talking impossible. Instead, she crossed the room—with far more grace than when she'd scrambled toward Branwen—and took her seat again by the fire. *Once we sail after the late morning tide, we'll never see her again.* She thought again— briefly—of pleading with Branwen to sail with them. *But she'll never leave Britain.*

She has a prophecy to fulfill.

"But," Tormond said, putting his coat back on and adjusting it over his sword, "ye're awake. I thought ye slept during the day."

Branwen smiled again and winked at him, causing a tear to fall from her eye. The tear fell upon a packet wrapped in brown paper, sitting in her lap. "Did you expect me to collapse into a deathlike slumber, only to awaken at Sunset?"

"Aye." Tormond let out a nervous chuckle. "I suppose I did. 'Tis nae as if we've ever *seen* ye sleep." He sat in his own chair by the fire, opposite Maebh. He struggled with the placement of the sword at his belt, trying to find a position that allowed him to sit, wear the coat, and be able to draw the blade quickly.

Maebh suppressed a smile. *He still struggles with how to wear that long weapon with those silly coats.*

But even though he's not wearing a kilt anymore, with those knee- britches and stockings, I still can at least admire the shape of his manly calves.

And, oh, he does indeed have fine calves.

Ah, the fashion of the times! Each waking brings new and frivolous vanities. And challenges.

Her lips twitched in annoyance. *Such as moving about in these ridiculous hooped skirts!*

Then she thought of the dear immortal woman who had provided the fashionable clothes they wore. She glanced at Branwen, and the lump in her throat returned.

"I can *only* Sleep during the day," Branwen explained, stroking the pommel of her ever-present short sword, "but I don't have to Sleep every day. I can easily do with Sleeping only once in a week. And there are days—like today—when I would much rather be awake."

"Because of the eclipse, aye?" Tormond said with a grin. "The one that the astrologer, Haley, pre—"

"Astronomer," Branwen corrected. "They are called *astronomers* in this age. 'Tis science they practice, not dubious soothsaying."

"Aye, Mother." Like a dutiful son, Tormond nodded his head in humble acknowledgement of the correction. "The eclipse that *astronomer*, Haley, predicted for half past nine this morning?"

"Tormond!" Fighting back tears, Maebh, eyed him with indignation and a little frustration. "Ye know quite well 'tis not what she means." *Men are so obtuse at times! Does he not see the tears in her eyes?*

Is his heart not breaking? As mine is?

Tormond bowed his head. "Aye. Forgive me, Mother."

Branwen chuckled. "Nothing to forgive, my son." She turned her eyes to Maebh. "'Tis the way of men—*some* men, at least—to cover sorrow with humor." She winked. "Forgive him, Daughter. 'Tis what people do when they love each other."

Tormond's cheeks flushed crimson, and he turned his face away.

Maebh grinned at Tormond, though he couldn't see it. *And I do love him. With all my heart.* "Always."

"Now, my son," Branwen said, "an eclipse of the Sun is a rare and wondrous thing. And it should not be missed if the opportunity arises."

"Aye." Tormond shot a guilty glance at Maebh before replying to Branwen. "I've nae seen one. But I assume ye have."

Branwen shrugged. "A few. God's celestial wonders are a reminder that He rules the Heavens. And the Earth."

"Aye," Maebh said, "He made the sun stand still for Joshua and go back ten degrees for Hezekiah."

Branwen beamed at her. "You amaze me, child! You have become quite a scholar."

It was Maebh's turn to blush.

"Did you know, my son," Branwen continued, "that she has finished reading the *entire* Holy Bible?"

Tormond blinked. "Truly? It has nae been so long ago ye could nae read a letter."

Maebh's blush deepened.

Branwen nodded. "Yes. Two nights ago. And she has started back again at the beginning."

A grin of wonder blossomed on Tormond's face, and unabashed admiration gleamed in his blue eyes. "Ye are indeed a marvel, lassie!"

Maebh felt as if her cheeks would burst into flames.

"Oh, stop that, girl." Branwen chuckled. "All that blood rushing to your face. You are making me" — her voice lowered almost to a growl — "hungry."

Maebh clapped her hands to her face, covering her cheeks. She turned her face away. "I'm so sorry!"

Branwen laughed heartily. "Oh, child, you have nothing to apologize for." She winked at Maebh. "My son, is she not lovely when she blushes so?"

"She's lovely all the ti—" Tormond's face flushed crimson again. "Will ye cease that, milady? 'Tis nae proper for me to say such things." He turned his face toward the window. "To look upon a woman with—"

"Truly?" Branwen rolled her eyes. "'Tis hardly *lust* to acknowledge a lady's beauty. And 'tis hardly improper. In fact, a *knight* should always be ready with a compliment for a lady."

A knight, perhaps, but not a religious. Especially, not a religious to a nun.

I may not think of myself as a nun anymore, but I'm certain that Tormond thinks of me that way.

And only that way. He will not allow himself to see me as a lady. As a woman.

Tormond turned to Maebh and gazed upon her with an unreadable expression. His eyes locked with hers, and she saw in his gaze great tenderness and never-spoken but ever-present love. Abruptly breaking eye contact, he bent his left leg and bowed low. "Truly, fair ladies, in all my unnaturally long life, I have ne'er seen such loveliness. The radiance of your feminine beauty outshines that of the sun."

Is he mocking me?

When he looked up once more, he was smiling, but there was no mockery in that smile—only a touch of sadness. Sadness and, perhaps, regret? "But," he said, "just as I cannae gaze directly on the sun—at least when he is not eclipsed—I dare nae gaze too long on your beauty, or else I may"—he paused, and his eyes bored into Maebh's—"burn."

Maebh recalled the words of St Paul—*"For it is better to marry than to burn."*

I burn too, my love.

"Very well spoken, my son," Branwen said. "You would make a fine member of the royal court." She lowered her voice to a barely audible murmur. "Not that King George would understand a word of it." She shook her head. "A German king who speaks not a word of English on the throne of Britain." She sighed, and a little louder, said, "Still, I suppose 'tis no worse than a French-speaking Viking king like William the Bastard." She chuckled. "But I suppose they call him William the Conqueror now. Did you know he was the bastard son of the Duke of Normandy and a tanner's daughter?"

Tormond nodded, grinning, his eyes finally breaking away from Maebh's. "Aye. I'm well aware of the story."

Maebh, however, was not aware of that particular bit of English history. She was, after all, Irish, not English, nor Scottish, as Tormond was. But as fascinating as the sometimes less-than-honorable history of kings and queens might be, she wanted to focus their attention elsewhere. And on some level—on some very selfish level—she resented that Tormond had turned his attention to Branwen. He was no longer gazing at Maebh, his blue eyes penetrating to her very soul.

Stop that, Maebh O Broin. He doesn't burn for Branwen. Nor she for him. He burns only for ye.

He loves only ye.

Though he cannot admit it. Not even to himself. Not yet.

But Branwen has promised—and Marcus has prophesied—that he will. Someday.

Branwen. Oh, Mother!

"We're never going to see ye again." She'd said it aloud and she didn't care.

Branwen's lips were drawn tight, and her eyes brimmed with fresh tears. She shook her head so quickly, it looked as if she were shuddering. "No, my darlings. Today is goodbye. 'Til we meet again beyond the veil of this mortal life."

"But ye are *immortal*," Tormond said.

"I too shall die," Branwen replied. "My death has been prophesied, as you know. And on that night, I shall at last be reunited with Marcus. And with Maelona. And eventually, with *all* whom I love so dearly." She rose from her chair, keeping well away from the sunlight. "I have a gift for the two of you." She held forth the brown-paper package.

"But, Mother"—Maebh wiped at her own tears—"ye have already given us so much." She thought of the chests full of gold and the trunks full of fashionable clothes already stowed aboard the ship waiting to take them to the New World. *In just a few more hours. The only thing ye could give us more, the only thing we desire of ye, is something ye cannot give us after today—your counsel and foresight. And your love.*

Tormond stepped toward Branwen, and she extended a hand to him. "We owe ye"—he paused, taking her hand and kissing it—"everything. Our very lives. But we desire only your love and guidance."

In spite of the gravity and sorrow of the moment, Maebh felt a stab of envy, like poisoned dagger thrust into her heart. *He has never kissed my hand. Not once.*

"But ye cannae go with us," Tormond continued. "Ye have your sacred mission to fulfill, milady." He gestured toward Maebh. "As do we. And ye have aided us already beyond measure."

"Oh, my son!" Tears streamed down Branwen's cheeks. "My love goes with you, across the ocean. And as for my guidance . . ." She held forth the package. "My guidance goes with you as well."

Tormond took the package from her, taking her hand once more and kissing it. "Thank ye, milady."

"Open it," Branwen said.

Tormond carried the package to Maebh. "We shall open it together." His eyes met hers. "As we do everything—as one."

The venom of jealousy evaporated from Maebh's soul. She smiled as she stood, her eyes never leaving his. "As one. Always."

And as one, they tore at the paper like children opening a present on New Year's Day.

They unwrapped a thin book, bound in red leather, and unadorned by even so much as a title.

Tormond relinquished the volume into Maebh's hands.

With trembling fingers, she opened the cover. The first page said in handwritten script—

> To my beloved children,
> to Tormond MacDonald, Executioner of God,
> and to Maebh O Broin, Shield-maiden of Christ,
> May this guide you
> in the trials and centuries to come.
>
>
> With all my love,
> Branwen Aquillius

Maebh turned the leaf and beheld more writing in the same bold script. Some of the lines were in Latin, but the bulk of them were in English.

"Mother!" Maebh said, her voice filled with awe. "Are these . . ."

"Yes, my children," Branwen replied. "I have copied all of Marcus's prophecies—at least the ones that pertain to you. They are in Latin, of course, as Marcus recorded them. I have added my own translations into English, as well as my thoughts as to their meanings. I have pondered and prayed long on this and have written as the Holy Spirit has directed me. You see, my love and guidance truly do go with you."

Maebh handed the book to Tormond, then dashed to Branwen's shadowed corner. She threw her arms around the immortal. "Oh, Mother!"

Branwen embraced her. "Daughter." She sobbed. "Beloved Daughter." The two women held each other and wept wordlessly, though not soundlessly.

Eventually, slowly, their weeping ceased. When they finally loosed each other from their embrace, Maebh kissed her adopted mother on the cheek, and Branwen returned the kiss.

Maebh turned and beheld Tormond.

He stood, clutching the red book to his chest, and it seemed to Maebh as if by embracing the book, he was holding Branwen herself.

"My son," the immortal woman said, "if you do not embrace me and kiss me goodbye, you will regret it for the rest of your days. As will I."

Tormond's eyes widened. "But the Rule! The Rule of the Templars!" He shook his head. "Not even our mothers! I could nae embrace nor kiss my own mother when I left for the Holy Land."

Maebh thought she could see the pain of that memory in Tormond's eyes, and his pain smote her heart. *Such a heavy price for his vows.*

Branwen growled. "Oh, damnation take your Rule! 'Tis the commandments of men, not of God. 'Tis the same wretched Rule that does not allow you to wear *shoelaces*, but you have long ago given that up!" She paused, seeming to collect herself. "I cannot come to you, Tormond." She eyed the sunlight warily. "Not unless I were to fly over the light and across the room." She waggled a finger at him like a mother scolding a boy who has been caught stealing a freshly baked pork pie. "Don't you make me do it, my son. Because I *will* do it and I *will* embrace you and I *will* kiss you. And there is naught you can do to prevent me!"

Tormond flushed crimson again. However, he reverently set the book down on the bed, then strode purposefully across the room and through the sunlight.

Maebh felt that stab of envy once more as Tormond embraced Branwen. There had been *three* times—in the cave, centuries before, when he held Maebh in his arms, comforting her—two times when she was frightened and a third when they mourned William's death. His arms about her, so strong, so warm . . . How she ached to be enfolded in those arms again!

Me. Not her.

330

Maebh was surprised by the sound of weeping.

Tormond? Tormond *is weeping?*

His shoulders shook as he held Branwen. "I shall . . . miss ye, milady." He took Branwen's face in his hands and kissed her cheek.

The toxic dagger twisted.

Branwen kissed Tormond's cheek as well. "Oh, my son! I am so proud of you." She looked at Maebh. "So proud of you both." Branwen's eyes flickered meaningfully at Tormond, then back to Maebh. Branwen mouthed, *Someday.* And she smiled through her tears.

The dagger faded away once more. *Thank ye,* Maebh mouthed in return.

"Now, my children," Branwen said, "you must take your leave. Your ship sails after the eclipse and the tide. You will need to break your fast and get your horses aboard and secured before then. I cannot help you. There is too much sunlight. And according to Master Haley, the eclipse will last for only a few minutes. So, this is *adieu.*"

Tormond once again made a courtly bow. "Farewell, milady. Go with God."

Maebh curtsied, her tears falling onto her hooped skirt. "Farewell, Mother."

Branwen waved from the shadows. "'Til we meet again in the Kingdom of Heaven. Where I shall introduce you to my husband and my sister."

Tormond picked up the red book of prophecy, then offered his arm to Maebh.

She took it, clinging to him. She did not look back. She could not bear to look back.

Together, Tormond and Maebh exited the inn room—Maebh's hooped skirt barely fitting through—leaving Branwen behind.

Leaving Branwen alone.

Maebh was certain she heard weeping coming from the room.

As they strode toward the stairs, Tormond whispered. "To the New World, Shield-maiden. To find and slay the Witches."

Maebh brushed away her tears. "To the New World, Sir Tormond."

"Together."

She smiled and leaned her head against his shoulder. "Always."

Chapter 30

Williamsburg, Province of Virginia: 1715 A.D.

"The Christ-killer whore?" Obadiah Thaddeus Worthy, Sergeant of the Temple, stared at the Executioner of God in utter disbelief and consternation as they stood in front of the nearly completed Bruton Parish Church. This? Obadiah thought. *This is how the Templar wishes me to serve him? Does he think that Jewess is connected with the Witches? Well, she is a Jewess. She could be a witch herself.*

The day had been chill in Williamsburg that autumn day, and Obadiah had worn his formal wig to meet with the Executioner, both to present a good appearance — the Templar never wore a wig himself — and to guard against the cold. But that night, the long, brown wig itched abominably. He suspected it might have become infested with lice again. He resisted the urge to adjust the wretched thing.

But why the Christ-killer? Surely, I can serve the Executioner in better ways. He shook his head. "Why in the name of all that is good and holy would you wish to have converse with that mongrel bitch?"

The Executioner's eyes narrowed, and in the last gleam of the setting sun, those eyes appeared to burn. Brother Tormond bared his teeth, and his lip curled as he uttered a low, feral growl. Like a wolf.

Obadiah trembled.

As a boy of six in his native England, barely past his breeching day — that day when he'd at last been allowed to wear his first pair of trousers rather than the dresses that unbreeched boys wore — Obadiah had once come face to face with a wolf. The terrible, gray beast bared its wicked teeth, then growled and sprang at him. That night, only his father's quick musket saved them. In his terror, young Obadiah wet his new breeches. To the lad's shame, his father insisted he be put back in dresses for an additional six months. "'Til you can better hold your water like a man," his father said with a disgusted scowl.

And now, more than four decades later, with the fearsome Executioner of God growling at him like a wolf ready to spring and rip out his throat, Obadiah felt as if he were once again that frightened little boy of long ago. He lost all control, and his knee-breeches grew warm and wet.

NO! Obadiah placed both hands over his crotch, but the spreading stain was already too large to cover.

Worsening his humiliation, he'd wet himself in front of the legendary and lovely Shield-maiden of Christ. He glanced at Sister Maebh. Perhaps he had hoped for pity, but in her ray eyes he saw only contempt.

"So, Sergeant," the Executioner snarled through clenched teeth, "ye *do* know of a Jewess in the vicinity. A Jewess, as I said, surrounded by books?"

Obadiah lowered his head and his eyes. He nodded. "Yes, B-Brother Executioner. The bookseller's daughter. On Botetourt Street, between Nicholson Street and Gloucester Street."

"Very well," the Executioner responded. "Ye will direct us to her."

Both the urine and his shame ran down Obadiah's left thigh, past his knee, and into his left stocking. *In this state?* His cheeks burned with his disgrace. "After I return to my home." *And change my breeches and stockings. Before it gets into my shoe!* "For just a moment."

The Executioner shook his head. "Ye will take us *now*."

"Tormond." Sister Maebh held Brother Tormond by the elbow.

The Executioner turned his fierce, scalding gaze away from Obadiah and looked at his companion—a lady far too pretty to have ever been a nun. Brother Tormond's terrifying expression softened. All his rage seemed to melt away. "Aye, milady?"

The Shield-maiden tilted her head in Obadiah's direction, but her eyes were fixed on the Executioner's face. "Allow him to . . . make himself more presentable."

The Executioner nodded. "As ye wish." He turned his face back toward Obadiah, and his eyes became hard and cold as iron. "Sergeant, ye will make yourself fit to introduce us to the lady, but ye will do it quickly, aye?"

Obadiah nodded vigorously. "Thank you, Brother Executioner. And you, Sister Shield-maiden." He shifted as if to sprint home like a naughty child, but the Templar's voice stopped him.

"Sergeant!" The Executioner's tone was midwinter ice. "Ye will ne'er again refer to one of the daughters of Israel as a Christ-killer. And ye will ne'er again refer to a lady as a whore or—What did ye say?—a *'mongrel bitch.'*"

Obadiah flinched at hearing his own words thrown back at him from the Executioner's lips. "I beg your f-forgiveness, Brother Templar."

"'Tis nae *my* forgiveness ye should seek, but God's."

Obadiah bowed his head. His wet trousers were warm no longer. The evening air made them chill as they clung to him. "Yes, Executioner." He hesitated, attempting to determine if he had at last been granted leave to go.

"Romans killed our Lord," the Templar continued, "and any Jews who might've borne some of the guilt for that heinous act have been dead for almost"—the Executioner paused, as if counting the passage of the centuries—"almost seventeen-hundred years. The Jews of this century are no more complicit in the sins of their ancestors than *ye* are in the foul pagan rituals your forefathers engaged in millennia ago. Did ye know your ancestors used to mate with donkeys to insure a good harvest, aye?"

Obadiah shuddered. *Mate with donkeys?*

Brother Tormond narrowed his eyes as if to drive the point home. "'Twould be better, would ye say, if none of us were held to account for the sins of our ancestors. After all, *ye* have never mated with an *ass*, aye? So why indeed should ye be guilty of the sins of your forefathers?"

"Of course not, Templar." *But what of Original Sin?*

I'd heard that the Executioner had acquired some revolutionary ideas over the centuries, but this — This sounds like heresy.

"D'ye nae think," the Templar continued, "that we should *only* be held to answer for our *own* sins?"

Our own sins? In that instant, Obadiah felt a creeping, sickening certainty that the Executioner was referring to Obadiah in a very personal manner. *But what sins?*

He cannot mean –

The Executioner's eyes bored into Obadiah's. "A woman, be she highborn or low, Christian or Jew or Mohammedan or pagan, bond or free, is *always* a lady until she proves herself otherwise. And any *man* of honor will defend a *lady's* honor to the death. Do ye take my meaning, Sergeant?"

Obadiah glanced at the hilt of the Templar's sword. The Executioner's left hand rested atop the pommel. It was not a particularly aggressive or threatening posture – in the weeks since the knight's arrival in Virginia, Obadiah had observed that the man's left hand always seemed to be resting on the pommel of his sword. If it had been his *right* hand on the hilt, rather than the left, ready to draw the fabled blade . . . Still, the Templar's fierce eyes made the Sergeant's knees smite together. "Yes, Brother Templar. I take your meaning."

"D'ye ken why the ancient Crusaders forsook all and fought in the Holy Land in the first place?"

Please, just let me go home! But he answered. He dared deny the Templar nothing. To do otherwise would be to face damnation and hellfire. "To liberate the land of our Lord's ministry from the Mohammedans." Obadiah had spoken the words as if reciting a line from a catechism.

The Executioner slowly shook his head. "Nae, Sergeant. We fought and bled and died, because for more than a century, Muslims had been abducting Christian *and* Jewish pilgrims on their way to and from the Holy Land, holding the men for ransom and selling the women and the lassies – and aye, the wee laddies as well – to their *brothels.*" The Executioner let that last word hang in the chill night air before continuing. "We fought to protect Christians *and* Jews from slavery and rapine. And I have nae patience at all for any man who demeans the very people I fought and bled – and my brothers died – to protect. And I cannae have the least regard for any man who demeans womanhood or holds another person in slavery. D'ye ken?"

"Yes, Brother Executioner!" Obadiah's quaking knees failed him, and he dropped to the dirt of the road. *Please don't kill me!*

"Ach!" The Templar's voice dripped with disgust. "Get up, man! I'm nae going to harm ye."

Unsteadily, Obadiah rose to his feet once more. He was about to brush the dirt from his knees, but he stopped himself, knowing full well he'd be unable to simply brush the dust from his wet left knee. "Forgive me, Brother Executioner. I meant no offense."

The Templar eyed him for a moment. His lips twitched as if they couldn't decide whether to scowl or to grin. Then the Templar's mouth twisted into a grin, but there was still something of the wolf in that smile. "Ye wish my forgiveness, aye? My forgiveness *and* God's?"

Obadiah nodded vigorously. "Yes, Brother! Anything you ask!"

The Executioner's grin widened, showing teeth. "And if I were to set for ye a penance? A way to make amends?"

"Yes, Brother Templar! Anything!"

The Templar stroked his unfashionable, short, yellow beard. "Or perhaps, since ye have offended womanhood . . ." He nodded. "Aye, Sergeant. I have the very thing. Since ye have offended womanhood, the Shield-maiden shall name your penance." The Executioner looked to the pretty nun — and winked at her.

He winked *at her?* Beyond the impropriety of a religious winking at a nun, Obadiah felt a creeping certainty that the two of them had planned this conversation in advance.

Like a cat that has cornered a mouse, the Shield-maiden smiled. "Ye own a tavern, do ye not?"

Obadiah blinked at her stupidly. "A tavern? You know I do. You were both there not two nights past."

She nodded. "Quite right. Now, have ye any slaves, Sergeant *Worthy?* Slaves that labor in your tavern?"

Obadiah blinked at her stupidly. *Slaves? You know I have.* "Yes."

She pursed her lips. "How many?"

"How many?" he repeated. "H-how many slaves?"

She nodded, smiling sweetly, like a mother instructing a painfully dim-witted child. "Aye, Sergeant. How many slaves?"

"J-just the one, Sister. That is, I have one black slave a-and two indentured servants."

She tapped a finger on her lips. "Oh, aye, ye have an African woman who works in kitchen, an Irish manservant, and your barmaid. She's also Irish, I believe."

"Yes."

She nodded again. "So, the kitchen woman is the slave—ye own her outright. Her name is Katy, I believe. The manservant is Abram. Ye recently acquired him?"

Obadiah nodded. "Yes, I just purchased his indenture from my cousin. He—my cousin, that is—needed money and could no longer afford the man. Abram has four years yet to serve me." *If the wretch doesn't die first. Work the Irishman to death if you can. Then there'll be fewer of them to breed and infest these shores.*

Worthless, degenerate scum.

"I see," the sister nodded. "And the *Irish* maid . . . she's the indentured lass. Ye do know that I myself am Irish, do ye not?"

Obadiah could only nod miserably.

"Tell me, Master Worthy, how many years does she have remaining on her indentures?"

"F-five years." The chill air on his wet breeches made him shiver. "Five of the s-seven."

"I see. And this maid—Rosy is her name, is it not? She is a *maid* no longer? This is the lass ye got with child, is she not?"

Obadiah gasped. *How does she know?*

In an instant, outrage smothered his fear.

That little Irish witch! She told the Shield-maiden? Shamed me in front of the Templar?

When I get home, I'll beat her! I'll horsewhip her is what I'll do! Then she'll be with child no longer.

The Executioner growled again. "*Did* ye get her wi' child, man?"

His outrage evaporating, Obadiah felt as if he might lose control of his bowels as well. "Y-yes!" Tears welled in his eyes. "God forgive me!"

"And your wife?" the Shield-maiden asked. "Has *she* forgiven ye?"

Obadiah hung his head, then shook it slowly. "She does not know."

"I see." Sister Maebh nodded. "And just so ye'll be certain sure, Rosy did not tell us. Your wife, Abigail, did. She knows, Master *Worthy*. She knows everything."

Abby knows?

"So, tell us, Master Worthy," the Shield-maiden continued, her voice freezing over like a January pond, "have ye *raped* your kitchen maid as well?"

Indignation flared again in Obadiah, and his lips curled in a snarl. "It is not *rape* to lie with my own property! It is my *right*, I tell you! My ri—"

The fist took him in the gut.

Obadiah crumpled to the ground and lay gasping, his stunned lungs clawing for the elusive air. His long wig had slipped from his head and obscured his vision. He could see nothing but brown hair as he struggled for breath.

The wig was yanked away and tossed into the dirt, and the Executioner squatted before him. "Listen carefully, Sergeant. I am the *last* Templar, aye? Nod if ye agree."

Obadiah nodded, trembling and gasping.

"And by default, that makes *me* Grand Master of the Temple, aye? Nod if ye agree."

Obadiah nodded again.

"And all Sergeants of the Temple are sworn to obey my word, aye?"

His breathe easing at last, Obadiah whispered, "Yes, Templar. We live to . . . serve the Temple and the . . . Executioner of God. All my life, I have looked forward to—"

"Very well, Sergeant. Then serve faithfully now. I give ye and all the Sergeants a new command which ye are sworn to obey. Are ye listening, laddie?"

Obadiah wheezed painfully. "Yes, Executioner."

"From this day forward, no Sergeant of the Temple shall *own* another person, another child of God Almighty. Nor shall he traffic in the slave trade in any of its abominable forms. All slaves and indentures held by Sergeants are to be freed immediately."

"Freed?" *Rosy still owes me for five years! And Abram four!* "But the law . . . In Virginia, freed slaves cannot—"

"The law?" The Executioner spat on the ground in front of Obadiah's face, splattering mud onto his cheek. "Damnation take any law that keeps men and women and children in slavery and allows *vermin* such as yourself to debauch women and girls — and aye, men and boys too, for some of ye have that inclination. Ye debauch women and men and girls and boys who cannae refuse. Ach, 'tis nae simple debauchery. 'Tis nae less than *rapine*. Nod if ye agree."

Obadiah nodded. *Vermin? The Executioner called me vermin?* A burbling sob exploded from his lips. *All my life I've dreamed of serving the Templar, and he thinks of me as vermin?* "I'm s-sorry. Forgive —"

The Executioner snarled, "I dinnae want yer thrice-damned apology. If I were to execute justice for yer crimes, death would be far too merciful for the likes of ye."

"P-please. Let m-me live." The words came out as a whimper.

"Oh, ye'll live, for ye must deliver the message, aye? Nod if ye agree."

Obadiah nodded, tears streaming from his eyes. "Thank you, merciful Executioner!"

"I dinnae want yer gratitude," the Templar growled, "only yer obedience." He paused, seeming to master his anger — and his contempt. Then he continued, "And when they are freed, the Sergeants will supply, from the vast wealth of the Temple — for I know ye control such wealth, beyond the treasuries of kings and emperors — five-hundred pounds sterling. Five hundred pounds to every man, woman, and child freed from yer contemptible slavery. I cannae free *all* the poor souls held in bondage in these lands, but with God's help, I'll free the ones I can. D'ye ken?"

He knows about the sacred treasury? "Five-hundred . . . pounds?"

The Templar nodded. "Aye. Five-hundred pounds *each*. And if a woman be with child, for her unborn child she'll receive an additional five-hundred pounds. And nae a shilling, nae a farthing less. D'ye ken?"

"Yes." *The Council will not be pleased about this.*

"And in addition to the money, freed slaves and indentures shall be given safe escort to wherever they choose to go, wherever they can make a life for themselves, free of the slavery and the depravities of their former owners. D'ye ken?"

"Yes, Templar."

"And ye'll deliver the message?"

"Yes, Templar."

"Remember, Sergeant, ye are sworn to obey. Any Sergeant who does nae obey will face the justice of God." The Templar patted the pommel of his sacred sword.

"I live to serve"—Obadiah swallowed down bile—"the Temple and the Executioner of God."

The Executioner nodded. "Good. I knew I could rely on ye. Turn to God, laddie. Confess yer sins to Him and to *all* ye have wronged. Make amends—such amends as ye can, though 'twill be far from sufficient. There can be no amends for robbing a woman of her virtue. Throw yerself on the tender mercies of Christ. There *can* be repentance, even for such atrocities. D'ye ken?"

"Th-thank you, Executioner." His mind seized on a relatively painless path to redemption. "I shall c-confess to a Chaplain of the Temple. We have one in—"

Another growl came from the Templar. "Ye cannae repent so easily, laddie. No Chaplain of the Temple, no priest grant absolution from sin. Only God can do that. D'ye ken?"

He denies the power of a priest to grant absolution? What heresy is this? But Obadiah nodded just the same.

The Templar's only acknowledgement of that nod came in the form of a contemptuous grunt. "Now, after the Shield-maiden and I conclude our business with the Jewess bookseller . . . Where was that shop now? Botetourt Street, between Nicholson Street and Gloucester Street, ye say?"

Obadiah nodded.

"What is the lady's name, pray?"

Obadiah swallowed. "Miriam. Miriam Cohen."

The Templar nodded. "I think we can find the way. After we have concluded our business with Mistress Miriam Cohen, we shall visit your tavern. Expect us before midnight. But whatever the hour, when we return, I expect to see and converse with Katy, Abram, and Rosy, and they are to show us their proof of emancipation—Katy, her writ of manumission, and Abram and Rosy, both halves of their writs of indenture. And there will be nae a single mark on any of them. D'ye ken?"

Obadiah nodded.

"Very well." The Templar stood. "Get yerself home, clean yerself up. And begin yer repentance. 'Twill nae be easy, I suspect."

Obadiah watched as the Executioner offered his arm to the Shield-maiden.

As she took Brother Tormond's arm, Sister Maebh said, "Let us go see Mistress Miriam Cohen then." Her voice sounded cheerful. "Oh, and, Sergeant," she said, "I strongly suggest ye make a full confession to your wife and beg her forgiveness."

And with those words, the pair of them turned and strode off into the night, leaving Obadiah weeping in the dirt and reeking of urine.

✠·✠·✠

Miriam Cohen eyed the Christians dubiously. A nobleman who carried a large, old-fashioned sword *and* a dagger—indeed, his left hand rarely left the pommel of the sword—and the pretty young lady whom he'd introduced as his cousin and ward.

The three of them—Miriam, Sir Tormond, and Lady Maebh were in the small sitting room, sipping tea from Miriam's best cups. The room was where Miriam had spent so many evenings reading with her father before his passing the previous year.

Why did I invite them in? And after dark, no less?

Though the knight was armed—and had the air of a man who could, at need, be quite deadly—Miriam had the distinct impression that he posed no threat to her. She was also intrigued by the fact that Sir Tormond was the only nobleman she'd ever met who did not wear a long wig in public—not even a *brown* one, though he'd certainly be entitled to wear a *gray* wig as befitted his station. He seemed a man capable of violence *and* humility—a contradiction in Miriam's experience.

And his accent! She'd met a few Scottish noblemen in her time, but most spoke as if they'd been born and educated in London. None spoke as if they'd been raised in the Scottish Highlands as Sir Tormond did. He was a man of contradictions.

And the Lady—Irish, to judge by her accent—if not by her eloquence and manners—spoke as if she'd been raised on a farm in the Irish countryside. She let her uncovered hair hang free—combed, but not coiffed. Surely no woman of rank would go about with her head uncovered, without a hat or a wig or both.

The knight and the lady were an odd and curious pair.

But, in the end, Miriam knew why she had invited this strange couple into her home. *I invited them in, because Papa would have done so.* Her father's words echoed in her memory. *"Treat all people as if they might be angels sent from Almighty God,"* he'd often said with the gleam in his eye that made him seem to be laughing at a secret joke shared only by himself and God. *"After all, remember the angels who came to Abraham and Sarah, appearing as traveling men. Always be ready to entertain angels in disguise, my child."*

The knight stood by her father's chair, while his lovely companion sat. He'd insisted Miriam not fetch a chair for him, saying he'd not sit in the presence of ladies. *The presence of ladies?* she thought. *I'm not nobility.* Her father had been well enough regarded — though they were the only Jews in Williamsburg — but no one, Jew or gentile, had ever referred to Miriam as a lady.

Miriam shook her head. "You say that *God* sent you to me? To enquire of *me*? Which god would that be? Your Christ?"

The man opened his mouth as if to answer, but it was the woman who spoke. "The God of Abraham, Isaac, and Jacob," she said in that lilting Irish accent. Miriam had never met an Irish *lady* before. All the Irish people she'd met in Virginia were indentured or — if free — penniless laborers.

A slow smile spread across Miriam's face. "'The God of Abraham, Isaac, and Jacob?' That's not a phrase I've ever heard from the lips of a Christian before." She felt a surge of warmth for this woman. "Where did you learn it, if I may ask?"

Lady Maebh grinned, though her cheeks reddened. "From the Holy Bible, of course."

Miriam tilted her head to the side and smiled. "Are you a scholar as well as a lady?"

Maebh's blush deepened.

Sir Tormond smiled like a proud father — though Miriam suspected, from the way he gazed at his companion, that his feelings toward the lady were more than fatherly in nature. "Aye. That she is."

"You know," Miriam said, "among my people, it is uncommon for a girl to be taught to read and write, much less to study the Bible."

Maebh grinned back at her. "Nor among mine, at least when I was a lass. *Tormond* taught me." She gazed up at the Scottish nobleman.

True affection shone in the Irish lady's eyes when she looked at Sir Tormond. Miriam took a sip of her tea to cover her own smile. *Much more than daughterly affection.*

He's older than she is, but not too much older. It would be a good match. Why haven't they married? They don't appear to be closely related. What obstacle is there between them?

Miriam pictured her own beloved. *We have our own obstacles, do we not? May the years pass quickly, my love.* She sighed and set her teacup on the small table next to her chair. "So, if God has sent you to me, may I be so bold as to ask why?"

Sir Tormond nodded. "Aye. We come seeking wisdom and knowledge."

Miriam pointed toward the doorway that led to the bookstore that occupied the front of her house. "Then you've come to the right shop. What type of book do you seek?"

The man shook his head. "'Tis the wisdom of a rabbi we seek."

Miriam laughed. "Then you know nothing of my people. I am no rabbi. Women cannot be rabbis. The nearest rabbi is in Pennsylvania."

The man furrowed his brow. "Then perhaps your father was more than just a book merchant? He was, perhaps, a rabbi as well?"

Miriam nodded slowly. "He was. In England. Not here. There is no congregation here. There is only me." *Me and one other. One dear, beloved other.*

"Who taught ye to read?" the lady asked. "Your father?"

Miriam nodded. "Yes."

Lady Maebh's eyes brightened. "Did he also teach ye the wisdom of your people? The wisdom of a rabbi?"

Miriam's eyes darted about the room as if searching for eavesdroppers. *Foolish girl! These Christians don't care if it was proper or not.* She lowered her gaze. "He was not supposed to. It went against . . . our tradition."

Lady Maebh sat forward eagerly. "But he *did* teach ye!"

Miriam met the lady's gaze. "Yes. He did."

The lady clapped her hands together. "Wonderful!" She put her hand on the Scotsman's arm. "Marcus was right! Of course, he was! Two prophecies in one night!"

Sir Tormond nodded. "Aye. And Branwen's interpretation was spot on."

Prophecies? Marcus? Who is Marcus? And who is Branwen?

Papa, I doubt these two are angels in disguise. Miriam blinked in confusion, shaking her head slightly. *But they have come seeking my aid. Only God knows why.* "How may I help you?"

Lady Maebh and Sir Tormond exchanged a glance, then the nobleman looked Miriam in the eyes. "We have seen a demoness."

Miriam felt the blood drain from her face. Without thinking, she raised the first two fingers of her left hand to her lips and blew three short puffs of air on them. She shuddered. "A demoness?"

"Aye," they both replied.

But fear gave way to anger. "You jest with me? Mock me? You come into my home and—"

Maebh held forth both hands as if imploring her. "No! We have seen a demoness. Truly! Ye must believe us. And we have come to ye, because . . ." Her voice seemed to fail her. She looked at Tormond as if for courage.

He nodded. "We have come, because God has directed us to do so. We need to know who this demoness is. We need to know how we may fight her. Her and her minions."

There was something about the man's eyes, the earnestness, perhaps— "This is no jest?"

He shook his head. "Nae. This is deadly earnest. We have opposed the demoness's will. And she has— She very nearly killed someone we dearly love."

Miriam hesitated, then nodded. "You *saw* her, you say? This demoness?"

Maebh nodded. "Several times."

"Very well." Miriam suppressed a shudder. "How did the demoness look? How did she manifest? What did she do? What did she say?"

Sir Tormond's shoulders seemed to sag as if with relief. "Thank ye. Thank ye for believing us."

Miriam shrugged and shook her head. "I'm not certain I *do* believe. But I'll help you if I can."

"Thank ye," Lady Maebh said. "I first encountered the demoness in Wales, many years ago . . .'"

☦·☦·☦

Miriam's finger traveled from right to left as she scanned through the ancient tome. Her finger did not actually *touch* the page—the parchment was far too delicate for that—but despite reading from the scriptures in Hebrew daily, most of what she read was in English, French, Latin, or Greek. So, when reading Hebrew, she used her finger to guide her eyes.

Her lips moved as she read, but in her mind, she translated the significant words.

Horns . . . adorned with gold . . . queen of heaven.. .

עַשְׁתֹרֶת

"I found her!" She pointed in triumph at the name.

Sir Tormond was looming over her in an instant, and Miriam stared up at him.

The knight peered at the word. "Ashtoret?"

Miriam blinked at him in astonishment. "You can read Mishnaic?"

He pursed his lips and shook his head. "Only a wee bit. Enough to work out the pronunciation. I dinnae know this word."

"Where did you learn to read Rabbinical Hebrew?"

He stared at the page, avoiding her eyes. "In the Holy Land."

"You were in the Holy Land?"

He nodded—curtly, it seemed to her. His lips twitched as if he were annoyed. "'Twas a very long time ago."

Who is this man? I've never met a Christian with this breadth of

346

knowledge.

"What was that?" Lady Maebh rose from her chair and glided across the room to stare at the ancient book. "What did you say?"

Sir Tormond looked at his companion. "I think Mistress Miriam has found the name of the demoness."

It's Miss, *actually,* Miriam thought with a small bit of annoyance. *At least for several more years.* "Yes. The description matches. Including the recumbent crescent moon atop her head."

Lady Maebh nodded. "What was the name again?"

"Ashtoret?" the man repeated. "Is that correct?"

Miriam nodded. "But I believe you would pronounce it 'Ashtor*eth*,'" she said, emphasizing the last syllable, "at least in English. She was one of the ancient Canaanite goddesses. The chief goddess, actually. The consort of Baal. The Queen of Heaven, she was called."

Lady Maebh gasped and put a hand to her mouth. "The Queen of Heaven." She shuddered.

"Aye," Sir Tormond growled. "The very same."

The lady's expression hardened, becoming resolute, but she grasped the man's arm with both hands as if borrowing strength from him. "What can ye tell us about Ashtoreth?"

"You say you have encountered her?"

"Aye!" both the knight and the lady replied. The truth of it — the *horror* of it — was evident in their eyes.

It was Miriam's turn to shudder. *I believe them. They have seen a demoness.* She took a deep breath to collect herself. *This is no mere scholarly exercise. This is deadly serious.* "She was a fertility goddess. She was worshipped with *carnal* rites. Worshippers would have *sexual congress* with the priestesses — or the priests — on her altars. To ensure a bountiful harvest."

"Were the . . . *priestesses*" — Lady Maebh spoke the word as if it were bile in her mouth — "willing or unwilling?"

Miriam shook her head, then shrugged. "I don't know. I suppose . . . But I cannot imagine *any* woman would be willing at first. Perhaps some were."

"No!" Lady Maebh shut her eyes. "Not at first. *Never* at first."

What happened to her? Surely not . . . "Were you . . ."

The lady shook her head with a vehemence that shocked Miriam. "No! I escaped. Fought my way free. But others . . ."

Sir Tormond patted Lady Maebh's hand. "How can we fight her? How can we defeat her?"

"Defeat her?" Miriam blinked at them, and suddenly, she realized she was angry again. *All of Papa's wisdom and knowledge for this?* She closed the book as if to hide the contents from mocking eyes. "Do you mean with a spell or a charm of some kind? I do not traffic in magics or amulets or arcane rituals. I traffic only in knowledge. In truth! I am no witch, no matter what some might say. If you seek magics, go and consult one of the Catholic priests in Maryland. I hear there's still one in Friendship. Perhaps he can sell you some holy water or a bit of communion bread."

Sir Tormond bowed his head. "I meant nae offense, milady." He met her furious gaze with humble, sincere eyes. "We seek only knowledge. This demoness has corrupted and enslaved so many over the centuries. And ye say she was worshipped by the ancients as well. We seek only a way to defeat her. To save innocents from her malice."

"Please," Lady Maebh said, "we were in earnest when we said that God sent us to ye. We believe ye have knowledge we lack."

"If there be any means whereby we can do ye good," Sir Tormond said, "ye have but to name it. If 'tis within my power to give, I'll give it gladly. Only, please, milady, tell us how we can defeat her."

Miriam's heart melted, and she sagged in her chair. She put a hand over her eyes, and released a shuddering breath. "Forgive me. I spoke in anger. And you did not merit it. I am so . . . *alone* here. We— my people—are so alone."

Sir Tormond dropped to one knee. "And ye have suffered cruelly at the hands of Christians, I know. But I, myself, have ne'er been a part of that."

Lady Maebh set a hand on the man's shoulder. "Tormond fought to protect your people. In the Holy Land."

Miriam huffed. "You make him sound like a Crusader."

The lady and the knight exchanged a quick, worried glance.

A Crusader? Impossible. Of course not. She looked again at the man's sword. It was no rapier, such as most noblemen might carry.

Nor was it the hanging short sabers that army officers wore, nor yet a naval cutlass. It was too big and bulky for that. It was a full sword. And on the pommel was an emblem—two Christian knights riding on a single horse, and around the emblem the words—

SIGILVM MILITVM XPISTI

She translated from the Latin—*Seal of the Soldiers of Christ!*

Not simply a Crusader, but a—

"Templar?" She gazed at him in wonder and awe.

Sir Tormond's eyes grew wide. He and Lady Maebh exchanged another worried look.

"You are a Templar." Miriam had not asked a question, she had merely stated a fact. "How *long* ago were you in the Holy Land?"

If the man's eyes had been wide before, they were now the size of teacups. "'Twas a long time ago."

"A long time ago, as if to say, last year? Or longer?"

Sir Tormond shook his head slowly. "Nae, milady. 'Twas much more than a year past."

Miriam tapped a finger to her lips. "There is a story told in my family of a pilgrimage to Jerusalem, of how a woman was abducted from her party by Mohammedan bandits. She was to be sold into prostitution. But she was rescued, delivered by a lone Templar on his way to join his brothers in the Holy Land. It was said, this lone Templar had hair and beard the color of gold and eyes as blue as sapphires. This woman—she was my ancestress. Her name was . . ."

"Hadassah." Sir Tormond's eyes softened. "Her name was Hadassah."

A thrill shot up Miriam's spine. "That was . . . in the thirteenth century. How"—she shivered—"How old are you?"

He smiled, standing once more. "Much older than I appear."

Miriam turned to the lady. "And you, Lady? Are you as . . . ancient as he?"

Lady Maebh laughed. "Not as ancient!"

Sir Tormond gazed at his companion with unabashed affection. "Aye, she's quite young. Merely fifteenth century."

"Angels," Miriam whispered in reverence. "Angels in disguise." *God be praised! But* Christian *angels?* "How?"

Sir Tormond chuckled. "'Tis a very long tale. For another night."

Another night? "But you'll tell me this tale?"

Lady Maebh nodded slowly. "Aye. But first, what more can ye tell us of this Ashtoreth?"

With trembling fingers, Miriam reopened the ancient book. She quickly found the relevant page. "Ashtoreth has manifested in many guises, under many names. Astarte, Ishtar, Anat. Others. She was worshipped by the Greeks as Aphrodite, by the Romans as Venus. But always she was a goddess of love, lust, and fertility. And also war—violence." She paused, afraid to read the next words aloud. "Some, it is said, worshipped her as the Virgin Mary."

Miriam looked up at Tormond and Maebh. But she did not see anger or offense in their faces.

"Aye," the Templar said. "She's been called that. But she is *nae* the Blessed Virgin."

The lady shook her head. "She is not the Mother of God."

Miriam found herself nodding in agreement. *At least not the mother of* Christ.

"So, how may we defeat her?" the Templar asked again.

"You can't," Miriam replied. "You cannot kill a demon. They are older than humanity." She paused. "They were cast out of Heaven at the beginning, before Creation itself."

"And they have nae bodies of flesh," Sir Tormond said. "So, she cannae be killed. I was nae speaking of killing her. Only of vanquishing her."

"No body of flesh?" Miriam had not considered that before. *Demons have no corporeal form?* "Perhaps, that would explain . . ." Her voice trailed off.

"Explain what?" the lady asked.

Miriam bit her lip. "Papa—my father—pondered on the mysteries, on the unexplained—particularly the nature of evil. He would say, 'Evil is motivated by hate, by fear, by lust, but most of all, by envy. This is why God gave us the Tenth and Last Commandment—Thou shalt not covet.' He said it was the driving passion behind most evil."

Sir Tormond nodded. "Aye. But what does that have to do with Ashtoreth?"

Miriam creased her brow. "You say she does not have a body of flesh."

Tormond nodded.

Maebh nodded as well. "We have that on very good authority, from one who . . . is far older than either of us."

Miriam shivered with excitement. *I must hear this tale as well!* "Yes, well, if Ashtoreth has no body, then she has never . . . *can* never know physical love, the love of the flesh. She covets what she cannot have." As she spoke the words, she knew them to be true. "So, she seeks to corrupt it, to twist it for her own ends. To make a mockery of it. To take it by violence."

Tormond nodded. "Aye." He nodded again with greater enthusiasm. "Aye! That rings true, milady!" He and Maebh locked eyes again.

Maebh nodded. "It rings true." She lowered her voice. "The whisperings."

Tormond grinned. "Aye."

The whisperings? Miriam shook herself. *For another time.* "And that is how you can vanquish her!"

Both her visitors turned their faces to her. "How?" they asked together.

"By taking away what she covets!" Miriam cried. "By denying her the worship she craves. By taking away her worshippers and their unholy rituals."

Sir Tormond blinked at her, openmouthed. Then he seemed to collect himself. "I am to slay *all* her acolytes?" He fingered the pommel of his sword. "All over the world?"

Miriam chuckled nervously. "Perhaps not *slay* them, but *persuade* them?"

"Persuade them?" Tormond seemed to be completely flummoxed, as if he could not understand the word. "*All* of them?"

The lady lay a hand on his arm. "Tormond, ye have been fighting her, frustrating her designs for . . . as long as I have known ye. Ye may be the Executioner of God, but ye can only do what ye can do."

Executioner of God? What is this?
Mystery upon mystery! I must hear more!

He nodded, his eyes resolute. "Aye, lass. I can only do what I can do. But it must be *all* that I can do." He smiled. "All that *we* can do."

Lady Maebh smiled back. "All that we can do."

As the two of them—the Templar and his lady—gazed into each other's eyes, it seemed as if they had forgotten that Miriam was also present. *Much more than fatherly and daughterly affection. Like Abraham, calling Sarah his "sister."*

Miriam pictured her own betrothed, longing for him, longing for the distant day when they could be wed.

A pounding came at the door.

Startled, Miriam jumped to her feet, her heart thundering in her chest.

"Miriam! Miriam!" The muffled shouts came through the stout oaken door. "Miriam!"

That voice? Can it be?

Grabbing a candlestick, she started for the door, but Sir Tormond cut her off, blocking her way. "Nae, milady." He drew his sword. "Let me deal with this late-night ruffian."

Miriam laughed. "This is no ruffian."

Careful of his sword, she pushed past Tormond. She gathered her skirts in her free hand and dashed to the front door. She set the candlestick on a small table, pulled the bolt, and flung the door wide.

And there he was. In the doorway. He looked disheveled and out of breath, as if he'd run the whole way from the tavern.

"Abram!" she cried. "What are you doing here?" She peered past him into the night. She grasped him by the arm and pulled him quickly inside, shutting and bolting the door behind them. She glanced out the window, expecting at any moment to hear the sounds of pursuing dogs or an angry mob. "Did ye run away?"

The tall, strong man took her hands in his. "No! I did not run away."

"Then why are you here? At night? He'll beat you for this! That beast! He'll horsewhip you!"

Abram shook his head, grinning from ear to ear. "No, my love. I'm free! Miriam, I'm free."

"But you have four years yet to serve. How is this possible?" In spite of her confusion, tears of joy spilled from her eyes.

He released her hand and dug in his shabby waistcoat pocket. He pulled out two pieces of paper, then held one in each hand. Both were torn along one edge in a jagged, irregular line. Carefully, he put the two jagged edges together, and they fit perfectly. "See, my love? Both halves of my indenture! My master gave me his half this very night. I ran all the way to show you! Now we can go to Pennsylvania, to Rabbi Levi, and be married! Not only that, but the master gave me *ten* pounds! He says there's more to come. A lot more. Five hundred pounds in all!"

As she gazed in wonder at the proof of Abram's freedom, she asked, "But why? Why would he do that?"

"It's a miracle!" Abram cried. "The Lord sent His angels, and now I am free." His eyes shifted, looking past her. He released one of her hands and pointed behind her. "And there they stand!"

Miriam whirled about. Her eyes focused on Tormond and Maebh. The lady held Tormond's arm and rested her head on his shoulder. And they were both grinning at Miriam and Abram. *Angels in disguise.* "You did this?"

"Yes!" Abram said. "Master Worthy said Sir Tormond and his lady purchased my freedom. Not only mine, but Rosy's and Katy's as well. We're all free."

Abram released her hand and strode toward Tormond and Maebh. He knelt and bowed his head. "Thank you, milord, milady. May the God of Abraham bless you."

Miriam approached and knelt beside her betrothed. "You truly are angels of God."

Tormond shook his head. "We are but His humble servants, milady."

Maebh smiled upon her. "As are ye, Miriam. As are ye a servant of God."

Miriam took Sir Tormond's hand and Lady Maebh's in each of hers and kissed them.

Then, casting propriety to the wind, she turned and threw her arms around Abram. After only a moment's hesitation on his part, she felt his strong arms around her.

And together they wept joyful tears.

✠·✠·✠

Obadiah Worthy wept bitter tears.

353

After the Templar and the Shield-maiden had come and gone, Obadiah sat alone in his tavern's deserted common room and drained his mug of ale.

"Vermin! The Executioner called me *vermin!*" He slammed the mug down on the table. "I am a *good* man! A servant of God! I have done nothing wrong! Nothing at all. God knows I have not!"

And Abby!

Abby had refused to allow him into her bed. And worst — *worst!* — of all, Rosy fled from his presence the instant he'd given her his half of her writ of indenture.

He rose and stomped over to the ale barrel, turned the tap handle, and poured himself yet another mug of his finest brew.

"She didn't even wait for the money!" He thought that if he assured her of the money, assured her of the thousand — thousand! — pounds, she'd have stayed. Stayed with him. *Now, I'll have to track the ungrateful bitch down just to give her the wretched money.*

It would take him weeks to obtain the bank notes to pay those ingrates.

The Council of Sergeants will be furious. They'll cast me out!

He drank another swig of the ale, then wiped the foam from his chin with his laced sleeve.

"No, they won't," he growled. "I know too many secrets." He pounded his fist on the table.

Then he sobbed. "I know too many secrets!" *They'll kill me if I reveal anything. Send the Executioner after me.*

And he'd do it too! "Lop off my bloody head, he would." He laid his head on the table, covering his neck with his hands as if to ward off the blow from the legendary Templar sword. "Vermin!" he sobbed.

He took another draft from his mug. As he lifted his gaze from the ale, his eyes peered into the kitchen and lit upon the door to Katy's room. The former slave was still in that small room, he was certain. *Katy's got nowhere else to go. Not yet.* The law demanded that manumitted slaves leave the colony, so, free or not, she couldn't leave until he arranged for her "safe escort" out of Virginia.

Katy will comfort me this night.

He stumbled toward Katy's door. Reaching it, he turned the knob and pushed.

But the door wouldn't budge.

Bolted? That bolt's only for my use. To keep Abby out.

He lifted his fist to pound on the door, to demand entrance. *How dare she? That black wench has no right to —*

She does now.

But Katy loves me. She didn't at first, but she does now. I know she does! She'll let me in. Comfort me.

Obadiah then did something he'd never done before, never in all the years he'd known her — he *knocked* at Katy's door. "Katy," he cooed. "let me in, Katy."

"I got a pistol," came the reply. There was no anger in Katy's voice. Only firm resolution. "An' I got a knife. An' you never goin' to touch me again. An' if you do, that Sir Tormond — he says he'd make you one o' them eunuch-fellas wi' no nethers." She laughed — *laughed!* "That'd fix you real good, that would. Now, go 'way, 'less you got my money and my safe escort out o' this wicked place. Go be wi' your wife. Only, she won't have you no more, will she? No, she won't. Now, go 'way and leave me in peace."

"You're lying, Katy. You don't have a pistol or a knife."

She laughed again. "Oh, yes, I do, Obadiah Worthy! That Lady Maebh — she gave 'em to me. Afore she left. You try comin' in here, an' I'll shoot you first, then make you a eunuch-fella myself. You don' own me no more. I'm free! A free woman. An' the first thing I'm a-goin' to do when I get that money you a-goin' to give me is buy my li'l girl, my li'l Janie's freedom, from that Mistress Polly you sold her to. An' we a-goin' far 'way from you. And I'm a-goin' to tell Janie wha' a bad man her father is. What did Sir Tormond call you? Vermin. He told me that means a rat. That's wha' you are. A rat. Now, go. Afore I shoot this pistol right through the door. Maybe I'll aim low and shoot your nethers off myself."

"Damn you, Katy!"

"Uh-uh," came the voice through the door. "That Sir Tormond says you has to speak nice to me. Proper to me. I'm a free woman now. Not your kitchen whore."

"Please, Katy," he whined. "Please. I — I *need* you."

She laughed. "Well now, that's just too bad, ain't it?" She laughed again. And her laughter grew until, at last, Obadiah slunk away from her door.

He stumbled back to the common room. He sat at the table, took a long draft from his ale, then buried his face in his hands. And he sobbed.

"Why do you weep, Obadiah?" a honeyed voice asked.

He sat bolt upright.

And beheld a vision.

She floated above a table at the other end of the common room, radiant, clothed with light. With light and nothing else. No, she wore golden jewelry. Her black, finely coiffed hair was crowned with a recumbent, golden crescent moon, the points sticking up like the horns on a cow. Or a golden calf.

And she was beautiful beyond description. And desirable. So very desirable.

"Who are you?" he whispered.

She smiled. "I am Mary, Mother of God, Queen of Heaven."

Obadiah crossed himself. First, he crossed himself in the Anglican manner—up, down, left, then right, ending by touching the center of his chest. Then he crossed himself again—without touching his heart—as the secret Catholic he was. He gazed up at her with adoration. And lust. "Oh, Blessed Virgin!"

"I ask again, Obadiah, why do you weep? Tell me. Hold nothing back."

He told her. He told her everything. The words came pouring out of him in a torrent of anger, frustration, and despair. And when he was done pouring out his soul to her, he finished with a plea. "Oh, Blessed Mother, Forever Virgin! What shall I do?"

She looked upon him with tender, sympathetic eyes. "Tell me, Obadiah—do you *burn* for these women? For Katy and for Rosy?"

"Yes!"

"Do you burn for them with Holy Lust?"

Holy lust? But he nodded. "Yes! I burn! I *need*. But they are lost to me. Lost!"

"Yes, my son. They are lost to you. They have served their purpose. They led you into Holy Lust, and you took them against their will, at least the first time. That is the true way."

"The *true* way?"

"Oh, my son, it has ever been thus. I, who am Forever Virgin, may only be venerated by the sacrifice of virginity and the purging of purity. Is this not so?"

"I— Perhaps."

"'Perhaps?' Obadiah, do you doubt my holy word? Where is your faith?"

Obadiah shook his head and raised his hands in supplication. "I do not doubt! How may I serve Thee?"

She smiled, and Obadiah basked in the radiance of that smile. "Oh, my son, you have already served me well, though you knew it not. But I do have a task for you."

"Name it, Holy One!"

"The Executioner and the Shield-maiden. They vex me. They do not serve me as they should."

Hope flared in Obadiah. *If I slay them, I can get Katy back. Or another wench. All I must do is wait 'til they drink the wine and sleep . . .* "Do you wish me to slay them?"

The vision's eyes darkened. "No! Their deaths would not satisfy me. I must have them. They must serve me." Her lips twisted in anger. "And they will."

"How, Blessed One? How will they be made to serve Thee?"

"The Executioner must *take* his pure Shield-maiden! If not by force, then they must both be so consumed with lust, with *Holy Lust*, that they break their vows of *chastity*."

That last word had been spoken with such loathing, such rage, it frightened Obadiah. "But the Executioner would never do that."

"Oh, he will, my son. He will. He will if they remain together long enough. It will not happen here, in this place, in this time, in this century, but it *will* happen. It is the way of those clothed in *flesh*." She said the word with a mixture of longing and contempt. "I do not care if it takes another *thousand* years, I can wait. I care not what Cernunnos desires. They must remain alive and together until they succumb." She grinned, and there was nothing beautiful in that predatory smile.

"Cernu— Who?"

She shook her head and waved a dismissive hand. "It matters not." Her beatific smile returned. "And so, Obadiah, my faithful son,

357

I have a task for you. Perform this task, and you shall find other women with which to venerate me, and your business will prosper. It shall prosper tenfold."

Other women? Tenfold? He felt as if could already count the gold and feel the soft flesh under his hands. "How may I serve Thee, Holy Mother?"

"You shall seek out other members of your order, other Sergeants of the Temple, and I shall visit them. Many of them served me in the past. But the Executioner slaughtered them. He slaughtered them in my own temple."

Obadiah nodded. "The massacre in Wales! In the fifteenth century."

She nodded. "Yes. I can see that you understand. You are clever and wise, Obadiah Worthy. That slaughter set me back generations, centuries. It takes time to find those who will embrace the *true* worship. But with your help, my son, more and more of your brother Sergeants shall serve me in the future. And when the Executioner and the Shield-maiden surrender, when they are consumed with Holy Lust, when they fall, then at last, I shall rise above all the others. Above Cernunnos and Baal and Molech. Even above that bitch Lilith herself! I shall be greater even than Lu —" Her voice cut off, and she gazed down at Obadiah, with eyes that were suddenly soft and alluring. "Will you serve me, Obadiah? Will you swear to me by your head?"

"YES!" he cried, his entire frame trembling in religious fervor. "By my head, I will serve Thee!"

"Blessed are you, my son. Here is what you must teach your brethren . . ."

Chapter 31

Placentia, Colony of Newfoundland: September 9th, 1775 A.D.

The Mother!" Tormond bellowed, though Maebh could barely hear him above the blasting wind. He pointed at the woman fleeing down the beach.

The woman in front of them clutched at her veil and hat with both hands as the mighty wind threatened to rip her covering away. As she dashed through the village of Placentia, heedless of how the storm whipped at her skirts, she turned her head to look back at Maebh and Tormond, appeared to stumble, then pressed on along the beach and toward the fort on the peninsula at the mouth of the harbor — Fort Frederick.

Tormond gripped Maebh's right hand so firmly it hurt as he dragged her along in pursuit of their quarry. But Maebh had no intention of letting go. She was certain that, if she did, the gale would knock her to the ground. She was surprised the woman they were following was able to keep her feet in the wind.

Why the veil? Maebh thought as she clutched Tormond's arm as well as his hand. Maebh's own bonnet had long ago flown away into the storm. Tormond's tricorn hat had been lost as well. *But this woman clings to her veil as if her very life depends on it.*

Perhaps it does.

Or perhaps she simply prizes her anonymity?

Could this truly be she? Could this truly be one of the Witches? The Mother?

The Sergeant in St. John's had described the Witch just so — a disfigured woman who never was seen abroad without her hat and veil. By the time Tormond and Maebh arrived in St. John's, Newfoundland — the colonial capitol — the Witches had already slaughtered their acolytes and harvested the magic fruit of their horrible, life-devouring tree. The Witches had only to flee to their refuge—wherever that might be—take a bite from the fruit, and sleep for the next sixty years. The Witches had apparently escaped. Again.

And so, once more thwarted in their mission, Tormond and Maebh journeyed to the other side of Newfoundland to fulfill yet another of Marcus's prophecies. There in the town of Placentia, they awaited the foretold sign—the arrival of the very maelstrom through which they stumbled—and that day, Tormond spied the veiled woman.

The running woman's wind-whipped hair—what they could see of it, trailing from under her hat—was honey brown. And her dress was of expensive green silk, though without the fashionable wide-hipped paniers or bustle. She was slight of build, unthreatening in any obvious way. These physical characteristics, combined with the veil, made the woman fit the Sergeant's description exactly.

But what is one of the Witches doing here, in this small fishing village? And where are the other two? The Maiden and the Crone? It makes no sense!

She can't be the Mother. She can't.

But what if she is? Maebh's heart began to pound faster. *Could it be she? Could this all be over soon?*

But this cannot be "the top of the mountains." That is where the sacred mission will end. That is what the prophecy says.

That is where Tormond will finally be ready to forsake his vows and marry me.

But first, we must survive this wretched storm!

"Tormond!" Maebh shouted. "We must seek shelter! The storm!"

"Nae!" he cried. "'Tis the Mother! The Witch, I tell ye!"

A sudden, more powerful gust struck them, and Maebh nearly fell. Only Tormond's strength kept her upright. But even as Maebh stumbled, she saw the woman's hat and veil fly away into the wind. Even through the storm, Maebh could hear the woman's scream.

The woman clutched at the wind, but the hat was far out of reach, flying over the harbor. Then she turned toward them.

When Maebh saw the woman's unveiled face, her breath caught in her throat.

One side of the face was normal, perhaps pretty. The other side was lifeless, dead.

The Mother!

Releasing Maebh's hand, Tormond drew his sword. In defiance of the howling storm, Tormond shouted a Templar battle hymn. "Crucem sanctam subiit —"

The Witch wheeled and fled.

Tormond charged forward, ripping his arm free from Maebh's grasp.

Maebh tried to follow, but she was barely able to keep upright against the wind. She stumbled. The wind caught her skirts like a sail and heaved her into the air. She screamed as she flew above the beach, then over the churning water of the harbor.

And as suddenly as she had been lifted into the air, Maebh fell. She drew a breath to scream. She struck the water hard, and the air was driven from her lungs. Water engulfed her. She kicked, her legs tangling in her skirts. She clawed toward the dim light above, toward the air. *Air!* For just a moment, she clenched her mouth against the crushing need to inhale, but her mouth opened of its own volition. Salt water flooded past her lips, down her throat, into her burning lungs. Her body spasmed once. Twice.

Darkness swallowed her.

✠·✠·✠

Maebh's first awareness was of pain — her lungs burned.

Warm lips encircled her mouth.

Air, blessed air filled her lungs.

Then the lips were gone.

She choked, then vomited saltwater.

Her nose was pinched shut by strong fingers. The lips returned. More air was forced into her burning lungs.

The lips were gone once more.

She was breathing. It was as if she could not remember how to breathe, as if she had never truly known how to breathe. But for that moment, breathing was all that mattered.

But it hurt. Her lungs still burned.

The wind howled around her. Rain beat against her face, against her body.

She opened her eyes. All was gray and blurred as if she had forgotten that color existed. But as she breathed — ragged, searing breath after ragged, searing breath — slowly the colors returned, and her vision resolved, clarified into a face.

Tormond's face — and his face bore an expression she had never seen there before — terror.

"Tor —" Her throat burned. "Tormond?"

His terror melted away, transforming into joy. "Ye're alive! Thanks be to God!" He crossed himself and closed his eyes. "I thank Thee, Most Holy Father! Oh, how I thank Thee!" His eyes opened again. "Ye stay right there!" he shouted. "Dinnae move. Just breathe! I'll be but a moment." He stood.

"No," she croaked. "Don't leave me."

But he was gone.

She lay on the beach, drawing painful, welcome, precious breaths. For the moment, breathing was all she could do. Breathing and waiting.

She counted each burning breath while he was away. *One. Two. Three...*

By the time she got to twenty-two, he returned, fastening his double-wrapped sword belt at his waist.

He laid aside his sword. To save me.

He was coatless, but still wore his waistcoat. He was shoeless, and one of his stockings was missing. The ribbon tying his hair back was gone as well, so his blond locks hung in a loose dripping curtain around his face. He was soaked and bedraggled from his head to his one-sock-off-one-sock-on toes.

And she had never seen a bonnier sight.

He knelt at her side, and his face split in a grin. "Still breathing, are ye?"

Somewhere she found the strength to smile back at him. "Aye."

"Then let's get ye someplace safe. Or safer." He scooped her up in his arms, then carried her through the wind and the rain, up from the beach, toward the higher ground of the village. Leviathan waves, more than twenty feet high, rose from the harbor and crashed on the strand. Each wave threatened to smash upon them and drag them back into the water.

Tormond struggled forward, but his progress was tortuously slow as he fought against the wind. It seemed he was making his way toward the fort the Witch had been running to — before Maebh was cast into the deep.

A wave smote them from behind, knocking Tormond to his knees. But he did not let go of her. With a barely audible roar, he lurched to his feet once more, still carrying her.

"Put me down!" she yelled, though it burned her raw throat. "I can walk!" She wasn't certain she could, but she couldn't bear the thought of Tormond's being swept out to sea, of his drowning. Like her.

He didn't respond. He simply staggered forward, step by painful step. The wind repeatedly caught him, then he stumbled and resumed his push forward.

"Put me down, Tormond MacDonald!"

He shook his head, a look of grim determination on his rain-spattered face. "Nae!" he roared. "I will ne'er let ye go! Ne'er again!"

She put her arms around his neck and clung to him — that and breathing took all the strength she could muster. She felt utterly helpless.

No. I am not helpless. He can carry me and fight the storm, but I can pray.

God, grant Tormond the strength to gain the safety of the fort. Don't let him die because of me.

On he struggled as the hurricane hammered at them, step by step, foot by foot. The water covered the ground, rising as Tormond splashed forward.

After what felt like an hour — but was probably considerably less — the walls of the fort appeared before them, looming black out of the blinding rain and sea spray.

Tormond fought his way toward the wooden gate on the southern end of the fort. Maebh squinted into the gale, attempting to pick out the smaller sally port in the midst of the gate. A new fear seized her. *Will there be anyone to man the gate? To open and let us in?*

She spied the sally port — a black hole in the darkness of the gate — but she needn't have worried about the door's being closed. The small door was gone, ripped from its hinges — another casualty of the storm.

As Tormond carried her through the doorway and splashed into the ankle-deep water in the bailey — the fort's courtyard — the wind howled and whistled after them as if the storm were furious at their escape, enraged by its own impotence to reach down and carry them away. But once Tormond and Maebh were inside the protective walls, the wind followed them no more. Though the hurricane bellowed, its winds were powerless to touch them so long as the fortress walls stood. The rain still pelted them, but at least it fell straight down from the sky, rather than sideways.

Tormond carried her toward a wall where a cluster of women and children — refugees from the storm — huddled, sitting in the water. There was no place to sit that was not submerged. Gently, he laid her on the ground, a dozen feet away from the group of refugees, propping her back against the stone of the wall. The water there was not as high — only an inch or so deep. Tormond stood and stripped off his drenched waistcoat and shirt. He knelt once more and wrapped sodden garments across her legs.

My legs! For the first time since she'd been brought back from the dead, Maebh realized she was clad only in her shift from the waist down. Gone were her wide skirts, petticoats, and the framework of paniers and bustle over her hips and backside — probably all lost at the bottom of the harbor. Even her shift had been ripped to mid-thigh.

"I apologize, milady," Tormond said, "for they'll nae keep ye dry. But 'tis all I have to give. At least they'll cover ye." But Maebh didn't care one whit about his rain-drenched garments or her bare legs — everyone and everything in the courtyard was exposed to the rain. Instead, her eyes were drawn to his bare, muscular chest and his mighty arms. He was shaped like an ancient — and very nude — Greek statue of Hercules she'd seen when they'd visited a museum in London in 1715. However, Tormond was not fashioned from cold, chiseled stone. He was flesh. Warm, living flesh.

Heat rose in her cheeks, but she could not make herself look away. "I'm" — she swallowed, heedless of the rawness of her throat — "I'll be fine. Thank ye."

He drew his dagger and placed the weapon in her hand. Then he stood. "I'll be back," he shouted above the howl of the wind raging overhead as he removed his remaining stocking. "Breathe, lassie. Just ye go on breathing. Can ye do that for me?"

Panic gripped her. "Where are ye going?"

His face hardened into a scowl. "Hunting." He drew his sword, then pivoted on his bare feet and splashed off into the rain.

No! Don't go out there again!

But he did not head for the gate. He went to the group of women and examined each face, then he moved on, disappearing into the sheets of rain.

The rainwater bombarding her was warm, but she shivered. *What magical powers does the Witch have? How does she protect herself? How can she harm Tormond? Can she strike him down with witchcraft?*

Merciful God, protect him!

I thank Thee for Thy preserving power that has delivered me from the storm, from the sea. Please deliver Tormond from the power of the Witch.

Maebh clutched the dagger to her chest in both hands. *God, please preserve him. Please. He left his quarry in order to save me. He saved my life.*

He is my life.

Please protect him.

At least the soldiers know him—know Sir Tormond. E'en without his shirt, they'll know his sword. They'll not attack him as he searches the fort.

I hope.

Please protect him!

As she waited in the deluge, she thought of the prophecy that had brought them to Placentia.

In pleasure in a newfound land shall the Executioner and the ever-faithful shield-maiden find their prey in the midst of the whirlwind. She shall drown in the depths. He shall lay aside his sword and he shall close her nose and breathe life into her cold lips. And he shall raise the dead. And thus shall he preserve his own heart.

Branwen interpreted the prophecy aright, at least so far as the place and the storm were concerned, Maebh thought, for thinking and shivering—and breathing—were all she could do. *She wrote that when the French established this town, they named it* Plaisance — *which means "pleasure" in the French, she said — and this is the Newfoundland.*

But Branwen thought — and we thought as well — that the "she" who would drown would be one of the Witches. None of us could conceive why Tormond would breathe life into the Witch's cold lips or raise her from the dead. But 'twas not her.

'Twas I.

I, myself — I am his own heart. In spite of the rain and the wind, warmth spread through Maebh. *I am Tormond's heart.*

As he is mine.

She grinned. *Tormond kissed me. Oh, aye, 'twas not a proper kiss. But his lips were upon my mouth.*

Perhaps I shall tease him about it.

But she shook her head. *No. No teasing. 'Twould cause him to perform some ridiculous penance. I'll not do that to him.*

She peered into the storm, looking for any sign of her beloved. *God, please save him from the Witch!* She gripped his dagger all the tighter as if holding his life in her hands. *Bring him safely back to me.*

The water inside the fort rose steadily. It was almost to her waist. Outside the fort, every building they'd passed had been partially submerged. She thought of the horses stabled in the village. *They must be terrified. If the water be rising here and 'tis lower there . . .*

Father in Heaven, while Thou art a-protecting Tormond, please comfort Fiona and Órd Dubh. They have been faithful steeds. 'Twould break Tormond's heart were he to lose Órd Dubh, and mine if I lost Fiona. Keep them safe. Please don't let them drown.

Please keep Tormond safe. A whimper broke past her trembling lips. *Please bring him back to me.*

She released the dagger with her right hand, just long enough to cross herself. *In Jesus' name. Amen.*

Then she clutched the dagger — Tormond's sacred dagger — in both hands.

And she waited and watched.

After what seemed an eternity, Tormond finally reappeared, emerging from the curtain of rain. He had sheathed his sword. He removed his sword belt, and sat in the water beside her, his back against the wall and the sheathed sword across his knees.

"Did ye find her?" Maebh shouted, but from his grim expression she could divine the answer.

He shook his head, the rain streaming down his bearded face. "She is nae here. I searched every room, every face. Even if she had changed her clothes — or donned men's clothes — there could be nae hiding that face."

Maebh shuddered at the memory of the hideous, half-dead countenance. "She has escaped again."

He nodded. Then he inhaled and let the breath out through clenched teeth. "But this be nae the prophesied place, aye?"

"No." *Not "the top of the mountains."* She laid a trembling hand on Tormond's bare arm. His flesh was so warm, at least compared to her own. How she longed for him to enfold her in his mighty arms and hold her to his bare chest. "But don't worry. That day will come."

He nodded. Then he looked at her and he grinned. "Aye. 'twill come. Some day. Some century."

She shivered.

"Are ye warm enough?" he asked. Then he growled. "I'm an idiot! Ye must be near tae freezin'!" He reached his arm behind her and pulled her to his side.

She shivered again, though not entirely from the effects of the weather.

He laid his sword aside, in the water, then put an arm under her knees. He lifted her into his lap and wrapped one arm around her. Then he retrieved his sword and sword belt from the water. "Hold this for me, lass."

She took the weapon and belt and held them to her chest.

He wrapped his other arm around her.

He held her, and in spite of the storm — or perhaps because of it — she melted into his embrace, laying her head on his shoulder.

And together they waited out the hurricane.

A part of her wanted the storm to never cease.

When at last the winds died down a bit — enough for them to talk without shouting — and the flood no longer seemed to be rising, Maebh asked the question that had plagued her since she'd awakened with Tormond's lips around her mouth, since he'd breathed life back into her. "Tormond?"

"Aye?"

"Why? Why did ye do it?"

"Do what?"

"Ye had the Witch in your sights. Ye could have killed her, fulfilled your sacred mission."

"*Our* sacred mission," he corrected.

She could not help but smile. "Why did ye let her go?"

"Hush now, lassie. Dinnae fash yerself 'bout it."

"Please, Tormond. Why?"

He sighed, and for a long moment, it seemed as if he might not answer. But at last, he said, "I had to choose. I could pursue the prey, or I could save ye, lass. I could nae do both. And for me, there was only e'er one choice. I chose *ye*, lassie." He gently kissed her forehead, making her shiver anew. "I will *always* choose ye, Maebh O Broin. Always."

✠·✠·✠

Giuseppe was at the end of his strength. The iron shackle around his ankle and the chain to which it was attached pulled at him. At the other end of the chain, below him, in the water — *No! I will not think of it. It is too horrible.*

He clung to the broken mast. It was all that was keeping him afloat. But soon his arms would fail him, and he'd slip beneath eerily calm waters of the harbor. He'd tried to push toward the shore, kicking with his free leg. Oh, how he'd tried! And the beach was no more than twenty yards away. But the distance might as well have been a mile. Giuseppe could not move, could not make the slightest progress toward the shore, because of the frightful anchor that at any moment would pull him down to a watery grave.

Please, Saint Elmo, he prayed to the patron saint of sailors, *please help me. Help me make it to land.*

But the saint had not heard his prayers.

Giuseppe prayed all through the storm — when he wasn't struggling simply to keep his head above water — ever since The Hungry Seamaid was smashed upon the rocks by the hurricane. Ever since he and Luciano fell into the roiling waters. He prayed, but no answer, no miracle had come.

Luciano prayed too. But Luciano sank beneath the waves and didn't resurface. And now Luciano threatened to drag him into the depths like some mermaid of legend, dragging sailors to their doom.

Soon it will all be over. Soon I shall drown, and my Bianca shall weep for me. O Blessed Elmo! If only I could see her face once more. I would never dream of going to sea again. I would settle down and be the cobbler she always wanted me to be.

Saint Paula, help my Bianca. Send her another husband to care for her, for I shall never return. And we shall never be wed.

He closed his eyes. "O Blessed Jesu!" he cried aloud, though it was no more than a croak. "Save me!"

Something gripped his arm—something wet and very strong. *A mermaid! Come to take me.* He almost welcomed the thought of surrender.

"I've got ye, laddie," the mermaid said—though her voice sounded nothing like Giuseppe had ever imagined. The voice was deep, masculine. A *merman?*

Giuseppe opened his eyes. A naked man—at least he was naked where Giuseppe could see—pulled his arm. The man hauled Giuseppe's arm across his bare shoulder. "I've got ye. Can ye hold me 'bout the neck? I'll need my arms to get us back to shore."

"Hold you? Back to shore?" Hope exploded in Giuseppe's chest. He nodded. "Si! Yes."

His blond-headed savior, said, "Good lad." The man turned around in the water, still holding onto Giuseppe's arm. With his back to Giuseppe, the man said, "With both yer arms now, laddie."

Giuseppe obeyed. With newfound strength, he locked his hands together in front of the swimmer's throat.

"Good lad." The man raised one arm out of the water and waved. "Dinnae choke me, lad."

On the shore, a woman waved back. She stood next to a massive black horse.

"Hold on tight, laddie," his rescuer said.

The two of them lurched forward.

Giuseppe yelped in surprise and terror, but then he saw what was gripped in the man's hands.

A rope!

Giuseppe looked to the shore. The woman was leading the horse away, and the rope — the blessed rope! — was attached to the retreating animal's saddle.

Tears of joy streamed down Giuseppe's face. "Blessed Elmo! I thank thee!"

Giuseppe heard laughter. *The man is laughing?*

"Thank God, not some Turkish martyr. Give thanks to God, laddie."

Forward they sped, the shore coming ever nearer.

His rescuer rose from the water, carrying Giuseppe with him. *Land! We are on land!*

The man released the rope, then turned and hauled Giuseppe to the beach.

Giuseppe could not walk. His leg was yet bound, and the chain dragged behind him.

His rescuer carried him forward as if he weighed nothing, then the man laid Giuseppe on the beach.

Giuseppe glanced behind.

At the end of the chain, Luciano's corpse lay at the edge of the water, his dead face staring up sightlessly at the darkening sky.

"Ye are safe now," his rescuer said. The man stood beside him, then gazed back toward the body. "Yer friend's dead, aye?"

Giuseppe nodded, panting as he lay on the beach. *He's not surprised at all. As if he knew Luciano would be there.* "Yes. Dead."

Giuseppe heard footsteps approaching, squelching in the wet sand. He turned his head and beheld the woman. From the waist up, she was clad in a proper bodice with half sleeves ending in bedraggled lace. But from the waist down, she was covered only in what appeared to be a sodden man's shirt tied about her waist. Her legs were bare below the knees. She led the great, black horse with one hand and in the other she held tools — a hammer and a chisel!

She released the horse's reins, and said a word in a tongue Giuseppe did not recognize.

The horse tossed its head, but stood still.

She then gave the hammer and chisel to the man.

"Find me a stone, lass," the rescuer said, kneeling beside Giuseppe. "Or a piece of wood. As big as ye can carry." The man was not completely naked — he wore dark knee-britches, but nothing else.

The woman grinned. "I have one ready, Tormond."

"Tormond?" Giuseppe asked his rescuer. "Is that your name?"

The man grinned. "Aye. Tormond MacDonald." He inclined his head toward the woman, who was returning, laboriously carrying a stone as large as her head. "And that be the Lady Maebh O Broin."

The woman set the heavy stone down near Giuseppe's shackled ankle. She smiled at him, and it seemed to Giuseppe that the sun itself shone in her countenance. "And your name is Joseph, is it not?"

Giuseppe gasped. *How could she know?* "You are the angels of God!"

She laughed—a very pretty sound. "Oh, no. We are but His servants. Ye are Joseph, aye?"

"Si. Giuseppe. Joseph."

Tormond lifted Giuseppe's foot and placed it on the stone. He positioned the chisel at the lock holding the shackle closed. He raised the hammer. "I'll have this off ye in a moment, lad." He struck the chisel with a mighty blow, and the lock shattered. In another moment, Giuseppe was free—and no longer chained to the corpse.

He stared at his torn and bleeding ankle. And then his eyes fell upon Luciano's pale body.

"What was his name?" the lady asked.

Giuseppe gaped first at her, then at Tormond, with wide eyes. "You don't know?"

Tormond looked at him with a blank expression and shrugged. "Why would we? We were sent to pull *ye* from a watery grave. God sent us to find *ye*, nae that poor wretch, more's the pity."

God sent you? To save me? "His name was" —he shuddered— "Luciano. He and I . . . We were struck over the head. I-in New York. Pressed into service aboard a merchant ship."

Tormond nodded, then growled, and his eyes seemed to burn with a cold, blue fire. "Aye. Slaves, ye were. Chained together during the storm, nae doubt, so ye would nae try tae escape." He shook his head. "Some things ne'er change. Nae in five centuries."

Five centuries?

"Ye must be hungry," the lady said. "And thirsty. There's food at the fort. And beer, but I doubt there's fresh water to be had anywhere in the village."

"Thank you," Giuseppe replied. "Thank you for saving me."

"Non nobis, Domine," Lady Maebh said. "Non nobis. Sed nomini tuo da gloriam."

Giuseppe stared at her mutely.

She grinned. "And here I thought a good Catholic lad such as yourself would understand the Latin. Give the glory to *God*, Joseph, not to us."

"Now, laddie," Tormond said, standing. He bent and offered a hand to Giuseppe.

Giuseppe took the hand, and the man hauled Giuseppe to his feet.

"Here now, laddie, put yer arm across my shoulders, and I'll help ye back to the fort. We'll get ye food and drink and warm clothes." He chuckled. "I could use some warm clothes myself."

The lady picked up the hammer and chisel, then took the reins of the great horse. The beast had waited obediently the entire time, precisely where she'd left him. "And as soon as may be," she said, "after ye've recovered from your ordeal, we'll arrange passage for ye back to — Where did ye say? New York?"

Giuseppe could only nod in reply.

She nodded as well, grinning. "New York, then. For ye must return to your Bianca. Ye must settle yourself and marry her and never return to sea."

Giuseppe gaped at her. "How do know this? Did God tell you?"

"Aye," Tormond replied. "Ye shall have a son, Joseph, and from his line — aye, from *yer* line — shall come a hero. Come. Let's go."

Supported by Tormond, Giuseppe began to limp forward. "A hero?"

"Aye," Tormond replied. "A warrior for God. A true servant of the Lord, Joseph Cavetto. And his name shall be Todd."

Chapter 32

Philadelphia County, Commonwealth of Pennsylvania: 1778 A.D.

Órd Dubh's muzzle nudged Tormond's hand, ripping the Templar from his magic slumber. The warhorse reared back and screamed.

Clad in mail and tabard, the Templar rolled off the wooden bed and onto the cave floor. "Who goes there?" he cried even as he leaped to his feet, his sword and dagger at the ready.

In the cave, a lantern shone, held by a man wearing a hooded cloak. The intruder wielded a wicked-looking yellow dagger that gleamed as if made of gold.

Órd Dubh reared to attack the invader. The man jumped back and slashed with the golden blade, barely missing the warhorse's flank.

"Órd Dubh!" Tormond commanded. "*Air ais!*"

The horse snorted, stamped, but obediently backed off, safely out of the reach of the intruder's weapon.

Tormond set his feet, ready to charge. "Who are ye?" he demanded. "Speak now or die!"

The hooded figure laughed, and that laughter filled the cave, echoing and reechoing like the cries of the damned. He lowered his lantern to the cave floor, lighting his face from below. His shadow grew against the far wall of the cave. It continued to grow long after he'd set the lamp down. And as it grew, the shadow's head sprouted horns like the antlers of a stag.

The horned shadow grew until there was only the darkness and the single point of lantern light. The shadow enveloped Tormond, smothering him, crushing him, sapping his strength. Tormond couldn't breathe, and his heart thundered in his chest. The sword and the dagger became heavy — too heavy to hold. The mail dragged him down. He was certain it would pull him to his knees at any moment.

Maebh. Must protect Maebh. Tormond clutched at that thought, even as he clung to his weapons and forced himself to stay upright by sheer force of adamant will.

"Who am I?" the hooded man cried in a booming voice. "I am John Fleming, High Priest of Cernunnos, the Horned God! Promised Consort to the Three—the Maiden, Mother, and Crone—whom you have hunted through the centuries. I am your death!"

Tormond felt a hand on his sword arm, pulling at him. With great effort, he looked to his right. Maebh clung to him with her left hand. In her trembling right hand, she held her pistol, aiming it unsteadily at the intruder. Tormond heard the click of the trigger, saw the spark as the flint struck steel—

But there was no flash, no booming crack. The weapon had misfired.

The intruder laughed again. "Your powder's too wet, you silly strumpet! You've been in this cave too long." He laughed soft and low. "But *my* powder is dry." As if he were in no hurry at all, the hooded man sheathed the golden dagger, then drew from inside his cloak a brace of pistols. "I can still put the nooses around your necks, smite you on your heads, then slit your throats *after* I shoot you in the guts. And you will let me do it. All of it. You are powerless." He cackled. "Even now, you are so overcome with terror, you cannot fight back. You cannot move, can you, Christian swine?"

Tormond felt his knees trembling. Any moment, he would fall. And if he fell, Maebh would be undefended. It was true—the terror was nigh overwhelming. But it was not a fear of the horned shadow or his priest or even of Tormond's own death. No, it was the thought that Maebh might perish as well.

"No!" Tormond snarled. "In Jesus' name"—he panted with the exertion of forcing words from his lips—"I adjure ye, demon. I . . . cast ye out."

The High Priest of Cernunnos threw back his head and roared with laughter. "You have no authority, no power to command my god! There is none on earth who can command Cernunnos! He is the Lord of Life Everlasting, Master of the Tree of Life and Death." He aimed one pistol at Tormond's gut, the other in Maebh's direction. "You cannot so much as lift your weapon against me."

Tormond lost his grip on the sword. It fell to the cave floor, ringing as it struck the limestone.

God, he prayed silently, *give me strength! And courage.* He shifted the too-heavy dagger from his left hand to his right, gripping the blade with fingers and thumb that felt cold and lifeless. *He's but twenty feet away. God, guide my arm. O Blessed Jesus!*

Tormond staggered forward. Even as he stumbled, he used the momentum to pull back his arm. With the last of his flagging strength, Tormond flung the dagger.

The dagger toppled end-over-end, then the point sunk deep into the intruder's left eye.

The man convulsed silently. His fingers jerked, and both his pistols fired.

Two shots boomed through the cave.

And then a third shot thundered.

Their attacker crumpled to the ground. He lay on his side, twitching with Tormond's dagger protruding from his skull.

A howl shook the cavern, as if some great beast of storm and shadow were bellowing out its rage and frustration.

The horned shadow vanished.

And suddenly Tormond could breathe once more.

Maebh!

He spun about, his strength returning. She was on the floor, but she was getting up, rising to her feet. Her useless pistol lay beside her.

That third shot! Where did it come from?

Tormond turned toward the still-twitching body. Blood flowed from a hole, the size of a chicken's egg, in the man's chest. *'Tis an exit wound. He was shot from behind.*

Tormond's eyes searched the cavern, even as he quickly picked up his fallen sword. "Who goes there?" he called. "Show yerself!"

From behind the massive skull of some strange and ancient beast, a human figure rose, then stepped into the lantern light. His weapon was lowered, and since it had just been fired, Tormond knew the single-barreled pistol would be no threat. The newcomer also wore a cloak, but without a hood. Atop his head sat a tricorn hat.

The man raised both hands above his head, along with the expended firearm. But with his left hand, he touched thumb to forefinger, extending the other three fingers. He slowly lowered the hand to his forehead, then tilted the hand slightly.

The Templar Salute!

"I am a Sergeant of the Temple," the man said, his voice calm and even. "My name is Peter Johnson."

Tormond sheathed his sword and growled. "Ye could nae have come a moment sooner, laddie?"

Maebh joined Tormond, taking hold of his elbow.

"Apologies, Templar, Shield-maiden," the Sergeant said. "I followed him into the cave" — he pointed at the no-longer-moving corpse — "but I had no light. I couldn't carry one, lest he see me following."

"Ye came just in the very nick of time," Maebh said. "We are in your debt."

The man swept off his tricorn hat, exposing a balding head. He bowed low. "It is my honor to serve God and the Temple." He walked slowly toward the corpse. "But I don't think 'twas my ball that killed him." He knelt and removed the dagger from the dead man's eye socket. He cleaned the weapon on the self-proclaimed High Priest's cloak, then gazed at the knife in awe. "The sacred dagger!" he said breathily. Still on his knees, he turned, bowed his head, and presented the dagger to Tormond. "Your weapon, Executioner."

Tormond took the dagger and sheathed it. "Thank ye, Sergeant. But please dinnae kneel to me. I'm neither a king nor a saint."

Peter Johnson stood. He eyed them both with joy. "I never thought I'd live to meet the Executioner of God! At least, not awake. Or the Shield-maiden of Christ! It is such a great honor. A-a-and a joy." He clasped a hand to his heart. "It is a miracle . . . I never dreamed . . ."

Tormond almost smiled at the man's enthusiasm, but this was not a time for rejoicing. *Might as well get it over with, aye?* "What be the year?"

The Sergeant's countenance fell. He swallowed. "1778. This is only the third year since . . ."

"1778?" Maebh cried. "No. No. No! We're fifty-seven years too soon!" She let go of Tormond's arm and slogged over to the wooden bed. She plopped herself down and sat dejectedly on the edge of the bed. "Fifty-seven. Not again!" She buried her head in her hands and wept, her unbound brown hair shrouding her face like a mourning veil.

"Aye," Tormond growled. He wanted to go to her, to comfort her in her despair. And to be comforted in his own. Instead, he focused on the Sergeant who stood with his head down, rotating his tricorn hat in his hands. "How did ye happen to be here, laddie? In the very nick of time, as Lady Maebh said?"

Peter shook his head. "But I *wasn't* in time! It was your dagger that slew him. I would've been too late."

Tormond resisted the urge to growl in his frustration. *Answer the question, man!* "Why were ye here at all, Sergeant?"

The Sergeant averted his eyes, suddenly appearing uncomfortable.

He just happens to follow an acolyte of the Witches? Follows him into the very cave where we are sleeping? "Answer me, Sergeant."

"It's the war." Peter sounded as if he were apologizing. He glanced at the corpse.

"War, aye?" Tormond shook his head slowly. *The rumors of rebellion in the colonies.* "So, 'tis come to that."

Peter nodded. "There is an army in winter quarters nearby. On your very doorstep. In Valley Forge." He grimaced. "When we selected this cave, we had no idea they'd encamp this close." He resumed turning his hat with shaking hands. "We've been keeping watch, to be sure you'd be safe. It has been difficult, what with the *Continental* Army so close."

In spite of the man's discomfort, Tormond had noted the contempt the Sergeant had given the word. "*Continental* Army, ye say? Is the whole continent at war then? And on which side of the war be this Continental Army? For the king? Or for the rebels?"

"Not the *whole* continent. From the Maine in the north—which is part of Massachusetts, if you didn't know—down to Georgia in the south. The Continentals, as they call themselves, are with the rebels."

And from the sound of it, ye are with the king.

"But," the Sergeant continued, "it's not much of an army. Washington—that'd be the rebel general—and he's not really a general, but rather a farmer playing soldier—has barely twelve thousand men. His Majesty King George has fifteen thousand well-trained troops in Philadelphia alone, and tens of thousands more elsewhere. The d-damned rebels are barely clothed, p-poorly armed, and starving. In the spring, the king's forces will crush them, I tell you, and George Washington . . . will be hanging from a gibbet." He shook his head. "That's if the Continentals"—his speech had slowed markedly—"if they manage to survive the winter." A violent tremor shook him, his breath steaming from his nostrils in the chill of the cave. "This is . . . the worst winter . . . I've ever seen!"

The Sergeant shuddered again, then blinked slowly as if he could scarcely keep his eyes open. "I . . . followed . . . that man . . ." His voice trailed off and he swayed as he stood.

Tormond reached out a hand and put it on the man's trembling shoulder. "Ye are soaked to the skin, laddie!"

For the first time since awakening, Tormond noticed the chill. With the excitement of mortal combat and the crushing disappointment of learning they'd been awakened early, the temperature hadn't yet truly touched him. But the Sergeant was freezing, quaking violently. Tormond said, "Ye need to get out of those wet clothes. Now."

"Nay," the man said, shivering more and more, "I feel . . ." A slow smile crept across his face. "I feel *warm*." He sank to his knees, then laid himself upon the limestone floor. "Rest. 'Sall I need. Sleep."

Tormond shivered, but not with the cold. *The man's in mortal peril!* He whirled about, retrieving his axe. "Maebh! Off the bed! Fetch our blankets."

Maebh leaped to her feet, racing to comply.

With the axe, Tormond set about hacking the bed to pieces. "Light the candle, lass."

"But the lamp?" In spite of her own question, Maebh lit the candle from the lamp's flame.

Between axe strokes, Tormond said, "Nae. I'll need the oil to start a quick fire." *But I thank ye, lass, for following my commands e'en when ye have reasonable questions.* He smote the bed again and snarled.

This wretched axe was made for hewing flesh and bone, nae wood. Aye, and this oak's so cursed hard!

Maebh returned with the lit candle, dripped some wax onto a rock, then set the candle in the solidifying wax. "The Sergeant—he's shivering so violently. I fear he may . . ."

Tormond continued hacking at the wood. "Aye. E'en with the oil tae start it, 'twill take a bit tae grow big enough tae warm him. If he goes tae sleep, he may ne'er wake again. *Ye* must do it."

"Me? Start the fire? But ye said—"

Tormond continued to hew the wood. "Nae, ye must *warm* him, or he'll die. Strip him of his wet clothes first."

Maebh's eyes were wide. "Strip him? Of his clothes?"

Tormond nodded. "Aye. Every stitch must come off. *Every* stitch, mind. If he resists, cut them off him. Then get him wrapped in the blankets. And be quick about it."

Without another word, Maebh set about her indelicate task.

Tormond could hear her as she urged, then pleaded with the Sergeant to remove his wet clothes. The man said nothing. A quick glance back showed Tormond that the fellow was unresponsive. A second glance, and he could see Maebh cutting the wet clothes away from the Sergeant with her dagger.

Ach! This wood is so stubborn! Break! Curse ye! Break!

God, give me the strength to hew this wretched oak! Keep the Sergeant alive.

He hacked at the bed until he had a small pile. *Enough to start a wee fire perhaps, but nae enough to feed it, to make it big enough.* He looked at Maebh—she was wrapping the naked, shivering man in the second blanket.

"He's all bundled up." Maebh's voice betrayed no emotion, no hint of embarrassment. "But he's so cold. How's the wood coming?"

"'Twill nae be in time tae save him."

"But what more can we do?"

May God and Maebh forgive me for what I must ask of her. "Ye must save him, Maebh. Ye must remove yer own clothes."

"*My* clothes?"

Tormond attacked the wood, putting all his anger, all his grief into his axe strokes. "Aye. Down tae yer shift. Yer shift be dry and thin enough as 'twill nae matter. But ye must strip down and get into the blanket with him. Keep him warm until I get the fire going. Then I'll take yer place in the blanket, and *ye* can tend the fire. Can ye do that, Maebh O Broin? Tae save his life?" Tormond didn't look at her. He didn't want to look at her, didn't want to see her pain. Instead, he focused his attention on the wood.

"Aye," she said, resolution strong in her voice. "That I can."

Thank ye, lass. Forgive me.

For a brief moment, he pictured her, nearly naked, wrapped in blankets with a nude man—another man—warming him with her body.

Tormond snarled as he hacked at the obstinate oak.

✠·✠·✠

"I come here to save your lives," Peter Johnson said, shaking his head, "and the two of you save mine." He shuddered, though not with the cold. He stole a guilty glance at the legendary Shield-maiden as she sat on the floor by the fire—on the opposite side from Peter. She was clothed again, wearing the same gown in which she'd awakened. Her luxurious brown hair was disheveled, but she was carefully working out the tangles with a tortoiseshell comb. *My, but she is a handsome woman!* he thought.

And to think I lay next to her, naked, with naught save her shift between us.

And I can't remember a bit of it.

More's the pity.

He shook his head. *I wouldn't know it had happened, if the Templar hadn't insisted on giving her the credit for saving me.*

Peter had awoken, wrapped in the arms of the nearly naked Executioner—the Templar was wearing only his smallclothes—rather than in the arms of the woman.

The Templar was also fully dressed once more. He sat next to the Shield-maiden as he read from a red, leather-bound book. He alternated between shaking his head and nodding. But he said nothing in response to Peter's words.

The Shield-maiden glanced at the Executioner. Then her eyes turned to Peter. *Such lovely, gray eyes.* She met Peter's gaze unflinchingly. Peter could find no hint of shame or humiliation in those haunting orbs. Only courage.

And kindness.

"Think nothing of it," she said. "Ye would have done the same for either of us." She smiled, and her smile stole his breath away. "As ye said, ye came here to protect us from yonder villain." She nodded her head in the direction of the corpse.

The Executioner had dragged the body well away from the fire, leaving a trail of blood on the limestone. When next the Templar and the Shield-maiden awoke, decades hence, John Fleming — High Priest of Cernunnos, Promised Consort of the Three Witches — would be nothing more than a pile of bones.

Yet another *pile of bones among so many.* The secret cave was littered with the bones of strange beasts. One of the skulls had once belonged to what must have been a massive beast with long tusks. Peter had once seen a drawing of an elephant in a book. On the great beast's back had been a man wearing a turban. This skull belonged to a beast several times that size.

"Thank ye," the Shield-maiden said, pulling Peter's gaze back. She continued to smile at him as she combed her long hair.

She is beautiful, but it's not simply her outward beauty, is it? The beauty of face and figure, yes, but it's more than that. It's her smile, her courage, her kindness.

Her unvarnished purity.

He smiled back.

She is not for you, Peter Johnson. You must remember that.

But how has he done it? How has the Templar resisted her charms all this time? He's not a saint. He's just a man.

"I think I've found it," the Executioner said, jabbing a finger into the red book. "The winter. We ne'er expected to be awake during a winter." The Shield-maiden leaned close to the Templar, reading where he indicated. "The rebellion. The farmer general."

The Shield-maiden and the Executioner locked eyes, and she said, "We were *supposed* to be awakened now." She stabbed her finger at the mysterious book. "Here. In this place. In this time." She smiled at the Templar.

The Executioner returned the smile. "We have a mission to fulfill."

Mission? What mission? Other than slaying the Witches? "What is that book? What does it say?"

She merely shook her head. "'Tis a gift from a dear friend."

"Dinnae fash yerself over it," the Executioner replied, closing the book.

What are they hiding? What's in that book?

"Are ye hungry, Sergeant?" she asked. "I'm afraid all we have are some apples, preserved in oil in wax-sealed bottles. They taste awful—like oil—but they're nourishing."

Peter shook his head. "No. My thanks, Shield-maiden, but no. They are for you."

"The biggest problem right now," the Templar said, rising, "is feeding the horses. I assume there be nae grass outside? Only snow and ice?"

Peter nodded. "I'll—" He could wear his shoes, even as wet as they were, but his clothes were rags now. He'd have to venture out clothed only in the blankets. *I'd be no worse off than those poor, deluded wretches the rebels call soldiers. Some of them don't have pants! At least, I'll have shoes.* "I'll go and get other men—other Sergeants. We'll return with hay and victuals." He extended a bare arm toward the fire, where the remnants of the bed were being consumed in the flames. "And wood. And candles. We'll have to sneak it in, on our backs, to get it past the Continental army—"

The Executioner laughed. "Nonsense, laddie. We'll accompany ye. I have some dry clothes that'll fit ye, and—"

"No!" Peter stood quickly. *That would be disaster!* "You mustn't leave the cave, mustn't go out."

"But why?" she asked. "Why would ye have us stay here?"

"There is a plague outside. Ravaging these colonies."

"A plague?" The Templar narrowed his eyes.

"Yes! It's called the smallpox! It's deadly to many. My sister's household contracted it. Three of them died. And those who survive—they are left scarred. And some go blind. The British army is protected—protected by God, it seems. They do not get the pox. But the Colonials—these colonies are being punished by God for their rebellion against King George. You must stay here."

"So, are we tae hide in this cave?" The Executioner asked. "Go back tae sleep? I say we must venture forth, man! We have something we must do."

"I understand, Brother Executioner." Peter did not understand. *Something they must do? Something they read in that book?* "But there is something I can do. I can protect you from the disease."

"How?" the Shield-maiden asked.

"It's called a variolation. A small cut is made in the skin. Then a thread that has been drawn through the opened pustule of an infected person is placed in the cut. You cover the incision with a piece of nutshell and bind the wound and—"

"Are ye daft, laddie?" The Templar looked at him as if Peter were indeed mad. "The pustule of an infected person? Ye mean the pox itself, aye? Ye mean tae place that in the wound?"

Peter nodded. "I know it sounds mad, but it is effective. Safe." *One person only has died due to the variolation, while thousands have been saved. But he did not tell the Templar or the Shield-maiden that.* "You will be sick with a fever for two days. You may develop a few pustules, but those are mild and do not leave a scar." The thought of such pustules or scars on the Shield-maiden's lovely face almost made him shiver again. "In as little as eight days, you will be as if you never had the disease." He drew the woolen blanket down from his shoulder, showing them his own variolation scar. "See? I had it done three years ago. I was sick for two days, but I recovered. If you'll let me do this, you can leave the cave in just over a week. I can return in a few hours. With wood and food and ale and the means to administer the variolation."

"Are ye a doctor, laddie?" the Executioner asked. "What makes ye competent to perform this?"

Peter stood a bit taller. "I am an apothecary. You can trust me with this. I have performed it many times. If you insist on going out, this is the only path."

The Executioner growled. He turned his face toward the Shield-maiden. They locked eyes once again and seemed as if they were engaged in wordless conversation.

At last, the Shield-maiden nodded. The Executioner then nodded as well.

She turned her haunting eyes on him. "Aye. We'll do as ye say. But it must be soon." She pointed at the fire. "We'll need the provisions ye mentioned as well."

Relief washed over him—relief so profound, it made his knees threaten to give way. He almost laughed. Almost. "If you'll lend me those clothes, I'll return in two or three hours. Four at the most."

✠·✠·✠

Ten minutes later, wearing dry clothes that barely fit him, Peter hastened through the snow-mantled woods. He took care not to slip and fall as he had before, on his way *to* the hidden cave. He'd fallen in that cursed stream, broken through the ice. That had been stupid. He had endangered everything. On his way back toward town, to the gathered Sergeants, he took great care crossing the same stream.

His fellow Sergeants would be waiting for him, ready with the supplies. Not too much at first. Just enough. And the materials for the variolation—they'd be ready too. They would have expected him hours ago, but that couldn't be helped.

"Peter." The voice was warm honey to his cold ears.

He halted.

There she was—the Blessed Virgin—standing in the air in all her alluring glory. The golden horns of the recumbent moon shone as if sending beams of yellow light into the night sky.

Peter dropped to his knees and raised his hands in adoration. "Yes, O Queen of Heaven!"

"Peter, my son. Is all well?"

"Yes!"

"Did you lead that fool disciple of Cernunnos to the cave?"

"Yes, I showed him the way, but I didn't slay him. There was no need. The Executioner slew him."

"And was Cernunnos there?"

Peter nodded vigorously. "Yes, he was! He was horrible. Terrifying."

"And the Templar overcame him?"

"Yes. He faced the demon and bested him."

"The mortal did *not* best Cernunnos. There is no mortal living who can do that. The Templar bested only Cernunnos's vessel, his *priest*." She invested the final word with the honeyed venom of contempt.

"Yes," Peter replied. "He did. He bested the vessel. Slew him."

The glorious being nodded. "I see. Very well. Perhaps that is better in the end."

"Yes, O Blessed One."

"And the Templar and his virgin whore suspect nothing?"

"No! They trust me completely." *The fools.*

"And have they agreed to the variolation?"

"Yes!" Peter felt the same elation, the same relief he'd felt in the cave, wash over him again. "It is all proceeding according to thy holy design."

The Queen of Heaven smiled upon him. "Blessed are you, my son."

Peter's body quivered in holy ecstasy.

Chapter 33

The fever burned in Tormond, and yet he shivered. His arm itched abominably, especially around the site of the wound where small pustules had formed. There were moments — very long moments — when it was all he could do to restrain himself from scratching. And he was so wretchedly tired.

But he dared not sleep.

For it was in sleep that the dreams came — dreams that drove him mad.

Two days. The Sergeant Apothecary, Peter Johnson, had said the fever would last two days. *Surely it has been two days by now.*

'Tis difficult to tell the passage of time in this wretched cave.

The fire was smoking worse than before. *The wood is too wet, too green.* The Sergeants — nigh two dozen of them — had brought the firewood, ale, beef, shriveled winter apples, carrots, turnips, and potatoes, along with hay and watering buckets for Órd Dubh and Fiona, carrying the supplies on their backs through the snow. The food had been good enough — for winter fare, at least — though neither Tormond nor Maebh had felt like eating after the variolation against the pox. But the wood...

In spite of Tormond's vast experience with firecraft, he could barely keep the wretched fire going.

"Ach!" he muttered. "At the least, wrestling with the fire keeps me awake." He growled. "For the most part."

His clothes were damp with fever sweat, clinging to him.

Maebh moaned in her fitful sleep, bundled up in woolen blankets — hers and his — for Tormond had insisted she use both. Tormond gazed upon her with a longing he could no longer deny — at least, not honestly. The longing had been growing stronger of late, the desire to be close to her, to touch her hand, to have her rest her head against his shoulder, to keep her safe in his arms. *Ever since the hurricane.* Even with her hair mussed and soaked with perspiration, her pale face drawn, her mouth slack, she was beautiful.

God grant me strength.

Tormond lurched to his feet, nearly tripping himself with his sword. He staggered toward Órd Dubh, pulling a fresh handkerchief from the cuff of his coat sleeve. Briefly, he patted the stallion's neck. The beast snorted and stomped the limestone with one hoof. "Soon, my old, ever-faithful friend. I'll take ye riding soon."

Órd Dubh tossed his head as if in scornful reply.

"I know," Tormond said. "I keep saying that. Tomorrow. After her fever breaks." *After my own fever breaks.*

Tormond stooped to soak the handkerchief into the warhorse's water bucket. Suddenly, the cave spun around him, and he nearly fell over. "None o' that, laddie," he snarled through clenched teeth. Tormond placed his hands on his knees, stabilizing himself. He took two slow, deep breaths to stop his head from spinning. "Ach, that's better. Steady now." He dipped the kerchief into the water, wrung it out, and straightened up.

Unsteadily, he shuffled around the pathetic, smoking fire and back to Maebh. He knelt beside the two stacked featherbeds—Maebh's atop his own—that the Sergeants had supplied. *Too thin. If I had my way, she'd be sleeping on a stack of such beds. Sleeping in queenly comfort.*

Gently, tenderly, he mopped her burning brow, cooling her forehead. *Our Father which art in heaven, Hallowed be Thy name. I ken the Sergeant Apothecary said this wretched fever would last but two days, and that we'd survive the fever, but I've ne'er seen Maebh so sick. Please, preserve her.*

Preserve me as well that I might protect her.

In the blessed name of Thy Holy Child, Jesus. Amen.

"Tormond . . ." His name escaped Maebh's lips as a barely audible moan.

"I'm here, Maebh. I'm here." He wiped her forehead again, then laid his fingers gently against her cheek. She still burned. As did he.

"Tormond," she whispered. "Don't leave me. Please, don't leave me." Her eyes were closed.

"I will nae leave ye, lassie. I will ne'er, e'er leave ye." *Ye are my heart. My very heart.*

"I love ye, Tormond. Oh, how I love ye."

Though he knew it was her delirium speaking, her words pierced his heart like a dagger. *I know ye do. God forgive me, but I love ye too.*

"Tormond, please."

"Aye?"

"Marry me, Tormond. Please. 'Tis been so long."

Tormond nearly wept at the pleading note in her voice. "I cannae. Ye know that, lass. I made a vow. A vow to God." *Not to the Order. Not to the Templars. The Templars are no more. To God.* "I made it of my own free will, lass. If we are e'er to succeed in our mission, if I have any hope that God will aid us in our long quest, I must keep my vow." *No matter how much I may ache for ye, my dearie, my love.*

And I do ache for ye.

"Tormond, I love . . ." Her voice trailed off.

He turned and sat beside her on the cold cave floor. "Aye, lass. I too."

He gazed at the guttering, hissing fire. *Worthless, wet wood. Did ye have no coal, Sergeants? Would a wee bit of coal have been too much to ask?*

He sighed, watching the low flames. *I ache. And I'm cold. And Maebh is so warm.. .*

Slowly, ever so slowly, his eyes closed.

Maebh was so deliciously warm. Everywhere her soft fingers traced, Tormond's flesh burned. How he loved the feel of her, the scent of her. The feel of her naked flesh pressed against his. The taste of her — of her lips, her tongue. She sighed as he kissed her neck.

"Take me, Tormond," a honey-sweet voice whispered. It sounded like Maebh's, yet also *unlike* hers. He'd never heard Maebh speak with such passion, with such need. "Be one with me, Tormond, my love. Worship me."

"With this ring I thee wed," he muttered between kisses, reciting the words of their wedding vows. "With my body, I thee worship."

Tormond woke with a start. His body was shivering, but he no longer burned.

His fever had broken.

The fire had almost gone out. A few spots of orange glowed weakly from the remaining embers.

He quickly lit a candle, then turned to Maebh.

She slept still.

Using great care to calm his trembling fingers so he would not wake her, he felt her damp forehead. It was cool to his touch. *God be praised!*

But the memory and the sensations from the dream lingered. A fire had been kindled within him — a burning that would never die. *With my body I thee —*

None o' that, laddie.

He turned his attention to the remains of the fire. He scrambled to the pile of firewood he'd left on the other side of the firepit to dry. *Still wet! All of it!*

Why would the Sergeants bring us wet wood?

If only I had nae let the wretched fire go out. I could have put wet wood on top of it to dry.

If only.. .

He growled. "If only" will nae save her. Deeds, nae words.

He scavenged what little he could from the wet wood — *not nearly enough!* — arranged it on the embers, and blew on the fire until he had revived it a wee bit. He was painfully aware that what he'd done would not last for long.

Must find dry fuel for the fire.

His clothes were damp, but he wrapped himself in his cloak, took his longbow, quiver of arrows, and axe, then hurried from the cave and into the snow-blanketed forest.

He dared not go too far. The rebel army, he knew, was close by. They would have picked over the surrounding woods in their never-ending quest for fuel and food. And he could not leave Maebh alone, especially not with soldiers about.

She's defenseless. God protect her!

He stuck the haft of his axe into his sword belt, slipped his head and arm through the long shoulder strap of the quiver so it hung at his left hip, over his sword, then drew and nocked an arrow. The forest was dark, and fresh snow was falling, covering the tracks the Sergeants had left two days before. *The only tracks out here will be my own. And they'll lead anyone who crosses them back to the cave. Back to Maebh.*

I thank Thee, Lord, for the fresh snow to cover my tracks, though 'twill make finding dry wood all the harder.

Guide me, Lord. Please.

Then help me find my way back.

He moved quickly, but with as much stealth as his fever-ravaged body could muster. And he shivered. His damp clothes clung to him, slowly freezing against his flesh.

None o' that, laddie! Move faster. That'll warm ye.

He spotted a dead and precipitously leaning tree that looked promising. Tormond hastened forward, even as his eyes scanned the forest.

But it was not his eyes that first detected the man and the horse — it was his ears. The voice of a man speaking. And any man out in these woods could be a danger to Maebh.

Tormond approached stealthily, which meant he was forced to move more slowly. *I'll nae do Maebh a bit of good if I get myself shot by a musket ball.*

The lone man knelt beside his horse. He wore a blue regimental coat with gold cuffs and lapels. A heavy, dark-blue cape, dusted by the falling snow, was draped over his back. The cockade on the bicorne hat sitting next to his knee identified him as a general.

Blue coat — nae red nor green. 'Twould make him a rebel *general.*

But what would induce a general to venture into these woods alone, at night, in the midst of a war?

Nae matter. I must get fuel for Maebh.

But as Tormond attempted to maneuver around the rebel officer, he caught the words the man spoke, and those words made Tormond halt to listen. The general pled with the Almighty, pouring out his heart to his Maker. He spoke of the desperate circumstances of his brave soldiers. He begged for relief for his men — for food, for fuel, for clothing, for shoes. He importuned for Heaven's mercy in the cause of liberty. And for himself, the general asked only for the courage and the wisdom to lead his men through their current crisis.

Though he did not weep outwardly, there was a profound sorrow and humility to his voice, and that sorrow and humility penetrated Tormond to his core. *This is nae a man seeking for power or glory. He is nae like Robert the Bruce — whom I admired — nor like any mortal king I have ever known. He is one such as Guillaume de Beaujeu.* The brave and humble de Beaujeu — the Grand Master of the Knights

Templar—had given Tormond the sword at his side. He had commissioned Tormond as the second Executioner only to fall to a Muslim arrow the very next day.

'Tis the "farmer general" of the prophecy. Washington. The one I am to "aid unawares."

A humble servant of God, or I have never known one.

And I have known many.

'Tis why he has come alone. To pray. To plead for the mercy of God and for the welfare of the men under his command.

Sergeant Peter Johnson holds this man in contempt. He says most Englishmen here in the Americas are loyal to the king. If only Johnson could hear this man pray as I do now, surely, he'd see the right of it.

There will be good and honest men on both sides of this conflict, and God only knows who will prevail.

God speed the right.

But the Sergeants, now . . . The Sergeants of the Temple are nae to involve themselves in the affairs of kings and queens. Or revolutions.

I must speak to Johnson, tell the Sergeants to remain neutral in this war. We fight only the wars of God.

Aye, laddie, the wars of God. But did ye nae fight for Robert at Bannockburn? Did ye nae lead Sergeants in his cause?

But that was to liberate Scotland from wicked King Edward's tyranny.

Is that nae what this Washington be doing? If we were to take a side in this war, it should be on the side of freedom. And the prophecy says —

A shiver ripped through Tormond. His sweat-soaked stockings had turned to ice.

The snow is getting worse. Soon 'twill be a storm.

I must go. Must save Maebh!

Tormond turned to leave, but a movement to the right caught his eye.

Not twenty yards away, another solitary man in a snow-blanketed cloak and tricorn hat knelt in the snow, intently watching the praying general. *Surely that man can hear the words as well. Perhaps he's a bodyguard after all. Aye, and there's his musket.*

A bodyguard.

The man turned, and Tormond was surprised to recognize him. *Peter Johnson!*

What be ye a-doing here, Sergeant? For certain sure ye are nae here to protect a man ye despise.

Ach! I dinnae have time for this! Maebh needs me!

Winking snow out of his eyelashes, Tormond glanced at Washington. The rebel general continued to kneel and plead with God, unaware of the presence of the two watchers. *Listen to this man, Sergeant. Then listen to yer heart.*

'Twill guide ye aright.

When Tormond looked away from Washington and back to Johnson, the man had shifted. The Sergeant was holding the musket to his shoulder. The weapon was cocked and ready to fire.

And it was aimed at Washington's back.

Nae!

Tormond whirled, drawing his longbow and aiming. He loosed, and his arrow sank deep into its target.

Peter Johnson slumped to the ground without firing a shot or uttering a sound. The snow around the Sergeant turned crimson.

Ever thicker fell the snow from the night sky as if to cover the dead Sergeant and his blood, spilled by Tormond's arrow.

✠·✠·✠

Maebh awoke alone, with only the light of a single candle to combat the cave's Stygian darkness. The fire had burned down to coals.

And Tormond was nowhere to be seen.

Terror seized her in its icy talons. She sat up, calling Tormond's name. The horses whinnied, but the only other answer was the echo of her own voice.

Maebh was cold. Her shift and stockings—the only clothing she wore—were wet, sticky.

But in her dream.. .

In her dream, she'd been warm. And Tormond had been so lusciously warm. In her dream, the two of them had been . . . and the words he'd whispered to her . . . and the words she'd whispered to him . . . and the way she had burned at his touch.. .

Maebh closed her eyes and shuddered. "Tormond! Where are ye! Tormond!"

"Maebh?" Tormond's voice sounded as if he were far away.

"Tormond?" She unraveled herself from the blankets.

She stood precariously on wobbly feet. The chill of the cave hit her as if she'd been doused with a bucket of well water.

"Maebh! Help me! Please!"

A claw of terror twisted in her gut. In all the centuries since she'd met Tormond, she'd never heard the mighty Templar's voice filled with despair or fear.

"I'm coming!" she cried. She plucked up one of her pistols, gripped her shift, and stumbled toward the exit.

Darkness closed around her as she wove, lurching between the bones of long-dead, ancient beasts.

"Hurry, Maebh!" Tormond called, his voice weaker, more distant.

She emerged from the cave, into a snowstorm. She could see nothing except snow, and even that was dim under the night sky. The wind whipped at her, sending her unbound hair flying, penetrating her wet, thin shift, leeching away her heat.

"Tormond! Where are ye?" She took a few halting steps forward. The snow was already well past her ankles, and her wet stockings gave her no protection at all. "Tormond!" she screamed into the storm.

"Maebh! This way! Help me!"

Maebh's body shivered violently as she trudged toward the voice. "I c-can't see ye!"

"Help me, Maebh. Please!"

Darkness and snow swirled about her. She turned along with them. "T-Torm-mond. I'm c-coming. I'm . . ." *Where? Where is he? Where am I?*

She fought to keep her eyes open. *Mustn't sleep. Why . . . sleepy . . . now? Must . . . find . . .* "T-Tormond?"

"Maebh. Come to me." His voice had lost its pleading, anxious tone. "Come to me, my love. Let me worship ye." His voice was warm. Warm and . . . high? Almost like a woman's voice.

The voice began to laugh.

Tormond? Why do ye sound like that?

Maebh wasn't shivering anymore. She couldn't feel the wind or the snow. Or her feet.

She was *warm*. Warm and tired.

Must . . . rest . . .

✠·✠·✠

Tormond witnessed her fall.

"Maebh!" he cried as he staggered through the snow toward her.

All his weariness vanished in that instant. The cold, the pain in his feet, hands, and face no longer mattered.

All that mattered — all that existed — was Maebh.

What is she doing outside? In naught save her shift and stockings?

She lay in the snow, on her side, her eyes closed.

Is she breathing? He scooped her up with his right arm and tossed her over his shoulder. In his left arm he still carried his load of firewood and his longbow. Bearing both his precious burdens — the potentially life-giving fuel and the woman whom he treasured most of all — he fought his way through the deepening snow toward the cave.

Once inside and out of the storm, he didn't stop until he had carried her back to her bed. He dropped the wood and the bow near the fire. Then he laid her gently on the woolen blankets. With all the haste his numb and swollen fingers could manage, he divested himself of his cloak, axe, quiver, sword belt, and sodden coat.

Forgive me, my love. He ripped away her icy shift and stockings — even the bandage covering the variolation site, for it too was wet — leaving her completely naked. *So cold. She's so cold!* He covered her nakedness with the blankets.

Quickly, he turned to the dying embers of the fire. He brushed the snow from the firewood, then tented it over the coals, drier-side-down. With quivering lips, he blew on the coals, rousing a few tiny tongues of flame. *Please, Lord, let that catch and burn!*

He stripped himself out of his own sodden and icy clothes, popping off buttons and ripping away cloth. Last of all, he tore off the bandage and the bit of nutshell over his variolation wound. Without the slightest hesitation, he opened the blankets, exposing Maebh's body once more, laid himself beside her, and wrapped them both in the blankets.

And only when they were both naked, her cold flesh pressed against his, did he at last check to see if she yet breathed. Her cold breath brushed against his cheek. He felt the expansion and contraction of her chest. He could feel her heart beating.

"She lives! I thank Thee, O God! I thank Thee!"

Tormond could not control his own shivering, but he did not care. *Even my shivering will serve to warm her.* Holding her against himself, he moved his hands, slowly rubbing her naked back. "Maebh. Wake up, lass. Please wake up."

Tears leaked from his shut eyes. "Our Father which art in heaven, Hallowed by Thy name. Please help me to wake her. Please dinnae take her to Thyself—nae at this time. Allow me to save her. Please, Holy Father." *Please dinnae take her from me.* "In Jesus' name. Amen."

Tormond gently moved his legs, rubbing them against hers—anything to generate more warmth. "Wake up, lass. Please." *Please dinnae leave me.*

"O God," he pled, "take my life for hers. Save her. My life for hers. My warmth for hers. I ken I hae been too familiar wi' her. I've held her close tae me. I've kissed her forehead. I should nae have done that, I know. But I hae been chaste. And so has she. We've kept our vows, Lord. In spite of the temptation"—a sob burst from him—"we've kept our vows!" *And, oh, how great be the temptation!* "Please dinnae take her."

Even after his shivering ceased, he continued to rub his hands along her back and to move his legs against hers. His fingers tingled, and needles of pain shot through them as feeling returned to them. And her flesh felt warmer under his tingling, painful fingers.

She felt warmer.

And as her body heat increased, his own, traitorous body responded to hers. Unbidden, images from his lust-filled, fevered dreams flooded back into his mind. To his horror and shame, he could not deny or hide his body's reaction to her warm, soft flesh pressed against his.

A moan escaped her lips.

"Maebh?" He turned his head to glance at her face. Her eyes were still closed, but her lips moved as if she were speaking in her sleep.

He turned his head away from her. "Please, lass, wake up."

Her lips continued to move against his ear, finally forming discernable words. Tormond recognized them from the Anglican Book of Common Prayer—words a bride would speak to her groom—words Tormond himself had spoken in his dream. " . . . this ring I thee wed. With my body I thee worship."

She stirred. Her hand, which had been limp and lifeless, moved. It moved against his back, as if in imitation of his own hands rubbing at hers. And where her fingers traced, Tormond's flesh burned. Her body pressed against his as if she would mold her soft, yielding flesh to his.

He jerked his legs straight and pulled and twisted his lower body away from hers as far as was possible.

But it was not far enough.

"Tormond?" She pulled her head back. Her eyes were wide open, and she stared at him. "What—"

"Ye're alive!" he cried, almost sobbing afresh. Then, more softly, "Alive." For a very long, very charged moment, they stared into each other's eyes. She was panting and trembling, and so was he. His hands stopped moving, and so did hers.

The urge, the *need* to kiss her surged within him. He inched his face toward hers. He could feel her breath on his lips, in his mouth. In a moment, their lips would touch.

And once they had crossed that threshold, they would do much more than merely kiss.

"Nae!" The word ripped from deep within his soul like barbed fishhooks tearing through his throat.

He fought his way out of the blankets, tearing himself away from her, fleeing the heat of her embrace—like Joseph fleeing from Potiphar's wife.

"Tormond?" she called after him, her voice filled with anguish and loss.

But he did not look back at her. He dared not look back.

He snatched up his wet cloak and wrapped himself in it, covering his nakedness. And his shame. "I'm sorry. I'm sae very sorry, Maebh." He went to the fire. It burned still.

Just as his skin burned at the memory of her touch.

Hastily, urgently, Tormond put more of the wood he'd brought onto the fire. He knelt and blew on the coals, fanning it into a small blaze.

"Tormond? Please. Look at me."

But he dared not comply. "This wood — the stuff the Sergeants brought — 'tis all wet and green. If I'm to get any of it to burn properly, I must get some of it on top, to dry it, or I'll ne'er keep the fire going." *Think of the fire. Only of the fire.*

"Ye saved me."

He closed his eyes, but when he did, all he saw was her body — her forbidden beauty. *Sae bonnie. More lovely than I e'er could've imagined.* His eyes snapped open.

Nae! Dinnae think of it. Dinnae think of her!

Think of something else. "I . . . I slew him."

"What? Whom did ye slay?"

He focused on his task — building the fire and drying the wet wood. "I slew Peter Johnson."

"The Sergeant?"

He nodded. "Aye. The very same. I was out, in the forest, seeking dry wood for the fire. Ye needed heat" — he nearly choked on the word and what it might imply — "and so I went out. A-and I came upon the rebel general. Washington. The 'farmer general' from the prophecy, aye? The one I was to 'aid unawares?'"

"Ye saw him?"

I saw ye. I saw yer naked body. I almost — We *almost —*

Dinnae think of it! Think of Johnson's body, bleeding on the snow. "Aye. But he did nae see me. He was praying. Alone in the woods. Praying for his men. And such a prayer!" He shook his head in awe of the memory — or *that* part of the memory. The other parts he would sooner forget. "Ye should have heard it, lass. Johnson was there as well. But he was going to murder Washington, shoot him in the back. Like a base coward. I had nae time to think. None at all. I . . . put an arrow through his heart."

"Johnson?"

Tormond nodded, placing another of the wet logs atop the fire to dry. *I almost —* "Aye. We're nae to take sides in the wars of kings and queens. Only God's wars. God's work. That's what we should be about." *God's work! Nae the lusts of the flesh!* He gritted his teeth and growled. "I am the Executioner of God, am I nae? And I am responsible for the Sergeants of the Temple. I had to kill him. To *execute* him. He left me nae choice. N-nae choice at all." His voice trembled with sudden grief. And with guilt as well.

She put her hand on his shoulder, startling him.

"Hush now," she said. "Ye did the right thing. The only thing ye could have done." Her voice was soothing, warm.

Everything about her is warm. He tried not to look at her, but out of the corner of his eye, he could see that she had wrapped herself in the blankets. "I . . . did nae *touch* ye, lass. I mean to say, I *did* touch ye, but I did nae . . . I would ne'er . . ." He swallowed. "I would nae dishonor ye so." *God forgive me, but I almost did.*

She removed her hand from his shoulder, then knelt beside him. Right beside him. "Ye saved my life."

He refused to look at her. *Sae bonnie.* He thought briefly of the demon, standing scantily clad before him. *Ashtoreth was beautiful, desirable . . . But nae beauty compares to Maebh's.*

Stop thinking on it! "W-why were ye out in the snow, lass? In naught save yer—" He could not bring himself to mention her undergarments—undergarments she was no longer wearing.

"I woke," she said, "and ye were not here. Then I heard ye calling me. Calling my name. Pleading for my help."

Finally, he turned to her. And her beauty smote his heart. "I did nae call ye, lass. I did nae call for help. 'Twas nae me." *But ye came for me all the same. Ye did nae hesitate. Ye came to save me.*

And nearly died for it.

Her brow furrowed in thought. "I was certain sure 'twas ye I heard. 'Twas *your* voice. At least, at the first 'twas. It changed. It became higher, like a woman's."

Tormond turned his face back to the fire, glaring at it with sudden fury. "Like a woman's, aye?" He growled. "The demoness. Ashtoreth. 'Twas her doin'. She planted thoughts . . . in my dreams. Possibly in yours as well, aye?"

She gave no answer.

The crackling and spitting of the fire and the sounds of the horses as they chewed their hay were the only sounds in the cave.

Those sounds—and the sound of her breathing.

He remembered her breath on his lips, in his mouth—the scent of her.

"Tormond?"

"Aye?"

"Thank ye for saving me. For saving my life. Ye risked . . . so very much. For me."

Tears spilled from his eyes. "Oh, lass! I thought . . . I'd lost ye. I cannae . . . cannae bear the thought of being parted from ye. I'm sorry for . . . what I had to do . . . to warm ye."

"I'm not sorry. Ye did the only thing ye could do. Ye did the *right* thing." She laid her head on his shoulder.

He resisted the urge to flinch away. He resisted also the greater urge to take her in his arms again.

She sighed. "Ye *always* do the right thing." She trembled, and he realized with a start that she was weeping. She took a deep, hitching breath. "Even when 'tis very, very . . . difficult."

He swallowed. "'Tis difficult for us both, lass."

"Please, Tormond. Please, hold me."

Dinnae tempt me, lass. I cannae bear it.

"I'm not asking for more than that," she added. "Truly, I'm not. I cannot deny that . . . th-that I . . . *desire* more. I do . . . desire more, but . . . not like that. Not until we can be . . . I simply . . . I need ye to hold me."

And I cannae deny that I desire more as well. So much more.

But I made a vow. And I must keep it.

Nae matter how much I may burn for ye.

But he worked an arm free of his cloak and put it around her shoulders, pulling her closer.

She melted against him, nestling her head on his chest. And for a long while, she simply breathed.

Tormond loved the sound of her breathing.

Our Father which art in heaven, Hallowed be Thy name. I thank Thee. She is alive.

And we are yet chaste.

She murmured something against his chest.

But he could not catch her words. "What did ye say?"

"I said that we defeated her."

"Her?"

She nodded. "Ashtoreth. We have defeated her. If this truly was her doing, if she created these . . . circumstances, this terrible trap . . . then we have defeated her. We have won. 'Tis because of ye, Tormond. Because ye are brave and strong. And true."

He smiled. "As are ye, Shield-maiden. As are ye." *And yet, I still burn for ye.*

And ye burn for me.

And, I fear, 'twill forever alter things between us.

God grant me strength.

God grant us both strength.

Suddenly, laughter filled the cave, making them both jump — making them cling all the harder to each other. "You think you have won?" crooned a honeyed voice. "Oh, foolish children. I have planted the seeds of your destruction. They have sprouted in your hearts, and they will grow. They will burn within you, hotter and hotter, until the flames of Holy Lust consume you. You may have won this battle. Perhaps." The demon laughed again, softer than before, and for all of its softness, her laughter was all the more sinister, all the more terrifying. "But I shall win the war. For the spirit is willing, but the flesh is weak."

"Begone, foul demoness!" Tormond snarled. "In Jesus' name, begone!"

Ashtoreth's laughter grew higher and higher, louder and louder. "You have no authority to banish me, mortal. There is none on earth that may command me. That power is fled. Gone. But *I* remain. I shall be with you to the end. And in the end, you *shall* yield. And then you shall be *mine.*"

Chapter 34

Philadelphia, Pennsylvania: April 1838 A.D.

A thrill ran up Thaddeus J. Westmoreland's spine as he stared openmouthed at the oddly dressed couple that had burst unannounced into his second-floor law office. Their clothing was at least half a century out of date. The man — tall, powerfully built, and sporting unfashionably long, blond hair and a rough, slightly darker blond beard — gripped the pommel of a large sword held at his hip by a belt adorned with brazen crosses. The woman, wearing a dress that would have been right at home in a stage production of Oliver Goldsmith's eighteenth-century farce, "She Stoops to Conquer" — a particular favorite of Thaddeus's — had a brace of ancient flintlock pistols thrust into a sash around her waist.

Could it be? Truly?

"Ye are Thaddeus J. Westmoreland, Attorney at Law?" the man demanded in a thick, Scottish accent.

Thaddeus nodded quickly. "Yes. I am."

The bearded giant grunted. "And that emblem in the corner of yer window outside? The red cross on a black square. That be yers?"

It is he! The Executioner of God! "Yes!" Thaddeus grinned widely as he made the secret Templar salute.

The man returned the salute, but he did not return the smile.

Instead, the Templar strode quickly forward and pounded his fist on Thaddeus's cherrywood desk, causing a stack of lawbooks to jump and the lamp to rattle. "Why did ye nae wake us, man? 'Tis three years too late! Three years!" He pounded the desk a second time. "Again!"

Fury burned in the Templar's eyes.

Thaddeus stood — slowly, so as not to further enrage the fearsome Executioner — and meekly bowed his head. "Forgive me, Brother Executioner, Sister Shield-maiden." He raised his head and met the Templar's eyes. "But we *lost* you."

401

The Executioner blinked. "Lost us?"

"Yes. We *lost* the cave. Between disease, the Revolution, and after that, a *second* war with England, so many of us—so many of the Sergeants of the Temple—perished. Everyone with first-hand knowledge of your cave's whereabouts was gone. We knew it was near Valley Forge, but . . . We've searched for *decades*." He shook his head. "But we couldn't find you. That's why I keep my office on this street and so close to the edge of town. We thought, if you came from Valley Forge into Philadelphia, this would be the road you'd enter on. And that, of course, is why I put the emblem in the window. It's larger than our wont—this sign is—but we prayed that you would find it. Find *us*." The words had spilled from his lips in an excited rush. So many times, he'd imagined what he'd say if the Executioner and the Shield-maiden found his office. He'd rehearsed and rehearsed the explanation, for, though every word of it was true, the Templar would—justifiably—demand answers.

Thaddeus grinned and clapped his hands. "And find us you have!" He sighed in happy relief and sank back into his chair. "We had almost despaired!" He laughed. "But you're here! God be praised!"

The Executioner and the Shield-maiden exchanged wide-eyed looks. Then the woman asked, "What of the Witches?"

"Yes!" Thaddeus pointed at them with both hands. "The Witches. Of course, the Witches! Last seen in Boston. In Massachusetts. One of the states. We have twenty-six—twenty-six states, that is. We're an independent country now! The United States of America. Oh, Brother, so much has changed in the last sixty years!"

The Executioner growled. "It always does."

Thaddeus leaped to his feet once more, unable to contain his enthusiasm. *The Executioner of God and the Shield-maiden! Right here in my office.* "But you must be hungry and thirsty! Are your horses outside? The legendary Órd Dubh and Fiona?" He pulled on a bell rope.

The lady smiled. "Aye. We are. And aye, the horses are tied up in front of this very building."

Merciful heavens, but she's lovely!

Someone knocked at the open door.

402

Thaddeus tore his eyes away from the Shield-maiden's captivating gray eyes.

Janie—a pleasant-looking black woman in a plain, brown, working dress and white apron—stood in the doorway. She appeared to be in her early thirties and had bright brown eyes and lips that seemed always to be on the cusp of a smile. "Yes, Mister Westmoreland?"

"Janie"—Thaddeus gestured at his guests as he sat once more in his chair—"I have visitors. Very *important* visitors. Run over to the hotel and get us some dinner. A bottle of wine as well, please. In fact, make it *two* bottles! French. The best they have!"

The Templar held up a hand. "One bottle will suffice, lad. We need to keep our wits about us." He smiled at the serving woman. "But a couple of mugs of cider would slake our thirst, good woman, if ye please."

Janie looked to Thaddeus for confirmation.

He nodded. "Wine and cider. Make that three mugs. And a fourth mug for yourself, Janie."

Janie gave a perfunctory curtsey, but even as she did so, her eyes never left his, and that hint of a smile was a *hint* no longer. "Yes, Mister Westmoreland. Right away, sir." With a rustle of skirts, she departed.

Thaddeus bit his lip to suppress a grin as he watched her go, then turned his attention back to the Executioner.

The Templar's eyes narrowed as he scowled. "A slave?"

Oh, my! Not that! "No, no! Brother Executioner! Janie is a *free* woman. She escaped from the South years ago. From Georgia—that's one of the Southern states. One of the *slave* states. She escaped, made her way north, and, well, she works for me now."

The Executioner's glare did not waver. "She *works* for ye?"

To Thaddeus, his office had suddenly become quite hot and stuffy. "Yes! I-I pay her a wage. Quite a generous wage if I may say so." A bead of sweat rolled down his cheek, and he resisted the urge to loosen his collar. "Th-the Sergeants of the Temple—we have followed your command to the letter, Brother Executioner. And slavery is *illegal* in Pennsylvania. As it is—at least technically—in most of the northern states."

The Templar's eyes softened. He nodded slowly, his brow wrinkling thoughtfully. "Free in the north, aye? But nae in the south?"

Thaddeus sighed. "Just so. In fact, slavery is at the root of most of the contention in this nation. I fear that someday it will lead to war between the North and the South." He shuddered. "I pray, as do most men, that it will not be in my lifetime. But . . . I don't know how much longer we can endure as a divided nation. Especially divided over such an evil as slavery."

The Templar fixed him with those piercing blue eyes once more. "Show us yer crucifix."

Thaddeus blinked at him in confusion. "My — My crucifix?"

The Executioner rose, approached the desk, and leaned over it, looming. "Aye, Sergeant Thaddeus J. Westmoreland. Show us yer crucifix. Or have the Sergeants of the Temple ceased wearing them? Have ye forsaken yer oath of service and obedience?"

Thaddeus shrank back. *So tall!* "No. I mean to say, yes. I mean"—he swallowed hard—"we still wear them. In secret, of course. We keep our oath." Hastily, he removed his stickpin, untied his cravat, and unbuttoned his collar, as well as the top of his shirt. Drawing on the string at his neck, he pulled forth an unadorned wooden cross.

The Executioner barely glanced at the crucifix. "Have ye another?"

"Another?"

"Another crucifix, man!"

Thaddeus shook his head. "Why would I have another crucifix?"

The Templar growled. "Show me yer neck, man."

Utterly confused, but anxious to obey, Thaddeus unbuttoned yet another shirt button, then pulled his collar back. "I have no other crucifix, Brother Executioner."

The Executioner nodded. "Aye." He sat once more, though his left hand went immediately to the pommel of his legendary sword. His lips twitched. "Yer pardon, Sergeant." He growled again, but there was no menace in the sound—merely frustration. "I'm beginnin' to suspect everyone."

The Shield-maiden gently placed a hand atop the Templar's right hand.

The Templar flinched, nearly jerking his hand away. He closed his eyes, inhaled deeply through his nose, then let out his breath slowly, as if he were attempting to calm himself. He opened his eyes, turned his face toward the Shield-maiden and gave her a tight-lipped smile.

The lady blushed — blushed! — then smiled awkwardly back, before facing Thaddeus. "Forgive us, Sergeant."

My, but her accent! That Irish lilt is enchanting! "There is nothing to forgive, Sister Shield-maiden." Thaddeus replaced the secret crucifix in its customary place against his heart, then rebuttoned his shirt as he continued to observe his guests closely.

The Shield-maiden squeezed the Templar's hand, and Thaddeus noticed that the Templar closed his eyes and again took a calming breath.

"Be that as it may," she continued, "we have come to believe that the Sergeants of the Temple have among them a secret cabal — one that serves, not God and the Temple, but a demoness."

Thaddeus gaped at her in astonishment — and not a little terror. "A demoness? Secret cabal?" *Among the Sergeants?* He barely stopped himself from making the sign of the cross.

She nodded. "Aye, Sergeant Westmoreland. And these wicked men wear a corrupted cross — with the top bisected by a recumbent sickle moon."

"Sickle moon?"

The Templar nodded. "Aye. We've seen this symbol afore. Centuries ago. I'm certain sure at least some of those wicked men — in the past — were Sergeants."

"Sergeants?" Thaddeus felt as if he might be sick. *It can't be!*

The Templar nodded again. "Aye. When last we were awake — in 1778 'twas — I was forced to *slay* a Sergeant. I stopped him as he was about to assassinate General George Washington."

Thaddeus gasped. "Peter Johnson! *You* slew him? We knew he disappeared, but . . ."

The Templar nodded. "'Twas I, myself. This Washington — ye've heard of him then?"

Thaddeus ran a hand through his hair, then laughed mirthlessly. "George Washington? He is the father of our country."

"Yer king?" the Templar asked. "He yet lives?"

"Our first president. We have no king." Thaddeus shook his head. "And no, George Washington passed away before I was born."

The Templar grunted, then wrinkled his brow thoughtfully. "No king? President?"

Thaddeus nodded. *The* Executioner *killed Johnson? But if Johnson was going to assassinate George Washington . . . George Washington!* The thought was almost too monstrous to consider. He shuddered. "I'm . . . certain you did the right thing, Brother Executioner."

The Executioner shrugged his great shoulders. "I did what God required of me at the time. As must we all. At *all* times. The next day—after I slew Johnson—I dragged his frozen corpse into the cave. About his neck, I found just such an unholy cross—the sigil of the demoness."

The Shield-maiden leaned forward, fixing him with her lovely, but intense gray eyes. "Have ye seen other Sergeants wearing this symbol?"

Thaddeus shook his head. "No." *Sergeants in league with a demon?* Then shook it more vigorously. "No! But from this day forward, I shall be on my guard, looking for this symbol, this . . . cabal."

The Shield-maiden nodded. "Thank ye, Sergeant." She smiled.

He smiled back at her. *She really is quite alluring. Those lovely gray eyes. The way her hair frames her face. And that handsome bosom.. .*

The Templar executed Sergeant Johnson in 1778. He saved George Washington! He cleared his throat. "Brother Executioner, do you realize what you have done? You saved our nation! Without George Washington—"

The Templar waved a dismissive hand. "The Almighty would have appointed another in his stead, I've nae doubt. I, myself, am a replacement. I am but the second Executioner."

Thaddeus laughed softly, shaking his head. *The Executioner saved America!*

The Shield-maiden squeezed the Executioner's hand again, smiling at him as if to say, *No one could ever replace you.*

Thaddeus suddenly envied the man. *What I wouldn't give to have her smile at me like that? What* any *man wouldn't give?*

Rather than closing his eyes and calming himself, the Templar merely sighed. Then he smiled ruefully at Thaddeus. "Laddie, I dinnae suppose ye can direct us to a tailor and a dressmaker? We are woefully . . . noticeable. We have some gold left. 'Tis mostly British pounds . . ."

"Gold?" Thaddeus shook his head. "Well, don't flash it about here. We use bank notes in these parts and a few, less valuable coins. Moreover, our currency is the *dollar* now, not the pound. And we have plenty of money laid aside for you and your expenses." He tapped his desk enthusiastically. "In fact, we have suitable, *modern* clothing for both of you. The latest fashions. The finest tailor in Philadelphia. And the dressmaker"—he beamed at the Shield-maiden—"is my wife's own seamstress. Nothing but the best!"

Thaddeus leaped to his feet and strode quickly to a large bookcase. He removed a copy of *Plutarch's Lives*, reached behind it, and tripped the hidden latch. He replaced the book, then easily pulled one side of the bookcase away from the wall, revealing the hidden room behind.

The closet held several racks of clothing for both the man and the woman, as well as chests, large and small. Thaddeus stood aside, watching their reactions carefully. "We used measurements taken from garments you've left behind in earlier centuries. They should fit."

The Executioner stood, then gave the Shield-maiden his hand, helping her to her feet. He then offered her his arm, and Thaddeus noted no reluctance on either of their parts. *But they are not touching each other—no flesh-to-flesh contact.* Thaddeus wasn't sure why that surprised him. *He is a religious, and she a nun, after all. But they seemed so awkward together a moment ago. And yet they have traveled and hunted together for centuries.*

Once inside the secret alcove, the Executioner pulled a silk top hat from its peg. He eyed it dubiously, then growled, "The vanity o' men." He chuckled, and turned to the Shield-maiden, showing the hat to her. "At least 'tis nae bedecked with ribbons or a buckle, aye?" He wrinkled his nose. "Or feathers."

She grinned back at him, pointing at her side of the closet. "Take a look at these gowns, will ye?" She turned to Thaddeus and scowled. "So thin-waisted. I suppose I'm to wear a corset underneath?"

Heat rose in Thaddeus's cheeks. "I, er, well . . . All your . . . *unmentionables* are in that box." He indicated one of the larger chests. "When Janie returns, she can help you dress."

The lady rolled her eyes. "*After* I eat. *Long* after. I want to be able to enjoy my food, not have it squished out of me along with half my innards." She pulled a gown from its hanger. And held it in front of her. Then she showed it to her companion. "Tormond? What d'ye think?"

He looked at the gown, then at her face. "Bonnie." He seemed to meet her eyes for a moment, then he swallowed visibly. "Lass, ye dinnae need to wear a corset. We'll get ye something that fits without one. Ye dinnae need to—"

"Do ye suppose *she* is wearing a corset? Right now?"

The Executioner glanced out the window.

Why out the window? Who is "she?"

Their mysterious companion from the seventeenth century? The one they called Branwen? And how would she be still alive? Is she . . . following them somehow? Is she here?

The Templar grinned, and it seemed to Thaddeus as if there were a twinkle in the fearsome Executioner's eye. "'The sun be set where she be. I would imagine so. She'd be wearin' a corset."

The sun be set? But it's daylight.

The Shield-maiden lifted her chin. "Then I shall wear a corset as well."

The Executioner winked—winked!—at her. "Ah, the vanity o' women, aye?"

She lifted her chin even higher. "What be the vanity o' women, as ye say, but what's forced upon them by men, aye?" She returned the wink and grinned.

Observing their interactions, Thaddeus was perplexed. *One moment, they act as if they are uncomfortable in one another's company, and the next, they seem like a courting couple. Or a long-married couple still deeply in love.*

Surely, they have not . . . They still hold to their vows, do they not?

"Tell me, laddie," the Executioner said, turning to Thaddeus, "what improvements have ye made in firearms in the last sixty years?"

"Firearms! Yes!" Thaddeus pushed between them. "Pardon me." He retrieved two flat, wooden boxes. He put the boxes on his desk, then opened the topmost. He pulled out one of two identical weapons and displayed it proudly to them. "It's called a revolver. It fires five balls in succession."

The Shield-maiden's eyes grew wide. "*Five* shots?"

Thaddeus nodded vigorously. "Without reloading."

She grinned and reached eagerly for the pistol.

"I have four revolvers," Thaddeus declared. "Two for each of you. Along with powder and shot, of course."

The Templar raised an eyebrow. "And I suppose every man out there be carrying one of these *revolvers*?"

Thaddeus shook his head. "They were only invented a couple years ago by fellow up in Connecticut. A Mister Samuel Colt. They are somewhat rare. They are seeing some use in the war with the Seminole Indians down in Florida."

The Templar nodded appreciatively. "Well done, laddie. Well done. I'm certain sure we can put these to good use."

Thaddeus beamed. He couldn't help himself. He felt as if his heart would burst from his chest. *Praise! From the Executioner of God!*

The Shield-maiden reverently returned the weapon to Thaddeus's hand. "Show us, pray, how 'tis loaded, this five-shot marvel." She smiled upon him.

She's lovely, but when she smiles, she's a vision. Thaddeus basked in the glow of that approval. "With pleasure, Sister Shield-maiden!"

"Ye must call me Maebh."

The Executioner of God put forth his hand, taking Thaddeus's hand and shaking it warmly. He grinned broadly. "And me Tormond, laddie."

I'm to be on a first-name cordiality with the Executioner of God! And the Shield-maiden of Christ! "I'm honored. And I am—of course—

your humble servant, Thaddeus." He bowed his head. "I live only to serve God and the Temple."

The Executioner—Tormond—nodded. "'Tis good to find a man we can trust."

✠ · ✠ · ✠

The hour was late when Thaddeus climbed the steps to his office. The Templar and the Shield-maiden were settled at their hotel. Their horses were stabled. *My, but that Órd Dubh is massive. The stories do not exaggerate!* The appropriate messages had been sent, informing the other Sergeants in Philadelphia of the glad news—*We've found them again! Or rather,* they *have found us, thanks be to God!* And his wife had been instructed not to wait up for him.

Janie had delivered that particular message on his behalf.

Thaddeus opened his office door and grinned to see that it was unlocked—just as he hoped it would be.

"Are our guests both tucked away, safe and sound?" Janie rose from his desk chair. "Not in that awful house across the street, I hope." Her nearly perpetual half grin transformed into a sour frown. "The food and beer is excellent, but the rooms are utterly revolting. Bedbugs!"

Thaddeus shuddered in disgust at the memory. "Of course not." He turned, locked the office door, pocketed the key, then, turning back to her, removed his top hat. "I put them up at the United States Hotel on Chestnut Street. Across from the bank."

Janie raised an eyebrow as she stepped around the desk and took his hat. "I *do* know the place," she said with a smirk, placing the top hat on the hat rack. She maneuvered behind him and helped him remove his coat.

He chuckled. "Of course, you do."

Janie hung up his coat. "Adjacent rooms?"

"*Adjoining* rooms—with a door between. The Templar insisted on it. So he'll be better able to protect her, he said."

She grinned. "Of course. To *protect* her. And, perhaps, for" — she licked her full, dark-brown lips—"*other* purposes?"

"No!" *The very idea!* Thaddeus's mouth twisted in horror. "He is a religious, as is she." He shook his head. "Quite frankly, I don't know how he has resisted her all these centuries. I'm quite certain he *desires* her." *And what man would not?* "And she desires him as well.

410

From what I observed today, I think they are madly in love with each other. But" — he shrugged, sighing — "the man must have a will of iron."

"A will of iron?" She laughed soft and low. "Unlike you, Mister Westmoreland?"

"I, my dear" — he grinned widely — "am neither *a* religious, nor particularly *religious*. Other than my sacred duty to the Temple, of course."

"Of course."

"Remember, Janie," Thaddeus said as he began to unbutton his trousers, "not a word about the Templar or the Shield-maiden to *anyone*. You're not supposed to know about any of this, of course."

"Of course not, Thaddeus. *Your* secrets are *my* secrets." She reached behind her neck and unclasped a gold chain under her hair. She furtively palmed the object at the end of that chain — just as she always did before one of their rendezvous.

Thaddeus had never gotten a good look at the trinket, but at such a moment, he had eyes only for her smooth, black skin.

Janie sat on the desk and began slowly drawing up her skirt and petticoats, grinning lasciviously. "You know you can trust me, Thaddeus. I wouldn't tell a *mortal* soul."

Chapter 35

Livingston County, Missouri: October 1838 A.D.

Blood stained the snow with every step Annie Morgan took. A few miles back—how many miles had it been?—only her right foot had bled through the rags bound around her shoeless feet. Now her left foot also left bloody prints behind. She'd ripped up a petticoat to wrap around her feet to protect her from the unusually early and heavy snow.

Each step was excruciating.

But I can still feel my feet. Take it as a blessing. Brother Joseph says we must acknowledge God's hand in all things.

I thank Thee, God, that I can still feel my feet.

When I can no longer feel them...

Please, God, don't take my feet too!

Annie's other petticoat was bundled around her infant son—Nephi, barely five weeks old. That petticoat was little Nephi's only protection against the cold. And the thin garment was already soaked around the baby's little bottom.

The child no longer cried. When Annie was driven from their home—without shoes or coat and with her small baby in her arms—in the dark of the night by a mob of nearly a dozen armed men, little Nephi had howled as only a distressed infant can. Annie had been forced to cover her son's mouth so the mobbers wouldn't hear them as she fled.

But for some time, Nephi had made no sound at all. He breathed—she clung desperately to the belief that her son yet breathed—but Annie couldn't hear it over the sound of her own ragged panting. She'd tried to feed him, even as she stumbled through the snow, but the babe wouldn't nurse. And his refusal to eat frightened her more than any horror she'd yet experienced that night.

Please, God, don't let my baby die! A sob wracked her cold body. *He's all I have left.*

Annie was certain her husband, her beloved William, was dead, slain by the wicked mob. She'd had to run, to protect their son, but grief and guilt threatened to leach away what little strength remained to her.

William! Forgive me! You told me to take the baby and run.

And I did. I ran. But —

William stayed behind, to distract the mobbers. Annie heard no gunfire, but the Missourians had knives too. One of them, their leader, had a sword.

William!

She'd heard about the atrocities perpetrated at Haun's Mill, what the mobbers did to the men and boys of that small village. The descriptions she heard of the massacre conjured up terrifying images in her mind. But in her imagination, each bloody, mutilated face was William's.

Annie didn't know exactly where she was going. She had a vague idea of making it to the town of Far West. Surely the Saints there would take them in — and the prophet was said to be there — but Annie didn't know the way. She knew only that the settlement was to the west of their little farm. But she wasn't certain they'd be safe, even among other Mormons, as the Missourians called members of her faith. She didn't believe anywhere in Missouri would be safe after the latest persecutions.

At least we might be out of the cold for the night.

Just survive the night and revive Nephi.

Please, God, don't take my son!

And please, if William is dead — she sobbed — *if William is dead, take him unto Thyself in Thy kingdom.*

I pray Thee, Lord, grant that his sufferings were brief.

Why am I praying to change something that has already happened — that is already done?

Past, present, and future are ever before Him. That's what Brother Joseph says.

She gave her son a gentle shake. "Wake up, Nephi. Please wake up. Aren't you hungry? I promise I'll feed you. Mama still has milk." *Even if I have nothing else! Nothing in this world!* She sobbed. "Only, please, Nephi! Please wake up!" But those tiny eyes, usually so curious and filled with wonder at the world, did not open.

Annie deeply regretted all the times over that last five weeks that she'd been annoyed — even resentful — when the babe deprived her of her sleep. At that moment, she would have given anything in the world to hear Nephi cry.

Why, Lord? Why? If we are Thy people? Why dost Thou not protect us? Why can't those wicked men just leave us alone?

Though they'd blackened their hate-filled faces with soot, Annie recognized each and every man in the mob. *They are all my neighbors! I know them. I know their wives!*

Thomas Bloodworth, the tanner, led them. Bloodworth, who leered at her every time she went into town — even when her belly was huge with Nephi. Bloodworth, who made those vile comments and wicked suggestions — things she couldn't repeat to anyone, not even to William — things Bloodworth said while his own wife, Mariah, looked on and said nothing.

And right behind Bloodworth when they attacked was Joshua Riley — schoolteacher during the week and Methodist parson on Sundays. Joshua was no less vile than his friend, the tanner, in his foul words and suggestions.

If we are Thy people, O Lord, why wilt Thou not send Thine angels to save me and my son?

Why didst Thou not save William?

"Whoop-whoop!" The horrible shout ripped the still night air.

Annie whirled about, and the night air froze in her lungs.

Six men on horseback came galloping across the snow toward Annie and her child. Most held aloft rifles. One pointed heavenward with a sword.

The mob!

Annie looked about, desperately searching for somewhere, anywhere to flee, to hide. A line of snow-covered trees glistened dimly to her right, more than a hundred yards away.

I'll never make it!

She ran anyway, abandoning the road and stumbling across the ice and snow as fast as she could force her half-frozen legs and bleeding feet to move.

"Whoop-whoop!" one of the Missourians shouted, the man with the sword. Others took up the triumphant cry. "Whoop-whoop!"

"She's bolting!" one shouted.

"After her!" another cried.

Annie glanced to her right.

The horsemen left the road and were closing in.

Annie sobbed as she stumbled toward the tantalizingly close trees. "God, help us!" But the trees seemed no nearer, and the mob was almost upon them.

"Mormon strumpet!" called the leader in a singsong voice— Annie recognized Bloodworth's voice. "Whoop-whoop, Mormon strumpet!"

In an instant, Bloodworth and his horse were in front of her, blocking her escape.

Annie screamed. She turned to the left, to the right, but she was surrounded by mobbers on horseback. She had nowhere left to run.

She clutched little Nephi to her bosom and sobbed.

The babe made no sound at all.

Bloodworth dismounted. "Thought you could get away from us, did ya?" He stank of whiskey, unwashed body, and the acrid reek of the tannery. "You and your Mormon brat?" He laughed, low and sinister. "Can't let a *nit* like that live. Nits grow up to be lice. And if that baby o' your'n grows up, he'll only grow up to be a *Mormon* like his dead pappy." He roared with laughter.

His friends echoed that fiendish glee.

William!

"Good one, Thom!" Joshua Riley said. "Can't let him grow up to be no Mormon!"

"Best bash his brains out now," Bloodworth said, grinning. "Not even worth a bullet. Hand him over, Annie. I'll take care o' him. Then you and me and the boys is gonna have us some entertainment!"

"No!" Annie begged. "I'll do anything. Just don't hurt my baby."

Bloodworth chuckled. "Sure. I'll treat him all"—he bent down, leering at her—"gentle-like." He reached for the baby with his left hand, while pointing the sword at her with his right hand. "Nice and gentle-like. Right up 'til I stomp on his skull!"

"NO!" She shrank back from his horrible, grasping hand. But there was nowhere to go. "God!" she cried. "Help us!"

"Gimme the damned brat!" snarled Bloodworth. "Gim—"

He froze. Then his whole body convulsed violently.

He collapsed to the snow like a rump-shot dog.

Something long and straight protruded from his right eye. It shook as he lay twitching on the ground—an arrow shaft, waving like the baton of an insane music conductor.

"Thom?" one man cried, but his eyes glazed over, and he toppled from his horse with an arrow protruding from his back.

"Injuns!" two of the remaining four shouted.

A third man fell from his horse, clutching at his throat as if he could somehow hold in the blood that fountained around the shaft of an arrow.

The three surviving mobbers turned atop their horses and fired wildly into the night. The three riderless horses scattered, galloping away in terror.

Five more shots rang out in rapid succession, but from further away. Another man crumpled in the saddle, then dropped his rifle and tumbled from his horse.

One man drew a pistol from his belt, but before he could aim it, he fell to the snow with an arrow in his back.

Four more distant shots, and the final mobber, Joshua Riley, the schoolteacher and part-time parson, fell, clawing at his gut with one hand. He lay on the reddening snow, squealing like a stuck pig, his wide-brimmed hat lying beside him. Somehow, he still gripped the reins of his terrified horse in one hand. The animal screamed. In panic and terror, the parson's wide eyes found Annie's. He reached for her with one gore-stained hand. "Help me! For the love of God, help me!"

Annie could only stumble backward, away from the grasping preacher.

Joshua's horse screamed again and reared, and the animal's front hooves landed on its master's chest and head with a pair of sickening squelches, sending the parson to his eternal reward.

The terrified horse galloped away.

All the horses were gone, and all her attackers were dead.

Annie, clutching her infant son, stood alone inside a ring of corpses and bloodstained snow. She stared, wide-eyed and panting, at the dead mobbers.

And at the arrows.

Indians!

She looked in terror toward the road.

But instead of Indians, she beheld a wagon, pulled by a single horse and driven by a woman, followed by a second horse on a lead. Galloping across the snow toward her was a third horse.

The animal was black as midnight, and above it floated a disembodied face.

Annie opened her mouth to scream, but the cry died in her throat.

Not a disembodied face—a rider clad in white.

An angel?

Horse and rider slowed abruptly, and the white-clad figure dismounted. He strode toward her, his white cloak billowing behind him. Across his body, he wore the longest bow Annie had ever seen. At his left hip, he wore a large sword, and at his right, a dagger and a quiver full of arrows. "Ye are Annie Johnston Morgan?"

Annie stood, trembling, unable to speak. *My name? He knows my name?*

The man unslung his great bow and laid it on the snow, then he whipped off his cloak and put it about her shoulders. He stared at her with fierce eyes—eyes that seemed to pierce like cold daggers. "Annie Morgan," he repeated, "are ye hurt, woman?" He took a step back and glanced at her feet. "Yer feet be bleeding. 'Tis how we followed ye"—his bearded lips sneered at the dead men—"ye and these devils."

He lifted his fierce gaze back to her, and those terrifying eyes softened. "I'll nae hurt ye, lass. Nae ye, nor yer wee bairn."

Annie at last found her voice. "My baby!"

With one trembling hand, she uncovered Nephi's face. But as her fingers touched the baby's cold cheek...

"NO!" she wailed. "No! You can't be dead!" She dropped to her knees in the blood-soaked snow. "Wake up! Nephi! Oh, Nephi! Oh, God, why?"

"Dead?" her rescuer asked. "He cannae be dead!" He paused. "How can he be dead? The prophecy — It cannae be."

Annie sobbed. "Nephi! Please. Open your—" She felt herself lifted from the ground by two strong arms, then carried with huge, jarring strides, across the snow, toward the wagon.

But Annie did not care. She held her dead child to her bosom and howled her grief to the cold, starry sky. *William! Nephi! Oh, God in Heaven, why?* "Why? Why?" *Oh, God! Take me too!* "William! My baby! My poor baby!"

As they approached the wagon, her rescuer shouted, "The babe! 'Tis dead!"

"Dead?" the woman on the wagon cried. "He can't be dead!"

Her rescuer carried Annie and her child to the back of the wagon. Annie looked up.

She screamed.

The wagon contained clothes, blankets, a pair of Annie's shoes.

And a man's body.

William lay in the wagon's bed. Unmoving. Pale as a corpse.

No mist issued from his nostrils or mouth.

For the last few hours, over uncounted miles of stumbling through the snow-covered road on bleeding feet, Annie had imagined his face. In her mind's eye, he had been bruised, swollen, and bleeding, with teeth knocked out or broken by the mobbers.

But his face was somehow whole—whole and perfect— perfect as a death-mask. There was blood, but it had dried, looking like nothing more than mud streaking his face.

Seeing him lying there, dead—and somehow unmarked by violence as if he were prepared for burial—pierced her with fresh grief as if a bayonet had been thrust through her heart.

"William!" she sobbed. "Dead! Why?"

Her rescuer set her gently onto the bed of the wagon, beside her dead husband.

She turned over and crawled, still clutching her dead son to her chest, to lie beside William's corpse.

"He is nae dead," her rescuer said. "He merely sleeps." The man sounded as if he were weeping as well.

"Touch him," the woman said. She was no longer in the wagon seat, but had come round to stand beside the white-clad man. "Touch him, and he will wake."

"Touch him?" Annie rose to her knees, staring at William's cold, pale face.

"Aye," the man said. "Touch his cheek. His hand. Flesh on flesh. And he'll awake."

"Kiss him," the woman said, and she too sounded as if she were weeping.

Annie looked at William's lips. They were not bruised nor broken. They seemed perfect. The soft lips she remembered, surrounded by three days' stubble.

She bent over him. Her lips touched his.

And he stirred.

He kissed her in return.

William sat up and enfolded her in his arms.

He was warm. And alive.

And mist issued from his nostrils.

"Annie!" he cried. "You're alive! I thought I'd never see you again."

"Alive?" She sobbed with joy. "William!"

She put one arm around him, but the tiny corpse was between them.

"The baby?" William asked.

"Dead!" The word ripped from Annie's ragged, dry throat. "Nephi's dead!"

She held the tiny body to her bosom and let her tears fall onto the sweet, innocent face. "My baby! My poor baby! Oh, Nephi!"

"I'm sorry," her rescuer said. "I'm sae very sorry, lass. If only I'd been faster. If only . . ."

The woman stood with the man. She had buried her face into his shoulder, and she sobbed. "Oh, Tormond! How can he be dead? The prophecy!"

The man named Tormond put an arm around the woman. Tears streamed down his cheeks. "We . . . We failed, lass. We failed. Marcus was . . . wrong. Or I was too slow. I was weak. I was . . . unworthy."

Gently, William pulled little Nephi from Annie's arms. He held the tiny, cold corpse to his chest, rocking their son as he had when the baby was fussy at night.

But that was before. When Nephi was alive. Before Annie's only child died in her arms.

"Nephi Moroni Morgan," William said, staring at the child's unmoving face, "in the name of Jesus Christ and by the authority of the holy Melchizedek priesthood, I command you to live."

Annie held her breath.

The tiny corpse moved.

A puff of steam issued from the small mouth. Little Nephi opened his eyes. Those small, curious eyes looked and found his mother.

And the baby smiled.

✠·✠·✠

"Are ye *certain* sure the babe was dead?" Maebh asked as she rode sidesaddle on Fiona, beside Tormond on the mighty Órd Dubh. *Perhaps we only* imagined *he was dead.*

"Ye saw for yerself, did ye nae?" Tormond swiveled in his saddle, looking back toward the wagon and the road. "The bairn was nae breathing. He was *white*, lass. Pale. I've seen *dead* aplenty. I know *dead* when I see it."

Maebh swiveled in her sidesaddle — the infernal contraption, with all its faults — *did* make such a maneuver much easier than it would've been in the high-canted saddles of centuries ago. As long as she turned to the *left*. She looked back at the little family. William and Annie rode in the wagon, bundled in clothing suited to the frigid night. Annie held her baby, nursing him. Her husband had one arm around her as he drove. As Maebh watched, Annie lifted her head and kissed her husband. *It seems as if every time I look, she's either kissing her husband or her babe.*

'Tis only natural — she nearly lost them both. No, she did lose them both. Only to have them restored to her. But the baby was not *supposed to die.* "The prophecy said nothing about the babe dying or being raised from the dead."

"Nae," Tormond said. "But perhaps that was because *we* did nae accomplish it. *We* did nae save the wee bairn. 'Twould seem our task was but to rescue the lass and deliver her husband back to her. So *he* could . . ." His voice trailed off.

"What he did . . . Was is it . . . witchcraft? Necromancy?"

Tormond shuddered. "Nae, lass. What we did — that was witchcraft."

Maebh closed her eyes, remembering the awful and wondrous scene —

They'd found William savagely beaten and lying on the dirt floor of the farmhouse — just as Marcus's prophecy foretold. William Morgan certainly appeared dead, and it was obvious his attackers meant to murder him. He had a nasty sword wound in his gut. By all rights, he should have been dead.

But his breath misted from his nostrils.

Acting quickly, Tormond forced a few drops of the Witches' wine — they'd brought a small flask as the prophecy directed — into the dying man's mouth. Then Maebh and Tormond watched in wonder as the bruises, the gashes, and even the gut wound healed. They watched as the man's broken legs straightened and mended themselves.

Maebh had never actually witnessed — not with her own eyes — the healing power of the magic wine. And she thought she'd never again see anything so marvelous. Then, while she gathered clothes and blankets, Tormond carried the man to the wagon — careful to not touch his exposed flesh — just as the prophecy directed.

"What *we* did," Tormond repeated, "*that* was witchcraft. But what we *saw* —" He shook his head in wonder. "'Twas a miracle from God. None but the power of God can raise the dead. That man — that William Morgan — he raised the wee laddie to life again. He called him, and the babe awoke. As our Lord raised Lazarus. He called for Lazarus to come forth from the tomb. And Lazarus came forth."

"Like Elijah and the widow's son."

"Aye, lass. None but an apostle or a prophet of God. Ach" — he waved a dismissive hand — "I've heard the legends, the tales of saints raising the dead. St. Vincent was said to have raised more than two dozen from the dead." He shook his head. "I cannae say as I've e'er believed a single one of those tales."

She looked at him askance. "None of them?"

"Nae a one. Save for the miracles in the Scriptures. These other tales ne'er . . . *felt* right. They smacked of fable and myth, a device to get the credulous to believe and obey the church. And 'tis nae as if the church has nae lied to us before, ye ken? Those tales . . . they were very . . . public. That, in and of itself—the public nature of those miracles—does nae make them untrue, but it does smack of . . . spectacle. Of staging. But this tonight was *private*. Nae but the four of us were witness to it. This"—he took a deep breath—"aye, this felt *different* from those tales of public miracles. It felt . . ."

Maebh shivered, but not with cold or fear. "It felt holy."

He smiled at her. "Ye felt it too, aye?"

"Aye." She returned the smile. "I felt it too."

Their eyes locked. For a moment. His eyes gazed into her very soul.

Abruptly, he looked away.

But Maebh did not. She stared at him, the longing that welled within her as painful and sharp as the head of a spear.

The excruciating awkwardness had returned. They'd shared a moment that night. A sacred moment.

But that *other* moment, in the cave, in 1778, before their last sleep—*that* moment when desire and lust had almost overcome them—*that* moment would never go away.

And now, every time he looks at me, every time we touch—even the briefest and most innocent of touches—there is always that moment.

I love ye, Tormond MacDonald, religious, Knight of the Temple.

I love ye with all my heart.

With my all heart and all the rest of me.

Do not torture yourself, Maebh O Broin. And don't torment him, this man ye love. That day will come. But 'twill be in God's way, in His time, and sanctioned by His holy sacraments.

And 'twill be in the top of the mountains.

Where'er and whene'er that may be.

"Tormond?"

"Aye?" He kept his eyes on the road before them.

"If this William"—she almost choked on the name, thinking of the dear, murdered boy with the same name, centuries ago in Wales—"if he can raise the dead . . . at least in this one instance . . . Did he not say 'twas by the authority of . . . the priesthood?

Melchizedek? I know that name. 'Tis both in the Old Testament and the New. In Genesis and St. Paul's Epistle to the Hebrews if I remember aright."

He chuckled. "*Ye* are the scholar, lass. Much more so than I." He gazed at her with affection and pride. He sighed and returned his eyes to the road. "Aye. Priesthood. Melchizedek. And this William did it in the name of Jesus Christ. He spoke as if he had the *right*, the *authority* to command the dead to live in that holy name."

"Could this be the restoration Branwen spoke of? The one Marcus prophesied should come?"

He pursed his lips and scratched his yellow beard. "Mayhap. I dinnae know. And this Brother Joseph they speak of. This *prophet*." He scowled. "There have been many *false* prophets, to be sure. Aye, false prophets and false *popes*. Our Lord said, 'Beware of false prophets, which come to you in sheep's clothing, but inwardly they are ravening wolves.'"

She nodded slowly. "Aye. But our Lord also said, 'By their fruits ye shall know them.'"

Tormond glanced behind them again, at the young family in the wagon. "By their fruits indeed." He shook his head. "But we cannae remain with them—William and Annie and Nephi—nor meet with their people. We must get them safely across the river."

"Into Illinois."

"Aye," he said. "Illinois. And after that, we must go to the new cave in Tennessee. And sleep. Perhaps next time we awake, we can learn more about these people and their faith. And their prophet. He'll most likely be dead by then. But we shall see what fruits have come of that tree, whether they be good or evil. But for now, we have our sacred mission. We have spent long enough in this foul year and this wretched country. Missouri sounds suspiciously like 'misery' to my ears." He grinned impishly, and his eyes twinkled in the starlight.

The beauty of his eyes and his smile made her heart ache. "Aye." *Anything that gets us closer to the top of the mountains.*

Anything that brings an end to this awkwardness, this distance between us.

So we may not be alone. *Separately and singly, even when we are together.*

"But one thing is certain sure," he growled. "The Sergeants best nae be late. Nae this time."

She sighed. "1895, not 1898."

"Aye."

They rode in silence for several minutes, then Maebh asked, "When ye went back to examine the dead men, did ye find . . ."

"The corrupted cross?"

She nodded. "Aye. Ashtoreth's cross."

He shook his head. "Nae, unless 'twas well hidden. They were evil men, aye, but they did nae carry the sigil of the demoness."

"If the Sergeants *do* fail to wake us . . ."

He growled softly. "Then we can only conclude that the *Sergeants* have been corrupted by Ashtoreth. And if they have . . ."

"Then," she said, "we would be truly *alone*."

Chapter 36

McCracken County, Kentucky: July 1895 A.D.

The Executioner and the Shield-maiden lay as if dead.

Ewan MacTaggart, Sergeant-commander of the Temple, stared in wonder at their unmoving bodies. *They do not even appear to breathe!*

He glanced quickly at the two horses—fabled Órd Dubh and Fiona—standing, asleep on either side of the wooden bed. *Even the horses don't appear to breathe.*

Surely, they must breathe – all of them. Just very, very slowly.

Of course, no one can ever know, for the instant they are touched, they awake.

Brother Tormond lay, clad in his full mail and tabard. His hands were folded at his breast, above the red cross on his tabard, and across the hilt of the Templar sword. The sword itself extended down his body, pointing toward his feet. The Executioner appeared ready for battle the instant he awoke.

When Ewan was in London, he visited the Temple Chapel where several Templars were buried. Those tombs were topped with carved, stone knights lying on their backs. Each knight held his sword and shield, some with their legs crossed in the medieval Christian fashion. Brother Tormond was the very image of one of those carved-stone knights, with the exception that he did not hold his shield, and his legs were not crossed.

Sister Maebh, however, conjured up another image entirely. She could easily have been mistaken for the Sleeping Beauty from Charles Perrault's fairy tale. Though her dress was not that of a medieval princess, it *was* a lovely gown from a bygone era. Rather than wearing her nut-brown hair up and in ringlets as had been the fashion back in 1838, she wore it loose so that it lay about her head and shoulders. She was a vision of loveliness, even if she was dressed as his grandmother would have been for a fancy ball.

Every bit as lovely as the tales say.

425

No, the tales do not do her beauty justice.

For a long moment, Ewan thought of waking her first—waking her with a kiss.

Those pink lips have never been kissed. By any man.

He envisioned himself silently, stealthily maneuvering past the horses and the Executioner to get to her—though the Templar had positioned himself in front of her so that such an approach was likely impossible, guarding her even in his magic sleep. Ewan pictured himself bending over her and gently placing his lips on hers...

Ah, but I am a married man. A happily married man.

A happily and faithfully *married man.*

And besides – he grinned – *the Executioner would kill me if I did.*

Still, she is lovely.

He sighed deeply.

"What are you grinning at?" The loud whisper came from behind Ewan.

He jumped, suppressing a squeak worthy of a startled mouse. He wheeled around to face his companion, Roger Mallard.

Roger was a solidly built man, with powerful muscles that the impeccably tailored suits he usually wore barely concealed. Roger stood, grinning at Ewan, as if he guessed the Sergeant-commander's thoughts. Roger nodded in the direction of their sleeping charges. "She's a rare beauty, isn't she?" he whispered. He shook his head, still gazing at the Shield-maiden. "I know a Sergeant of the Temple shouldn't admit to such things—especially a *married* Sergeant, but if I were the Templar, I'd have taken her long before this. Married her, at least. From all accounts, she loves him." He chuckled softly. "The man must be a saint. Or a eunuch."

Ewan gaped at him. "You shouldn't say such things!"

Roger rolled his eyes. "I know. I just admitted as much, didn't I?" He exhaled sharply through pursed lips. "She's probably never even been kissed. Look at those lips! I could do the honors. Wake her with a kiss?" His grinned again. "What do you think?"

"She's a nun!" Ewan was spluttering. "It's our duty to preserve—"

Roger's grin became positively lascivious. "A nun, huh? Not dressed like that, she's not. You've heard the stories about the two of them. You've read the Chronicles. Those two may be religious — *and* keeping their vows — but she's dressing that way to catch his eye, is what I say."

Ewan's eyes narrowed even as his cheeks flushed. "That's enough of that, Sergeant. Besides, keep your voice down. We'll wake them soon enough."

Roger put up his hands in defeat. "All right, Sergeant-commander," he whispered. "But if the noise of us hauling in all their supplies didn't wake them, I doubt a few soft-spoken words would."

"I don't want to wake them until everything is in place, until everything is perfect. Did you get the last of the boxes? The money?"

Roger nodded, all levity — and leering — vanishing in an instant. He was suddenly all business, as befitted a man of his worldly station and occupation. He was, after all, a bank president. Roger knew how to handle money. "Yes, I did, Sergeant-commander."

"What about the . . . *special* box?"

Roger pointed back to the cave chamber entrance. "On top of the money chest." He shook his head, a wondering expression on his face. "You actually met *her* when you were over there, didn't you? In England? You met the vampire?"

Ewan looked past his friend. In the light of the lantern, he could barely make out the wooden box sitting atop the money chest — the wooden box with the large A carved into the lid. "The wax seals are still intact?"

Roger nodded. "Intact." He turned to gaze at the box. "The stories said it used to contain gold. Back in Britain, in the old days. But it didn't feel heavy enough to contain sacks of gold. And it's not as big as the stories say." He shrugged. "Might not be the same box. It certainly doesn't look as old as it should. Probably a new box." He turned to his commander. "You must've wondered what's in it. Wondered what could be so important that she would risk contacting you over there to make sure it got to *them*."

It was Ewan's turn to shrug. "Best not to speculate." *But I have been speculating. That's all I've done since returning from England with the box.*

That and guarding it with my very life.

427

Roger grinned at him. "I don't know how you resisted. You could have pried off the wax seals with a hot butter knife."

Ewan sighed. "I thought about it. Truly, I did. For about two seconds." He shook his head. "Branwen is not a lady to refuse. Ever." *Or to disobey.* He shuddered at the thought. "Trust me on this, Roger."

Roger threw his hands in the air once more. "I believe you. We all have women in our lives we must appease. Our wives, for example. Still" — he paused — "I wish I could meet her. Tell me — is she as beautiful as the Chronicles say?"

Ewan lifted his eyebrows and nodded. "Oh, yes."

Roger pointed at the Shield-maiden. "More beautiful than her?"

Ewan glanced at the sleeping woman. "Yes." He grimaced. "No. I don't know. Having seen both of them, all I can say is . . . they are both beautiful in their own way. It would be like comparing the loveliness of the most beautiful, perfect flower you've even seen to the loveliness of the full moon on a cloudless night."

Roger sighed. "You're a lucky man, my friend."

A sudden shivering tore through Ewan. "Lady Branwen is beautiful. So beautiful. But she is terrifying as well. Beautiful and deadly."

Roger seemed to consider that for a moment. "I think I understand. At least, a little."

"Well," Ewan grinned and rubbed his hands together. "You are about to meet *one* of them."

He turned back toward the low, wooden bed on which the sleeping legends lay. "We're about to meet the Executioner of God and the Shield-maiden of Christ!" A thrill ran up his spine. "And just think! This time, we know *exactly* where the Witches are! We have their address in California! I know it's all in the urn over there — all the information — just as has always been done. But this time, we get to tell them ourselves! In person. It's almost over, Roger! Victory is at hand. Our sacred mission will at last be fulfilled."

And perhaps, when it is all over, Tormond can finally marry his one true love.

I could never say that aloud, not even suggest it. But . . . what a tale that would make!

Ewan, you are a romantic.

"All I have to do," he said, his palms suddenly moist, "is reach out and touch them. Well, touch *him*." He shook his head. "I wouldn't *dare* touch *her*."

"Just get on with it, why don't you?" Roger said. "Quit making speeches. Just do it."

Ewan grinned widely. "Just *do* it." He took a step forward.

Ewan felt a hand on his shoulder.

He saw a flash of steel.

He barely felt the slice at his throat.

Ewan clutched at his neck, vainly attempting to hold in the crimson spray of his life's blood. He fell to his knees, then collapsed, rolling onto his back. His friend stood over him with a knife in his hand.

Roger? Ewan's lips formed the name, but only gurgling blood escaped his mouth.

"I'm sorry, Ewan," Roger said. And indeed, his expression was one of sorrow. "I really am. But the Queen of Heaven commanded it."

Queen of Heaven? Even as Ewan's eyes dimmed, the cave filled with light. Then his sight faded entirely.

The last thing Ewan heard was a honeyed, female voice. "Well done, Roger, my son. Now, leave before you wake them."

Chapter 37

McCracken County, Kentucky: 1898 A.D.

Was he a Sergeant?" Maebh held the lantern aloft and watched as Tormond examined the corpse on the cave floor. The desiccated body was certainly badly decayed, but it did not look as if it'd lain there for decades. *Not like Da,* she thought, suppressing a shudder.

"Aye." Tormond lifted a small crucifix from atop the man's chest—at least Maebh assumed the deceased had been a man and not a woman, judging by the remnants of clothing—trousers and a shirt—and the cracked leather shoes. Tormond held up the cross for her to see.

The simple crucifix appeared to be wood, lacquered dark brown, but it was otherwise unadorned, not even with a figure of the crucified Christ.

"'Tis painted," Tormond said. "'The lacquer probably preserved it from rotting with the rest of the corpse." He scraped away a bit of the brown with a thumbnail, revealing a brighter color. "See. Underneath, 'tis red."

Maebh wrinkled her nose. The corpse didn't stink—not really—but neither did it smell particularly pleasant. It smelled . . . musty. "Red, aye, but what does that signify?"

Tormond turned the cross over with his fingers. "Because only the Sergeant-commander wears a lacquered crucifix. And 'twas always painted red."

"Sergeant-commander? Ye mean, he was the commander of the Sergeants?"

Tormond nodded. "Aye. Under the Templars, of course. Under me."

Maebh knelt beside Tormond, holding up the lantern and taking care to pull her skirts away from the corpse. "How did he die, d'ye suppose? And here, right in front of us? Without waking us?"

Tormond grunted. He transferred the crucifix to his left hand, then reached to his left and picked up another object—a badly rusted knife. "Murdered."

"By whom? Not by another Sergeant!"

"Who else? One in league with Ashtoreth, I've nae doubt."

Maebh opened her mouth to object, but Tormond continued. "Think about it. He was killed *here*." He pointed with the rusty knife at the chests and boxes stacked neatly near the chamber entrance. "The murderer left all this behind. Nae a bit of it disturbed nor ransacked. Nae, he murdered the Sergeant-commander, but left the stuff intact. He could have killed us while we slept—or at least he could've killed *me*, for I've nae doubt ye'd have awakened and put a ball through his heart with one of your pistols. But he did nae kill us." He scratched his beard. "He did nae wake us."

Maebh nodded slowly. "Ashtoreth wants us to live. She wants us to"—she closed her eyes, vainly attempting to shut out the image, the memory of lying naked in Tormond's strong arms—"to fall." *Like David to Bathsheba.*

Like Bathsheba to David.

Maebh almost reached for his hand—so strong, yet so gentle. So warm.

Abruptly, she stood. She glanced at the corpse, then swallowed down bile. "This man, this Sergeant-commander, must've come to wake us, after leaving our supplies. And he was . . . prevented—stopped before he could wake us."

"Aye." Tormond stood as well. He looked at her, and their eyes met. His eyes were so blue, so tender. He opened his mouth to speak, then paused as if changing what he might've said. "I'm glad, lass, that ye're here. With me."

Oh, Tormond! She wanted to fling herself into his arms—even if they were standing in the presence of a corpse, but she couldn't. She dared not. Instead, she smiled at him, though she could not keep the sadness from her smile or her voice. "'Wither though goest, I will go.'" *My love.*

He gave her a barely perceptible nod. "'Thy God shall be my God.'" Then he broke eye-contact.

He strode toward the supplies left by the Sergeants. He stopped before a pile of what once might have been hay for the horses. But the fodder was mostly rotted away. He grunted. "We'll need to get Órd Dubh and Fiona outside to drink and graze." He knelt and picked up the customary urn with its lacquered top, bearing the Sergeants' mark. He smashed the vessel against the limestone floor, then retrieved the scroll from within.

Holding the lantern, Maebh knelt beside him and looked over his shoulder as he unrolled the message. The message was written in Latin—at least most of it appeared to be—as was customary. And with the message in Latin, she could read it only haltingly.

So she waited patiently—or perhaps not so patiently—for Tormond to translate it.

His lips moved silently as he read, then they curled, and he snarled with rage. "*Magairlean!*"

Maebh didn't know that particular word—though it sounded similar to a crude word from her native Ireland—but she was reasonably certain it was not to be used in polite company. She had never heard Tormond utter a foul word, and his use of a curse at that moment frightened her. "What is it?" *Indeed something truly awful.*

Tormond's hand shook with rage. "They *had* them! The Witches. They found them. They knew precisely where they were. Right down to the thrice-damned address in"—he looked at the message—"Sacramento, California, where'er that be." He pounded his fist against his armored thigh as he shook the parchment. "In 1895!"

Maebh covered her mouth with her hands. *No! This could all have been over!*

"And now, 'tis 1898, nae doubt." He bowed his head and covered his eyes with one hand. "1898." He had uttered the year as if it were an epithet, fouler even than the brief curse he'd used before.

Haltingly, Maebh reached out a hand and laid it upon his mail-covered forearm. "Tormond, I'm so sorry."

He gently placed his hand atop hers and turned his face to her. His eyes showed no hint of anger, only sadness. "Nae, lass. 'Tis I who am sorry. I should nae have cursed, especially nae in front ye—ye or any woman. But ye most especially. Forgive me, milady. Please."

Maebh smiled. And then she laughed.

Tormond gazed at her in astonishment, then smiled as well. "What's sae funny? I've just now told ye we have missed the prey yet again, when we were sae close, and ye are laughing? Have ye gone daft, woman?"

Maebh couldn't answer. All she could do was laugh all the harder.

His eyes softened. "Aye, but 'tis good to hear ye laugh, lass."

Maebh at last got her mirth under control. "Ye big, Scottish oaf! Ye act as if I've ne'er heard a man swear afore. I grew up on a farm, surrounded by uncouth Irishmen. I'm not so delicate a blossom as I can't abide a rough word now and then." She grinned at him. "Ye mighty lummox, ye!" She laughed again.

And that time, he laughed along with her.

The horses neighed, as if they too were joining in the merriment.

When the last echoes of their laughter finally died away, only the smiles remained.

Aye, but 'tis good to hear ye laugh as well, Tormond, my heart.

Perhaps, this year, things won't be so awkward between us. Things cannot go back to the way they were, not exactly as they were for certain sure, but they cannot remain the way they are.

Even together, we are alone.

Reluctantly breaking eye contact, she pointed at the parchment. "What else does it say?"

He sighed and uncrumpled the parchment. "Aye, well, it says we can get to this Sacramento" — he paused, and his eyes widened — "on the other side of this vast continent by . . . railroad."

Maebh blinked at him. "Railroad? Ye mean a train? That loud, smoke-belching, foul-smelling contraption we saw in Baltimore?"

"Aye," he said with a grimace. "It says, we can take passage by train at St. Louis, Missouri, and travel to Sacramento, a distance of nigh" — he blinked — "*One-thousand seven-hundred miles, in a week!*"

"One-thousand, seven-hundred? In a week?"

"Aye." He shook his head. "I can scarcely believe it. What's next? Will men be a-flyin' like falcons over the mountains?"

"Well, there are those balloons we've heard tell of."

"Nae. Those can but drift with the winds. They're nae fast, nor can ye steer them — at least nae well." He paused, examining the

Sergeant's message again. He growled softly. "If only we'd been awakened. They knew *exactly* where the Witches were." He shook his head. "If only. If only. Aye, well, there's naught for it now."

"So should we go to this Sacramento?"

He scratched at his beard. "Possibly. Let's see what the Red Book tells us, aye?" He stood, then offered his hand to assist her to her feet. She gladly accepted his hand and his assistance.

She relished the warmth of his hand in hers, and at the same time, dreaded the feelings—the longing—she always felt at his touch. *'Tis just a hand. A knight offers his hand to a lady. 'Tis a courtesy. Nothing more.* She stood. "Let's go consult Marcus."

He offered his arm, and she took it. Together, they strolled to the small boxes Maebh and Tormond had left behind. In one of those chests lay the Red Book that Branwen had given them. But Maebh's eyes strayed to the wooden chests of supplies left by the Sergeants. *I wonder what marvels those contain? What gowns and shoes?*

What amazing advances in firearms? She grinned eagerly.

Her eyes alighted on a small wooden box atop one pile.

A box with a single letter boldly carved into the lid.

A capital letter "A."

It can't be! She froze. "Tormond! Look!" She pointed at the box with a trembling, yet eager hand.

Instantly, Tormond's arm ripped away from her hand, and he drew his sword. "What is it?"

Without answering, she hastened forward and lifted the box, tilting it so he could see the lid.

His eyes widened. Then he looked about the cave. "Branwen? Branwen? Are ye here?"

Maebh could hear the hope in his voice.

But the only reply was an impatient snort and hoof stamping from Órd Dubh.

"She's not here." Maebh was surprised at the emptiness she felt, the depth of sorrow, as the pain of their parting from her adoptive mother came rushing back. *Of course, she's not here. She would never leave Britain.*

Maebh's eyes found Tormond's. Fresh grief was written in those fierce, yet tender, blue eyes. "Aye, well, *somehow* she contrived to get this here. She must've entrusted a Sergeant with it." He gestured behind them, at the corpse. "Probably that poor laddie."

Maebh did not look toward the dead man. Instead, she focused on the box.

"Set it on the ground, lass. Carefully, now." There was a note of fear in his voice—fear for her. "Touch it nae more than ye have already. Let me check it for traps."

Branwen wouldn't— But it's been handled by someone else, hasn't it? Carefully, Maebh knelt, gingerly setting the box on the cave floor.

Tormond knelt beside her. He examined the box without touching it. "'Tis sealed with wax. 'Tis her signet, her A. Aye, and the seals appear to be intact." After his customary inspection, probing with his dagger, he broke the seals and opened the precious box to reveal the treasures within.

The topmost item was, of course, a letter.

When Tormond removed the letter from the box, he uncovered a framed picture—a photograph.

Maebh's breath caught.

Branwen's serene, unsmiling face stared up at them. The monochromatic portrait did not capture the fiery red of her hair, nor the emerald green of her eyes, but it did capture the nearly perpetual smile of those ancient, ever-young eyes.

Tears rolled down Maebh's cheeks. "Oh, Mother!"

She reached into the box and carefully extracted the photograph. A quick glance at Tormond revealed that he was misty-eyed as well. Maebh's own gaze returned to the portrait.

"'Tis very like her," Tormond said. "The science of photography seems to have advanced much since our last waking."

"I miss her," Maebh said, gazing at the unsmiling, yet somehow smiling face. *How I wish ye were here to embrace me and tell me all will be well.*

Tormond touched the edge of the frame. "Aye. I thought we'd ne'er see her again."

"'Tis a miracle. A gift from God." Maebh brushed away a tear. "'Tis as if He—and she—are saying we are not alone in this strange world." *Oh, Mother!*

"Aye." Tormond paused. "What's this, now? A book? More prophecy?"

Maebh tore her gaze from the portrait and looked at what he'd removed from Branwen's box.

He held a brown leather-bound book. He turned it so the stylized gilt lettering on the spine was visible. "Book of Mormon." He wrinkled his brow. "Mormon? Is that nae what William and Annie Morgan called themselves? The name of their people? Mormons?"

Maebh nodded. She looked back into the box. At the bottom lay an envelope. "What is that?"

Tormond handed her the book, then retrieved the envelope. The back of the envelope bore two wax seals, side-by-side. One seal was impressed with Branwen's sigil "A," the other resembled the sigil on the pommel of Tormond's sword—two Christian knights riding a single horse, with three words circling the rim of the seal—

SIGILVM MILITVM XPISTI

The Templar sigil!

Tormond turned the envelope over. On the front was written in Branwen's bold hand—

Tormond,
The letter inside is for your eyes only, my son.
Show its contents to no one else, not even to Maebh.
Trust me in this.
Remember the night you became a Templar.
Remember your sacred oaths.
After you read the letter, burn it.
With all my love,
Branwen

Maebh stared at the writing, then she turned her eyes to Tormond. "Why not me? Why can't I read it?"

Why would Branwen exclude me? Betrayal slithered like a viper up her spine.

Tormond didn't meet her eyes. He turned the envelope over again and stared at the Templar sigil. "'Tis for my eyes only."

"But we are together in this," she protested. *Why would Branwen forbid him to share it with me?* "We share everything, don't we? We have no secrets between us."

His expression hardened. "Nae, lass. Some things cannae be shared. Nae e'en between us."

"But—"

"Nae." His voice was cold as an iron wedge left outside in the dead of winter—a cold wedge driven between them, pushing them apart. "We'll speak nae more on this."

Chapter 38

Weber County, Utah: 1898 A.D.

A week had passed since Tormond burned the envelope and its contents. Branwen was absolutely correct — committing the papers to the flame was the only acceptable course of action, the only thing he could do.

I have honored my sacred oaths, but I ne'er thought doing so would come at so dear a cost.

The papers were gone, burned before they left the cave, but the words and the drawings were seared into his brain. And those words vexed him.

But that vexation was nothing compared to his distress at the pain he'd caused Maebh.

But what else could I have done? She didn't understand, and he couldn't explain what he did, nor why he did it.

I'm sorry, lass. I'm so sorry. I would rather give my life than hurt ye.

He gazed at her as she sat opposite him in their Pullman railroad car drawing room. Her nut-brown hair was done up in the latest fashion, piled upon her head with wee curls here and there almost as if they were there by accident — which, of course, they were not. He had decided the coiffure was bonnie and lent Maebh a certain elegance, but he preferred her hair cascading down her back. Hers was a natural beauty that didn't require enhancement, at least in Tormond's unbiased opinion.

She was, of course, reading The Book of Mormon in her lap. Her precious Bible lay open on the seat next to her. Occasionally, she would consult the Holy Bible, comparing passages in both books or searching through the Bible, investigating something she read in the new book.

Tormond, of course, read from The Book of Mormon as well, and at night, when there was nothing to see outside, save the moon and the stars, they read the book together, taking turns reading aloud. Parts of what they read resonated within him. Particularly the chapters about the valiant Captain Moroni and his war against the Lamanites and against corruption within his own nation. That part sang to his soul.

Other parts, though . . . *Isaiah has ne'er been one of my favorites — may God forgive me for even thinking so — and this Book of Mormon quotes him. Extensively. Although there are some variations, some differences...*

A hint of a smile flickered across his lips.

Aye, and Maebh is very good at detecting and pointing out those variations. She has a keen mind, that one.

One particular phrase in the quoted Isaiah chapters caught his attention.

> *And it shall come to pass in the last days, when the mountain of the Lord's house shall be established in the top of the mountains, and shall be exalted above the hills, and all nations shall flow unto it.*

" . . . in the top of the mountains . . ."

"What did ye say?" Maebh looked up from her reading.

Did I say that aloud? How did she hear me above the constant clack-clack and rumble of the train? "I'm sorry, lass. I did nae mean to disturb ye." He smiled. "So, tell me — what have ye gleaned from yon book today?"

She blinked. "Gleaned?" Her eyes brightened. "Ooh! It says that our Lord appeared to them! To the Nephites and the Lamanites. In America!" She tapped the book with her finger. "After His resurrection, of course."

"Aye? Truly?" He glanced at the book and how few pages — comparatively — remained. *She is so far ahead of where we were last night.*

"Aye." She grinned. "Truly."

Her smile, so rare since they'd awakened — since he'd hurt her feelings — smote his heart. *I cannae speak to ye of the fiendish letter. I gave my oath to God. And I cannae break it. Nae e'en for ye.* "And how d'ye feel about this that ye've read? Branwen said to listen to our hearts, to listen to the whisperings of the Holy Spirit."

Maebh bit her lower lip and briefly turned her eyes away. A tear spilled down her cheek. Her tears had been far too frequent of late. She drew a deep breath, then sighed. "I feel . . ." She looked at him, and though more tears fell, those lovely gray eyes were smiling. "Oh, Tormond, I feel *good*." Her eyes bored into his. "How do *ye* feel about it, about what *ye've read*?"

How do I feel? He swallowed, but did not shy away from her intense gaze. "I feel . . . good as well. Aye. But my heart has been in such turmoil . . . this entire journey. And the constant noise of this infernal train . . . it will nae leave me be."

Sadness softened her eyes. "'Tis that letter. That wretched letter." She took another deep breath, and Tormond braced himself to once again bear the rough side of her tongue. She'd shown her Irish temper aplenty that week. But instead of tearing into him, she lowered her gaze. She closed her book and laid it aside.

She scooted forward as if she were about to stand, but she surprised him by sliding to the floor and kneeling in front of him. She brushed away tears, then looked at him. "Tormond, please forgive me."

He blinked at her in confusion. "Forgive ye, lass?"

She nodded, but her eyes never left his. "I'm reading . . . Well, our Lord is teaching the people—in the book—the same things He taught in the Holy Land. The Sermon on the Mount as 'tis called, aye?"

"Aye."

"Well, Tormond"—she bit her lower lip—"dear Tormond, I haven't been *kind* to ye lately."

"Oh, lass! Ye are the kindest soul I've e'er—"

"Tormond, please. Let me finish." She grimaced and brushed away another tear. "'Tisn't easy for me to admit . . . my sins."

"Sins, lass?"

She let out a shuddering sigh. "Aye. My sins. I have been *angry* with ye"—her lip quivered, and her tears flowed freely—"angry with the one person I love above all others in this world. I have been cross and have said . . . harsh words. Words I would take back if I could. But I cannot. They have been spoken, and I cannot recall them. I've hurt ye. And I beg ye, Tormond, my heart, my dearie, please forgive me."

Love. Heart. Dearie.

Would that I could say such tender words to ye, my love. My heart. My dearie.

But I cannae. I dare nae.

Carefully maneuvering his sword, dagger, and six-shooter, Tormond slid to the floor and knelt with her.

She had lowered her head and was weeping softly.

He ached to take her in his arms, to comfort her—to be near her. But instead, he did something he hadn't done since before he'd held her naked body close to his—he reached for her hands.

When he touched those dainty, soft hands—*so warm!*—she flinched, but then she yielded. Her trembling hands clung to his as if she were drowning again and his hands were the only things keeping her from sinking beneath the waves.

He lifted her precious hands and gently kissed each. "Nae, lass, 'tis I who must beg yer forgiveness. I did nae mean to hurt ye. I simply cannae speak of it. Ever."

Tenderly, she pulled his hands to her lips and kissed them. Then she pressed his left hand to her tear-wet cheek and closed her eyes. "Then *don't* speak of it. Never, ever speak of it. I understand."

"Nae, lass, ye cannae under—"

"I have guessed some of it. No, please do not speak. I'm not looking at ye. I'm not looking at ye a-purpose. I don't want even your face to betray ye. But please, let me say what I have guessed. 'Twill show ye that I *do* understand."

"Very well, lass. Say on."

Her lips curved slightly. "I said, don't speak. Ye don't listen, do ye?"

Tormond could not help but grin. A little. But his grin quickly faded.

"That's better." She nodded. "I saw the envelope. I saw what Mother had written there, on the outside. And I saw the Templar seal. Branwen instructed ye to remember the night ye became a Templar and to remember your sacred oaths."

In spite of the Utah desert heat, Tormond felt a chill.

"I also saw," she continued, "the expression on your face as ye read the letter. Ye looked astonished. Ye looked . . . horrified."

I was horrified.

"And then ye were angry. When ye burned the letter, ye were enraged. I've seen ye in combat, my love. I've seen ye fight. I've seen ye cut down the enemies of God. But I have never afore seen ye enraged."

Aye. That I was, lass. So very angry.

"So, what ye read," she continued, squeezing his hands, "was Templar business, Templar secrets. Thus, the seal. And 'twas sacred to the Templars. All religious — Templar knights, monks, and nuns — when they first take their vows, there are . . . ceremonies, rites." She blushed. "Even *I* went through such on the night of my induction into . . . into that foul order. But I tell ye true, Tormond, the initiation rites I experienced gave no hint of the . . . *true* nature of the order. Nor the horrors to come."

She shuddered, then continued, "The night ye became a Templar, there was a rite, a sacred ceremony. Don't say anything. There must have been. And ye were bound by sacred oaths to never reveal it, to never speak of it. And this letter, the one ye burned . . ."

Tormond's eyes grew wide.

"Tormond, I have a wee confession to make. Ye could only read the secret letter by lamplight. And ye know how afraid I am of the dark. So ye did not go far." She brought his left hand to her lips and kissed it again. "Bless ye for your kindness, but ye did not go far enough. And though ye tried to conceal it, I did get a glimpse of the letter. Just a wee glimpse, mind. I saw Branwen's writing on one sheet, but the bulk of it was in another hand. And at the top of one such page, I saw large letters. They read, 'Satanic Rites of the Mormons.'"

A shudder ripped through him. *She saw that wicked letter? Did she also see the blasphemous drawings?*

"I saw no more than that," she added, and Tormond's relief caused him to tremble again. "Just those words, mind. Naught else."

Ye have keen eyes, lass.

She took a deep breath, let it out, then continued. "So, Branwen sent ye . . . something. A letter. And with it, something else. Another letter, perhaps? But 'twas not something she herself had written — that much is for certain sure. 'Twas something she told ye to read and to burn. And though it said, 'Satanic Rites of the Mormons,' I think . . . I *guess* that what ye saw described your

442

Templar ceremony. Your initiation ceremony. And that is why ye cannot and will not speak of it. Because 'tis sacred to ye. Because of your sacred oaths."

My sacred oaths. He recalled Branwen's words, for indeed, they were also seared into his mind —

My son,

I intercepted this manuscript and its villainous author. The man intended to have it published in order to disparage the Church of Jesus Christ of Latter-day Saints, which I believe to be the Lord's church restored at last. I questioned this man, as only a Child of Lilith can, and discovered that he had been excommunicated from the church for many acts of adultery. The manuscript purports to describe the sacred rites to be had only in the latter-day temples of God.

I do not know if the descriptions are accurate or scurrilous or a mixture of truth and lies. By the time I was baptized nineteen centuries ago, temple ordinances had ceased to be performed. My husband never discussed them, if indeed he had ever received them. He would not have discussed them, for they are sacred, and he was not authorized to administer them to others.

But, my son, I do know the tale of how the Templars found scrolls under the site of the ancient temple in Jerusalem and of how the Templar knights based their initiation rites on the descriptions in those scrolls. Since you are the last of the Templars, the last living mortal to have undergone the Templar rites, I will leave it for you to decide if the descriptions in this manuscript are accurate or not, at least according to your knowledge.

But if there is some similarity to what you experienced as a Knight of the Temple, ask yourself, my son, how did Joseph Smith come to know the true and ancient ordinances that have been lost for centuries or at best distorted? The answer could only be that he was a prophet of God.

Read it. Ponder and pray. Then burn it.
All my love,
Branwen

Aye, he thought, *they were similar. Disturbingly similar. How else would Joseph Smith have known? And why would the author of the manuscript reveal them? Did he nae fear the wrath of Almighty God?*

Just thinking of a such a sacrilegious betrayal set his blood to boiling in fury. *That wicked traitor. That cursed Judas.*

"Did ye hear me, Tormond?" Maebh was squeezing his hands, but her eyes were still tightly closed. "I do not ask if I have guessed aright. Please don't say anything about that. But do ye forgive me?"

Tormond smiled. "Aye, lass. I do, freely and with all my heart. But ye must forgive me as well. I should have been kinder." He paused. "Open yer eyes, lass." *Yer beautiful, gray eyes.* "And say ye forgive me as well."

Her eyes flew open, and her face brightened with joy. "Oh, Tormond! I do!" She let go of his hands, leaned forward, and threw her arms about his neck. "I do! I do forgive ye." She sobbed, her body trembling against his.

Tormond had not held her — had barely touched her, not since that night in the cave one-hundred and twenty years before — but slowly he encircled her in his arms. It felt so good to hold her.

Too good.

"Oh, my love," she said, blubbering, "let us never be cross again. I promise, I'll never, ever be cross with ye again."

My love. If only . . . He chuckled. "Dinnae make promises ye cannae keep, lass. I am, as ye say, stubborn as a pig bein' led to slaughter. Ye *will* be cross with me again, aye? For I'll provoke ye. 'Tis part of yer nature. And I would nae have ye change a thing."

She laughed. "Ye big lummox, ye." She squeezed him tight. "How I love ye."

I love ye too, lass. But I cannae say it aloud.

Part of him wished she hadn't said it aloud.

Part of him rejoiced in hearing it.

Aye, but it does feel so good to hold ye.

"I'm glad" — he paused, vainly attempting to dislodge the lump in his throat — "things be mended between us, lassie." *At least as far as may be.* "So very glad."

"I too."

A knock sounded at the drawing-room door.

Tormond and Maebh jerked apart like guilty children.

Tormond leaped to his feet, steadied his sword, then assisted Maebh to stand. She turned away from him as she dabbed her tears with a handkerchief.

The knock came again. "Mr. MacDonald? Miss O Broin?"

"Aye?" Tormond said, turning toward the door. "Come in, Charles."

The door opened partially. The porter, a mustachioed man who looked to be in his mid-forties, stuck his head in the door. His dark cap displayed his name, "CHARLES," above the bill. His black skin contrasted sharply with his crisp, clean, white coat. He grinned, showing a mouthful of gleaming teeth.

He pinched the bill of his hat and tugged it slightly downward. "Mr. MacDonald." He tugged on his cap again. "Miss O Broin. We'll be coming into Ogden in about five minutes. That's the end of the line for the Union Pacific. You'll need to change trains to the Southern Pacific Railroad to get to California. But they'll take real good care of you, I'm sure. They have the same type accommodations, the same sleeping cars, and they added a dining car a few years back."

"Thank ye, Charles," Tormond said. "Ye have served us faithfully."

"Thank you, Mr. MacDonald," he replied with a grin. "Now, I'll get your bags transferred over to your new car. And your horses will be transferred too. I don't know much about the horse cars on the Southern Pacific, but I know they've got 'em. And the conductor says he'll be sure they get transferred."

Tormond opened his mouth to say something, but Charles cut him off. "I told 'em, Mr. MacDonald. I told 'em. You'll be there to observe the transfer in person. They're taking good care of your horses, sir, miss. Real good care. I gave each of the men those hundred-dollar bills, just like you asked. Yes, sir, I gotta tell you, they were mighty glad to get 'em. They almost never get tips back there.

No, sir. They were mighty glad. You're mighty generous. They've taken real good care of those fine horses."

Tormond nodded. "Thank ye, Charles."

The porter looked past Tormond to Maebh. "You'll have about forty-five minutes to stretch your legs or get a sarsaparilla in the station if you like, Miss O Broin, before you need to board. And I managed to sneak a couple of big carrots from the dining car." His grin widened. "Just like you asked, Miss O Broin." He stepped into the drawing room and presented a small bundle wrapped in white paper. "Here you go, Miss—" His eyes widened, and his brow creased in concern. "You all right, Miss O Broin? I-I'm sorry, but you been cryin'? This desert air—it can irritate the eyes. I know it can."

Tormond looked at her, and though her cheeks were dry, her eyes were noticeably red.

She smiled. "Oh, I have been a-crying. But 'twas a *good* cry. And long overdue. Thank ye for asking."

He grimaced. "I shouldn't-a said anything. I'm not supposed to be— Passengers' business and all, but you both've been so kind to me. Polite. Not like I'm just an old negro porter." He chuckled. "Which, of course, I am, but . . .'"

Maebh strode forward and kissed the man on his cheek. "Thank ye, Charles, for being so kind and attentive." She took the bundle from him. "And thank ye for the carrots!"

Charles put his hand to his cheek. His lips lifted in an astonished grin. "I've never been kissed by a passenger before." He shook his head and chuckled. "Sure am glad nobody saw that. What'll my wife say when I tell her? Kissed by a passenger!"

Maebh's cheeks bloomed scarlet. She looked at Tormond and tilted her head in the porter's direction. "Tormond, don't ye suppose the man deserves another tip?"

Tormond grinned widely. *A wee bit more of the Templar money put to good use.* "Aye. Well done, lad." *Lad? Ach! Should nae have called him that. 'Tis too like the other passengers calling him "boy" or "George."* Why the other passengers referred to the porters as "George," Tormond had no idea, but he knew that "boy" was meant to be demeaning. Tormond reached into his coat and pulled out his money clip. He extracted a bill. "I mean to say, well done, *sir*. Well done." He placed the money into the porter's hand.

Charles appeared to struggle against the urge to look down, to look at the money. But after a moment, curiosity won out over propriety. His eyes widened. "Oh, my! Another hundred? But you already gave me a hundred." His hand trembled, but he extended it and the hundred dollars toward Tormond. "Mr. MacDonald, you must've forgotten."

Tormond enclosed the porter's hand and the money in both his hands. "Nae, Charles. I did nae forget. 'Tis for ye." He winked. "Use a wee bit of it to help that new granddaughter of yers."

Charles nodded. "Thank you, sir. I will." He stuffed the money into a pocket in his white coat. He nodded again, grinning. "I, uh, have to go notify the other passengers." He tugged at the bill of his hat again. "Mr. MacDonald." Another tug. "Miss O Broin." Then he hastened from the drawing room, closing the door after him.

Tormond was certain he heard cheerful whistling from the corridor. He grinned. "Aye. Good use indeed."

✠·✠·✠

Even with the much narrower skirts in fashion in 1898, it was impractical for Maebh to enter the horse cars. Still, she would have enjoyed giving Fiona the carrot in person. She and Tormond had agreed that the carrots would help Órd Dubh and Fiona settle in their new car so soon after being freed from the old one. *A carrot is such a paltry reward for enduring the train ride in that stuffy car.*

Maebh opted to forgo the sarsaparilla in the station restaurant, preferring instead to "stretch her legs" while carrying her unfashionably large—and heavy—handbag, while she gazed in wonder at the mountains of Utah.

"Aye, but they are huge!" *They put the mountains of Ireland and Britain to shame. But the land here — 'tis so barren. So few trees.*

How do people live without green?

Passengers began to board the new train, particularly those who rode in the coach cars, those who'd have to sit up on the benches night and day. *They seek to find a choice seat, I suppose.* Those, like Maebh and Tormond, who rode in the sleeper cars seemed less anxious to reboard.

Maebh and Tormond had ridden in the coach cars on the two shorter train trips they'd taken across Missouri—west and then north—before boarding the transcontinental railroad at Council

447

Bluffs, Iowa. But after boarding the Union Pacific Railroad in Iowa, they traveled in a luxurious Pullman Sleeper car's private drawing room. There were less expensive accommodations, to be sure, and both she and Tormond, as Templar and nun, could easily have tolerated more ascetic conditions, but Tormond insisted on the drawing room.

He said it was so he could best protect her. And while Maebh was certain that was a factor, it had ever been Tormond's habit to do all he could to ensure her comfort. Even when she was cross with him — and she had been very cross — he was ever considerate of her needs and wants.

Well, not all my needs and wants. But that must wait until we awaken in "the top of the mountains."

She sighed. *Best be making my way to the new train. Best to be sure our bags are there.*

Her pulse quickened at the thought of seeing Tormond again. They had been separated for less than fifteen minutes while he attended to the horses, but she longed to be reunited with him. She found even short separations nigh unbearable.

Just as she found close proximity to him maddeningly tempting.

But we have *been separated for the last several days — by more than the walls of a horse car and a few hundred paces. And now that we are reconciled...*

More than a dozen soldiers, clad in their blue uniforms and carrying rifles, were preparing to board the train. Maebh had heard rumors of impending war between the United States of America and Spain, and she supposed the soldiers were being sent west to California — in case those rumors became reality. Several soldiers were saying their farewells to sweethearts and families. One soldier kissed his young wife while she carried a babe in her arms. Two more small children — a boy and a girl — clung to their father's legs. The woman smiled at her husband, but did not attempt to hide her tears.

I wonder if they shall ever see him again?

A pair of surly-looking men lounged on the platform, near one of the coach cars. They leered at Maebh surreptitiously. She pointedly turned to glare at them with a withering look, and they quickly turned their heads. The pair boarded the train in Kansas City and made lewd comments to her at the time. Lewd comments that Tormond overheard.

Tormond showed them the error of their ways, and none too gently. The fading purple and green patches on their faces testified eloquently of Tormond's method of instruction.

As Maebh strolled toward the Pullman car, another couple saying their farewells caught Maebh's eye—a man and woman, although they were most likely not sweethearts, nor closely related. The man, well dressed, tall and thin, had snow-white hair and a thick mustache. The woman was much younger—and much shorter. Her gray dress was stylishly cut, with a bell-shaped skirt, a high neck, and sleeves that puffed out from shoulders to elbows, then were formfitting to her wrists—very much like Maebh's own dress. The young woman's black hair was piled around her head in the style that Maebh had seen in a ladies magazine. "Gibson Girl" the style was called. The maid in their Pullman car had coiffured Maebh's hair in the same style the previous day.

But it was the young passenger's face that caught Maebh's attention. Her skin was a dark red, like a flint.

Maebh had seen a few individuals from the native tribes of the United States, but she had never seen one so dark-skinned.

I wonder—could she be a descendant of the Lamanites in The Book of Mormon? Is this what is meant by "dark skin?"

Wasn't the dark skin intended to be repellant?

'Tis not repellant in the slightest.

'Tis striking. Lovely.

The pair shook hands, then the older gentleman bent at the waist in an almost courtly bow and kissed the young woman's hand. He withdrew his hand, turning as if to leave. The young woman dropped her bag, then launched herself forward and wrapped her arms around his chest. "Thank you!" she cried, loud enough for Maebh to hear. "Thank you, Doctor Svenson! For everything! I *will* study hard. I will! I will make you proud."

The old gentleman—Doctor Svenson—chuckled, but he did not return the embrace. Rather he kept his hands well clear of her as if fearing the appearance of impropriety. "I know you will, Miss Nephi. You have made me proud already."

Miss Nephi? That name can't be a coincidence. She must be a Lamanite!

Something tugged at the back of her mind. A thought or a memory she couldn't quite grasp.

"You have been an excellent nurse — if not a licensed one," the white-haired doctor continued. "And you've served your people well. I'm certain you'll make a fine doctor. And then you'll be an even greater blessing to your people, long after I'm gone." He finally put a hand on her shoulder. "Now you better get on board, Miss Nephi."

She nodded, then released him. She craned her neck to look up at his face. "I'll write to you every week, doctor."

He nodded. "And I'll look forward to reading about your progress. Now, get on board. Medical college won't wait." He tipped his hat to her, then pivoted and strode away. As he walked, his back straight, his eyes staring straight ahead, Maebh was surprised to see a tear on his wrinkled cheek.

The young woman waved at his back, then picked up her suitcase, turned, and hurried toward the coach car.

The pair of Missouri ruffians eyed the young woman, exchanged a glance, and followed Miss Nephi onto the train.

That cannot be good.

Maebh glanced quickly toward the end of the train where the horse car was located and was relieved to see Tormond approaching.

She waved frantically at him.

He waved back.

Maebh hefted her handbag, then wheeled and hurried to the coach car, trusting that Tormond would follow her.

✠·✠·✠

Yellow Moon Nephi was terrified.

She'd traveled by train before — when she came north from Provo, after graduating from Brigham Young Academy. Doctor Svenson insisted she travel by train. And of course, he paid for her ticket.

Just as he paid for everything.

He paid for her college tuition, her books, and her room and board in Provo. He was paying for her to attend medical college in

San Francisco. And though he never said so, Yellow Moon was certain he'd twisted a few arms to get her admitted.

Probably more than a few.

Yes, she'd traveled by train before, but never so far. And never out of the state. If fact, she'd never set foot outside Utah in her entire young life.

However, that wasn't what truly terrified her. What frightened her was the monumental task before her.

What if I fail him? What if I'm not capable of becoming a doctor? They've admitted me, but will they really accept me?

She did well in college, graduating with honors. But that was Brigham Young Academy, where they were at least somewhat accepting of her as a Ute woman. The College of Physicians and Surgeons of San Francisco was different. She had no reason to expect that the medical college would be particularly friendly to or accepting of Mormons, women, or Indians.

What if I fail my people?

First Ute *doctor? First* Ute *woman* doctor? First Mormon Ute woman doctor. So many "firsts!" How can I possibly hope to succeed?*

Father in Heaven, please don't let me fail! Not just for me, but for my people.

For dear Doctor Svenson.

The coach car was mostly empty. Yellow Moon chose a bench at the back of the car. She had to stand on her toes to get her bag stowed in the rack above the seat. She barely managed to get it up there. But once she had released her grip on the bag, she almost immediately regretted it. The bag slid back, out of her reach.

A chill of panic struck her like a blast of winter air coming off the Duchesne River in the high Uintah Basin. "No!" *Now I'll never get it down!*

Everything she owned in the world was in that suitcase and in her handbag.

Yellow Moon looked frantically for someone, anyone to help. *Someone taller than me.*

Which would be just about anyone.

The only other passengers were a woman in the forward half of the train sitting between two children. The tops of the children's heads were barely visible above the bench.

Yellow Moon opened her mouth to ask for help —

"Somethin' wrong?"

Yellow Moon turned quickly toward the voice.

Two large, burly white men stood behind her. Both of them had badly bruised faces as if they'd each been kicked in the head by a mule. One of them grinned, showing gaps in his yellowed teeth.

Something in that grin reminded Yellow Moon of a coyote.

As a young child, she'd lost her twin brother, Winter Hawk, to a coyote. She'd seen the beast rip out his throat and shake him like —

She forced a nervous smile. "No. I-I'm fine." She swallowed, then resumed her strained smile, dipping her head slightly. "Thank you." She sat on the bench and lowered her eyes. She squeezed her elbows against her sides, trying to make herself appear as small as possible.

Please go away. Go away. Go away.

She thought of calling for help.

She thought of the knife she *used* to carry in her shoe, or more recently, her stocking. She hadn't needed a knife in Provo. It was packed away in her suitcase.

"A pretty young thing like you shouldn't be travelin' all alone. What d'you think, Horace? Should she be travelin' all alone?"

A guttural chuckle, then, "I reckon you're right, Tim! A lady needs protectin'. That's what I say."

"But *she* ain't no lady," the one called Tim said. "She ain't nothin' but a Injun *squaw!*"

Yellow Moon tensed, ready to leap to her feet. Ready to run.

Ready to fight for her life and her virtue.

Out of the corner of her eye, she saw the woman at the front of the car hurry her two children out the front exit.

"Ye two don't learn, do ye?" a new voice said — a strangely accented female voice.

Yellow Moon's head snapped up. An elegantly dressed white woman, holding a very large handbag, stood well behind the two brutes. They wheeled to face her.

"You!" Horace said. "The *Mick* bitch."

Tim laughed. "Lost the Irish dandy, huh? Come for a couple-a *real* men, ain't ya?"

The woman laughed. She neither looked nor sounded frightened in the slightest. "*Real* men, aye? 'Tis *men* ye think ye are? Preyin' on defenseless women? That doesn't make ye *men*. It makes ye no better than a pair of rabid dogs." She smiled, and in contrast to her words, that smile appeared guileless, almost sweet. "*Stoneless* dogs."

"I'll show you stoneless, ya Mick bi—"

The woman reached into her handbag so quickly, Yellow Moon was surprised to see a revolver appear in the lady's hand. "Do ye know what I love about modern firearms, Stoneless?" She grinned like a cat that has caught two mice under one paw. "Firearms make a wee lady such as myself more than a match for a pair o' cowardly brutes like ye." She nodded her head toward the exit at the back of the car. "Now get off the train."

Horace chuckled, moving confidently forward. "You ain't even cocked it."

The lady's grin widened, halting him in tracks. "Ooh, brainless as well as stoneless. Well, allow me to educate ye. 'Tis an 1878 Colt Lightning. Double-action." She shook her head. "I don't *need* to cock it." She aimed the weapon at Horace's heart. "All I need do is pull the wee trigger." She winked at Tim. "Twice."

The grin vanished, and Yellow Moon saw in those narrowed, gray eyes the cold look of a woman who had killed before and would not hesitate to do so again. "Now. Get. Off. The. Train."

"But we got tickets!" Tim said, whining like a frightened boy. "We got jobs in California!"

"Ooh, tickets, aye?" She chuckled. "Jobs in California? Bad luck for ye two. Ye can take the next train. Ye are going to miss this one." Her toothy grin hardened and became simply a baring of teeth. "Now, go." She lowered her aim a bit. "Afore I shoot ye where your stones are supposed to be. Ye have to the count of three. One."

The two large men scrambled over each other in their haste to escape, looking like a pair of whipped curs caught in the house, clawing desperately for traction over a freshly waxed floor.

The lady watched them go, scowling, then returned her gun to her handbag. When she looked up at Yellow Moon, both the scowl and the murderous look had vanished. Only kindness remained. "Are ye all right, miss? They didn't hurt ye, did they?"

Yellow Moon shook her head. "No. I'm fine."

But she wasn't fine. Her legs quaked, and she felt as if she might fall. Yellow Moon had never swooned in her life, but the room seemed to spin around her.

"Oh, ye poor, wee thing, ye!" The lady embraced her.

Yellow Moon clung to her savior, shuddering. "Th-thank you."

"Maggots!" came a shout from outside the train. "I told ye!"

Yellow Moon heard a yelp and a very unmanly scream. She pulled away from the lady, then turned and hurried to the window.

The two hapless brutes were running away from the train, pursued by a well-dressed man with a drawn sword. The pursuer, however, stopped after a few yards. He sheathed the gleaming weapon in a scabbard at his hip. Then, he wheeled about and sprinted to the train car.

She heard him bounding up the steps before he appeared at the back of the car. His eyes were fierce, almost blazing with righteous anger from his yellow-bearded face. But when those fierce, blue eyes alighted on the lady, they softened. "Ye're all right, then?"

The lady smiled, and that smile was tender with unmistakable affection. "Oh, I'm safe as can be."

The man jerked a thumb in the direction of the fleeing brigands. "Those two blackguards?"

The lady chuckled. "'Twas nothing I couldn't handle myself." She gently shook her great handbag. "With a wee bit o' help from Mr. Samuel Colt, aye?"

The man's eyes turned to Yellow Moon, and she was surprised at how kindly those eyes were. "And ye, milady? Ye're all right? They did nae . . ."

The lady stepped forward and kissed the man's bearded cheek.

He seemed startled, then he blushed.

"We're both fine," the lady said. "Right as rain."

"I'm glad to hear it." He bowed — bowed! — to Yellow Moon, bending his leg and stooping low. "I am Tormond MacDonald, and if I can do aught to serve ye, milady, ye have but to name it."

The lady extended a hand to Yellow Moon. "And I'm Maebh O Broin." She glanced at the man. "He is my cousin. My *distant*

454

cousin." She'd said the word "distant" as if to emphasize that they were not so closely related that they could not marry . . .

Yellow Moon's legs threatened to collapse again, but she took the lady's hand and shook it. "I'm Yellow Moon. Yellow Moon Nephi. And I . . . I must sit." And sit she did. Barely in time.

The lady—Miss O Broin—sat beside her. The woman was not tall, but she was taller than Yellow Moon, and the lady put a motherly arm around her. Yellow Moon suddenly missed her mother very much. She leaned against Maebh. "Thank you."

The man—Mr. MacDonald—went to the window. He looked left, then right. "I dinnae see them, but 'tis a beastly long train. They could've reboarded at another car."

From outside came the conductor's customary shout. "All aboard!"

Miss O Broin nodded. "Aye. Perhaps I should've shot them anyway."

Mr. MacDonald chuckled. "Who's the Executioner here, aye?"

"Tormond"—the lady pursed her lips—"ye don't suppose we should . . ."

He nodded. "Aye. 'Tis the only thing to do, short of me prowlin' the entire train, huntin' them down like—what do they call those wee wolf-like beasties we read about?"

Miss O Broin said, "Coyotes."

He nodded. "Coyotes, aye." He rubbed his hands together. "Well, then, Miss Nephi, if I may be so bold, we have an extra berth in our drawing room. We'd be honored if ye'd travel with us—as far as ye are going. That way we can keep ye safe."

Yellow Moon's eyes widened. "Travel with you? Drawing room?" She was about to protest when the lady cut her off.

"'Tis settled then. Mr. MacDonald will take care of the extra fare and make the arrangements with the conductor and the porter."

Yellow Moon shook her head. "But I—"

"Is that yer bag up yonder?" Mr. MacDonald pointed at the luggage rack. When Yellow Moon didn't answer, he stepped past her and retrieved the suitcase.

"Stop!" Yellow Moon shook herself free of Miss O Broin's arm, then she stood—as tall as she was able. *These years among the whites have made me soft.* "Please. Stop. I'm grateful. I am. But you're asking me to trust you? Travel in your drawing room? Sleep there? That's a kind offer, but I don't know you. How do I know I can trust you?"

MacDonald set her bag down. "Ye have the right of it, milady. Ye dinnae know us. And I'll nae force a lady to do anything 'gainst her will."

"I'm *not* a lady. I'm a Ute woman. A *mumuch*. I'm not white. I'm—"

"Forgive me." He bowed his head. "I did nae mean to give offense. I am— We are strangers in this time and place. We dinnae know the customs." He straightened, standing tall. He gave her another bow such as she'd read about, such as she'd imagined, in the courts of Europe. "But on my honor as a knight, ye have my word— nae harm shall come to ye while ye are in our company and under my protection."

A knight? As in Ivanhoe?

Miss O Broin shook her head. "Ye don't know us. But, if I may be so bold, what does your *heart* tell ye?"

"My heart?" Yellow Moon thought for a moment. And then she quickly prayed. *Heavenly Father, God of my ancestors, can I trust them? They are so strange, but they* have *helped me. Can I trust them?*

A feeling of peace washed over her. A slow smile crept across her face. "My heart says yes."

Miss O Broin clapped her hands. "God be praised!"

The man bowed once more. "Thank ye, milad— I mean to say, thank ye, fair Ute *mumuch*." He reached forward, then abruptly jerked his hand back and straightened.

Yellow Moon had the distinct impression that Mr. MacDonald had been about to kiss her hand. Mr. *MacDonald? Or would that be* Sir *MacDonald, or perhaps, Sir—what was his Christian name? Tor-something?* "Thank you? For what?"

"For allowing me the honor of serving and protecting ye." He smiled. "For a wee bit, at least."

"Have ye eaten?" Miss O Broin asked suddenly. "Supper will be in a few hours. We would love to have ye as our guest in the dining car." She bounced on her heels as if she were genuinely delighted at the thought. "And for every meal for the remainder of your journey."

Yellow Moon thought of the corn frybread in her handbag—all she'd brought along to eat. "You're already doing so much for me . . ."

Miss O Broin grinned. "Nonsense! Ye can repay us by telling us all about yourself and your people."

"My people? You want to know about my people?" *No one wants to know about my people. They want us to act white. Or stay on the reservation.*

"Aye!" The woman looked as if she might explode with girlish excitement. She reached forward and took Yellow Moon by the elbow as if they were sisters. "Tell me, Miss Nephi—"

Yellow Moon was overwhelmed with the woman's attention and apparently genuine friendliness. "Uh, please call me Yellow Moon."

Miss O Broin trembled with glee. "And ye must call me Maebh! We're going to be good friends, I just know it."

Yellow Moon laughed and shook her head. "I suppose we shall . . . Maebh." She looked at the man. "What should I call you? *Sir Tor*—?" *Oh, what was his name?*

He grinned. "Ye may call me anything ye choose, but *Sir Tormond* feels a wee bit stuffy for my taste. Call me Tormond if ye like. Or laddie. Or hey, ye big lummox!" He winked at Maebh.

Yellow Moon curtsied as she'd been taught. "Thank you, Tormond, Maebh."

Yellow Moon's use of the lady's Christian name seemed to delight her. "So, tell me, Yellow Moon Nephi, are ye a Lamanite?"

✠·✠·✠

"Our original family name was Cuch," Yellow Moon said over a sumptuous main course of mutton chops with tomato sauce, accompanied by green corn, stewed new potatoes covered with walnut ketchup, and preserved apricots. "But when my grandfather and grandmother were baptized as Mormons, they adopted the surname Nephi." She took a bite of her mutton.

"So," Tormond said, "ye are a baptized Mormon."

Yellow Moon nodded, smiling. She chewed quickly, then swallowed. "My father baptized me when I was eight."

"Eight?" Maebh raised an eyebrow. "Not as a babe?"

Yellow Moon blinked. *As an infant?* "Why would anyone baptize an infant?"

Maebh and Tormond glanced at each other, exchanging looks as if she'd said something truly remarkable.

Then the knight asked, "No baptizing of infants?"

Yellow Moon shook her head. "Infants are saved by the blood of Christ. A child must be at least eight years of age to be baptized. Otherwise, how could they *choose* to be baptized?" When neither the man nor the woman replied, Yellow Moon added, "The Book of Mormon teaches in Moroni that infant baptism is an abomination."

Tormond's eyes brightened at that. "Moroni? Captain Moroni?"

Yellow Moon shook her head. "No. Not that Moroni. Another one. At the end of the book."

Maebh nodded with a thoughtful look in her eyes. "We haven't gotten that far. But"—she turned to Tormond—"Branwen said that would be one of the signs."

Yellow Moon asked, "Branwen? Who's that?"

Tormond smiled, but there was sadness in that smile. "A dear, old—very old—friend. A member of my family."

"I see." Yellow Moon did not see, of course, but they were straying from the subject. "My brother, Winter Hawk, died when we were six. He did not need baptism."

"Ye had a brother?" Maebh asked.

Yellow Moon nodded. "My twin."

"But he died?" Maebh asked. "How? If I may be so bold?"

Yellow Moon's voice softened. "A coyote killed him."

Tormond nodded slowly, his fierce eyes soft. "I'm sorry, lass."

"Life on the reservation is hard. Children die. Adults too."

"And that," Maebh said, "is why ye are to become a doctor?"

Yellow Moon nodded. "To help my people."

"Your people," Tormond said, stroking his yellow beard, "Aye. The Utes? They must be a noble people indeed to raise up a young lass with such a strong sense of duty."

Yellow Moon smiled. She smiled too easily—a trait she'd picked up from the whites. Still, a smile seemed to charm white people, to soften their hearts. "I like to think so."

Maebh swallowed a bite of potatoes. "What does it mean? Ute? The name of your people?"

"It means, 'high up,' but the whites say it means, 'people of the mountains.' And that is close enough to the actual meaning."

"'People of the mountains?'" Maebh sighed. "Sounds poetic." She pointed out the window at the darkness. "And your mountains are indeed very 'high up.'"

Yellow Moon grinned, pointing east, behind Tormond and Maebh. "*My* mountains are that way."

"And this land?" Tormond waved his fork in a small, encompassing circle. "This state. 'Tis called Utah, aye? Named after the Ute people? Your name for this place."

Yellow Moon nodded. "Yes and no. In our language, we call ourselves the *Noochi*. 'Ute' comes from an Apache word, *Yuttahih*. The Spanish shortened it to *Yuta*. All these mean, 'people of the mountains.' So, it could mean, 'the land of the people of the mountains,' but the best translation — the one closest to the real sense of the word — is simply 'the top of the mountains.'"

Both Tormond and Maebh gasped, their eyes widening. They dropped their forks onto their plates. Then they turned to each other, clasped their hands together, and cried at the same time, "The top of the mountains!"

Maebh burst into tears.

Chapter 39

Calaveras County, California: 1955 A.D.

Tormond woke when the bullet slammed into his chest.

At first, he felt no pain, only the impact, as if he'd been struck by a mace. He sat up, gripping his sword. Blood frothed and bubbled from his chest.

Pain exploded within him. Tormond tried to suck in air, but couldn't seem to draw breath. He tasted blood.

Gunshots echoed in the cave. The twin stenches of the modern battlefield — gunpowder and gore — filled his nostrils.

Protect Maebh!

He glanced to his left. Maebh lay undisturbed, still asleep in spite of the cacophony of the gun battle.

Tormond rolled to his right, gaining his feet. His chest was molten agony. He shook his head to clear his vision.

A cold light filled the chamber, emanating from strange lamps sitting atop a pile of boxes and chests.

Dead and dying men littered the cave floor. The screams of the dying punctuated by gunshots. One man yet stood, his back to Tormond, shielding the Templar with his body, firing at two assailants. The enemy crouched near the chamber entrance, behind a pile of corpses, firing back.

Órd Dubh and Fiona stood on either side of the cave, their heads down, still insensate in magical slumber.

"Brother Executioner!" their defender shouted. "Stay down!"

Another bullet struck Tormond, glancing off his left pauldron. The blow nearly toppled him. Numbness shot through his left arm.

Two more shots, and one of the attackers doubled over with a cry.

Then Tormond's lone defender fell, struck by gunfire.

In spite of the agony, the wet inferno of his collapsed lung, Tormond staggered forward, stumbling between dead and dying men, raising his sword in his hand. His left arm hung useless at his side.

His remaining assailant rose from his crouch, gun in hand. And as he stood, his shadow grew and grew, filling the cave – a man-like shape with stag's horns rising from its head.

The shadow enveloped Tormond, sapping his faltering strength. His sword arm grew unbearably heavy. He lowered his arm, the sword nearly slipping from his grasp.

Cold filled him. And despair. *Please, God. Let me defend her. Give me strength. In Jesus's name. Amen.*

The attacker laughed. "At last, Hunter!" His voice was as the sound of rushing waters, the howling of a woodland storm. "The victory of Lord Cernunnos is complete! For this I shall be consort to the Three." He gestured with his gun past Tormond to where Maebh slept. "But first I shall take your woman! The Huntress shall be mine, and when I'm done with her, I'll slit her throat." He pointed the weapon at Tormond and leered. "Maybe I'll slit it *while* I'm in the very act of defiling her."

Tormond gripped his sword tighter, forcing his leaden arm to raise the sword once more. *Give me strength.*

Protect Maebh.

My life for hers.

As he staggered toward the demon's avatar, Tormond tried to sing a battle hymn. But all that came out his mouth was a gurgling wheeze.

And blood.

"Crucem . . . sanctam . . . subiit – "

Another bullet struck him in the chest.

Tormond stumbled, then lurched forward again, closing the distance with his foe. "Qui . . . infer – "

Another bullet slammed into him.

"Die!" snarled the attacker, striding toward Tormond. "Just die!" The man fired again, but the hammer clicked on an empty cylinder. He looked down at his weapon in astonishment.

And Tormond lopped off his head.

Bereft of his mortal avatar, the demon fled, howling in rage.

With the demon's departure, Tormond felt a surge of strength. Wheezing and gurgling, acting by instinct and centuries of

461

training, the last Templar wiped his sacred blade on an unstained portion of his tabard. Then he turned back toward Maebh.

She lay unharmed and unmoving.

Tormond stumbled toward her. *Please, God, let me die at her side. As she has e'er been at mine.*

The brief surge of strength collapsed. His vision blurred, darkening. Gore dripped from his lips.

Somehow, he reached the bed and fell upon it. He rolled onto his back, and lay staring up at the cave ceiling. *Keep her safe.*

The pain was fading. All that was left to him was weakness. Weakness and the final struggle for breath.

Tell her I loved her. With all my heart.

The chamber was silent save for Tormond's death rattle.

But then he heard something else. Movement.

One man yet lived.

Friend or foe?

Defend Maebh.

Tormond looked to his right and tried to lift his sword, but it lay at his side. He hadn't the strength to raise it.

A wounded man was crawling away from them.

Defender. Thank God.

Won't hurt Maebh.

God, protect her.

Tormond closed his eyes. *I love ye, lass. My heart. My dearie.*

"Forgive me" — a wet cough — "Brother" — more gurgling coughing — "Executioner."

Tormond forced his eyes open once more. Dimly, he saw a face above his. A man's face. Though he'd not seen it, Tormond knew it was the defender's face.

Tormond tried to force his lips to move, to push air out of his mouth. "Pro . . . tect . . ."

"Only way," the defender said. Coughing up gore, he hefted a round object.

Wine cask.

Witches' wine.

Liquid spilled from the cask. Onto Tormond's lips.

Into his mouth.

He tasted sweetness, mingled with his own blood.

Oblivion took him.

Chapter 40

Calaveras County, California: 1958 A.D.

Maebh awoke to absolute darkness and tomblike silence.

No, not complete silence—she could hear the horses breathing.

But she could not hear Tormond.

"Tormond?"

Órd Dubh snorted loudly, followed by a whinny from Fiona.

But Tormond did not respond.

Alone!

In the dark!

She could *feel* the darkness like the ocean swallowing her, drowning her.

"Tormond!" She sat bolt upright. She groped in the blackness, feeling the spot next to her on the wooden bed where Tormond should've be. Her fingers felt only wood.

Empty!

"TORMOND!" Her scream echoed off the walls of the cave.

Órd Dubh whinnied. Fiona screamed.

Maebh rolled onto her knees. She felt for him again. Her fingers touched cold metal—a mesh of steel rings.

His armor!

"Tormond!" She groped with both hands, touching his mailed arm, his tabard-covered chest. She could feel the rings of his mail beneath the linen. But the linen was crusty, stiff.

Something sharp pricked her questing fingers.

With a cry, she snatched her hands back. She put her wounded fingertips to her mouth.

And tasted blood.

"Tormond?" She felt again.

On his chest, in the midst of the linen-covered mail, she found the sharpness again.

Shattered steel rings.

Shattered?

A hole? A bullet hole?

In that horrible instant, she realized what it was that crusted Tormond's normally immaculate tabard.

Blood!

"TORMOND!" Her fingers probed his chest.

The sword? Where is the sword?

It was not on his chest as it should be with his hands curled around the hilt.

Her fingers found more shattered mail, another bullet hole.

"Ye can't be dead! Ye can't!" She sobbed. "God in Heaven! Ye cannot take him! Please! Please-please-please. He cannot be dead!"

She groped farther up his body. Her fingers touched hair.

His beard!

She knelt over him, placing one trembling hand on his unmoving chest. She patted his bearded cheek. "Wake up! Please, wake up!" Her tears rained from her eyes.

She slapped him. "Wake up!"

He remained unmoving, lifeless.

"NO!" She laid her head on his chest and sobbed. "Ye cannot leave me. What shall I do? Heavenly Father, what shall I do without him? Am I to go on alone? I can't! Not without him!"

She spread her arms around his chest. She shook him.

But he did not respond.

"Why? Why, God? Why did ye take him?"

Black despair, blacker than the cave that had become her beloved's tomb, crushed her. *Why? Why hast Thou forsaken me?*

She remained with her head on his chest, sobbing. Her sobbing slowly gave way to a quieter weeping.

"I love ye, Tormond, my heart, my dearie. I love ye." She swallowed. Determination rose in her. Determination, but not hope. "I shall go on. I shall fulfill your sacred mission. *Our* sacred mission. For *ye*. But I don't . . . know how. But I will honor *ye*, my love." *Will the Sergeants still help me?* "God will help me."

Why did Ye take him? Why? Why have Ye left me alone in this strange, wicked world? A world without hope?

A world without Tormond?

She moved her hands along his chest, until she found his beard once more. She paused, steadying herself, mustering the courage to say the words — the words that would be a cold, iron spike driven into her heart. "Goodbye, my love."

She lowered her face in the dark and kissed his cold, unmoving lips.

His lips moved.

She screamed, jerking away.

"Maebh? Are ye all right, lass?"

A thrill shot through her. "Alive? Ye're alive?"

He chuckled. "Aye."

She heard the metallic rustling of his mail as he sat up. She felt his hands feeling for her, touching her. Then his arms were around her, holding her.

Trembling with her.

"Alive," she whispered. "ALIVE!" She threw her arms around him. "Alive! Alive!"

"Aye, lass. Though I should nae be. I was —"

"Shot! Ye were shot!"

"Aye. Four times."

"I felt the bullet holes." She laughed. "Thank Ye, God! Thank Ye, Heavenly Father, most merciful and kind!"

"'Twas the Witches' wine. It healed me."

"Light the candle, Tormond. Let me see your face."

"Aye, lassie. Give me but a moment."

He let go of her, and though she had told him to light the candle, though she feared the crushing darkness, she feared even more the loss of his comforting arms.

Tormond struck a match, and light flared in the blackness. The match flame was so bright, it hurt her eyes. But there he was. She could see his dear face.

Another sob, one of profound relief, burst from her. He lit the candle, blew out the match, then turned toward her.

And he was smiling. "All is well, lass."

She wiped away her tears. "All is well *now*."

She ached for him to hold her again. But he did not.

She examined his chest. Three holes in his mail. Most of his tabard was the rust color of dried blood. "Ye said ye were shot four times."

"Aye." He tapped his left pauldron, and Maebh saw the fourth hole in the plate mail. "Took me in the shoulder." He flexed his left arm, rotating it. Then he nodded, seeming satisfied. "I think it shattered my shoulder. But the wine healed that as well, of course."

"Then ye are well?"

"That I am. Ready and able once again to slay the enemies of God."

"Tormond, what happened?"

He raised the candlestick higher. "A battle."

Maebh squinted, surveying the scene. Corpses littered the cave.

"I got shot." Tormond pointed to a bullet hole. "'Twas that as woke me." He paused, probing the area of the healed wound. "What's this, aye?" From underneath the damaged rings, he withdrew a small, misshapen object pinched between his thumb and forefinger.

"Is that—" Maebh gaped at the object. "Is that the *bullet*?"

Tormond grunted. "It must be. As my body healed, this must have been . . . pushed out. 'Twas pinned under the chain." He extended his hand as if to give her the bullet.

She shuddered and pulled back.

He set the bullet on the wooden bed between them. He probed the other holes and found one more bullet. "The rest must have fallen elsewhere. Or they're still inside. Nae, if two were pushed out, the others must've been as well."

"Who were they?"

His lips curled in a mischievous grin. "Who? The bullets? I dinnae think they have names, lass."

She narrowed her eyes at him. She wanted to punch him in the arm—not hard, but . . . She also wanted to kiss him.

Again.

Instead, she growled. "Ooh! Ye are joking with me? At such a time as this?"

His grin widened. "What's a wee jest between the two of us. We're alive, lass. Thanks be to God. We're alive."

She sighed happily. "Aye. That we are." *Ye are alive. And we are together.*

He turned his face away and pointed at the piles of boxes stacked beyond the horses. "My guess is these poor lads—the ones near us—were Sergeants. They brought us supplies. I think they were attacked while preparing to wake us. That would have been in 1955, if they were here to wake us as instructed. Since *ye* awakened undisturbed, I assume this is 1958."

And we have missed the Witches yet again.

Tormond pointed to the entrance. "Those blackguards yonder were soldiers of Cernunnos—the demon whom the Witches serve."

Maebh shuddered, remembering their encounter with the horned demon and his avatar in 1778. The darkness seemed to close in around her again, like the demon's shadow on the wall. "H-how do ye know?"

"One of them—the last one standing—declared himself so. He shot me at least two times. I relieved him of his head." He pointed at a round object on the cave floor.

"He shot ye twice?"

"Aye. At least two of the bullets were his. If not more. There were at least two of the villains when I awoke. They could have both shot me. I dinnae ken."

"And yet ye still managed to cross the chamber and behead him?" Maebh imagined Tormond, mortally wounded, charging through gunfire to slay an enemy of God.

"Aye."

"But then ye also managed to get to the Witches' wine and heal yourself?"

He shook his head. "'Twas nae myself as did that." He waved his arm toward the corpses. "'Twas one of the Sergeants. *He* saved me. Put me to sleep again." He lowered his head, then made the sign of the cross. "He was badly wounded himself, the poor, brave lad. I've nae doubt he lies here among the dead."

He turned and swung his legs over the edge of the bed. "What's this?" He slid off the bed, then knelt beside it.

Maebh lifted her skirt a bit and crawled awkwardly to the edge of the bed.

Tormond leaned over one corpse that lay crumpled next to the bed on the cave floor — one corpse among many others.

But unlike the others, that particular body showed no signs of decay, though his shirt showed two bullet holes and huge rust-colored stains of long-dried blood. He looked young, barely twenty, if that. He was clean-shaven, with very short, brown hair. His body was twisted awkwardly, and one hand lay atop a small, wooden cask — a wine cask.

A thrill rippled up her spine. "Is he . . ."

Tormond reached out and touched the hand atop the empty cask.

The eyes in the young face fluttered open. He blinked. Then his mouth opened wide. He sat up so quickly, Tormond was forced to jerk back.

The young man stared at Tormond and then at Maebh with wide eyes. "Brother Executioner! Shield-maiden! Forgive me!" He wrung his hands like a wee lad caught filching a pasty before a feast.

Tormond glanced at Maebh, then eyed the lad. "Forgive ye, lad? Ye saved me. Ye administered the wine to me. Ye defended *us*."

"But we must have led them right to you!"

"Perhaps," Tormond said. "But 'tis nae the first time an agent of the demon Cernunnos has discovered our hiding place. And ye defended us. And ye paid with your lives. We have ye to thank —"

"But I drank the sacred wine! And the rest of it" — he looked in horror at the empty cask — "I spilled it!"

"'Tis nae sacred." Tormond reached forward and clapped a hand on the young man's trembling shoulder. "From the look of ye, laddie, 'twould appear ye needed the Witches wine as much as I. And we still have the one cask left." Tormond pointed at the single remaining wine cask, sitting apparently undisturbed with their other gear.

The man glanced about the chamber, gazing at the decaying corpses. He looked as if he might be sick. "They're all —" He looked straight at Tormond. "Jeepers! Wh-what year is it?"

"'Tis 1958," Maebh answered. "Since we — that is, since *I* went to sleep in 1898 and then awoke undisturbed . . ."

"Aye," Tormond said, "1958. 'Twould be the year."

The young eyes closed in anguish. "Then we failed you again! Again!" He buried his face in his hands, and Maebh could hear him weeping. "We were so sure we had it right this time. We were gonna be here to wake you and— Aw, nuts! I'm sorry."

"Dinnae fash yerself, laddie. Ye saved us. We have lived to serve God another day." Tormond let out a single chuckle. "Another day, another century, aye?"

The young man nodded, then quickly wiped away his tears with his sleeve. "I'm sorry, Shield-maiden."

Maebh blinked in confusion. "Sorry? To me? Why would ye be sorry to me?"

With his head still bowed, he said, "It's not very . . . *manly* of me to cry. 'Specially in front of a lady."

Maebh laughed. She couldn't help herself. "Is that so, Sergeant? Ye are a Sergeant of the Temple, aye?"

He nodded.

"Well," she began, "Sergeant— Do ye have a name?"

"Edward. Edward Masters. But . . . only my mom calls me Edward, and usually only when she's mad at me. Most folks call me Eddie."

Maebh smiled. "Well, then, Eddie—or is it Sergeant Masters I should call ye?"

"Just Eddie, ma'am."

"Well, then, Eddie, where I come from"—she paused— "where and when I come from, men weep when they have need. There's nothing unmanly about it." She winked at Tormond. "Just ask the fearless and manly Executioner here."

Tormond shook the lad's shoulder gently and smiled. "Aye, laddie. There be nothing unmanly about a man who weeps. For even our Lord wept."

Eddie lifted his head. "Thank you." Then he laughed nervously. "But that's not how it is in the good old U. S. of A. Not in 1955. I mean, uh, 1958." Suddenly his eyes grew wide. "Jeepers! 1958! Sally's gonna kill me!"

"Who is Sally?" Tormond asked. "And why would she—"

"My girl!" Eddie looked at Maebh with helpless, pleading eyes. "We had a date this weekend. Aw, jeepers. That was three years ago! Aw, man! I was gonna take her to dinner and the movies and ice cream a-and . . . and I was gonna propose!" He groaned. "By now she's probably gone and married Charlie Brewer! Dang it!" Eddie shook his head. "Not that I'd blame her. Or even Charlie. Not after I upped and disappeared for three dang years." He lowered his voice to a murmur. "Even if he is a girl-stealing putz." He sighed. "She'd be older than me now. Probably married with a kid — if Charlie had anything to say about it. What a crazy world!"

✠·✠·✠

"Where's the rest of it?" Maebh sounded distressed to Tormond's ears. "This can't be right."

Tormond had been examining the simple, full-length trousers and the long-sleeved, buttoned shirt the Sergeants had left for him. He thought the clothes very practical, and they looked as if they'd be easy to put on and take off — not fancy at all, which was much to his liking. The belt, the stockings, and the shoes he understood. But he could not make any sense of a long, thin strip of black cloth.

He looked up at Maebh. She stood, holding in front of her the blue, floral-printed dress the Sergeants had provided.

The cause of her distress was obvious, at least to Tormond.

He shook his head. *Poor lass. She must be mortified.* "'Twill nae cover the ankles."

"The ankles?" Color blossomed in her cheeks. "'Twill leave half my calves exposed! I'll be practically naked."

Naked? Hardly. I've seen ye naked, lass, in all your glory, and.. .

Dinnae think on it, laddie.

But still, 'tis indecent to expose a lady's legs.

Eddie paused in his grisly work. He'd been clearing away the bodies as best he could, dragging them — wholly or in pieces — mostly in pieces — away from the entrance. Some of the dead must have been his brother Sergeants, perhaps his friends, but he seemed oddly at ease with the gruesome task.

The young Sergeant looked at Maebh and grinned appreciatively, as if imagining her in such an indecent garment.

Have a care the way ye look at her, laddie.

Suddenly, Eddie's eyes grew wide as if her realized what he was doing, and he gasped. "Th-that's not really a sh-short skirt. Not at all. I've seen . . . a *lot* of ladies wear them even shorter. Right up to th-the knee! And in the movies and on TV —"

471

Maebh's jaw dropped. "The knee?" She turned her astonished gaze on Tormond.

Tormond felt his own cheeks burning. "The fashion of the times, aye?"

She rolled her eyes. "I'd wager *she* wears such skirts."

Tormond suppressed a smile. *If Branwen could wear such skirts, Maebh will nae hesitate to imitate her.*

Eddie said, "When ladies go swimming, they wear skin-tight swimming suits, with nothing at all on their legs."

"Skin-tight?" Maebh looked horrified. "Completely bare legs? In front of men?"

"Uh-huh." Eddie seemed to be amused by Maebh's discomfort. "But it's no big deal, Shield-maiden. Besides, my *mom* wears dresses—I mean, skirts like that."

"Your mother?" Maebh was almost spluttering. "Skirts th-that bare the *knee*?"

The young Sergeant shook his head quickly. "N-no!" He pointed at the dress in Maebh's hands. "Like . . . like that one. Below the—" His jaw dropped. "My mom! Jeepers! She'll be worried sick! She probably thinks I'm dead."

"Oh, your poor mother!" Maebh paused, then furrowed her brow. "Why didn't she come looking for you? It's been three years, after all."

Eddie hung his head. "She . . . doesn't know about the Sergeants. She wouldn't have known where I went. Or why. Only that I never came home. And even if she *did* know about the Sergeants, the location of this cave was top secret, even among the Sergeants. Every man who knew the location . . ." He looked pointedly at the corpses.

Maebh raised her eyebrows. "Ah. I see. 'Tis an order for men. For men only."

Eddie nodded. "My mom must've been worried sick. And now . . . You see, ever since my dad died this spring—three years ago, now—Mom's been trying to run the family business all by herself. That's why I came home from college for the summer. To help her."

"Your father," Tormond said, "he was a sexton, ye said. Before he suddenly passed. 'Tis a respectable position, sexton. Aye?

And his wife—your mother—would have to be a respectable woman, aye?"

"Sexton?" Eddie looked confused. "Oh, yeah. I *did* say, 'sexton,' didn't I? Because I thought you'd—you know—*understand* that word. But a sexton works for a church. My dad was a funeral home director. He was an undertaker. Do you know that word? Undertaker?"

Tormond nodded. "I know the word. Still, as an undertaker, as an official funerary, he would've been a respectable man, aye?"

Eddie chuckled and shrugged. "Yeah, I guess. We always had to 'behave ourselves' in public. 'Act with decorum,' is what he used to say. But a lot of folks—well, they just thought it was creepy. You know—morbid?" His lips curled into a sheepish grin. "Me, I don't mind so much what they thought. I actually used to help my dad with the bodies sometimes." He looked down at the partial corpse he had been dragging. "That's why this stuff doesn't bother me so much, I guess." He chuckled again. "Might also explain why I like horror movies."

Maebh lowered the dress. "Horror . . . *movies*? What is a *movie*, pray tell?"

"Moving pictures?" Tormond suggested. "Like that kinetoscope we saw in Sacramento?"

Eddie grinned. "I've seen one of those! In a museum. It was really short, though. No, a movie is so much longer. And better. Moving pictures. With sound! And color! And music! Whole stories, not just a few seconds of some guy pedaling an old-timey bicycle over and over."

"Truly?" Maebh's eyes were alight with wonder. "And must ye go to a museum to see such a marvel?"

"No!" Eddie cried. "We've got movie theatres. Big screens! Last year, Sally and me"—his voice hitched only slightly when he said the lass's name—"well, not last year, I guess, but in 1954, Sally and me went to see *20,000 Leagues Under the Sea*. It's a movie. A really great movie."

Tormond eyed him dubiously. "20,000 leagues? *Under* the sea?"

"Yeah! It's about a submarine. They filmed parts of it underwater! It's a Disney flick. Walt Disney makes the *best* movies."

473

"Aye, Tormond," Maebh said, "ye remember we read about a submarine. The Huntley, was it? The Civil War? 'Twas lost at sea, ye remember."

"Aye." Tormond stroked his beard. "I do remember. To be certain sure, there'll be marvels aplenty in this age, as there are each time we awake. But can they help us find the Witches, aye? Sergeant, can any of your technological miracles help us find the accursed Witches?"

Eddie nodded, his expression suddenly sober. "We have radios and telephones and even televisions. We can send and receive sounds and pictures—moving pictures—across great distances."

"Over wires?" Maebh asked. "Like a telegraph?"

Eddie nodded vigorously. "Telephones use wires, yeah. You can talk to someone across the country. You can even talk to someone in Europe, but that uses a radio connection. Radios and televisions—they don't use wires. The signal moves through the air."

Europe? Tormond's excitement rose. "And Britain? Can we talk to someone in England or Scotland? Or in Wales or Cornwall?" *Where'er she may be.*

"Yeah. But overseas is *really* expensive. Heck, talking to someone in the next town over is expensive. But not as bad as overseas. But that's how the Sergeants communicate now. Instantly. That'll help us find the Witches."

Tormond looked at Maebh, and their eyes locked. "Branwen," they said together.

"Branwen?" Eddie's head swiveled from Tormond to Maebh and back again. "The vampire?"

Maebh gasped.

Tormond rose to his feet. He strode to the young Sergeant, ignoring the partial corpse in the lad's hands, and gripped him by the shoulders. "What do ye know of Branwen?"

Eddie blinked, confused. "All the Sergeants know about Branwen the vampire. She was your mentor for centuries. She's a legend. A *living* legend. Well, an *undead* legend, maybe? That's what they call vampires in the movies—undead."

Tormond's eyes bored into Eddie's. "And are the Sergeants *friendly* with Branwen?"

Eddie swallowed nervously, but he didn't look away. "Friendly? That's not the word I'd use. Not exactly. But we're not *unfriendly*, you know? It's just that we can't seem to get any information about her. And we—the Sergeants of the Temple—well, it's our job to gather information, intelligence." He quickly added, "And to serve the Executioner of God."

Tormond nodded. "Aye. But ye . . . dinnae ken *where* she is." He was disappointed, but he was also relieved. He released the Sergeant's shoulders.

Eddie blinked in apparent confusion. "Dinnaken?"

"He means," Maebh said, "ye do not *know* where she is."

"Oh." Eddie shook his head. "No, we don't know where she is. But I think she left a message for you."

Maebh clapped her hands with the dress still in her arms. "A message? Where is it?"

"Aye, laddie." Tormond grinned. He hadn't seen a box from Branwen—not that he'd expected to find one—not that time. "Give us the message, Sergeant. Where's the letter?" He held out a hand to Eddie.

Eddie looked at Tormond's open hand, then met his eyes. "Letter?" He shook his head. "There was no letter."

"Ye said there was a message." Tormond growled in vexation.

Eddie flinched at the sound. "It was just a phone call—you know, a telephone call? At least, we *think* it was her. She identified herself only as 'Mother.' She called for my dad—he was Sergeant-commander for California at the time. Before he died, that is. But I was the one who answered the phone and took the message."

God grant me strength. Will ye get on with it? "Speak, Sergeant. What did she say?"

"We didn't understand at first—because of what she said. Because of the *year* she mentioned. It didn't make sense, 'cause we were planning on waking you in 1955." His lips twitched. "And that didn't exactly work out. Anyway, I memorized the message. She said, 'Tell Tormond and Maebh it's Mother. Tell them the first of June 1958, 8:00 PM Daylight Savings Time, the Multnomah Hotel, Portland, Oregon. Be in Tormond's room.'"

Tormond growled again. "It could nae be Branwen." He did not even attempt to hide the disappointment in his voice. "She would nae travel to the Americas. She *cannae* come here." He clenched his jaw and spoke through gritted teeth, "'Twas one of the thrice-cursed Witches, laddie. The Mother, perhaps." *The one I let escape me.* "Or one of their acolytes. One of Cernunnos' servants." He jabbed a thumb at one of the corpses. "Like those bas— I mean to say, like those poor, deluded souls. Trickin' ye she was, laddie."

Eddie shook his head again. "Begging your pardon, Brother Executioner, but I don't think so. Besides, she's not *coming* to the U.S. She's going to *call* you. *Talk* to you. On the telephone."

Then we shall get to speak to her! All the way from Britain. A technological miracle indeed. "Oregon is north of here, aye?"

Eddie nodded. "About six-hundred miles. We have some intel—uh, I mean, intelligence that suggests Portland was the next destination for the Witches. In 1955."

Tormond grinned fiercely. "And Branwen has determined that on her own." *Of course, she has. There was that mention of "the land of the port" in the Red Book—in Marcus's prophecies.* "What intelligence had ye received?"

"Well, you see, there were some inquiries in Portland for a breeder of ravens. The Witches always require a mated pair of the birds."

Tormond nodded. "Aye. But the Witches will be gone by the time we get there, of course." *Again.*

There's nothing for it, but to go on. Go on as we always do.

"But we *will* talk to Branwen," Maebh said, holding the dress up to herself once more as if imagining herself wearing it.

Tormond imagined her wearing it. He imagined seeing her ankles and legs always on display. *Such lovely—*

God grant me strength. "Aye, lass. That we will. Tell us, Sergeant, be there a train that goes to Portland?"

Eddie nodded. "You *could* take a train, I suppose. But an airplane would be faster. You could be there in as little as two hours—I mean, once we took off."

"Two hours?" Tormond furrowed his brow. "Are we to sprout wings and fly? Even a bird could nae fly so fast as that."

476

The young Sergeant grinned. "An airplane can. It's a flying machine. The Order owns one—a DC-7. Last I knew, it was hangered at Sacramento Muni Airport, ready for your use."

Órd Dubh snorted and stamped impatiently.

Easy, old friend. We'll get ye outside soon.

"What about the horses?" Maebh asked. "Can they ride aboard your . . . DC-7, did ye say?"

"Oh, yes!" Eddie replied. "We planned for Órd Dubh and Fiona. We had padded horse stalls put in the plane just for them." His eyes brightened. "Hey! Since it's 1958 already, maybe we have a *jet* by now!"

Tormond was struggling to follow all the strange, new words. "And what, dare I ask, is a *jet*, laddie?"

Eddie grinned. "Oh, Brother Executioner! Jets are the coolest! Just last week—I mean three years ago—I saw Jimmy Stewart in *Strategic Air Command*. Jets are even *faster* airplanes! A B-52—that's a *big* jet—can fly halfway around the world unre—"

"Faster than a"—*what did he call it?*—"a DC-7?" Tormond asked. "Six hundred miles in less than two hours?"

Eddie rubbed his hands together eagerly. "Yeah! In *one* hour. Just think of it! Jeepers! I've never flown in a jet!"

"Well, Eddie," Maebh said, "that makes *three*

of us." She grinned, shaking her head in wonder. "Five, counting the horses."

Flying machines? Six-hundred miles in an hour? Truly an age of marvels. But.. .

Dear God in Heaven, we've missed the prey again. How are we ever to find them in this strange world full of marvels and things I dinnae understand?

And when we do find them . . . how are we to fight them?

I feel old, Lord. Sae very old.

And useless. He fingered one of the bullet holes in his mail. *My armor is nae protection against the weapons of this world. 'Tis a relic of a bygone age.*

Like me.

The Witches have their magic. Their acolytes have their guns.

How can I fight guns with a sword?

Chapter 41

Pull over, Tormond!" Maebh shouted — a wee bit too loudly — in order to be heard over the roar of the rain beating against the convertible top of the Chevrolet Bel Air Impala. "Pull over!"

Tormond slowed, signaled to go to the right, glanced quickly over his right shoulder through the plastic rear window and through the passenger-side windows, and checked his mirrors. Then he pulled the car over to the curb on SW Pine Street.

At least I remembered to signal that time, he thought, silently bemoaning the complexity involved in driving "the infernal machines," and the ever-present possible threat posed by policemen scrutinizing his driver's license. The Sergeants had provided both Tormond and Maebh with the documentation so necessary to simply get around in the twentieth century, but Tormond was uncomfortable with the idea of presenting his license with its fraudulent birthdate to a policeman. Again. However, were Tormond to disclose his *actual* birthdate to an officer of the law.. .

"Back up," Maebh said, softening her tone. "Can ye back up a wee bit?"

"What's going on?" Eddie Masters asked from the backseat. "What's wrong?" He was barely audible over the rain.

Tormond shifted the automatic transmission into reverse and did as Maebh asked. Twisting in his seat to look behind as he backed the car up, Tormond said, "Laddie, if there be one thing I've learned in my long life, 'twould be that when the Shield-maiden tells me to do something, 'tis best to be doing it — and that right quickly."

"Stop here." Maebh reached for the door handle as if she were about to exit the vehicle and venture into the downpour.

"Wait, lassie." Tormond laid a hand on her arm, stopping her. "What be the trouble, aye?"

Maebh pointed out her window. "They'll be soaked to the skin!"

Tormond followed her urgently pointing finger. He spied two women — one tall and one short — huddling under a single umbrella as they tromped down the puddle-strewn sidewalk through the unseasonably heavy storm. "Aye, lass. I'll handle it."

Leaving the car running, Tormond looked out his window, checking for oncoming traffic. His eyes went to the guitar case propped on the bench seat between Maebh and himself — the case that contained, not an instrument of music, but two instruments of death — his holy sword and his dagger. He almost reached for the case's handle. Instead, he patted his long duster coat over the spot where his shoulder holster was hidden. *I'll just have to trust to the firearm.*

E'en though I'd rather trust to the sword.

Probably nae need for either. How much danger could two wee damsels-in-distress be, aye?

Tormond opened his door and quickly exited the vehicle. As he shut the door, he realized he'd left his hat on the seat. *Too late now — hair and beard are already drenched.*

He hurried around the car through the downpour. *Hardly a cloud in the sky when we were out riding and shooting, and now this?*

Welcome to Oregon, laddie.

The two women halted, appearing to cling to one another. The single umbrella provided little protection from the rain, but Tormond knew they weren't huddling for fear of the rain.

Ye've frightened them, ye gallant lummox. Ye are a strange man confronting two ladies in the middle of a storm. Tormond squelched his urge to bow. *Nae one in this benighted century seem to appreciate or understand the courtesies anymore.* He spread his arms, displaying his empty hands. "Ladies! May we be of assistance?" He gestured toward the car. "May we offer ye a ride?"

"We're fine," the shorter of the two said. "But thank you, sir."

"Please, ladies, I know ye have nae reason to trust us, but we'd be honored if ye would allow us to assist ye."

They both shook their heads. "You're very kind," the short one said, "but we need to be on our way."

The two started forward again, giving Tormond a wide berth.

Out of the corner of his eye, Tormond saw the car door open. Maebh emerged. She wore no raincoat nor used the ubiquitous umbrella so often necessary in Portland. Her long ponytail and floral dress were soaked in an instant.

Tormond suppressed a growl of frustration. He'd hoped to protect Maebh from getting drenched. But there was no stopping her if she thought she was doing the right thing. That very stubbornness was one of the many things he admired in her.

"Ladies, please!" Maebh cried. "We wish only to help ye."

The women halted once more, glancing from Maebh to Tormond. Then they looked at each other. They hurriedly whispered together. The shorter one closed her eyes, but her lips continued to move.

She's praying.

Tormond waited silently. *Leave it to God, laddie.*

While the shorter woman consulted with the Almighty, the taller woman eyed Tormond warily as if seeing him as a potential threat.

I'm nae e'en carrying the sword. She cannae see the gun.

And they have nae idea that I'm a knight — that a knight would lay down his life for any lady.

The shorter woman appeared to shudder briefly, then her eyes opened. She and her companion exchanged another quick, meaningful look. Then she turned to Tormond. She nodded quickly, and her face split in a grin. "Thank you, sir, ma'am. We'd really appreciate a ride. Cats and dogs and all that."

Cats and dogs? What be the meaning of that? But he grinned, then hurried to the car. Maebh stood aside and pulled the back of the passenger seat forward.

The two ladies quickly clambered into the backseat with Eddie. Soon Maebh and then Tormond were safely inside the car as well.

Tormond turned in his seat to get a better look at the women. He noted that they were both young — Eddie's age or perhaps slightly older. They were certainly no older than Maebh's *apparent* age. He gave them what he hoped was a disarming smile — he well knew that he often instinctively presented himself as a warrior, rather than as a gentleman. *Nae wonder they saw me as a threat.* "I'm Tormond MacDonald. This be my cousin, Maebh O Broin." He pointed to Eddie. "And this fine lad is our friend, Eddie Masters."

"I'm Tormond's *distant* cousin," Maebh added. "His very distant cousin."

Tormond suppressed a chuckle. *Establishing your claim again, lassie?*

The shorter of the two young women, sitting between her companion and Eddie, extended a hand to the young Sergeant. "I'm Sister O'Flanagan," she said with a grin. "You're a godsend!" In spite of her Irish-sounding name, Tormond detected no trace of an accent. And there was something decidedly un-Irish about her features — something *almost* familiar, though Tormond couldn't place it.

The other woman extended a hand to Maebh. "I'm Sister MacGregor." Tormond noted the woman's strong Scottish burr. The taller young woman grinned and shook hands with Tormond as well. "'Tis a blessin' to meet another Scot here in the States, though ye dinnae sound like any MacDonald I've ever met. Yer accent is passin' strange."

"Well met, milady," Tormond said smiling. "My family hails from the Isle of Skye." *But 'tis nae my mother's birthplace, but rather my century as defines my manner of speaking.*

"Ah," the MacGregor lass said. "The Isles." She nodded as if that explained everything.

"Thank you for the ride," the woman said who'd called herself Sister O'Flanagan.

"Aye!" the Scottish lass said. "Thank ye ever so much."

"Where can we take ye?" Maebh asked. "And why *Sister* O'Flanagan and *Sister* MacGregor? I don't mean to be impertinent, but ye do not look even a wee bit like a pair of nuns."

Sister O'Flanagan laughed. "We're not nuns."

"Good!" Eddie said with a flirtatious wink and a smile. "You're both too pretty to be nuns."

Sister MacGregor smiled, but did not return Eddie's wink. "Well, we're no'. No' nuns, that is. We're missionaries for the Church of Jesus Christ of Latter-day Saints. Ye've heard of the Mormons, have ye no'?"

Eddie's grin vanished. He abruptly leaned away from the pair as if he'd just gotten a whiff of something rotten.

Eddie's reaction barely registered on Tormond, as Tormond and Maebh looked at each other with wide eyes.

Maebh then turned to the lady missionaries. "And ye, Sisters, are an answer to our prayers. Tell us, have ye eaten yet?"

✠·✠·✠

"Are you out of your doggone mind?" Eddie Masters growled at Tormond as the two of them sat in the Arcadian Grill, the posh restaurant in the Multnomah Hotel.

"What's that, laddie?" Tormond noted the young Sergeant's angry tone—just as he'd noticed the lad's reticent contempt all evening—but Tormond's eyes were intently focused elsewhere. He fought down the urge to grab the guitar case, march over to the entrance of the "Ladies Lounge," and stand guard there until Maebh and the two lady missionaries emerged. He knew, however, such a course of action would only attract unwanted attention. He hated having Maebh out of his sight, where he could not get to her in seconds if danger threatened.

In their suite of rooms in the hotel, the "Presidential Suite" — apparently a number of American presidents, a Romanian queen, and some ridiculous singer named Presley had stayed in the very rooms where Tormond and Maebh were currently living—Tormond was much more comfortable, knowing he was never far away from her. She, of course, needed her time away from him—and from all men—but that was different. It felt safer. *Why is it lassies prefer to visit the necessary together?* He'd never understood the custom. *But at least there be safety in numbers.*

Nae one would harm them if they be together, aye?
And Maebh has her gun. In her purse.
She'll be safe.
She did take her purse, did she nae?

"Sergeant," he said, never taking his eyes from the ladies lounge entrance, "check by the Shield-maiden's chair. See if she took her purse."

"You can't be serious!" The belligerence in Eddie's voice was growing. As was his volume.

"Lower yer voice, Sergeant," Tormond growled, "and obey my command."

With a grunt, Eddie leaned from his chair. "No, she didn't."

Tormond felt like cursing. Instead, he prayed. *Heavenly Father, protect her. I ken 'tis only the necessary, but please keep her safe. This world is so strange and full of danger. And I've been so uneasy of late.*

Please keep her safe.

In the name of Thy —

"You can't be serious!" The Sergeant had lowered his voice, but his anger remained. "You told those *Mormons*" — he imbued the word with sufficient vitriol to sour even the sumptuous dinner the five of them had just consumed — "that you want to be baptized."

"Aye, laddie. And as soon as possible."

"But we're Catholic!"

"Nae, Sergeant." Tormond kept his voice low and even, but he enunciated every word clearly. "I have nae been Catholic since the accursed Pope Clement the Fifth declared me and all my Templar brothers heretics in the fourteenth century. I am a Knight without a church. I'm nae Catholic, and neither are *ye*, Sergeant."

"What? You're looney. I've been Catholic all my life!"

"Ye serve the Poor Fellow-Soldiers of Christ and of the Temple of Solomon, aye?"

"Of course! But —"

"Ye keep yer affiliation with the Templars secret, even from yer parish priest. Ye make yer *true* confession only to Temple Chaplains. And why d'ye do that, aye? Why d'ye keep it secret? Because, if 'twere known ye are a Sergeant of the Temple, ye'd be excommunicated in the blink of a papal eye."

"But — But the Mormons! They're . . . heretics." The last word had come out almost as a whimper.

"Aye, laddie. Heretics. As am I. As is the Shield-maiden of Christ." He paused. *Hurry up, ladies! Be safe in there.* "Tell me, Eddie Masters, Sergeant of the Temple, have ye read The Book of Mormon?"

"No! Of course not."

"Well, I *have* read it. I encourage ye — I dinnae *command* ye — I would nae e'er command ye in this matter — but I do *encourage* ye to read it as well. Ask God if 'tis His word. He'll tell ye. And I tell ye true, 'tis the word of God. And I have" — *though I'll nae talk about that* — "received proofs *other* than the book itself. For one, the Holy Spirit has borne witness to my soul." *And to Maebh's as well.* "I intend to be baptized into Christ's restored church. Perhaps then I'll finally be ready to find and kill the Witches. I'll finally be armed with the truth, protected by the 'whole armor of God,' as Saint Paul puts it." *Perhaps I ne'er was ready before. Perhaps 'tis why the Witches have eluded me all these centuries.*

And when 'tis finally done.. .

The ladies lounge door opened, and Maebh, Sister O'Flanagan, and Sister MacGregor emerged.

Tormond let out a relieved sigh. He felt as if he'd been holding his breath the entire time Maebh was away from his protection. Still, his eyes never left the three ladies. He noted with some amusement all three of them had taken yet another opportunity to brush the rain-produced tangles from their hair and freshen their makeup. "Ye should read The Book of Mormon, laddie." He grinned. "I've nae doubt the sisters could lend ye a copy. In any case, ye *will* treat them with the respect due to *all* ladies. Am I making myself clear, Sergeant?"

"Yes, Brother Executioner." He paused. "I'm sorry."

"Apology accepted, laddie."

Out of the corner of his eye, Tormond noticed that the singer and the band had assembled on the Grill's small stage and were preparing to provide music for the diners. He heard the introduction to a song that had become a favorite of his ever since he first heard it on the car radio. *Dennis Day — now there's a proper singer. Nae that Presley fellow.* The singer crooned in a joyful Irish accent —

There's a tear in your eye,
And I'm wondering why,
For it never should be there at all.
With such power in your smile,
Sure a stone you'd beguile . . .

As the three women approached, Tormond finally allowed himself to look at the Sergeant. He expected to see anger or consternation or perhaps annoyance on the young face. But Eddie's expression was sober, thoughtful.

"Yer crucifix, laddie," Tormond said.

Eddie nodded. He reached into the neck of his shirt and pulled out his small wooden cross.

Just a plain Templar cross. Tormond knew all the lad had to do was keep the corrupted cross, Ashtoreth's cross, hidden — if he were actually wearing one — and show the uncorrupted crucifix to Tormond. But the trust ritual had been established, and there was something comforting about the young Sergeant's ready willingness to display the symbol at a moment's notice.

"Same as always," Eddie said.

"Thank ye, lad."

Eddie stuffed the cross back into his shirt and gazed at the women. "You really think I should read it? The Book of Mormon?"

Tormond laid a gentle hand on the young fellow's shoulder. "Aye, laddie. I *do* think ye should. But I dinnae *command* ye to do so."

Eddie nodded. "Yeah. I get that." The hint of a smile curled the corners of his mouth. "I appreciate it — that you're not *ordering* me to." He chuckled softly. "If the Executioner of God can read it, maybe I can too."

Tormond squeezed Eddie's shoulder. "Ye are a good lad, ye are. I'm grateful ye're here to be our faithful guide in this century." Tormond winked. "*And* to teach us to how to drive." *To drive those infernal, overly complicated machines with their annoying turn signals.* He gave his full attention back to Maebh.

She was smiling, and her eyes gleamed, embodying the song.

Tormond stood and moved around the table to pull out Maebh's chair, and as he did so, he found himself softly singing along to the chorus.

When Irish eyes are smiling,
Sure 'tis like a morn in spring.
In the lilt of Irish laughter,
You can hear the angels sing.
When Irish hearts are happy,
All the world seems bright and gay,
And when Irish eyes are smiling,
Sure, they steal your heart away.

Eddie stood and pulled out both chairs for the two missionaries.

"What have ye two men been a-gossipin' about?" Maebh's tone was playful, but the gleam in her eyes had dulled as she looked pointedly at Tormond, tipping her head—almost imperceptibly—in Eddie's direction.

Tormond winked at her. "Ach, ye know we men and our gossip. When 'tis nae about war and women, 'tis for certain sure about truth, heresy, and other weighty matters of the soul."

Her eyes brightened once more.

Sure, ye steal my heart away.

'Tis a shame to chastise her, e'en a wee bit. But I must.

As she sat, Tormond leaned forward and whispered in her ear, "Ye left yer purse, lassie."

Maebh nodded, and turned her face toward his. "Ye're right. I'm sorry."

"I just want ye to be safe."

"I know." Her enchanting smile returned.

Their eyes met, and for a long moment, the rest of the world faded away—except for the song. *When Irish eyes are smiling . . .* Tormond was seized with an urge to close the inches between them and kiss her. His gaze shifted to her lips—parted and slightly open —and so very tempting.

"Are ye no' goin' to kiss her, laddie?" a female voice asked.

Tormond blinked, then straightened with a jerk. The voice, of course, belonged to Sister MacGregor.

"Go on, then," she said. "'Tis no' as if we've ne'er seen two people in love a-snoggin' before."

He shook his head quickly, feeling the heat rising in his cheeks. Out of the corner of his eye, he could see that Maebh had flushed crimson as well. "'Twould nae be . . . fittin'." He made his way back to his own chair.

"Ach, now!" Sister MacGregor grinned as she sat with Eddie's assistance. "Just because *we*"—she pointed to herself and then to Sister O'Flanagan, who had also resumed her seat—"can no' kiss the laddies or get married while we're out on our missions, we *do* believe in love and marriage."

"Aye," Maebh said, a mischievous grin on her face, "so ye Mormons believe in celibacy *while* ye are on your mission, but not *after*? Once your mission is fulfilled, then can ye marry?" She turned her impish grin in Tormond's direction. "Imagine that, will ye?"

I have imagined it. I imagine every day. And I dream of it each and every night.

But my mission — our mission — is nae fulfilled, my love. And I cannae see the end. Nae until we awaken in the top of the mountains — in Utah. And only the Lord knows when that'll happen.

The Scottish missionary's eyes twinkled. "Precisely. I have me own deary back in Inveraray. We're to wed when I return in October. In the London Temple, no less. 'Twill be dedicated this very year."

"Yes," Sister O'Flanagan said, beaming. "And marriages sealed in the temple of God are not just for this life — not just 'til death do you part — but for all eternity."

"Truly?" Maebh's eyes sought Tormond's, but he avoided her gaze. "Married forever? After death? In . . . Heaven?"

Sister O'Flanagan nodded vigorously. "In the resurrection. For time — that's this mortal life — and all eternity — that's the next life. Eternal marriage is an essential part of the plan of salvation. Would you like to know more?"

Maebh chuckled. "Oh, Sisters! We've already said we wish to be baptized. Of course, we wish to know more. Anything ye can teach us."

The two missionaries exchanged a grin, then Sister MacGregor said, "Is there someplace we could go that's a wee bit more private? We, uh, need space to draw. Draw a wee diagram."

"Perhaps," Maebh suggested, "we could have dessert delivered to our rooms, upstairs. We have a large front room in our suite." She glanced at Tormond, and he nodded. "And perhaps a wee bit of champagne? I noticed ye didn't take any wine with dinner." Maebh indicated her own half-empty wine glass. "Or coffee perhaps? Tea?"

They're obviously teetotalers, lass. Dinnae offend them. He was about to flag down their waiter, Henri — who, Tormond suspected, was not really French at all — standing stiff as a soldier a respectful distance away, but the expressions on the Mormon ladies' faces caught his eye.

Far from appearing to be offended, the two missionaries looked eager, and though Tormond didn't know why, he had the distinct impression that the ladies were about to reveal some new pearl of truth about the restored church. Forgetting the waiter, Tormond leaned forward in anticipation.

"We don't drink any of those things," Sister O'Flanagan said. "No coffee, tea, or alcohol."

"No tea?" Eddie piped up. "No coffee?"

The dining room seemed suddenly chill. Tormond and Maebh locked eyes. "No wine." she said.

And if we cannae drink the magic wine, we cannae pursue the Witches.

"You've gotta be kidding me," Eddie said. "No wine? Not even for communion?"

"No," Sister MacGregor said. "No' e'en for communion. We use water in the stead o' wine."

Tormond swallowed, but his eyes never left Maebh's. "Is this a missionary custom, Sisters? Or is't for all members of Christ's restored church?"

"All members," Sister MacGregor replied. "'Tis called the Word o' Wisdom. 'Tis the Lord's law o' health."

"Oh . . . my . . ." Maebh said, the color draining from her face.

"Aye," Tormond groaned in reply.

At last, he turned to the missionaries. "Sisters, there be somethin' we must confide in ye, somethin' ye must know."

"No!" Eddie shook his head vehemently. "You can't. Brother Exe— Brother Tormond, you can't tell them."

"Laddie, I must. But nae here." He stood, glancing around the room as if expecting to see demon-acolyte spies lurking in the shadows. Or perhaps a horned shadow on the wall. The waiter seemed to be standing closer, perhaps a wee bit too close. It appeared to Tormond almost as if the man were making a show of *not* listening. *The best of servants can be nosey at times. 'Tis likely nae more that than, but* . . . "As ye said, we should go somewhere with more privacy. Sisters, would ye be so kind as to accompany Maebh and me— along with young Eddie here— to our rooms so we may talk?"

✠·✠·✠

"Ooh, she's sae bonnie." Sister MacGregor indicated one of the two framed photographs sitting on the sideboard table in the Presidential Suite's drawing room. "Who is she?"

Maebh smiled. "'Tis complicated. But let's just say she is a very dear friend." *And we will be speaking with her tomorrow night! From across the world. Oh, Mother! I can hardly wait!* "She's family."

Eddie stood near the door as if he were guarding it—which, Maebh supposed, was precisely what he was doing. He snorted. "Family?" he mouthed.

Maebh realized that they'd never explained to the young Sergeant the precise nature of their relationship to Branwen. *We're about to tell these relative strangers everything, and poor Eddie doesn't know who Branwen is to us. And who we are to her.*

We'll need to rectify that.

Tormond picked up Branwen's picture. "She is my ancestor's wife. My step-great-grandmother, if ye will. But that's nae what we must speak with ye about. Ye see, 'tis about wine. We have . . . an obstacle. We must—"

Sister O'Flanagan gasped loudly. Her sharp intake of breath had sounded almost like a squeak. She picked up the second framed photograph and stared at it with wide eyes, her mouth agape. "I— I know this picture. I've seen it before. Where did you get this?"

"'Twas taken"—*is that the proper word? Taken?*—"when we were in San Francisco, visiting"—she sighed—"visiting an old friend."

"Tell me, Sister," Tormond said, "where have *ye* seen it?"

Sister O'Flanagan glanced at the picture. "On my grandma's mantlepiece. It was one of her most prized possessions."

"Yer grandma?" Tormond asked.

"What was your grandma's name?" Maebh asked, but the thrill running from her head down to her heart told her she knew the answer already.

"O'Flanagan. Same as me, but her maiden name was Nephi."

"Nephi," Tormond said at almost the same instant as the missionary.

"Ooh!" Maebh squealed in delight and clapped her hands. "Yellow Moon was your grandmother?"

"How?" Sister O'Flanagan trembled. "How do you know my grandma?"

Tormond and Maebh locked eyes again. He appeared to be as thrilled as she felt. "She must've married that other medical student!" Maebh cried. "The one she was going on about."

Tormond nodded. "The Mormon laddie." Tormond turned to Sister O'Flanagan. "Harold was his name, aye?"

The young woman clutched the photograph to her chest as if it were a shield. "How do you know my grandma?" she repeated.

Tormond laughed. "I thought ye looked a wee bit familiar. Ye have her cheekbones, lass! And her eyes."

"Is she still alive?" Maebh asked, barely suppressing the urge to jump up and down in her excitement. She noted the awe—bordering on terror—in the young woman's eyes. "We knew your grandmother."

"Aye," Tormond said. "Such a noble lady. Tell me, lass, did she realize her dream of becoming a physician? Did she return to her people to serve them?"

Sister O'Flanagan nodded slowly, but said nothing.

Sister MacGregor put an arm around her companion. "Will someone please tell me what's goin' on?"

Maebh took a deep breath. They had intended to confess everything to the missionaries, but now that the moment had come, she hesitated. *Ye've come to the precipice. Might as well leap.* "Look at the picture, Sister. Look closely."

Sister O'Flanagan blinked, then her eyes dropped to the photograph. Slowly, hesitantly, she lowered the framed picture away from her chest, turned it around. She stared at the faded image. Her eyes widened. She looked up, and her gaze flitted from Maebh to Tormond and back to the picture. "I don't understand. You look just like them." She turned the picture toward them. The old photo showed a light-haired, bearded man and a dark-haired woman standing on either side of a young Yellow Moon Nephi.

Maebh sighed. "We look just like them, because we *are* them."

Yellow Moon's granddaughter shrunk away from them, dragging her companion back a step. "B-but this was taken . . ."

Tormond nodded. "Sixty years ago, aye. 'Twas part of what we needed to tell ye. We wish to be baptized. And we'll nae lie to ye about who . . . and *what* we are. If ye'll take a seat"—he gestured toward one of the sofas—"we'll explain."

"And what are ye?" Sister MacGregor was quaking. "Immortals? Are ye . . . *vampires*?"

Maebh stifled a giggle. Eddie snorted again. And Tormond burst into unabashed laughter.

✠·✠·✠

"Can ye no' *boil* the magic wine?" Sister MacGregor suggested. "Surely, 'tis no' the alcohol that gives it magical properties."

So many new rules to follow, Maebh thought. *Comes with having current-day prophets, aye?* "Is that permitted? To drink boiled wine?"

"To be sure." Sister MacGregor waved dismissively. "Me mam makes *coq au vin* all the time. Though me *faither* does no' like that she keeps burgundy wine in the house. But the *coq au vin* is all she uses it for."

Tormond chuckled. "And just like that, our dilemma is solved."

"What's *coq au vin*?" Maebh asked. "It sounds French."

"Aye." Tormond nodded. "'Chicken in wine'—'tis what it means."

"Aye." The Scottish missionary nodded. "Me mam's specialty."

Tormond chuckled again, shaking his head and stroking his short, yellow beard. "With all we've told ye this evening—our fantastical story—ye seem to have taken it all in proper stride."

The two missionaries exchanged an amused look. Sister MacGregor shrugged. "I'll admit, 'tis passin' strange, yer tale. But there is the photo. And Sister O'Flanagan here is especially sensitive to the Spirit. And if she believes ye, then so do I."

Yellow Moon's granddaughter blushed. "I'll admit, your story sounds like a load of malarky. But with the photo . . . well, I've prayed about—silently, of course—and I *do* believe you." She rolled her eyes. "Now, we've just got to get the mission president to believe you too." She nodded resolutely. "But we will. Grandma Yellow Moon was very sensitive to the whisperings of the Holy Spirit. It kinda runs in the family. In fact, I'm named after her. My middle name is Yellow Moon."

"Oh," Maebh sighed. "'Tis a lovely name. I always thought so."

"Thank you." Sister O'Flanagan's blush deepened. "Grandma Yellow Moon and Grandpa Harry settled up near Duchesne, near the reservation. They served Grandma's people 'til the end of their lives. They never got rich doing it, but it was her dream. And Grandpa found joy in it as well. They were very happy together. And because they were sealed in the temple" — she sighed — "they *still* are. Happy and together, that is."

"What a lovely tale," Maebh said. "And ye say, since they were married in the temple of God, their marriage is forever?" *I just want to hear it again. And again. And again.*

"Yes!" both missionaries answered, nodding and beaming.

"Then that" — Maebh placed her hand atop Tormond's, and for once he did not flinch away, though he did not grasp her hand in his — "is where I wish to be married. In the temple of God."

"I *knew* it!" Sister MacGregor exclaimed. "I *knew* the pair of ye were in love." She laughed, shaking her head. "'*Distant cousins,*' ye said! '*Very* distant cousins.'"

"But" — Sister O'Flanagan's smile faded, her eyes narrowing — "to be married in the temple, you must wait a full year after baptism. And the two of you seem so anxious to — "

Tormond withdrew his hand from underneath Maebh's. "I cannae marry — I have made my vows to God. And I must keep them."

"Brother MacDonald," the Scottish missionary said, "God does no' require lifelong celibacy. Marriage is ordained of God. Surely ye ken that now."

"A while back" — Maebh chuckled — '*Tis so liberating to be able to talk without obfuscation!* — "centuries ago, ye see, Tormond was — how shall I put it — bargaining with the Almighty, if ye will, to get Heavenly Father to spare my life. Tormond renewed his vow of celibacy at the time. To save me, ye see. And I'll not ask Tormond to break his vow. To ask him to do so" — Maebh deliberately reached across and took his hand again, and he allowed her, though he seemed to be pointedly staring ahead, away from her — "'twould be to ask him to be less than he is. And I won't do that." She squeezed Tormond's hand. "I would *never* do that. But when this is all over . . ."

Sister O'Flanagan nodded. "When the Witches you spoke of are no more? When your sacred mission is fulfilled?"

Maebh nodded. *After we awaken in the top of the mountains. In Utah. Whenever that may be.* She opened her mouth to speak, but couldn't force any words past the lump that had suddenly formed in her throat. Tears spilled from her eyes.

492

"How soon"—Tormond's jaw clenched as if he were wrestling with emotions he could barely control, and his hand trembled as he gently squeezed Maebh's hand—"may we be baptized?"

Sister O'Flanagan's brow creased as if she were in deep thought. "Well, we—the four of us—must talk a few more times, to make sure we've covered everything—all the basics. A few more lessons, you see. *And* your case is . . . unique."

Unique. That's one way of putting it, as the saying goes.

"So," Sister O'Flanagan continued, nodding gravely, "we'll need to consult with the mission president. And of course, you'll need to meet with the bishop. But"—a smile blossomed on her face—"how does next Sunday evening sound?"

✠·✠·✠

The knock at Eddie's hotel room door came just before midnight, and Eddie Masters was ready.

He drew his Smith & Wesson Model 39 from his shoulder holster and stood to the side of the door. He knew better than to look out the peephole. That would alert whoever was in the hallway that Eddie would be standing right behind the door, making him an easy target. Instead, Eddie thumbed off the safety on his semiautomatic and said, "Do you have any idea how late it is?"

"Room service, *Monsieur*," was the muffled reply—accented and far too cheery.

"I didn't order room service."

"I have a bowl of *vichyssoise for Monsieur*."

"Cold potato and leek soup?" Eddie responded, hoping he remembered correctly. "Sounds disgusting."

"*Oui, Monsieur.* As you say. But that is what *Monsieur* ordered, *non?*"

Eddie let out a breath he hadn't realized he'd been holding. He thumbed off the safety, holstered his gun, and unlocked the door.

Henri, the waiter from the Arcadia Grill, stood there, dressed in his crisp waiter's uniform and spotless white apron, holding a tray with a covered bowl of soup. Henri locked eyes with Eddie for a moment, then Eddie stood aside, allowing the waiter to enter.

Eddie locked the door behind them.

493

Henri placed the tray on the small table. He immediately began moving about the hotel room that had been Eddie's home ever since the young Sergeant—along with the Executioner and the Shield-maiden—arrived in Portland that spring. Using a small flashlight, the waiter checked behind the curtains and under the table, chair, and bed. He shone the light inside the lampshades. Then he made a quick search of the bathroom.

Henri turned on the water in the sink and tub, and the small bathroom filled with the noisy gurgling of running water. Then the waiter silently motioned for Eddie to approach.

Eddie entered the bathroom and whispered just loud enough to be heard over the water, "You sweep my room for bugs every day, don't you? We've never found a single one."

Henri tugged on the jacket of his crisp waiter's uniform, straightening imaginary wrinkles. "You know the drill, kid." Henri— or rather, Hank—had finally dropped his faux French accent. "The agents of Cernunnos and his Witches could be anywhere. And we don't want another disaster like in 1955, now do we?"

Eddie nodded. *But* you *weren't there.* You *didn't get shot.*

You *didn't almost die.*

And you didn't lose your girl when you lost three years of your doggone life, either. Eddie didn't like Hank. There was something about the older Sergeant, his liaison to the Order, that bothered Eddie. But Hank was Eddie's superior, and liking Hank wasn't a job-requirement. "You got my message."

Hank rolled his eyes. "Obviously, kid." He pulled a comb from his pocket and ran it through his Brylcreemed, black hair, then across his pencil mustache for good measure. "Next time, ask for *bouillabaisse.*"

"*Bouillabaisse.*" At least Eddie had heard of that one, unlike *vichyssoise.* "Got it. Fish soup, right?" *It's gonna stink up the room.*

The waiter pocketed the comb. "Fish *stew.*" He shook his head, one corner of his mouth lifted in a half sneer. "Honestly, kid. Your mom never cooked you any fine French cuisine, did she? Meatloaf and mashed potatoes every dang Friday night, huh?"

Eddie decided to ignore the other Sergeant's contempt and the less-than-subtle jab at Eddie's mother—at least outwardly. *You fake-French pig.* "*Bouillabaisse* it is."

Hank smoothed his mustache again with a thumb and the knuckle of his forefinger. "So, kid, what do you have to report?"

Eddie hesitated for just a moment, but he hoped Hank didn't notice. Eddie *hated* this part of his mission. It made him feel like a tattletale, like a snitch in a gangster movie—the ones who'd "sell their own mother down the river for a five-spot." But he *had* to rat them out to Hank. "You were right. They're planning on joining the Mormon church. They're getting"—Eddie's voice broke as he nearly choked on the word—"baptized. In eight days."

Hank shook his head. Then he swore softly. "I *hate* it when I'm right."

No, you don't, you smug jerk. You love it. "So, what are my orders?"

Hank closed his mouth and breathed in noisily through his nose. Then he let his breath out slowly—and just as noisily. "We can't let that happen. We just can't let the Executioner and the Shield-maiden become heretics. No matter what."

But aren't we all heretics? Including the Sergeants? That's what Tormond said. And it kinda made sense. At least, it did when he said it. "But how can we stop them? I mean, if they *want* to do it . . . should we even try to stop them?"

"We have no choice. It's for their own good."

"But isn't the Templar our commander? Isn't Brother Tormond the *de facto* Grand Master of the Temple? We're sworn to obey him without question."

"Listen, kid," Hank snarled. "We've worked too darn hard for too darn long to fail now. We're so close! We know where the Witches will be next time."

"We do? That's great news!"

"Yeah, it is. But it'll all be for nothing if the Executioner turns heretic on us."

"But what can we do?"

Hank grinned, showing a mouthful of perfect teeth—the best orthodontic work the Order's money could buy—and that wide, perfect grin made Eddie's stomach roil. "We got a contingency plan. We've had it ready for a while—just in case this happened."

"What contingency plan?"

495

"If the Executioner's so hell-bent on becoming a Mormon, we're just going to have to *distract* him."

"Distract him?" *I don't like the sound of that.* "How?"

"Tomorrow. At the farm. They'll be out riding and off their guard. They'll feel safe. But we're gonna need your help, kid, so, I guess it's time we gave you *this.*" Hank reached into his vest pocket and removed a small, golden object. "Hold out your hand."

Eddie complied, but it was all he could do to keep his hand from trembling.

Hank placed the object into Eddie's palm—a small gold crucifix with a recumbent sickle moon bisecting the top.

Eddie gazed at the symbol with awe. *Finally!*

"Keep it hidden," Hank said. "Above all, don't show the Templar or the Shield-maiden."

"Oh, yeah." Eddie shook himself. "Uh, I mean, of course not."

Hank's grin widened. His eyes gleamed with a feral, hungry light. "Welcome to the Council of Sergeants, kid."

Light blossomed behind Eddie, in the outer room, and a thrill shot through him. *This is it!* Eddie turned.

And beheld her, shining and floating in the air.

"Kneel, you moron!" Hank whispered.

Eddie knelt, clutching the horned crucifix to his heart. He couldn't take his eyes off the radiant vision. He forced his eyes *not* to linger—at least not for too long—on her perfect, alluring form, focusing instead on her lovely face. "Holy Mary, Mother of God! O Blessed Virgin, Queen of Heaven!"

"Edward, my son," a voice like warm honey said, "blessed are you!" Her exquisite lips curled in a luminous, beatific smile.

Chapter 42

Portland, Oregon: June 1st, 1958 A.D.

We're almost on our way." Coming over the phone, Eddie Masters sounded as frustrated as Hank felt. "The Shield-maiden insists on changing out of her Sunday clothes and into her riding clothes at the *hotel* instead of the farm. So, it'll be another hour. At least."

Hank Boykin cursed loudly. Then he swore again. The other three Sergeants in the ranch house office stared at him in shock. As Sergeant-commander of the Temple, Hank rarely used foul language — at least not the really bad words, at least not in public, and never in front of the other members of the Council, and never in his persona as Henri, the French waiter — he had an image to maintain, after all. But at that moment, he didn't care who heard him. Swearing was the least of Hank's indulgences.

Hank covered the telephone mouthpiece with his hand. "Another hour!"

His three companions reacted with a groan, a snarl — one even thumped his fist loudly against the oak-paneled wall — but none of them swore. And that simple act of forbearance on their part infuriated Hank all the more.

It had been such a simple plan. A good plan.

But it can still work.

He uncovered the mouthpiece and snapped, "What the hell took so long?"

"Church!" was Eddie's reply. "Mormon church. They've had *two* meetings already. Something called 'Priesthood,' which the Shield-maiden wasn't invited to, and Sunday School."

Hank looked up at the horseshoe-shaped wall clock. "It's already 1:35. You'd think they'd just have mass in the morning like any sensible Catholic and be done with church for the whole week."

"Well, they're *still* not done," Eddie growled. "They've got something called 'Sacrament Meeting' at five. Or 'Fast and . . .

497

something-or-other Meeting.' I'm a little confused on that. Apparently, that's where they have their version of the eucharist. But they already had their eucharist in Sunday School. I just don't get it. Anyway, they're planning on going back, leaving the farm, at four — you know — for the five o'clock meeting — so they're only planning on taking the horses out for a quick ride."

Hank grinned and smoothed his pencil-thin mustache. "But they won't be making it back for any five o'clock meeting, now, will they?"

"Gotta go!" Eddie whispered.

Hank heard the click of the phone connection terminating. He slammed the receiver down. Then he unbuckled the antlered helmet he'd been wearing and laid the helmet on the desk.

The other three Sergeants removed their horned helmets as well.

"I hate this thing," Don Morales said as he set his helm on the desk beside Hank's. Don poked his fingers into the eye slits of his helm. "It itches and you can't see and it doesn't look anything like what our spies described anyway. I don't think the Templar's gonna be fooled. He's not gonna think we're agents of Cernunnos, just 'cause we're wearing antlers on our heads."

"He's not stupid," Corey Petersen said. "Out of date, out of time, yeah. But not stupid."

"Even if he's not fooled," Jason Morgenthaler said, "at least he won't know it's us."

"Yeah." Don lit up a cigarette. "That's the important thing — that they don't know who's behind this. That they think it's the bad guys."

Corey lit up a Salem as well, took a long drag, then leaned back. "So, where's she getting" — he grinned — "broken in? Here? Or are we sending her overseas?"

Jason chuckled. "You *wish* she was getting broken in here." He wasn't one for smoking but got up and poured himself a shot of whiskey. "Imagine that, will ya? Being the one to *finally* take the Shield-maiden of Christ." He downed the whiskey, grimaced briefly as the alcohol burned his throat, and gave out a loud, wistful sigh. "What I wouldn't give . . ."

"Morons," Hank muttered. "Bunch of morons. Maebh O Broin is not going to be *taken* on the altar. Not here. Not anywhere. And she's not going to be sold to some Commie official in Moscow or East Berlin. No, sir. The bitch is *special*. The Queen of Heaven wants the bitch to *fall*. She wants the Shield-maiden and the Templar to break their vows together of their own free will. After all the times the Executioner and the Shield-maiden have thwarted her over the centuries, *that* would be the ultimate revenge."

Don took another long drag on his cigarette. "The ultimate revenge." He nodded. "Still, it's a shame. Maebh *would* be the ultimate sacrifice, don't ya think?"

Jason poured himself another shot of whiskey. "Sure as shootin'!" He shivered as if in anticipation. "One *fine* sacrifice." He downed the whiskey.

"Hold off on the hooch!" Hank snapped.

"Why?" Jason retorted. "We got an hour." He began to remove the white robe that—along with the antlered helms—constituted their Cernunnos-acolyte disguises.

"Leave it on," Hank ordered. Jason started to protest, but Hank didn't give him the chance. "Just leave it on." The Sergeant-commander heaved himself out of his chair and stomped toward the bookcase.

It was such a lovely bookcase, filled with books about horses—everything from horse-breeding and equine veterinary medicine to the novels of Mary O'Hara. *Books, books, books. Horses, horses, horses. As if that's what this place is really about.* He pulled on the copy of "My Friend Flicka," then heard the click and whoosh as the bookcase swung back, revealing the hidden chamber beyond.

The lights came on automatically and glinted off the cache of weapons—rack upon rack of American and Soviet-made semiautomatic sidearms, M3 submachine guns, Kalashnikov automatic rifles, boxes of ammunition, grenade belts, and half a dozen M2 flamethrowers sitting on the floor—everything a growing boy and his spunky pals might need. Hank wrinkled his nose at the ever-present scent of gasoline from the M2s, but it wasn't the arsenal that drew Hank's attention at that moment. No, Hank's eyes went straight to the altar.

The stone altar was cushioned on the top, with a padded shackle below two corners — one for each wrist. And above the altar hung the horned cross — symbol of the Queen of Heaven.

Hank imagined Maebh O Broin on that altar, chained down and wearing a spotless, white nun's habit, her legs held by two strong men. He imagined her — as he so often had since the first time he'd posed as "Henri, the French waiter," serving her and Tormond in the Arcadia Grill. She'd be pure and virginal and screaming and pleading for deliverance — just like all the others he'd taken there. And, oh, he'd give her deliverance. Yes, indeed, he would. A fine *sacrifice*.

But not for you, Hank, old boy. Not for you. Not her.

A grin crept across his face. *But I get those two Mormon missionary bitches. They're promised to me.*

As soon as the Executioner is distracted.

"So, if she's not gonna be broken in here" — Corey's voice came from behind him — "and she's not gonna be sold overseas, where are we gonna keep her?"

"The idea" — Hank began — "is that the Executioner will be so busy searching for her, he won't have time to turn heretic. You know how he is when it comes to her."

"Yeah" — Corey paused — "completely obsessed." Corey paused again, as if drawing in a deep breath.

Drawing a deep breath or taking a long drag on —

The blood froze in Hank's veins. He spun around.

— a cigarette! In the vault!

"Get back!" Hank waved frantically at the other Sergeant and the lit cigarette dangling precariously from his lips. "Get that damn thing out of here!"

Corey's eyes went wide as teacups, and the cigarette fell from his lips to the floor. He stomped on it desperately, putting it out. "Sorry! Sorry!"

Hank let out a stream of curses, ending with, "Damn moron!" He shoved Corey out of the chamber, sending the white-robed man sprawling on the office floor.

Hank gave Corey a vicious kick in the ribs. "Idiot!"

Corey grunted in pain.

Don and Jason were on their feet, but they did not interfere.

Hank aimed a kick at Corey's groin.

Corey screamed like a little girl. When Hank kicked him again — in the same place — Corey's scream rose another two octaves.

"Kill us all!" Hank bellowed. Then he turned his blazing eyes on Don and his dangling cigarette. "I thought I told you to fix that gas leak. M2's leaking! I told you. I told you!"

Don lifted his hands in a placating gesture. "Sorry, Hank. As soon as this is over. Tonight. I promise. After we —"

The office door burst open. Tormond leaped into the room, a pistol in his hand and his sword at his hip. He was followed by Eddie Masters, also holding a semiautomatic sidearm.

Hank shoved his hand into his white robe, desperately reaching for his own weapon. But the robe, the disguise, got in his way.

"Do it, Hank!" Eddie snarled. "Give me an excuse."

Traitor! Hank raised his hands in surrender. "You said we had an hour." Even to his own ears, he sounded ridiculous.

Eddie shrugged. "I lied. I'm pretty sure God'll forgive me."

"The four of ye," the Executioner ordered, his voice hard and cold as winter iron, "against the wall." He gestured with his gun.

Hank, Don, and Jason moved to comply, but Corey could only whimper on the floor, clutching at his groin with bloodied hands.

"The one on the ground," the Executioner said, "get his weapon."

Eddie handed his own gun to Tormond, then knelt beside Corey.

The injured man offered no protest as Eddie ripped open Corey's robe and retrieved his sidearm. Eddie set the weapon on the floor next to Tormond's feet.

"Now," the Executioner said, "ye will rip open yer own robes in like manner, aye? Keeping yer hands well away from yer weapons, aye?"

Hank's gaze flitted about the room, seeking a way to escape. *If I go for my gun, he'll shoot me.* He glanced at the no-longer-hidden chamber and the bounty of weaponry there.

"Dinnae e'en think of it, laddie," the Executioner said. "I may nae be as good a shot as the Shield-maiden ye" — his voice dropped

501

to a growl—"sought to abduct and defile, aye? But at this close range, I'll be certain sure to put a bullet in yer heart. Now open yer robe."

Hank complied. He heard Don and Jason ripping their robes open as well.

"As they say in the movies," Tormond said with a cold grin, "hands up. Again."

Hank, Don, and Jason obeyed.

"Sergeant Masters," Tormond said, "get their weapons."

Eddie stepped up to Hank and reached into Hank's shoulder holster, relieving the Sergeant-commander of his Smith & Wesson.

"Traitor!" Hank snarled. "I *trusted* you!"

Eddie raised an eyebrow. "You seriously expected me to betray the Executioner and the Shield-maiden? To betray God? You really are an idiot. Even worse, Hank, you're"—Eddie paused, then imitated Hank's faux French accent, "a pretentious jerk."

Tormond chuckled softly. "I think ye did the French voice a wee bit better than he did, Sergeant."

Hank swore under his breath.

As Eddie moved down the row and gathered up Don's and Jason's weapons, Hank whispered, "You betrayed the Virgin Mary."

Eddie stepped back with the guns in his hands, keeping well out of Hank's reach. "That *thing* was never the Blessed Virgin. And you know it."

"What are you going to d-do with us?" Jason's voice trembled and took on a petulant note. "E-execute us?"

"'Tis what I should do. 'Tis what ye deserve. And I am the Executioner of God, aye?"

"It'd be murder," Jason whined. "Cold-blooded murder! Please! M-mercy!"

A low growl filled the room. The Executioner had bared his teeth. His gaze was fixed on Jason.

Hank was suddenly grateful those fierce eyes were not focused on him.

"Tell me, ye vile worm," the Executioner snarled, "did *they* nae beg for mercy, the innocents ye ravished on yon altar? How many was't? How many innocents did ye defile? HOW MANY?"

Jason sobbed. "I—I d-don't know."

"Liar!" The Executioner shifted his burning focus to Hank. "How many, dog? Each one brings ye the sentence of death. HOW MANY?"

Hank's bowels churned as if he might soil himself. But in the midst of his terror, from somewhere deep inside himself, he found the spark of another emotion.

He found rage. "How dare you?"

"Eh?" The Executioner seemed taken aback.

Hank forced his trembling body to stand a bit straighter. "How dare you? I serve the Queen of Heaven!" He gathered his outrage, channeling it into his voice, steadying it. "I have served her all my days! Well and faithfully! What are you? The Executioner of God? Of Jehovah? You've been pursuing your prey for centuries and YOU NEVER FOUND THEM! Some Executioner. Some hunter. I've been a better, more valiant servant of the Blessed Virgin than you have ever been to your pathetic Christ." He lowered his voice, meeting the Executioner's hard gaze. "At least I've *had* women. At least I'm not a *eunuch* like you."

"Had women?" Eddie sneered at him. "You've *raped* women. That doesn't make you a man. It just makes you an animal."

"If y-you let us go," Don said, the cigarette finally falling from his quivering lips to the floor, "we won't tell a s-soul."

"Shut up, Don." Hank shook his head. *If we betray her . . .* "He knows that's not true. He *has* to kill us. To keep the secret." He sneered at Tormond. "Don't you, Executioner? You *have* to kill us."

Tormond shook his head. "I would nae kill ye merely to protect the secret. 'Twould indeed make me a murderer. If ye are any indication of what the Sergeants have become, this entire, corrupt Order can burn in Hell for all I care."

"So, what are you going to do with them?" Eddie asked. A corner of his mouth lifted in a half-smile. "Tie them up and call the sheriff?" When the Templar didn't answer, the smile faded. "Tormond?"

The Executioner was silent for what felt like a very long time, though his intense gaze never faltered. Hank felt those cold eyes boring into his.

He wouldn't do that.

He couldn't.

A shiver ran up Hank's spine. *He would!* "You can't! You don't know what she'll do to us! To me! To our families! Death is no escape!"

"She?" The Executioner appeared confused. "The demoness?"

"The Queen of Heaven!" Hank cried. "Kill me!" Hank pleaded in mortal fear. "Please just kill me! Don't leave me to *her!*"

"She cannae touch ye after this—"

Hank feinted forward, as if he were about to attack. Instead, he leaped to his left, toward the lovely bookcase filled with books about horses. He dashed toward the open chamber door.

The Executioner fired once, twice, missing Hank both times.

Hank seized a grenade and yanked the pin. He dropped the grenade and reached for another.

From the office, he heard Eddie shouting. "Tormond! Run!"

Hank pulled the second pin. "Goddess, forgive me." He pulled a third.

And the world ended in fire.

✠·✠·✠

On the way back to the hotel, battered, dust-covered, and bloody, Tormond drove in silence, wrestling with his own dark thoughts. *Would I truly have spared them and walked away from the Sergeants? They cannae all be corrupt. Young Eddie is nae. He came to me as soon as they approached him.*

"We're not all corrupt, you know." Eddie ran his hands along the guitar case that hid the holy sword.

Tormond glanced at the young man. "Ach. Of course, nae. *Ye* were true. Although, when ye first showed me the demoness' cross . . ."

"I *had* to show you. Just like you asked me to. To show I was holding nothing back."

Tormond laid a hand on the lad's shoulder. "Aye. Ye did." He paused. "What ye did took courage."

Eddie shrugged. "I suppose. Maybe. I . . . suppose doing the right thing does take courage. *You* taught me that."

Tormond raised an eyebrow. "*I* did?"

"Yeah, you did. In a million little ways, but . . . You were ready to walk away from . . . *everything* the Sergeants can provide. Because it was the right thing to do."

Tormond grunted. "Aye. The right thing to do. Always. At least, I pray 'twill always be so—that I will always choose the right."

"Tormond?"

"Aye, laddie?"

"I want you to know . . . I mean, I will do whatever you ask me to do. Because I know you won't ask me to do something wrong."

"I'm nae God, laddie. I'm nae infallible."

"Nope. Nobody is. But I trust you."

Tormond, his lips drawn in a curious smile, glanced at Eddie again. "I trust ye as well, Sergeant."

Eddie paused, opened his mouth as if to speak, then shut it again. Suddenly, he blurted, "Just come right out and ask it. Please? I know you want to. But you're afraid. Afraid for *me*. And so am I. I'm scared. But I promise, I *will* do it."

Tormond sighed. *He's guessed it.* "Aye, well, I have a task for ye then, Sergeant Eddie Masters. A most dangerous task. I need ye to be my eyes and ears *within* the Council of Sergeants. They dinnae know that ye were with *me* and nae with *them* at the farm. They'll still think ye are one of them."

Eddie nodded. "I can do that. I can't go with you—into the future—but I can pave the way. I can pretend to be one of them. Gather intelligence. Spy on them."

"Ye are a brave lad. But ye must nae join in their obscene rituals. And save as many of the innocents as ye can."

"And I'll be there to awaken you in 2015."

Tormond gave him a sad smile. "That ye cannae promise, lad. Ye'll be in your late seventies by then. Nae matter what else ye may do, ye cannae promise to live longer than your allotted span of years. But who knows? Ye might make it."

"Fair enough. But I'll try." He paused. "If I'm not still alive to wake you, how will I pass you the information? Tell you what I've learned?"

Tormond smiled. "Leave it in a sealed wooden box with the letter A carved into the lid. The Sergeants have nae e'er disturbed such a box."

Eddie nodded. "Sounds like a plan, man!"

Tormond's grin widened. "Aye, a plan, man." He chuckled. "Or should it be 'a plan, daddy-o?'"

Eddie laughed long and hard. "Hey, not if an old geezer like *you* says it."

Tormond chuckled as well. "An old geezer like me."

"Do you suppose . . . when *she* calls tonight . . . at eight o'clock . . ."

"That ye may speak with her? With Branwen?"

Eddie's cheeks darkened. "Yeah. I only got to speak to her the one time. And she probably thought I was a complete idiot."

"I'm certain she'd be honored to speak with ye, laddie. After all, ye are the bravest Sergeant I have ever known."

✠·✠·✠

"Tormond, my son!" Branwen said, her laughter coming through the speakerphone. "You still haven't lost that *dreadful* Scottish accent! You do know you're the only Scotsman I've met in a thousand years who speaks that way, right?"

Tormond laughed right back at the phone. "Aye! So I've heard!"

Maebh elbowed him. "There's a missionary — a sister missionary — from Scotland who's here in Portland who said as much. And do ye know what Tormond told her?"

"No! What did he tell her?"

"That his family was from the Isle of Skye!" Maebh nearly fell over laughing.

"Well," Tormond said, his cheeks flushing crimson, "'tis true. My mother was from Skye!" He chuckled. "But 'tis nae matter. We have confessed everything to them. They know precisely who and what we are."

"So," Branwen said, her voice sobering, "you are going through with it?"

"Next Sunday," Tormond said. "We met with the bishop this evening, after sacrament meeting. Confessed all."

"And he believed you?"

"Aye," Maebh said. "One of the sisters recognized us from a sixty-year-old photo. There were other proofs as well. And frankly, whether he completely believed us or not, he cleared us for baptism next Sunday. 'Tis all that matters."

Tormond quickly added, "After we have a few more lessons with the missionaries this week."

506

"I'm so very happy for you, my children." She paused. "We're to get a temple here in London. This fall. I'm going to be endowed. Do you know what that means? Endowed?"

Tormond sat up straighter. His eyes pointedly avoided Maebh's. "I ken what it means. The sisters explained it, at least in the broad strokes."

Maebh suddenly clapped her hands. "Oh, Mother! They said 'tis possible for *ye* to be sealed to your husband, though he be dead. Is that true?"

The only sound was the crackle of the phone.

"Mother?" Maebh prompted.

"No, my children," Branwen replied. "At least not now. Because I was married so very long ago and because I have no *record* of my marriage—no marriage certificate"—Branwen let out an audible, shuddering sigh—and Maebh was sure she could hear weeping on the other end—"it cannot be done now. The Brethren have not given their approval. My sealing will . . . just have to wait."

"Oh, Mother!" Tears fell down Maebh's cheeks too. She reached for Tormond's hand.

He did not pull away.

"It will happen," Branwen said. "Marcus said so. It *will* happen. Someday."

There was a long pause, and the uninterrupted crackling became unbearable.

"Mother," Tormond said, "there's someone here I'd like ye to meet. We have a new ally in our struggle."

"That's wonderful!" Branwen said. "Introduce me, please!"

"Mother, this is Eddie Masters, Sergeant of the Temple. Eddie, this is Branwen Aquillius."

"I'm very pleased to meet you, Eddie Masters," Branwen said.

Eddie's ears turned pink. "Actually, ma'am, we've met before."

"We have? You've been to the UK?"

Eddie chuckled nervously. "No, ma'am. It was on the phone. You called a few years back. To talk to my dad. He was Sergeant-commander at the time. You called to arrange *this* phone call."

"Oh, yes!" Branwen exclaimed. "I remember you!" She chuckled. "You were quite nervous as I recall."

Eddie loosened his collar. "Still am. Nervous, that is."

"Well, don't be," Branwen replied. "I *do* bite, but not *usually* my friends." She laughed. "Sorry. Vampire humor."

"That's all right, ma'am. I'm very pleased to meet you. Again."

"Likewise, Sergeant Masters. Tormond says you are his new ally. So, tell me, exactly how are you going to aid my children?"

"I'm going to be a spy."

"A spy? That sounds dangerous."

"Aye," Tormond said, "'tis very dangerous." He explained Eddie's mission.

"Well, Sergeant Masters," Branwen said, when Tormond concluded, "you sound very brave indeed. You know, Tormond, it has been on my mind for some time that you may no longer be able to trust the Sergeants."

"Aye." Tormond breathed out slowly. "We have come to the same conclusion, but we must trust them for a wee bit yet. Until our mission brings us to Utah." He locked eyes with Maebh.

Then 'twill be over, Maebh thought. *When we awaken in the top of the mountains. In Utah.*

"Oh, yeah!" Eddie snapped his fingers. "Something else I found out last night. We know where the Witches will be next. It's gonna be in—"

"UTAH!" Maebh, Tormond, and Branwen all exclaimed together.

"Yeah!" Eddie laughed nervously. "How did you know?"

508

Chapter 43

Utah County, Utah: 2014 A.D.

One more year to go." Eddie Masters's chest hurt. It seemed like his chest always hurt lately. *Not my chest. My darn heart.* "I'm not sure I'll make it." He chuckled softly. Then he coughed. He was doing a lot of that lately as well. The beam of his flashlight wavered, causing eerie shadows to dance across the sleeping faces and the walls of the cave.

Tormond and Maebh lay face-up and side-by-side on the wooden bed in the cave. They didn't look like the bodies Eddie had seen in his dad's funeral home so many years ago—all plastic and sunken—no, they looked very much alive, as if they were about to awaken from a night of refreshing sleep.

A night that had lasted fifty-six long years. So far.

"You look so darn young." He sighed. "And I'm so darn old. Older every year. Imagine that." He chuckled softly, then ran a hand across his nearly bald, age-spotted scalp. "I doubt you'd recognize me." He glanced at the horses—first at Órd Dubh and then at Fiona—standing in their magical slumber on either side of the bed. "I wonder if *they'd* recognize me—if I smelled the same. Probably not. I got old-man smell. In spades. And I changed aftershaves a couple decades back. I'm an Old Spice man now." He smiled wistfully. "My Angie likes it. Well, she *liked* it. She passed a couple years back." He chuckled again, shaking his head. "But I told you that last year, didn't I? That's one thing about you two—you're great listeners. You never complain if I repeat my stories. My wife and kid used to *roll* their eyes . . ."

Eddie patted the wooden box beneath his bony rear. "I updated it again. All the new stuff. Just like I do every year. Yessir, new stuff. New, new stuff. I put in other things. Things you'll need this time around. Driver licenses, bank cards. And, of course, the intel—the *information*. I hope it helps." His wrinkled face hardened. "I hope it helps take these monsters down." He shrugged. "You're going to need help with some of it." He grinned. "A lot of it. Computers, huh?"

He nodded. "My boy, Jerry—now, he was good at computers. He helped me get some of this stuff. Hacking, they call it. I tried to learn—Jerry tried to teach me—but Jerry had a talent for it. I never brought him in, though—not all the way. I didn't want him touched by all this."

Realizing what he'd just said, Eddie quickly waved a hand—the hand not gripping his cane. "Not by you! Oh, no, not touched by *you*. I wish he could've known the two of you. Not touched by the *Order*, I mean." He shook his head. "It's so bad now. Ashtoreth is in control. Complete control. And everybody in the Order knows it, not just the Council. It wasn't like that when I joined. Only some on the Council were corrupt. But now it's everybody. Amazing, *horrifying* how much it's changed in just my lifetime. Just two generations."

He sighed. "But I've kept my hands clean. With God's help, I've kept my hands clean. And I kept Jerry out of it. *Mostly* out of it, anyway. God only blessed Angie and me with one child. And Jerry and his wife, Connie—they couldn't have kids. And—as I told you before—he was taken from us. Connie too. Random gang shooting, they called it. But me? I think it was the Order. They never said so—never even hinted at it—but I think it was to punish me. For not recruiting Jerry into the Sergeants."

The silence of the cave closed in around him, pressing on his aching chest. The shadows reached for him like the restless ghosts of his lost family. "But at least we're sealed together as a family. Sealed in the Salt Lake Temple." He winked, grinning. "You should try it."

His smile faded away. "I hate to think if one or both of you dies, before . . . without . . ."

He swallowed, then coughed again. "Anyway, so it's just *me* these days. And I don't know if I'll make it one more year. And if I don't, the Order has no intention of waking you, I can tell you that much. Ashtoreth wants— Well, you know what she wants. And that's not gonna happen if you succeed, if you slay the Witches. Your failure would drive your despair. And your despair would drive . . ."

He leaned forward and rested both hands and his chin atop the handle of his cane. "I'm tempted, you know. I really am. Never been so tempted by anything in my life. To wake you now. It'd be a year early, but so you age another year. No big whoop, right? You're both so young. So darn young. And the truth is, I *miss* you. I'm all alone now. I would love to talk to you one last time." He grinned. "And have you talk back. I think that's what tempts me the most."

He sat up straighter, squaring his shoulders. "But no. I've prayed about it. And I'm not gonna wake you early. 'Sides, I gave you my word. And even if I don't make it . . . well, I'm at peace with that. The Spirit says you're gonna be okay. 'Cause this is it, right? The fulfillment of the prophecy? You awaken in 'the top of the mountains,' and it will all end. Right?"

Eddie wiped away a tear. "Tell me it's gonna be all right."

He paused as if hoping for an answer.

But of course, the sleepers remained silent.

"Anyway, I told a friend of mine to be on the lookout for you in 2018—you know, in case I don't wake you in 2015. He doesn't know about this place. Or a whole lot about you. But he knows what to look for. You'll like him. He's a former Catholic priest who married a former nun, though she's passed too." *Just like my Angie.* "Member of the Church now. Big into history. I know he'd just *love* to pick your brain. Real swell Joe." Eddie chuckled. "That's not his name—Joe. It's actually— Yeah, like you're gonna remember any of this. Anyway"—Eddie sighed, coughed, then clutched at his aching chest—"it's all in the box."

Eddie stared at the knight in his armor, clutching his sword, and the lovely, former nun, wearing riding clothes that were more than a half century out of style. His labored heart swelled with affection for both of them. *Wish I could talk to you just one more time.*

If I make it just one more darn year . . .

"Well, I'd best be going. It's a long hike down to my SUV, and I'm not so good at hiking at night anymore. Or hiking at all, for that matter. See ya laters, alligators."

Eddie Masters got painfully to his feet. But the ache in his arthritic joints was nothing compared to the ache in his heart. *I'll probably never see them again.* "Goodbye, my dear friends. Thanks for listening all these years. You were a real help when . . . my family was taken."

He turned and shuffled toward the chamber exit.

Once he was out of the main cave, the tunnel narrowed and lowered. He remembered how they'd almost failed to get Órd Dubh inside, but if anyone could coax that huge animal into a dark and tight spot, it was Tormond. The Executioner was surprisingly gentle with the warhorse, and of course, Tormond was always tender and chivalrous to Maebh.

Set an example for me, with my marriage. Always strove to be like Tormond.

He peered into the darkness, but the only light came from his flashlight. *How much farther? Should see the exit by now.*

He glanced at his watch. *Only 3:34. Should still be light outside. Storm maybe? Naw, if it was gonna rain, I'd've felt it in my knees.*

So dark! The light from his flashlight seemed to be failing. He could barely see two feet ahead. The darkness closed in on him again. The restless dead grasping for him.

Could go back. Get the lamp and light it. Then go get the other flashlight in the car.

Yeah. That's the ticket.

He turned and shuffled back toward the chamber.

But if I get the lamp and go all the way to the car, I'll just have to turn around and walk all the way back again to bring the lamp back. Then I'll have to walk all the way back down to the car.

He halted, leaning on his cane and breathing heavily, trying to decide between getting the lamp or just pressing on to the SUV.

In the end, he knew his aching knees would decide for him. But still he hesitated, facing toward the chamber and his sleeping friends. *I just put new batteries in today, doggone it.* He shook the failing flashlight to no avail. *Darn Energizers! So much for truth in advertising!* "God, give me light!"

"I prefer to be addressed as Goddess," a honey-sweet voice said. "But your prayer is granted."

Light blazed in front of him, driving back the Stygian blackness.

There she floated, in the midst of the light. She was clothed this time, dressed in her guise as Mary. And she smiled down upon him. "Eddie, Eddie, Eddie. What are you doing here? You didn't come to wake them, did you? You know I have expressly forbidden that. It would not suit my purposes."

She thinks I'm on my way in, not my way out! He shook his head. "N-no! I was just gonna check on them." His knees trembled and his chest felt as if an elephant were sitting on it. "I-I do it every year!"

"Eddie." She shook her head like a disappointed parent. "Did I tell you to do this thing? Did you receive this command from any of my disciples?"

Eddie shook his head quickly. "No! I took the initiative myself."

"I see." She pursed her perfect lips. "Well, perhaps it is a good idea after all."

Even knowing *what* she was and *who* she was, her words of approval made him quiver with unwanted pleasure. He couldn't help it—the Lust-Demon had that effect on people. On men particularly. *I don't do it for you, demon! I've never done any of it for you. I bear the Melchizedek priesthood. I have the authority to banish you in the name of Jesus Christ. Not forever, but at least for now.*

His right arm began to rise of its own accord. *No!* He forced it back down to his side. *I gotta play my part. To the end. Be true to the end.* "Thank you, blessed one."

Her beatific smile widened, showing impossibly perfect teeth. Eddie had never seen lips so luscious, nor teeth so perfect.

Angie's teeth were never that perfect, that white. But then, Angie was human. Angie had a body. An imperfect mortal body. And I loved—I love her glorious, mortal imperfections.

Loathing bubbled up within him. *Everything about you is fake, you monster, because you'll never be mortal. You gave that up when you followed Lucifer, when you rebelled against Heavenly Father. When you gave up everything that truly matters.*

"You have served me well, my son." The demon smiled, and chills rippled through him—chills of pleasure and revulsion.

"Thank you, blessed one." *You'll never know the fragrant scent of a rose or the cold, sweet taste of vanilla ice cream or the exquisite pleasure of a gentle caress. You'll never know the joy of human love, the sacred, glorious intimacy between a husband and a wife. You'll never know any of the things you lust after, all the things you seek to corrupt. Because they are eternally beyond your reach.*

In a way, maybe I should pity you. Just a little.

But I don't. Not one darn bit.

513

I hope Tormond and Maebh kick your flawless, never-born butt. "I live to serve."

"Dear, dear Eddie. I know you wouldn't betray me, would you, Eddie? Betray your oath?"

"No. No! I wouldn't." *I've dedicated my life to betraying you, to fighting you. And I never actually took your rotten oath.* "I would never betray you!"

"Because, Eddie, you *know* what awaits those who've sworn to me and betray me. I've shown you before, given you just a taste." She winked at him. "Perhaps, you need another taste. Just as a *gentle* reminder."

Not again! "No! Please!"

Flames encircled him—a searing wall of fire. He'd felt the heat of those flames before.

Not real! All in my mind!

But he felt the searing inferno all the same. And he knew that so long as his *mind* believed in the heat, his skin could still blister. It had happened the first time. His arms still bore the scars. "Please!" he shrieked. "No! Make it stop!"

Banish her!

No! God, give me courage to endure!

The fire crashed into him. Eddie was aflame. Every hair of his body was consumed. His skin bubbled and charred and melted. His eyes burst in their sockets.

Not real! Not— Eddie screamed. He fell to the tunnel floor and writhed in hellish torment.

"What are you doing here, Eddie?" the demon cooed, like a loving mother singing a lullaby to her babe. "Were you here to wake them?"

"NOOOO!" he howled in his agony. Some small part of his mind knew he should not be able to scream, let alone speak if he were truly burning.

Banish her!

No! Hold on! Be true!

"I want to believe you, Eddie, my son. I really do. But, sweet child, it has occurred to me that I have never seen you take part—not once—in the *true* worship. I have never seen you join in the rites of Holy Lust. Why is that, Eddie?"

Eddie tried to give voice to one of the many excuses he'd used over the decades — excuses he'd used to avoid participation in those evil rituals — but in that moment, in his torment, he couldn't recall a single one. Instead, he focused on the victims he'd managed to save over the decades. He could recall each of their faces — faces filled with wonder and gratitude at their deliverance.

One face appeared in his mind — a twelve-year-old girl he'd managed to sneak out of the clutches of the Order, managed to return to her family. So innocent. So terrified. In his anguish, he couldn't recall her name, but he focused on her face.

"Eddie, my child, think of your wife. What was her name? Angie? Yes, Angie."

In his mind, the girl's face morphed, turning into Angie's. Sweet, beautiful Angie. She was young again, wearing her wedding veil, just as she had when the two of them had been sealed in the Salt Lake City Temple. Eddie reached for her.

"Angie is mine now, Eddie."

Angie's face twisted in horror and agony as the flames enveloped her. She screamed as her face melted.

"And your beloved son."

Jerry appeared before him. He was ten again, wearing his baseball glove, ready to play catch. But Jerry wasn't grinning, eager to play. Little Jerry looked terrified. "Dad! How could you, Dad?" Fire consumed the boy. Jerry shrieked. "Tell her! Dad! Please!"

Then Connie appeared. She scowled at him in rage. "Selfish bastard! If you had given the Goddess what she wanted, then maybe I'd have given you grandchildren." She too was consumed by demonic fire.

"NO!" Eddie screamed. "True! I was true!"

And suddenly, it was all gone. The flame, the burning, the horrific visions. Everything.

Eddie lay, panting, wheezing on the ground, his heart feeling as if it would explode at any second.

He forced his eyes open. His eyes. He still had eyes, of course. He gazed up at the demon.

Not real. Not real.

She doesn't have them. Beyond her reach.

Banish her!

515

If I do, she'll know. She'll know everything. Must hold on!

"Tell me, Eddie," crooned the demon. "If you *have* betrayed me, just tell me. And all will be forgiven. I'll release your family from eternal flame. And when your time comes, you shall join them with me, in Heaven. We shall all be one, together in blissful Holy Lust. Eternally."

Eddie's heart thundered. Each too-rapid beat was a burst of agony. He could hear blood pounding in his ears, feel it pulsing in his brain.

Tell her!

No. Please, God. Help me hold on. Don't let me betray them.

Banish her!

No. Just hold on. Be true. To the end. "True," he wheezed. "I was true."

"Very well, my son. I believe you. But just in case" — she smiled — "another taste . . ."

Eddie wasn't certain he could endure another round. *Help me, Heavenly Father!*

He felt pain in his left arm. Then numbness.

In spite of the agony in his chest, Eddie almost laughed. He almost smiled.

Thank you, God. I kept my promise.

Help them. Guide them.

Eddie's heart exploded.

Faithful to the end of his long, lonely mission, Eddie Masters, Sergeant of the Temple, was finally at peace.

Chapter 44

Mapleton, Utah: April 2018 A.D.

Whore! Whore! Whore!" Little eighteen-month-old Lucy Cavetto squealed happily, pointing at the road with her small fingers. She toddled across the backyard toward the wooden fence. "Whore, Mama! Mama! Whore!"

Moses Abbot—Moe, to his friends—looked up from the large sheet of white-painted plywood he'd been about to nail to the roof of his brand new, never-occupied horse stable to watch Peggy Cavetto chasing after her rambunctious daughter. Peggy was a statuesque woman of thirty-three, and little Lucy was her first and only child—so far. Most folks wouldn't call Peggy beautiful—until she smiled, that is, and her whole face lit up—but marriage and motherhood had made the lady blossom.

Her husband, Todd, looked up from the propane grill where he was cooking, his body taut as he gazed after his wife and daughter. There was an air of danger and wariness about Todd Cavetto—the kind of vibe one got from Secret Service agents, guarding the president or someone else of great importance. And to Todd Cavetto, there was nobody in the world more important than Peggy and Lucy. Todd had already dropped the grill tongs, and his hand was under his arm, resting on the handle of his Glock 9mm in its shoulder holster. Todd hadn't drawn the weapon—yet—but anyone—even a complete stranger—observing Todd at that moment would realize one thing down deep in their soul—Todd wouldn't hesitate to kill if it meant protecting his family.

Moe watched as Peggy scooped up her squealing child. Lucy twisted in her arms and kept pointing at the road. "Whore! Mama! Whore!"

"Yes, sweetie!" Peggy laughed, holding the squirming, wriggling toddler. "Those are horses! Horses! Can you say, 'Horse?'" Peggy emphasized the "S" in the word.

517

"Daddy! Daddy!" the child shouted. "Whore, Daddy!" She even looked up at Moe. "Unca Moe! Whore!"

Moe finally followed the child's frantic gestures.

And his jaw dropped. "Holy —"

Two people on horseback rode slowly along the road sloping down from the east — from Hobble Creek Canyon — the horses clip-clopping just outside Moe's backyard fence.

One rider was a woman, wearing an old-fashioned equestrienne riding skirt, atop a gray horse. At her waist, she wore a gun belt that sported two holstered sidearms.

The other rider looked like something straight out of a movie or the Renaissance faires that Moe so often attended — a medieval crusader atop a massive, fully armored, and white-draped warhorse as huge as a Budweiser Clydesdale. The knight bore an impressive array of arms. A white heater shield, with a simple, bold, red cross painted on it, hung from the guige strap across his white cloak and tabard. A two-handed axe hung within arm's reach at the great, black horse's right shoulder. An unstrung longbow and quiver of arrows hung at the beast's left shoulder. At the knight's left hip, on a double-wrap belt, hung a sword. At his right hip was a dagger and — quite incongruously — a gun belt and holstered sidearm. The knight held a sugarloaf great helm in the crook of his left arm, while his head was covered with a chainmail coif that appeared to have blackened with age.

"Now will you look at that?" Moe said to himself, hardly believing his eyes. He got to his feet, careful not to slip off the roof. He raised one hand and waved, while pointing with the other at the sign he'd been about to attach to the stable roof. The sign read —

"TORMOND & MAEBH"

I guess he didn't have any room on that horse for any 1950's-style clothing. Probably didn't see a reason to keep it. He needs his arms and armor — for what I'm not exactly sure. Eddie didn't say. But the critical thing is they're here. Just as Eddie said they'd be. "Sir Tormond!" Moe shouted. "Tormond MacDonald! Lady Maebh O Broin!"

Both riders looked up and reigned in their horses. The lady shielded her eyes with one hand, though the sun was barely past its zenith. The knight raised his right hand, palm forward, and cried, "Who be ye? State yer name and yer purpose!" The thick accent sounded reminiscent of a Scottish burr, though different from any Moe had ever heard, but the tone and intent were unmistakable. Moe had little doubt that if he were to answer amiss, three things would happen in rapid succession—the helm would drop to the ground, the longbow would be strung and drawn, and an arrow would bury itself in Moe's heart.

"My name is Moses Abbot! I was a friend of Eddie Masters. He told me to watch out for you!"

"*Amicus noster es?*" challenged the knight.

Moe translated from the Latin—*Are you our friend?* He thought of the designated response, the one Eddie had written in his bizarre letter. The word was in Arabic, and Moe hoped he had the pronunciation right. "*Insh'Allah!*"

The crusader slumped slightly in his saddle as if in relief. "God be praised."

The lady waved a hand, smiling. "Well met, Brother Abbot!"

Moe grinned widely. "Call me Moe!" He glanced at Todd. The man still gripped the handle of his Glock, though he hadn't drawn it yet. "Todd! Stand down! It's them."

Todd nodded, removing his hand from the weapon, but still keeping his eyes on the strangers.

"You folks arrived just in time!" Moe called, dropping the no-longer-necessary plywood sign over the side of the roof, and running a hand through his close-cropped, graying hair. "Hope you're hungry! Todd's grilling his famous fajitas."

The lady grinned widely. "We're starving! We haven't had a bite in, ye might say, *decades!*"

✠·✠·✠

"Beef or chicken?" Todd Cavetto studiously kept his voice casual. He made it a point to avoid the Templar's gaze as he offered the man two platters—one filled with seasoned beef and the other with equally seasoned chicken—across Moe's dining room table. Of course, there were two separate platters—the two meats would never touch, at least not in the context of Mexican food—as long as Todd had anything to say about it. Technically, Todd knew, fajitas were *Tex-Mex*, not Mexican, but the *Test* still applied. And in spite of the fantastic story Moe had shared about the newcomers—and everything Moe, Todd, and Peggy had done to prepare for their arrival — Todd needed to *know*.

The bearded knight had showered and changed into a pair of jeans, a flannel shirt, and a pair of sneakers — all previously procured by Moe, using the sizes provided in the mysterious Eddie's equally enigmatic letter. But the man known as Tormond still carried himself like a warrior. In spite of the change in wardrobe, the knight wore the double-wrap sword belt, with both sword and dagger, and under his left arm, he sported a sturdy-looking, older-model Smith & Wesson in a shoulder holster.

At least, Todd thought, *he left the axe, bow, and arrows in Moe's guestroom. And the shield too.*

I didn't see a lance. Did thirteenth century knights have lances?

If he passes the Test, I'll ask him.

Todd knew the amazing story, of course. Moe had shared the letter with them, and Todd, Peggy, and Moe had been preparing for this day for months. And given all that the three of them had been through together, he shouldn't really have been surprised. But . . . *An actual Templar Knight!*

Why is he still wearing the sword? I mean, he's got a semiautomatic.

Todd pictured the scabbard sticking out behind Tormond's chair. *Lucy's gonna trip over that thing.* He risked a quick glance at his daughter — safely in her highchair, happily smashing her fingers through her mashed potatoes. Occasionally, a bit of the pureed tuber would actually make it into her mouth.

The knight had stood guard — *stood guard!* — outside the bathroom while his lovely companion — the Lady Maebh — bathed, changed into a modest, mid-length blue dress that Peggy helped Moe buy a week before, and did her hair and makeup. Todd could relate to a man standing sentinel over the woman he loved — and it was obvious to anyone with eyes how much Tormond loved his lady. She wore her brown hair loose but neatly brushed into long waves that flowed down her back — just like Peggy's. Her eyes were a striking shade of gray. Peggy had helped the lady with her eye makeup, showing the lady a more modern style. Peggy was especially talented with eye makeup — perhaps a little obsessed — and never left home without it, often claiming that her eyes were her best feature. Maebh was a striking woman, yes, but Todd had noticed one thing right off the bat—her teeth had never been straightened by an orthodontist. Not that her teeth were horribly crooked—they weren't—but they reminded him of another woman's slightly crooked teeth—Elaine Morrigan's.

He suppressed a shudder at the very thought of Elaine.

"Which do you prefer, Sir Knight?" Todd insisted again. "Beef or chicken?"

"I dinnae know the custom nor the form of this meal," the knight said. "I've ne'er tried it afore. Fajitas, is't? D'ye eat beef or chicken or d'ye mix the two?"

"Which do you prefer?" Todd asked. *Come on. Come on.*

He felt a sharp kick against his foot under the table. "Todd!" Peggy said through a forced smile. "Be nice!"

Todd turned to his wife, an expression of perfect innocence on his face. "I *am* being nice. I'm offering the man a choice."

"Watch yourself, mister," Peggy replied, narrowing her enchanting, brown eyes.

"Aye," Tormond replied, oblivious to the hidden meaning behind Peggy and Todd's exchange, "if 'tis all the same, I'd prefer beef."

Good man.

Peggy rolled her eyes, then her *forced* smile became utterly genuine. And when Peggy smiled.. .

. . . she stole Todd's breath away. *You are so beautiful.*

Todd couldn't help smiling as well.

Tormond scooped a helping of the seasoned beef onto his plate. "Smells delicious, laddie."

"Aye!" Maebh inhaled deeply. "I've never smelled the like." She winked at Tormond. "Much better than roasted dog."

Roasted dog?

A question for later. After the Test. Todd turned his attention to Maebh. "And for you, milady?"

Tormond cocked an eyebrow at that. "I've nae heard anyone use that title for centuries—save myself, of course. And ye called me, Sir Knight." He grinned.

Peggy chuckled. "Todd's a bit of a nerd. He talks like that a lot, at least when the mood takes him. Comes from his days of playing D&D back at college."

Maebh looked at her curiously. "Dee-an-dee?"

"Dungeons and Dragons," Peggy replied. "It's a game where you pretend to be knights and warriors and wizards and—" She blushed. "I suppose that sounds pretty silly to you two."

Maebh grinned. "A game of knights and warriors and wizards? And did ye play this game as well, Peggy? Do ladies play?"

Peggy laughed. "All the time! That's how I first met Todd—playing D&D."

Maebh cocked her head. "So, warriors and wizards, but no ladies?"

"Oh, there are ladies in the game," Peggy replied, "but the women are all warriors and wizards too."

Maebh gave her a skeptical look. "Why, that doesn't sound like much fun to me. Where's the fun if men and women are the same?"

Peggy laughed. "They're not the same—not exactly—but . . ." She shook her head. "But it's all just pretend. I can explain it later."

"And speaking of later, "—Todd gently shook the two platters—"Milady Maebh, beef or chicken?" *It's not as important for a woman, Cavetto. And this lady obviously watches her figure.*

Maebh glanced at Tormond's plate. "Beef, if ye please."

Todd grinned. *I like her.* He set the chicken platter down and presented Maebh with the beef. She served herself a portion. Though not as large a portion as the knight's, it was *all* beef.

I like them both.

Moe burst out laughing. "Same old Todd. You never change, thank heavens." He thumped the table with his forefinger. "Congratulations, Sir Tormond, Lady Maebh, you just passed Todd's test of character."

Tormond raised an eyebrow. Again. "Aye? And what test of character would that be?"

"It's foolproof." *And I will not apologize for it. Or for the chicken that nobody's going to eat. It can all go into the trash for all I care.* "And you *both* passed with flying colors." He set down the beef platter. *The rest of you can serve yourselves if you're going to mock the Test.*

Peggy rolled her eyes again. "He calls it the 'Mexican Chicken Test.'" She paused, then took his hand and squeezed it affectionately. "Well, it's *your* silly test. *You* explain it."

"Okay." Todd grinned. "It works like this. Chicken in Mexican food is disgusting. No arguing—it just is. Now, a lady might choose chicken over beef if she's watching her figure. So, there's a little wiggle room for women. But now, a *man* . . . Any *man* who willingly chooses chicken over beef or pork in Mexican food is not—I repeat—*not* to be trusted."

"Aye, I see." Tormond stroked his beard, then nodded. "Well, I thank God we passed. Ye see, laddie, I have my own test of character. 'Tis how a man treats a lady. *All* ladies, nae just his own."

Chivalry. Makes sense. "And do I pass?"

"So far, laddie. Ye certainly treat your lady wife as a queen."

Todd turned toward Peggy and smiled. "She *is* my queen."

Peggy smiled back, setting Todd's heart aflutter. *Every dang time.*

"I have a question," Maebh said, a very serious expression on her face. She looked at Peggy. "What, pray tell, is a *nerd?*"

Todd, Peggy, and Moe burst into peals of laughter.

✠·✠·✠

"We must go back to the cave," Tormond said, staring intently at the charred tree stump in Moe's backyard. "Retrieve Eddie's body. Give him a proper burial."

Moe, standing on Tormond's left, said, "I'm sure he'd like to be buried next to Angie. I'll arrange it. Do you have other possessions in the cave you'd like to retrieve?"

Tormond shook his head, but his eyes never left the stump. "Nothing of consequence. The Sergeants left nothing for us. Just as Eddie predicted."

The charred stump was the lone evidence that life—even corrupted life—had ever existed inside the circle of death. No blade of grass intruded inside the irregular ring, no insect crawled. The hard-packed earth was lifeless, barren. Eternally corrupted.

Tormond knew the stump would not rot away on its own—the natural forces of decay never seemed to operate on the wood of the accursed tree. Only the effects of weather and time would erase the remnants of that vile wood.

Órd Dubh and Fiona, grazing in Moe's spacious backyard, avoided the cursed spot. Even the wee lassie, Lucy, instinctively avoided the area as she toddled and waddled around the yard.

Peggy and Maebh chased the child around, playing with her, making certain she didn't get too close to the grazing horses. Or the "presents" the horses left behind. Whenever Lucy cried, "Whore! Whore!" one of the two ladies would scoop up the girl and carry her closer so Lucy could pet the beasts. Neither horse seemed to mind the attention.

Tormond knelt at the edge of the dead area. He felt no need to enter it. Though he had long ago given up the custom of drawing his sword and holding it before him, hilt up, as a cross when he prayed, he still rested a hand on the pommel. The sword grounded him, reminded him of who he was and what he was called to do. "Heavenly Father, have mercy upon the deluded souls corrupted and murdered by the Witches. They were deceived. In Jesus's name. Amen."

I have missed them again. They'd be three years gone by now.

But 'tis "the top of the mountains." 'Tis the prophesied place.

How am I to find them and kill them if they be sleeping? Will I perhaps be led to their hiding place?

"Todd tried to save some of them," Moe said. "When they — the Witches' acolytes, as you call them — were drugged with the magic fruit and left to die, Todd pulled a bunch of them out of the burning house." He gestured back toward his house. "Not *that* house, of course. I rebuilt on the ashes of the old, after I acquired the land. And of course, *my* house looks *nothing* like that monstrosity. It's just a house. But I wanted some good to come out of . . . of all that. What with my family — my *ancestors*, not me — being complicit for centuries, and all. Good thing too, since this is the address Eddie gave you. Anyway, Todd was there — here — to save Peggy. She wasn't an acolyte — not at all — but she and her best friend were meant to be sacrificial victims. But she managed to get herself and her friend out. And Todd went in over and over, pulling people to safety, but . . ."

"But it didn't do any good," Todd added, standing on Tormond's right. He wasn't looking in the direction of the dead space, but rather back at the ladies, ever vigilant for the safety of his wife and bairn. "They were all murdered *after* I pulled them out. Throats slit. Every one of them."

But that's what the Witches do. Murder their followers. Sacrifice them to their pagan god — to Cernunnos. Tormond stood. He laid a hand on Todd's shoulder. "Laddie, if there be one thing I've learned in my long life, 'tis that God values righteous effort. The struggle, the fight be more important than the victory. We crusaders lost the Holy Land in the end, aye, but good came out of it too. The lives spared, the hostage pilgrims delivered."

"But I didn't save them!" Todd snarled. "They died anyway."

"But did ye nae save Peggy in the end? Not here, but in the Witches' cave? That be what Moe tells me."

Todd nodded. "Yeah. I saved Peggy in the end."

Tormond squeezed Todd's shoulder. "Then ye have been richly rewarded. Your Peggy — she is a remarkable lady."

Todd grinned. "Oh, yeah."

Peggy was holding her wee daughter and talking to Maebh, as the little girl patted Fiona's neck.

Those two seem to be getting along quite well. It gladdens my heart that Maebh has found a friend in this century.

"Speaking of remarkable ladies," Moe said, "when are you going to marry yours?"

Tormond's heart ached. "I cannae marry. Nae 'til my sacred mission — *our* sacred mission, Maebh's and mine — be accomplished."

"Yeah." Moe rubbed his chin. "You know, Eddie was vague about that — your mission — in his letter. He never said what it was. He never said why you've been traveling through the centuries. He asked me to help you, to get you set up in this century. But he never said why."

Tormond blinked. *Of all the things for Eddie to hold back . . .* "I am the Executioner of God. I was given the office and commission to hunt down and slay a trio of Witches — the very Witches that planted yon evil tree and fed it with human blood to appease their foul god, Cernunnos. "Tis been my life's mission —"

Maebh screamed.

Tormond drew his sword.

Todd drew his gun.

Maebh ran toward them. "Tormond!"

Tormond sprinted to meet her, looking everywhere for threats, but seeing nothing. "What is't? What be amiss?"

Maebh threw her arms around him. "Oh, Tormond! 'Tis over!"

Taking care to keep the blade safely away from her, Tormond searched her face. He was astonished to see that she was weeping. Weeping and smiling.

"What d'ye mean, lass?"

"The Witches!" she cried. "They're dead!"

Chapter 45

Dead?" Tormond gaped at her. "When? How?"

Maebh squeezed him all the harder, trembling with joy. "'Twas in 2015! Todd and Moe killed them. They're gone!" Maebh pulled back, barely able to contain her happiness. How she wanted to kiss him right there, before God and their new friends. Their first *real* kiss.

But when she beheld Tormond's stricken expression . . . *What's wrong? Why isn't he happy?* "Do ye not understand, my love? 'Tis all over. Todd and Moe killed them."

"Well," Todd said, holstering his sidearm, "if you're talking about the Morrigans, technically speaking, Moe and I didn't do the killing. But we were there. We saw it happen."

Moe slapped Todd on the back. "He's being too modest by far. It wouldn't have happened without Todd. *I* was the one who was *just there*. Along for the ride, so to speak. And Peggy was there too."

"Todd saved us all," Peggy said as she joined them, carrying Lucy on her hip. "And you, Moe, were very brave." Her voice bore pride and affection for both men. "I was *asleep* the whole time, remember?"

But the words barely registered on Maebh. She released Tormond and took a step back.

He kept his eyes on the ground as he wordlessly sheathed his sword. Then he turned away from her.

"Tormond?" Maebh trembled. *We should be happy! Everything we've dreamed of . . .* "What's wrong?" She maneuvered around him until she could once more see his stricken face, his fallen countenance.

He stared beyond her with despairing eyes.

She followed his gaze.

He's staring at the stump. Where the tree was.

Slowly, deliberately, Tormond unbuckled his sword belt. He let it drop to the earth. The sword Tormond always carried lay on the ground. Abandoned. The sacred weapon that had never been far from his hand, even in sleep.

With a cry of confusion and dismay, Maebh knelt and retrieved the fallen belt, the dagger, and the sacred sword.

When she looked up, Tormond was walking away. He shuffled toward the charred stump like a lost soul. Upon reaching it, he turned, sat on the stump, and buried his face in his hands.

Maebh followed him. When she came to the edge of the circle—lifeless, save for the man she loved sitting in its center—she hesitated for the briefest of moments, but then she joined him.

She knelt before Tormond, heedless of the dirt on her dress or the unclean feel of the place. She laid the sword across her lap. She lifted her eyes, watching his hands covering his face.

And she listened.

He's not weeping. He's not . . . doing anything.

She opened her mouth to speak, then stopped herself.

Give him time. He'll talk when he's ready.

'Twas the death of the Witches. 'Twas that which upset him.

But we've dreamed of this day — the day the mission would be over. When we could finally —

No. Don't think of that right now. Think of Tormond. Of what he needs.

What is it, my love? What do ye need? How can I ease your sorrow?

Tears spilled from her eyes as she sat in distressed silence.

She heard whispered voices behind her. Being inside the unholy circle, she could well imagine the ghosts of the dead gathering behind her, round about her. She felt gooseflesh rising on her arms. But if she were to glance back, she was certain she'd find Peggy, Todd, and Moe talking together. *'Tis they and none else.*

She did not glance back.

If Tormond uncovers his eyes, let the first thing he sees be me. Let him know I am here for him.

And so, she waited. And her tears continued to fall. And the whispers continued.

Please, Heavenly Father, comfort him. I don't know precisely what is wrong, but . . . Is there aught I can do to help him?

"You should not have died at Acre." The words blossomed in her mind, and she recognized the still small voice of the Holy Spirit.

And so, she repeated the words she'd been given. "You should not have died at Acre."

Tormond flinched as if she'd struck him. He dropped his hands and looked at her. His eyes were puffy, red, and wet with unshed tears. "What did ye say?"

She shook her head quickly, flinging teardrops to either side. "Not my words. But ye should *not* have died at Acre."

"Did I say that aloud? I was thinkin' that—I *should* have died at Acre. With my brothers."

"No, Tormond, my love. Ye said nothing. Not aloud. But ye should *not* have died at—"

"But what was it all for?" His jaw clenched, and his eyes narrowed in rage. "I gave up everything! Father, mother, family. The joy of hearth and home. And love! Then I *abandoned* my brother knights at Acre. How many died because I was nae there to fight beside them on the walls. How many could ha' been spared if I'd been there? And for what?" He lifted his face to heaven. "For what? I've done as Thou hast asked. *All* that Thou hast asked. I've hunted them through the centuries. I . . . I hunted them." He lowered his face into his hands again. "And now they are gone. Slain by another hand. I've failed. Failed God. Failed in my sacred mission."

Someone cleared a throat behind them. "Uh, excuse me," Peggy said, "but you're wrong."

"Aye?" Tormond uncovered his face once more. The rage was gone, but he had the look of a man who'd lost all hope. "What's that?" He paused, then added a hasty, "Milady."

Peggy, holding her child, stepped forward, but remained just outside the edge of the dead circle. "Maebh was telling me about you. About the two of you. The things you've done over the centuries. The lives you've saved. When we met, I don't think we gave you our last name, did we? Did you know my husband's family name is Cavetto?"

Cavetto? Why does that name sound familiar?

And like the light of a match, suddenly flaring in the darkness, Maebh remembered. "Todd Cavetto!" She reached forward and gripped both Tormond's hands in hers. "That Italian lad in Newfoundland! The one ye pulled from the bay!"

"Holy—" Todd cried. "All those stories you told—I never put it together. You're the *angels* that saved my ancestor! Joseph Cavetto. Or—or maybe you knew him as Giuseppe. He was pulled from the sea by two angels—a man and a woman in ragged clothing. And a big, black horse!"

Maebh shook Tormond's hands. "Do ye not remember, Tormond? Ye told Joseph Cavetto he'd have a descendant named Todd. 'A warrior for God,' ye said. 'Twas in the Red Book. Marcus's prophecy! Do ye remember?"

Tormond blinked, then took a shuddering breath. "I remember. Aye. The hurricane. 1775. We told him we were nae angels. Only servants of God."

"Yeah," Todd said, laughing and waving a hand in dismissal. "Angels. Servants of God. Whatever. Listen, Sir Knight, without *you*—without *both* of you *and* your big, black horse—I wouldn't even be here. And for that matter, if I weren't here, neither would Peggy or Moe. Lucy would never have been born."

Moe stepped into the circle—just a foot or so, but inside. "If that was your mission, Tormond, to kill the Morrigans—uh, I mean the Witches—then you succeeded. Because of what Todd did, because of what *you* did centuries ago, they're dead. Without you, son, they'd still be out there right now, hidden and sleeping, ready to wake in another . . . almost sixty years, to wreak corruption and death upon the world again. Don't you see, Tormond? *You* succeeded where no one else could have."

Todd entered the circle and stepped right up to Tormond. Then he knelt on one knee and laid a hand on Tormond's shoulder. "What was it you told me, Sir Tormond? 'God values righteous effort?' That the good fight is more important than the victory? Something like that."

The hint of a smile played at the corners of Tormond's mouth. "Somethin' like that. Aye."

Tormond pulled his hands out of Maebh's, then eased himself off the stump. He knelt, facing her. She lifted the weapons from her lap and offered them to him. "Your sword, my love."

He smiled. "Thank ye, lassie." Shuffling around on his knees, he turned to face the stump. He drew the sword from the scabbard, then, like a knight of legend stabbing a dragon's back, he drove the blade point-down into the accursed wood. He grasped the blade and turned his eyes to the hilt—the hilt that formed a cross. "Heavenly Father, forgive my presumption. And my despair. I thank Thee that Thou has brought us together this day, this century, in this place, that I might yet serve Thee. I am grateful for our new friends who have given us food and shelter and clothing and the knowledge that my life—*our* lives—have nae been lived in vain. And most important of all, for the *hope* that I may yet fulfill my holy mission."

His holy mission? But the Witches are already dead! A quick glance around showed Maebh that Moe and Peggy had also joined them in prayer—though Peggy merely bowed her head and remained standing outside the circle, holding her daughter.

"I thank Thee also," Tormond continued, "for my dearest companion. She has been brave and faithful and valiant in all things. Bless us both that we may continue to be brave and faithful and valiant to the end of the quest."

But we are at the end of our quest!

"In the blessed name of Thy beloved Son, Jesus. Amen."

Leaving the sword in the stump, Tormond rose. He wrapped the sword belt about his waist, then fastened both buckles. He wrenched the sword from the wood and, with a practiced, decisive motion, sheathed it. He offered Maebh his hand and pulled her to her feet.

"But Tormond," she said, "we *have* finished our mission. We can be . . ."

He shook his head slowly, but firmly. "Nae yet, my love. Nae yet. I am still the Executioner of God. And I see now why we have been preserved for such a time as this. I see it clearly. For the first time in my long life, I see it clearly. I know my purpose."

Maebh's heart ached as the hope of love and marriage guttered like a candle flame in the wind. "Why, Tormond? What yet have we to do?"

He smiled, and a fierce beauty shone from his face. "'*We,*' ye said. Aye, '*we,*' my dearie. *We* must destroy the Order of the Sergeants and the power of the demoness Ashtoreth."

"But how, Tormond? There are just two of us."

"God, lassie. God will show us the way. As He always has."

531

"Hey," Peggy said, "it's not just the two of you anymore. You have me and Todd as well."

"That's right," Todd said, standing. "We wouldn't miss this."

"You're not leaving *me* out!" Moe grinned as he too stood.

Wee Lucy wriggled in Peggy's arms, reaching for Tormond. "Unca Tormo! Unca Tormo!"

The Executioner of God laughed, filling the circle of death with the blessed sound of joy. "Ye see, beloved Shield-maiden? Already, we are an army."

Chapter 46

New Canaan, Utah

Carl! Come take a look at this, will ye?" Moira MacDonald Morgan reached for the remote control to pause the local evening news report. "Hurry up, laddie!"

"I'm coming! I'm coming!" Carl Morgan called as he minced onions and carrots for Korean pogum-pap—his customary Saturday night dinner. "Hold your horses!"

"Horses, Mama! Horses!" Two-year-old Maighread squirmed in Moira's lap, pointing at the TV.

At the mention of horses, five-year-old Sergei looked up from playing with his diecast toy airplane—a B-52H, naturally, just like Daddy used to fly—and gave his attention to the television as well. When his father walked into the room, drying his hands on his shirt, the boy cried, "Look, Daddy! Horses! And a knight!"

"Well, I'll be," Carl said. "Back it up, sweetheart."

"Daddy," Maighread said, a reproachful frown on her cherubic face, "say please."

Sergei looked up at his father and giggled.

Carl chuckled. "You're absolutely right, Mai-mai." The child's frown vanished. Carl paused for effect, then laid on the sugar. "*Please* back it up, Moira, sweetheart."

Moira managed a small grin as she used the remote control to rewind the news broadcast thirty seconds or so.

"Well, check this out, folks." the KSL-5 female news anchor said. "This cellphone video was captured by a Mapleton resident this morning and sent to KSL." A bracketed video appeared on the screen showing two people on horseback. "This looks like something out of Hollywood."

"That's right, Ashley," the male co-anchor replied. "KSL news specialist, Alex . . ."

As the report continued, Moira felt a chill ripple up her spine. Without pointing at the mounted knight on the screen and the accompanying equestrienne, who was wearing a more traditional — if old-fashioned — riding habit, Moira said, "Laddie, if ye were to guess, what period and culture would ye say his regalia represents?" She attempted to keep her voice even, glancing at Sergei. *Dinnae want to excite the wee laddie. Sergei is so sensitive to anything . . . unusual.*

But the little boy's eyes were glued to the screen. He'd set his toy bomber on the floor.

On the television, the reporter continued, " . . . no film permits issued for Utah county at this time . . ."

Carl said, "*You're* the expert on European history, my love."

Moira shook her head. "But ye are the one who's passionate about *military* history."

"Roger that. Well, I'm no expert on the Crusades, but . . ."

Crusades. Moira shivered. *It cannae be.*

" . . . if I had to guess," her husband continued, oblivious to her mounting fear, "I'd guess thirteenth century. That's chain he's wearing under that tabard. And that helm he's carrying — it's a Sugarloaf. See the conical top, rather than a flat top? That's right at the end of the thirteenth century, into the fourteenth. And if I'm not mistaken, that's a Templar surcoat and cloak he's wearing."

"Alex," the female news anchor said, "could they have been practicing for a Renaissance faire?"

The reporter shrugged. "Well, Ashley, there is a faire up north in Marriott-Slaterville on weekends next month, but not down here in Utah County. I caught up with Mapleton resident and Roman reenactor, Moses Abbot, who was up at the faire last weekend . . ."

A kindly-looking man with short-cropped, graying hair appeared on the screen. He stood before a display of Roman armor and weapons.

"Moses," the reporter said, "you've seen the video. What do you make of it?"

Moses grinned. "Well, the armor looks pretty authentic to me. Most of the time, faire goers and reenactors prefer plate mail — if they wear armor at all. That's a couple centuries later than what this guy's wearing. Better for jousting, you know."

"I've seen the jousting," the reporter said. "It looks brutal."

Moses shrugged. "It can be. But it draws the crowds. Now, some faires are trying to depict a specific period or culture. For instance, there's a fantastic annual faire up near Spokane, Washington, that depicts a different year from the reign of Henry the Eighth. Each season, it's a different year." He chuckled. "With a different queen or mistr—uh, different *woman* for King Henry. It's all pretty cool."

The man's face was replaced by footage of the Marriott-Slaterville Renaissance faire—jousting knights performing to cheering crowds of fairgoers dressed mostly in very modern-looking T-shirts and shorts.

"Other faires," Moses continued, "welcome any and all comers. Including wizards, witches, fairies, and pirates. I mean, my Legion—the group I'm affiliated with—the Roman Military Historical Society—I'm the centurion, by the way—reenacts the late-first-century Roman army."

The jousters were replaced by a formation of men marching in Roman armor, followed by a shot of Moses wearing his own Roman armor and holding his red-plumed centurion's helmet in the crook of his arm. "We don't get invited to perform everywhere—only at faires that are open to various periods. So, I wish this fellow luck."

The image shifted back to the smiling reporter. "Pretty interesting stuff. Back to you, Ashley and—"

Moira paused the playback.

"Holy—" Carl breathed. He placed a hand on Moira's shoulder.

Moira nodded slowly. "Aye." She reached for her husband's hand. Their fingers intertwined. Carl's hand leant her courage, calmed her trembling.

"I wanna see the horses!" Sergei whined.

"Me too!" Maighread cried.

"Aye," Moira said. "Of course, my bonnie bairns." She lifted her voice. "Rolf? Sarah?"

Nine-year-old Rolf and seven-year-old Sarah appeared from their respective rooms. "Is it dinner time already?" Rolf asked, though he didn't seem particularly eager—Korean food wasn't his favorite.

Sarah held a stuffed sloth under her arm. "What's wrong, Mama?"

"Nothing's wrong, sweetie," Carl replied.

Moira squeezed Carl's hand. *'Tis nae* precisely *a lie. Heaven knows we've come through worse.* "I need ye to do me a favor, Sarah." She extended the remote control to her oldest daughter. "'Twas merely a story on the news. It involved horses. I need ye—one of ye—to run it back and show wee Sergei"—she let go of Carl's hand and gently eased Maighread off her lap—"and yer sister the horses again."

Rolf rolled his eyes. "Horses, is it?" He didn't have a trace of a Scottish accent, but Rolf, more than any of their other three children, tended to mimic his mother's speech patterns. "I should hae known." He stepped forward and took the remote. "I'll do it."

"There's a knight too!" squealed Sergei.

"Thank ye, laddie." Moira rose, then took Carl's hand. "Mama and Daddy will be right back."

Hand-in-hand, Moira and Carl retreated to their bedroom. Carl closed and locked the door behind them, while Moira opened a large and heavy fireproof box in their closet. Reverently, she withdrew a large, fragile book. The cover read, "Holy Bible."

Moira sat on the bed and set the ancient tome in her lap.

Carl sat beside her and put his strong and comforting arm around her. "We're in this together," he said.

She nodded and gave him a sad smile. "Always. But there are times . . . Laddie, have we nae earned the right to live the rest of our mortal lives in peace?"

Carl sighed, then he chuckled. "Oh, my love. When we married, it was on the eve of battle. Then came the war. And then . . ." He squeezed her, then kissed her cheek. "The war against evil is never over. You know that. We've known this day would come. We've known for months now."

"Aye." She leaned her head briefly against his shoulder. Then she lifted her head and kissed him. Deeply. Passionately. As if it might be the last kiss they'd ever share. "D'ye remember the first time we kissed?"

He grinned. "Yeah. You'd just punched me in the jaw. Broke it, as I recall."

She narrowed her eyes at him. "Ye deserved it, as *I* recall. Flyin' off like that. Leavin' me alone. *Alone.*" Her eyes softened. "Whate'er comes, we'll face it. Together."

He nodded anyway. "Together. For time and all eternity."

"Aye." She turned her attention back to the ancient family Bible. She opened the book, carefully searching through the yellowed, fragile pages at the back—the pages covered with various handwritten scripts. She skipped past the genealogies, the family records, until she came to the many pages written in a single hand—all in Latin.

Where was that entry? She could almost quote the words. But needed to *see* them, to read them once again. Exactly as they had been transcribed centuries earlier.

When she found the entry, she let out a shuddering sigh. "Here 'tis."

"Go on," Carl prompted. "Read it. But in English, please."

She gave him a halfhearted smirk. "Ye really should learn Latin, laddie. Ye really should."

"I know. I'm working on it. Now go on. Read it."

And so, she read it. Everything was there—the Crusader and the lady, riding out of the canyon—the Roman centurion who was *not* a centurion—"Maple Town"—obviously, Mapleton—and what was to come after.

Just as Marcus Aquillius prophesied almost two millennia ago. And the last time we were involved in fulfilling some of Marcus's prophecies . . . She shuddered, thinking of the terrible price that had been paid. Tears spilled freely from her eyes. She wiped at them with her sleeve to make sure none fell onto the fragile pages and the transcribed prophecies.

"They're here," she said. "*Carnifex Dei et Christi Innupta Scutae.* The Executioner of God and the Shield-maiden of Christ."

"Roger that." Carl sighed. "I guess we'd better go to Mapleton and see this Moses Abbot."

"Mama!" Sergei called, suddenly pounding on the bedroom door. "I wanna see the knight again!"

"Horses! Mama!" Maighread wailed.

"Just a minute, laddie," Moira said, rolling her eyes and putting away the precious family Bible. "Rolf! Run it back again."

"Aye!" Rolf shouted, obviously annoyed. "I already showed it to them twice!"

"Thank ye, laddie," Moira replied. She pulled out her cell phone. "I'll call the sitter and order a pizza."

"Roger that," Carl replied.

"Must make sure we give the bairns a kiss goodbye." Moira wiped away more tears. *Must nae show fear to my bairns.* "Just in case."

"Yeah." Carl nodded grimly. "And then I'll get the swords."

Chapter 47

And ye say this automobile is ours?" Tormond eyed the low, sleek sedan, painted white with a simple Templar cross on the hood. It had a metal framework on the front that reminded him of the cowcatcher on the front of an ancient steam engine, though he rather suspected it was designed for ramming into other vehicles, rather than cattle.

Moe chuckled. "Who else would it belong to? If it'd been up to me, I would have opted for a more subdued paint job. Maybe black, with no cross, you know? But Eddie was very specific in his instructions. If it got to be 2018, and I didn't hear from him, I was to use your bank account—Eddie gave me power of attorney for it—to order a bulletproof police cruiser—no lights or sirens, of course—with a custom paint job. He said you'd want the enemy to know exactly who you were." Moe pointed to what was obviously a horse trailer, painted white, with a red cross on the side. "That's yours too."

Tormond stroked his bearded chin. "Bulletproof, ye say?"

"Yep. 2018 Dodge Charger Hellcat armored police cruiser. Fully loaded. Even the glass is bulletproof. The tires, if hit, will still run flat for about sixty miles. Per Eddie's instructions, the horse trailer is armored too. Well, as much as possible. It's got run-flat tires as well. Wherever it is you're going, Eddie wanted you to be able to make it there alive."

Eddie, ye thought of everything.

Tormond walked slowly around the vehicle, his hand on the pommel of his sword. "D'ye know, laddie, that a while back, when an armorer would make a suit of plate mail, he'd deliberately fire a pistol at the breastplate. The ball—the bullet—would leave a dent in the plate." He bent, peering into the car. "That dent was called the 'bulletproof,' and was to show the armor could stop a bullet. So, all the best suits of armor came with a dent in the breastplate."

Moe came to stand beside Tormond. "I noticed you have a dent in one of your pauldrons. Was that the armorer's bulletproof?"

Tormond smiled sadly. "Nae, but the pauldron did indeed stop a bullet. Saved my life." *'Til the infection nearly took me. Then 'twas Branwen who saved me from death.* "'Twas a gift from a friend. A faithful Sergeant." *William. I miss ye, laddie.* "Back when some of them—perhaps most—were still faithful." *So very many have served faithfully and nobly to get us to this place, this time. So many sacrifices.*

Eddie was perhaps the noblest of them all.

Moe put a hand on his shoulder. "Want to take it for a spin?"

"The car?"

"Yeah. I had to drive it to get it here from the dealership. It was a special order, like I said. But it drives like a dream. So fast. It's a real beauty."

Tormond grinned. "As far as cars go, I suppose she is a handsome machine, aye." He looked toward the house. Maebh, Peggy, and Todd sat on the front porch, talking and playing with wee Lucy. The lowering sun caught Maebh's chestnut hair, and the light made it shimmer. "But I've beheld true beauty, Moe. I'll call nothing else fair so long as I live."

Maebh wore the same dress she'd worn at their late lunch. It exposed her legs to the knee. In a bygone century, she would have considered showing half her legs to be positively scandalous. *D'ye remember that gown Branwen left for ye in Carmarthen? The one that exposed so much of your chest and back? How mortified ye were?*

D'ye remember how my fingers trembled when ye needed me to tighten the laces in back?

He waved at her, then beckoned for her to join him.

She smiled, and the loveliness of that smile made his heart race. *When Irish eyes are smilin'...*

"I know what you mean," Moe said. "You are a lucky man."

Tormond laughed softly. "Luck has nary a thing to do with it. I am blessed." *And cursed. Here we are, in "the top of the mountains," and we still cannae marry.*

Not until the mission – the true mission – be complete.

Maebh glided toward him, her long hair dancing in the lowering sunlight.

Moe sang softly to an old tune —

She looked so sweet,
From her two bare feet,
To the sheen of her nut-brown hair
Such a coaxing elf,
Sure, I shook myself,
For to see I was truly there.

"That's from an old Irish folksong," Moe said. "It's about an Irish maid and the lad who falls in love with her. Today we use the same tune in church. The hymn is called, 'If You Could Hie to Kolob.' It's a song about the eternal nature of, among many other things, love. It was one of my Joan's favorites. Especially after they started using that old tune. She had chestnut hair too, my Joan. I used to call her my Joan of Arc."

As Maebh closed the last few yards, she began to skip, almost to dance.

Tormond sighed. *The eternal nature of love.*

Maebh's smile widened. "Aye, my dearie?"

Tormond gave her a courtly bow. "Would milady care to take a spin?"

She laughed. "Surely, ye are not asking me to dance, are ye, Tormond MacDonald?"

Tormond grinned. "Nae, my love." *Aye, but it feels good to be able to say that openly. E'en if it cannae be fully realized. Yet.* "I meant, would ye care to take a drive in our new car?"

She clapped her hands in delight. "Oh, aye! Peggy tells me there's an ice cream parlor in Provo—wherever that may be—called Cold Stone Creamery. She says there may be a closer one in Spanish Fork—wherever *that* may be. We could all go together. But Peggy, Todd, and Lucy can go in their car. And we could take ours." She pointed at the cruiser. "I do assume that's ours—the one with the Templar cross. And Moe can ride along to give us directions."

And here I thought we might have a few minutes alone. But he maintained his grin. "Aye, that sounds grand."

Maebh cocked her head. "And later, perhaps, the two of us can go for a moonlight stroll." She winked.

Tormond's smile widened. "Aye, now that *does* sound grand."

"I'll just take a wee moment to tell the others." She curtsied, then spun and skipped away.

Tormond gave a shuddering sigh. *God grant me strength.*
And show me how I may vanquish the enemy quickly.

Moe slapped Tormond on the back. "A very blessed man."

"Aye." He turned to Moe. "May I have the keys?"

Moe fished in his pocket and pulled out a pair of black, oblong, plastic shapes, not much larger than a pair of flattened plums. "Here you go." He placed the objects in Tormond's hand.

Tormond eyed them dubiously. "These are the keys?"

Moe nodded, grinning. "They're called key fobs. One is for you, and the other is for Maebh."

Tormond looked at the car door. "But I dinnae see the key in this key fob nor anywhere to insert it."

"You put it in your pocket. Then you walk up to the door and insert your hand into the door handle and —"

Both men looked to the end of the property where a small, odd-looking — at least to Tormond's eyes — vehicle pulled into the driveway. It appeared to be a small van of some kind. Tormond and Maebh had seen one such vehicle on their ride from the cave.

Tormond spotted two silhouettes in the vehicle. "Friends of yers?" Tormond asked, his hand going immediately to the hilt of his sword.

Moe shook his head. "I don't recognize the car, at least. And I'm not expecting any more visitors today. But I can't imagine that anyone driving a minivan could be much of a threat."

Todd was suddenly at Tormond's side, his hand on the weapon in his shoulder holster.

Should have worn a gun myself. "Todd, move to the left a few paces, laddie. Let's present them with multiple targets. Moe, ye move to the right."

"I'm unarmed," Moe replied, but he sidestepped to the right.

"See that ye correct that in the future, man," Tormond said. "We live in perilous times. And as long as we're with ye, ye're a target."

Suddenly Maebh was on his left, holding her handgun.

"Get behind me, lassie."

"We stand together," she replied.

"Aye, well, at least stand on my right so I can draw my sword."

"Aye." She crossed behind him and stood at his right hand.

The driver-side door of the minivan opened, and a man emerged. He was dressed simply, in a T-shirt and blue jeans. But he carried himself like a warrior. He quickly moved around the front of the van and opened the passenger door. A woman emerged. Slender and lithe—but there was also something about her stance that suggested she too could be dangerous, even lethal. She likewise wore a T-shirt and jeans. But what caught Tormond's attention more than anything else was her hair. Long and red.

She reminded him of Branwen.

The sun's still up. They cannae be vampires.

The man opened the van's side door, reached in, and pulled out two objects—both long and thin and loosely encircled with some kind of wrappings.

The man handed one object to the woman.

Swords!

The two newcomers fastened their sword belts about their waists. Their movements were practiced and fluid as if the wearing of swords were commonplace. The weapons were full-sized and had metal baskets around the hilts. The man's steel basket had a red tassel dangling from the end. The woman's basket was black.

The newcomers looked at each other, then joined hands. Together, they walked slowly toward Tormond and Maebh.

"Who are ye," Tormond challenged, "that come here bearin' weapons."

They halted about ten paces away, still holding hands.

The man spoke. "My name is Carl Morgan. This is my wife, Moira MacDonald Morgan."

MacDonald?

The woman lifted her voice. "And if we are nae very much mistaken, ye"—she pointed toward Tormond and Maebh—"are Tormond MacDonald and Maebh O Broin, the Executioner of God and the Shield-maiden of Christ. We are yer distant kin, Sir Knight, milady. We too are descendants of Marcus and Maelona Aquillius."

Maebh gasped. She gripped Tormond's arm, trembling.

Together, the man and woman stepped forward once more, only to halt two paces away.

Tormond's grip tightened on his sword, but he did not draw it. "Why are ye here, Carl and Moira Morgan?"

"We have come," the man said, kneeling and drawing his weapon and holding it forward, his right hand inside the basketed hilt, and the other holding the blade, "to offer you our swords and, if need be, our lives in the coming battle."

His wife knelt also, and presented her sword in like manner. Except for the brass cat's-head pommel, the entire sword, including the blade was a shiny black. "If by life or death we can aid ye, we will."

"Tormond!" Moe cried, suddenly appearing to the right of Maebh. "I know these people. I mean, I don't *know* them, but I know who they are." He took a step forward. "You're the Morgans. The vampires! The ones who defeated Lilith and her armies! A decade ago. It was all over the news."

"I remember you!" Todd said, stepping closer and finally taking his hand off his weapon. "You're the vampires! On the news."

Carl Morgan nodded, lowering his sword. "That's right."

"They can't be vampires," Maebh said. "The sun's still up. Vampires burn in the sun."

"I know that," Moe said. "But they *used* to be vampires. There aren't *any* vampires anymore, anywhere. They're all . . ."

Moira Morgan lowered her sword as well. "We're all mortal again, thanks be to God. The curse is broken."

Moe pointed at the kneeling couple. "Tormond! Maebh! These are the *good* guys! The heroes! Holy — Mr. and Mrs. Morgan, it's such an honor to meet you!"

Vampires are nae more? The curse is broken? Tormond relaxed his grip on his sword, but he didn't let go. "*Good* vampires, ye say? Aye, good former vampires?" *Is Branwen mortal once more? Can she come to America now? Could we go visit her in Britain when this is all over?*

Maebh let go of his arm. She took a step forward, clicking on the safety and lowering her sidearm. She knelt before Moira. "I know 'tis silly of me to ask—'tis a wide world, after all—but did ye, by any chance, know Branwen? Branwen Aquillius? The vampire?"

The Morgans exchanged a glance and a shadow passed over their faces. A shadow of pain. And of loss.

Tormond's breath caught in his throat. "Branwen? She cannae be . . ."

"I'm so"—Carl choked on the words—"so sorry." A tear spilled from his eye.

"Branwen," Moira said, tears spilling freely down her cheeks, "is dead."

"No!" Maebh wailed. "She can't be dead! She can't!"

"She is," Carl said. "She fell in battle. Last year. In England. Defending the two of us." He swallowed. "She died well and honorably and in fulfillment of prophecy. Marcus's prophecy."

Tormond released his sword and knelt beside Maebh. He put his arms around her. She embraced him as well, and the two of them wept together like suddenly orphaned children.

"I'm sorry," Moira said. "We loved her too. But we didn't know her as long as ye did. We only had—" She sobbed. "I'm sorry. Her wound was . . . I'm a doctor! A surgeon! And I . . . I could nae save her."

"T-tell me," Maebh said, "if ye can, if ye know— Was she ever sealed to Marcus? In the temple? For eternity?"

Moira nodded, smiling through her tears. "Aye. That she was. We were there, with her, in the temple. She was killed shortly afterward. But she *is* sealed to Marcus."

Maebh sobbed. "At last she had that. She had that!" She squeezed Tormond all the tighter. "Now they're together again!"

"Aye, my love," Tormond said. "She's reunited with him at last."

Chapter 48

Hearing another vehicle enter the driveway, Tormond ripped himself from Maebh's embrace. He leaped to his feet, his hand reaching for his sword once more. He stood between her and the new potential threat.

The car—a small, blue sedan—halted at the end of the driveway. By the time the engine shut off, Maebh stood at Tormond's side again, her weapon in hand. Carl and Moira Morgan stood beside Maebh, their right hands on the hilts of their sheathed swords.

Our wee army grows, Tormond thought. *Heavenly Father, I thank Thee. Now what be this new threat?*

The driver-side door opened, and a rather ordinary-looking bald man wearing a three-piece suit emerged. He had very dark, almost midnight-black skin and sported a white mustache. He appeared to be armed with only a briefcase.

He could still have a pistol in a shoulder holster. Or hidden in yon briefcase. With a quick glance to his left, Tormond saw that Todd Cavetto had his hand on his still-holstered firearm as well. *That laddie will stand down, drop his guard, only when he's dead. After what he went through protecting his Peggy against the Witches and their minions, I cannae blame him.*

If the newcomer was disturbed at all by the heavily armed reception, he showed no sign of it. Barely a dozen yards away, he buttoned his suit jacket, smoothed his mustache, then strode confidently forward. "Good evening!" he called, waving genially. "I'm looking for Sir Tormond MacDonald and Lady Maebh O Broin." His accent was distinctly high British—without the lisp so common in the previous century. His smile seemed genuine as he glanced at each of them, but he quickly focused on Tormond.

He does nae look like a Sergeant, but I've seen many a warrior who outwardly played the courtier. "I am Tormond MacDonald. Who would ye be? And what be yer purpose here?"

The man stopped and bowed his head in acknowledgement. "Sir Tormond." His smile widened. "And you must be Lady Maebh.

546

You are as lovely as you were described to be." He strode quickly to Tormond, then extended his right hand. "I am Alistair Shipley Fitzcairn of Bradley, Fitzcairn, and Stoker of London."

Cautiously, Tormond took the man's hand and shook it. Fitzcairn's grip was firm, but not aggressively so. "And how may I help ye, Mr. Fitzcairn of Bradly, Fitzcairn, and Stoker of London." Tormond released the man's hand, then rested his own on the pommel of his dagger.

Fitzcairn extended his hand to Maebh. "Lady Maebh."

Maebh hesitated, then transferred her Smith & Wesson to her left hand, and took Fitzcairn's hand in her right.

Rather than shake her hand, Fitzcairn bowed his head again and lifted her hand to his lips. He kissed it, released it, then grinned widely, showing a mouthful of gleaming white teeth. "I say! It is an honor to meet you both, my lady, Sir."

"Aye," Tormond said, cocking an eyebrow, "I dinnae mean to be rude, Mr. Fitzcairn, but ye have nae arrived at the most opportune moment. And ye have yet to state yer business. How may we help you?"

Fitzcairn's smile vanished, his expression sobering. "I'm afraid there is no opportune moment for business such as mine. But as for helping me, it is I who may be of some small assistance to you. To the both of you. I am a solicitor" — he glanced left and right to the others present — "what you fine people on this side of the pond would call a lawyer. I am here, representing the *estate* of Mrs. Branwen Aquillius. I regret to inform you that Mrs. Aquillius is deceased."

Pain burned afresh in Tormond's chest. "Aye. We've already been informed." He heard Maebh choke down a sob.

Fitzcairn nodded. "I see. Allow me to offer my most sincere condolences on her passing. She was" — the corner of his mouth twitched — "a remarkable woman. I had the honor of serving as her solicitor for almost thirty years."

"How did ye" — Maebh paused, clearing her throat — "know we were here, Mr. Fitzcairn?"

The others — the Morgans, Todd, and Moe — closed in around them.

"Ah." The solicitor's eyes brightened, utterly unperturbed by the armed party encircling him. "Mrs. Aquillius left explicit instructions. I have been in the States for a week now, carefully watching the local news on the telly. She told me what to watch for. When I saw the video of a Templar Knight and a lady riding horses—one of them a massive, black warhorse in Templar barding, the other a gray mare—into Mapleton, Utah, I knew it was you." He turned to Moe. "Mr. Abbot, your interview was most useful in helping me determine exactly where to find you."

"Well," Moe muttered, "so much for me trying to be clever."

Carl Morgan nodded. "We used the same news report to locate you."

Moe looked genuinely upset, ashen. "If the news led *you* to us"—he looked directly at Tormond—"that means the Sergeants will know where you are. Where *we* are."

Tormond scowled. "The Sergeants have always known where we—Maebh and I—have been. If they wanted to kill us, they could have done so while we slept. But our deaths would nae serve the purposes of their demonic mistress. At least, nae yet."

"Yes," Fitzcairn said, "well, jolly good. I do know something about this. And as I said, I am here to help." He pointed toward the house. "If we might retire to the house, I have a prerecorded message from Mrs. Aquillius for you, Sir Tormond, Lady Maebh."

"A message?" Maebh gripped Tormond's arm, and she was trembling. "From Branwen?"

Fitzcairn nodded and a smile reappeared on his face. "Quite so. If we may retire to the house, hmm?"

✠·✠·✠

They all sat around the dining table—Peggy included, with wee Lucy in her lap—as the solicitor set up a small, flat, rectangular device he referred to as a laptop computer—though he set it on the table, not on anyone's lap. The screen on the device reminded Tormond of a television, only it was far too small. Then Fitzcairn sat back, allowing everyone else a better view.

Branwen appeared on the wee screen, looking as if she were very much alive.

Maebh gripped Tormond's hand, putting the other to her mouth to stifle a sob.

"Hello, my beloved children," Branwen said. "If you are seeing this, I am dead and I have at last been reunited with Marcus and Maelona." She smiled. "Know also that I am very happy. I know mourning is a part of life. But please, do not mourn for me." She wiped away a tear. "According to prophecy, I *will* be sealed to my beloved Marcus before I pass beyond the veil. It has not happened yet. It is not possible yet, but someday soon, I have faith it will be. With my passing, you will feel sorrow, my darlings, but know that I will *finally* have what I have dreamed of for almost two thousand years."

Branwen paused, wiping away fresh tears. "My endless loneliness is coming to an end—just as my endless night is over." She paused again, pulled a tissue from somewhere off-camera, and blew her nose. She chuckled. "I have to say, blowing my nose is *not* something I missed about being mortal. It's so . . . undignified." She laughed again. "I actually had a *cold* last month." She shook her head. "Not fun."

She sighed. "Anyway. I kept back a few of the prophecies about you. Please don't be cross with me."

How could I e'er be cross with ye? Tormond thought. *Ah, Mother! How I miss ye. I pray God ye are happy with yer long-lost love.*

Maebh squeezed his hand, and Tormond sensed she shared the same sentiment.

"For example," Branwen continued, "I have known from the beginning that the Witches you have pursued through the centuries would not be slain by your hand, but rather by the hand of another. I held that back, because I didn't want to break your spirit. But by now—it's now the spring of 2017—you will already have discovered that. But you should also know it is because of your actions in the past that the Witches were finally vanquished and their evil—including the Cult of Cernunnos—ended. That part of your mission has been a great success, though it may be a bitter pill to swallow after your relentless hunt. But you should also know by now that you have a much greater, more powerful enemy to vanquish. Yes, I'm quite sure you do."

Branwen sighed. "You will need new allies in 2018. Yes, I have determined that 2018 is when this will all come to a head, when you will finally confront the Sergeants and their mistress, the demoness Ashtoreth—though you've faced her before. And I have also determined that *I* will not live to see it." A sad smile crept across her face. "But I'll be watching you from the other side of the veil. Marcus and I, and of course, Maelona—your true ancestress—we will be watching over you."

Branwen shook herself. "But enough maudlin stuff. As for your allies . . . Two of them will be former vampires, like me, though not near so ancient. Trust me—*nobody* alive is as ancient as I, not even the apostle John or the Three Nephites." A small smile curled her lips. "The prophecies call these two the Unwilling and the Penitent. Marcus never revealed their names, but after some very publicly televised events a few years back, I've finally identified them. I know their names. They are Carl and Moira Morgan, and they live in New Canaan, Utah. Alistair has their contact information. You saved one of their mutual ancestors on the isle of Oronsay in 1617—Elspeth MacKinnon, who married Malcom Macfie."

Moira gasped. "I know those names! From the genealogy chart." She and her husband exchanged knowing looks.

"Do you remember Elspeth?" Branwen continued. "Of course, you do, my darlings. That was right before we met. And you saved some of Carl's ancestors in Missouri in 1838—William and Annie Morgan."

Carl nodded, and he stared in awe at Tormond and Maebh.

"I've never met them," Branwen said, "Carl and Moira." She smiled. "But I will." Her smile took on a wistful quality. "Soon. Also, there are Todd and Peggy Cavetto. You saved Todd's ancestor, Joseph Cavetto, in Newfoundland in 1715."

Todd nodded vigorously.

"I don't know where the Cavettos live," Branwen continued. "But I have their names. Oh, they must be in Utah somewhere. I'm sure Alistair can find them. He is a marvel."

Fitzcairn sat a wee bit taller.

"And there is an abbot—or perhaps a *former* abbot—named Moses." Branwen paused, and Moe chuckled. "I'm fairly certain he was a Catholic *priest* at least, but he's now a member of the Church, I think. I'm not sure where he fits in. But you need him."

Moe beamed. "Well, you've got me."

"And finally, my children, if you will accept him—even if he's not in the prophecies as far as I can determine—there is my faithful solicitor, Alistair Shipley Fitzcairn."

The solicitor bowed his head. "At your service, Sir Knight, my lady."

Branwen continued, "He's former MI-6—that's the British intelligence service—though he still has contacts there. He's a formidable hand-to-hand combatant, an expert marksman, and a good friend." Branwen smiled.

Fitzcairn bowed his head again. "Thank you, my Lady Branwen."

Branwen's smile vanished. "You're also going to need resources. Tormond, my son, I have made you my sole heir. I know that long ago you took a vow of poverty, but I'm assuming, now that you're a member of the Church, that vow is moot." The hint of a smile played at the corners of her lips. "Don't worry, Maebh. Once you marry, you'll share in his inheritance. And you *will* marry. Marcus has prophesied it."

Maebh squeezed Tormond's hand.

He squeezed back and winked. "Marryin' me for my fortune, aye?"

She gave him a mock-glare. "Ooh, ye—"

"Alistair will give you the details," Branwen said, "but last I checked, I have at least two-hundred and thirty-three-million pounds deposited in various banks around the world."

So much! After this is over, I must find a way to help others with this.

Nae, Maebh and I must find a way to help others.

"Holy guacamole!" Moe whispered.

"It's a bit more than that now," Fitzcairn intoned, pausing the video message. "A considerable bit more."

Maebh gave Tormond a sly look. "Definitely the money." She winked and squeezed his hand again.

Fitzcairn pressed a button on the computer and the message resumed. "Vampires"—Branwen grinned—"have few actual living expenses, and I've been able to save a wee bit over the last nineteen centuries."

A wee bit, aye!

"Now, Tormond," Branwen said, her expression suddenly grave, "I have kept the worst for last." She paused, taking a deep breath. "You must have faith, my son. Things are going to get very dark before the end. Very dark. Do you remember my . . . crisis of faith beneath Rosslyn Chapel? You told me that you have doubts every day. That sometimes you cling to your faith by your fingernails." She leaned forward. "Well, my son, a time is coming, a crisis for you, when you will feel that all is lost—that everything you have hoped for and lived for is gone, ripped away from you. In that moment of despair, have faith." She lifted her hands and squeezed them into fists. "Cling to your faith with all your might. God will not abandon you in your hour of darkness."

Tormond felt a chill twisting his guts. *An even* greater *crisis of faith?*

Branwen unclenched her hands. "You have one asset now that you did not have before. You bear the priesthood of God, the authority to act in His name. Remember what you have seen done in His name and by His divine authority. Cling to your faith, my son, and you *will* come through this. You will come off conqueror."

In spite of the icy claw twisting inside him, Tormond nodded. *I will, Mother.*

Branwen's smile returned. "Maebh, my daughter, for someday you *will* be my daughter"—the smile faded again—"you must have courage. You have always been very brave, but your courage will be tested as never before. You must have the courage not just to face death, but to *leap* into the abyss. To sacrifice all." Branwen wiped away fresh tears. "For you will be called upon to sacrifice . . . everything. But you *will* do it." She smiled through her tears. "I know you will. I have faith in you, my daughter."

Maebh's hand gripped his more tightly. Tormond looked at her. She was trembling, her face ashen, but resolute.

"I love you, my children," Branwen said. "Have faith and have courage, and all will be well. And I *will* see you again. Not in this life, but beyond the veil." The tears flowed freely down her cheeks. "And it will be a glorious and joyful reunion. And you will finally get to meet Marcus and Maelona. Until then, God be with you."

Branwen reached toward the screen, and the image froze.

Tormond heard sobbing. He turned to Maebh, and though she wept, the sobbing did not come from her.

Moira and Carl clung to each other, shaking as they wept.

"Ye loved her," Tormond said. "Ye loved her dearly."

Moira nodded. "Aye! We loved her. How we miss her still!"

Carl nodded as well. "The wounds are still . . . raw."

The room fell silent, except for wee Lucy's soft snoring.

Eventually, Fitzcairn said, "My sincere condolences for your loss." He turned to Tormond. "Sir Tormond, Lady Maebh, will you accept my humble service, such as it is?"

Tormond nodded. "Aye. Gladly."

Someone cleared their throat. "Mr. Fitzcairn," Todd said, "I'm sure you must be starving. Have you had anything to eat? We were going to go out for ice cream, but I bet you could use some *real* food. We have tons of leftovers from our late lunch."

The solicitor's stomach rumbled loudly, and he grinned sheepishly. "I, uh, am a bit peckish, I suppose."

Todd grinned. "Super. Mr. and Mrs. Morgan? How about you?"

Carl chuckled as he pulled out of his wife's embrace, both of them wiping away tears. "Yeah. We kinda had to run out the door to get here. I was starting to make dinner, but we ordered pizza for the kids."

Todd nodded. "Kids? You have children?"

"Aye," Moira said. "Four wee ones. And I do have to admit, I am fair to starvin'."

"Great!" Todd rubbed his hands together. "We have fajitas I can warm up. Tell me, do you prefer steak or chicken? We have plenty of both."

"Todd," Peggy growled under her breath.

"Ooh," Fitzcairn said, "that sounds absolutely smashing. Steak for me if you please."

"How about for the ex-vampires?" Todd asked. "Red or white meat?"

"Todd," Peggy growled again, a bit more loudly. Wee Lucy stirred in her lap.

"Yeah," Carl said, "steak for me too, if it's all the same. I've never really appreciated chicken in Mexican food."

Moira nodded. "Aye, red meat for me as well."

Todd beamed. "Excellent!"

Peggy rolled her eyes, but she smiled as well, softly patting her daughter's back.

Tormond and Maebh exchanged sly grins.

I suppose that means we can trust them, aye? "And while ye sup, we can discuss strategy. We can begin formulating our battle plan. But just in the broad strokes, mind ye." He winked at Maebh. "I promised a certain shield-maiden a walk in the moonlight."

Maebh's smile melted his heart.

But the icy claw of fear returned, chilling him again. *Everything I have hoped for, lived for, gone? Ripped away? And Maebh must leap into the abyss?*

What did Branwen mean? What more did she nae tell us?

Chapter 49

The nearly full moon hung low in the western sky, dipping toward the mountains, as Maebh and Tormond strolled down the deserted road, meandering through Hobble Creek Canyon. Tormond held her hand, their fingers interlaced.

This is different, she thought. *Nice.* A smile curled her lips.

He'd held her hand before. He'd even kissed it. But this intertwining of fingers felt more intimate and tender than anything she'd ever experienced.

"What be ye a-thinkin', lassie?" Tormond brought her hand to his lips. Then he smiled. "Or as they say, a penny for yer thoughts?"

She sighed happily. "Ooh, 'tis nothing. I was just thinking, ye've never held my hand this way."

His smile vanished. "Is't too familiar?" His hand jerked slightly as if he might pull it away.

"Don't ye do it, Tormond MacDonald! Don't ye dare let go of my hand. Not now. Not ever."

He relaxed, and his smile returned. "I will nae let go. Nae e'er." He patted the pommel of his sword with his free left hand. He winked. "Unless I must draw my sword to protect ye, milady."

Maebh did not regret leaving her purse—and thus her pistol—behind, in the car. She'd wanted to simply enjoy the night and their time together and not think of the ever-present danger. Or the impending battle. *I have Tormond, and he has his sword. And his dagger. And his firearm.*

Of the three weapons, it was the sword that comforted her most.

There had been no recurrences of Tormond's crisis of faith since that April afternoon. The incident had terrified her, but the sword's presence was a token of Tormond's renewed resolve.

The man I love is back. Ready to fight and slay the enemies of God. And I do love him. With all my heart.

She squeezed his hand again. "'Tis as if we're on a date. A *real* date. Just ye and me. Under the moon. Under the stars. Just a lassie and her laddie."

"For it tae be a date, I thought I had tae buy ye dinner. Perhaps take ye tae a movie after, aye?"

"Oh, aye, ye've done that. Many, many times."

"Ye must admit," he said, winking, "the *movies* are a relatively *new* thing for the two of us, aye? But we have been to the theatre many times. And 'tis true I bought ye ice cream at that Scottish hamburger drive-thru."

"Aye, ye did that." She smiled, remembering the sweet, soft, and airy ice cream—and the fact that Tormond never referred to the fast-food restaurant as by its name as if he were distancing himself and his clan from the place. "But this . . . way of holding hands feels different." She wiggled her fingers for a second. "More . . . intimate."

He chuckled softly. "More intimate? As I do recall, there was an occasion where we were"—he cleared his throat—"well, there was that time in the cave. In 1778. Inside the blanket. I mean, well, I *have* seen ye naked, lass. We have been . . . a wee bit more intimate than a-holdin' of the hands."

Maebh felt the blood rise in her cheeks. "That was different." She tried to push away the memory of how her body had reacted to his. *None of that! Not now. Do not spoil this sweet moment!* "Ye were only doing what ye had to. To save me." Ye always are there to save me.

"And ye, lassie—ye have saved me as well. Dinnae forget that. I certainly will nae forget." He sighed. "I'm sorry 'tis so late. Our meeting tonight took sae long. But we are almost ready."

She shook her head. "I'm not tired. Are ye?"

He chuckled again. "Lassie, we've slept through the centuries, sixty years at a time. I think I can handle a wee midnight stroll."

It was Maebh's turn to chuckle. "'Tis a fair bit past midnight, ye big lummox!"

She thought back on the meeting earlier that night—

The twice-a-week war council at Moe's house had lasted well past midnight, as they so often did of late. There was always so much to plan and centuries' worth of information to exchange. Carl and Moira Morgan—the ex-vampires—knew little of Tormond and

Maebh beyond what they managed to glean from studying the prophecies. Apparently, the Morgan's had a copy of all Marcus's prophecies—transcribed into Moira's family Bible—not just the ones Branwen transcribed into the Red Book. And it seemed that Branwen never told the Morgans about Tormond and Maebh.

Todd and Peggy Cavetto soaked up history like a sponge. Especially Todd.

Carl's and Todd's skills and resources would be of great importance in the coming battle, but the timing of their actions needed to be precise and executed flawlessly. "It's not like you see in the movies and on TV," Todd said. "These kinds of logistics take time to set up. And any number of things can go wrong."

"Yep," Carl said. "And we need to have all our assets—and their backups—in place. Once the enemy figures out what we're doing, we can't allow them time to react."

Alistair showed up that night having shaved off his white mustache and offered no explanation other than a toothy grin and, "It would be a hindrance." He turned out to be a veritable fountain of information and did indeed have contacts within British intelligence—and he made good use of them. Between what Eddie wrote and what the former-spy-turned-solicitor provided, Tormond felt certain they could confront the Sergeants in a matter of a few weeks.

"There are yet many preparations to make, aye," Tormond said, "but I'd venture we may indeed have a wee chance of survival. Perhaps e'en a chance of victory, Insh'Allah." He grinned when he said it, but Maebh noticed the worry in his eyes, the doubt.

Earlier that night, when they took a short break to stretch their legs and sip Peggy's delicious hot chocolate with marshmallows, Moira pulled Maebh aside. "If I may offer ye a wee bit of advice, lassie," the ex-vampire said, "get married. Now. Before ye march intae this final battle. Carl and I were married, sealed in the temple, before we went intae battle. That way we knew, nae matter what happened, we'd be together in the eternities."

Maebh gave the woman a sad, wistful smile. "Aye, but ye see, Tormond won't break his vow—not 'til our mission is complete."

"But I'm certain ye could convince him otherwise. 'Tis far more prudent tae make certain ye are sealed before—"

"But 'tis the very problem, ye see," Maebh said. "We cannot be sealed in the temple until we've been baptized for at least a year. And I will not marry any other way, unless 'tis eternal. Unbreakable. I mean, what would be the point? To have Tormond for a short while and then to lose him forever?"

Moira shook her head. "Lassie, ye said ye were baptized in 1958. 'Twas sixty years ago."

"Aye, and there's the rub. Ye see, we were baptized in June of that year. We waited 'til December before we started our long sleep. We have only been members of the Church — active members of the Church, as they say — for a wee bit more than nine months. We still have three yet to wait." She sighed. "Three more months. And we cannot dilly-dally another three months before we make our assault on the Sergeants. This waiting, the preparation is taking long enough. Sealed or not, we must face the Sergeants as soon as may be."

"But," the former vampire protested, "they've been around for nigh a millennium. Surely —"

"Every day they exist, more women, more girls, more boys are abducted, violated in their obscene rituals, on their vile altars. And those victims that are spared the rituals are sold as virgins to wicked men around the world." Maebh shuddered at the ancient memory of what had almost happened to her —

Being held down on the altar, fighting for her life and virtue. Kicking Sir Guy in the stones. Escaping, running.

She growled through clenched teeth. "We must attack as soon as we are ready. I'll not allow another innocent to be sacrificed while I sit idle. Not if I can help it."

Moira nodded and placed a comforting hand on Maebh's arm. "Aye, lassie. Dear, brave lassie. I well ken yer meanin'. I do." She fixed Maebh with her intense, green eyes — so reminiscent of Branwen's. "And Carl and I are with ye 'til the end. Whate'er that end may be."

Maebh placed a hand atop Moira's. "I thank ye." She swallowed, fighting back sudden tears. "We'll just have to trust in God and Marcus's prophecies."

But, Maebh thought at the time, *what of the dark prophecies Branwen revealed in her video? I must leap into the abyss? How am I to do that? What does it mean?*

Late though the hour was, neither Tormond nor Maebh was anxious to return to Moe's home — *their* home for the last couple of months. *But if we stay out here much longer,* Maebh thought, *alone under the moon and stars like this, we'll never want to go home. And if we never go home, we'll never have to face the coming battle. Never have to face . . . the end.*

But beyond the end lies hope of the temple of God. And all the joy that implies.

Assuming *we survive.*

Assuming we both *survive. Survive to be married, sealed for eternity.*

But if we don't —

After all these centuries, all the horror . . . to be separated — eternally *separated at the end . . .*

No! Don't dwell on that!

We will *succeed. We* must *succeed.*

Please, Heavenly Father, let us succeed.

But if we don't . . . if we get to the end and after all this, we cannot be.. .

I have to "leap into the abyss." Sounds a lot like death. Or Hell.

She covered a shudder by squeezing Tormond's hand.

He squeezed back.

Stop that. Cherish what we have now. *In this lovely moment.*

They approached the parked white car with the red cross painted on the hood. After getting ice cream cones in Springville, they'd returned to Mapleton and driven up the canyon. They'd parked the bulletproof car at the side of the road so they could stroll along the deserted canyon road. Alone. Together. Under the moon and stars.

She pressed her head against his shoulder as they walked, lingering there. *I wish we could linger in* this *moment just a wee bit longer.. .*

Tormond fished in his pocket, then removed the key fob. He pressed a button twice to start the engine remotely. The car beeped twice in answer. Then the engine purred to life. "Remarkable bit of technology, this. Like magic."

"Aye. Like magic." *But now we must go home. To our separate rooms.*

As they drove toward the house, Tormond switched off the vehicle's lights.

"Tormond?"

He pointed down the road. "D'ye see those vans?"

Maebh peered into the darkness.

Four black vans were parked along the dark road. Though their headlights were off, their taillights shone red and white.

"Their engines are running!" she said.

"Aye." Without signaling, Tormond turned the corner, drove a dozen yards, and parked the car. He handed her the key fob. "Stay here. Lock the doors. If things go badly, drive away, escape. Go to Todd and Peggy's."

"I have my gun! I can help!"

"Stay here, I say. Ye'll be safe here. E'en if there be gunfire." He gripped his sword belt and exited the car.

"Tormond! I can help! I want—"

"Stay in the car, woman!" He jabbed the lock button, then closed the car door.

Maebh watched in helpless frustration as Tormond buckled on his sword belt, drew his sword and pistol, and charged off into the night. "God," she prayed, "please protect him!"

In spite of her skirt, she quickly maneuvered herself into the driver's seat. She drew her weapon from her purse, thumbed off the safety, and peered into the darkness. She lowered the driver-side window just a crack—enough to hear what was going on outside.

She spotted Tormond easily. He was not dressed for stealth, and his light-colored shirt and sword caught the starlight.

But there were other shapes out there that blended better into the darkness. They were dressed all in black. More than a dozen men crept toward the house. Moonlight glinted off their weapons.

Then Tormond was upon them, attacking from the rear. His sword flashed.

Black-clad men screamed and fell.

Some of them wheeled and fired wildly, their muzzle flashes briefly illuminating the scene. But Tormond was in their midst, firing his weapon until his magazine was empty. He dropped the firearm and continued to attack with sword and dagger.

Other black-clad men came running from around both sides of the house. They converged on Tormond.

"Tormond!" she cried. "Look out!"

Another black shape moved in the darkness, emerging from the house. It attacked the others, dropping several of them. The newcomer moved like a shadow, black on black, and as he moved from man to man, whomever he struck with hands or feet crumpled to the ground.

The door of the house opened again. Out came Moe, brandishing his short Roman sword. He charged at the nearest assailant and thrust him through. Then he stabbed another.

Tormond swung and stabbed and hacked, whirling from opponent to opponent.

In moments, it was over.

Dead and dying men littered the backyard.

Only three remained standing—Tormond, Moe, and one other—Alistair. The solicitor had apparently stripped to the waist, and his dark skin blended into the night.

Tormond and Alistair knelt beside a fallen man, as if they were questioning him.

"Well, that certainly didn't go as expected," a male voice said. "Good thing we have a backup plan."

Maebh started, nearly discharging her weapon.

Outside the car, a black-clad man wearing a black ski mask, leaned across the white-and-red hood of the car. He held a long rifle with a rather large telescopic sight on it. The gun's barrel rested on a short bipod and was aimed at the scene below.

Aimed at Tormond.

"Tormond!" Maebh screamed, fumbling with the door in her terror. *Must warn him!*

"I wouldn't do that, if I were you," the voice said, "not unless you want Frank, here, to shoot the Executioner. Frank can shoot the butt off a fly at three-hundred yards. And that's a night-vision telescopic sight he's using."

The voice had not come from the sniper, but from Maebh's left.

Another black-clad-and-masked man stood outside the door. He leered down at her. "One word from me, Shield-maiden, and the Executioner dies."

"I have the shot," Frank said, his voice like ice.

Maebh glanced at the sniper, then at Tormond. "Please," she said, her voice trembling. "Please don't kill him."

The other man shrugged. "I do only as the Goddess commands." He bowed.

With a start, Maebh realized she was not alone in the car. A thrill of terror clawed its way up her spine.

A woman sat in the passenger seat. Or rather, she *appeared* to be sitting in it. She was clad only in gossamer blue and her gold jewelry. The demon smiled at Maebh. "Greetings, my daughter." Ashtoreth's grin widened. "My sacrifice." She caressed the word like a lover.

No! Please! Not that!

The man at the window said, "You have two choices, Shield-maiden. You can come with us, or the Executioner dies. It's that simple."

For one insane moment, Maebh lifted her weapon, ready to fire at the marksman on the hood. But the same bulletproof glass that shielded her would protect the sniper.

"Drop it," the man at the window growled. "Now."

God, please protect Tormond. Maebh tossed her weapon into the passenger seat—at the demon.

The gun passed right through Ashtoreth's insubstantial, demonic body, vanishing beneath her.

"That, foolish child, was blasphemy," Ashtoreth said. Her perfect smile did not waver. "And blasphemy is punished."

Flames erupted around Maebh, consuming her. She screamed, writhing in agony. Her hair turned to ash. Her flesh bubbled, cracked. Her eyes exploded from their sockets. The flames poured down her throat, into her lungs.

And suddenly, the flames were gone. And the pain was only a vivid memory.

Maebh shuddered, panting. *Not real. Not real. God, help me!*

"That was just a taste of my power," the demon said, her voice sweet, "a taste of the flaming abyss that awaits those who defy me."

Through the haze of remembered agony, Maebh's mind locked onto one word. *Abyss?*

"Now," Ashtoreth said, "you will do as commanded, or your precious Tormond dies."

"Get out of the car," the man said. "You're coming with us." He held up a black hood and a pair of handcuffs.

"Tomorrow night," Ashtoreth said, "when the full moon is high, you will finally adorn my altar. Again. And this time . . ."

Maebh trembled. *Please, God, no! Deliver me!*

Light burned in the demonic eyes. "You will submit to Holy Lust. And you will do it willingly. Or your beloved dies. Make your choice, my daughter."

Maebh tasted bile. *Must save Tormond. No matter the cost.*

I must leap into the abyss.

Maebh nodded. "I'll go with you. But Tormond will come for me."

"Yes, my daughter, my willing priestess, he will." Ashtoreth licked her perfect lips. "I'm *counting* on it."

Chapter 50

Tormond tore the black ski mask from the dying Sergeant's head, then ripped the corrupted crucifix from the man's neck. He knelt beside the man and brandished the cross with the crescent moon in the man's face.

The Sergeant clutched for the symbol with one blood-drenched hand, even as his other hand covered the gaping wound in his abdomen, vainly trying to keep his intestines from spilling out. "No!" the man whimpered as Tormond kept the crucifix just out of reach. The Sergeant's weak, ineffective movement caused fresh blood to well in a large shoulder wound. White fragments of bone protruded from the hole.

"What was yer objective?" Tormond snarled, shaking the crucifix. "Speak, man! And I'll give ye back yer cursed talisman!"

"Please!" the man gasped, struggling for breath. "I must . . . have it . . . on me. I swore . . . an oath."

"An oath, aye?" Tormond growled. "Ye swore an oath to obey *me*. To serve the Temple."

"I swore . . . to Mary . . . the Blessed Vir —"

"'Tis nae Mary! 'Tis the demoness Ashtoreth. But ye ken that full well, d'ye nae? Now tell me! What was yer objective this night?"

"I — I can't!" He whimpered, reaching again for the demonic symbol.

Around them, other Sergeants — those not yet dead — moaned and cried out — some of them crying for their mothers. But more of them cried out to their "goddess."

"Why won't he talk?" Moe asked, crouching beside Tormond. Gore still dripped from the point of his short Roman sword. Like Tormond's, Moe's clothing was splattered with dark blood.

"He won't talk," Alistair said in a matter-of-fact tone, "because he's terrified." The solicitor knelt on the other side of the dying Sergeant. "You read what that chap Eddie wrote — we all did. The demon can conjure the pains of hellfire, making them suffer. It doesn't matter that it's all in their minds — it still *feels* real." From the way the Englishman spoke, he could just as well have been discussing the finer points of estate law. "Even worse, she can make them watch as their loved ones seem to be burning as well. This bloke's more terrified of Ashtoreth than he will ever be of us."

"They couldn't have been here to kill us," Moe said. "It makes no sense. If that's all they wanted, why sneak into the house with such a large force? Or for that matter, why not just blow the house up? Or set fire to it?"

All this talk . . . The man's wounds are mortal. There be nae time! "Answer me, ye traitorous villain!"

"If I may, Sir Tormond?" Alistair asked, his beatific voice calm. "I have some training in time-sensitive advanced interrogation techniques."

Ye mean battlefield torture, aye? Tormond nodded. "Do it."

Alistair jabbed his thumb into the Sergeant's ugly shoulder wound.

The man screamed.

"That smarts," the ex-spy said. "I know it does. But in a moment, you'll convince yourself that you can handle the pain. That you can endure it. That all you have to do is hold out until you die. Or until your demon comes to save you." He paused while the Sergeant panted. "See? Even now it feels just a little bit better. The acute agony is passed. You can hold out. You know you can. Because the alternative—what your so-called goddess can do to you and yours—is far, far worse."

Then Alistair twisted his thumb in the wound.

The Sergeant screamed again.

"But you can't," the solicitor said. "You can't hold out. As soon as the pain begins to subside, it will get worse." He twisted again. "Much worse, I'm afraid."

The Sergeant howled in agony.

"Your goddess has abandoned you," the solicitor said. "You must throw yourself on the mercy of God. Before it is everlastingly too late, old son. Beg forgiveness for your sins." He twisted again.

The man screamed clawing at Alistair's hand.

Moe turned his head away as if unable to watch.

Tormond had seen enemy prisoners put to the question in the Holy Land, but only when timely answers were necessary to save lives. He had also known men—Christians and Muslims—who seemed to enjoy inflicting pain on others, who readily volunteered for the task.

Such men made Tormond ill.

Alistair, however, did not appear to be one of those twisted creatures. He was merely a soldier, doing what timely necessity dictated and no more.

Moe emptied his stomach onto the blood-soaked lawn.

"The woman!" the Sergeant cried. "We were to"—he panted—"take the Shield-maiden!"

Maebh!

"Why?" snarled Tormond.

"Ritual. T-t-tomorrow night."

But she's safe. In the car. God, please let her be safe in the car! "I'm goin' to see to Maebh," he said, rising.

Alistair nodded. "And I'll see what more I can get from him. And from some of the others."

"Shouldn't we call an ambulance?" Moe said, wiping at his mouth with a quivering hand. "A *lot* of ambulances?"

"Too late for these devils," Alistair replied. "I doubt any of them . . ."

But Tormond was no longer listening as he sprinted toward the car, sword and dagger in hand.

Ritual. Tomorrow night.

She's safe. She must be. Please, Heavenly Father. Let her be safe.

"Maebh!" he called as he approached the white-and-red car on the unlit road. "Ye can come out, lass!"

There was no response, no movement from inside the car.

Tormond felt the hair rise on the back of his neck. "Maebh?"

He peered through the bulletproof glass.

The car was empty.

Terror gripped him like a wake of vultures ripping at his guts.

He pivoted, scanning the empty road for danger, for any sign of Maebh. He circled the car. He looked toward the house. *Did she pass me in the dark?*

Impossible.

"Maebh!" *What could have made her leave the safety of the car?* "Maebh!"

There was no answer, save a distant warbling. *The constabulary.* The siren was getting louder.

"Maebh!"

A single piece of paper lay on the driver's seat. He sheathed his dagger, then wrenched the door open and snatched up the paper. By the dome light of the car, he could see that the message had been typed out, as if it had been written in advance of the raid.

Tormond read —

To the Executioner of God —

We have the Shield-maiden. The Goddess has reclaimed her.

Tomorrow night, under the full moon, in the sacred grove, and before the sacred asherah pole, the virgin sacrifice will be offered upon the altar.

Do not look for her before that. She won't arrive at the grove until after nightfall. Until then, she will be held at a secure, secret location.

No harm will come to her before the ritual.

We have been looking forward to this glorious night all our lives. There have been many rituals and many sacrifices over the millennia, but through the Shield-Maiden of God, we will at last be joined, united with the Goddess, the Blessed Virgin, in the purest form of Holy Lust.

We have no fear of what man can do. After the ritual, all the earth will be ours.

Come, Brother Executioner, and join us.

The Goddess has promised that you may be granted the honor of taking the virgin's purity. But if you refuse, that honor will fall to others.

Many, many others.

Until then, Brother Executioner, I am your obedient servant,

Sergeant-commander of the Temple and
High Priest of the Queen of Heaven

Tormond's knees trembled, threatening to buckle under him. Fear and anger warred in him—terror such as he'd never known in all the centuries of his long life, and rage beyond anything he'd ever faced on any battlefield.

My life for hers!

Heavenly Father, protect her. Protect her until I can — "Until I can slaughter them all! Until I can send every last one of them straight tae Hell!"

The siren—multiple sirens—were louder and closer, all coming from the west.

"Please protect her."

With one last glance inside the empty car, Tormond rammed his sword into its scabbard, then sprinted toward the house.

Moe and Alistair dashed to meet him.

"Where's Maebh?" Moe called as he slowed to a halt.

"Taken!" Tormond cried. "They've taken her!"

Alistair bared white teeth, his veneer of lawyerly composure slipping. "I couldn't find out where they've taken her. A 'safe house' is all I could get from them." He gestured at the corpse-littered yard. "All dead or too far gone, beyond help in this world."

A silver pickup with police lights strobing blue and red skidded to a halt in front of them. The door burst open, and a single female police officer emerged. The constable, clad in black and silhouetted against the lights of her truck, leveled a black, semiautomatic rifle at Tormond and his allies. "Police!" she yelled. "Drop your weapons!"

Moe's sword fell to the lawn.

Tormond had his hand on the hilt of his sword, ready to draw. He was willing to cut through any obstacle that dared stand between him and Maebh.

"A Templar ne'er surrenders," he growled. "They've taken my lady!"

"Please, Sir Tormond," Alistair whispered, "do as she says. You'll not help your lady by getting yourself shot."

"Drop the sword!" the constable ordered again, her rifle aimed at Tormond's chest. "Now!"

Two more police vehicles arrived. One white, one black. Both vehicles disgorged rifle-bearing officers.

With an audible snarl, Tormond unfastened both buckles of his sword belt and let the sacred weapons fall to the ground.

God, please protect her!

✠·✠·✠

Strobing lights of blue, red, and amber from more than a dozen police vehicles cast bizarre and shifting shadows around the normally quiet Mapleton neighborhood. A few ambulances had arrived as well, adding white and more red to the strobing lights, but the paramedics had given up on finding survivors — other than the three handcuffed men sitting on the lawn.

"Come on, Susan," Moe said. "You *know* me. I taught your boys in seminary. This is *my* house. I have a right to defend it!"

Mapleton Police Officer Susan Kosminski — a fit, attractive woman in her mid-forties — shook her head. "Sorry, President Abbot. Just doing my job. You know that. You got a right to defend your own home. Of course, you do." She waved behind her where more than a dozen law-enforcement officers from various jurisdictions — including the Utah County Sheriff's Office and a lone Utah Highway Patrol trooper — had the area sealed off and were actively preventing a small crowd of onlookers from entering the property and disturbing evidence. "But we got twenty-nine bodies here. Twenty-nine *dead* bodies. And you three" — she swept her hand in the general direction of Moe, Alistair, and Tormond — "are the only ones still standing. And all three of you are covered in blood."

"But *they* attacked *us*," Moe continued to protest.

"Look, President, you were my kids' seminary teacher for years, like you said. And you're in the stake presidency and all, but I gotta keep you three here until the detectives arrive. And we have to get them outta bed. They don't usually work the night watch, you know? Not in Mapleton. They'll get here, ask you a few questions, and then you'll probably be free to go. But until I hear otherwise, I have to detain you on-site for questioning."

Moe grimaced. "I understand, Susan. I do. But could you maybe take the cuffs off?"

"I can't, President." She nodded her head in Tormond's direction. "Not while Mr. MacDonald over here poses a potential threat."

"My lady has been taken," Tormond growled for the hundredth time. "And we dinnae know where the villains have taken her. And ye are keeping me from pursuing them."

"Right," Officer Kosminski said, "you keep saying that, but I gotta ask you, if you don't know where they, whoever *they* are, have taken your lady—Miss O Broin—then where would you go, even if we released you? I mean, we've got an Endangered Person Advisory out for her—you gave us her description—but we don't even know what to look for. We got no description of any vehicle or any suspect. I mean, look—I sympathize, I do, but we don't know where to look. And according to you, neither do you."

"It's true," Alistair said. "You don't know where to look for her."

Tormond growled. "I could follow the whisperings of the Holy Spirit. I could go to that foul compound of theirs. I could tear that unholy place apart with my bare hands. And anyone who gets in my way—"

"And *that*"—Officer Kosminski gave an emphatic nod—"is *exactly* why I can't let you go, Mr. MacDonald. You keep telling me how you're going to kill folks with your sword—like you did back there. I've seen your work. You're one scary dude. Now, if you could just calm down for a—"

"Calm down?" Tormond snarled, lurching to his feet, though still in handcuffs. "Calm down? They've taken her! They intend tae commit *rapine* on her! D'ye nae ken what that means? D'ye nae speak English in this wretched century?"

Officer Kosminski aimed her rifle at Tormond again. "Sit down, Mr. MacDonald. Or I'll put leg shackles on you as well. I'll lock you up in the back of my truck. And then you're not going anywhere."

"Sir Tormond, please," Alistair said. "This isn't helping. We must wait."

"It's all we can do," Moe said. "And pray. We can pray."

"Then pray I shall." Tormond dropped to his knees. His face was twisted in pain, frustration—and terror. "Will ye join me, lads?"

"Of course," Moe said.

"Most certainly," Alistair said.

"Uh" — the police officer lowered her weapon — "may I join you?" She appeared suddenly embarrassed. "I mean, I gotta stand here and keep my eyes open, but I'd like to pray with you too, if that's okay."

Tormond's lips were drawn into a tight line, his jaw was set, but he nodded. "Aye, constable. I'd be grateful."

✠·✠·✠

Tormond knew enough about the FBI to understand that they were a national-level police force. And by and large, the agents of the Federal Bureau of Investigation had been portrayed as decent, worthy officers of the law in the television shows and movies he'd watched with Maebh — though there *had* been exceptions.

Tormond suspected Special Agent in Charge Arthur Ritter might have been one of those exceptions. No sooner had Tormond and his allies — he'd come to consider Officer Susan Kosminski among them — finished their prayers, than a long train of cars and vans arrived. The occupants all wore navy blue jackets with "FBI" emblazoned in yellow on the backs. As far as Tormond could tell, they were all men. And in the modern age where female law enforcement officers were not uncommon, Tormond thought it odd that *none* of the federal agents were women.

And those men were led by Special Agent in Charge Ritter of the Salt Lake City Field Office.

Immediately upon his arrival, Ritter had taken charge, claiming jurisdiction, that the assault on Moe's home — for the past few months, Tormond and Maebh and Alistair's home as well — was "part of an on-going investigation into an international human-trafficking operation."

The Holy Spirit whispered to Tormond that he could trust Officer Kosminski — even if she could not release him. But Tormond felt the polar opposite in the presence of the FBI agent.

Officer Kosminski seemed to share Tormond's disklike of Ritter and his handling of the situation.

"How the heck did you get here so darn fast?" she demanded of SAC Ritter. "Salt Lake's almost an hour away."

Ritter smirked at her. "That's on a need-to-know basis. All you need to know is it's part of an ongoing investigation."

"Yeah," she replied. "You keep saying that. But here you are with every fed in the state and then some, less than twenty minutes after the nine-one-one calls came in. It's like you were waiting for this to happen."

"Like I said" — Ritter waved dismissively — "you don't need to know. But this is a hell of a lot bigger than a local gang shootout in small-town, Utah. Anyway, we're here and we're in charge. So, get over it, officer."

"I'm calling the chief," Kosminski replied. "We'll see what he has to say."

"You do that, officer. Your chief will confirm my authority here. You may not like it, but as of right now, you and the other locals here are on crowd control. Keep them away and don't interfere with my investigation."

A nearby Utah County Sheriff's deputy and a Utah Highway Patrol trooper watched the less-than-cordial exchange with resentful scowls. "Feds!" the trooper growled. He made it sound like an epithet.

Ritter sneered at the disgusted state trooper. Then he turned to one of the many men wearing FBI jackets. "Morales, set up a command post in the house. I want these three suspects put in separate rooms for interrogation."

"They are not suspects," Kosminski protested. "They live here. This is Mr. Abbot's home. The other two are his houseguests. Whatever else this was, these men had a right to defend —"

"Whatever else this was" — Ritter stepped close to the female constable, looming over her — "is not your concern, Officer Kosminski. Are we clear, on that?"

"Clear as mud," she replied. "This isn't over, Ritter."

Ritter grinned. "It is for now. So, do as you're told like a good little county mounty, or I'll have you arrested for interfering with a federal investigation." With that, he'd walked away from her, but Tormond caught the leer on the man's face as glanced at the female officer.

Once Ritter had the suspects separated into different rooms for interrogation, he sat across the bedroom — Maebh's bedroom — from Tormond, staring at him with a smirk on his face. The man's blond hair was close-cropped like a soldier's. His features looked as if they'd been chiseled from granite. His blue eyes glinted at Tormond with amusement.

Tormond's hands were cuffed behind his back. He sat on Maebh's bed—a place he should not be—while the FBI agent watched him without saying a word.

"Are ye nae goin' tae ask me any questions?" Tormond demanded. "Can we nae get this farce of an interrogation over with? I did nae but defend our home."

"I ask the questions. You give the answers." Ritter's smirk widened into a jackal's grin. "That's how it works here, Sir Tormond."

"Sir?" He kens I'm a knight? Tormond glanced at the holy sword and dagger lying at the side of Ritter's chair. "I heard from the Mapleton constable that ye had to confiscate my weapons as evidence. But there they lie." *Nae confiscated, but out of reach.* "If ye are going to use them as evidence, why are they here?"

"I told you—I ask the questions. But fair enough. Your weapons are here, Sir Tormond, because I intend to return them to you. Just as soon as we've finished here."

"Then return them, man! Return them and let me go. I must find my lady. The blackguards have taken her."

"But you don't know where, do you?" Ritter's grin faded, replaced by what might be mistaken for a look of concern were it not for the amused look in the man's eyes.

"Nae." *'Tis maddening!* "All we know is she's to be held at a safe house. Somewhere."

"But you don't know where?" Ritter repeated. "No idea?"

Tormond shook his head. "But I can find it! I know I can. The Holy Spirit will guide me tae her. All I must do is—"

Ritter laughed, throwing his head back. "Oh, this is too much! The Holy Spirit?" He laughed again, shaking his head. "You still think you're guided by God? Worse, by the *Mormon* God? Not even the *Catholic* God anymore. You still think He talks to you?"

Why is he mocking me? Mocking the sacred? "Aye. I *know* He does. He has guided me many times."

"Ooh," Ritter said, his eyes filled with mirth, "many times over the *centuries*, you mean."

"The centuries?" I did nae tell him that. "Who are ye?"

But Tormond already knew the answer.

"I am Sergeant-commander of the Temple, High Priest of the Queen of Heaven. But I see you've already figured that out. And since you've answered the only real question I had for you . . ." He reached inside his jacket and withdrew a pistol, but a gun such as Tormond only had seen in movies and television.

Tranquilizer dart?

Tormond leaped to his feet, charging at Ritter.

The dart took him in the chest.

Tormond continued forward.

Ritter was on his feet as well. He evaded the charging Templar.

God grant me strength to burst my bonds. Like Nephi of old. Even as he pivoted after the Sergeant, Tormond roared, pulling at the handcuffs with all his strength.

The cuffs bit into his wrists, but the chain burst asunder, freeing his hands. "I have ye now, villain!"

Ritter's eyes grew wide in sudden terror. "Goddess!"

Tormond charged again.

But the room spun around him. His feet were sluggish. His arms felt like lead. He staggered like a drunkard.

But he still managed to reach Ritter. Even as the Sergeant attempted to defend himself, Tormond punched Ritter in the gut. Hard.

The air exploded from the Sergeant's lungs, and he fell to his knees.

Tormond fell upon him, his fingers locked around the man's throat. "Where is she?" He shook Ritter like a wolf shaking a rabbit. "Where is she? Where have ye —"

The lights in the room faded to shadows — shadows reaching for him with inescapable claws.

Maebh!

"Where . . ."

The shadows took him.

Chapter 51

I may be a prisoner, but I am not helpless. I can still resist.
And Tormond will come for me.

Maebh was certain she was not at the compound, not at the orchard that she and Tormond and the others had been studying for months. She'd had a hood pulled over her head once she was in the Sergeants' van. Unable to see, she listened and paid attention to the motions of the van. They stayed on smaller roads, bumpier roads with lots of stops and starts, never driving on the Interstate, and they didn't drive long enough to reach Ashtoreth's grove.

She caught the phrase, "safe house."

Then she was taken from that van and forced to walk, but not far. It seemed she wasn't being held in the crescent-shaped building at the orchard compound — According to Eddie, all the cells were in the basement.

But compound or no, her cell was obviously meant for one nefarious purpose — it was a rape room.

The sound-proofed cell had no windows and only one door — securely locked, of course. A single ceiling light illuminated the room. The cell had no furniture other than a bed bolted to the floor — with four padded shackles attached to the wall — and a commode. A video camera and a speaker were mounted on the wall, too high for her to reach. A single wooden peg stuck out from the wall. On that peg hung a white dress, full-length with long sleeves and a high neck — a modest, pure white dress.

Though Maebh had never been inside a Latter-day Saint temple, she knew what the dress was meant to be — a temple dress.

'Tis meant to be a mockery of the temple, of purity and chastity. Instead of a nun's habit, a temple dress.

So far, they had not fed her nor given her aught to drink.

They had left her to wait.

To wait while they watched.

Maebh looked up at the camera with its small, red light aglow. "I'm hungry and I'm thirsty. I'm fairly certain ye wish me to keep up my strength for the ritual tonight."

There was no response.

Maebh shrugged. "Very well. Maybe ye want me weak and helpless. Ye probably have never had a woman who could fight back."

The speaker crackled to life. "Step back from the door. Sit on the bed."

Maebh complied. "I'm sitting on the bed. But ye can see that. I'm no threat to ye. I'm just a wee lass, after all."

The door opened, and in stepped a man. He carried what appeared to be a fast-food hamburger wrapped in paper and a can of orange soda. He bent and set the burger and soda on the floor, to the left of the door. He straightened, leering at her. "The burger's cold, and the soda's warm." He shrugged. "But hey, you didn't ask until now." He licked his lips. "You're pretty. I'm gonna enjoy taking you tonight." He stepped toward her. "You won't be *pure* when it's my turn — not by a longshot — but . . ."

Maebh suppressed a shudder and forced a smile. "That's true. But I am pure now. Maybe ye can't *have* me — not just yet — but . . ." She forced her smile wider. "Ye know, I've never even been kissed. Not once. I have, as they say around here, virgin lips." She stood slowly and took a languorous step toward him, spreading her arms invitingly. She even managed a wink. "I want to know what it's like to be kissed. Just once. Would ye like to taste my virgin lips?"

He hesitated, glancing behind him. Then he focused on her.

"But please," she said, "be gentle."

He chuckled. "Gentle?" His leer widened. "Hey, baby, I can be gentle." He stepped forward eagerly, reaching for her.

She reached for him as well, took his head in her hands.

And drove her thumbs into his eyes. Deep into the sockets.

He screamed and fell back, clawing at his ruined eyes.

Maebh kicked him hard in the groin.

He crumpled to the floor, screaming.

Maebh sprinted for the door.

But she skidded to a halt when it opened.

A man stood in the doorway. He leveled a strange-looking gun at her and fired. The gun made a whooshing sound, not like a firearm at all.

She felt the impact, in her chest, just below her collarbone. She looked down to see a tube sticking out of her chest—a tube with small feathers at the end.

Tranquilizer dart.

She stumbled back, almost tripping over the screaming blind man on the floor.

Strong arms caught her. She looked into the face of the man who'd shot her. She clawed at his eyes.

He turned his head away, so she grabbed one of the hands holding her. She brought that hand to her mouth and bit down. Hard.

She tasted blood. Still biting down, she twisted her head and felt flesh tear away from the hand. *The rabbit becomes the wolf.*

The man howled in pain, while the blinded man continued to scream.

Maebh spit the flesh from her mouth.

"Bitch!" the bitten man roared, letting go of her.

She fell. She caught herself on the floor for a moment, and then collapsed and knew no more.

✠·✠·✠

When she woke, she was lying on the bed. The blood had been washed from the floor and from her face.

She could still taste the blood, though her mouth felt as if it were filled with cotton.

"Finally. You're awake." The male voice came over the intercom. "Put on the dress." The dress in question still hung from a peg, apparently untouched by the earlier mayhem.

Maebh sat up, fighting grogginess and nausea, and looked at the camera. She shook her head. Simply, without inflection or emotion, she said, "No."

Don't show fear.

Don't give them – don't give her – the satisfaction.

"If you're worried about your modesty, we'll turn the camera off for a couple of minutes."

In spite of her terror, she forced a laughed. "No, ye won't. Even if that wee, red light on the camera goes off, I'm certain sure ye have other cameras hidden elsewhere."

"Put it on, or we'll come in there and put it on you by force."

577

She laughed again, and that time, the laugh was genuine and full of scorn. "Oh, no, ye won't."

"*Yes*, we *will*." The voice sounded annoyed.

"*No*, ye will *not*. Because ye could send ten men in here, and I'd still fight ye. I'd claw ye and bite ye and kick ye in the nethers. And I know ye could overpower me, but ye'd *bruise* me. Ye'd *damage* me. And your demonic mistress will not tolerate that. She wants me *pure* for the ritual tonight. Undamaged. Ye forget—I've been in this situation before. I know what she wants."

Maebh stood. "And I'll not give myself to ye undamaged. Ye may force me onto the altar, kicking and biting and screaming, but I'll be bruised and damaged by the time ye do." She grinned savagely. *Not helpless. I can still resist. To the end.* "So, no, ye will not force me into that dress."

She sat down on the bed once more and defiantly folded her arms.

Wee victories.

God, grant that Tormond is safe.

And grant me my wee victories.

A light blazed in front of the cell door. The light narrowed vertically, a slash of fire in the air. Then it took shape. Curves. Colors.

The glow resolved into a woman, floating in the air above the floor. Ashtoreth appeared to be wearing the same style of white temple dress that hung from the peg on the wall.

But she still wore the recumbent, golden, crescent moon above her perfect, black tresses.

The demon smiled. "Oh, daughter, you disappoint me."

Maebh stood once more, her hands balled into fists—as much to appear defiant as to mask the way her hands trembled. "Stop calling me that!" she snarled. "Only two women have *ever* had the right to call me daughter—my mother and Lady Branwen Aquillius. And ye are neither of them."

"I think," the demon said in a voice like honey, "you need a reminder of what I can do, of what awaits those who disobey their goddess."

Not that! Please, no! "Go ahead! Put me in hellfire. I'll scream and I'll writhe in pain, but unless you intend to kill me or drive me mad, ye cannot keep it up forever. Go on, show me Tormond burning. I know 'tis not real. I can endure it." *Please, Heavenly Father, give me strength to endure it. I spoke brave words, but I'm so terribly frightened.* "There is *nothing* ye can do to me to force me into that dress. I will not mock of the temple of God! Ye cannot make me do it."

Ashtoreth's perfect smile vanished. Her lips writhed in fury. "Oh, can't I? I have walked this earth since before Adam and Eve were cast out of the Garden. I cannot force you? You willful, ignorant, little bitch. Behold my power!"

Maebh squeaked in surprise and fear as she was lifted as if by unseen hands off the floor. She fought to move her arms and legs, but though she struggled, she could not force her body to obey. Her clothes were ripped from her and shredded to rags before her eyes. She floated naked in the air, helpless and utterly exposed to the men watching through the camera on the wall.

The white dress floated off the wall peg and toward her, climbing higher until it hovered above her head. Maebh's arms were forced up. She struggled, but she was powerless to stop her body from being manipulated by the demon.

The dress settled over her, clothing her nakedness. The zipper closed of its own accord. The buttons at her sleeve cuffs fastened themselves.

Her arms were forced down to her sides again, and she was lowered until her feet once again rested on the cell floor.

Maebh fought down sobs, but she couldn't stop the tears of rage and fear spilling from her eyes. She trembled, but she remained erect, facing Ashtoreth.

"You think you can defy me?" the demon crowed. "I can force you to do anything—*anything*, I choose. Do you feel *that*, child?"

A sudden chill infused Maebh's body, and gooseflesh rose all over her skin. She shivered uncontrollably.

"You are cold, aren't you?" The demon snarled. "*I* did that. And now, heat!"

The chill was instantly replaced by a searing heat. Sweat dripped into Maebh's eyes, stinging them.

"I can make your body do anything I desire. And speaking of desire . . ."

The heat was gone, and in its place was a different type of heat.

"That's physical arousal. Yes, I can make you feel that as well. " Her smile returned, though it had a savage edge. "You think your Tormond will save you? When he comes, *if* he refuses the honor of taking you on the altar" — she licked her perfect lips — "I can *force* him to take you. Just as I forced you to wear that dress. And to feel the sensations you're experiencing."

"S-sens-sations ye can n-never feel, d-demoness. Bec-cause ye have no body! Ye n-never have!"

Ashtoreth's eyes narrowed. "But I can make *you* feel them. I can make your body and his body do *anything* I choose. This world is *mine*. And *you* and your precious, chaste lover are mine. Tonight, at last, I will have you both."

The demon floated a step closer. "Think on that, *daughter*. Meditate on it while you prepare for the ritual, the Union of Holy Lust. And afterward? My acolytes will have you. *All* of them. And Tormond will watch. And then I will burn your precious Tormond — your *fallen* and *corrupted* Tormond — to death while you watch. You, *daughter* — you will live and serve me for the rest of your miserable mortal days. You are powerless before me."

Powerless.

Ashtoreth vanished with a flash of light.

Maebh was left alone. She collapsed to the cell floor, sobbing.

Don't come, Tormond. Please, don't come. Leave me to my fate.

Helpless.

Chapter 52

This stinks to high heaven. Mapleton Police Officer Susan Kosminski glared at the back of SAC Ritter as the FBI agent left President Abbot's house. The man was hunched over as he walked, one hand pressed to his gut. In the morning sunlight, he looked pale. And he appeared to be in pain.

A lot of pain.

He reminded Susan of an auto accident victim she'd once encountered on State Street. That man tried to refuse medical attention, but was eventually taken away in an ambulance, suffering from what turned out to be a ruptured spleen.

What the heck happened in there? It's not like Ritter got T-boned by a truck. He was fine when he went in.

Well, fine for a class-A jerk.

For a brief moment, in her mind's eye, she imagined that massive Scotsman, MacDonald, somehow overpowering Ritter and giving him a perhaps-not-undeserved trouncing.

She almost smiled at the thought. Almost.

Like that's gonna happen. MacDonald is in cuffs.

If I hadn't seen Ritter's credentials, I would never have believed he was legit. I'm still not sure.

In her nearly two decades as a police officer, Susan had never had the displeasure of dealing with a more unprofessional law enforcement officer. Or a more haphazardly handled crime scene. Van after unmarked van arrived, and the dead were taken away by men with "FBI" emblazoned on the backs of their jackets. They took pictures of the scene, but not near enough. They collected all the weapons and "policed the brass" — gathering up the brass shell casings — but she was positive a lot of the brass and some of the firearms were handled improperly. She was certain several of the guns had *not* been placed in evidence bags.

It's like they don't even care.

Like this is more of a cover-up than an investigation.

She glanced from Ritter — who was conferring with other FBI personnel — to Moe Abbot's door. There was no sign of President

Abbot or his two houseguests. And as far as Susan could tell, no FBI agents—or any other law enforcement officers—were left inside the house.

If Moe, Fitzcairn, and MacDonald are being detained in the house, wouldn't they be guarded? Are they free to go?

She'd checked with her chief of police, waking him, and he said to leave everything to the feds—in fact, he was quite adamant about it. Susan had obeyed orders, but nothing about the situation felt right.

She noted that most of the unmarked vans were in the process of buttoning up and clearing out—or had already left.

They can't be done already.

And where are Moe and the others?

Ritter looked as if he too might be getting ready to make his exit. *Like Snidely Whiplash—exit stage right!*

Susan marched over to him. "Hey, Ritter, are you *leaving*?"

Ritter leaned against the passenger door of the unmarked vehicle he'd arrived in. He turned toward her.

Susan nearly flinched at the sight.

Ritter's ashen face was a mask of agony. "What?" he snarled through clenched teeth. "What do you want?"

In spite of her annoyance at the Special Agent in Charge, Susan asked, "Are you okay?"

He shook his head, grimacing. "Bellyache. Bad lox."

Bellyache? Like heck. "You look like you need to go to the hospital." She glanced around hurriedly, but the ambulances were long gone—no survivors to treat. "Someone should take you to the ER."

"I'll be fine, dammit!"

"No way." She turned to one of Ritter's men. "You better take him to Utah Valley Hospital. Now."

The agent glanced at his boss, then nodded. He went to Ritter and pulled on his arm. "Come on, sir. Let's get you to the hospital."

"I can escort you," Susan said. "With lights and sirens. Clear the way."

Ritter groaned, clutching his abdomen. "No!" He grabbed his subordinate by the lapel in a white-knuckled grip. "Take me to *her*."

Her?

The man nodded. "Yes, Sergeant-commander."

Ritter glanced at Susan, then back to his man. "Let's go." He growled under his breath, "Idiot."

Ritter whimpered as he painfully forced himself inside the car.

Susan watched them drive away.

Sergeant-commander? What does that mean? Who the heck are these people? If this is an official FBI investigation, then I'm Jack the Ripper.

She turned toward the yard. Darkening blood stained the lawn, but all other physical traces of the carnage were gone. All that remained were the police officers from various jurisdictions keeping the small but growing crowd back.

The last FBI agent was gone, along with the bodies and the bulk of the evidence.

She turned and strode toward the house. She hadn't seen the three detainees taken away. *Must still be inside.*

As she searched the house, she called out their names. "President Abbot? MacDonald? Fitzcairn?"

Only her voice and footsteps disturbed the house's crypt-like silence.

She found three locked doors—presumably, bedroom doors. *One apiece.* She knocked and called at each door but received no answer.

She pressed her ear against the third door. *Was that a moan?* She pounded harder at the third door. *They must be in there.*

She drew her weapon and shouted, "Police!" Then she kicked in the door.

MacDonald lay on the floor, unconscious, a pair of cuffs still locked around his bloodied wrists. The chain that should have connected those cuffs was broken. *He broke the chain?*

On the floor lay a tranquilizer dart. And MacDonald's belt with the sword and dagger.

She holstered her sidearm, then knelt beside him, reaching for her radio to call an ambulance.

MacDonald's eyes fluttered open. They zeroed in on her. "Constable?"

She nodded. "Mr. MacDonald, are you okay?"

He took a deep shuddering breath. "Aye. I think so." He glanced about the room. "Ritter? Where is that black villain?"

"Gone."

"He's got my lady," MacDonald snarled. "He and his men."

Susan felt only mild surprise at that revelation.

"He's nae FBI."

Disgust churned in Susan's gut. "Yeah, he is. But I'd bet good money the rest of his crew were not." *It was a cover-up. This is big. Something really big. And it's like Ritter doesn't care that we know.*

MacDonald grimaced, then sat up. "Where are Moe and Alistair?"

"Probably in the other two locked rooms."

Susan's radio crackled to life. "Kosminski," a male voice said, "this is Deputy Trujillo. Susan, you inside the house?"

Susan grabbed her radio and answered. "Affirmative."

"We've got a woman out here. Says she's a doctor." A pause. "Say's she's *MacDonald's* doctor."

Susan locked eyes with MacDonald. "What's her name?" she transmitted.

Another pause. "Dr. Moira Morgan. You know. *That* Dr. Moira Morgan."

MacDonald nodded quickly. "Aye."

That vampire woman? "Send her in."

"Copy," came the reply.

MacDonald nodded again. "Thank ye, Constable. Pray, go find my friends. They were probably sedated as well." Still wearing the handcuffs with the broken chain, he got quickly to his feet, swaying only a little.

"You okay, sir?"

He nodded. "I'm grand. 'Tis my lady needs rescuin'." A look of pain—mingled with fear—twisted his features.

As Susan headed toward the broken door, MacDonald picked up the belt and buckled it on. "I'm comin' for ye, Ritter, ye blackguard. I'm comin' for Maebh."

I knew Ritter was dirty. In this up to his eyeballs.

✠·✠·✠

"Ashtoreth has forced our hand." Moe shook his head. "We're not ready, and she knows it."

"We *have* to be ready." Carl Morgan looked over the battle plan spread out on the table. It was hand drawn, of course. They had all agreed early on that they didn't dare put the plan anywhere near cyberspace, anywhere remotely hackable.

"We can't put this off," Peggy agreed. "Of course, that's easy for me to say, since I'll be the only one of us not *physically* there. Me and Lucy."

Todd turned to his wife. "Your part in this is just as important as anyone else's, honey. *More* important. But for the first time in a long time" —his jaw worked as he appeared to struggle with sudden terror—"nobody will be there to protect you."

Peggy put a hand on Todd's arm. "It's no different than when you leave on your Guard duty weekends." She looked around the room. "Lucy and I stay here with Moe," she explained. "Only, it'll just be me and Lucy and my Glock" —she looked pointedly at Moira and Carl—"and your people in New Canaan." She smiled at her young daughter in the playpen nearby. "We'll be fine, won't we, Lucy?"

Lucy, for her part, happily bounced her new plush toy horse—all black like Órd Dubh, of course.

Todd nodded quickly. He clenched his hand into a fist and looked as if he might pound the table. "We're outmanned and outgunned." He thumped a spot on the battle plan. "And we won't have the gunship, because I can't possibly get an Apache here tonight." He growled through clenched teeth. "But what choice do we have? They have Maebh. And that horrible ritual's *tonight*." He glanced out the window at the lowering sun. "In just a few hours."

"Worst of all," Moira said, "they know we're comin'. We've lost the element of surprise. They've picked the time and place of the battle."

"'Outmanned and outgunned,'" Tormond repeated, gripping the hilt of his sword with his left hand as he paced around Moe's dining room table like a lion in a cage. "Aye, that we are. And no gunship—no air cover." *God, please protect Maebh!* "But we've known from the start 'twould be so, aye? We've known we cannae win this war by force of arms alone. There'll be killin', aye. There'll be slaughter aplenty. Some of us may nae survive. And the price the survivors may pay could be very dear." He swallowed. "Perhaps too dear."

Please protect Maebh. My life for hers, Lord. Please, Heavenly Father, my life for hers!

Branwen's words burned in his mind. *"Everything you have hoped for and lived for is gone, ripped away from you."*

Maebh has been ripped away.

"In that moment of despair, have faith. Cling to your faith with all your might. God will not abandon you in your hour of darkness."

But they know *we are coming. We cannae win. 'Tis hopeless.*

Nae, with God, nothing is impossible.

But my friends. . .

Tormond took a deep breath, held it a moment, then said, "I release ye" — he looked at each of his allies — "every one of ye, from your promises. I cannae — "

"Ach, now!" Moira slapped the table. "Are ye daft, laddie? Ye shall nae go it alone. And *ye*, Tormond MacDonald, dinnae have the power to release *me* from *my* promise! We shall nae abandon ye."

"And neither shall I," Alistair said, rising to his feet. "Half a millennia ago — if the legends are true — you stood alone in that horrid abbey. You fought the darkness against impossible odds. Alone. And you won. Because God was with you. But you are not alone now. Not any longer. We are with you 'til the end, Sir Tormond. We will follow you into fire, into darkness, into death. Into Hell, itself."

Moira stood as well. She drew her sword and pointed it toward the ceiling. "We stand with ye, laddie."

Carl drew his sword, following his wife's example. "Absofraggin'lutely."

Todd, who, of course, carried no sword, stood as well, placing his hand on the table. "And we *will* rescue your lady."

Moe joined them. "We *will* come through this. *All* of us. God will provide a — "

The doorbell rang, startling all of them.

Carl and Moira quickly flipped the paper of the battle plan over, then held their swords at the ready.

Todd drew his Glock and put his body between Peggy and Lucy and the door.

Moe strode toward the door.

Alistair drew his Walther PPK and took up a position on Moe's right.

Tormond unsheathed his sacred sword and guarded Moe's left.

Moe, of course, carried a Glock as well, but he did not draw it. He glanced at Tormond and then at Alistair, put his hand on the doorknob, and opened the door.

Outside stood Officer Susan Kosminski. She was not in uniform, but she wore a Kevlar vest and carried a Glock at her hip.

And she was not alone.

Another dozen or more men stood behind her, all similarly armed. Tormond recognized some of the faces from earlier that morning. *More constables. Nae the false FBI.*

"Susan?" Moe said.

"President Abbot," she replied, her expression grim and determined. "Mr. MacDonald. Mr. Fitzcairn." She nodded toward Carl, Moira, Todd, and Peggy. "Dr. Morgan. Mr. Morgan. Folks I haven't met yet."

Tormond resisted the urge to force his way in front of Moe, putting his sword and his body between Moe and the police. "Are ye here to arrest us, Constable? Now is most definitely nae an opportune time. Come back tomorrow, please." *When Maebh is safe. Please, Lord, keep her safe!*

Kosminski glanced at his sword, then shook her head. "No. We're not here to arrest you."

"Then why?" Moe asked.

"We can't be here in any *official* capacity," she said. "Look, President, I tried talking to the chief, but he says this is the feds' case now. *Ritter's* case." Her expression had soured as she uttered the villain's name. "The chief says to stay out of it. Heck, I'm sure all the other chiefs, the sheriff, and so on, would say the same. We've got no jurisdiction here. But me and the others"—she locked eyes with Tormond even as she pointed over her shoulder with her thumb—"we smell a rat. A dirty cop. A *really* dirty cop. And that pisses us off. We wanna help. We're here to help get your lady back. And if we take down Ritter in the process, I don't think that would bother any of us one bit."

Tormond met her unflinching gaze. "Ye have nae idea what ye're saying, Constable. Nae idea what we're facin'. 'Tis bigger than ye imagine. Beyond yer ken."

She bared her teeth in a savage grin. "Then, *Sir* Tormond—that's what the Brit calls you—bring us up to speed. Because you're not going anywhere without us. We're sticking to you like ugly on an ape."

"You need them." The words formed in Tormond's mind, and he recognized the whisperings of the Holy Spirit. He returned Kosminski's grin. "D'ye know who ye remind me off, lassie?"

"No, *laddie*. Enlighten me."

"Robert the Bruce, King of Scotland—though ye are much bonnier than he, for certain sure. 'Twas said of him and his men, 'These are men who will conquer or die.' And, aye, they were badly outnumbered too *and* outgunned, so tae speak—facing a vastly superior enemy led by that ponce, Edward the Second." His savage grin returned, wider and fiercer than before. "And we conquered, aye. We *routed* proud Edward and his *vastly superior* army at Bannockburn. We conquered, aye, because God was with us."

Officer Kosminski chuckled mirthlessly. "You make it sound like you were there."

Moe laughed. "Actually, Susan, he was."

The constable huffed, giving Moe an incredulous sneer. "You're kidding."

Moe grinned. "No, I'm not." He stepped aside. "Come on in. All of you."

Tormond sheathed his sword, then bowed. "Enter, milady constable, and welcome. Welcome to our wee Army of Light."

I need them.

But we're still less than two score against hundreds.

Hold on, my love. I'm coming.

Please, God, my life for hers!

Chapter 53

You know," Arthur Ritter said, "you could have avoided all this simply by getting married." His voice came over the headset Maebh had been forced to wear. Even through the intercom, he sounded as if he were shouting to be heard over the whirring roar of the helicopter and the air rushing through the passenger compartment as they flew. The Sergeant-commander's face was deathly pale and gaunt, like the visage of a corpse, as if he were in horrific pain — pain he seemed utterly oblivious to. With sunken eyes, Ritter gazed at Maebh from across the passenger compartment. Dim red lights made her and Ritter appear as if they were both awash in blood. "I mean, if you and the Executioner had just gotten married — and had your wedding night, of course — the Goddess wouldn't have any further use for you. So, in a sense, you brought this all on yourselves."

"Liar!" Maebh shouted, though she doubted the fiend could hear her. Unlike Ritter, her hands were bound, so she had no way to push the "talk" button wired to her headset.

Ritter's grin widened into a leer. "You're right, of course. You wouldn't be a *sacrifice*, per se, since you'd no longer be *pure*. But even if that were true, the Queen of Heaven still wants her revenge. She will *still* put you into her service as a Priestess of the Sacred Grove." He shrugged. "Perhaps *High* Priestess of the Sacred Grove. You'll still be *serving* — servicing me and others — for the rest of your *useful* life. But the *first* time wouldn't be as" — he licked his lips — "painful." He shrugged again. "Or as enjoyable for the one who gets to take you. Pity it won't be me. It'll be your precious Tormond. Oh, won't that be glorious? The high-and-mighty and oh-so-pure Executioner of God being the one to initiate you?"

Maebh forced herself to glare back at Ashtoreth's High Priest. Her defiance was involuntarily mute, but she put all the contempt, all the loathing she could into her stare.

Anything to mask her terror.

Show no fear.

She was staring into the eyes of the man — one of the many — who was planning to rape her. But as much as that horrified her, the coming ordeal was not what she feared most.

Please, Heavenly Father, keep Tormond away. Protect him!

Take my life, please. Only save my Tormond.

"Tell me, Shield-maiden of *Christ*" — from Ritter's lips the name of Deity dripped with scorn — "was it simply the Executioner's ridiculous vow of chastity? Or could it be that he's simply not" — he chuckled — "capable? Maybe he doesn't care for women at all? We do have *boys* — or effeminate priests — if that's what he prefers. Maybe he's not really a *man* at all."

Maebh spat at Ritter, hitting him right in one of his sunken, hollow eyes.

Ritter jerked back, his mouth agape. His lips writhed as he snarled out a string of curses Maebh could not hear. Then he wiped at his eye, his gaunt face hardening into a scowl. "You'll pay for that."

Maebh turned her face away. *I know I will. But I shall be defiant to the end.* A tremor ripped through her. *Or will I be so broken, so degraded, that I will . . . embrace my fate? Will there come a day when I will no longer have the will to defy . . . Please, God, grant me strength.*

Outside in the twilight, the ground rushed by. Ritter had ordered the pilot to stay low to the ground as they approached the grove. The mountains seemed to pass by slowly, but the scrubby vegetation and the occasional building careened by at a dizzying speed.

The moon was just peeking above the Wasatch Mountains to the east — the moon under which Maebh would be offered as a sacrifice to a demon of lust.

Please, Lord, protect him.

I leaped into the abyss. To save him. Please, do not let my sacrifice have been in vain.

Marcus prophesied.. .

Another tremor rippled through her. But not one of fear.

I believe, Lord. "Help Thou mine unbelief."

She closed her eyes, embracing and kindling the ember of hope that had once again begun to glow in her heart. *I thank Thee, Lord. I will trust in Thee.*

"What are you smiling about?" Ritter said, scowling.

To her surprise, Maebh realized she was indeed smiling. She opened her mouth to answer, then shut it again and shrugged. And kept right on smiling.

Ritter leaned forward and picked up the wire that went to her headset. He pressed her mic button.

Her smile widened. "Do what ye will to me, ye pathetic excuse for a man. Are ye even capable of being with a woman ye have not taken by force? With other men there to hold her down? Aye, do what ye will with me—in the end, ye will fail. God will triumph." She leaned closer to him, staring him in the eye—remnants of her spittle still glistening at the corners of it—her confidence building with each word she spoke. "And His Executioner will triumph in His blessed name. And Tormond will give God all the glory. For Christ is mightier than any demoness. Mightier than all her deluded, pathetic, impotent minions."

She drew a deep breath and lifted her voice in Tormond's favorite battle hymn—

> Crucem sanctam subiit
> Qui infernum confregit.
> Accinctus est potential.
> Surrexit die tertia. Alleluia!

Ritter tossed the headset control away, but her voice still carried over the intercom.

She laughed. "Ye left it in the hot-mic position, aye?"

He lifted his hand to strike her, but she laughed again. "Ye mustn't damage the sacrifice, aye? Ye wretched coward! And in case ye no longer understand the Latin, here 'tis in English—"

> He bore the holy cross
> Who shattered Hell.
> He was girded with power.
> He rose on the third day. Alleluia!

Ritter snarled in rage and frustration. He clawed at her mic button, fumbled with it, and finally cut her off.

"Hey, Ritter," came the voice of the pilot over the intercom, "can you keep it down back there? We're about to land."

"Just shut up and do your damn job!" Ritter snarled.

"Listen, man," the pilot said, "this is a night landing without proper landing lights or a marked helipad. Those torches your boys are holding down there distort the landing picture, not to mention creating an updraft. I told you it was going to be tricky. And expensive."

"I'm paying you enough," Ritter snapped.

"Only twenty-five percent so far."

Ritter's hand shook with fury. "The rest after we land. Wired to your account. As agreed. I have my tablet right here. Ready to send your money. Until then, *I'm* in command. You will do as *I* order."

"Negative. Until we land, I am the aircraft commander. I am the *law*. Hell, as long as we're in the air, I am *God*. All your talk of gods and goddesses doesn't mean squat to me. The only god I believe in is money. And all the money in this world won't do me any good if I'm not alive to spend it. We're on approach now. So, shut. The hell. Up. Copy?"

Maebh laughed again as Ritter fumed in mute impotence.

And she kept right on singing.

✠·✠·✠

Tormond adjusted his earpiece and microphone yet again. It wasn't that he didn't *trust* the modern technology—he did—for the most part. He and the others had tested the communications equipment several times. He'd just never tested it under his helm. And he worried that once he put on his steel helm, the headset might become dislodged at a critical time.

He sat in full armor atop Órd Dubh, his helm in the crook of his left arm. The great warhorse was fully barded as well. To his left, Moe rode Fiona, Maebh's mare. Fiona had been equipped with armor as well, but much lighter than the stallion's barding. The mare was no warhorse, but Tormond wanted her as protected as could be. *Maebh would mourn her loss. And Maebh will need a mount when 'tis all over.*

She will need a mount. She will be alive to need a mount.
Have faith. Cling to that faith with all yer might, laddie.
Heavenly Father, let her live. Please. My life for hers.

Alistair and Todd sat atop a pair of black-painted electrical four-wheel all-terrain vehicles to Moe's left. Two more such vehicles sat riderless on Tormond's right. Those two ATV's had no riders, because Carl and Moira Morgan stood atop the cabin of one of four black-painted trucks—military-style two-and-a-half-ton trucks—"deuces," as they were called in the Air National Guard, according to Todd. Both Carl and Moira watched the grove—Ashtoreth's grove—with high-powered night-vision binoculars.

Alistair, Todd, Carl, and Moira all wore white tabards emblazoned on the chest with a red cross, specially made for them by Peggy. But underneath those tabards, they wore Kevlar vests.

Of course, Tormond's armored car and trailer were parked there as well—they'd been needed to transport the horses after all.

The trucks blocked the access road—the *only* road—to the Sergeants' compound. They'd used the trucks to transport the ATV's, but by blocking the road, they managed to turn away hundreds of cars, SUV's, and pickup trucks—all of them presumably carrying Sergeants. The idea for the roadblock was proposed by Officer Kosminski and Utah Highway Patrol Trooper Ray Harrison. "You've seen Utah traffic," Harrison said, and Kosminski added, "Yeah, it's way too easy to bring everything to a complete halt around here."

The Holy Spirit said I'd need the constables, and I do. I thank Thee, Lord, for sending them to me.

Tormond patted the stallion's neck. "Ye've served me well, laddie. I pray ye come through this night. And I pray ye live to sire many foals on Fiona." In all the centuries they'd spent together, the mare had not come into heat, but Tormond suspected that, without the Witches' wine, next spring, she would. And the great, black warhorse and the gray mare had often been seen trotting together around Moe's yard, sporting and playing. "Ye've earned the rest, laddie. And the joy." He patted Órd Dubh's neck again through the barding. "One last battle, my true and faithful companion."

Tormond locked his headset talk button to the "on" position, so he'd not need to touch it again.

"Ripper, this is Mjölnir," he said. "Do ye copy?"

"Affirmative, Mjölnir, Ripper copies," Susan Kosminski said over the radio. "Lima-Echo-Oscar is in position."

"Roger," Tormond replied. "Stand by."

"Roger, Mjölnir. Ripper and Lima-Echo-Oscar standing by."

Susan Kosminski and the other LEO's—law enforcement officers—had chafed—to put it mildly—at the idea of acting under Tormond's command, but when Tormond stubbornly refused to "bring them up to speed" without their first consenting to the Templar's leadership—even when some officers threatened him with detainment and additional delays—they all agreed. "But as soon as we have the site secured," she said, "I'm calling dispatch." Without the gunship, Kosminski and her LEO's would provide the badly needed second front of the attack.

The full moon rose in a sky overflowing with stars unhindered by the electric lights of civilization. The grove—the battlefield—lay ahead, to the left of the unilluminated, crescent-shaped building that housed the international headquarters of the Sergeants—and in the basement, a number of the Sergeant's victims. *Call it what it is, laddie—the temple of Ashtoreth and the Order of the Queen of Heaven. And the slave brothel beneath.*

Nae her temple. Her true *temple—as 'twas anciently—be the grove itself, with the vile altar and the corrupted cross at the center.*

Tormond lifted his own night-vision binoculars to his eyes. By the ghostly green light, he surveyed the scene.

Scores of dark-robed-and-hooded men—the demonic cross emblazoned on each robe—filled in the clearing behind the building, milling around the altar and the demon's cross that loomed over it. Moe had called the cross an asherah pole—an idol—such as the idolatrous Israelites and Canaanites had used to worship Ashtoreth in antiquity.

Many of the robed Sergeants had combat rifles slung over their robes. Tormond was certain the rifles were fully automatic weapons—AK-17's, AK-47's, M-16's, M-4's, and the like. Many Sergeants were so armed, but not all. *Perhaps only half. That might even the odds a wee bit, but we dinnae know if the rest carry sidearms under the robes.*

We be outnumbered and outgunned.

Even with all the wealth at Tormond's command, he and his allies hadn't been able to *legally* obtain fully automatic weapons. And Tormond steadfastly *refused* to break the law. *If we want God to be with us, we must obey the laws of the land as our Lord commanded. "Render unto Caesar the things which are Caesar's." And as the prophet Joseph Smith said, we believe in obeying the laws of the land and in honoring and sustaining the law.*

But that night, with Maebh's life — and virtue — in danger, Tormond almost regretted his stance.

Almost.

Trust nae in the arm of flesh. Trust in God.

Ye cannae win without God.

And no matter what they do to her, Maebh will always be pure and virtuous to me. Pure as the day I met her.

Please, Heavenly Father, protect her!

Some of the robed figures carried burning torches — not a single flashlight was to be seen, no electric lights anywhere. *Torches? In this age of technological wonders?*

Even more surprising was the circle of torches around the helicopter landing site. A few weeks earlier, Tormond and Todd had flown a reconnaissance mission over the site in a rented "chopper" — with Todd, an Air National Guard pilot, at the controls. They discovered the makeshift helipad — a simple, circular patch of bare earth — but they saw no lights around the circle. "Gonna be a tough spot for a night landing," Todd said at the time. "You need the lights and the big letter 'H' — which they don't have — to judge the size of the pad and the distance to the ground. Maybe they'll add it soon."

Let her land safely, Heavenly Father.

Carl, the former B-52 pilot and vampire, surveyed the skies with his binoculars. "Bogey at twelve o'clock low."

Incoming aircraft, straight ahead, low to the ground.

"Is it a helicopter?" Moira asked.

"She's low and slow," he replied. "Could be. Can't tell by the running lights."

"Is there more than one bogey?" Todd asked. It had been the plan for Todd to pilot an Apache helicopter gunship, coming at the enemy from the north — the opposite side — but since they'd been forced to move up their battle plan, the gunship was out, and Todd was relegated to being just another part of the ground assault team that night.

"Negative," Carl replied. "Just one bogey." He paused. "It's on approach. Tally on the chopper. Confirmed. That's our bird."

Maebh's on that aircraft. God protect her!

Give me – us – the strength to deliver her.

If they've hurt her...

Dinnae think on it. Think only on the battle.

Ye'll do her nae good if ye give in to fear.

Trust in God, laddie. E'en when – especially when – everything ye hold dear has been ripped away from ye.

However, his fear felt like a massive spider made of ice, crawling in his gut.

Please, Heavenly Father, keep her safe!

"Bogey has landed," Carl reported.

"Aye," Tormond said. "Todd, give the signal."

"Roger," Todd replied, "wilco." He lifted a handheld radio to his ear – the ear opposite the headset earpiece. The Sergeants used cell-phone suppressors in the area, so radios were the only choice for communications. "Agent Carter, this is Captain America. Do you copy?"

"Affirmative," came Peggy's radioed reply. "Agent Carter copies."

"We are *go* for November Tango," Todd said. "I repeat, we are *go* for November Tango."

"Roger that," Peggy said. "Executing November Tango."

November-Tango. N-T. Tormond thought of the ridiculous movie he and Maebh had watched. *"National Treasure."* Supposedly *about a hunt for the treasure of the Templars.*

The world kens so little of us.

Aye, but we were a secretive order.

Please, Lord, grant that this works. Grant that Eddie's information was correct, that his sacrifice was nae in vain. And grant that Peggy's legion of young computer people – Carl's employees under her command – can do this all at once.

Through his night-vision binoculars, Tormond watched four robed figures with rifles approach the helicopter. The aircraft's blades slowed to a stop. In moments, the four Sergeants dragged a woman wearing a light-colored, full-length dress from the helicopter.

Maebh!

She fought them, but her hands were bound. They were large men, and she was so small in their brutish hands.

Hold on, my love!

I'm coming.

My life for hers, Lord!

Another robed figure followed Maebh out of the aircraft. He carried a glowing, flat object, which he appeared to be furiously jabbing at with a finger. Tormond recognized the object as a computer tablet. And by the light of that tablet, the man's unhooded, gaunt face was clearly visible. In spite of the man's drawn face, Tormond recognized him.

Ritter!

"Captain America," Peggy said over Todd's radio, "this is Agent Carter."

"Go ahead, Agent Carter," Todd replied.

"November Tango is complete. I repeat November Tango is a success." The excitement in her voice was obvious.

"Yesss!" Moe hissed. "Good old Eddie!"

"Excellent," Alistair said. "Jolly good."

Tormond allowed himself a brief sigh of relief. *I thank Thee, Lord.*

And I thank ye, Eddie. Ye did well, Sergeant and friend. "Now for the battle."

"I count eighty-one," Moira said. "Not hundreds, but 'tis still eighty-one tae sixteen."

"Seventeen," Tormond corrected, observing as Maebh struggled against her captors. "Dinnae count Maebh out of this fight just yet."

"Seventeen," Moira agreed. "Aye."

A man who wore no robe exited the helicopter from the pilot's cabin. He gesticulated, pointing animatedly at Ritter.

Aye, it did indeed work. Well done, Lady Peggy. Tormond grinned. "Prepare to advance!"

Carl and Moira jumped down from their perch atop the truck cabin. They mounted their electric ATV's.

Tormond glanced at his troops. *God preserve these brave men and women.* He had seen so many mighty and holy men fall in battle. *Sae many brothers. Sae many friends. Including Maebh's own ancestor, Declan.*

He slipped his arm into the straps of his shield. He placed his helm on his head, careful not to dislodge his earpiece and mic. He drew his sword and pointed it like a lance at the assemblage of corrupt Sergeants.

"Forward, Soldiers of Christ!" he commanded.

"Ripper copies," Kosminski said. "Lima-Echo-Oscar advancing."

Tormond gave his horse's flanks a light kick. Órd Dubh leaped forward eagerly.

With a battle hymn in his heart, though not on his lips—because his microphone was activated—the Executioner of God led the last charge of the Templars.

✠·✠·✠

"Ritter!" the pilot bellowed, holding up a computer tablet of his own. "Where the hell's my money?"

Ritter flipped through screen after screen on his tablet. His agitation and horror mounting with every new, devastating screen. *How?* "It can't be!" *Every account?*

Maebh laughed at him. "What's the matter, Ritter, ye base coward, ye?"

How? When? It was all there when we took off!

"Could it be," the woman crowed in triumph, suddenly pausing her efforts to free herself from the two Sergeants, "that all your treasure, all the vast wealth of the Templars is *gone*?" She laughed at him again. "'Tis like magic, aye? Poof! With the wave of hand, like a magician's rabbit. Gone! All of it gone."

Ritter stared in horror at the tablet's damning display of zeroes. *Gone?* He continued to flip through the screens. *Switzerland? Germany? China? Canada? Grand Caymans?*

Gold certificates? He checked screen after screen. *Minerals? Lands? Stocks? Bonds? No! No! NO!* "It can't be! How can it all be gone?"

"In truth," the captive said, "I can't say as I entirely understand how 'twas done, but 'tis done, aye? And all your treasure, all the power that money can buy is now lost to ye. Even your own private accounts, aye? The money ye absconded with?" She laughed. "And 'twas all due to Eddie Masters, the last true and faithful Sergeant of the Temple."

Ritter looked up at her. "Masters? Old Eddie? A traitor?"

"Hey, Ritter!" the pilot demanded. "Is what she says true? Are you broke?"

"Shut up!" Ritter roared. He tossed the perfidious tablet aside, strode forward, and pulled a sidearm from the holster of one of Maebh's guards. He thumbed off the safety, pulled back and released the slide, chambering a round, spun, and fired twice into the pilot's forehead. The man crumpled to the earth. "Shut up!" Ritter emptied the weapon's clip into the pilot's chest. "Shut up! Shut up!"

Ritter wheeled back toward Maebh. He tossed the empty pistol aside and snatched the sidearm from Maebh's other guard.

Ritter switched off the safety on the weapon, chambered a round, and pressed the deadly end of the barrel against Maebh's forehead.

"Sergeant-commander, no!" the other guard cried. "The sacrifice!"

✠·✠·✠

Gunfire! Maebh! Tormond had seen the flashes, then heard the pops. But he'd felt no impact. He twisted his head, checking his white-tabarded troops.

None had fallen. And no report had come from Kosminski and her constables.

The shots were nae directed at us.

Fighting among themselves?

'Twould nae be the first time.

God, preserve Maebh!

"Hold yer line," he ordered in a calm voice that belied the wriggling terror in his gut. "Continue the advance."

✠·✠·✠

Maebh forced her eyes away from the gun pressed into her forehead. *Look beyond it. Look at* him!

Ritter's face was pale, drawn, as if he were sick, in mortal agony. But his gaunt expression showed only rage. "Where is it?"

"The money? The Templar gold? The lands, the—"

599

"WHERE IS IT?" The gun trembled in his hands, digging into Maebh's skin.

Maebh swallowed, but glared at him in defiance. "Where it belongs — in the hands of the last Templar. And he shall use it to ease the suffering of innocents." She pressed her head forward, pushing the gun back. "To ease the suffering of *your* victims."

Ritter howled. He quaked.

But he did not fire.

"Arthur," a familiar, honey-sweet voice said, "do not kill her."

The voice had come from behind Maebh, as did golden light, illuminating Ritter's twisted visage.

"She is not yours," the demon said. "She is mine, though you *will* have her. In the proper way. On my sacred altar."

No fear! If I die — God save Tormond!

Ritter lowered the weapon, and Maebh nearly collapsed as relief washed over her. Her forehead still hurt from where the instrument of death had indented her flesh.

"But he's taken it!" Ritter's voice was a wail. "All of it!"

"Oh, Arthur," Ashtoreth cooed, "have I not power to restore it to you? I am the Goddess of Lust and Fertility. All the riches of the Earth are mine to give. Do you doubt me now? When my triumph is at hand? Where is your faith?"

Ritter shook his head slowly. "No, Goddess, Blessed Virgin. I do not doubt you."

"Then perform the ritual, my son. Perform the ritual, take the sacrifice, and reap the reward."

Ritter bowed his head in reverence. "Yes, O Queen of Heaven!" Then he lifted his sunken eyes and leered at Maebh. "Put the sacrifice on the altar!"

The two Sergeants who held her arms dragged her toward the altar.

And in that moment, in her mind, she was back in 1497, back in the abominable abbey. She fought. She screamed. She tried to bite, to kick, to claw, but it was useless. *Hopeless.*

In moments, she was on the altar, her wrists bound, her ankles held in the iron grip of two strong men. The idolatrous asherah pole loomed over her.

And above her floated the demon, wearing a white dress like Maebh's, with the golden recumbent moon—so like the horns of a cow—upon her perfect black hair. Ashtoreth smiled down upon Maebh. "The time has come at last, my daughter. We await but one final player in our mystery play. One final participant. The star." She rotated in the air, turning to the south. "Welcome, Tormond, my son."

Maebh turned her head.

And there he was. Tormond. Her Knight. Clad in his white tabard, the red Templar cross on his chest, he rode atop Órd Dubh, sword and shield in his hands. Knight and warhorse thundered toward her.

The others—her friends and allies—were there as well, riding their electric steeds, but Maebh had eyes only for Tormond. *God save him! My life for his!*

The demon laughed.

And Tormond was yanked off his horse and up into the air.

"Come, Tormond, my son," cooed the honeyed voice. "Come and taste her, the woman you love so dearly. Taste the fruits of Holy Lust."

Flailing, slashing ineffectually at the air with his sword, Tormond floated toward Maebh. Then his flailing stopped. His arms were forced slowly to his sides as if by powerful, invisible hands.

"I told you, daughter," Ashtoreth said, "I can make him do anything. He is my puppet. His body is mine to control. And now I shall make him take yours."

The demon floated down to stand beside the altar, beside Maebh. She bent and whispered in Maebh's ear, "And when he does, you shall both be mine."

Chapter 54

Tormond!" Maebh's anguish rent the air. "Please, God, no!"

Ashtoreth laughed. "Look upon him as he takes you, daughter. Look upon his tortured face."

Tormond's helm lifted off his head and dropped to the earth.

But as Tormond floated closer, he was smiling.

Is she forcing him to smile?

"Ashtoreth," Tormond said as he approached, hovering a few feet above the ground, his arms still pinned to his sides, "ye once told me that I had no authority to banish ye. Ye said that power was no longer on the Earth. But I say unto ye, by the grace of God, that power and authority has been restored. And by that authority, I command ye to depart, demoness, in the name of Jesus Christ, my Master."

An ear-splitting shriek filled the grove. It shook the ground, the trees. Ashtoreth and her unholy light vanished.

And Tormond dropped to the earth.

He landed on his feet and sprang toward Maebh and her captors.

Another scream rent the night.

Maebh turned her head to see Ritter writhing on the ground, clutching his suddenly swollen belly.

Maebh kicked with both her legs, freeing them from her captors. But her wrists were still bound.

The men who'd held her legs, stepped back in shock. One drew his weapon, aiming it at Tormond.

With a mighty stroke of his sword, Tormond relieved the man of his arm. The Sergeant dropped to his knees, screaming and holding his bleeding stump.

The second man fired his gun, hitting Tormond in the chest.

The Templar was knocked backward, hitting the ground hard.

Maebh cried out his name, yanking on the fetters that bound her wrists.

She unclipped a radio from her belt. "This is going to be one heckuva mess to clean up. And that's not even mentioning all the ones we turned back on the road. At least we have their names, thanks to you."

Tormond nodded. "Aye, Officer Kosminski. Ye and yer compatriots have my undying gratitude. And there be the many captives to liberate in yon building, in the basement." He wiped his sword on his cloak—one of the few spots that was not drenched in blood—and sheathed it.

Then he took Maebh in his arms, ignoring the pain in his bruised and possibly broken ribs. He held her tight. "Are ye truly all right, my love?"

She laughed, clinging to him. "Aye! Is it truly over?"

"Aye, my love! Aye. God has triumphed. Praise be to God!"

A sob of joy burst from her. "I love ye!"

Rather than respond in kind, he pulled himself free of her embrace.

"Tormond?"

He knelt. On both knees. As if he were praying to the Almighty. He pulled back his mail coif, revealing his arming cap. He untied and removed the padded cap. Then he placed both hands over his heart. "Maebh O Broin, Shield-maiden of Christ, will ye marry me?"

Proposing on a battlefield? While covered in blood? Why not? Maebh smiled. "'Tis about time, don't ye think?"

She didn't hear the bullet that ripped into her back. She only felt her heart explode.

Chapter 55

MAEBH!" Tormond wailed as he held her corpse in his arms. "NO!"

Susan Kosminski kicked the gun out of Ritter's hand. She rolled him over and zip-tied his hands behind his back.

Ritter screamed in agony.

Kosminski shook her head. "You should have gone to the dang hospital." She paused. "Arthur Ritter, you have the right to remain silent . . ."

Moira Morgan ran to Tormond's side. She knelt, ran her fingers over the gaping exit wound in Maebh's chest. She felt for a pulse at Maebh's neck. "Oh, Tormond! I'm sae sorry."

"Maebh?" Carl knelt beside his wife. "Is she . . ."

"She's gone," Moira said. "Shot right through the heart."

Todd ran up. So did Alastair and Moe. All three knelt around the grieving Tormond, staring in mute anguish.

"Ye cannae be dead!" Tormond sobbed. "Ye cannae be. Oh, my dearie! Oh, my poor, poor dearie!"

"Hey, doc," Kosminski said. "I'm sorry about Miss O Broin, but Ritter's still alive. He needs you."

Moira dashed away her tears as she left to attend to the wounded villain.

Tormond rocked back and forth, smoothing Maebh's brown hair away from her pale face. *Why, God? Why? I did as Thou asked. I served Thee with all my heart. She served Thee faithfully. Why take her now? Why now?*

He caught a few words Moira spoke. " . . . ruptured spleen . . . kept alive by the demon . . . nothing I can do . . ." And finally, "He's gone."

Ritter—Maebh's murderer—was dead, but his death was no comfort.

Tormond's tears fell on Maebh's face. Tenderly, he brushed them away. "Oh, my love. If only we had married. Then we could be sealed, even after ye are dead. Oh, my love. I'm sae sorry." *Why, God? Why didst Thou let this happen? Why?*

"Maybe you still can be," Moe said. "We could petition the First Presidency. They could allow you to be sealed." His voice dropped to a whisper. "Worth a try."

"That's nae what the prophecy said!" Tormond snarled. "Nae what . . ."

Moira had returned. "Tormond, I'm sae sorry. I—"

"The prophecy!" Tormond cried. "Marcus said . . . He said . . . The top of the mountains. We did as Thou asked, Lord! We—"

Moira laid a trembling hand on his arm. "Tormond! Aye! The prophecy!"

He turned his anguished face to her. "Marcus said we'd be married! He prophesied—"

"Nae that prophecy," Moira said. "The one Branwen mentioned. In her video."

"Branwen?" Tormond shook his head in confusion. "Video?"

Moira nodded. "When all is lost . . . when everything ye hoped for and lived for is gone . . . ripped away from ye. In that moment of despair . . . cling to yer faith, Tormond. Yer faith, laddie. God will nae abandon ye in yer hour of darkness."

"What?" Tormond stared at her through his tears. "God will nae . . . nae abandon . . ."

And then it came to him. A snow-blanketed night. A dead baby. A grieving mother. A father with faith enough to.. .

"Aye." He nodded his head. "Faith. Aye. Both hands. Aye." Gently, he laid Maebh's corpse on the ground. He placed both his hands on Maebh's head. He looked to Moe, to Carl, to Todd, to Alastair. "Will ye join me, brethren?"

Carl shook his head. "Tormond, it's too—"

"I've seen it done," Tormond said. "In 1838. I saw a dead babe raised back tae life. If my faith is strong enough . . . And God wills it. Insh'Allah. Insh'Allah! Will ye join me?"

Carl nodded. He placed his hands atop Tormond's. Moe, Todd, and then Alastair did the same.

Tormond closed his eyes. "Maebh O Broin, by the power and authority of the holy Melchizedek priesthood which we hold, and in the name of Jesus Christ" — *Faith. I have faith* — "we command ye to live. We command ye to be healed. Maebh O Broin, live!"

Live, my love. Please, God. Give her back to me.

Maebh's chest moved, rising and falling. Her eyes fluttered open. They fixed upon Tormond's.

And she smiled.

Chapter 56

Maebh was caught again—not between the devil and hell, but between two opposing angels.

Moira and Peggy were arguing—perhaps "arguing" was too strong a word—were having a *spirited discussion* about wedding dresses.

"A full train," Peggy insisted. "It can be pinned up for the temple."

"Nae," Moira countered, "a *court* train, with a full skirt and petticoats underneath, to make her look like an Irish princess. And this one"—she pointed at a decidedly Celtic-looking gown—"with the laces up the back, 'twould nae need alterations. 'Twould fit her today."

"That'll be too hot," Peggy replied. "She'll sweat to death under all that."

Moira shook her head. "The wedding is nae 'til October. She'll appreciate the extra warmth!"

Maebh suppressed a weary sigh. *It could be worse, aye? Susan could be here as well.*

Indeed, the Mapleton police officer had *wanted* to come on this, their fifth excursion. She'd been with them on the last four, but had to be out on patrol that morning. Not that Maebh would've *resented* Susan's presence—she'd come to consider the constable a dear friend—Maebh simply didn't relish the idea of *three* sets of conflicting opinions about her gown.

I mean, whose wedding is this, anyway? Maebh's lips curled into a smile. *'Tis mine. My wedding. Mine and Tormond's.*

She let out a weary sigh as she ran her fingers over a dress with far too much lace. *Even if 'tis yet nigh three months away.* She eyed the rows and rows of wedding gowns wistfully.

The *spirited discussion* suddenly ceased.

Maebh looked at her friends.

They were gazing at her with obvious concern.

"Maebh, lassie," Moira said, "what's the matter?"

"It's us," Peggy said, her cheeks blossoming with pink. "*We're* arguing over *her* wedding dress."

Moira blushed as well. She reached for and grasped Peggy's hand as she smiled at Maebh. "What do *ye* want, Maebh? Ye've . . . uh . . . *heard* our advice. But what do ye want?"

Maebh smiled, throwing an arm around each of them. "I just want to be married. Sealed. To Tormond. For eternity. 'Tis all I want. All I've wanted for centuries." *And I've been waiting* patiently *for all those centuries. Well,* mostly *patiently. Mostly.* She stepped back, taking one of Peggy's and Moira's hands in each of hers. "And I don't care what my gown looks like. So long as I can wear it in the temple. I'm certain sure Tormond will think me bonnie in anything."

Peggy's eyes suddenly gleamed with unshed tears. "Of course, he will."

Moira nodded, misty-eyed as well. "Aye. That he will."

Maebh sighed again. "I just wish 'tweren't so far away."

"Three months isn't *that* far away," Peggy said. "We've got so much to plan."

"I don't care about any of that," Maebh said. "And three months feels like a century. *Another* century." Heat rose in her cheeks. "And"—she glanced guiltily at the salesclerk waiting patiently nearby and lowered her voice to a whisper—"'tis getting harder and harder for Tormond and me to be *alone* together."

"Alone together?" Moira's expression showed her confusion. "But ye are together every day. All day. And every night."

Peggy cleared her throat. "Uh, I think she means, it's getting harder and harder for them to, uh . . . *wait.* You know—for the wedding night."

Maebh felt as if her cheeks would burst into flame. "Aye. If 'tweren't for the work of helping the survivors, the Sergeants' victims"—*so many women and girls and boys!*—"and the plans for the Templar Survivors Foundation . . ." *To help other victims of human trafficking around the world.* "If 'tweren't for those . . . distractions . . ." She bit her lip. "I mean, 'twas *ye,* Moira, who advised us to get married right away. To *not* wait." *To* not *torture ourselves.. .*

Moira gave her a kindly smile. "I forget, sometimes, how it can be. Carl and I were married sae quickly. Once we'd made the decision . . . Well, there was nae time to waste. And there *was* a moment . . . perhaps more than one . . . when . . . Aye, well, but we endured. We passed the trial unscathed." Then she muttered. "Barely."

Peggy coughed again, discreetly steering the ship of their conversation into slightly less stormy seas. "Have you decided where you're going on your honeymoon?"

Maebh grinned. "Aye! Ireland. Tormond has never been there. And I want to see Kilkenny again. See how it has changed over the centuries. See if I can find my mother's grave."

"Ireland!" Peggy sighed. "That sounds *so* romantic!" She giggled. "Well, except for the part about the grave."

Moira stifled a giggle as well.

"Well," Maebh said, "it sounded romantic when Tormond suggested it." And suddenly, she was giggling too.

"There's a lovely pub in Kilkenny," Moira said. "Ye must visit it. 'Tis centuries old. Founded by a *witch*. Well, she was nae a *witch*, ye ken. Just a woman whose husbands —"

The door of the bridal shop burst open. Tormond stood in the doorway.

It was still so strange to see him without his sword — he never carried it anymore — almost never — but lately he carried a Glock in a hidden shoulder holster.

Tormond's eyes scanned the store. And then they alighted on Maebh.

And his face split in a wide grin. "Maebh! Ye're here, lass!"

He strode to her, swept her up in his arms, and twirled her about, laughing as he did so.

"Tormond!" she cried, laughing as well. "Are ye daft? What be ye a-doin' here?"

He grinned. "I'm sweepin' ye off yer feet, lass! That's what I be a-doin' here!"

Their eyes locked. Her pulse quickened. For one brief, mad moment, she thought he was going to kiss her. They had agreed that their first kiss — their first *real* kiss — would be across the altar of the temple, but at that moment, she would have yielded. She would have kissed him right there. In the bridal shop. In front of the salesclerk. In front of Moira and Peggy. In front of God.

They stared at each other, panting. She felt as if her heart would thunder its way out of her chest.

"Maebh," he said, his voice soft and breathy, "I came tae tell ye . . ."

When he didn't continue — when he appeared to be lost, gazing into her eyes — she swallowed. "Tormond, my love, ye are not supposed to be here. Ye are not supposed to see my wedding gown before the day of our wedding."

"Aye?" He chuckled. "Well, that day, lass . . . that day be *today*. If ye'll have me."

She blinked. "Today? What?"

He nodded. Slowly, but definitively. "Aye. 'Twas Moe. He arranged it. Cleared the way. He is in the stake presidency, ye ken. He said nary a thing 'bout it 'til today. Did nae want to get our hopes up. Said he received permission from Salt Lake this very morning. We have special appointments with the bishop and then the stake president in the next few hours. To get our temple recommends. We'll have to go to their places of business, but . . ." He smiled, and it was as if the sun shone from his countenance. "Moe has arranged it all. We can be wed today! In the temple. For eternity! I called and made a reservation. In the Provo City Center Temple. For six o'clock. This very afternoon. What d'ye say, lass? We have a reservation! Shall we keep it?"

Maebh was dimly aware that both Peggy and Moira were bouncing up and down, squealing with delight.

"Six o'clock?" she asked. "This very day?"

"Aye, my love. Please say aye!"

She nodded. "Oh, aye! Aye!" She squeezed him tight, joyful tears streaming from her eyes. "A hundred, a *thousand* times, aye!"

Somehow, she kept herself from kissing him. Barely. But she stared into his eyes as she said, "Moira, please tell the salesclerk that we'll take the Celtic gown. The one that will fit today." She grinned. "I suppose we must get a marriage license, aye?"

And later that afternoon, shortly after six o'clock, surrounded by their friends — including several police officers — and wearing the Celtic gown that made her look like an Irish princess, Maebh and

Tormond, as husband and wife, shared their first *real* kiss over the altar of the temple.

And that first kiss was very sweet. It was soft and tender, yet promised so much more. It stole her very breath away, sending delightful shivers through her body.

It was everything she had dreamed of.

"Tell me, milady," Tormond whispered, beaming at her, "was it worth the wait?"

She smiled. "Aye, milaird. Worth the wait of centuries."

She leaned forward and kissed him again.

The End

Acknowledgements

This has been a massive project, especially in terms of research. While I do enjoy the research, I was definitely sailing in (for me) uncharted waters. I am profoundly grateful to Father Christopher Gray of St. Mary's Church and seminarian Joseph Baldwin for their invaluable help in understanding Catholic faith, doctrine, and sacred ritual. They graciously provided insights (and gentle corrections) I would not have gleaned on my own. While I am obviously writing from a Latter-day Saint perspective, these two good brethren helped me to depict medieval (and later) Catholicism with (I hope) accuracy and respect.

Essential law enforcement expertise was provided by Detective Christian Belt of the Las Vegas Police Department, Lt. Phillip Bringhurst of the Mapleton Police Department, Sgt. Spencer Cannon of the Utah County Sheriff's Office, and Sgt. George Hansen of the Utah Highway Patrol. I thank them for their assistance and for putting their lives on the line to serve and protect a too-often ungrateful citizenry. These men are heroes.

As always, Eric D. Huntsman, PhD, of Brigham Young University helped me with Latin and ecclesiastical matters. Bishop Josh Richey also assisted me in matters of church procedure. Christopher M. Flood, PhD, of Brigham Young University provided Middle French translations, and Seba Jean-Baptiste assisted with more modern French. Thank you, brethren.

My friend, Dawn "Red" Johnston of Aberdeenshire, Scotland assisted with the Scots Gaelic and colloquial expressions. Thank ye, milady.

Loralee Evans, novelist and educator, provided expertise on the Utes and their language. Thank you, my friend.

Sara Graham Stuflick, equestrienne extraordinaire, and Dr. Willie Lanier, D.V.M., assisted with all equine matters. Thank you to you both.

Olya and Joseph Goodrick gave me two books on the Knights Templar, including a translation of "The Primitive Rule of the Templars" by Bernard of Clairvaux and Hugues de Payens. Olya and Joe, your contribution was priceless.

My dear friends, Ric Buhler and Malachi Hall, let me talk their ears off. Sounding boards such as they have helped me greatly, especially when I was stuck on a plot point.

None of this would be possible without the assistance of my editor and friend, Elizabeth Petty Bentley.

When I was little, my dad, William David Belt, told me stories about a superhero/detective he made up just for me called "Darkman." Darkman dressed all in black and used the dark color of his skin to blend into the night so he could combat the forces of evil. Darkman is, in large, part the basis for Alistair Fitzcairn. Thank you, Dad. I miss you.

My mother, Mable Belt (who, by the way, is most definitely *not* a fan of horror), is my standard when it comes to writing horror. If she cannot read it, it doesn't go into the book. (Although, it might make her squirm on occasion.) She has been my first line of defense as a proofreader. Other proofreaders and reviewers include the wonderful horror authors, Brandon Bluhm, Crystal Brinkerhoff, and Daniel Earl, and romance author, Jenny Flake Rabe, and historical fiction author Marie Woodward. And of course, I could not have done any of this without my dearest, lovely, and faithful eternal companion, Cindy Belt. She is my editor, my friendly critic, my one true love, my heart, and the inspiration for all my heroines. She is also my best and truest friend.

I am often asked (sometimes by people who cannot quite — or will not even attempt to — disguise their, shall we say, horror), "Where do you get your ideas?" The answer is, quite simply, prayer and, as Tormond would put it, "the whisperings" of the Holy Spirit. I pray for guidance when writing my stories, and my Heavenly Father provides me with that guidance. When the Spirit is not there, the words do not flow. I acknowledge God's hand in this work.

Non nobis, Domine. Non nobis. Sed nomini tuo da gloriam.

A joyful, humble, and sincere thank you to all of you.

C. David Belt

About the Author

C. David Belt was born in the wilds of Evanston, Wyoming. As a child, he lived and traveled extensively around the Far East. In Thailand, he once fed so many bananas to a monkey, the poor creature swore off bananas for life. He served as a missionary in South Korea and southern California (Korean-speaking), and yes, he loves kimchi. He graduated from Brigham Young University with a BS in Computer Science and a minor in Aerospace Studies, but he managed to bypass all English and writing classes. He served as a B-52 pilot in the US Air Force and as an Air Weapons Controller in the Washington Air National Guard and was deployed to locations so secret, his family still does not know where he risked life and limb (other than in an 192' wingspan aircraft flying 200' off the ground in mountainous terrain). When he is not writing, he has been known to sing in the Tabernacle Choir at Temple Square, and works as a software engineer. He collects swords, spears, and axes (oh, my!), and other medieval weapons and armor. He and his lovely wife have six children (and a growing number of grandchildren) and live in Utah with a cat that (as the family scape-cat) patiently and unashamedly takes the blame for everything in the household.

C. David Belt is the author of *The Children of Lilith* trilogy, *The Sweet Sister*, *Time's Plague*, *The Arawn Prophecy*, *The Whole Armor of God*, *The Witch of White Lady Hollow*, *The Witch and the Devourer of Souls*, and *The Executioner of God*. For more information, please visit www.unwillingchild.com .

www.ingramcontent.com/pod-product-compliance
Lightning Source LLC
Chambersburg PA
CBHW021832010726
47493CB00005B/1366